PENGUIN MODERN CLASSICS

The Penguin Book Of Dutch Short Stories

JOOST ZWAGERMAN (1963–2015) was a novelist, poet, essayist and editor of several anthologies. He started his career as a writer with
bestselling novels describing the atmosphere of the 1980s and 1990s,
such as *Gimmick!* (1988) and *False Light* (1991). In later years, he
concentrated on writing essays – notably on pop culture and visual
arts – and poetry. Suicide was the theme of the novel *Six Stars*
(2002). He took his own life just after publishing a new collection of
essays on art, *The Museum of Light*.

D1354477

The Penguin Book of Dutch Short Stories

Edited and with an Introduction by JOOST ZWAGERMAN

PENGUIN BOOKS

PENGUIN CLASSICS

UK | USA | Canada | Ireland | Australia
India | New Zealand | South Africa

Penguin Books is part of the Penguin Random House group of companies
whose addresses can be found at global.penguinrandomhouse.com.

This edition first published in Penguin Classics 2016
001

Introduction copyright © the estate of Joost Zwagerman, 2016
Chronology copyright © Prof. Dr Marita Mathijsen, 2016
Author Biographies copyright © Victor Schiferli / Dutch Foundation for Literature, 2016
The Acknowledgements on pp. 550–55 constitute an extension of this copyright page.

The moral rights of the authors and translators have been asserted

This book was published with the support of the Dutch Foundation for Literature

Nederlands
letterenfonds
dutch foundation
for literature

Set in 10.25/12.25 pt Adobe Sabon
Typeset by Jouve (UK), Milton Keynes
Printed in Great Britain by Clays Ltd, St Ives plc

A CIP catalogue record for this book is available from the British Library

ISBN: 978-0-141-39572-2

www.greenpenguin.co.uk

Contents

Introduction

INTRODUCTION

One day in 2007, the American translator Damion Searls had a meeting in Brussels with the Dutch novelist Tommy Wieringa, several of whose novels – such as *Joe Speedboat* and *These Are the Names* – have now appeared in translation in many countries. Searls asked Wieringa who he believed was the greatest Dutch writer of the past one hundred and fifty years. Wieringa's answer was Nescio (1882–1961), the author of a small but highly cherished body of short stories, including the two crystalline miniatures 'Young Titans' and 'Little Poet'. Nescio's stories outshine many a fat Dutch novel, in Wieringa's opinion and that of numerous Dutch writers. Searls read Nescio's stories in German translation and was blown away by his seemingly plain yet unapologetically lyrical style. It was hard for him to reconcile this lyricism with the popular image of the Dutch as level-headed, hard-working people.

Searls went to the editors of the New York Review of Books Classics series to advocate an English edition of 'Young Titans' and Nescio's other stories. The editor Edwin Frank was equally thunderstruck by Nescio's sprightly, melodious mode of story-telling, and *Amsterdam Stories* appeared in 2012 – almost eighty years after Nescio's book had been published in the Netherlands. Nescio, the pseudonym of J. H. F. Grönloh (an office clerk by day), had at last won a place in the ranks of the world's great short-story writers. One might well ask whether that was what Grönloh wanted; at first, he did not tell the public that he was Nescio the writer, because 'if people find out that you write, they think you must not be qualified for your "real" work'.

Nescio's American editor has spelled out the strengths of the story 'Young Titans': 'It's about the melancholy of young men, but subtly laced with the melancholy of an older man looking back on the particular, *bygone* melancholy of his youth. While the young friends in the story experience that period of their lives as constrained, the narrator, grown older, realizes what immense opportunities they had back then. Each of the young friends failed, in his own way, to seize those opportunities. The hell of constraint, as experienced in one's youth, is transformed – with an appropriate degree of unrealistic idealization – into the heaven of seemingly boundless possibilities. It's a turn of thought and emotion with which everyone can identify. And then there are the wonderful descriptions of the Dutch landscape. It's a remarkably beautiful, lyrical work. But "Young Titans" also has an intriguing social component, besides which it touches on what may be the ultimate Dutch dilemma: the impossibility of reconciling, either in fact or in imagination, the prosaic spirit of commerce with poetic dreams of a life that transcends the mores of trade and business. All these facets are interlinked in one short story, which, furthermore, is written in a suggestive style, laconic and evocative in equal measure.'

Often, as in this case, it takes an outsider to explain to us here in the Netherlands why a particular work of art deserves its place in our national canon. We love the young men with dreams that are bound to perish, such as Bavink the painter, who is so determined to 'paint the sun'. Yet it took an American reader to point out one of the story's most attractive features: the fateful tension between a life spent *in* trade or business and a life lived *for* art. Dutch readers feel this tension but don't always realize that it not only underpins the story but also resonates in the author's style.

And as far as trade and business are concerned, I know full well that the Netherlands has a reputation, to this day, as a small but industrious nation shored up by the unrelenting activity of merchants and businessmen like Grönloh. Fortunately, Nescio offered a glimpse of the other side of the Netherlands: a country that, generation after generation, has given birth to scores of headstrong 'Young Titans', energetic innovators in art, music and literature, many of whom swing between moods of hushed serenity and outbursts of unadulterated *Weltschmerz* or experimental ruckus. Not what you might expect from this supposedly hard-headed country. The prototypical Dutch writer creates protagonists that are – excuse the contradiction in terms – contemplative arch-romantics, reserved iconoclasts. Keep this prototype in mind, and you will understand the personalities of more than a few of the authors in this collection.

Other writers in the NYRB Classics series are also included here: Maria Dermoût and Marcellus Emants, with whose story 'An Eccentric' the collection opens. Emants (1848–1923), who belonged to the circle of Dutch naturalist authors, felt a strong kinship with Émile Zola and Ivan Turgenev and kept up a correspondence with Turgenev for years. Yet for Dutch readers, Emants is an admired but distant figure, as are A. Aletrino, Frans Coenen and other naturalists of the same generation, even though they were active less than one hundred and fifty years ago. Readers in France, Germany, Russia, England and the United States can still easily read 'their' authors from the not-so-distant past. Present-day French readers can appreciate Victor Hugo's *Les Misérables* without a dictionary, and for a child in Manchester required to read *Macbeth*, Shakespeare's writing is not nearly as impenetrable as a book written in Hebrew or Hindi.

In contrast, the Dutch language is constantly in the throes of change so radical and sweeping that Dutch linguistics and literature departments at universities in the Netherlands offer courses in 'diachronic linguistics', in which these changes are the topic of investigation. Many great works of seventeenth-, eighteenth- and nineteenth-century Dutch literature have to be translated into modern Dutch to make them accessible to the average reader, to whom eighteenth-century Dutch – and I do not exaggerate – seems almost like a foreign tongue, as exotic and indecipherable as Hindi.

Consequently, even cultured Dutch readers generally pay mere lip service to their country's literary canon. In secondary school, we are introduced – however briefly – to the leading literary lights of our Golden Age, Joost van den Vondel and P. C. Hooft, but only a small number of academics are still equipped to read Vondel's play *Lucifer* in its original form. By now, it has been through at least four rounds of translation and modernization.

Even nineteenth-century Dutch authors are now drifting away into the abstract, inaccessible backwaters of the canon, at the same time that Dutch readers have a wide choice of recently translated nineteenth-century stories and novels by great writers in major world languages, such as de Maupassant, Tolstoy, Dostoevsky, Flaubert and Henry James. A new Dutch translation of Joyce's *Ulysses*, published in 2014, received more publicity and attracted more readers than a new edition of a Dutch masterpiece, Multatuli's *Max Havelaar* (1860), about an eccentric loner's battle against the corrupt colonial regime in the Dutch East Indies.

The growing impenetrability of our own canon, combined with a long-established interest in classic literature in major world languages, has unmistakably influenced our image of our own literary culture. In fact, many Dutch readers have almost completely lost touch with our own classics. Fortunately, however, there is still a widespread awareness that our literary tradition measures up to those of the most influential and widely spoken world languages. The world knows about our windmills, our footballers and our drugs policies (no longer as libertarian as they once were), and the Dutch literati are especially proud of our world-famous artists, such as Vermeer, Rembrandt, Van Gogh, Mondrian and Marlene Dumas. Their importance is universally recognized, and the canon of Dutch art is integral to Western art history. Our literature likewise merits recognition as an integral part of world literary history.

Only about twenty-five years ago, when the Netherlands and Flanders were the Guest of Honour at the Frankfurt Book Fair, did a relatively large number of Dutch-language novels begin to be published in translation elsewhere in Europe. Since then, many books have been translated by major authors such as Cees Nooteboom, Margriet de Moor, Harry Mulisch, W. F.

Hermans, Arnon Grunberg, Leon de Winter and Connie Palmen, most of whom have a short story in this collection.

Leading German newspaper *Die Welt* comments, 'How is it
possible that, until now, we never discovered the élan and
esprit of literature from the country next door? In comparison
with the average German author, Dutch writers are bundles of
energy, life and healthy curiosity about the world around them.
We have to make do with writers who fill page after page with
their own little lives and problems, spelled out in excruciating
detail, while *they* write with such freshness and agility that
they seem to be in the thick of life. In Dutch novels, we find
characters who give every impression of being real people,
down to the innermost layers of their personalities, rather than
mouthpieces for grandiloquent effusions. These true-to-life
characters inhabit a dynamic society, and in many novels that
society is unmistakably part of a larger world, a world of tur-
bulence and unfathomable diversity that infiltrates the literary
sphere. Dutch writers place their characters in settings that do
justice to the social, political and personal dynamics which
keep our lives in constant transformation. Here in Germany,
literature seems to have gone rigid; Dutch literature, on the
other hand, is in flux and ferment. Personal fascinations and
obsessions blend seamlessly into sketches of times and places,
leaving room for ambiguity and, in the words of one of the
greatest Dutch writers since the Second World War, magnifying the riddle of our lives, partly thanks to the irresistible
stylistic ingenuity and tremendous eagerness with which Dutch
writers dare to tell stories and conjure up images.'

In the United States, John Updike called *The Assault* by
Harry Mulisch (1927–2010) 'a perfect novel'. The book describes
a German raid during the Second World War in the city of
Haarlem, North Holland, and its impact on the neighbourhood over a period of decades. Updike's review opens with the
words: 'The chance of birth gives a writer his language; if the
language is a small one, like Dutch . . . the writer must be more
than merely good to receive international attention.' Updike
continued to follow Mulisch's career after this first review, and
he commented on the novel *Last Call*: 'Mulisch is a rarity for

these times – an instinctive psychological novelist . . . He builds his plots with a dense architecture.' When authors such as J. M. Coetzee and Milan Kundera followed in Updike's footsteps, publishing essays on Dutch novels in translation, it forever changed the one-sided conversation that Dutch writers had always held with the rest of the world. Finally, the world was talking back. This was the start of a modest literary dialogue, and the Netherlands earned a place on the map as a literary hot spot.

An even more crucial step in the dissemination of Dutch literature in a growing number of languages was the enthusiasm of the illustrious Polish-German critic Marcel Reich-Ranicki for the novel *The Following Story* by Cees Nooteboom (b. 1933), part of the same generation as Mulisch: 'This book made a deep impression on me, and I deeply regret having overlooked, and not read, all of Nooteboom's books until now. He is a very important European author, and this is one of the most important books, perhaps the most important book, that I have read in years . . . The book touched me deeply . . . I recommend it because it is true literature . . . I like to talk about false bottoms, the hallmark of literature, and here we find a false bottom, here are literature and poetry. I am deeply impressed with this Nooteboom; look, the Dutch, too, have an author like this!' These words of praise were followed by many translations of *The Following Story*.

The international praise for Mulisch and Nooteboom opened the way for translations of novels by younger writers from Marcel Möring to Connie Palmen, and from the above-mentioned Tommy Wieringa to Arnon Grunberg. But while increasing numbers of Dutch novels are available to readers in major world languages, our eloquence in another literary genre, the short story, remains more or less undiscovered. Some critics in the Netherlands believe that three great Dutch writers of the past century – F. Bordewijk, Willem Frederik Hermans and Harry Mulisch – are at the peak of their ability in their short stories, showing their most radical sides. Their radicalism finds expression in their stylistic experiments and fanciful forms, the joyous anarchy of their narrative voices, their blend of taut description and slippery surrealism, and their mastery of that vital technique of the short story: namely, omission.

Some of our greatest short-story writers seem to have felt the need to apologize for working in this genre. Remco Campert (b. 1929), another Dutch master of the short story (and a well-loved poet), once said in an interview: 'I'm not sure the novel is really in my system. My only ambition has been to write good stories, in the tradition of F. Scott Fitzgerald or Truman Capote.' As if it were a trivial matter to craft a tale in the tradition of those two authors. Campert is not only one of our greatest but also one of our most modest writers, and would never make sweeping claims about himself. So others, like me, have to make them on his behalf: Campert's body of work can hold its own against either Scott Fitzgerald or Capote. Campert's stories now cover a period of five decades, and some of them convey a subtle sense of historical period: while Fitzgerald is the icon of America's Roaring Twenties, Campert is the great chronicler of the oppressive Dutch climate of the 1950s and the country's sexual and social 'liberation' in the 1960s and '70s, and his stories track the sometimes rocky development of Dutch sexual and social mores. Yet at the same time his style is a miracle of clarity, nothing short of timeless. Campert's evocations of time and place always cover up the same underlying dynamics of slight psychological shifts and subtle social relationships. Campert is the master of finely honed observation, of dialogue whose natural sound conceals its ingenious refinement. Of all the writers mentioned here, Campert may be Nescio's most gifted heir. In any case, his idiom is deceptive in its simplicity; it will be a long time before the language of his stories needs updating. 'The Kid with the Knife', included in this anthology, shows that Campert, like Fitzgerald and Capote, is capable of evoking an atmosphere and historical setting that can keep the entire story aloft. 'The Kid with the Knife' also contains one of the finest opening sentences in the history of the Dutch short story: 'You only had to snap your fingers and it was party-time.' That sentence is followed by a quick, atmospheric sketch that brings to life that age of unbridled festivity. In a single compact and lyrical image, Campert underlines its sublime nonchalance: 'At 3 a.m. anything was possible: you could do a handstand on a genever bottle.' But in the same opening sentences, he also recalls the dark side of that epoch of euphoria and intoxication: 'Your thoughts had disintegrated into isolated words – key words, which you kept on mumbling, because you were afraid you would cease to exist if you forgot these words as well.' Light-hearted whimsy and a subtle portrait of fear in two brief opening paragraphs – and then Campert spins his story of the boy who brought a knife to a party, twisting together strands of comedy and tragedy, conveying both the whimsy and the fear, and never letting on to his readers whether he's drawing them into a sunny or a sinister tale.

Jorge Luis Borges called the short story 'the essential form of writing', and he lent his name to one of the two types of stories identified by the American critic Harold Bloom: the Chekhovian story and the Borgesian story. (Obviously, the other variety is named after Anton Chekhov.) Bloom argued that Chekhovian stories begin fairly abruptly and end without a plot, and that they refer directly to a familiar reality. According to Bloom, Borgesian stories emphasize, above all, that they are linguistic constructs bearing no direct relationship to reality.

The miraculous thing about many Dutch short stories is that they combine the best of both genres. Belcampo wrote hundreds of stories that begin in a Chekhovian mode, rooted (loosely, at least) in the realities of Dutch life, only to branch out into a mix of magical realism and burlesque surrealism. Their most distinctive feature is the self-referential use of language, which was also the trademark of the *Revisor* generation. This group, which emerged in the 1970s, was named after the literary magazine in which its members published (which in turn was named after a short story by Gogol). All four of them – A. F. Th. van der Heijden, Frans Kellendonk, Oek de Jong and Nicolaas Matsier – have stories in the present anthology.

Frans Kellendonk summed up the literary credo of the

Revisor group: 'When we tell a story, we hold the form of that story, the form of the communication, up for debate, so that the reader knows what he is reading and can therefore remain critical.' This point of view incensed writers like Maarten 't Hart, who became embroiled in a ferocious debate with the *Revisor* writers. 't Hart, the leading exponent of the neo-naturalistic Dutch story, called the *Revisor* stories 'chandeliers that won't light up'. So here we find at least a temporary dividing line between Dutch writers of Borgesian and Chekhovian stories.

But as I mentioned, many other writers have no regard for that dividing line, instead combining the best of both genres. For example, Harry Mulisch once said that his stories always 'begin somewhere in the real world and always end somewhere else'. That is undeniably true of the Mulisch story in this volume, 'What Happened to Sergeant Massuro?', about a soldier who undergoes a gradual metamorphosis. From its Chekhovian beginning, the story shifts into a purely Borgesian mode, in which dream and waking, hallucination and reality, seem to flow into one another.

'What Happened to Sergeant Massuro?' is set in New Guinea, and contrary to the old misconception that Dutch literature is inward-looking and set within our national borders, many of these stories unfold outside the Netherlands. 'Green', by A. Alberts, for instance, takes place on an unnamed island in the Indies. The settings of Arnon Grunberg's stories (both fiction and non-fiction) vary widely, from Hungary to Afghanistan and from Berlin to New York. 'Glass', by Willem Frederik Hermans, is situated in post-war Germany and may represent the confluence of the Chekhovian and Borgesian traditions; it begins as a realistic narrative in a hospital ward for wounded soldiers, but winds up as a surreal tale of suspense, characteristic of early work by Hermans, who began his career as a writer of short stories that were equal parts surrealism and nihilism.

We often find indications in Dutch short stories that the authors are in conversation, both stylistically and compositionally, with kindred spirits who worked in other languages.

Remco Campert mentioned Capote and Fitzgerald. Emants felt a bond with Zola and Turgenev. Mensje van Keulen shows a similar family connection to the prose of Patricia Highsmith and Flannery O'Connor. Nicolaas Matsier's story 'The Minnema Variations' plays with reality and imagination in a lucid manner reminiscent of Italo Calvino. Maarten 't Hart has frequently pointed out his affinity with Anthony Trollope. Arnon Grunberg, who couches the relentless darkness of his world view in deceptively chirpy prose, has been tipped in the Netherlands as the great successor to Hermans, who referred to his own literary approach as 'creative nihilism'. Grunberg himself, although clearly influenced by Hermans' early novels, has repeatedly suggested that his work can also (or even primarily) be read as a dialogue, and sometimes a debate, with the oeuvre of J. M. Coetzee. Sanneke van Hassel's stories reflect the formative literary influence of the generation of American authors known as dirty realists: Raymond Carver, Richard Ford and Tobias Wolff. The youngest author in this anthology is Joost de Vries, who has been heralded on the Dutch literary scene as 'the new Mulisch'. De Vries, an author and critic, fashions his stories with a playfulness and an interest in formal experimentation reminiscent of his generation's most idiosyncratic American writer: David Foster Wallace.

Almost all the authors in this collection have similar ties to authors working in major languages, ties which are essential to their creative process. It is rare for Dutch writers to place themselves in a strictly Dutch tradition; their literary horizons almost always lie beyond the bounds of their language and nation.

Of all the contributors to this anthology, Maarten Biesheuvel may take his kinship with foreign authors to the most radical extreme. Biesheuvel's stories are elusive, irresistible nonsense arias, both ludicrous and filled with despair, and the literary universe that they paint is unique to its very core. Although Biesheuvel is as Dutch as writers come, he also holds a literary passport from nineteenth-century Russia, a supernatural connection to three authors – Gogol, Chekhov and Dostoevsky – whom he has described as reincarnated and peacefully co-existing within himself. This may seem like an awfully self-aggrandizing statement. But if you read one of Biesheuvel's stories, you will realize that statements like these are inseparable from the unique music of his nonsense arias.

What, other than length, distinguishes a short story from a novel? One major characteristic that separates the two is that many short stories offer a place of refuge, a sanctuary, for fictional loners, for eccentrics, hermits and outcasts, for incorrigible fantasists, vintage nutcases, introverts, reclusive dreamers, darkly romantic criminals and other misfits. The American writer Frank O'Connor felt that this was a vital aspect of the genre, so much so that in 1962 he called his classic study of the American short story *The Lonely Voice*.

This lonely voice addresses the reader not as an ally, but as a sounding board who, in reading, creates the setting for the voice. Short stories thus demand a more active form of reading than do novels. While a novel reader always expects to be rewarded for his or her tendency to identify with the main character – the mark of a philistine, Nabokov tells us – the reader of a short story must be prepared to fill in the details of the world left out by the writer for lack of space. This is because an effective short story often relies on the hint, the open question, the missing link. The story is embedded in a larger textual world created by the reader, based on bits of information carefully meted out by the author. While the novelist fills in, making the reader's job as easy as possible, the author of a short story rubs out, leaving all sorts of work for the reader to do.

Milan Kundera has written, 'Novelists draw up the map of existence by discovering this or that human possibility.' A short story presents a scrap, a shred of that 'map of existence'. And it is not the writer's task, but the reader's, to draw the entire map, with nothing more to go on than that small slip of paper.

I have mentioned that in remarkably many short stories, these shreds of the map of human existence are extended to us by 'a lonely voice', a misunderstood outsider. This is a second prompt to readers to use their own imagination, first of all by asking the question, 'Whose voice am I hearing in this story?' Often, the author does not supply a straightforward, neatly packaged answer. How unreliable is the narrator in the average short story? Far more unreliable than the main characters in plenty of novels; that much is clear.

On the fundamental shiftiness of many 'I'-figures in short stories, D. H. Lawrence wrote, 'Trust the tale, not the teller.' In this anthology, many a narrator is troubled by a feverish brain. Is the poet Minnema, in Matsier's 'The Minnema Variations', right to suspect that he does not really exist, that he's merely the puppet of a nightmarish being with whom he carries on a correspondence, real or dreamed? Is the poet Minnema *writing*, or *being written*? This question fills Minnema with an existential horror that drives him to the brink of madness.

Again, madness. While it forms the very fabric of Maarten Biesheuvel's writing, madness also plays a role in many other stories, from Emants's 'An Eccentric' to Grunberg's 'Someone Else'. Hallucinations, the fear of insanity, an overheated intellect, *la folie*, a short circuit in the brain – elements like these set the tone and form the marrow of numerous stories in this collection.

Dutch writers frequently explore the vague borderland between delusion and reality, often sketching the disturbing process of delusion eating away at those borders and ultimately conquering the entire territory. In this respect, Nescio's celebrated story 'Young Titans' may form the blueprint for the characteristic, half-mad Dutch short story. One of the characters most cherished by Dutch readers of 'Young Titans' is the painter Bavink, who ends up in an asylum after failing to achieve his dream. Bavink's simple, innocent ambition also happens to be extravagant and practically unattainable: he wants to paint the sun on a piece of painters' linen. Not an image of the sun, or an imagined sun, but the sun itself. This ideal, as I said, is both naive and arrogant: to succeed, wouldn't Bavink have to unseat God from his throne? Incidentally, the God we encounter in 'Young Titans' is no Old Testament tyrant, but something more like a Buddha adapted to fit pragmatic Dutch notions of give-and-take, a 'lonely voice' from an unknowable reality, a voice of detachment that offers the young men in this story a Zen-like state of Being. 'Young Titans', as I mentioned, dates from the early twentieth century, and its spiritual dimension is anything but sappy and sentimental – subversive and surreptitious would be more accurate. The 'Young Titans' are fundamentally Dutch cousins of the two good buddies in Kerouac's *On the Road*, except that Nescio's young men embark on their journey without actually lifting a finger. In perfect repose, they hurtle through the heavens at high speed. If *that* doesn't open the door to madness just a sliver . . .

In the mental institution, Bavink often sits staring into the sun for so long that his eyes start to burn. The nurses tell him not to stare at the sun, but that doesn't stop him. 'Do you understand what the sun wants from me?' Bavink asks his old friend Koekebakker.

What does the sun want from me?

The average cool-headed, calculating Dutchman is immune to the power of this High Romantic question. But to Bavink, it seems only natural that the sun wants something from him – he just doesn't know what. His question, in all its compact force, may exemplify the most striking ambition of the short stories in this anthology: to capture the world of madness in words. To give a voice to madness. To show madness itself, lurking beneath the surface of the story. To embody madness in language. Just as Bavink wanted to show the sun itself, on canvas.

Joost Zwagerman
Haarlem, September 2014

Translated by David McKay

Chronology

1588 Founding of the Republic of the Seven United Netherlands. The States General are the decision-making body and the government is led by a grand pensionary, while military leadership is in the hands of a stadtholder. Although it has been seven years since the Spanish king was deposed under the Act of Abjuration, the war with Spain has not abated. Calvinism is gaining ground at the expense of the Catholic Church.

1602 Establishment of the East India Company, a shipping company set up by the States General to coordinate the lucrative trade with the Far East.

1612 The first sizeable polder to be drained is the Beemster, by means of forty-three windmills.

1621 Establishment of the West India Company for trade with North and South America.

1626 Publication of a collection of political songs, entitled *Dutch Sounds of Remembrance* (*Nederlandtsche gedenck-clanck*), of which one, 'The Wilhelmus', will later become the Dutch national anthem.

1637 Publication of the States Bible (Statenbijbel), which will remain the official bible translation of the Reformed Church until 2010, exercising a powerful influence on the standardization of the Dutch language.

1638 First performance of the play *Gijsbrecht van Aemstel*, written by the country's most important tragedian, Joost van den Vondel. It is traditionally performed on New Year's Day in the Amsterdam Schouwburg.

1642 Rembrandt completes *The Night Watch*.

1648 Peace of Münster. After eighty years of war, Spain recognizes the Republic as a sovereign state.

1654 Performance of Vondel's tragedy *Lucifer*, about the fall of the archangel. The play is banned after three performances.

1655 Completion of the Town Hall on Dam Square in Amsterdam by architect Jacob van Campen. Amsterdam is now the most important mercantile city in the world. It has more than 100,000 inhabitants.

1672 'Disaster Year', with the start of the Third Anglo-Dutch War (1672–1674) as well as declarations of war against the Republic by France and by two German bishoprics.

1677 Death of Spinoza. Publication of *Ethics, Demonstrated in Geometrical Order* (*Ethica, ordine geometrico demonstrata*), about his pantheist worldview in which God is equated with nature. A ban follows, but the treatise is distributed across Europe and becomes hugely influential, as do Spinoza's other writings. This is regarded as the start of the Radical Enlightenment.

1685 Flight of 70,000 Protestants (Huguenots) from France to the Republic, many intellectuals among them. They integrate with the Dutch and establish their own periodicals.

1689 In the Glorious Revolution, William III, who is married to the daughter of James II, king of England, becomes the Dutch stadtholder, remaining so until his death.

1691 Balthasar Bekker writes *The World Bewitched* (*De Betoverde Weereld*), in which he maintains that witches and devils do not exist.

1697 Tsar Peter the Great of Russia arrives in the Republic to learn shipbuilding.

1775 Start of the American War of Independence. The Americans receive financial support from the Dutch Republic. Their Declaration of Independence is inspired by the Republic's Act of Abjuration of 1581.

1781 In the night of 25 September, anonymous pamphlets are distributed across the Dutch Republic entitled *To the People of the Netherlands* (*Aan het Volk van Nederland*), in which the population is urged to rebel against the politics of the stadtholder and his regents. The Patriot movement arises, made up of citizens who, based on Enlightenment ideas, want greater involvement in politics. Society becomes divided between the Orangists (loyal to the stadtholder) and the Patriots.

1782 Publication of the epistolary novel *The History of Miss Sara Burgerhart* (*De historie van Mejuffrouw Sara Burgerhart*) by Betje Wolff and Aagje Deken. It is the first Dutch novel to focus on the middle classes.

1784 Foundation of the Society for Public Welfare, which aspires to spread Enlightenment ideas through a system of schools, libraries, readings, school textbooks and debates. The aim is to abolish social evils and cultivate good citizenship.

1785 The Patriots take power in several cities. The stadtholder flees The Hague and withdraws to his summer palaces.

1787 The wife of the stadtholder, sister to Frederick William II, king of Prussia, is detained and held by Patriots on her way to The Hague. At her request a Prussian army comes to the aid of the Orangists and defeats the Patriots. Many Patriots are imprisoned or flee to France.

1789 Start of the French Revolution.

1793 France declares war on the Republic, where the stadtholder is William V.

1795 Since the rivers are frozen, the French army is able to advance into the northern Low Countries, with the help of returning Patriots. The country becomes a vassal state to France. Stadtholder William V flees to England. The Batavian Republic is established.

1797 Appointment at the University of Leiden of the first professor responsible for the teaching of the Dutch language and rhetoric, Matthijs Siegenbeek.

1798 Introduction of the first Dutch constitution, the *Staatsregeling voor het Bataafsche Volk*.

1806 Emperor Napoleon of France appoints his brother Louis Napoleon as the first king of Holland. Through his brother, Napoleon wishes to exert greater influence over the country.

1810 Louis Napoleon is deposed by his brother for being too favourably inclined towards the Dutch. Napoleon turns the Dutch kingdom into a province of France.

1813 After the Battle of Leipzig, Napoleon's power is broken. A Russian army arrives to help liberate the Dutch. The stadtholder has meanwhile died, but his son returns from England and declares himself sovereign prince of the United Netherlands.

1814 The Congress of Vienna decides to unite the Southern Netherlands with the Northern Netherlands to form a strong buffer state against France.

1815 William I becomes king of the United Netherlands and introduces a new constitution.

1816 The Dutch East Indies becomes the official name for all the Dutch colonies in the Malay Archipelago. Dutch is made their official language.

1830 The Belgian Revolution. The southern provinces of the United Kingdom of the Netherlands rise in revolt against the policies of King William I, forming an independent Belgium.

1837 Establishment of De Gids, the first fully-fledged Dutch literary magazine.

1839 The Netherlands' first railway is built, from Amsterdam to Haarlem.

1848 Introduction of a new constitution that limits the power of the king and turns the Netherlands into a constitutional monarchy.

1859 Under the pseudonym Multatuli, Eduard Douwes Dekker writes the novel Max Havelaar, which denounces colonial abuses in the Dutch East Indies. Max Havelaar has since become one of the most translated novels of Dutch literature.

1863 The Law on Secondary Education introduces a new type of school, the Higher Civic School, to train children for senior positions in trade and industry.

1871 Aletta Jacobs becomes the first woman to be admitted to a Dutch university (Groningen).

1874 Samuel van Houten's Child Protection Law bans child labour before the age of twelve.

1885 Establishment of *De Nieuwe Gids*, an important and innovative literary magazine, featuring writers and artists who are adherents of naturalism, impressionism and symbolism.

1885 Opening of the Rijksmuseum in Amsterdam.

1890 Suicide of Vincent van Gogh. In 1888 he painted his famous *Sunflowers*.

1890 Publication of Louis Couperus's debut novel, the naturalistic *Eline Vere*, which has a powerful impact on readers and is much translated and reprinted. Couperus is said to have been one of the most frequently read authors of the period.

1894 Establishment of the Social Democratic Workers' Party. Support for the socialist movement had been increasing for several years.

1899 The first international peace conference is held in The Hague. The decision is made to establish a Permanent Court of Arbitration, to be based in The Hague. American philanthropist Andrew Carnegie finances the building of the Peace Palace, which is completed in 1913.

1900 Education is made compulsory for children aged six to twelve.

1914 Start of the First World War. The Netherlands pursues a policy of neutrality. A million Belgian refugees find temporary refuge in the Netherlands.

1917 Establishment of the modernist periodical *De Stijl*. Those involved include Theo van Doesburg, Piet Mondrian and Gerrit Rietveld. Their aim is the complete overthrow of traditional art.

1919 Historian Johan Huizinga writes *The Waning of the Middle Ages* (*Herfsttij der Middeleeuwen*), a book that soon meets with worldwide acclaim.

1935 The last building by architect H. P. Berlage is completed, the Municipal Museum (Gemeentemuseum) in The Hague. Berlage combines the notion of a synthesis of the arts with a modernist style.

1940 German troops invade the Netherlands, which capitulates after the heavy bombing of Rotterdam.

1941 Establishment of the Dutch Chamber of Culture (Kultuur-kamer). Writers and artists must become members of the Chamber before they are allowed to publish or exhibit their work. They are required to declare themselves in agreement with National Socialism.

1944 Piet Mondrian dies in New York before completing his abstract *Victory Boogie-Woogie*, in which he attempts to distil music and painting into blocks of colour. It will become one of his most famous canvases.

1945 End of the Second World War.

1947 The father of Anne Frank, who died in the concentration camp Bergen-Belsen, publishes her diary of her years spent in hiding (1942–4), under the title *Het achterhuis*, 'The Annexe'.

1947 Gerard van het Reve publishes *The Evenings* (*De avonden*), regarded as the most important novel about the atmosphere prevailing among young people immediately after the war.

1948 Surrealist-expressionist painters from Copenhagen, Brussels and Amsterdam form the group CoBrA. Its Dutch representatives, Constant, Karel Appel and Corneille, are joined by poets who will later become famous as the Vijfti-gers, writing spontaneous, free verse. The leading figure among them is Lucebert.

1949 The Netherlands recognizes the independence of Indonesia, four years after the colony declared itself independent in 1945.

1951 First Dutch television broadcast.

1953 Flooding in the province of Zeeland causes 1,835 deaths (in fact 1,836 – one newborn child drowned before its birth could be registered).

1956 The cabinet under Willem Drees introduces the General Old-Age Law, giving all citizens the right to a pension from the age of sixty-five.

1958 Publication of *The Darkroom of Damocles* (*De donkere kamer van Damokles*), the most highly regarded novel by prominent author Willem Frederik Hermans, about appearance and reality during the Second World War.

1966 A turbulent year, especially in Amsterdam, with the Provo movement and the start of student protests.

1969 Formation of Dolle Mina, a women's emancipation movement. Meanwhile Aktie Tomaat and Aktie Notenkraker protest against the conservative repertoire of theatre companies and orchestras.

1982 Publication of *The Assault* (*De Aanslag*) by Harry Mulisch, the book that will make him one of the most translated of Dutch authors.

1985 The Schengen Agreement abolishes border controls between European countries.

2000 Paul Scheffer writes 'The Multicultural Drama' (*'Het multiculturele drama'*), an article in which he foresees the creation of an underclass of second-generation immigrants who will not integrate and will become radicalized.

2001 Same-sex marriage is recognized in law.

2002 The euro replaces the guilder.

2004 Murder of writer and filmmaker Theo van Gogh by a Muslim extremist.

2005 Establishment of the Party for Freedom by Geert Wilders, which will enter the Lower House of parliament for the first time in 2006. The party attracts a great deal of attention and represents a large number of dissatisfied voters, marking a turn towards intolerance and the extreme right in Dutch politics.

2009 Publication of *De Nederlandse en Vlaamse Literatuur vanaf 1880 in 250 verhalen*, a 1,600-page anthology by Joost Zwagerman, hailed by the Dutch press as 'a monumental publication' (*NRC Handelsblad*) and a 'treasure trove' (*Het Parool*).

2015 Suicide of author Joost Zwagerman, a leading figure among a new generation of writers of Dutch literature in the 1990s as well as an essayist and compiler of anthologies of Dutch literature, including this Penguin anthology.

THE PENGUIN BOOK OF
DUTCH SHORT STORIES

I

MARCELLUS EMANTS

An Eccentric

Een zonderling

Z. was sketched at a debating table in the club. So it is possible he never existed. But the description was as follows: according to Z. creation was an insane act of the Absolute, as a result of which we are doomed to live in absurdity, act in absurdity, endure absurdity. Z. does not trumpet that doctrine about. On the contrary. Usually he refuses to speak about it; he is almost never talkative. As a result Z. has no friends and only very rarely comes into contact with his acquaintances. Many people therefore consider him a fool, an ass or a poseur; but those unwilling to judge from a distance and by appearances do not believe that Z. deserves such an unfavourable judgement. There are also those who see him as a brilliant thinker who unfortunately lacks sufficient ambition to publicize his ideas. That he is an eccentric, no one denies, and in the empty streets of the quiet town he lives in, Z. cannot venture out of his house without being the target of jokes, or at least giving rise to a conversation. The greengrocer, giggling all the while, tells the kitchen maid who opens the door to him that he has just seen that old duffer with his big floppy hat and his eternal raincoat. The schoolboy asks his classmates who on earth that man is, who always walks alone and looks straight ahead as if he is furious. The visitor to the club enquires of his fellow members: what kind of individual is Z., what does he do and what does he live on? With his long beard and long hair he looks like a street preacher; but he never preaches.

There are also those who classify Z. among the deaf mutes.

The truth is that Z., who ekes out a poor living from a small capital sum, does nothing, wants nothing and that most people cannot imagine such an existence, while for Z. this way of life is the only way of acting with as little absurdity as possible, of spreading as little absurdity as possible and having as little bother from absurdity as possible. So – someone once said to Z. – you are a philosopher. However, Z. denied this as firmly as possible. Of all the absurd people – and according to him no one living is entirely free of absurdity – he calls philosophers the most absurd of all, as they try to make sense of nonsense, which is impossible anyway.

Z. seldom allows himself to be talked into giving a more extensive exposition of his view of life. If things get that far, he begins as follows: What is the first thing that a newly born human does? Suck. Why does it do that? To stay alive. Now isn't it absurd that someone who knows nothing of life in general and in particular does not know whether his own life will turn out to his taste, still immediately wants to maintain that life? And human beings, who are and remain blind to the future, continue with that absurdity until the last ounce of vitality in them is used up. If he can no longer see or hear virtually anything and no longer has any limb of his body properly under control, if he, from morn till night and often all night long, has nothing more to do but suffer pain and endure misery, he still tries to prolong his dreadful existence with all kinds of remedies. Isn't that absurd? Isn't it also absurd that we condemn, abhor or lament suicides – the only truly sensible people?

And what does a person do as soon as he gains the least bit of awareness of a world around him? Play. Isn't that absurd too? He wraps a rope around the arm of a chair, sits behind it with a whip in his hand and imagines that, in a horse-drawn carriage, he is making headway. Not nonsense? He rocks dolls in his arm, dresses them, gives them food and drink and pretends they are children. Not nonsense? When he has grown a little older, he has to cram his head full of thousands of so-called useful facts, which he will never bother about later or call them incorrect and discard by the time when he might have use for them. It must be said to man's credit that in his youth he himself finds this extremely absurd and only does it ... because older fools, i.e. foolish parents, force him to, for fear of cultivating a generation that would in an unbiased way see the absurdity of all this. But before he has finished his studies, he immerses himself in the greatest possible absurdity when he falls in love and wants to marry. Love! Our senseless art lives on it; but I ask you: can anything crazier be conceived than love? Look around where you will and you will see that people do not differ greatly, either outwardly or inwardly. Apart from a few hunchbacks, freaks, rare abnormalities and great criminals ... and even in them the human type can be easily recognized ... individuals display only minor physical and mental differences. Yet a person in love suddenly hits on the insane idea that one being, of whom he did not even suspect the existence yesterday, is in all respects inwardly and outwardly an ideal, elevated high above all beings of the same species. And in order to show his stupidity clearly, he presumes to claim a kind of right of possession over that idea. He can no longer imagine his own existence separately from that other being, and dreams of the most wonderful delights if only he can be united with it for his whole life. All that this other possesses: eyes, nose, mouth, hands, indeed, even those parts he has not yet seen, make him swoon with rapture and without a trace or shadow of proof, he ascribes to the one he adores all the qualities of mind and heart, which in daily life qualify as beautiful, noble and good. That a person is not responsible for his actions in this period of confusion is generally recognized; but no one realizes that love must be seen only as a temporary intensification of the enduring malady: vitality.

Once married – in other words, given possession of the object of his crazy affection – he does everything possible to increase the burdens and pains of his life, although he constantly bewails those burdens and pains. He also maintains that those burdens and pains have been imposed on him, for the sake of his moral improvement, an improvement which those around him may enjoy but he himself never could. He mainly achieves this increase of burdens and pains by producing children, who continue his madness, who torment and taunt him with it, while they cannot yet stand on their own two feet and leave him to his own devices as soon as he expects recompense from them for all he has spent on their upbringing and all he has endured for their sake. If only this stupid longing brought him to the point of buying or renting them! Then at least he would be able to assess what he gained. But that would not be absurd enough. A woman who refuses to buy the smallest item of merchandise without having felt it first and tested it for durability does not shrink at all from braving the most appalling pains to have children, though it is completely uncertain whether they will be affected with the most dreadful disorders of body and mind. And both parents love these creatures before they have ever seen them. They would not sacrifice a single guilder to a lottery of millions of duds and a single prize; but they give up the relative quiet, the relative freedom and the relatively carefree existence of the whole of the rest of their life with the greatest frivolity for the highly problematic chance of being able to enjoy a small amount of pleasure from their children.

And while the wife is occupied with the children, the husband toils and sweats to demolish what their predecessors built up and to produce new works for his fellow men, which his successors will in turn destroy just as contemptuously. Unless those works are themselves not completed and no one cares any longer for the decaying piles of rubble. That a man is actually envied during this labour by idiots, who are even sicker than he is, is still belittled and disparaged by those just as crazy, who perceive only the sickness of their fellow man and not their own malady, he himself sees only a necessary evil native to all labour, and in his blindness he curses the do-nothings, who, slightly less crazy than he, have asked themselves: why should I shoulder all those burdens; isn't it bad enough to have to be alive? If the worker receives from the government – which he of course hates, because no one wants to be ruled – a patch of ribbon in his buttonhole as an honour and a reward . . . then he proves . . . the man who laughs at other people's decorations . . . not one jot more sensible than in his childhood, when seated on a wooden hobby horse, he imagined that the nanny took him for a general.

Oh, Z. would then conclude, consider frenzied human activity where you like and if you are not too intoxicated by the delusions of a crazy life instinct, you'll see the insanity of it all soon enough. Look, for example, at how human beings constantly fight against the maladies that undermine them and at the same time do their best to keep the sick alive, by whom those maladies are perpetuated. Listen to them eternally arguing and proving, although they admit they know nothing. See how they honour truth as something sacred, and constantly lie to and cheat each other on a small and a grand scale. Notice how everyone is praised after his death, but is disparaged, thwarted and even persecuted during his lifetime. Consider that people regard earthly life as the most valuable thing they possess, the sine qua non for enjoying everything else, and consider how frivolously they behave with that life, risk reckless adventures, shorten it through their behaviour, sacrifice it for figments of the imagination like a love, the fatherland or honour. Wherever you look, you see absurdity, nothing but absurdity, and it's just as well that man is finally coming to realize that. Many years ago we began treating the worst criminals as insane; in our age we are considering setting up so-called asylums for degenerates, and it may not be long before the whole of society is constructed on the model of a gigantic madhouse with a system of wards.

Probably this will herald a period of relative happiness for mankind; but for as long as human beings try to introduce sense into nonsense their work is inevitably doomed to failure.

When the narrator finished telling them about this philosophy of Z.'s, most members of the debating table could not come up with a better response than a pitying or contemptuous laugh. However, one said: What the man is maintaining is not as daft as all that. Whoever admits that he is insane undoubtedly is and whoever doesn't admit it is probably already too insane to see his situation. The others' view of this one speaker was: another madman.

Translated by Paul Vincent

2

LOUIS COUPERUS
The Opera Glasses

De binocle

It was about five years ago in Dresden that a young tourist, a
Dutch Eurasian journalist, a bright chap, of a slightly nervous
disposition, very mild-tempered despite his tropical blood,
bought a ticket for the opera one morning, for a seat in the
front row of the fourth tier, to hear *The Valkyrie*. At the time
the fourth tier was where all the foreigners who could not
afford the luxury of a box of their own sat; indeed, even those
who could often preferred the fourth tier to the third or
the second, though the abyss of the wide auditorium opened
up between that tier and the stage. It was a splendid day; the
parks were clad in golden leaves; a sweet sense of *joie de vivre*
floated through the ample sky and the young tourist, in his
melancholy-tinged loneliness, was happy to wander through
the beautiful city, walk into a museum, have lunch in a sum-
merhouse somewhere by the sun-drenched waters of the Elbe.
And he had the happy expectation of hearing *The Valkyrie* that
evening, an opera he did not know, for which he reproached
himself, adoring Wagner as he did.

The hours passed without him speaking to a soul except the
waitress and the tram conductor. He had a cup of tea and a
bite to eat, since as the opera began very early he knew there
would be no time to dine. And then, satisfied and gently,
quietly happy, as was his nature, he walked calmly – he had
plenty of time – to the Opera House. A few shops in Prager-
strasse were already closing for the day and he saw an optician
instructing his assistant to put up the shutters in front of the
window, when he remembered that he didn't have any opera

glasses. It occurred to him in a flash that the fourth tier, where he had often sat, at the back, was a long way from the stage and that opera glasses would come in handy. He also reflected that he had had a cheap day and that his seat cost only three marks and now his eye happened to catch that of the optician on the lookout for custom, he waved to him, as if by inspiration, hastened his step and called out, while still on the pavement:

'Is the shop closed? Do I still have time to buy some opera glasses?'

Grinning good-naturedly the tall, thin optician nodded and motioned to him to enter the already half-darkened shop. And scarcely had the tourist got inside when it flashed through his mind that he was making a mistake, and would be better advised to leave the shop, as the face of the shopkeeper was like an unpleasant bird mask. But the flash was so quick, unmotivated and vague that it did not penetrate his logical consciousness. So the young man stayed and went on:

'In that case, I'd like some opera glasses, simple ones, not too expensive.' The optician showed him a few and pointed in a laudatory way to their manufacturers' names.

These were too small, said the young man shyly; being small and delicate himself, he liked large dimensions in personal effects, unconsciously feeling he was making an impression with an outsized handkerchief or gloves that were too big for him.

'Take these, then,' urged the shopkeeper.

'Those are more binoculars for racing,' laughed the tourist. 'They're rather heavy too . . .'

He looked through them for a moment, turning the knob until the lenses were focused. He could see quite clearly into the street.

'I do like them, though,' said the tourist. 'How much are they?'

The price came as a shock. If he bought the opera glasses, it would be an expensive day. But how sharply these glasses brought the street scene into focus!

'All right,' said the tourist, 'I'll take these.'

He paid. And left with the opera glasses in their case. Now he had to hurry. Suddenly he remembered that he had found the optician's birdlike face really unpleasant. But he dismissed that foolish aversion; he frequently had those strange antipathies and sympathies too, and they were often bothersome in everyday life.

Now he made haste. There was the Opera, where the black-silhouetted opera-goers were already streaming across the evening square into the wide illuminated entrances. Nervously, although he knew he was not late, he hurried along, tripped nimbly up the many flights of stairs, while other people laboured, and quickly found his seat, in the front row. He sat down, in happy anticipation of enjoying the music. He took the opera glasses out of their case and placed both in front of him on the wide ledge. Next to him, to left and right, and behind him people were quickly taking their seats: it was filling up as always. Below, too, the tiers of boxes and the stalls were filling up.

Suddenly it struck the young man that the opera glasses might fall into the now dimly lit auditorium and he put them on his knees. The performance began, full of rapt concentration and devotion to Wagner. In the large, full auditorium, besides the huge waves of the music, there was scarcely any sound or movement, scarcely a cough, just a hand holding opera glasses.

The young tourist also trained his opera glasses on Siegmund, whose voice vibrated blissfully through him, in order to bring him closer.

Suddenly, through his pleasure it flashed through him that the auditorium, seen from up there, was an abyss and that the opera glasses were heavy. At the same moment, some distance away, a programme floated down. It distracted him: he saw the programme flutter down and land on the grey, coiffured head of a lady, whose hand had grasped the programme like a bird. Next to the lady sat a gentleman with a shiny bald pate.

But Sieglinde again enchanted the young tourist. The blond Germanic maiden fascinated him, ensnaring his submissive soul in an enchantment of song; he found her touchingly poetic, with Siegmund in Hunding's hut. The opera glasses weighed heavily on his knee. Again he put them on the ledge, above which the black glasses loomed like twin towers. And yet they were safe enough there.

The young man leaned forward, in amused concern, to see who was sitting exactly below him in the auditorium. And who the opera glasses would land on . . . should they fall.

It was a mischievous curiosity, welling around the quick conception of an event that was almost impossible. Since now it had occurred to him that the opera glasses *might* fall, they would not do so.

He could not see clearly who was sitting there, perpendicularly below him. The auditorium was very dark. But precisely because of the darkness in which the outlines of the audience were blurred, he again saw more clearly over there the previously noticed dove-grey lady who had grabbed the fluttering programme. And beside her . . .

His bald pate gleamed. Among the thousands of rapt silhouettes sitting closely together, the coiffured women's heads and the bald-headed men, that distant skull gleamed . . . It gleamed roundly, like an obsessive full moon, sunk among all those darkened figures: attentive backs of heads motionless with concentration. It gleamed like a goal, like a target, it gleamed white, it gleamed . . .

The young tourist was annoyed at his strange distractedness – it bothered him – and forced himself to give his attention to Hunding. He greatly enjoyed the Liebeslied, the brilliant tenor voice, which sang of an outpouring of love and of spring. But he could not forget the shiny pate down there and could not make himself invisible any longer. His distracted gaze kept returning obliquely to the skull, which seemed to be gleaming in the dim light of the auditorium, now as a huge billiard ball!

A spasm of impatience and annoyance at himself went through him. At the same time he grabbed the opera glasses with the sudden panicky feeling that they would fall. And the glasses did not fall, and the hands of the young man gripped the opera glasses more firmly than was necessary . . . And he pointed them at Siegmund and Sieglinde.

Then it was as if he could no longer control it ... As if a powerful imperative was forcing him to hurl the opera glasses high through the abyss of the auditorium, aiming at that alluring globe, that giant billiard ball, the shiny target down there, three-quarters of the distance between himself and the stage ...

In a violent motion of resistance, he threw himself backwards ... And, trembling, he just managed to put down the opera glasses ... The effort was almost too great for him. Then he pressed his arms to his sides. So as not to grab the opera glasses and hurl them at the round target. Which was down there, gleaming.

The lady in the next seat shot him a sideways glance. He reacted to her movement as if it were a motherly act of rescue.

'I do apologize,' he mumbled, pale and half-crazed. 'I don't feel well. I feel really ill. If you'll excuse me, I'd like to leave.'

The first act was coming to an end. He got up; trembling, but without a sound, he slid past the legs of the five or six people between himself and the end of the row.

'You're forgetting your opera glasses!' the lady in the next seat whispered after him.

'That's all right, madame. I'll be back shortly, I hope.'

He stumbled down a few steps; there were angry hisses of, 'Sh!' Then the curtain closed, the house lights came up, and there was applause. He had deliberately left the opera glasses there, afraid of the things. Now, in the interval, he regained his composure. How stupid he'd been! In the now brightly lit auditorium the obsession of a moment ago struck him as a foolish, ridiculous impulse to which he would never have given in! He wasn't a lunatic! Hurl his binoculars into the auditorium?! Come on, he would put the crazy notion out of his head with a minimum of will-power and common sense. He felt hungry and went to the bar for a roll and a glass of beer. That would calm him down after that nonsense of just now.

However, when the second act began and the house lights dimmed, he decided that what had surged through him had been a kind of giddy delirium induced by heights, what the

French call *vertige de l'abîme* . . . Although he had felt no compulsion to plunge down himself. Perhaps it might be better not to sit so far forward in that first row, so high above the abyss of the auditorium . . . No, it would be better if he stayed back here, in the aisle. Even if the obsession had been nonsense, it might take hold of him again in that seat and so detract from his enjoyment of the music.

He stopped. Down there his seat remained unoccupied and the twin towers of his black opera glasses rose sarcastically but harmlessly on the wide ledge in front of his empty seat. But if he stood on tiptoe, he could just see the white pate in the auditorium, gleaming like a target . . .

He shrugged his shoulders in annoyance, dismissed that annoyance with a 'tut-tut' sound, and gave his full attention to Brünnhilde's exultant cries, atop the rock on which she had appeared. And became calmer. And was transported.

The magic fire motif overwhelmed him and his pure rapture completely restored his equilibrium.

Still, when the opera was over, he determined never again to sit in the first row of the fourth tier. At any rate, never again with such large opera glasses in front of him. And also not to take the opera glasses with him . . . since their weight had felt so strange in his hands and together with the sense of depth, and because of that stupid target down there, might have triggered that crazy obsession . . . to leave them there . . . with their small twin black towers . . . on the wide ledge . . . outlined against the void of the auditorium, now emptying below and on all sides.

And he more or less fled right down the stairs, frightened that someone would call after him that he had forgotten his opera glasses.

Five years had gone by. He had been successful in his career. He was married. He had been on short trips in summer and winter, for his work and for holidays. He had not been back to Dresden, but this year he found himself there by chance. In early autumn when the parks are clad in golden leaves. The opera posters announced a series of performances of the Ring cycle. That evening they were performing *The Valkyrie*. He remembered the beautiful performance of five years before. The memory of his obsession had faded until it had become no more than the vaguest recollection of vertigo, about which he had sometimes since smiled and shrugged his shoulders. He would definitely go and see *The Valkyrie* again this evening. But at the box office he was told that the show was sold out.

He was sorry. He turned away. When at that moment someone approached and told the box-office clerk that he was selling his seat, booked in the front row, fourth tier, for that evening. He was unable to come.

The young man eagerly took the seat and wondered where he had seen that unpleasant bird face before. Come on, it was the front row of that high fourth tier again, but he wouldn't get as dizzy again and wouldn't allow himself to be thrown by an idiotic notion. Come to that, he wouldn't even take any opera glasses. He didn't have any with him and he wasn't going to buy any.

He went rather late that evening. The auditorium was already dark and full; the music had started. He hesitated to disturb the listeners in his row, but the usherette thought he could easily get to his seat past only four people. So he shuffled past their knees, muttering apologies, and sat down.

Then the usherette leaned over him and in a whisper offered him some large opera glasses, asking:

'Would you like to hire some opera glasses? For one mark?'

He thought he detected a sarcastic tone, started and looked at the opera glasses she was holding out to him. They were his, from five years earlier, left behind here, never reclaimed, not taken to the police station and constantly hired out by the usherette, whenever she could. They were his opera glasses. Before he could refuse, a hand irresistibly grabbed the things. Angry voices called out 'Sh!' and the usherette withdrew, saying he could pay later . . .

So it happened that in the middle of Siegmund and Sieglinde's duet, high up, in the front row of the fourth tier, someone writhed, screaming, as if overcome by an attack of epilepsy, as if struggling with a force stronger than himself, and a hand hurled through the auditorium, where the audience was startled out of its rapt attention, a heavy object through space, which plunged in an arc into the abyss.

And down below, where next to a dove-grey lady a bald-headed gentleman sat, someone else, although not aimed at or noticed, was fatally injured and roared in his death throes, as the brains spattered.

Translated by Paul Vincent

3

ARTHUR VAN SCHENDEL
The Green Dream

De groene droom

Life can be as singular as a dream – a dream of happiness that turns a minute into a century, or a nightmare from which you cannot wake too soon. But a dream can also seem so real that you wonder whether you are really dreaming and whether the world is seen most truly by waking or sleeping eyes, and even if the healthy mind draws a line between fantasy and reality, it must admit, if it is healthy enough to look into the matter, that the distinction between the two is often a mystery.

But whose mind deserves to be called healthy? Is the man who has never dreamed, and doesn't even know what delusion is, the only one whose mind is free of flaws? In that case, we can be certain there are few people in this world whose minds are perfect and unblemished. Men who never dream appear to be very rare indeed, and as for their minds, a scholar once said that such men must be missing something essential, because the power of thought depends on the power of the imagination. He went on to say that, in fact, new ideas are born of dreams and fantasies.

On the other hand, it seems doubtful that a man who dreams a great deal is perfectly healthy. There are people whose minds are so eager to flee from everyday reality that they need only close their eyes to see dream images. It is not normal, you must admit, this mental compulsion to flee from the world of one's fellows to another of unreal beings; it is immoderate, irregular. Those who do it are fantasists, dreamers, and they may be ordinary, healthy specimens of their kind, but in human society they are as orchids among flowers, exotic quirks of nature.

When Cloverleaf, dreamer and fantasist, was still young, he was set apart by his many eccentricities. Food and drink that everyone enjoyed, like currant bread and milk, revolted him. Sights everyone agreed were beautiful, like a Sunday suit or a parade, were ugly to him. The things that inflamed passion in every heart, like a comely young woman or a glass of red wine, made his spirits sink. He did not care for *this*, he did not care for *that*, and what he *did* care for were things he had never really known, things beyond his grasp, like fairies and ambrosia. That Cloverleaf, people said, he's an odd one, there's no pleasing him. In truth, he had no desire for pleasure. The only thing he enjoyed was sitting by himself, or better still, walking by himself, because then the fantasies in his head were not disturbed.

These fantasies were a process independent of his will. They began to run through his head as soon as he opened his eyes in the morning, and when he closed his eyes again in bed at night, they continued in a slightly different fashion. Sometimes he fought them, because he grew weary of them or because he believed his heart needed something more. Then he would seek diversion, and his extreme behaviour would surprise people. Yet although his head would stop its picture show for as long as he remained frenetically active, no sooner had he stopped than it would take him by surprise with a new show, more vivid and colourful than the last. Once in a while this turned into a battle between Cloverleaf and his mind. Then he would talk and laugh with friends so much and so uproariously that his mind had no way of playing its games. But he couldn't keep that up for long; his mind would ambush him in his sleep, when his will could not protect him. Dreams, strong and burly, overpowered him with images beyond counting, presented to his inner eye for centuries at a time, while Cloverleaf was aware of lying powerless, a toy, an object that drifted on mists.

Maybe I'm giving you the wrong impression of Cloverleaf's fantasies. Who put on these picture shows? He himself? His mind? That was what he believed in his youth, and that was why he resisted when he'd had enough. Later, once he'd learned that even the most ferocious opposition could not liberate him from his fantasies for any more than a moment, he began to suspect some other mind or spirit of possessing him and using him as its plaything. Perhaps this was merely another delusional idea, slightly further removed from reality than the previous one, because this delusion went so far as to involve the supernatural. You will understand how easily a man enslaved by his imagination could come to believe such a thing. Whatever the case may be, Cloverleaf ultimately had no doubt that his head was merely a playground for all sorts of spirits, who communed with each other there, usually without taking any notice of him, although he sometimes seemed to amuse them.

Now, another eccentricity of his was his strong preference for certain colours, sounds and smells and an equally strong aversion to others. The sound of a cat or a tenor caused him pain, he said, while the sound of an infant or a dog was music. Of all colours, he was most attached to blue, so much so that he was never seen dressed in anything but blue – navy blue, or a touch lighter, in winter, sky blue in summer. There was also a colour that he detested, a colour that sent vicious pains stabbing through his head: green, in all its shades. You might think this an unnatural character trait, since nature loves to dress in green, but while he admired the colour in trees and grass, he rejected it anywhere else in the world as false, venomous and pernicious. Green is envy, he would say, green is hate, the heart of the devil, and when he saw someone dressed in green, he would avert his eyes. He believed that heaven was filled with a radiant blue light, while hell burned with green flames that gave off green fumes. Little wonder that many people thought Cloverleaf a man of outlandish tastes and distastes, and those who learned of his fantasies pitied him, saying that he must harbour a diseased spirit.

And one day he had a dream, an illusion, a hallucination, whatever you might call the phenomenon, after which he himself feared that his mind might be poisoned.

When he left home that Saturday around four in the afternoon, he was still in a waking state. It was late June, oppressively hot and humid. Over the roofs he made out a greenish glow of the kind you sometimes see before a storm, and over the bricks that lined the street he also detected some hint of green in the shadows. The air he breathed reminded him of the smell of pickled gherkins. He could normally tolerate that odour well enough, but now it so disgusted him that he made a detour into different streets. By the time he reached the outskirts of the city, the sky had become overcast, with a yellow glimmer here and there. What a strange place, Cloverleaf said to himself, imagining that he had lost his way. Then he froze in astonishment. On his lavender-blue trousers, from top to bottom, and his darker blue jacket, especially on the sleeves, he saw tiny yellow stars and flowers whirling rapidly. He wanted to brush them off with his hand but noticed that this left stains, green like canal water. It made him shudder. When he looked up, a coachman stood before him in a green jacket, with moss-green whiskers, beckoning him into a coach of a dark, dirty green. This is a bad idea, Cloverleaf thought, but he climbed in anyway. Inside it smelled of sulphur, and he noticed that he was riding down a steep slope. The coach came to an abrupt halt, and the coachman, looking a little slimy by this time, loomed up outside the door and ordered him to run away quickly, because it was becoming dangerous there. I knew it, thought Cloverleaf, who felt as if his throat were being pinched. He ran down the hillside through soft reeds of some kind, and as he was running he realized he was dreaming. Well, then, he thought, I have nothing to be afraid of. It must be some spirit playing another mean trick. He stopped and, since his head was growing heavy, lowered himself onto some bushes, which smelled as if they had been painted. The spot where he sat was still on the same slope, with trees below him whose round tops had an enamelled look, dark against the sky. From the right and the left, fleeing in panic, came women in veils who sat down all around him, keeping their faces covered.

He examined them one by one and thought every one of them beautiful, a thought that gave him pause, for they were all wearing green veils, in a greater variety of shades than he had ever seen – sea green, translucent green, from light to dark and all the way to greenish-black, bronze green, emerald green, mackerel green, spruce green – and he could peer through all the veils and see the green hearts. Although he knew they could not be beautiful, he felt drawn to them. Looking at one, he longed to look at another, and once he turned to the other, he was drawn back to the first. That's how love begins, Cloverleaf said to himself. I never thought I would have anything to do with love, and I'll be amazed if some stupid spirit can change that. Has my time come after all?

He spread his arms and was about to stand up and wrap them around one of the figures, but he could not. She straightened and rose, the veil falling from her head, her large malachite eyes gazing into him. Two braids slithered over her shoulders, two green snakes. The mouth opened and the voice was like waves crashing on the rocks: Here is the green man. He has stolen the colour from all the grass in the world, all the trees and all the seas, for his own use. He has drunk all the light of the sun. See how he glitters in his green glory, a tree of peacock plumes. We must sit in his shadow or we shall turn pale and wilt.

It's true, thought Cloverleaf, I am what I abhor.

All the figures rose and paced in slow circles around him, in their trembling veils. The one who had spoken approached, sank down before him and laid her hand on his knee. Around him blew a rustling wind of sighs. When he held out his hands to her, he saw that they were as green as emerald. It made him cold, and he did not dare to touch her. Shivering with fear, he took off his jacket and tore off his shirtsleeves. His arms were the colour of stems growing in the dark, with streaks and patches of faded green. His chest was oak bark covered with a thick layer of chilly moss. He thrust his hand into it, pulled out his heart and saw that it was a heavy piece of green marble. He grew angry, hurled it far away and heard it fall with a clap like thunder beyond the trees.

Yes, said Cloverleaf, sitting at home, that was a very bad dream. But why do I still feel as though I am green on the inside? The malachite eyes were not real, I know that – I haven't lost my mind. Yet somehow they have found their way inside me; their spirit has latched onto mine. Is it a game or vengeance? And am I really in my right mind? Who can tell me that? If I go to a psychologist, he'll ask me a thousand questions, and even then, he won't know. Maybe he'll explain that it was only a dream and I shouldn't let it worry me. And if I say I can still feel the green eyes here inside me, he'll tell me not to let my fancy run away with me. And so on and so forth, and meanwhile I'll be no closer to the truth. But I'll find it in the imagination, and it must be blue.

Translated by David McKay

4

NESCIO

Young Titans

Titaantjes

I

We were kids – but good kids. If I may say so myself. We're much smarter now, so smart it's pathetic. Except for Bavink, who went crazy. Was there anything we didn't want to set to rights? We would show them how it should be. 'We': that meant the five of us. Everyone else was 'them', the ones who didn't see it, didn't get it. 'What?' Bavink said. 'God? You want to talk about God? Their pot roast is their God.' Other than a few 'decent fellows' we despised everyone – and, secretly, I still think we were right. But I can't say that out loud to anyone now. I'm not a hero any more. You never know who you might need later. Hoyer also thinks you shouldn't offend anyone. No one ever sees or hears from Bekker any more. And Kees Ploeger talks about the good-for-nothings who led him down the wrong path. But back then, in our crazy days, we were God's chosen ones, we were God himself. Now we're sensible, again except for Bavink, and we look at each other and smile and I say to Hoyer, 'What did it all get us?' But Hoyer doesn't see it that way, he's a lost cause, he's turning into one of the bigwigs of the Social Democratic Workers' Party and all he does is raise his hands in doubt and shrug.

We were never clear about what we were going to do exactly, but we were going to do *something*. Bekker had some vague idea about blowing up all the offices, Ploeger wanted to make his boss pack his own clocks and then stand there watching him with a cigar in his mouth, cursing at people who can never do anything right. We were *unanimous* that we had to 'get out'. Out of what, and how? The truth is we did nothing but talk, smoke, drink and read books. And Bavink went out with Lien. Looking back, I think we were a magnificent bunch of young men, we deserved a fortune but despised 'having lots of money'; Hoyer's the only one who started to think a bit differently about that before long. Bavink didn't understand why some people could ride in carriages whenever they wanted and wear expensive coats and order other people around who weren't any dumber than they were. You didn't see many automobiles yet in those days.

We spent whole summer nights leaning against the fence around Oosterpark and talking and talking. We could have earned enough for a whole living-room set if only we'd kept track of it all. People write so much nowadays.

A lot of the time we were less talkative. We sat on the kerb until long past midnight, right on the street, and were melancholy and stared at the bricks and then up from the bricks at the stars. Then Bekker said that actually he felt sorry for his boss, and I tried to write a poem, and Hoyer said he had to stand up because the cold from the blue limestone kerb was seeping into him. And when, in that short, balmy night, the darkness turned pale above our heads, Bavink sat with his head in his hands and spoke of the sun, almost sentimentally. And we thought it was a shame to have to go to bed, people should be able to stay up for ever. That was one of the things we'd change. Kees was asleep.

And then we were off to the Zuiderzee to watch the sun come up, except for Kees, who went home. Hoyer complained about the cold but Bavink and Bekker didn't notice it at all. They sat on the stones down on the dyke with eyes half closed and looked through their eyelashes at the little arrows of dancing gold that the sun made in the water. The sight made Bavink go mad; he wanted to run across the long, long, glittering stripe all the way to the sun. But he stopped at the water's edge after all and stood there. I remember one day when we, Bavink and I, went to the seaside and half the sun lay big and cold and red on the horizon. Bavink hit his forehead with his

fist and said, 'God, God, I'll never paint that. I'll never be able
to paint that.' Now he's in a mental hospital. When we came
back from the Zuiderzee we couldn't see anything except yellow spots for a long time and our bosses didn't like these
excursions of ours at all. I was half asleep at the office afterwards and Bekker, who could handle it better than I could, sat
at his desk daydreaming about the sun all day and looked out
at the lit-up treetops on the far side of the garden more than
usual and longed for six o'clock more desperately than ever.

We were also big on excursions after work to the ring of
dykes around the city. We sat in the grass down on the dyke,
among the buttercups, and inquisitive cows came up to us with
their big eyes and looked at us and we looked at them. And
then it was a sure bet that Bavink would start in about Lien.
One way or another those cow eyes must have had something
to do with it. And then the twilight started to shimmer, the
frogs started croaking, one frog made a horrible racket right
next to my shoe, my foot was almost in the ditch. You could
hear other frogs softly, far, so far away. The cow that in the
half dark you could hardly see any more you could still hear,
trimming the grass. One started mooing pitifully in the distance. A horse ran back and forth, you could hear it but not see
it. The cow near us snorted and started to get restless. Bekker said: 'It's nice here. If only it stayed like this.' Bavink
stood up and spread his arms wide and listened, and then sat
down again and said that we didn't get it either, and we never
would, he himself didn't get it, and really we were not much
better than everyone else, and I think he was very nearly right
about that.

No, we didn't actually do anything. We did our work at the
office, not all that well, for bosses we despised – except Bavink
and Hoyer, who had no bosses, and who didn't understand
why we went in to see ours every day.

But we were waiting. For what? We never knew. Bekker
said: 'For the Kingdom of God.' At least that's what he said
once, without explaining any further. Bavink always talked
about 'the end that is also a new beginning'. We knew exactly
what he meant and said nothing more about it.

2

That summer we met almost every night at Kees's attic. Kees had decided he needed a 'place' too. His place was the biggest and the easiest for all of us to get to. The neighbours didn't like everybody going up and down the stairs every night. Kees's father didn't see the point of the whole thing. Now Kees's father greets me very politely and calls me 'Mr Koekebakker', because he's seen my name in the *Handelsblad*.

Bekker told Kees how he had to decorate it. They bought cheap wallpaper with a little flower pattern for three cents a roll and then glued it to the wall reversed so that the plain green backing faced out. Bekker wrote out a proverb in calligraphy and stuck it to the wall next to the door: '*J'ai attendu le Seigneur avec une grande patience, enfin il s'est abaisse jusqu'à moi.*'

I don't know any more where he got that from. Kees couldn't read it. But Kees did contribute something, he made a shovel and Bekker managed to attach it to the wall pointing at the proverb. It wasn't clear at first what it was supposed to mean, but later it turned out that Bekker wanted to go and live on the heath someday and work a little piece of land, and never have to go back to the office. Bavink thought that was a good idea but was afraid Lien wouldn't agree, and Hoyer preferred to hang around in bars.

Then we sat there and tore everything to pieces. Or almost everything. I remember that Zola and Jaap Maris came out more or less unscathed, maybe one or two others. Bekker read to us from Dante, he knew Ecclesiastes and the Song of Songs and the Book of Job by heart. It was very impressive. Not much of the outside world made it into Kees's attic. The only window was almost shoulder-height off the floor; when you sat at the table, you couldn't see much more than a sliver of sky, the colour slowly draining out of it, and a few stars when it was dark out.

Paint? Who still knew how to paint nowadays, to hear Bavink tell it! You could palm anything off on people today, literally anything. I should paint a picture myself – he was talking about me, Koekebakker. He would tell me what to do. 'Paint two horizontal stripes, one on top of the other, same width, one blue and one gold, and then put a round gold bit in the middle of the blue stripe. We'll write in the catalogue #666: *The Thought, oil on canvas*. And we'll submit it under my name: Johannes Bavink, Second Jan Steenstraat, number so-and-so, and we'll price it at eight hundred guilders. Then you can just sit back and see everything they come up with. They'll discover all sorts of things in there that you didn't have the slightest idea of.'

Bavink was still very young back then. Later on, Lien came over too sometimes and made tea. One time, she scrubbed the floor and dusted everything, but that was very unpleasant. It caused some embarrassment for Kees when she came over, because his old man had definite misgivings about the young lady, and Bavink was never the way we liked him when Lien was around. He was always giving her little squeezes and pinches. It was annoying.

Luckily he started to leave her at home before long, because he thought she was making eyes at me. Bekker said, 'Girls, they're not worth it,' and puffed on his clay pipe with especial satisfaction the first time she didn't come. And that evening it was really nice too. We sat for hours in the dark. The lamp got fainter and fainter, then went out. We just stayed there sitting and smoking, for hours. Every once in a while someone said something. Bavink decided that painting was the dumbest thing anyone could do. Kees didn't understand anything, as usual. 'You have to just sit quietly and stay like that,' Bavink said, and looked up at the sky. A big greenish star twinkled. 'You have to just sit quietly and stay like that and long with all your might, without knowing what for.' He filled a fresh pipe.

3

It was a strange time. And when I think about it, I realize that that time must still be happening now, it will last as long as there are young men of nineteen or twenty running around. It's only for us that the time is long since past.

We were on top of the world and the world was on top of us, weighing down heavily. Far below us we saw the world full of activity and industry and we despised those people, especially the important gentlemen, the ones who were always so busy and so sure they'd got pretty far in the world.

But we were poor. Bekker and I had to spend most of our time at the office and do whatever those gentlemen said, and listen to their ridiculous opinions when they talked to each other, and put up with the fact that they thought they were much more clever and capable than we were. And when they thought it was cold then all the windows had to be shut and in winter the lights had to come on much too early and the curtains had to be pulled shut so we couldn't see the red sky and the twilight in the streets and we had no say in it at all.

And we had to live on streets that were too narrow, with a view of the oilcloth curtains across the street and the tasselled fringe and the potted aspidistra with an impossible flower on top.

Oh, we took our revenge, we learned languages they had never even heard of and we read books they couldn't even begin to understand, we experienced feelings they never knew existed. On Sundays we walked for hours on paths where they never went, and at the office we thought about the canals and the meadows we had seen and while they ordered us to do things that we didn't see the point of we thought about how the sun had set behind Abcoude on Sunday evening. And how we had thought our way through the whole universe, without words; and how God had filled our head, our heart and our spine, and how stark raving mad they would look if we told them about it. And how, with all their money and their trips to Switzerland and Italy and God knows where else and with all their clever hard work, they could never feel such things.

But still, they had us in their power, they confiscated the greater part of our time, they kept us out of the sunshine and away from the meadows and the seaside. They forced us constantly to fill our thoughts with their incomprehensible business. Even though that only went so far. They chewed us out; at the office we were totally insignificant. 'Ah, Bekker,' they said to each other. The gentlemen had been well brought up; the woman on the third floor said, 'That hare-brained idiot,' but the gentlemen were too well brought up for that. And they were bright, much brighter than the woman on the second floor, whose husband was a lamplighter, a good job that didn't need much education. My boss asked me if I wrote poetry by any chance. Bekker thought that a man like him shouldn't utter the word *poetry,* shouldn't be allowed to. 'What did you tell him?' I hadn't said anything. I only looked at his face and saw what a thick skull he had and I thought: He doesn't know who he has standing here in front of him, he hasn't got the brains. And they paid us badly, the gentlemen did.

4

And we were in love. For months Bekker went out of his way to walk down Sarphatistraat every morning. He was in love with a schoolgirl of about seventeen or so, and he walked fifty steps behind her or on the other side of the street and he looked at her. He never knew her name, never said a word to her. Over the Christmas break he was unhappy. In February he took an afternoon off to wait for her when school got out. He stood there on the quiet canal-side street in the snow and a man rode by on a white horse wearing a blue smock and a straw hat. How odd, that on precisely that afternoon he had had to see something so ludicrous. But Bekker left at five minutes to four, he didn't dare stay. He walked slowly away, and on Weteringschans she caught up with him. She was laughing loudly with a friend, another girl. I don't think she ever knew Bekker existed.

Bekker wanted me to tell him where this was heading; it couldn't go on like this. And it didn't either. After the summer vacation she never came back.

'Girls,' Bekker said, 'they're not worth it ... She had a spring in her step when she walked.' He turned the lamp up a bit and turned the page in the book he was reading. 'Where do you think she is now? Do you think she's kissing someone?' A little spark fell from his pipe onto the book. He put it out with his matchbox. 'Damn, a hole, that was stupid.

'It's better this way, girls aren't worth it, they don't get you anywhere, they only distract you. They're pretty at a distance, to write poems about.'

He read. After a short pause he looked up again ... 'You know what the strange thing is? When she caught up with me that afternoon she walked past me, right next to me. She only just missed me. There was, so to speak, nothing separating us, a little clothing on her and practically none on me.' (Bekker went around summer and winter with only an over-shirt covering his bare chest.) 'That's not much, you know?' I said it wasn't much – there was a lot more between the Naarden tower and Bekker's room, for example. 'Between the Naarden tower and this moustache,' Bekker said, 'is much less, *much* less, than there was between her shoulder and mine that day. No comparison, Koekebakker.' He turned another page, looked into the light, and said, 'That's how it is,' and went on with his reading.

5

And so it was: God showed his face and then hid it again. You never got anywhere, especially if you only looked at the girls from a distance and let other men kiss their pretty faces, the important gentlemen they, as a rule, liked a whole lot more than us. They were so much more respectable and spoke so well. And we were bums.

There was nothing to hope for from God – who goes his own way and gives no explanations. If there was something we wanted we had to take care of it ourselves. But we realized that it was easy for Bavink and Hoyer to talk, they had talent, they could really accomplish something in the world, but we – Bekker and Kees and me – the only difference we'd ever make was as socialists and it did seem a bit weak, after sitting at God's table, to address envelopes or join the Kastanjeplein Neighbourhood Association. And nothing came of life on the

heath either, because even when Bekker did get a little money
his shoes needed repairing. Maybe we could join Van Eeden's
commune, but when we walked out to Bussum one Sunday,
four hours on foot, we saw a man strolling around in a peasant
smock and expensive yellow shoes, eating sponge cakes out of
a paper bag, hatless, in inner harmony with nature as people
used to say back then, with crumbs in his beard. We couldn't
bring ourselves to keep going, we turned right around and
walked back to Amsterdam, walked along the Naardern canal
in single file, singing, and a farm girl said to a farm boy, 'There
wasn't nothin' about it in the paper, in't that somethin'? D'you
know about that?'

6

So we didn't do anything. No, actually, that was when Bekker
wrote his first poem.

I still remember it perfectly. It was on a Sunday, of course,
because whenever anything happened it was on a Sunday. The
other six days a week we spent dragging our chains around
from nine to six.

I was out looking for a job in Hillegom, a job with a bulb
dealer with fat red clean-shaven cheeks. The others decided
right away to make a day of it. Bavink, Hoyer and Bekker had
all said so many times that they wanted to go to the Museum
of Antiquities in Leiden, this was the day. Kees had to come
too; he did whatever the others did. I was going to meet them
in Leiden.

It was December. I stood at the back of the tram, all the way
at the back. It drove through the country and stopped and
started again, it took hours, the countryside was endless. And
the sky got bluer and bluer and the sun shone until it seemed
like flowers would have to start sprouting out of the country
bumpkins. And the red roofs in the villages and the black trees
and the fields, most of them covered with straw, had it nice and
warm, and the dunes sat bare-headed in the sun. And the road
lay there, white and smarting, it couldn't bear the sunlight,

and the glass panes of the village streetlamps flashed, they had trouble withstanding the glare too.

But *I* got colder and colder. And the tram ran as long as the sun shone. It's a long ride from Hillegom to Leiden and the days are short in December. By the end, a block of ice was standing there on the tram staring into the big stupid cold sun that was flaming red as though the revolution was finally starting, as though offices were being blown up all over Amsterdam, but still it couldn't bring a spark of life back to my cold feet and stiff legs. And it kept getting bigger and colder, the sun, and I got colder and stayed the same size, and the blue sky looked down very disapprovingly: What are you doing on that tram?

Bekker wrote his first poem that afternoon. When I got to Leiden, as they were lighting the gas lamps, and I found the immortals sitting in a row on a long bench in the third-class waiting room at the train station, near the stove, it was my turn to undergo the poem. It was beautiful. No title? Bekker shook his head. But Bavink and Hoyer shrieked that they'd seen something written at the top. A well-dressed gentleman said 'Louts' to the man who punched his ticket at the door. Bavink snatched the sheet of paper out of Bekker's hands. What was written at the top? Was it even a question? 'To her.' Just what I would have guessed.

Bavink thought the stove could use more coal but he couldn't find the scoop. They always take the scoop out of the waiting rooms, otherwise the public uses too much coal.

So Bavink tossed lumps of coal into the stove with his bare hands, and got into an argument with a guy in a white smock.

It was fun that night. Kees and Hoyer fell asleep on the train. Bavink chatted with a girl from The Hague and inhaled the smell of heliotropes given off by her dear little frame.

Then Bekker started talking about the heath again. How he wanted to live there in peace and wait and see what God had planned for him. And not have to *do* anything. He was deeply melancholy. I had an objection to the heath: it's so dry out there. And I asked Bekker what exactly he planned to live on, office workers don't usually do too well on the farm, except in

America (we believed all kinds of lies about America). But he wasn't worried about that. He didn't need anything.

Now he knows better. Only God doesn't need anything. That is precisely the fundamental difference between God and us.

So life on the heath came to nothing too.

7

Four of us sat in the fine white sand at the foot of the dunes in Zandvoort and looked out at the ocean. Kees wasn't there. It was late July. The sun was still high above the ocean at seven o'clock and it made, again, I can't help it, it's God himself who keeps repeating himself, it again made a long golden stripe in the water and shone in our faces.

A tugboat was puffing on the horizon. It rose and sank; when it sank we could only see the steam pipe.

Bekker was going to Germany the next day. His knowledge of languages had got him a job as a clerk in a factory handling foreign correspondence. And Hoyer was off to Paris, to paint.

Bekker, in particular, was deeply melancholy again. He wished he had never taken that job. He couldn't understand why he'd done it. He was in that miserable factory town for two hours, for the interview, and got sick, homesick. He fled back to the train station as fast as he could. The rails still lay there, luckily running straight to the horizon and beyond, back to Amsterdam. He had already bought his ticket, and on it was clearly printed, right there: 'To Amsterdam.' And the train came on time and carried him home along the rails, and when he got off at Centraal Station his heart was so full of emotion that he struck up a conversation with the engineer and gave him a cigar, an expensive cigar, and even stroked the locomotive with his hand and thought: Ah, nice locomotive. And then he took the job anyway. It brought in a lot more money than he was making here. Now he had to go away and not see the ring of dykes around the city again. All that time the rails would be lying there, but he would only be able to go stand on the platform and watch the trains pull out in the evening, and all day Sundays, many times a day.

The sun was lower now, and red, the golden stripe was gone. It was a warm, still evening. The red water rippled a little, the waves rolled slowly in with a gentle hiss.

Bekker had a theory that he would save money and come back and live on the heath. But in his heart he didn't believe it himself. We tried to believe it, even Hoyer tried, and we convinced ourselves that that's what would happen, but we didn't believe it. And it didn't happen either. Bekker came back a year later, he had saved a couple of hundred guilders and he walked down Linnaeusstraat at half past eight every morning again with his sandwich in a bag from home. There's a lot a person needs.

But we weren't thinking about reused bags that night. We were doing our best to believe that we would still manage to accomplish something, really something. We would shock the world, unimpressive as we were, sitting calmly there with our legs pulled up and our eight hands clasping our eight knees. Hoyer had decided to paint all kinds of ordinary things. He had read an article in a magazine about the social duty of the artist, and now he was all in favour. He started to argue with Bekker about the heath. It was a miracle of erudition. He tried to convince Bekker that it was a mistake to withdraw from the world and go off to the heath, which he would never do anyway. An artist belongs at the centre of modern life.

Hoyer wanted to hear what *I* thought. I just said I'd never thought about it. I didn't know what Hoyer wanted either – he *knew* it already, why did he need to know what I thought too?

Bavink was the only one who didn't say anything; he just sat with his chin on his knees and took the sun into his heart. The sun was as flat as a lozenge now, and dull red, almost gone.

Hoyer couldn't sit still. He jumped up and took Bekker with him. They walked along the beach and from a distance we could hear Hoyer screaming, he was obviously worked up. Bavink and I stayed sitting there for a while, then sauntered slowly after them. It wasn't very nice to have a worldview, it seemed to me. Hoyer was screaming so much.

Bavink and I stopped and looked down at the tips of our shoes and the waves rolling in over them. The sun was gone, the red shimmer on the water began to fade, a bluish darkness rose in the south. It smelled of mud. In the distance, near the village, the arc lamps suddenly came on along the beach.

'You understand all that?' Bavink asked. 'About social duty?'

I shrugged. 'What kind of guy d'you think wrote that article? Do *you* have a Sense of Responsibility, Koekebakker?' Hoyer had talked about that too.

'Hoyer sure talks nice,' Bavink said. 'Awfully nice. *I* don't have a sense of responsibility. I can't be bothered with that. I need to paint. It's not a walk in the park. What was it he said again?'

'Who?' I asked.

'The guy in that book; what was it he said artists were?'

'Privileged.'

'You know what I think, Koekebakker? That that's the same guy who wrote the train timetables. I've never understood how anyone could write those either. Privileged . . . God is everywhere, Koekebakker? Or isn't he? They say that too, don't they?'

I nodded. The darkness started to rise up everywhere from the water; the horizon to the north-west still glowed a yellowish green, the last light was leaving from over our heads. There were no clouds.

'So, he is everywhere,' Bavink said. 'There, and there, and there.' He pointed all around us with an outstretched arm. 'And there, beyond the sea, in the land we can't see. And over there, near Driehuis, where the arc lamps are. And on Kalverstraat. Go stand with your back to the water there and listen. Can you stay out of it?'

'Out of what?'

'Out of the ocean?'

I nodded yes, I certainly could.

'I can't, or just barely,' Bavink said. 'It's so strange, having that melancholy sound behind you. It's like the ocean wants something from me, that's what it's like. God is in there too.

God is calling. It's really not a walk in the park, he is everywhere, and everywhere he is he's calling Bavink. You get sick of your own name when it's called so much. And then Bavink has to paint. Has to get God onto canvas, with paint. Then it's Bavink who's calling, 'God.' So there they are, calling each other. It's just a game to God; he is everywhere and without end. He just calls. But Bavink has only one stupid head and one stupid right hand and can only work on one stupid painting at a time. And when he thinks he has God, all he has is paint and canvas. It turns out God is everywhere except where Bavink wants him to be. And then some guy comes along and writes that Bavink is privileged and Hoyer memorizes it and goes around blathering it at Bekker. Privileged, right. You know what I wish? I wish I wrote timetables. God leaves people like that alone; they're not worth the trouble.'

I offered Bavink a cigar and suggested we walk to Driehuis. I felt like a coffee. I didn't think it was very nice of Bavink to put down a useful fellow like that who was just doing his job. Behind us, Hoyer and Bekker came walking back; they were still going at it.

At eleven o'clock that night we were back on the beach. The wind had picked up, the waves hissed. A little something to drink had driven off the gloominess and melancholy. A new age was about to dawn. Bekker, in the solitude of his German boarding house, would translate Dante as he had never been translated before. Bavink had a great painting in his head, *A View of Rhenen*, he had been there once and could see it all clearly in his mind. And Hoyer was going to go and work on his social duty – he would show them. And I tried to believe it all.

The cool wind blew around us. The ocean made a complaining sound, the ocean that complains and doesn't know why. The ocean washed woefully up onto the shore. My thoughts are an ocean; they wash woefully up against their limits.

A new age would dawn; we could still do great things. I did my best to believe it, my very, very best.

8

I stood in the twilight in Rhenen, on the bridge over the rail-road tracks, and looked north. Far below me were the rails, running out to the horizon, with the hill rising up steep on either side, overgrown with light green grass and dark green gorse covered in yellow flowers. I looked at how the slope of the hill got lower and lower until, far away, it became the flat plain.

Again the darkness started creeping stealthily up out of the ground, the way I had seen it do so many times before. The last light of day rested on the mountaintop, nervous and afraid, while the valley was full of darkness, and a red light came on on a post by the tracks. The sky was coated in grey and looked colourlessly down on the beaten, defeated day.

I had been away for six years and now I was standing there, just back in Holland, in the place I had thought about so often, which they had described in almost every letter they wrote to me (every year Bavink wrote to me at least twice, Bekker a bit more often). Back at the hill that Bavink had sent me seven drawings of over the years and Bekker had written two very short poems about.

I had come back to Holland to suffer poverty and write art-icles and stories in the neighbourhood where I had lived for so long. And I wanted to go through my last two rijks dollars in the city that for a while, in my absence, had been the centre of the world.

In the north the darkness was gulping down the light, the mountain was nearly swallowed up, the day's last escort fled to the north-west and I stood on the little bridge on the edge of nothingness, enveloped in infinity.

I leaned my elbow on the railing and propped my chin in my hand and looked into the darkness and thought about the flat red sun that had set long ago into the green waves of the Atlantic – waves that rose up with sharp edges and scooped out sides and fell and rose and were rising and falling even now. About the yellow lights in the shops in the poorer neighbourhoods of Amsterdam, which I would shortly see again, which had shone every night while the ocean never stopped moving.

And the vague expectations from back then rose within me again, and the longing, without knowing what for.

But I also had a feeling I hadn't known before. All those days had passed and many more days would pass as well, and on every one of them my expectations would remain unfulfilled and my longings unsatisfied. Bavink had worked for years, on and off, on his *View of Rhenen* – on the river, the mountain, the Cunera tower, the blossoming apple trees, the red roofs of the city, the chestnut trees with their red and white flowers and the brown beeches between the houses in the distance, and the little windmill somewhere up on the mountain. For years Bekker had spent every Sunday in the cabin on the mountain that Bavink rented, translating Dante and writing little poems now and then, for years I had drifted around the world. And what did it all mean? For the world, for God, or even for us?

I stood on the Rhenen tower and looked into the distance, and my heart went out into the distance, to the red sky in the west. But even if I could have flown off the top of the tower into that distance, I would have found only the distance nearby, and my heart would have gone out to the distance once more. And what good did it do me – the wisdom that taught me that nothing would ever change, it would be like this for ever?

Every day we longed for something, without knowing what. It got monotonous. Sunrise and sunset and sunlight on the water and behind the drifting white clouds – monotonous – and the darker skies too, the leaves turning brown and yellow, the bare treetops and poor soggy fields in the winter – all the things I had seen so many times and thought about so many times while I was gone and would see again so many more times, as long as I didn't die. Who can spend his life watching all these things that constantly repeat themselves, who can keep longing for nothing? Trusting in a God who isn't there?

And now the gorse was blooming again, and the lilacs and
apple trees and chestnuts, and the sun was blazing down on
all of it. Full of emotion, I had seen it all again. And while I
was thinking about it, my vague longings and expectations
faded away.

God lives in my head. His fields are immeasurable, his gardens are full of beautiful flowers that never die, regal women
walk there naked, thousands of them. And the sun rises and
sets and shines low and high and low again and the endless
domain is endlessly itself and never the same for an instant.
Broad rivers run through it, curving and meandering, and the
sun shines on them and they carry the light to the sea.

I sit quiet and content beside the rivers of my thoughts and
smoke a clay pipe and feel the sunshine on my body and see the
water flow ceaselessly into the unknown.

The unknown doesn't bother me. I nod now and then to the
beautiful women plucking the flowers in my gardens and I hear
the wind rustling through the high pines, through the forests
of certainty, of knowing that all this exists whenever I decide
to think it. I am grateful that this has been given to me. And I
puff on my pipe in all humility and feel like God himself, who
is infinity itself.

I sit there aimlessly, God's aim is aimlessness.

But to keep this awareness always is granted to no man.

9

When I arrived in Amsterdam, about nine the next morning,
and stood on the square in front of Centraal Station, I saw lots
of electric streetcars, which I had never seen there before, and
taxis, and policemen with caps instead of helmets. But they
hadn't filled in the Damrak yet, I saw the backs of the houses
on Warmoesstraat right on the water and the Oude Kerk spire
up above. So that was all right.

And the same fine gentlemen were still walking around,
their hair was perfect and there was not a crease in their jackets or a speck of mud on their shoes. They still looked like they

knew absolutely everything and felt that they'd pretty much
succeeded in life. They were friendly and polite to each other,
as always. Their clothes were slightly different from a few
years before, but basically the same. You could see that they
had everything figured out: a suit was a suit, same as ever, and
a jacket was still a jacket, and a respectable woman was still a
respectable woman and a girl was a girl. It all worked out perfectly. And they also knew perfectly well who and what were
beneath them, I had no doubt about that. The Damrak would
certainly be filled in too once they got around to it.

I took Tram 2 down Nieuwezijds Voorburgwal. So it was a
good thing they'd filled it in after all, otherwise the tram probably couldn't drive down it, and now you could cross from one
side to the other wherever you wanted.

Tram 2, the line par excellence for fine and important gentlemen. A couple of terribly important gentlemen were on the
tram, I was *nothing* next to them. The good old sun was shining happily down on Voorburgwal, the buds on the trees were
still pale green, and I saw that the shadow of Nieuwe Kerk
didn't reach the other side of the street, not by a long shot. And
I remembered that years before, in late May, I had seen the
same shadow looking exactly the same. And that on a sunny
winter day, when there were no trams on Voorburgwal yet, I
had walked through the shadow of the church which covered
the whole width of the street. Now it didn't even reach the
rails, the tram drove past the church in the sunlight. In a few
months the same tram (it was still brand new) would be driving in the same place through shadow. And when I looked
back at the two terribly important gentlemen, I decided that
the whole time Rhenen had been the centre of the world, this
world had hardly changed at all.

I thought about when these two gentlemen would die, and
stand naked at the Last Judgment, and be forgotten down
here. And about terribly important gentlemen coming and taking their place. Would they still have their silent self-possession
when they arrived up there without their nicely polished shoes?
And what would become of the perfect part in their hair?
What about their idiotic air of superiority, might their faces

not show a hint of modesty when they got there and saw the
other, even more important men they had looked up to for so
many years, and they were naked too?

And how many idealistic young people down here would
have written essays by then, and written little poems and painted
little pictures, and got angry and got excited about things? And
kissed? And then grown important too, perhaps, and been forgotten as well?

Then a girl with a violin got on the tram and looked at the
tips of her shoes with her dark eyes, and I looked at the rounded
curves of her summer coat and forgot all about the elegant
gentlemen.

10

Hoyer was home. He had a very proper apartment in a side
street behind the Concertgebouw and he received me in a sitting room I hardly dared walk in because the carpet was so
expensive. His curtains were velvet, his chairs were uphol-
stered in yellow moquette, a black pendulum clock and
candelabras were on the mantelpiece and I think I saw a bronze
horse somewhere, all things from expensive shops. I didn't
dare to really sit down either, I sat on the edge of the chair the
whole time, but I don't think Hoyer noticed a thing.

Hoyer had had an amazing stroke of luck. They had made
the same old stupid mistake and refused one of his nudes. He'd
named the lady *Lust* and I must say, since I am writing for a
respectable publication, that she did look 'very nice'. And now
Hoyer was living large in furnished rooms managed by an elegant widow with an aristocratic name, along with a female
lawyer and a colonial official on leave with his wife and child.
Hoyer ate out since the widow was far too elegant to cook for
her boarders. Shoeshines cost extra.

And I sat on the edge of my chair the whole time and looked
at the ornamental table legs and the gilded frame of the mirror.
It was deadly. I had to tell Hoyer about my trip, of course, but
I didn't know what to say, I heard myself talking and listened,

scatter-brained, to the sound of my own voice. The light in the
room was dim and gloomy; I think the widow was afraid of
people looking in. I just wanted to leave, and I looked around
at the three walls I could see without turning around in my
chair but they didn't dissolve, I couldn't see through them. I
looked at the door – I couldn't help it – I sat there staring helplessly. My eyes were just drawn to the door. I had vague visions
of Cunera, of the Grebbeberg with its river, of the sunny square
in front of Centraal Station and the clock face gleaming on the
Oude Kerk spire, and through these semi-transparent visions I
saw the painted grain of the fake oak wood on the door. Someone was talking the whole time, oh, right, Hoyer. Then I myself
answered, or not actually my self, but my tongue did move and
sounds did come out of my mouth, I could hear them loud
and clear.

Hoyer didn't notice *anything*. His studio was upstairs. Shall
he lead the way? I numbly followed. 'This must be the lav-
atory?' I thought something along those lines was the proper
thing to say when a gentleman was showing you his house.
Hoyer didn't notice *anything*. 'No, that's a closet,' he said. And
I thought, Why didn't he say, 'I beg your pardon, that's a
closet'? Surely that's what he would be saying within a year
or two.

The hall was a tight squeeze, the runner was narrow, the
stairs proportioned accordingly, there was a thin banister with
slightly turned posts, but everything was very fine and in good
taste, I have to admit. Hoyer still didn't notice anything.

Upstairs I recovered a bit, at least there was light, the famous
'studio light'. The easel stood empty. There was an expensive
chair in the studio and I sank into it. Never in my life had I sat
in such a chair. Hoyer was painting portraits these days, of
ladies and gentlemen, all in elegant clothing. He showed me the
portrait he had just started of the lawyer in the building. She
was travelling at the moment. Hoyer used to have his studio in
another building, but the lawyer had convinced 'Madame' to
allow part of the attic to be converted into a studio. They had
had a hard time persuading her and managed to only when she
heard that Hoyer was going to paint a portrait of a young lady

from Willemsparkweg, in winter hat, boa and muff. And the rest of her clothes, too, of course. And that he had been put forward as a member of Arti et Amicitiae.

Did Bavink ever come by? No, never; he'd never been here. Had he heard anything about Kees? Yes, Bavink had run into Kees on the street a while back and they had talked. He had gone through three or four jobs in the past couple years, with long stretches unemployed in between. His father had finally found him something with the gas company.

'He walks around now in a uniform and a cap, he has Amsterdam's three white Xs and "AmGas" on his head and a little book under his arm. And another guy with him, with a black bag.' Bavink found it quite a sight. His job is to go around emptying the two-penny coins out of the gas meters; the other guy's job is to carry them around in his bag. And after they've got the coins out, Kees has to go and ask the lady of the house if she wants the two-penny coins back again as change for the meter. Bavink spent a while with him; he had never walked along with someone doing that before. But it got boring fast. He never did it again.

I gazed at the Bokhara carpet lying in front of the club chair and saw clearly before my eyes the deserted cobblestones of Linnaeusstraat and the blue limestone kerb and the seam where two stones were set next to each other, and the bricks of the pavement. I saw us sitting there in the summer night. Bavink and Bekker and Kees and Hoyer and me. I saw that the cobblestones and the dust on the street were wet, the watering cart had been by, there was a wet sheet of newspaper somewhere. And I heard Hoyer say that he was standing up, the cold from the stone was seeping into him. Now I was hearing the same voice, only a little more refined, more modulated, saying: 'You must excuse me, Koekebakker, I have a consultation at eleven.'

Outside, the spring sun shone down on the cheerless street. My God, how could a street like this exist? I was absolutely not allowed to kiss the girl in the tram but a street like this was allowed to exist. *That* was allowed.

11

On one of the grand canal streets I stood on the stairs and read on the door: 'P. Bekker, Agent, Sales on Commission'. I rang the bell and waited. It took a long time. Then the top half of the door swung open and I saw a young man with a blockish head. 'Is Mr Bekker in?' That sounded strange. While the young man opened the bottom half of the door, not without some difficulty, I remembered how the front door used to open without my seeing anyone, there was a cord he could pull from upstairs, and I would yell, 'Hi, Bekker!'

'Is Mr Bekker in?'

Mr Bekker was with someone at the moment. A large roll of carpets was lying in the marble passageway. 'Who may I tell him is here?'

'Koekebakker.'

'Would you follow me, please?' The young man went first, up a narrow staircase that changed direction too many times to count.

Upstairs, at the end of a dark narrow hallway, he stopped. In the dim light I could just make out the words 'Samples Room'. 'Is this where I'm supposed to wait, friend?' I asked, pointing at the words. I could tell that Friend found me a bit odd. 'We've just never changed the sign, sir.' He knocked.

I heard Bekker's voice call out, 'Yes.' The friend went in and the door shut behind him and there I was.

Would I be so kind as to wait here? I was led to a small back room with a view of a blind wall. A massive roll of packing paper hung on a bar from the ceiling, with the end of the paper hanging down above a large, empty packing table. The young man went and sat at a little desk by the window, with his back to me, and started to tap on a typewriter. I looked at the packing paper hanging there, I saw that it had been torn off at an angle. I looked at the office worker's broad, bent back and bony shoulders and at the blind wall out the window. One of the bricks was broken and dark red inside; that crumbled piece of brick was the most beautiful thing I saw.

The worker typed away at God knows what. Whenever he stopped for a moment I could hear two men's voices through the closed door, and recognized Bekker's voice without being able to make out any words. I sat there for twenty minutes, dying. *Per me si va nella citta dolente.*

Then the door opened and Bekker appeared. He was nervous and embarrassed. How was I doing? I looked good. He was terribly sorry. He was with a client, from Bordeaux; the man had come especially to see him. He didn't think he could get rid of him before late that evening ... 'You understand – man, you sure look good. Just back from Algiers?' I understood perfectly. Yes, back from Algiers. 'Where are you staying? If I can I'll come by and see you at nine tonight.' I wasn't staying anywhere, I was out of money, but that's not something you can say in an office with a stranger standing right there. So I said I didn't know yet. I'd drop by again later. 'Better luck next time!' I knew he'd say that. It's one of those things that fine men and women say to each other where you don't even need to listen.

He took me to the front door. He thought it was a damn shame. I looked at the little sign, 'P. Bekker, Agent, Sales on Commission', then into his eyes. And I saw that he suddenly heard it too, the cow mooing, the cow in the twilight ten years ago that you could hear but not see. We shook each other's hand. *'Per me si va tra la perduta gente,* Koekebakker.' He held my hand tight and put his other hand on my shoulder. 'Let me know if you need any money, okay?'

I went down the front stairs. The client was standing at the window with his hands on his hips, legs spread wide, looking out at the street. He looked rich and well-fed. I respectfully doffed my hat to him and he returned the greeting, politely and graciously.

12

I'm coming to the end now, slowly but surely. Thank God, someone will say. Ach, I knew before I started that this wouldn't amount to much. What does the life of an Amsterdammer ever amount to, these days? When I was young there were so many times when I wished something would happen, anything. But nothing ever happened. We never even changed address. And later . . .

Only Hoyer knows what it all adds up to. He inherited some money, now he's loaded. He's a member of the Social Democratic Workers' Party, and he reads *The People*.

In the evening he sits in the reading room and leafs through the *Berlin Tageblatt*. He doesn't paint any more. And he has a reason why he doesn't paint, too: it's because we live in an age of decline. A new art is coming, he is sure of it, and waiting for it to arrive. Meanwhile, he brings Art to the People – how, I don't know. A bricklayer asked him once: 'What does all that nonsense get me?' Hoyer had an explanation for that too: 'We Social Democrats know only too well . . .'

He says loads of things that are absolutely true, and when you start to think, Now *this* is getting interesting, that's when he stops. One afternoon in Café Poland he had a whole lot to say about 'proletarian sentiment' and 'bourgeois ideologies'. I just listened. One time I said to him, 'It's wonderful how you understand everything so well.'

At that he started right in again and I couldn't get a word in edgewise for half an hour. And it really is wonderful, to someone who has to do what other people tell him his whole life without understanding much about it himself, and who is constantly being snarled at and has to eat margarine and live in stuffy little apartments. If I was allowed to keep even the slightest doubt I would join the Social Democratic Workers' Party too. One good thing, though: the people who always end up in stuffy apartments don't need me. And maybe they'd manage, somehow, without Hoyer too. I should check if it is allowed: doubt.

Things went badly with the agency, sales on commission. The sales on commission part was total nonsense, Bekker had just put it there because it sounded good, and someone who has translated Dante and written poems, even if there were only thirteen of them, should not be an agent for domestic and foreign firms. On a rainy December day, with the lamps lit

along the canal, I found Bekker leaning on his desk with his
head on his hand. The room was half dark. He was motionless.
I turned on the gaslight. There was three days' mail, unopened,
in the waste-paper basket behind him. He'd shoved the whole
pile in with his elbow, deliberately, without looking at it. He
had got rid of his employee months ago. They'd taken away his
phone. There he sat. A list of steamship departures hung on
the wall; the most recent one had long since returned and set
sail again, several times. On the mantel was a thick book: a
deluxe edition of the *Divina Commedia*.

The lamps were burning outside, pale and strange in the last
light of day, like some unaccountable mistake. The way they so
often did. Everything seemed like an unaccountable mistake.

Bekker is back working in an office now, with a good boss,
who respects him for having translated Dante. On days when
the weather is fine he lets Bekker leave early, so that he can
walk around a bit in the sun.

Bekker didn't turn to drink. He solves chess problems or
sleeps. He has no vision of the future and no longings, not even
for six o'clock. What good are they anyway? He takes a melancholy pleasure in collecting his salary, and a melancholy
pleasure in using it to buy neckties and shoes. His clothes are
properly brushed. Sometimes he feels a little pleased with himself for having 'lived the life of the mind' once.

He still goes and looks at a painting every once in a while. I
ran into him recently. He told me about *The Arrival of Queen
Wilhelmina at Frederiksplein,* Eerelman's painting, the one
with the ad for ODOL mouthwash painted on it so naturally.
Wouldn't that be a lovely painting to hang in a fancy phar-
macy? he said.

Kees is still working for the gas company and living in one
of those stuffy little apartments I mentioned. He doesn't know
where they'll find room for the next kid to sleep. The children
are still small but in a year or two they'll be squabbling every
morning over the one faucet and the one bathroom, the way it
always goes in District III neighbourhoods. He struggles with
what Hoyer calls 'the chronic shortages in working-class
households' and buys cigars only on Saturday nights. On

Sunday he has to keep the children in line. He gripes about
how he'd be doing so much better if he had only listened to his
father sooner.

His wife is good to him. He gets a clean handkerchief in the
middle of the week. But she wouldn't awaken desire in anyone
who isn't used to her like Kees is. It was different six years ago.

In his father's attic, where Kees used to have his 'place', his
sisters' underwear is hanging up to dry.

13

And Bavink?

In the battle against the 'goddamed things', Bavink lost, or
surrendered. The things that wanted to be painted and then,
when you thought, Well, in that case it'll have to happen,
turned out not to want to be painted after all. He was just
starting to become famous when the struggle came to an end.

Two months after my return he came and told me, in a very
calm voice, that he had cut his *View of Rhenen* to pieces. And
so he had. The river, the mountain, the Cunera Tower, the
blossoming apple trees, the red roofs of Rhenen, the chestnut
trees with their red and white flowers, the brown beeches and
the little windmill somewhere up on the mountain – into
sixty-four identical rectangles 15 by 12 1/2 cm each, with a
blunt penknife. It was hard work too.

The thing just wouldn't stop pestering him. It was worthless, totally worthless garbage. He wanted me to tell him why
anyone would paint. What's the point? He didn't know anything any more. He stretched out his arm and waved it around.
There, that's where the things are. He hit his forehead with his
fist. And *here*. They want to come out, but they don't come
out. It's enough to drive you out of your mind.

Almost a year later I saw him at Centraal Station, seeing
someone off on the eight o'clock train to Paris, a hairy guy
with long black curls and a huge beard, more hair than man,
and a high forehead with nothing behind it. The setting sun
shone big and red, it was at the edge of the glass and metal

roof, there was a reddish light in the window panes and the varnish on the train cars. Bavink was drunk. The train pulled away, slid out from under the station roof and curved to the left. As it turned, the light flashed brightly on the cars.

We strolled to the end of the platform. We came to a man with a signal lamp and I saw that as he passed us he looked at a conductor standing on another platform and made a drinking movement with his hand near his mouth. We stopped past the end of the roof and looked at the sun. 'You see the sun, Koekebakker?' The sun was especially clear, right in front of us, close by, bigger and redder than I had ever seen it. It almost touched the rails, it didn't flash brightly on things any more, there was a dull glow only on the frosted window panes of the train shed to the right of the track.

'You think I'm drunk?' I did indeed. 'It doesn't matter, Koekebakker, when I'm sober I don't understand anything anyway.

'Do you understand what the sun wants from me? I have thirty-four setting suns leaning against the wall, one on top of the other, all facing the wall. But every evening it's there again.'

'Unless it's cloudy,' I said. But he wouldn't let himself be distracted.

'Koekebakker, you've always been my best friend. I've known you since – how long has it been?'

'About thirteen years, Bavink.'

'Thirteen years. That's a long time. You know what you need to do? Do me a favour. You have a hatbox?'

I didn't say anything.

'Put it in a hatbox, Koekebakker. In a hatbox. I want to be left alone. Put it in a hatbox, a plain old hatbox. That's all it's worth.'

Bavink blubbered drunkard's tears. I looked around helplessly. A man in a uniform with a yellow stripe on his cap came up to us and spoke to me.

'I think it would be better, sir, if you took the gentleman home.'

I saluted and held out my arm for Bavink. He came willingly. He fell asleep in the taxi and woke up for a minute on

Nieuwezijds Voorburgwal when we drove over a pothole, and he wanted to start in on the hatbox again. But he fell right back asleep.

One morning he sat staring blankly in front of his last sunset. I arrived at his place with Hoyer. He didn't recognize us. He just looked at the sun, a big cold red sun setting behind the clouds.

'It just looks at me; neither of us knows what to do with each other.' He didn't say anything else.

Now he's in an institution. It's very peaceful there and he's calm. He just looks up at the sky, or gazes at the horizon, or sits staring into the sun until his eyes hurt. He's not supposed to do that but they can't get anywhere with him. They can't get him to talk. His paintings fetch a high price nowadays.

And old Koekebakker has turned into a sedate and sensible man. He just writes, receives his humble wages, and doesn't cause trouble.

God's throne is still unshaken. His world just takes its course. Now and then God smiles for a moment about the important gentlemen who think they're really something. A new batch of little Titans are still busy piling up little boulders so that they can topple him down off his heights and arrange the world the way they think it should be. He only laughs, and thinks: That's good, boys. You may be crazy but I still like you better than the proper, sensible gentlemen. I'm sorry you have to break your necks and I have to let the gentlemen thrive, but I'm only God.

And so everything takes its little course, and woe to those who ask: Why?

Translated by Damion Searls

5

F. BORDEWIJK

The Briefcase

De aktetas

It was already nearly ten years since the liberation. In that time Mr Kars had seen his family increase, he was approaching middle age and he was still working – after some previous uncertainty in employment – in one of those government offices concerned with the liquidation of war damage and restoration of rights, and intended to be self-liquidating. Thus he had finally become a civil servant.

But Mr Kars, who had quite soon risen to a senior position, was not at all afraid of his own liquidation. He had done too much creditable work for the government not to want to keep him on. He knew his value and fortunately the man at the top knew it too, so that in due course he would be sure to find reasonable state employment elsewhere.

He did a lot of extra work at home in the evenings, taking difficult files with him to study them at leisure. He came from a long line of civil servants, and remembered tales told by his grandfather, in whose day there were no such things as briefcases. The gentlemen of the various departments walked empty-handed, or with at most a stick or an umbrella, to and from the office. They devoted the evenings to their part-time jobs. Part-time jobs were very necessary in those days. It was impossible to say what had come first: low civil-service wages or the part-time job; anyway, no one worried their head about such matters.

But Mr Kars, without the time for or need of a part-time job, did need a briefcase. This had become so much a part of his public persona that his wife often had to relieve him of his briefcase before the start of a Sunday walk. It had only been absent-mindedness, and yet Mr Kars didn't enjoy the walk as much as he did during the week, although he recognized the compensation offered by the presence of his charming other half.

On this delightful May afternoon at slightly after five o'clock, Mr Kars was making his way home from work. He always walked. It wasn't far, about twenty minutes, from his office, in a large high-rise block, to his house in the same neighbourhood. Exercise was good for him, as he had a tendency to corpulence, and he liked walking. He was a fairly small chap, a fraction stooped, and usually paid little attention to his surroundings as he walked along, with his thoughts focused mainly on his files, as was the case this afternoon. He had never had much of an eye for young greenery, unless Mrs Kars pointed it out to him. She knew about his slight absent-mindedness and constantly warned him to be careful in traffic. In reply he appealed to the animal instinct for self-preservation, but, feeling that this reassurance was not quite sufficient, he added that he also kept a sharp lookout.

Mr Kars's route always, and hence also today, took him over a complicated junction. Somewhere close to his house he had to cross a large highway consisting of various lanes: a footpath of fine gravel, an asphalt bicycle lane, a clinker roadway, two tram lanes with overgrown grass between them, another asphalt bicycle lane, and another footpath of fine gravel. All these lanes were separated from each other by single lines of thick trees, which made the avenue very attractive but also obscured the view, so that a pedestrian could not make do with looking in each direction in turn as they crossed but definitely had to peer round the trunks as well. And in the place where Mr Kars used it the highway had a further feature, which made it a junction: it was used by another double tram lane for an S-shaped crossing.

At about quarter past five Mr Kars, coming from work that afternoon, crossed the avenue, which was carrying heavy traffic in both directions. Somewhere along the way he had the oddest sensation he had ever experienced. It couldn't be put into words in any language, nor could it be translated into a sound or an image or expressed in gestures. It was beyond the realm of sensory perception and at the same time it had something omnipresent about it. But the strangest thing was that he instantly forgot it.

He walked on. He had crossed the avenue. There ahead of him lay the winding cross-street through which the other pair of tram rails meandered. From now on he would follow the old familiar route: at right angles across this road then along a footpath with a small hill and gates at the beginning and end to keep out cyclists, then the residential area where he and his family rented a couple of rooms and he would definitely be home in five minutes.

However, once he had made his way across the second thoroughfare and was standing safely on the other pavement he was compelled by an inexplicable force to look back, and the first thing that struck him was a stationary motor vehicle between the rows of trees along the big avenue, at the front of which a group of spectators had already formed. That front swelled, and Mr Kars, who was standing there perfectly safely, with the entrance to the hilly footpath at his back, saw more and more curious people come running up and cyclists and moped riders dismount and cars stop. He saw it clearly from this short distance away and at the same time with a certain lack of interest. By nature he was not someone to want to be confronted by a traffic accident at close quarters. However, for a moment it recalled his strange sensation of just now. Had it perhaps been a kind of premonition that something was about to happen? Because look, hadn't it been in more or less the same place? And yet it was not so much the accident that fascinated him, as the impact it had on those around it, and the reaction fascinated him more than usual, though he wasn't aware of it.

He saw people asking questions feverishly, latecomers standing on tiptoe, everyone packed more and more together; he noticed the advantage of those with a large build, he saw buses slowing down in which the rows of heads suddenly turned towards the same spot and necks craned as far as they could. Meanwhile, another tram came sliding along the road where he was standing and when it followed its S-shaped line across the avenue where the accident was he saw all the passengers get up from their seats as if in response to a command, and rush to the windows as if the vehicle were a full pleasure-boat in rough weather.

Not thinking at all of the unfortunate who was undoubtedly lying there under the cowcatcher, Mr Kars watched with a slight amusement, which had come on slowly and was not at all in keeping with his character. Then came the blare of a police siren from somewhere. Mr Kars caught a glimpse of the closed horse-drawn carriage, but the throng was such that he lost sight of the rest and continued calmly on his way home. He would soon have something to tell his wife, tonight he would hear more about it on the radio and tomorrow morning he would read the report in the paper. Now, though, they were scarcely reports, since as accidents increased in number, their individual size decreased. The jokes column of the old daily had been replaced by the accident column of the present paper, and the typeface had remained the same.

Reflecting on these matters, not without some secret satisfaction at this comparison, Mr Kars climbed the gentle hill of the footpath, which was very little used, manoeuvred his way through the first gate with his customary routine, which required no more than three steps and three twists of the hips, and a little later manoeuvred in the same way through the gate on the other side of the hill. As he negotiated this second obstacle something unusual happened in that a strapping young man negotiated it at the same time, from the other side. The gates were daily witnesses of politeness and rudeness, of courteous invitations and stiff nods in reply to slight greetings and momentary smiles, frowns, curses under the breath and out loud, and besides the psychological clashes physical ones too. However, it escaped Mr Kars, who had not seen any reason to give right of way to the strapping young fellow, that on this occasion a mysterious feat had been achieved.

Mr Kars was now in the first avenue in the residential quarter. Four minutes and he would be home. It was quiet, and in the distance Mr Kars could hear four notes in a regular rhythm, melodious and melancholy. The signal stopped abruptly. It must be the ambulance.

It was not this four-note signal in itself that suddenly made Mr Kars go cold, nor was it the fact that – for the first time – he associated the sound specifically with death – it was that at the same time he became aware of his briefcase and, realized, he did not know how, that the case was dead. It gave him a feeling of unimaginable cold. Yes, it really was his briefcase, really his briefcase, quite scuffed from use, but tough and stuffed with files. He carried it as always in his left hand, he had not let go of it for an instant, and yet the briefcase no longer had any weight, it was not actually dead, but more, or less; Mr Kars was carrying a ghost. For a moment he considered taking his fingers off the handle, but he didn't dare. He was afraid; he knew that the briefcase would go on floating. Then he felt huge beads of sweat breaking out on his forehead and at the same time felt that they were not there. And he heard, he did not know from where – inside him or outside him – words that he had perhaps once read, or overheard, caught in passing in the street: death does not immediately free itself from the earth.

Mr Kars stood there like a statue. And saw it in front of him. When he went home he didn't need the key, he could pass straight through the closed front door, through the door of the room, and no one would know. His wife would pick up the telephone and hear an unfamiliar deep voice:

'Madam, highway police here. I regret to inform you that I have some very grave news. We'll be with you shortly.'

Perhaps his wife was holding the receiver to her ear at this moment. Yes, she was. She was ashen. And, oh God, his children were there too.

Translated by Paul Vincent

6

MARIA DERMOÛT

The Sirens

De sirenen

The story goes . . .

It was not a man but a woman who bought the proa, a beautiful proa, carved, gaily painted, on the stem the single, wide-open, 'all-seeing' eye, tall masts of bamboo, which could be lowered when the wind would not come, triangular sails of plaited leaves, brown and red, which could also be lowered, or could serve as an awning in storm or shower, or when there was too much sunlight or too much moonlight.

A proa with a broad bamboo wing on one side, and of shallow draught to get through the straits between the drowned lands, with here, there and everywhere small islands, one large island far away on the one side, and a great continent far away on the other. Where?

Once everything had formed part of that continent: the single large island, all the little islands, the drowned land in between, all one land. The Land of the Tiger had been its name, long ago.

The Land of the Tiger was there no more.

The sea was still there, as of old.

The woman did not buy the proa because she loved the sea. She did not love the sea. She was afraid of the sea.

She loved the great continent she had never seen but where she longed to go; she must! She should! That was the reason she had bought the proa. That was the reason she had left the one large island, her home.

Where along the river, on the edge of the woods, under the trees, stood the 'longhouses' (which belonged to the women), built on high stilts, with beautiful carved beams, with beautiful carved flights of steps leading upward.

Where every night torches were lit, exactly half an hour after midnight, and the men had to leave the women, going down the steps of the longhouses, down a dark path to their own quarters, some distance into the woods.

Where she, too, lived in a longhouse with her mother, who was the head of the family, of all the families in the longhouse. The women and children in the houses, the men on their own in the woods.

And she the eldest daughter!

Where life could have been good, waiting for her turn to buy, for so many sarongs and headcloths woven with gold or silver thread and weighed on the scales, a man she liked; waiting to bear children, preferably female children! Listening to the roaring waters, the tall rustling trees, and at half an hour after midnight the crackle of blazing torches, and the sound of the men's voices coming through the dark, as they climbed down the stairs of the longhouses, complaining as they went. Waiting for her turn to become the head of the family, of all the families in the longhouse, after her mother had died.

But this woman had not awaited her turn, she had bought a proa with everything that went with it, and a young man for her shipmate; and a cat, a striped cat, yellow and black, for the mice. She was afraid of mice. And she had put to sea on the proa, with the man, with the cat, sailing through the straits between the drowned land and the myriad small islands, which she visited one after the other – with the one large island where she would never return to one side – to search for the great continent on the other. For days, for months, for years.

She never found the continent, the story goes.

In the marketplaces on the little islands the villagers drew in their breaths, and stared at one another.

The woman! A heavy, full sarong woven of real gold and silver threads, a black girdle around her waist, a cloth of black silk swathed about her breasts, her black hair combed tightly back and oiled; moving easily, her shoulders pulled back, looking straight ahead of her, and always in front.

Behind her came the man, beautifully dressed like herself, a straight sarong tied high up under the armpits, a headcloth, both rich with gold and silver, a present from the woman in all probability, a flower tucked behind his ear. He kept his distance, and carried a basket containing their provisions. He was a young man, younger than the woman, but not young enough to be her son. Too old for a son? Too young for a husband?

Who was he? What was he?

Relation? Shipmate? Lover? No one could tell from his appearance.

Beside the woman walked a large yellow and black striped cat, who would meow from time to time and stroke his flanks against her sarong until the woman said 'Pssh!' to him and he returned to his place at her side.

At the markets on those little islands the woman bought provisions. Fresh, clean water for the earthenware bowls on the proa; charcoal for cooking when at sea; oil for a lamp at night and food for herself, the man and the cat, rice and tubers, red peppers, coconuts and lots of lemons, dried meat and fish which would keep a long time, and sweetmeats, tobacco and perfume. She was fond, too, of buying flowers, flowering shrubs in pots, which lasted well, even on a boat. Most of all she liked the hibiscus, with its red flowers. The man wore a red hibiscus flower behind his ear.

He must be the woman's lover!

For the cat she bought raw meat, still red with blood. Cats like blood. The woman paid in cloths of gold or silver thread, large and small.

Afterward she dealt out some sweetmeats and tobacco and stood talking with the villagers in the marketplaces on the little islands; about the weather and the wind and the straits and about the drowned land – she stared straight ahead of her – and . . . about the continent.

The villagers would nod; they had heard about it.

Some said they knew where it was. One man said he had been there.

But when the woman asked, 'Where? Where?' they pointed

north and south and east and west, to the four silent Sheikhs
at the corners of the earth, to all four at once.

'Ah, bah,' said the woman and shrugged her shoulders.

The young man and the cat stood there silent, the one
behind her, the other at her side. They took no part in the conversation. They listened.

Was the young man the woman's lover?

The young man was the woman's lover.

It had come about like this.

Not all at once, not in the beginning. In the beginning the
woman slept on her beautiful, painted wooden couch behind a
matted sail, while the mate slept here and there in the proa, on
a little mat.

The cat tried to find a place to sleep on the woman's couch;
sometimes she would allow it, not every night.

One day, when they had been sailing for a long time around
the little islands, around the drowned land, without finding
the continent, the woman called the shipmate and told him
that he should share her couch at night. Then she would give
him the trunk full of beautiful men's clothes, the gold and silver sarongs and the headcloths; not only for him to wear on
special occasions, for the market, but for keeps. He could
weigh the clothes on the scales if he liked, to see their worth.
And she would give him the flowerpots on the stern with the
red-flowered hibiscus, for him to keep as his own. The man
gazed at the woman as she spoke.

He had often gazed at her; the way she would squat on a
mat, the way she would lie on the couch, the way she rose and
walked away, the way she halted, paused; he had often gazed
at the way she held her head and looked straight ahead of her
as she was speaking.

He, too, had come from the one large island, but in his part
there were no longhouses. There a woman walked and stood
and held her head in quite a different way. There a woman did
not look straight ahead of her and say what she pleased: that a
man may come and share her couch at night. There a man said
such things to a woman. Like that. And walked and stood and
held his head, like that, and looked straight ahead of him.

The mate thought the woman beautiful, in her golden sarong, black girdle, black breastcloth, with black knotted hair, looking straight ahead of her, as she stood by the rail of the proa, the sky a nocturnal blue, the moon and stars behind her. And the sea under the white moonlight, he thought beautiful, too; and the horizon silvery, hazy, far away – was there land over there? Or was there no land over there? And the proa, too, he thought beautiful: the masts, the purple sails, all its carved woodwork; and the gold and silver clothes in the trunk as well, the sarongs and headcloths, and on the stern the flowerpots with the hibiscus and its red flowers. He was fond of red flowers. He was fond of all these things.

'All right,' he said to the woman, 'as you wish.'

It was not the first time he had shared a woman's couch. He liked doing so.

The mate, the young man, Tuangku So-and-So, or whatever his name might be, liked quite a number of things.

The only thing he did not like was the cat.

It was as though the woman noticed it.

During the day the cat would be lying somewhere on the proa in the sun, licking itself clean with a curly pink tongue, blinking its yellow eyes against the light, yawning, and dozing a little. But at night when the man and the woman were lying on the couch, the cat would be gone. Sometimes, absent-minded, the young man would ask: 'Where is that cat?' not because he cared; he did not. And the woman would say she had put the cat down in the hold where there were mice. He would catch them in the dark.

Sometimes, when it was a still, windless night, and the proa was quiet on its anchor stones, and the man and the woman quiet on their couch, they could hear the cat.

A dull thud like a cat jumping, peep, peep, and then nothing more but the sound of crunching, for a second, a second, no more.

The young man drew in his breath between his lips. 'Ugh, cats love blood!' he said and shuddered. 'Yes,' said the woman at his side, 'cats love blood.'

Every day, in the late afternoon when work was finished,

when the proa was washed down and scrubbed for the night, they would throw out their anchor somewhere on the lee side, near the drowned land, not so near that the proa could run aground, still out in the deep water. Then they washed and scrubbed themselves down to be clean for the night. They liked to be clean, all three of them. The cat washed and licked itself almost every moment of the day and night. He was always clean.

The woman hung up a sail to act as a screen and washed herself behind it with fresh water from a bowl; she always used oils and perfume and lemons, then she was clean, and fragrant too.

The young man took a daily plunge in the sea. He was a good swimmer. Every day the woman tried to restrain him, but he would not listen to her.

He laid aside his flower, his headcloth and his sarong, and dived into the sea over the railing of the proa.

With a few short, powerful strokes, he put the deep water, full of sharks who like blood – he knew that well enough! – behind him. He always said he swam faster and better than the sharks.

And then he was above the drowned land, it was not deep there. Vast plains under the water, covered with algae like grass, green and brown and very wet. And in these meadows cattle were grazing, as they should be.

In the meadows of the sea, the sea-cattle were grazing. They grazed in herds on the floor of the shallows, large and black, with tails like fishes, with round black heads, round black glimmering eyes, round mouths with protruding white teeth, with which they nibbled at the algae. They were mammals, with breasts like a woman's with two long fins to the right and left, on which they would lean, as though they were arms, whenever they lifted themselves up. And this they often had to do, to breathe in air above the surface and to gaze out over the sea.

Not in the fierce sunlight. In the dusk, in mist, or at night. They looked like women, these sea-cattle. And they lowed.

Accompanied, muted, sometimes drowned by the noise of sea, waves and wind, they seemed to sing, these black women under the water – the Sirens, as they have been called from ancient days.

The young man went up to them, wading through the shallows, and stood at their sides, sat down among them. Or, if the water was very shallow, he would lie down on his back, in their midst.

They came nearer, forming a circle around him. They did not harm him, they were only curious. They lifted their bodies, their heads; they looked at him, and they sang to him.

After a while he came back, wading through the shallows, swimming very powerfully through the deep sea where the sharks lay in wait, and climbed back into the proa. He felt clean after his swim. He took a fresh sarong and headcloth, plucked himself a new, red flower.

And then the woman said: 'Why do you swim in the sea every day? What is the point of it? Those sea-cattle will do you harm. One day they will kill you and drink your blood!'

The man laughed. 'Since when did cattle drink blood? Cats like blood, and sharks.' And drawing away from the woman, he gazed back upon the drowned meadows, green and brown under the water, and at the black, recumbent forms there, and pointing to them, he said: 'Those creatures over there aren't cows. They're women.'

The woman stood there in that way of hers, her shoulders pulled back, her head held high, and looking straight ahead of her.

'Ah bah! What beautiful women!' she said scornfully.

'I did not say they are beautiful,' said the man, 'no one could say that the black women under the water are beautiful.' After a pause he added: 'They can sing. Didn't you ever hear it? If you were to listen carefully, you could hear it, too.'

'Ah bah!' said the woman. 'Cows are cows, on land and under the sea. Cows do not sing, they low!'

The young man did not answer. He stood beside her in his gold and silver garments, the red flower behind his ear, looking beyond her and smiling.

He liked the green and brown meadows. And the black women. And their singing.

Every day, at dusk, as night began to fall, this scene would be repeated. The woman said this, the man said that, and at night they lay side by side on the couch.

The woman always wore – all the women of the longhouses did – a pin, as thin as a gold thread from her sarong. Nobody could see she was wearing it.

Not at once, gradually, the woman got into the habit of rising in the night from the man's side, carefully!

He lay, as he always lay when asleep, flat on his back, his arms at his side to left and right, one hand hanging over the edge of the couch. He slept, sound and deep, and dreamed.

The woman walked, as she always walked, but very cautiously now, along the one plank that did not creak, to the trapdoor covering the hatch and opened it – the hinges were well-oiled – whispered, 'Puss,' and the cat – very cautiously too – came up from the hold and together they walked back, the woman on bare feet, the cat on velvet paws, along the plank that did not creak. The woman bent down, took the sleeper's hand – he did not notice it – and pricked the tip of his finger with the little gold pin, so quickly, so carefully, he did not feel anything. She kept hold of the hand, as slowly, drop by drop, the blood started to flow from it.

'Puss,' she said, without moving her lips; and the cat opened his mouth and the drops of blood fell onto his tongue, not a drop was spilled, and the man did not feel a thing. After a time the blood stopped flowing. The woman dried the man's hand gently and laid it on the couch at his side. He slept on; he had felt nothing.

The cat licked his mouth clean and the woman conducted him back to the hatchway, fastened down the trapdoor after him and went back to lie down beside the man on the couch again, so quietly that he did not notice a thing.

The same scene was repeated every day, in the evening twilight . . . during the night . . .

One day when the young man woke in the early morning and lifted himself up on the couch, he saw that the sun had coloured everything a rosy red: the woman and himself and the proa and the drowned land and the sea-cattle and a little

island somewhere and the far horizon, and he stroked his hand
over his eyes, his head.

'I sometimes have very queer dreams,' he said to the woman.
'Not at all pleasant. Always the same dream, but I can't remember what.' He looked pale in the morning light. And the woman
said, 'What is the use of all this swimming in the sea? It's making you ill, and one day . . .' And the man said . . .

So now they said these things twice a day, at early dawn and
late in the evening.

The young man loved both – the morning and the evening;
the day, the long and lovely day . . . and the night? He no longer
knew whether he loved the night.

In the past he had loved the night as well. And his dreams.

Her shipmate did not rise from the couch that morning; the
woman had left it long before he woke. He pulled himself up
again, stroked his hand once more across his eyes, his head,
and said: 'I remember now! I dreamed of the cat. All these
nights I have been dreaming of the cat!' He cursed savagely. 'I
don't like dreaming of that wretched cat!'

He seemed to be talking to himself, not to the woman, who
made no reply. He fell back on the couch; he looked pale and
kept falling asleep. That day the woman left the proa riding at
anchor. She managed to do all the work. She hauled up a sail to
prevent the sun from annoying the man. She cooked and brought
him food and drink. But he cared for neither food nor drink.

She asked if he would like her to wash him down? 'No,' he
said. What he wanted was a clean sarong and headcloth. She
fetched them and plucked a fresh, red hibiscus flower for him.

'Thank you,' he said. He looked at the flower, sniffed at
it – hibiscus flowers have no scent – put it in his hair and fell
asleep again. At sunset, in the dusk, he got up and leaned
against the rail. He could still have managed, he thought, to
walk in the meadows, under the water, in the vicinity of the
sea-cattle, but he knew for sure that he could no longer swim
faster and more powerfully than the sharks.

And so the woman no longer said this, the man that. Why
should they? The man lay down again on the couch, closed his
eyes, slept, dreamed.

In the evening, at night, he no longer dreamed of the cat. The woman no longer lay down at his side – why should she? She slept somewhere, anywhere, in the proa, on a mat; she did not get up in the night, she did not use her pin, she did not open the trapdoor for the cat. Why should she? The cat meowed a little, down there in the hold. The man did not hear it. The woman feigned not to hear it.

Never before had it been so dark – no moon, no stars and no oil left for the little lamp. The proa lay at anchor, the man lay silent on the couch, the woman silent on her mat, even the cat fell silent down in the hold, when late at night the wind rose, not a strong wind, not a storm or a typhoon or anything of that sort – just the wind – and the proa swayed a little, as if a strong current was drawing it through deep waters, so deep that the anchor stones could no longer reach the bottom. The woman squatted on her mat. What if they ran onto the submerged land and capsized and were drowned? What if they were thrown up on a high shore or on the rocks? But none of these things happened –

Slowly the proa was propelled forward towards some destination; its anchors afloat, all through the night. A slight shock. The proa lay still.

The woman got up. She walked, groping through the dark, to the couch to rouse the mate. She could not rouse him. She caught hold of the hand that lay at his side on the couch. The hand felt chill in her own hand. She placed it back where it had lain.

Suddenly the cat growled, again and again, down in the hold. 'Be quiet!' the woman whispered to herself and propped herself up against the couch to wait for the daylight. She waited for a long time. Why did it have to be so long? The mate did not move. Now and then the cat meowed, and every time the woman caught her breath.

At last, in the first murky grey light long before the dawn, the woman saw that the proa was near land, that on one side it was touching it, the broad bamboo wing on the other side lying on the water.

A steep shore, rocky and dark, and behind the rocks a

forest – never before had she seen so dark a forest – and, in the distance, hills and further forest. A land! Dark. A dark continent.

The woman looked at the ship's mate in the grey light. He was deathly pale. He was, in fact, dead. Down in the hold the cat meowed and growled so loud it was as if every now and then he screamed, and he kept jumping up against the trapdoor.

'Quiet!' the woman cried.

First of all, she washed herself; she combed her hair, brushed her teeth, powdered her body; she opened a trunk and got out her most beautiful golden sarong, her most beautiful breast-cloth; she pulled sarong and breastcloth tight about her and put on a broad girdle. Then she walked to the couch, bent down and took her shipmate up in her arms – he was not very heavy – walked with him to the railing of the proa, not on the side of the continent, on the other side, near the drowned land. She drew herself up and, arching her body she threw him over the side, beyond the bamboo wing, into the meadows under the waters, the fields where the sea-cattle graze. Then she turned away.

The cat was now growling incessantly and jumping up incessantly at the trapdoor. The proa seemed to be creaking in all its joints.

'Yes, yes, all right!' said the woman. 'I'm coming.' And she opened the trapdoor; the cat came up out of the hold, lashing his tail to and fro. His burning yellow eyes took everything in at one glance: the woman, the proa, the drowned land on the one side, the sea-cattle – where the man was lying – the continent on the other side, the woods, the hills, the mountains, the forest all around, and again the woman – he growled and in one spring he leaped out of the proa and stood on the high rocky shore, a full-grown tiger, golden yellow with black stripes, terrible to behold.

The woman climbed, awkwardly, hampered by her golden sarong, first over the railing of the proa and then up the steep rocks, to join the animal, which was waiting for her there. Then they walked on together, the tiger first, the woman following, to the forests on the hills, to the mountains of the great continent, their destination . . .

The beautiful proa was left abandoned (even the mice deserted it) on the shore of the continent, until the storm wind should come and dash it to pieces.

Every night, in the light of the moon, in the light of the stars, perhaps even in the dark – but then no one can see – a young man, Tuangku So-and-So, or whatever his name may be, lies in a drowned meadow somewhere near Malaya.

In a gold and silver sarong, strung up high under the armpits like a taut sleeve around his body, a narrow gold and silver cloth wound tightly around his head, a red flower, a hibiscus flower, behind one ear.

He lies straight and quiet among the moist brown and green algae. Yet he is not drowned. Neither is he asleep. He lies quietly on his back, his arms at his sides.

He keeps his eyes closed, like one who is listening. He keeps his eyes open – then he is looking through the water. Around him, in a circle, are the black women, the Sirens, singing to him.

They are singing about something, about anything, about everything.

They are singing about a proa and a woman and a ship's mate and a cat. They are singing about a great continent, somewhere, and about a tiger. But it is all an old story to him.

Sometimes he cannot help but laugh at what they are singing; but not always.

He lies very quiet, listening –

He is a lucky man, that Tuangku So-and-So, or whatever his name may be.

He will never grow old; he will never have to die again.

Not only does he like the songs of the Sirens, he understands the songs of the Sirens –

So the story goes.

Translated by Etty Kist and James Brockway

SIMON VESTDIJK

My Brown Friend

De bruine vriend

I remember virtually nothing of the immediate surroundings of my parental home, a bulging forehead above the crumbling teeth of a shop, although I must have played there from childhood on. Fissures run through the house itself, the front seems to have been cracked by hardship, which in fact we never knew. What a host of contradictions! Instead of the rooms simply leading into each other, they (so I imagine them) fit into each other in a lopsided way, as if they had to take turns in serving as each other's box beds. In my memories of childhood, games are delayed by mighty thresholds; the beds on the other hand are small, shrunken, as if burnt out. A pear-shaped brass lamp, gleaming with paraffin (as a small child I spoke of 'parraffa', with a throaty r-sound that my elder sister imitated; 'parraffa' for me was both paraffin and associated with snakes, but perhaps also with a variety of biting fish, one or more of which I suspected in the green, parchment-covered jars that the boys took home with them after a long afternoon's fishing on the ditches around the town), in the evenings that lamp then illuminated very strongly and harshly the bald back of the head of my prematurely aged but lively father, who at that time usually sat at his shop accounts in clouds of tobacco smoke, drumming his feet with impatience when he couldn't balance them, so that the sailing ship in the bell jar on the clothes cupboard clattered along with him, as if it were suddenly full of half cents and my father was prepared to give up that one half cent. In my memory my mother is beautiful and dark, but has allowed herself to become bourgeois, and prematurely aged, and even my

sister seemed to be struggling against an approaching weight
of years. She sang long songs passionately in the kitchen, in her
room on summer evenings, when other girls grow quiet. She
was always running about and in uproar, always on the point
of doing something intense and decisive, a step for life. With
bright-red cheeks and sparkling black eyes she flew back and
forth among the neighbours, making dates for evening get-
togethers. Although at the time my story begins she had only
just turned nineteen, she wanted to be the life and soul of every
party; she saw her youth as less of an obstacle than one more
incentive, and then there was that general trait in our family:
feeling disadvantaged, imagining we were despised by the little
town and for that very reason trying to vie with the elite of the
town dignitaries. Although well-to-do and a respected citizen,
my father could of course not expect the Hon. So-and-So with
his Irish setter to greet my mother in the street. He understood
that, and so did my mother, although it remained a thorn in
the flesh. My sister, however, celebrated her nineteenth birthday with a tantrum, because that setter had passed with a
non-greeting Hon. So-and-So. She inculcated manners in me,
gave me messages to deliver to Revd Kalmans about the church
choir, which relied on her clear soprano, and gave me slaps
under the table when I teased her about young men or young
people who in her eyes were too inferior to free her from her
obsession with the Hon. So-and-So. I still loved her, though.
Her face enchanted me, and I still believe that she was too
beautiful for the town. She was not vain, in the sense normally
attached to the word, not big-headed, she was open and honest; it was just that she expected the world would bring her
what she would not make any effort to attain for herself! The
fact that she deliberately dressed less well than other girls, was
rather an instinctive gesture than a sign of false humility. The
only ambiguous attitude that I occasionally caught her out on
in this respect was her complete lack of interest in my
grammar-school education. But in those days secondary
schools did not yet form part of girls' education and I can only
assume that she was jealous of an axiomatic privilege and
demonstrated it in this way.

For me the whole of the rest of the town is built around that grammar school. It was, as it were, its Burgos Cathedral. A huge sea inlet – huge in my imagination – that created and interrupted horizons, gave birth to islands almost volcanically from the fog and then made them sink again like sandbanks in a spring tide, had made the town itself so temporary and provisional that the large, shiny building with its systematic knowledge and the mostly very energetic teachers was definitely necessary to make one believe in a permanent human settlement with a clearly circumscribed life plan. Nature squashed the town, scattered it into slums, came to an alarmed halt before the historic-town-hall, but behind its back denied it with a particularly dirty livestock market, where it glugged its way down brown gutters to the single shopping street with that strangely stuffy, suffocating, vaguely sexy smell of textiles, which were measured between thumb and index finger in no less than four different Jewish shops (my father did not know these people, although he was himself mainly a manufacturer) – and apart from that kept to the really elegant and shady quays, far too good for the ramshackle rubbish within them. In front of the country house of the non-greeting Hon. So-and-So built not so long ago (he lived there with an elder sister who was known as 'the Hon. Miss Sticks'; not content with this distortion, at the grammar school we talked about 'the Hon. Miss Acheron', secretly horrified by her appearance; she was large and muscular, with a burnt-out look and a skin like grated cheese), nature spread out obligingly in a single sward of pleasure, but that was immediately the end of it, and it already reverted vengefully via views of improbably lush green meadows grazed by cows, low dunes, piles of old rust and rubbish, crooked windmills, whitened bones of rebels against the Spanish, to a horrifically bleak sea, which misty, breathing with a hollow sound, moved past basalt like a canal widened a thousand times, separated itself into a muddy little harbour, a gathering point for Calvinist skippers weakened by inbreeding, and then flowed back into itself with a couple of eddies, without surf, without horizon, scarcely any fishing boats, but lots of crabs on the dyke walking sideways, and over everything the indescribable stench of rotting jellyfish and periwinkles, which, although with an entirely different origin, most resembled in its effect on the mind that smell of yellow cotton in the high street, through which we as boys trooped, after having played at the sea for an afternoon, tired and dusty and a little anxious because, once again, everything had turned out to be so endless and futile. An old gateway with some coat of arms or other on it was the conclusion of the grey, wide, square-like extension of the shopping street. Old fishermen leaned against it and spat over massive yellow butcher's dogs. Yes and here the sea began again, which just now one thought one had escaped. It was everywhere. On three sides of the town one saw sea (or mist); who has ever heard of such a thing? The only difference was that at the gate it stank of dried dab rather than rotting jellyfish – and that suddenly, God knows where from, like a brand-new world in the chaos of mist, a lighthouse loomed up, exactly on the corner of the harbour, black and yellow, striped like a zebra, long-necked like a giraffe, and at night of course sweeping its light. For a long time I did not know the exact rhythm with which that light went to and fro; I always thought that it was not visible from land anyway and not even from close by on the sea, but that one would have to go a long, long way into that wretched element to catch sight of it like a diplomatic wink intended for the far side of the conference hall. Perhaps as far as the Gravel Bank, which was submerged at high tide, and which boys sometimes rowed around looking for shells. But the Gravel Bank was also a misty concept to me, something that was there and then not there, something that represented danger and yet consisted of ordinary sand . . . No need to say, after all this, how much I hated the sea. I hated the sea, because it always wanted to be different from usual, I hated it for its famous past, still present with us, that exuded the stink of dead periwinkles, for its inert anger, its nervous multiform ponderousness and the inhospitable way in which it deposited home-made boats on the dyke. If it had not been for the grammar school, I should have despaired of life, but as it was it was all right, until I was fifteen or sixteen.

So for me conscious, demonstrable human existence began

with my entrance exam, an event that had already shone its
illuminating rays years in advance. A wonderful time, in which
one discovers things! Probably one doesn't even feel that much
happier than later, but one is more mobile, looser, more alert,
more open, which the grown-up then confuses with happiness
and cheerfulness. I remember young madcaps who inside were
melancholics. My friend Gerard Steierman was an exception to
the extent that he combined precisely a calm and sedate presence with a cheerful nature, but of a very odd kind, and
definitely unyouthful in its imperturbability. With his surprised childlike eyes, his sing-song and pedantic Overijsel
dialect – he seemed ingenuous; however, one gradually found
out that he was a philosopher and clever in an unsuspected
way. But he also always remained top of the class, without
much effort, and his sceptical philosophical bent made him
anything but a teacher's pet. Later I lost sight of him. He probably became a surveyor, as he always said; he was too modest
for university; anyway, being able to continue your studies was
an exception in those days. After the other boys realized that
their teasing and imitation of his Overijsel dialect could not
make the slightest difference to the expression of those big,
grey-blue circles, he immediately became popular, although on
the sports field, unlike me – we played mainly rounders – he
found it hard to keep up. But besides sport and homework, he
had a third world!

At first he was very secretive about the 'atomic theory' that
he had invented; it took me three long evening walks before I
heard him say in a strangled tone: 'An atom is a *vertebra* in
the ether' – for the first time emotionally, for the first time
solemnly! – though he was always solemn, and I should have
known what was coming. There followed months of weighty
philosophizing, first about matter then mind, then about both,
then about girls, but that didn't last long, because Gerard was
so horrified at the things I confided to him – although I found
his confidences much worse – that he said nothing for days and
just stared and stared, attentive and cheerful, though without
any evil intent. Still, there was a slight estrangement, and from
then on we philosophized only in catechism class, that is under

direction. How much I would have liked to hear more about those atoms! It seemed to me a theory worthy of being hatched out in a misty place like ours. Mobile and omnipresent as they were, in the sea water, among the basalt stones, among the tobacco juice of the old fishermen, those mysteriously turning particles made up for municipal monotony almost as much as a haunted house, but I never managed to extract anything clearer in outline from Jard (as we called him, in the Zeeland way), and perhaps he had forgotten the whole theory.

I see the teachers all as young chaps with springy steps, bursting with *joie de vivre* and facts they wanted to impart to us; even the headmaster can't have been older than forty. Disorder was unknown. There were murmurings about a model school, with iron discipline, maintained playfully. It was true that strange figures turned up among the pupils in the senior classes: boys who couldn't keep up at other schools or had been expelled for worse reasons. We had them from all parts of the country. Every year, on the first day before school began, it seemed as if we had acquired some more new teachers in a pair of those surly pipe-smoking types who don't fit into third-form desks and had their heads full of the sea or pubs or girls. Because the newcomers for all their antics were remarkably well-disciplined, the grammar school did not suffer much from its designation as a deportation colony. The outsiders, though, were highly respected by us younger boys, despite the fact that they ignored us entirely; their heroic deeds were retold, exaggerated and later attributed in turn to others who had nothing whatsoever to do with them – but for real outbreaks of wickedness, which might have been feared, there was too much Zeeland peasant blood in our classes: industrious, rather narrow-minded roundheads, nice lads for the most part, not high-flyers, not demons! Solid Dutch, with a touch of Spanish blood, so they say, blood that is used to controlling itself and being controlled. And except for the teasing to which Gerard Steierman was subjected for a while, I never noticed any kind of unpleasant tone among the local pupils; even the Jews were left unmolested. And obviously the discrimination about which my parents complained, and which, real or imagined, had left such a deep mark on my sister, passed me by without a trace.

My actual story begins in the autumn between the second and third form; the new term was preceded by a carefree long vacation with lots of fresh air, lots of conversations with Gerard Steierman and the occasional love affair of the kind one has as a boy, not very profound and fully part of the general emotional atmosphere of unfounded excitement. I was thoroughly rested and very open to new impressions. The new term was due to start in a week's time when one afternoon Gerard and I and some other boys were walking to and fro outside the grammar school, perhaps out of impatience. Sea, meadow and canals had no more attractions for us; we had become jaded by rowing, pole vaulting and fishing; to put it bluntly we were longing for books and a teacher's voice above our heads. Although we called the school names – of course – it was with a secret love. We discussed the possibilities of the deportation colony: what guest would we be accommodating? Look, there, Gerard's finger pointed in the direct of the terrace of houses next to the grammar school building. Out of boredom all of us now peered in that direction, but at first noticed nothing but a few fourth-formers, who were standing in a huddle smoking. Four figures separated from them and came strolling towards us; I did not have the feeling this was very significant. Anyway, I recognized three of the four when they got closer: two outsiders from last year, Jelte Veenstra, a lad from the north of the country, who had hit a teacher up there with a knuckleduster, a gloomy John Bull by the look of him, with loutish drinker's eyes, and the impudent, slim, Charles Desmet with immaculate hair, about who we were wont to whisper about light fingers; and finally the son of one of the Jewish shopkeepers from our high street, who was generally called Rusman, although I believe his name was Heiman Asser Polak. This Rusman, four-square in build, but with a supple gait and strikingly dark appearance – hence his nickname, which on our lips had something flattering about it – had acted for some years as a mentor to new batches of exiles, to whom he was able to remain faithful as, deliberately lazing about, he never went up from his fourth form; I had long relished the thought of being in the same class next year. Commanding respect through a kind of taciturn restraint, he did not fall at all within the category 'Jew', which involuntarily always invoked an element of noisiness. In addition Rusman really had a handsome face; I still remember, at about twelve, watching the rounders game, when a man behind me, a kind of skipper with rings in his ears and a grey fringe of beard stained with tobacco juice around a weak mouth hanging open, said to someone else: 'That's a fine-looking young chap!' Although there were five or six boys playing, I knew at once who was meant. It was the first time that I heard one male praised by another for his physical attractiveness, and in some way that insignificant incident took deep root in me, although I don't think one should look for anything else in it but the joy of hearing the admiration we felt for a schoolmate confirmed by a real grown-up.

So that because all three of the boys had a more than usual significance for me, I was unprepared to find something between them, that easily outstripped them, and according to quite different criteria than they represented. The group strolled past us at a distance of ten paces, with that further member in the middle who had a limp: that was the first thing I saw about him. I thought: A boy with a limp – what's he doing with Rusman, Desmet and Jelte Veenstra? At the same instant a look full of derision reached me, transmitted above the unfortunate hobbling movement which just became apparent. The cold self-control that his whole being expressed, the well-proportioned shape of his slim body, which seemed to bear the affliction proudly and stoically as an eternally imposed gymnastic exercise, the trait of rebelliousness and the sneering aggrieved expression around that sharply etched mouth, made no less of an impact on me. I did not know what all this meant. A tightly clenched wave of emotion rose in my throat, when the bitter image of the cripple, who was no longer paying any attention to me, had passed by. Why should that boy pay attention to *me*? I could still see the pale, haughtily sneering face, slightly ginger with faint summer freckles; the nose fine, short and flat; the bags under the brown eyes which peered coldly and contemptuously – and finally I saw nothing else but that seeking and groping, in a face that I had already forgotten. There is something copper-coloured about that boy, I thought. There he strolled in the distance, limping, his short brown jacket flapping in the wind and yet with such inimitable distinction in my eyes, that it was as if a prince in exile, surrounded by rough retainers – two nobles and the dragoman! – had left behind his weariness and his derisive revolt. But why had that derision been aimed at me, who knew I was inferior to no one on earth!? I may be small and quite ugly, but I am straight-limbed and muscular enough, and I think that those transition years were far from showing me in the least flattering way, as is often the case with other boys. Despite my dislike of the sea I was an excellent fisherman and swimmer; this summer I had rowed three times to the Gravel Bank! And I wasn't stupid either, even Gerard Steierman, although he sometimes called me a fool, looked up to me! As I called the indifferent troop to mind again, I searched and searched and suddenly had the thought that Rusman, who knew everything about every boy, might have said something about it to me, just before that look hit me. I went off looking for the rest of the day, in a vague anxiety, a dark enchantment. Gerard and the others didn't even know his name.

Three days or so later, for want of anything better to do, we had gathered at one of our ditches, just outside the town, Gerard Steierman, myself and the two Evertsen brothers: Henk, a good-natured tree of a fellow, and the slightly younger Boudewijn, who was much smaller and a little vicious. Gerard was just attempting the run-up, holding our only pole ahead of him, when I saw on the other side of the meadow opposite the same threateningly indifferent band from three days before. Waving their arms, legs wide apart like sailors on deck, they approached, with the limper in their midst, his loose jacket flapping around him in that unusual, almost birdlike way. My heart was beating fast. But Gerard too seemed to have smelled a mysterious rat: he slowed down, stopped just before the canal, and began poking the pole in the water, as if he wanted first to kill some deep-sea monsters, before venturing across.

At the same moment he turned a stone whooshed between
Henk Evertsen and me: the dancing arms of the limper had
been looking for a target! Nothing had changed in the listlessly
strolling limp, the faintly contemptuous smile appeared on the
coppery face, and then another stone came towards us, which
plunged into the water, and another, which almost hit Gerard
Steierman's right arm. 'Stop it!' shouted Henk Evertsen calmly.
But I thought: Don't shout. It's not intended for you, that stone.
It's a gift from that boy to me . . .' Because I had seen it: the
movement of throwing, without any effort or design, almost as
a component of the limping ritual, again expressed the same
contempt; it was the movement with which one shoos away a
dog, with which the French marquesses of the *ancien régime*
threw mouldy bread to the rabble . . . I hadn't for a moment
noticed him pick up the stones; perhaps those with him handed
them to him unobtrusively . . . 'Come on, Jard,' said Henk
Evertsen abruptly and yet calmly. The attackers had stopped –
but after all it was ridiculous to think of attackers here; it was
simply unheard of with us, it wasn't that kind of school! Blinking at the sky with his round eyes, Gerard also seemed to be
engaged in this sum of experience, resulting in a theoretically
absolutely guaranteed safety on the other side of the canal.
Nevertheless he made his run-up slightly longer now, so that
all three of us expected to see him swerve aside at the very last
moment. A cry went up from the four of them, as he set off at
a jog; the boy with the brown face limped forward, almost to
the fringe of mud that separated the canal from the higher
meadow, slipped on the edge and stopped there. The idea was
that the jumper should land on the higher section. 'Come on,
Jard!' Gerard Steierman, who really had turned back for the
second time, nodded reassuringly, as if he now knew exactly
how to tackle this ditch. Meanwhile, I could make out the face of
the boy with the limp well; it was open to me as it were, although
he wasn't looking in my direction. The dark brown eyes were
squeezed shut in concentration, at the corner of his mouth
was the taunting smile, but the whole face, held backwards in
anticipation, had something so tender and feminine about it,
that one would have attributed the strange ginger-brown glow

to nothing as much as shame. His shoes were almost entirely in
the water. The other three, who kept at a distance, jeered in
turn: 'Who's next?' – and Henk Evertsen kept yelling back: 'For
goodness' sake, stop it. Who's done anything to you?' – fairly
senselessly, since no one was throwing any more, and the boy
with the limp stood there as if he was going to catch sticklebacks with his bare hands. To loud cheers, Gerard, who had
gone beetroot red at the cries of encouragement with which
Henk Evertsen alternated his yells, took the long run-up for
the third time. After entering the water at an angle, the pole
seemed to settle deeper in the mud on the bottom than usual –
too deep. Legs slightly thrashing Gerard floated against a
steep, recalcitrant slope, but he had already passed the dead
point and his own weight must now deposit him if not on the
edge of the meadow then on the mud a few metres to the side
of the newcomer. Suddenly the latter leaped up, leaned far forward, stretched his right arm out straight and grasped the pole
between the two places where Gerard's hands were gripping
the thing. For a moment the arm bent a long way, then, trembling and tugging, it was stretched out again, vertically. The
fist, compressed till it was white as a sheet, held the pole at an
angle of forty-five degrees so firmly that the jumper's only
option was to slide down slowly into the muddy water. It *was*
something for a philosopher. He wriggled to and fro like a
monkey! I wasn't able to see the attacker's face properly again,
but I am sure that it had not lost that mocking expression and
that strangely feminine, slumbering in anticipation, and that
glow of shame. Fortunately everything turned out better than
one could have imagined. What we witnessed next was a tour
de force. On the point of sinking helplessly into the water,
Gerard was grabbed by two strong fists, swung in one go and
deposited on the middle of the dry area of the fringe of mud;
the pole was left trembling, and then leaned a little to the left.
All of this was done so quickly and with such dexterity, that
we could not help giving in to the impulse to join in with the
cheers from the other side. Only Henk Evertsen swore under
his breath and had one foot forward, as if he were going to
help the victim with a free jump over the ditch. Not a hair on

Gerard's head had been harmed, though. Without a splash on his clothes he was able to scramble onto the meadow, where the other boy, after having wiped his hands on each other, had already preceded him. And there he was, hopping around, accompanied by the other, a strange brown insect in that flapping jacket. True, Desmet and Veenstra were still yelling mocking words at us, but their leader seemed not to want to spoil the effect of his intervention; they were also too far away for us to hear. Or had Boudewijn Evertsen caught something! As we went slowly home, talking things over – with the pole, which had been difficult to retrieve, as a nearly dishonoured trophy between us – he suddenly said to me, 'Did you hear what they called out about your sister?' I shook my head and saw his brother silence him with a dig in the ribs. Completely full of the spectacle on the canal bank, I didn't give it any more thought: the well-known boy's attitude of ignoring sisters outside the home was still very much mine; apart from which, I knew that Boudewijn was not averse to malicious inventions.

Three days later school began. The first few weeks following this were so dominated by the figure of Hugo Verwey – that was his name – that I noticed hardly anything of the other things happening around me. It was said that he was the son of a senior army officer and must already be over eighteen. No one knew where he came from, but the cause of his deportation could not remain a secret. Drink, women, stealing: those were the three cardinal sins, besides the usual street and school violations, and in this case it was 'women' – girls. But who? Well, I don't have to repeat all those stories; let it suffice to say that amid the most scabrous bluster of his comrades, a rude word never crossed his lips, and that may prove more than a whole list of peccadilloes. Those obsessed by women don't talk about them. Anyway, at Hugo Verwey's age all this is determined less by unsatisfied sensuality, that must be expressed at all costs, if necessary in words, than the urge to act, courage and enterprise, and that he possessed those, everyone could convince themselves with their own eyes.

Our gymnastics teacher, a moustachioed ex-sergeant, would have gone through fire for him, and certainly not because his father was a former superior, because he didn't give two hoots about that. Rather it was his exploits in the gym, up the double giant swing, to which his physical handicap gave a very special glory. With everything involving that one paralysed group of muscles, he of course dropped out: he was an excellent oarsman but could swim scarcely if at all. Our sergeant called him 'a courageous sportsman with his arms, a crane, boys!' – he said this in a hoarse and emotional tone. And then, if one was reluctant to be impressed by this, there was still the school: his behaviour in the fourth form, which could be admired at second hand by the lower forms. As far as I have been able to ascertain, his main speciality was teaching our teachers manners – our young, alert, good-natured teachers! Mr Ramacher, a short, fat chap who taught Dutch in a lively carefree way, was in the habit of sitting on the table in front of the class with his legs crossed. Since he had once thought of himself as a man of letters, he wore his hair long. He had small, insignificant, unseeing eyes, but that doesn't explain why Hugo Verwey, sitting at his feet in the front row, was able to grab one of those long blond hairs from the fat thigh with impunity and, pulling a face, dropping it on the ground between his thumb and forefinger! No, the teacher had seen it, but didn't dare stand up to his groomer: that was our explanation, and I still believe it was the right one.

But here I must add that at the time such evidence of his impudence made scarcely any impression on me. I was satiated with impressions; I was satiated with Hugo Verwey himself, with his image. I dreamed of him not because of what he did, but what he *was*! It would actually have been more agreeable to me if he had not been at the centre of general attention: now I didn't have him all to myself! He never paid attention to me any more, when he hobbled up and down before school in his brown sports jacket, with his small retinue milling around him, whose swaying bodies seemed to express as much dislike of the offensive chore to which this young prince was condemned, like the clearing of the throat and spitting out of curses, that one would never hear from him; for that matter he spoke so little that I can't even remember his voice from that first period. Never again did I stare into those cold, alert eyes with the bags under them. But the more inaccessible he seemed, the more he filled me. It caused me a tantalizing fear to summon up that face disguised with freckles, which had been focused on me for a moment, as a challenge, an order, a condemnation. I pondered with great concentration, as if my thought had to bore through that strange, supercilious mask. Who was he? What had the boy been through? What did he feel and think? His eyes pursued me, mocking, searching, indicting, hiding and revealing secrets at the same time. Each meeting was a new surprise, became an anxious festive event, something that could only happen once – and yet it repeated itself. I abandoned myself to strange daydreams in which I found Hugo Verwey alone, on the seafront, and walked and talked with him, as I did with Gerard Steierman. No others there, no retinue! Because I realized vaguely that in that case the newcomer would be quite different, that he might tell me what had driven him to this town and why he wore such a mocking expression, so stiff and also listless, and why he despised me. Had *thought* he despised me – because there could of course be no question of contempt now! A friend? Yes, for the first time I longed for something of the kind – Gerard, the philosopher, had always been more of a pastime, an intellectual game on the surface, for which anyone is suitable. This exceptional Hugo Verwey, however, was intended for me alone, though he was two or three years older than me. I never set out to get to the bottom of this feeling, but I know now, I know, as if it is written in a book: it was love, it was precisely the same thing one can feel for women, just without the sensuality. The lack of focus that characterizes Eros at that age: I experienced it physically – no, not physically: in my mind.

To lay everything at his feet, to make myself his slave for all eternity, this burning desire took my thoughts to bolder heights than atomic theories! The image of Hugo Verwey gave my life at the time a breadth only apparently belied by the poignant, sharp-pointed nature that characterized that image. It was as if a narcotic fluid that blurred everything entered me though a sharp hypodermic needle. When I looked at him I had the definite sensation in my mind of itching or mild pain, very localized, on the right or left. But when I thought about him in solitude, everything became wide open and happy, with an indescribably ethereal tingle, which one feels when one is about to undertake a journey or is contemplating a huge turnaround in one's life.

The very fact that I was not ashamed and kept my condition secret so as not to have to trouble anyone with riddles, proves my complete lack of awareness of the abysses that this obsession contained within it. I would not have been able to explain it, and I did not even consider 'love' as a possibility. If someone had carefully described to me what I was feeling, I would have been grateful to him, even though he would immediately know everything. After about a month I suddenly thought that my sister knew, because she was so cheerful, but perhaps she had caught that cheerfulness from me, so I thought, and it came as quite a surprise when she said: 'What a long face you're pulling' ... After that I adopted a forced exuberance for twelve hours, without, though, being able to compete with her in any way. She sang as if she wanted to crack the walls; she went round the whole time with urgent messages, which did not yet exist, or still had to be formulated; her bustle was equalled only by her fury if one cast doubt on the point of it. Cause: the soprano part, which she had been assigned in the Christmas cantata for the first time, an idiosyncratic composition consisting of psalm texts set by the singing teacher Balkom to his 'own' music! Was she not now the equal in edification of Revd Kalmans himself, and of 'the Hon. Miss Sticks', the president of the small Protestant church choir, and in weightiness of stiff admonitions? That's what she herself thought (I found out later that not even this was true: it was just the reflection of our teasing, which shaped the receptive nineteen-year-old from outside); but when she came dashing into the room feverish with *joie de vivre*, she looked more like a Maenad with her hair up, and my mother had to raise her hand, and my father looked at the sailing ship, which stood rattling in its case like an oracular genie from the Arabian Nights in its jar. And although I saw little of her, because I saw only the other person, her dark-red cheeks and moistly glistening eyes sometimes bored their way through everything, and what else could I do but complete the triumphantly booming line: 'To us with love our God looks down', with the loudly bleated: 'And Sophie in the tub will drown' – whereupon she would chase me through the whole house, until the shop assistant came upstairs to say that the children mustn't play in the shop any more as a roll of twill had fallen over.

She surprised me most when, one long October evening, she started talking about the grammar school; that had never happened before. The two of us were sitting at the living-room table, I with my schoolwork. She stretched out her open hand and said sarcastically: 'How learned you're going to be, Henk. Professor Mannoury!'

'Hasn't that got a ring to it? Oh, but Gerard is much more learned; he thinks up things about physics, doesn't he, and about atoms! We never even had that subject at school.'

'Wouldn't you prefer to be an officer?'

'An officer?!'

'Then you can ride back and forth to Breda, or can't you do that? Or a naval officer – oh no, you hate the sea, and on land you're not happy either . . .' Cheerful and excited, she started going on in her usual way, then she stretched out her arms so that the material of one of our finest silk blouses stretched across her bosom (she had never worn silk before, I suddenly saw it and thought of the cantata), breathed deeply and seemed to be listening. I heard a step in the shop, a few words were exchanged with the assistant, who had the evening off and was about to leave, and then there was the same step on the stairs.

'There's Mother!' cried Sophie with delight. She leaped towards the door singing and was gone. A little later her voice sounded from the kitchen, alternating with my mother's calming sound. In the falling dusk, which turned my paper blue in the gloomy frame of the worn plush, in which there were still a few crumbs sticking, I went on working. The tobacco smell of my father's snorting pipe was something static, something dead, but softly and insistently the sailing ship rattled on the wardrobe, carried in waves that rose from the kitchen. I couldn't get Sophie's unfortunate allusion out of my mind and

more than ever I was aware of the sea surrounding all this. Perhaps I was scared of the sea; if I could not row and swim so
well, I would have been predestined to drown, or to taste death
by drowning to its extremes, like that fisherman on the Gravel
Bank covered by the sea at high tide, who pulled off his boots
under water and started seeing all kinds of lovely flowers and
himself as a boy. Then they stumbled upstairs again; the door
was flung wide open, and a clarion call dispelled the dreams:

'Cakes! Cakes, Henk!'

'What are you talking about?'

'Cakes! Next week! You mustn't eat anything in the
afternoon . . .'

Not until a day later did I find out that the next rehearsal of
the choir was to be held at our house. There weren't enough
funds to keep renting rooms and our front room was spacious
and high-ceilinged. As she not only presided, but also actually
joined the altos, 'the Hon. Miss Sticks' was also coming. Distinguished visitors, then. Various changes were made to our
collective wardrobe; a first pair of long trousers for me, for it
was of course quite possible that this person or that would
bump into me, although my part was confined to the cakes. I
vaguely understood that Sophie, instead of informing me
immediately, so exposing herself to my mockery, had first
wanted to express her enthusiasm in a different way, and I was
strengthened in this opinion by her further behaviour: Mr
Balkom and the Honourable Miss Acheron were now the
trump cards, in regard to me too; there was no more talk of the
officer and the naval officer.

I can still see in that spick-and-span front room our chairs with
the addition of a few borrowed ones standing in three rows, I
can see the glasses, the piles of cakes on the sideboard, and the
winks that my sister directed from me to those cakes and then
to her mother, to whom she paid more attention than usual at
this critical moment. My father sat smoking his cigar in his
shirtsleeves, to save his dress coat. Meanwhile it was unlikely
that any of us would be shown to the visitors, unless there was
a sudden fire. In the ball gown she was wearing Sophie looked

beautiful and distinguished to me, and most of all happy. After all, all the ignominy caused her by non-greeting dignitaries would be erased! I can still see the white cloth she threw over her head during the final dusting; I can still smell the sausages in the kitchen, I can hear the sailing ship rattling in alarm at every hurried step, until my father picked it up and put it on the floor, revealing for the first time how old and dusty it had become under the jar. And then I heard that first ring at a quarter past eight, loud, triumphant, hungry – it was a lad who had come to settle a bill, for which my father had to go downstairs, to his office for a while – and suddenly I knew that no one would come, no one! It wasn't a powerful and irrational premonition, not a mysteriously predicting voice; no, it could be deduced perfectly logically from our gleaming paraffin lamp, from my father's shirtsleeves, from the discount the lad would be given, from the sand over the signature on the seal! I no longer dared look at anyone. I had identified so intensely with them that the strings had suddenly snapped; the uncertainty and the inferiority complex, which usually tormented them, now invaded me. I was overwhelmed by the groundless fear of the dependent child, who cannot intervene when its parents are threatened. A piercing pity for my sister was added to it, something I had never known before. Perhaps this was the moment when I freed myself from the context of youth and became an adult – if such a moment exists . . . But then everything was over again, as suddenly as it had begun – and I imagined as stubbornly how 'To us with love our God looks down' and the rest of Psalm 68:10 points to it, having sprung from the brain of Mr Balkom, would nevertheless ring though our rooms, and that when a second bell rang I was already prepared to make an obligatory bow to 'the Hon. Miss Sticks', who I saw come rustling in in a kind of dress with a train. This time it was a farmer's wife who had come to buy three yards of corduroy at the last moment.

I prefer not to remember the half-hour that followed; for me it is laden with ominous tragedy, which far surpassed my own gloomy forebodings. Trivial things particularly, in my memory magnified into blows of fate, affected me deeply. It was almost gruesome to see my father creeping through the rooms in his dress coat, with which he hoped to control events, no further than two paces into the untouchable front room, and then to hear him mumble: 'They'll be here, child.' Although I finished everything in advance, I had started on my schoolwork, already without pulling up my trouser-legs when I sat down, and my mother was dithering by the sausages. Not until my sister, who ran through the whole house like an animal at bay, as if they were all hiding somewhere, after pulling a cloak on hastily had gone to see a girlfriend who lived a few doors away from us and sang with the mezzo-sopranos, did we know where we were.

'Oh, then it's been postponed for a week,' said my father soberly, when my sister had already gone upstairs, 'if she didn't know anything, then ... it's been postponed for a week,' he continued to my mother, who had come in with the sausages and pushed a cake in my direction that tasted of sand. 'Gerrit Barends' Nel had got a notification.'

'And Fietje hadn't?!'

'Must be a misunderstanding . . .'

The following morning, in the middle of a wild dream, in which my sister like the Little Mermaid from Andersen's fairy tale swam under water to lay flowers on a row of church chairs, I was woken by my mother, who put her head round the door: 'Be quiet now, Henk. Sophie's not well.'

I immediately got out of bed and followed her down the hall to ask more questions. After putting her finger to her mouth, she disappeared into my sister's bedroom. I noticed that I had a pounding headache. Before I went to school, my mother told me that at breakfast Sophie had read an explanatory letter from the Hon. Miss Sticks, but had then become unwell and could not stay up. She gave me details of vomiting and the rest in a tone of lament, as suited her plodding character. My father was not at home. Probably he had, with his carefree cheerful nature, fled the house, the new chilly arrangement of the rooms, which had all assumed something of the aspect of waiting rooms. But that I would be henceforth barred from the sickroom turned out to be a misapprehension. After breakfast my mother brought me a request from Sophie to come and see her, 'to keep her company'. With a strange feeling of embarrassment I went upstairs on tiptoe and hesitated even after I had turned the doorknob. The smell in that girl's room was like that around a deathbed; the doctor and the apothecary's assistant had already been, and my mother sprinkled lavender water on such occasions. I had to walk right round and bump into something twice before I saw the face of the patient, which was not pale as I had expected but dark red, and possibly even more beautiful than the previous evening, about that embroidered nightdress closed up to the neck. Her frequent habit of stretching out her right hand with the thumb completely to one side, seemed to be more imperious now than beseeching, but there was also a theatrical note to it, of which I became vaguely aware, as I sat by her bedside.

'Henk,' she said in a loud voice, which made me look round involuntarily at the door, which had been left open, 'you are the only one who must know. I'm not ill. It was all a sham. You are the only one who can help me. But first you must read this letter, Henk.'

As she said this, she pushed a large sheet of paper towards me, which felt thick; a vague water mark, furtive, constantly and randomly interrupted in an extremely distinguished way made a much greater impression on me than the far more obvious aristocratic coat of arms. I read in proud, spindly writing that hurt the eyes, and as I did I suddenly saw not the muscular Hon. Miss with the grated-cheese cheeks, but the Irish setter of her brother who did not greet:

> *Young Lady. We have heard from a reliable source that you have been seen a number of times in the evening around our town in the company of a scholar. Without wishing to embark upon a judgement of your behaviour in the present case, we find, after long consideration, that we cannot justify offering you a solo part in our Christmas cantata. On behalf of the committee, A. M. M. Strick van Landsweer.*

I sat there speechless, with the paper in my hand. This document far exceeded my scanty experience of life. I wasn't even sure I knew what a 'scholar' was, and I thought rather of one of our teachers than of a schoolboy. Meanwhile, the silence was becoming oppressive. Sophie took the letter back from me and hid it away. Finally I said gormlessly:

'Is that the Hon. Miss Sticks?'

'Who else?' she burst out, pounding on the bedclothes and sliding powerfully forward with her whole sitting body. 'Such an insult! But it'll be the death of me; if you don't help me, I shall drown myself!'

'No, don't do that,' I stammered clumsily, very worried, but suddenly she took my hand and pulled me towards her, bursting into tears. I smelled hair, lavender; I felt a wet, warm cheek, and did not know what to do. I still remember very well that I was mainly moved by her token of trust and because she did not want to play on my sympathy by pretending to be sick. Luckily just then my mother's voice came from downstairs. I jumped up and went to the door; behind me I heard Sophie's whispering: 'Say it's doing me good!'

After communicating this to my mother, who called up that I must not tire Sophie out, I went back to my chair, wanting more light to be shed on all these mysteries. The light was as unexpected as it was appalling. Eyes open wide, turning round completely to face me, my sister asked:

'Do you know Hugo Verwey?'

She went on looking at me for some time, but, instinctively concerned to keep a secret which under other circumstances and better prepared I would have been glad to share with her, I didn't say a word. This precaution acted completely beyond the control of my consciousness. I had started to feel so completely empty and vacant, that for that very reason nothing noticeable can have shown in me. The name Hugo Verwey stripped something bare and paralysed something in me. With my mind empty of thoughts I stared straight ahead, without even making any connection between the name and the scholar with whom my sister had been seen around our town and who was responsible for the Hon. Miss Sticks' letter. Sophie seemed to have assumed that I knew him, that at least I gradually began to understand. She now spoke very fast, and only afterwards was I able to establish a connection between the fragments I picked up. About two weeks ago Hugo Verwey had spoken to her in the street; since she felt pity for his physical handicap and deduced from his behaviour that he was not common, she had mellowed and had walked along with him; the fact that he was at the grammar school and maintained he knew me was yet another point of contact. Since then she had met him twice, always in the evening. He had not kept his age or his 'scholarly' status from her, although neither could constitute a particular recommendation for a girl of almost twenty. As far as I could judge, she had succumbed thoroughly to his charm; but obviously the period of their acquaintance was too short for what one might call more intimate contact; I now write this with certainty: at the time I did not even think of the possibility of such a thing. I was much more interested in who had seen them and betrayed them, a question Sophie was as unable to answer as I was, although I remembered Boudewijn Evertsen's remark about what Veenstra or Desmet had called out about 'my sister'. Only much later, knowing relations in our town, did I come to a conclusion based on assumption, which focused mainly on the animosity in the cloth guild. Just as my parents felt slighted by the mayor, squire or district judge, so the Jewish merchants in bombazine were hostile to my father, because he walked past them without greeting; in addition – and in this case this seems to me decisive – a Sara Polak was once voted down by the choir, who was supposedly a sister or cousin of Rusman! So the line from Rusman to Hugo Verwey, to whom he may have pointed out my beautiful sister, ran, after those three walks, back from Hugo Verwey to Rusman, to Sara, to Rebecca, from whoever you like to the Hon. Miss Acheron; that seems to me the diagram of that slander, but who then in heaven's name was the 'reliable source'? Oh, let us assume that the pair were noticed by others, let us assume it was the squire's Irish setter.

When my sister thought I had understood everything, she looked at me with those same big eyes, as if she expected something from me, an outburst of rage, or a long story to comfort her or to justify the 'behaviour' of my 'fellow pupil'. I had a vague feeling that our whole school was involved, the grammar school, which Sophie had until recently so haughtily ignored, but actually I did not do much except repeat to myself: Hugo Verwey, Hugo Verwey – half anaesthetized by that unforeseen fact: that someone else had spoken his name . . .

'You must go to him,' Sophie finally said decisively.

I started. At last everything dawned on me, although I understood nothing of the task with which she seemed to want to entrust me. Was it fear or happiness or embarrassment that made the blood rush to my cheeks? I was all a-tingle, not from a desire to help my sister, but because I was being offered the opportunity to come into contact with him! . . .

And yet I knew that I wouldn't dare, I knew that I must not assume this burden, however much I wanted to, with one part of my being . . .

'What must I do then?' I stammered, inaudibly, to gain time. Her eyes flashed angrily over me; then, after a desperate raising of her eyebrows, her mouth and lower jaw set stubbornly and she started explaining patiently to me that her only chance of rehabilitation was for Hugo to go to the Hon. Miss Sticks or to one of the other committee members and make a personal declaration that would remove any suggestion of a dishonourable intention from those evening walks. To my question why did she not write to him or go to him herself, she replied that she did not know where he lived; after the last walk they had made no further assignation, and she did not wish to expose herself again. With a trembling voice, frightened that she would guess my true fear, I told her Hugo's address, which I had heard of by chance; like a student he lived in rooms, in a side street not all that far from us, and I kept insisting that she should write to him at that address, and explain everything, then everything would be all right and she would be able to sing again! She nodded in agreement at those zealous words, but, whether it was because I said nothing about Hugo himself and acted as if I had never seen him before, or maybe it was because of the feeble way I dismissed her request, she seemed thoroughly disappointed in me. I had far from taken sides when I finally left the room, glad to be free of the conflict! Up to now my feelings for Sophie had been easily neutralized in that solution of rivalry, familiarity, selfishness and teasing: the usual binding and dividing medium between brothers and sisters. And it occurred to me even less to expunge the slur on her good name, since the insult came from people so unassailably far away and grown up, so venerable, and sympathetic too, like Revd Kalmans (whom I lumped together with the choir committee), so aristocratic like the Hon. Miss Sticks – while that other, vague insulter in the background was superior even to them in unassailability . . .

When after three or four days, on which I saw Hugo Verwey before and after school limping past like a dangerous young god without taking any notice of me, nothing had changed in Sophie's condition, I realized I wasn't free of her yet. Because our parents had to be kept out of it, she had determined to stay ill until her honour was restored; that was indeed the best course of action for her, and our old, good-hearted family doctor, who had brought us all into the world, including my mother, was in on the plot. I did not go into the sickroom much any more, but on the fifth day after the tragically failed evening, the bomb burst. Sophie's face was now very pale and taut, her hand strayed plucking across the covers, like that of a typhus patient, she swallowed a few times, and then handed me another letter, a thin, casually folded sheet this time, which smelled of cigarettes. The manuscript was just as casual, but equally sharp and precise, and in it I read the following:

Dear Miss –. I regret that it is impossible for me to fulfil your request. Apart from the fact that I do not know and do not wish to know the Honourable Lady you mention, I absolutely refuse to defend my behaviour against such unfounded accusations (or accusations founded on prejudice). In that way one is acknowledging the rights of petit-bourgeois thinking. Moreover, my reputation is such that the Honourable Lady would probably not believe a word of my explanations. I can only hope that you will regard this incident with the same contempt as me. Sunt pueri pueri, pueri puerilia tractant. *Finally I give you my assurance that I retain the most pleasant memories of our evening walks. With regards, your humble servant Hugo Verwey.*

It was a perfidious act by the young god. But of course I did not see through him, for me he remained where he was: on his pedestal. The unspoken accusation of petit-bourgeois standards against my sister too, the cowardly withdrawal, the genial allusion to the evening walks, as if talking to a shop girl, which now collectively constitute one of my bitterest memories, were completely lost on me; I was simply impressed by the cool, clear language, the unheard-of turns of phrase, the supercilious Latin – and mainly frightened of what would follow.

Still pale and taut, Sophie whispered to me that I might as well tear up the letter. As I was putting it away, I resolved to read it five times over. I was still not thinking of taking sides.

'You must go to him, Henk,' I heard her cajoling.

Head bowed, I remained looking at my shoes and gradually felt able to take my mind off the letter. I knew how stubborn she was. I also knew that she had every right to appeal to me. Moreover, I had seen all this coming, for days. Before I realized I had agreed, but not from joyful self-sacrificing chivalry! It was a sentence pronounced against me, I was in the power of an avenging goddess, with no will of my own, despairing like King Gunther, when he was ordered to kill Siegfried. It surprised me that Sophie could not read my assent in my face. Why, I thought, does she keep bending forward, does she wring her hands so theatrically, when she has complete control of me anyway? Why does she start talking about the water again now? It relieved me inexpressibly, when those twitching movements, which I could not really bear to look at, finally stopped:

'So you'll do it, Henk?'

'Yes,' I said dully.

'Promise me?'

'Yes.'

'You mustn't ask if he is going to see the Hon. Miss Sticks, but the vicar. I *hate* her too much.'

'And if he doesn't want to?'

'Then . . .' She stopped for a moment, drew me to her with a grand gesture, so that I was standing over her against the edge of the bed like a horse over the trough, and finished her sentence with a blush: 'Then you must *avenge* me. Do you promise me that? Do you swear?'

The words tickled my ear as if I had all kinds of tiny hairs there. The word 'avenge', which I knew only from books of cowboys and Indians, meant absolutely nothing to me. But 'swear' was already more comprehensible and probably I would have let her have her way if she had talked Greek to me: to be finished with it, no longer to feel the hard wood against my knees, and perhaps because of so many other things. For however oppressive and uncomfortable I was in that embrace, in which I finally 'swore', now I look back on it, I know that the whole situation bore the stamp of a sensual encounter, that must have affected me deeply. Unawakened as I was, my soul carried with it nevertheless the almost-awakened state, the should-have-been-awakened state, down to today, and the imagination makes up for what reality was not ready for. I see my sister, long since dead, before me again, as a girl with her black, glowing eyes, her blushing cheeks and firm chin, who hugs me to her and traps me in the scents of her bed, as unconscious as I was of all this ... But whatever the case: I had sworn.

'*Big* Henk?' asked Revd Kalmans, turning his lively blond face with the Van Dyck beard to Henk Evertsen, and briefly bouncing on his toes, which always made him look so young and sporty, without any ceremony, albeit slightly puppet-like. Henk Evertsen thought for less than a second:

'Love, of course, Vicar!'

'Good,' said Revd Kalmans, and then slowly came towards me via a couple of boys from the trade school and Gerard Steierman. It was a long, bare room in which these questions were asked. Only a faded map of Palestine was visible on one of the walls, in the yellow gas light. On chairs that had undoubtedly borne the weight of many church council members before being considered just good enough for the catechism room, we sat in the usual comfortable disorder, which must not be called disorder here officially – but actually I was not sitting with them, although I knew precisely that I would *not*

say 'love'. I saw everything through a haze. I had not slept for
two nights. What awaited me after this catechism class, I did
not want to contemplate – but in any case that I should not say
'love' was the minimum requirement, the first step! If I had
once practised on the grown-up, the boy would be no trouble.
That is why I had wanted to wait until after the weekly religious instruction from Revd Kalmans, which was connected
with the church choir and hence was partly responsible, to
which Hugo Verwey had to come, according to my sister's will,
which for me was law, since I had sworn. Although I liked
Revd Kalmans, for the time being I had focused all my hatred
on him; I scarcely knew the Hon. Miss Sticks by sight, and she
was in the nobility . . . But my sister was in bed, and my father
was not sleeping well and kept asking what was going to happen about the choir, and twice a day I was summoned to the
sickroom to be reminded of something . . . No, I'd be damned
if I would say 'love'.

'Jard?' asked Revd Kalmans in a popular tone. He had been
held up slightly by the trade school boys with the black smudges
over their faces, who got confused about definitions.

'Love, Vicar.'

The object was to give a description of God. These definitions were the nicest things in the catechism, because you
could think for yourself and sometimes debate with Revd
Kalmans, and that was why, in all my misery, it disappointed
me that Gerard Steierman had not been able to think up a
more original reply than 'love', which all the others had come
out in favour of, down to the most stupid fisherman's boy –
and anyway was the fruit of the previous week's instruction. I
remember one evening when Gerard, almost despite himself,
chose pantheism from theism, deism and pantheism, his main
argument being that 'if God was everywhere, he wasn't actually anywhere', and then in addition confused Revd Kalmans
by asking whether pantheism had anything to do with the
pagan god Pan – all in good faith, of course. Unfortunately, the
vicar, even when most heatedly contradicted, always gave you
the benefit of the doubt in some complicated way, without con-
ceding that he was right, which in the long run was bound to

have a paralysing effect, and after all I couldn't blame Gerard Steierman because love inspired him less than pantheism . . .

'*Little* Henk?' asked Revd Kalmans.

That was me. I waited for a moment, and then said slowly and bluntly:

'*Not* love, at any rate.'

Later I found out that Revd Kalmans had not even known about the Sophie affair, let alone been a party to it; since he was considered 'liberal', he was excluded from the obscurantist activities of the church choir. But although there was nothing in his face that indicated he was aware he had an adversary in front of him, for me the victory was complete. In my overexcited state he seemed to me stupid, superficial, smiling inanely, ready with conciliatory words, but he wouldn't catch *me*! Surprised muttering had spread along the rows of chairs; Gerard Steierman's safe round eyes focused on me, as if the penny had dropped and he had wanted to retract his reply. I was so cured of my sleepiness that I did not even think of Hugo Verwey . . .

'Hmm . . .' Revd Kalmans bounced on his toes, and tugged his silver-blond goatee. 'So do you perhaps have another answer, Henk?'

He had spoken calmly, happily and confidentially, as if the two of us were alone in that room. Instead of sticking to my negative answer until he had asked for an explanation, I began looking for something new, to crush him even more. So I fell into the trap and the attack on the God of salvation was no longer difficult to repulse.

'Well?' he asked, bouncing rather impatiently on his toes.

'Justice,' I said grumpily, mentioning the first abstract concept that occurred to me. Only abstract concepts were valid, as we had decided that amongst ourselves: that God was a quality, a being, not a 'person', despite the majority of votes for theism in the past.

'And how do you imagine that God of justice, Henk?'

Long silence. The slim, black-clad figure moved urgently up and down, and the gold watch was produced, as it was almost eight o'clock, and it was necessary to expand on love; perhaps

Revd Kalmans would otherwise have liked a comparative discussion on the God of the Old Covenant and that of the New
Testament. With an amicably reproachful frown he glanced at
the other end of the table where the mumbling wouldn't stop.
But I already saw no more of all this, and no words took shape
in my feverish brain; I felt only the draught that crept coldly
under the doors and seized my heart. It was the quiet, cool
October evening that I felt around me in that oblong catechism
room, the petty-minded town where the grown-ups displayed
lack of understanding and hostile intentions – and in it that
one street I had to go to after this hollow victory . . .

'Well, boys, I believe that *big* Henk had the right end of the
stick! God is of course so mighty and inexpressible, and open
to different interpretations, and yet . . . *love*. The personal,
intimate relationship with God . . . *our* God . . .'

Outside I waved away the noisy questioners and hurried
towards the street where we lived. The moon, almost full, was
above the houses on my right, the fine mist, which at seven
o'clock had still been swirling around, had lifted. I did not
know what was more ominous: the shops that had already
closed or the shops that were still open. From a direction
impossible to identify came the sound of a foghorn. Above our
dark shop more dark, and above it, at the top, the yellowish
light of Sophie's bedroom, where a paraffin lamp had been
put. I thought of the sailing ship, which was still on the ground
in the living room; perhaps it would stay there for the time
being and only start clattering again when I had fulfilled my
task and Sophie was better . . . Teeth chattering from the damp
night air, I turned into the first side street I came to; the street
I was making for, and which ran parallel to it, I could reach by
a linking alley a few minutes away. The second street, which I
walked through quickly, without realizing that my objective
was now right in front of me, was narrower than I had thought,
quite dark, and full of handcarts and coils of rope in front of
shops. After about twenty paces I made out in the distance
outside one of the houses under vague yellow light a group of
two or three people; I also thought I caught the sound of their

voices now and then. Not from fear, but because I wanted to
be certain of the numbers, I turned round, and began right at
the far end of the street, where number one was. Praying and
pleading that that bunch would not be standing outside his
door, I approached; I did not for a moment think of waiting till
they had gone. I counted, mechanically, in a dream, every
house, every workplace I passed, and would still have made a
mistake, but I was already where I had to be, with right ahead
of me the face of Jelte Veenstra, with sleepy, wide cow's eyes in
the darkness; I didn't dare pay attention to the others. I immediately walked around them in an arc to be able to look upstairs
unnoticed further on, where the light was coming from and
where his room must be. There was gas, a couple of gold flames
against dark wallpaper. Behind me the voices resumed their
conversation, far away, businesslike, paying no regard to me.
When I turned round, the voices fell silent. A hostile silence
reigned, there, just six or seven paces from me. Next to Jelte
Veenstra I made out not Charles Desmet or Rusman, but a boy
from the sixth form called Lodijzer, an import too and the
commonest sort: a puffy little fatty with bad teeth. The third
person was Hugo Verwey, without a hat or cap; the light fell
precisely on his dark-brown curly hair, which had a touch of
red in it. I saw that he had crossed his legs, but there was nothing wrong or deformed about them, and the way in which he
held his right hand with the bent wrist under his brown jacket
lapel seemed to me distinguished and charming. As I knew
Jelte Veenstra best of the other two, I turned to him:

'Does Verwey live here?'

Coming closer, I smelled the drink fumes from his mouth;
he said something with a slur; the others said nothing. With
repugnance I asked the vulgar Lodijzer:

'Does Hugo Verwey live here?'

Lodijzer looked over my shoulder towards the end of the
street, then slowly, very slowly, took out from one of his trouser pockets a wooden pipe, with the stem of which he pointed
to the third man, who even now I didn't dare look at. Then he
put the pipe in his mouth and sucked air through it, smacking
his lips.

At that moment something happened that distracted my attention completely. Jelte Veenstra's slurred mumblings had turned into guttural song: one line of a text I didn't know, which he kept stupidly repeating:

'What a gor-geous wo-man's body!'

He sang it seriously and with a certain devotion. But the words seemed to me so abject, with its grotesque emphases (where the tune, of a popular street song of the time, jumped up and down again in a lively way), that I felt the ground giving way under my feet. While Lodijzer started laughing with the pipe between his teeth, Hugo Verwey took a step forward:

'What have you come about?'

'I wanted a word with you,' I replied shyly, with my eyes fixed on the ground; now I was not looking at him, he seemed to me made of granite, broad-shouldered, and infinitely bigger than me, although in reality he came just above the shoulder of the tall Jelte Veenstra.

'But I don't even know you.'

Of course he knew I was Sophie's brother. Besides which, hadn't he said to her at the time that he knew me? It would have made everything much simpler for me if I had pointed out that contradiction to him; then I would immediately have introduced Sophie, as it were in passing, what had seemed the most difficult thing from the very beginning, and then like that with that bunch standing there. But in order to think up such things, I would have had to be much less in awe of his voice, which I had never yet heard properly, and which for all its soft-ness and musicality, was easily audible above the continuing bluster of Jelte Veenstra. Holding on to that unexpected voice, I looked at him pleadingly and was then borne up still more by the absence of the usual taunting trait round the corners of his mouth. There was no contempt in the narrow, mobile face, whose features seemed carved from a fine-flecked raw material with a metallic sheen. It was a face composed of ginger ribbed shells, which ran together, the eyelids, the bags, the flat nose – a seaworthy face, fine and at the same time weathered, repulsive and at the same time of an indescribable charm there in the dark, under that yellow light from his room.

'I don't know you,' he repeated calmly.

'Can I speak to you alone?' I asked in a trembling voice, doing my very best not to listen to that disgusting song or to Lodijzer's giggling, and to concentrate solely on him. He threw his head back a little and crossed his arms over his chest.

'If it's about that letter, no.'

At that point Lodijzer involved himself in the conversation: 'Now you're in for it, Hugo, she's sending . . .'

'You understand that I won't be forced, Mannoury,' said Hugo Verwey, without paying attention to the other boy, and in a much louder voice than at first. 'If I make someone's acquaintance, I don't want to be punished by being sent to some Honourable Lady.'

'But there's no need for that,' I stuttered zealously, putting out my hand to him, 'preferably not, in fact . . . If you'll just go along to Reverend Kalmans and say . . .'

The other two seemed to have been waiting for this. Jelte Veenstra interrupted his song about the woman's body and started laughing deeply like a drain, gently waggling his vast trunk, while Lodijzer raised his pipe in the air and went on shouting: 'That's a good one! Reverend Kalmans. Reverend – what did he say? – Kalmans! Ho, ho, ho, ho!' They danced and swayed, to the right behind me I saw their great, cowardly shadows moving back and forth. But despite that I held on to the idea of an audience! Just a momentary upsurge that resembled anger, and again I was hanging on the lips of Hugo Verwey. After all he had not laughed, he didn't look sarcastic, rather there was a hint of pity on his ginger face.

'That makes no difference to me,' he said.

'So you don't want to?' I asked subserviently, on the point of turning round, away from that terrible din behind me.

Suddenly this was stopped (it turned out to be coming only from Lodijzer; Jelte Veenstra had choked and was hiccupping at intervals) and Lodijzer came forward. Orating with his pipe he explained:

'If she'll marry you, Hugo, I'll testify that she . . .' And he concluded with an obscenity, which I have by no means forgotten, but which I have excluded from these pages. I turned round and kicked him with all my might in the groin, so that he shot back howling and stood there bent double, with his hands over his stomach. I had not said or shouted anything. But, despite the lightning speed with which all this happened, the feeling of humility towards Hugo Verwey had not yet had time to disappear: it was not a transition that took place in me, it was two halves into which I fell, and even in that fleeting moment a rational link must have been established between the two spheres: anger and slavish adherence. Because I can still clearly remember that I felt I was fighting not for my sister, who was being insulted here, but for *him*, and not to show him my courage or strongly developed sense of honour, but to defend him, heaven knows from what . . .

Just as Jelte Veenstra, who was leaning against a bollard, began his song about the body again, between two hiccups, the sickly, deadly feeling in the belly of the cringer – I knew it from experience – began rising in my own belly. A hand was laid on my shoulder, I looked into a contorted face, heard the words muttered almost with a sob: 'I'll teach you, you wretch.' I received two or three blows on my cheeks, with the flat of the hand, not very hard; two fists bent me slightly forwards and a sharp but sustained kick up my backside took me one house further on, on my knees in front of a different doorstep. He must have done it with his left leg, the non-crippled one. I stayed there for almost half a minute, expecting more. When I got up, the tears were running down my cheeks, but the door was already shut, the street empty. High above me, from his room, where the curtains hung down, there was the sound of muffled voices. Each time the voices grew a little louder, I cringed, but I stayed there, not knowing where to go! Sleeping on the same floor as Sophie was out of the question. The conversation with him still had to take place, there was nothing to be done about that; that was why I had come, and that's why I was staying, since I now remembered only the disturbance created by Jelte Veenstra and Lodijzer, and his refusal scarcely at all. I went across the street and hid in the entrance to an alley, from where I could keep an eye on the house. As soon as the other two had gone, I would ring the bell and again ask to speak to him.

The moon had already climbed so high that the glow on the alley walls that were very close together was tangible, when after some stumbling on the stairs the door was flung open. In the darkness of the street two figures came out, first Jelte Veenstra, very much sobered up to judge by his gait, and then Lodijzer, who seemed to be limping, then after a slightly longer interval, a third figure. I now realized that the second figure must be the limping Hugo Verwey, who was going with the others; Lodijzer, who had closed the door behind him, was walking normally again and was not even being supported. When they were ten houses away, I crept from my hiding place in order to follow them at a steady distance. From quite close by a church tower struck nine o'clock. At first sleepy and chilled from standing against the wall for a long time, I gradually brightened up from this new movement, the changing aspect of the streets. To be sure that they were still walking there, I bent right forward from time to time, enabling me to see their heads outlined against the row of houses on the other side, which were more clearly illuminated by the moon, where the street, close to ours, made a turn with strikingly white gables. But this background too glided past, and now they were almost about to enter our street. Hugo was limping in the middle, as if between his seconds. He was not wearing a cap or overcoat; it had become noticeably close once the mist had lifted. Stationed behind a handcart, I saw them dawdling on the corner; hands were shaken, I caught the sounds of farewell, and Jelte Veenstra disappeared, recognizable from his size, off to the right, while the other two turned left. I immediately ran on tiptoe to the corner on the left, to make sure that they did not elude me in some side street, but the impulse was more attributable to the joy of shortly meeting Hugo Verwey alone, without an escort. It was clear enough: he was going to take Lodijzer, who was either still or no longer in pain, home – in any case it was the obvious thing to do to take someone like that home, after an incident like that. Under the trees of our street I saw them continuing unhurriedly, constantly lit by the street lights. Again I passed my house with the yellow lamp-light at the top, the house that banished me until I had kept my promise. But now I had hope again; it was only a matter of minutes, I knew where Lodijzer lived, and yes, they turned into the street that gives the shortest route to the high street. Lodijzer lived not far from Rusman.

Hidden in a shallow doorway, I had to rely entirely on the noises just round the corner where Lodijzer lodged with a grocer. I could not understand any words; fortunately, it did not last too long. After the door banged I expected to see Hugo walking back past me or in any case past the end of the side street, but the footsteps moved further away, merging with the footsteps of other pedestrians and then vanished, just at the point when I hesitantly turned the corner. One glance in the high street told me that he must have disappeared. Fighting back my despair, I first looked for Rusman's house, above one of the cloth merchants. All dark. Past the twill and the unbleached cotton, which I couldn't smell now, I ran to the next side street, looking round the whole time. Just when I had established that no one was walking there either, I heard a door behind me, voices, another farewell, I dashed away, huddled against a low garden gate that sprang back a little, and listened to the footsteps, to see if they would come closer or go in the opposite direction. The former was the case. After a few moments Hugo Verwey limped past my side street, further down the high street, in the direction of the square-like extension of it, which from a distance looked dark and became even darker after the last street lights. Behind me to my left the moon was becoming clearer, seeming to surge from my direction against the houses, where our shadows floated on, his bending, shrinking, as it were, nodding in contemplation at each limping movement. Although the number of walkers had considerably reduced here too, I had the feeling I was still in the centre of the town. Moon and stones – I didn't think about the sea. Gradually, and according to a kind of calculation, I quickened my step: only catching up one after each three steps – I was about fifty paces behind him – so a hundred and fifty was the time difference – that was perhaps two minutes. Suddenly, threatening and surly, lit as it were from the wings by a pale lemon-yellow wall lamp, the old gate loomed up, by which the skippers always stood spitting and the yellow butcher's dogs lay on the cobbles. No one was standing or lying now. The distance between us had shrunk to no more than fifteen paces, when he disappeared into the dark gateway fleetingly lit brown on both shoulders. The coat of arms above the gate was foreshortened, two crossed hands faded into gloves that had been taken off: I had also hurried in, quite prepared to bump into him on the other side. I forgot all precautions; I left my fear, my despair behind me; I didn't know what I would say to him, but because it was dark there, I couldn't care less about being hit or kicked again ... A cool westerly wind, a damper atmosphere, the furthest wink of the elegant lighthouse announced the sea. Unexpectedly I saw him at extreme left, on his way to the little harbour, which surrounded by two short piers, was scarcely worthy of the name, sanded up as it was. Fishing boats could never get more than halfway, the other half was navigable only for rowing boats, which were also usually moored there, as common property, particularly of the young. All one needed, as a strapping lad, was to make friends with an arbitrary idling fisherman, to become the hirer of one of those boats. The grammar-school boys at least were always exempted from a hire charge; even wear and tear was not charged for. As I followed Hugo over the sandy section that led to the north pier, constantly stumbling over pieces of wood and barbed wire that had come loose, I still hadn't a clue what he was planning. The moon shone so brightly that beyond the harbour mouth silvery blue stripes could be followed almost to the horizon, but there was a distant ethereal mist whipped up by the moon and blown back again by the wind, or perhaps generated automatically by the ambiguously rising or falling water around the Gravel Bank, which was a half-hour's row out to sea and was covered at high tide. Although I had been there often enough, the sand bank took a more mysterious meaning for me than usual, simply because in that direction the sea revealed itself so unexpectedly far, without being directly shone on like the twinkling water of the harbour, past which the figure of Hugo Verwey was limping. But not before at the beginning of the harbour he began to descend one of the crude sets of steps hewn out of the basalt did I realize that he must have been attracted by that mysteriously changing island out to sea. Perhaps he was longing for the fresh air, water splashing on his cheeks, the company he had just left . . .

I crouched down behind a fat bollard painted black and white that smelled of tar and waited to see what he was going to do. It was a strange sight to watch that crippled figure stepping into one of the boats, fixing one of the oars and pushing off with the other. The water rippled as far as both piers; the splash of oars was the only sound in the deserted harbour. He was now rowing quite fast. He might be away for an hour, or less – but also half the night, till the moon set! I couldn't wait here. And until I had asked my question a second time, I couldn't go home either . . . That was why I decided to follow him in one of the other boats, observe him, speak to him on the Gravel Bank or out at sea (this appealed to me not because I would be safe from a second hiding, but because of the romantic aura, of which I was gradually becoming aware), and in the most unfavourable case to follow him home, after which I could buttonhole him on land. When after the rhythmic splashing of the oars in the harbour mouth had died away I hurried in the same direction as him, towards the rowing boat that was most in the shadow, I began to be filled with reckless confidence. The firmer my resolution grew, the more I became free of the despair that had dominated me on my journey through the town. Far out to sea he could no longer despise me, that was impossible. He would understand how seriously I took it, and that there was no other way, because of Sophie. He would respect my daring; he would refuse me nothing! Finally I might even bring him back to Sophie's feet . . . With my head burning, I cast off and stepped into the boat. The water level was falling, in an hour it would be low tide, the distance between the tidemark on the basalt steps and the surface of the water was already over a metre. I tried to row as fast as he had done. Under my bent knees swayed a rectangle of water, on which the moon would soon be shining, like on a coat of arms I was carrying with me. I could almost have cried with joy, as I pulled hard on my oars, but just outside the harbour, with on my left the first full beams of the lighthouse, I kept looking over my shoulder so as not to catch up with him too fast . . .

My exultant mood lasted for the first ten minutes of my voyage to the Gravel Bank; after that everything became more confused and no longer completely accessible to my memory. Water, splashing around me, the singing wind, the creaking of the oars, together formed the accompaniment to my happiness. From one side of the sky to the other the lighthouse rolled its eyes. I had to steer a slightly southerly course, because of the current. I almost loved the sea, because it wasn't the sea but moonlight on sea, and in it two people who would find each other. But then sleepless nights went to my head like wine, suddenly and irresistibly; I thought I would tumble forwards, but kept rowing and when I turned round felt the wind full in my face, and mechanically scanned the horizon where the grey-yellow line, with waves lapping gently around it, must appear. I couldn't see his boat, but where else can he have gone but the Gravel Bank? And if he wasn't there, I would imagine he was: limping, leaping like a light-brown insect on that round bank with the gleaming shells, which shrank and disappeared at high tide, to re-emerge at low tide, six hours later, and then he would still be on it waiting for me and saying for the first time what united our hearts. Didn't we row as well as each other? Weren't we at grammar school together? . . . No, none of that contorted face, Hugo Verwey, none of those contemptuous words! . . . Away with that copper-coloured face that attacked me here in order to restrain me, threatening, searching, accusing – and it did disappear, and it blurred in the outlines of the sand bank onto which I climbed with the rushing waves. Perhaps the three of us should sing together in Revd Kalmans' church choir, on the hard pews, and I would take back all my reservations about the God of love. If his boat was not there . . . But his boat *was* there, although there was no sign of him on the low island, which must be almost at its largest now, a quarter of an hour's walk around it. Just after I felt the first impact of land, I noticed the long black mark, on my right, not very far away. The boat lay there without a rope attached to a metal peg: he must know too that it was low tide and high tide only in six hours. Far up in the sky the moon shone on the slightly sloping surface with the scattered constellations of shells; I let my own boat run aground between two of them, and there lay the two boats on the sand, as if they would never part. If he was not on the island, I would of course have to take his boat back with me, to show him what I was capable of ... Yes, I must do that, that must be done, what need did he have of a boat?! It seemed to me more difficult than anything, but perhaps it would be straightforward. I was already itching to do it; it was the last task I had to accomplish to find peace, to be able to sleep. Where was the rope? Was it long enough? How strange, those oars that I did not need and so could place carefully to one side. Pushing his boat back towards the water, securing the rope in the right place to mine, and then floating both boats, it was a splendid exercise, and only now was I aware of the lighthouse, which waved back from far away. Yes, I was making headway. He could stay there for ever, limping in the moonlight. If he wanted to go back, I would come and get him, the same way, but first his boat must be taken to safety. Or perhaps he would not even want to come with me, because what friends did he have on shore? ... In any case, I had defended him against his enemies; at school he would have a quiet life with me, and he would know everything, understand everything ... How the wind was blowing from behind me after all, playing with the boat that was tugging at mine, and scarcely cooling my forehead. It all seemed so peaceful, a good end. And yes, there was the lighthouse, half-size, and there right before my eyes was the second boat, which wanted to go left or right of the direction in which the ever-receding sandbank lay, or occasionally stayed in the middle and then whenever I looked round, the lighthouse again, under which I would eventually be able to go to sleep, when the lights went out, at daybreak, in the town six hours later ...

No, he didn't drown, though no one could have hoped for his rescue, myself included, in those days when our old doctor spoke of 'brain fever' and consultation and observation. My sister sat next to me day and night, until she also had to take to her bed. And the Christmas cantata became so insignificant besides all this that it was not even talked of any more, when I went back to school and heard about the outcome. No one ever knew what really happened, no one suspected that it was me who took the boat off the Gravel Bank, not even my sister, despite my wild utterances in my delirium. The two boats, which I had brought back to their place in the harbour in my half-somnambulant condition, were still tied together by a rope, but there was never an investigation, as far as I know. In fact, people spoke only of the miraculous rescue. Hugo Verwey must have struggled heroically against the rising tide, for hours and hours, at first with his clothes on, then naked, in turn swimming and standing on tiptoe where shells made the sea-bed firmer. At five in the morning he was spotted by fishermen and pulled chilled and exhausted into a rowing boat. Pneumonia followed, a cure in Davos – but it's quite possible he's still alive, although he never came back to us. I am still proud that he coped so well in the element that I hate, since he was, after all, my friend. And just because he was my friend, I did what released me from my passion and left no room for myself. Only for that reason. Anyone who thinks I brought the boat back out of revenge – revenge for my sister, or revenge for the hiding he gave me – has understood nothing of my story, and perhaps that is the best way to read it – the best way for myself, who for years afterwards, at least till I was twenty or twenty-one, when my feelings for him had long since disappeared, had to suffer the punishment of dreaming about Hugo Verwey: how I rowed after him, caught up with him, lay next to him on an endless golden expanse of sand, where supernatural voices sang far above our heads, where there was no place for separation and no way back to the town, to which I, alone, had fled.

Translated by Paul Vincent

8

BELCAMPO

Funeral Rights

Uitvaart

By two men who did not speak his language but who could clasp his arms in an immovable grip, he was chucked down the stone stairs into the darkness. There he lay and bled. With a booming blow the iron hatch slammed shut above him.

By the reverberation he gleaned that he had been cast into a large space. It could be a hall. He was lying on a stone floor; he could feel damp sand here and there. There was nothing he could see; it seemed pitch dark there. He could hear something. Shuffling sounds now and then, other ones too occasionally, as if a paw was being put down, a body turned over. Breathing, too.

He was not alone there. Animals? Would he be eaten later on? Had they already smelled his blood? His teeth chattered with fear; his knees began to tremble and he no longer had the power to subdue them.

Though he did not know yet whether the end of his life was imminent, his fear was already accompanied by the feeling of complete desolation each dying human being experiences in his last moments of consciousness. No one any longer could do anything for him; all of humanity had turned away from him: he was alone. All his past experience appeared to have been deception. To be betrayed by life itself: this is the bitter end of every man.

Yet, the space he was lying in seemed gradually to clear up a bit; perhaps his eyes, blinded at first by the sudden darkness, were slowly getting used to it. He began to discern something, to distinguish between things in the dark. The pale gleam of limbs, it would seem. Dim movement, here and there. He recognized human forms, mainly lying down, a few sitting up. No, he had not ended up in an animal pit but in a human one. It grew ever clearer. The entire floor of the subterranean hall seemed covered with a curious life form, with a layer of the living.

Slowly, the terrible truth penetrated his tortured brain: here, in this bottommost darkness, the warriors of vanquished peoples were left to their own devices.

No one any longer spoke a word; not even the whispers between two of them could be heard; all were completely cast back upon themselves. Language had ceased to exist. Nothing else remained but resignedly to undergo the decline of the body.

A movement seldom came, and extremely slowly even then; movement had become precious, it took away from the only thing that remained to them and upon which their lifespan depended: their reserves of strength.

He had a number of wounds but there was no point in examining them; nothing could be done about them anyway. Just wait and see whether he would still survive the healing of his wounds. It was turning into a contest.

There was nothing to do except cling to life. Escape was out of the question: that which walled them in was the impenetrable rock of the earth itself. And concerted action could never again go forth from this realm of shades: at best, concerted death would. In the feeble dusk which grew no clearer, he distinctly saw attitudes of dull resignation all around him, of surrender to the waiting, the waiting for nothingness.

He, too, settled himself down as comfortably as possible on the warm rock in such a way as to benefit most of its support, closed his eyes and did the only thing he was still capable of doing and which they all did: in his thoughts he returned to the past, to where his freedom lay. He had a sudden urge to re-experience his entire past life, more clearly, more consciously than the first time, to realize, before the end, an inner flowering of the images of his memory the way a tree, too, wastes its last strength in an uncommon flowering.

Particularly the first part of his life, before the start of the war, was what he would remember at leisure: when they were still happy and had feasts, when the world was still a friendly dwelling place to him. The darkness turned out to help him in this; in the dark he could bring those images clearly to mind, and the silence, too, allowed him to hear the sounds of the past more clearly. This, to all, was the only thing that remained.

He managed to lull himself within his memories to such an extent that, occasionally, he would catch himself out smiling. In this pit that seemed like a blasphemy, its negation. It would only happen when he felt little pain. Each time when, as a result of lying for too long in the same position, his wounds began to smart, his thoughts would stray to the war, to his life as a warrior: they became searing.

Besides the fact that the business of war itself is pervaded with deep suffering, there had moreover been the certain realization of fighting against a superior force, in this case, of having to experience the fall of his tribe. To die without issue is already a double death, but to leave a world behind in which your language is being annihilated is the most bitter thing of all. And not because of an inner decline but because of a foreign power.

What splendid people they were! Full of strength and agility; rich in ingenuity, in making use of nature. And their women: so elegant and so stubborn at the same time, as good helpmeets in battle as pleasure grounds of passion in times of peace. No, they had not been brought low by better opponents but by more numerous ones.

And how many tribes such as the one he belonged to had gone this way and were still going? During the transport here he had soon not seen a single fellow tribesman any more. They were being mingled in. As regards those who must die, too, did they still conduct their policy: the extermination of the foreign tongue? Gods were preserved but languages were exterminated: thus was the conqueror's will.

On one occasion it did occur to him that there was still *something* he could do: crawl out of reach of the big stairwell above him. Stairwell in two senses of the word: the well of all their empty stares. By touch, he slowly moved himself forwards.

He could easily have gone upright, stepping over the others; though he had indeed been weakened by his injuries, he could still draw on a large quantity of reserves of strength even so. They had been given food during their transport, extras too, occasionally, from women along the way. He still had muscles, he still even had fat. If he preserved his energy as much as possible, he could hold out a good while yet. But why, really? Merely to let his thoughts roam for a week, a month longer. Absurd was what it was.

When he was out of reach of those to come after him – his descendants, he thought bitterly – he abandoned himself to his memories again. To bring each family member and every friend to mind yourself, and to recall words passed between you, to call up each human image from the past and be in its company. And meanwhile he felt how, slowly, his body disappeared. Down to the bone. To take leave of himself.

He had been lying like that for days on end now. Days? There weren't any, not any more. Time ran on in a straight line. The alternation of day and night was something from his previous life, something of which only now did he realize the splendour.

The trace of murky light continued to prevail; the adjustment of the first hours had soon reached its peak. Perhaps, when the senses themselves were affected in the end, a short period of clarity might come through a last hyper-sensitivity of his eye.

The only thing left to him of the world was the stretch of ground he covered with his body, the one he could feel his way across by touch. That, in a way, was still his. It was still so kind as to bear him. This was really his entire fatherland now. Passing his hands over it, he would sometimes imagine a river valley at each little groove, a mountain at every rise. He felt like caressing this ground because it still bore him.

This was the way they were lying there, together, like a pale fire slowly glowing to extinction. No one any longer knew how long they had been lying there like that. They couldn't care less any more, either. An imprisoned criminal continually counts the days, even though he has got twenty years, scratching long ladders of numbers into the wall of his cell. Time, in fact, becomes all-controlling to him. Here, time had been suspended for ever, nothing was expected from outside any more.

Was that something approaching in the air? Was his gaze struck by growing light? Or were his eyes already being affected? Impossible. That only happened at the very end, and he was still possessed of all his strength. Slowly, a soft dusk spread overhead, the vaults of the cavern began to glint here and there. Dusk burgeoned to light, the inconstant light like that of torches, ever increasing like that of torches being carried in.

This turned out to be the case. Up above, at the base of the vault, corridors seemed to terminate and enemy servants appeared there with big torches, which they placed in iron baskets fixed to the rock face.

Now that the entire space was lit up, the prisoners saw one another for the first time: their corrupting bodies, their eyes, and a general revulsion arose. This communal suffering gave no feeling of solidarity, no mutual sympathy; things were too far gone. The dead lay between them, and those who merely breathed, who didn't react to the light from above.

Many, however, still looked round and up above, like he did. What did this mean? Did they want something more of them?

It would soon become clear. The enemy servants who had placed the torches – they wore the clothing of the victor – had disappeared down the corridors through which the fumes of the torches was being sucked away as well, and now they began to go back and forth to a large balcony, shaped by nature or by man, protruding from the rock face. The smell of food pervaded the space.

He saw there was a long table on the rock balcony and people were busy carrying a feast of food to that table: huge tureens, salvers piled high with meat, dishes full of vegetables and bowls laden with fruit. And many buckets of wine. Everything was clearly visible; lamps and candles were being put among the fare all the time.

Was this a vision? Was he dying?

Not yet. It went on. Men with stringed instruments now arrived. They arranged themselves to one side and began to tune up. Because of the resonance in the cellar vaults, this jangle of scrawny sounds acquired a certain fullness.

Were they going to serenade them? The serenade of the dying? But why, then, all that food?

No, the guests stepped forward. A jolly company of men and women decked out most richly, the women mainly with their own abundance, gathered at the table. In the centre, on the tallest chair, a copious *matrone* sat herself down. She had the allure of supreme power. The wife or mistress of a stadtholder or war lord, herself perhaps even an empress, she seemed to be the soul of this revel. She gave the signal to be seated, one more for music; she gave the signal to gorge. And together they gorged themselves at length, bringing meat and wine to their mouths by turn.

And as they drank, their mood became more exuberant. It seemed as though they were not being whipped up by the music and the wine alone, but also by the deep humiliation they wished to inflict on the captured enemy. To have him perish of want in sight of their plenty, to let him die in sight of their joy in life.

If this truly was their intention, then it utterly misfired. The mental state of these prisoners could no longer be fathomed by a healthy, free human being. Deeper humiliation was no longer possible for them. On the contrary, each sound, every glimmer they could still allow to sink in, was welcome. Something was going to happen after all, there was still *something* to come. And that music, the most heavenly thing on earth, resounded then: solace and rapture in one!

Who cared whether it was being played to mock them now; not by the musicians: they simply had to and, who knows, perhaps they were making an extra effort in fact – to do them a last kindness.

By no means everyone experienced it in this manner. Many would only hear it in the distance, as sounds calling them from the other side, singing of their release from their suffering. Others, less far gone, looked up the while, mistaking it for the opening up of heaven to reveal an image of what awaited them there. Some, with their last remaining strength, stretched out their arms towards it.

Only those who were intact discerned the full reality. He, too, who had been cast inside last and was the least dilapidated therefore, who still had command of almost all his strength, for his wounds had much improved. Nothing escaped his notice. After all that time of enforced deafness and blindness, the use of his senses was an intense experience in itself: to assuage the hunger of his eyes, to slake the thirst of his ears.

While everything remained motionless below, as though in a petrified world, he saw how the binge up above became ever more impetuous, the voices rising continually above the music. The guests no longer merely groped for food and drink but for one another too. Their movements became wilder, their sounds, even their laughter, more bestial. From time to time, a bone, gnawed clean, would carelessly be tossed down, over the balustrade.

As spirits rose this happened more frequently. Not just bones, but bones with meat still on them too. The musicians were exhorted to louder and faster playing, the guests directing more and more of their attention towards the realm below them. Some were already hanging over the balustrade. One raised his glass in space and then drank to them.

The true meaning of this junket now became clear to him. They sought to amuse themselves with them. Like with animals. To have them fight for the scraps from their table. And possibly then to see them devour each other in consequence. They had first drunk themselves into a conscience-less state so as to be able to play this game with full abandon.

More and ever larger chunks of food they cast down, emitting cries such as those one exhorts dogs with. A large piece of pie came down right beside him; he did not stretch out his hand towards it.

They did not stop at scraps. Entire platters of meat, just brought in, flew down amongst them, leaving an arc of vapour in the air.

But not one of the prisoners moved: they went on being that

petrified group. Many were incapable of rousing themselves but the strong, too, it seemed, carefully weighed up the effort a general struggle would cost them against the advantage of capturing a chunk. The only thing he saw was that they would look round occasionally, at the food and back at each other again, only moving their eyes in doing so. Predatory it was.

No matter what was going to happen, he would never join in with that. He'd done with everything for good. He would calmly undergo the decline of his body. He would give the enemy no power over this decision and in so doing he would preserve a final independence. Or was he able to decide this because he still had his resistance? And would his will desert him too, before time? So that then he would do things which still shamed him now? He shuddered at this.

They had broken up the symposium. Bar a few, the entire company had openly turned to the arena of death. While the music was silent, one of their number made a long speech to them of which he could understand not a word but which had to be very droll for the speaker was always being interrupted by general hilarity. He was probably mocking them for their refusal to show interest in the food they had been thrown, asking ironically whether they were too sated perhaps, or so spoiled that these dishes were not to their taste.

The oration was addressed to them but only intended for the ladies and gentlemen on the balcony who amused themselves, moreover, by taking aim at individual prisoners. A big, ruggedly hairy warrior formed their target more than the others. He did not move a muscle. No one did.

This general rigidity could be interpreted as contempt, and anger began to rise in the company the way anger does in a donkeyman when his beast baulks, its legs stretched out, and it can't be driven on, no matter what.

Then they played their final, trump card. The centre of the balcony was cleared for a moment and as the music speeded up and grew into a pandemonium, a tremendous roast boar, suspended by servants from its spit, was dumped into the arena.

With this the spell was broken. This was too much. Those

who were first to reach it might sate themselves for months.
The chance of living on beckoned from afar again. A general
stampede ensued. Groaning, the foremost struck their teeth
into the mound of roast flesh. Atop and beneath one another,
they thronged from all sides now, like piglets to the sow, and
the moment they struck lucky they adopted the voracious
movements of larvae.

The strong smell pervading the entire vault, the exciting
music and the jubilant shouts of encouragement from the balcony left not a soul untouched. The weakest, too, tried to get
there; they sacrificed their last remaining strength for this.
Only the dead remained behind, as did he, the one still intact.
His soundness rendered him as inviolable as the dead.

He wasn't affected but he had changed. In this deluge of
events, his attitude of resigned waiting was lost. He had a part
in it, a most grievous part. The enemy's scheme of depriving
them of all dignity, even of that of suffering, to render them
like animals, like the least among animals, had succeeded. To
let them murder each other. For this was happening. He saw
how gradually a bulwark of fighters and vanquished formed
round the boar.

Unhindered, he polished off a few separate chunks of food
lying within his reach, the piece of pie, too. These chunks were
still lying all around, untouched: once the great trek to the
boar had begun, no one had bothered about them any more.
Many now fighting themselves to death there could have sated
themselves with these without any trouble, but nobody any
longer possessed the small amount of reflection necessary for
this. As far as he could see, he was the only one to have preserved his independence.

He was also the only one to keep an eye on the balcony, who
saw their jubilation, the way they were drinking there, the way
they took ever fiercer delight in the meat and the bloodbath
beneath them. It was striking the way they no longer inter-
vened in any way, how the throwing and hollering had ceased
immediately once the forces had been unleashed. Seeing how
these forces would burn themselves out gave them the greatest
satisfaction apparently.

The more deeply the mob gnawed its way into the boar, the wilder things became. Those who felt their powers return now formed a likeminded force of occupation and together they defended the boar against the weaker ones all around. A division arose between those who were gaining more and more strength and the ones who were losing theirs continually. The swine seemed like a lifeboat, already laden with the ship-wrecked, which those in the water are still trying to clamber into from all sides and who have to be prevented from doing this with force. And the more the boar was being eaten away inside, the more it began to resemble a boat, with its rostrum and ribs. Bones were laid bare. One or two from the occupying force broke off a rib and in this they had a weapon to batter away with: at hands clamped round the boar, at shoulders ris-ing up from the waves, at faces distorted with craving.

The music was way past having anything to whip up any more: it merely followed. All the sounds together formed the voice of the deity who had created this inferno.

But gradually everything returned to calm again. Many had died, others were sated, the boar was finished, only its skeleton was still being gnawed at. On the balcony, too, passions had abated. The men and women had joined in pairs and silently they conducted their amorous dialogue. The end of the great upheaval seemed nigh and he who had kept himself apart all the time wondered whether, after this deepest of humiliations, there would now be an end of it. He was filled with an intense sadness. That glorious life boiled down to this and that others took delight in such an end, to him this was a dislocation of all coherence. But no: he erred in his view. Life did not begin for the sake of its end. The end is not a final outcome but merely the last thing. The journey was the essence, not the manner in which you disembark; it was a delusion to despise one's entire life because of the way its end was now.

He was suddenly amazed at finding the strength for such thoughts and for such a feeling. Had all these events stirred something within him after all? Or was this simply caused by his having eaten again? Then the others, the ones who had devoured the boar, would have to sense a dawn among the ashes of their sensibilities too. And lo: something happened that appeared to be connected with this.

The music fell silent, the guests on the balcony grew quite mute, a deathly silence set in. The servants who previously had carried in the torches now came with long stakes with which they moved the light baskets that turned out to be fixed to pivoting arms, moving them a good way out from the wall. Because of this, parts of the vaulted rock above them, having remained in darkness until now, were suddenly illuminated. All looked up and kept their gaze trained upwards, for what they saw they had never expected to be there.

Oval holes had been hacked out at regular intervals in the vaulting and in each opening, accessible from the outside apparently, arms and legs resting on its edges or possibly supported by cords, was a young woman. The unsteady light of the torches played around as many as twenty such floating bodies. At first sight, they seemed to be statues, ceiling ornaments, but this wasn't Greece and such statues could only have existed there.

The music began, a soft, sweet lingering melody; the suspended women now addressed the world beneath them with movements, like in a dream at first, more emphatically as the music grew, with enticing gestures of arms, head and legs. Everything about them seemed to say: Come to us, we are intended for you and there is nothing we would more dearly like to do than to fulfil that purpose.

Meanwhile, the balcony had become a complete pleasure ground.

Dash it all. Not satisfied with the havoc they had wrought, they wished to continue their amusement with those who had survived it, whose drive for food had been assuaged and who through this had regained their strength, to continue it by baiting them as regards their second drive. While they themselves were fornicating freely there, they attempted to whip up their prisoners one more time to acts of fruitless rage. Slave girls served them to this end. Perhaps they had been promised their freedom for playing this role, for they vied with one another in seductive movements of love. They gyrated, they sang and smiled down at the men, and with their arms they pretended to draw them up to them.

With despair, he saw that this devilish intent succeeded too. His cave-mates kept their eyes riveted on the sirens above. They got up in order to be closer to them; they paced back and forth, restless, as though in a fever. He saw some of them stretch their arms aloft as if to say: Let yourselves drop, we'll catch you. But the other ones laughed and beckoned and gyrated their bodies.

One now tried to climb up the steep rock face. It was rough; here and there one could gain a hold. Followed by all eyes, the balcony's too, he went on climbing. Halfway up, his strength failed him or a support gave way. He plummeted down and lay there.

Others, too, attempted it, chose the most charming of the women or the roughest ascent and began their daring journey, encouraged by a chorus of cries. The start to the vault, only a few metres removed from the desired goal, when the hands stretching out from either side almost touched, was nearly always fatal. Each time someone dropped down, the music would suddenly fall silent so the thud could clearly be heard.

Once, he saw a man – wasn't he that big hairy one? – almost succeed. He was already clutching the edges of the oval gap. But the same white arm that first had helped him get that far now thrust him down unexpectedly.

Never before had there been such cheering in the cave as when this happened.

The longer he viewed all this, the more his soul unravelled. He felt himself go quietly mad. He felt regret over the food he had taken, for he wished to die. He stretched himself out on the rock floor, closed his eyes and resolved not to open them ever again. He wept over the sight the world still proffered him now on parting. He would turn away from it for good.

That's the way he lay there a little while, the goings-on around him forced back to a distant clamour. Then a droplet fell on his chest. The unexpectedness, the strangeness of this cleared his mind completely and made him abandon his resolve at once. He opened his eyes and looked straight up above. And lo: there was a slave girl right above him. And regarding her closely, things became clear to him at once. She wept.

Oh, what is it, that powerful thing that suddenly can come into being between two people? A current? A force field? An invisible ladder, in this case? He saw that, among all those women, she was different. No less charming, but dazed and desperate like him. He was the only one who saw this in the midst of the hellish uproar. He could not see that she wept but her tear had reached him there. A second one fell, on his shoulder.

A great desire quivered throughout his being. If ever two people must be united in this wilderness, they were the ones. He jumped up and stretched his muscles, felt his strength return to him as though by magic. Did she see him too? He looked up and thought she did. Was that a smile breaking around her mouth? Was that a gleam in her eye? Was it the case that they only existed for one another now?

With the eye of a hunter, he explored the steep rock face. Every fissure, every ledge he perceived and then he plotted his way accordingly, like in the past, when reaching a nest of young vultures was at stake. He gave a sign she would have to understand if the same fire had been kindled within her. And she did understand, for in reply she crossed her arms in front of her chest, thus indicating that she would pray for him the while.

Now the alliance had been sealed. Who knows, she may already have noticed him much earlier on, and her tears had been a call.

Slowly, and uncertainly at first because of his emotion, he began the ascent. As he rose higher and more perilously, the placement of his hands, of his fingers, the support of his feet, the transfer of his weight demanded all his attention. He was inconspicuous doing this: he was one of the many. Only later on, at the edge of the vaulting, did he attract general notice.

Each time he had found sufficient support, he would rest for a moment and look up, and the more clearly he could see her, the more glorious she seemed to him. Now he could read his own, huge desire in her face. No, it wasn't a game with her like it was with the others, a game of cat and mouse, for beyond the radiance of her love's glow he could see the fear, the fear of failure, of him falling. But the others had to think that she, too, was luring him to his death.

There had been one perilous moment; not when, for the first time, he saw her lips, her teeth, her nostrils, the wave in her hair, not even when he could distinguish the pupils in her eyes, when they switched focus from their faces to their eyes. All this was just glorious.

Dangerous was the moment when, for the first time, they could call out to each other. He began, and when she answered him she did so in his own language. She was one of his tribe!

By a whisker, he avoided toppling right over backwards. His entire body a-tremble, he clung to the rock and waited like this until he'd calmed down.

His language, his language! His language had not yet died: it was still alive. It revived between the two of them, which was the most important thing, the *only* important thing. Now, she was completely like him.

Who cared the way the others spoke? Nobody existed for him any more, except her. What he had wished to do when he believed to be closing his eyes for ever, to banish all that surrounded him from his thought, that same thing happened to him now. To him, she was all that truly existed.

This was no trembling with fear, but trembling with happiness, which was why it could change into strength and control. No more abandoning himself to tenderness now, no more words now except the ones trapeze artists will cry out to each other in the circus: no taking an advance on their happiness as long as it hadn't been captured yet.

The most difficult part of all came at the edge, where he must surmount the incline. He now avoided looking at her on purpose; the sight of her so close by would be as deadly as that of Medusa, would make him fall at once.

Measure for measure, he progressed. He, too, began to incline, over backwards: he had to grip the stone tightly. Softly, almost at a whisper, she gave instructions. 'Bit more to the left – a little further – no, not there, that bit's loose – yes, there's a hollow there – now raise your foot: there's another ledge there – slide along very slowly – let go your left hand and stretch out as far as possible.'

Yes, she gripped him: Let go!

Now those who were following him with bated breath from below and from the balcony saw him float through the air but to their amazement, he did not fall, though the music had already ceased.

Quite how it was done, no one could really tell: a few seconds on, they saw the prisoner and the slave girl in deepest embrace up there.

She had truly drawn him to her.

Now they were together. Now they could behold one another, say sweet nothings in each other's ears, melt their joys and their sorrow into one and entrust one another with their bodies.

Both wept with happiness, but they knew, too, that it would not last, and that all that can be between man and woman must be encompassed in that short time.

The sense of this brevity was the only thing that remained within them of the mayhem in the cave; all other things had been completely obliterated by their mutual possession.

Every word, each gesture proved to them that they were alike to an unfathomable depth.

They hurled themselves into the abyss of one another.

Amazement soon turned to anger in those who beheld this. They began to hurl abuse, to shout, to rant. Rage took all in its grip, the prisoners as much as the others. The empress shrieked. Like a fishwife.

None of this got through to the loving couple.

It took a long time before the order had been passed down the line and its execution came into effect.

Then the servants reached them with their stakes and pushed them down.

They still remained united in their fall.

On the ground, she was torn to pieces over his broken back.

Translated by Richard Huijng

9

A. ALBERTS

Green

Groen

The whole morning it has been nothing but coastline, an exceptionally pleasant and neat coastline, a real piece of nature with palm trees, but they don't wave. I would like it even more if they did, and if I did not know that the thick, white line under the palm trees becomes more and more dirty and dingy as you get closer, and that filthy huts appear under those same palm trees. I know all that, and I say goodbye to the captain, which is not necessary at all because in an hour he will also be going ashore, and I step into a prahu and we row to the shore.

The sea is filthy, which does not surprise me, and so shallow that we are scraping the bottom. The rowers jump out to push the prahu further, and we are probably still a mile from shore. At first they wade up to their waist through the water, but the sea becomes more and more shallow and I can already see the legs of the biggest one, who is walking right next to me. Finally we are permanently stuck.

I see a bunch of people standing under the palm trees, not doing anything, just standing there, but then I also see that two men are on their way towards me with a litter. They come alongside the boat. The litter is a worn desk chair, nailed to two bamboo poles, with no paint left on it, and with a hole in its cane seat. I sit in it and we wobble towards the beach and a little later I am standing on the sand that is just as filthy as I thought it would be.

Opposite me a man who introduces himself: Peartree. He is a colleague of mine, also living on the coast, but sixty miles further west. Two days' walk, he says, and I express my admiration at such a pace. Yes, you've got to be able to walk around here, he says, and then he asks what I brought with me. And also some beer and gin, I conclude, because I don't know yet what his attitude is towards beer and gin. How much? he asks. The amount is more than he expected even though I only report half of it, otherwise he'll be here for another two weeks, and while it is possible, if not probable, that a month from now I will throw myself at any sweaty European as the only white man I have seen for some time, I've had enough for now.

This is the village chief, Peartree says, and he points at the front bearer of my chair, and I give him a friendly nod. And now you probably want to know where you're going to stay. He has obviously decided to become more cheerful because he can look forward to beer, gin and a landsman who provided them. I now also notice from his tone and manner that he is nervous; in fact, his nerves are all shot.

We walk on through the palm trees, because my house appears to be beyond the palms in a more ordinary forest. Those palms are like a screen of about a hundred feet between the coast and the forest.

I see my house. It isn't so much a house as a part of the forest, under a lean-to roof, and partitioned into a couple of compartments. There are chairs and a little table in front, and for a moment I imagine that the glasses are already on the table, but it isn't quite as bad as that yet, even though it won't be long now.

The place looks cool and is cool and also quite pleasant. A couple of villagers are watching. They are your servants, says Peartree; your predecessor left them behind. Who was it? I ask. I had met my predecessor some time ago and I know that he's on leave now, but I think it's better to act ignorant like a green-horn on occasions like this.

Can't remember his name, Peartree says. As a matter of fact, he drank himself to death. I say: That so? And a little later again: That so? Now he knows that I know that things are tough around here. And perhaps I'm showing that I can handle it, as well as future problems, by starting to drink right on top of this. Given the situation, that seems tactless enough. So

I say: How about a beer? And we sit down at the table. Perhaps my predecessor didn't quite drink himself to death, but his servants certainly know all by themselves how to find a crate of beer in my luggage, to break it open and to open the bottles. After things have got a little friendlier between Peartree and me, I feel that I can leave him alone for a while.

Inside my house I've got to take a breather and I lie down on my bed, that is to say I lie down on the bed in the room where my luggage is. For the first time since my arrival I experience a feeling of loneliness. I lie back on my bed with my hands folded under my head, though, naturally, I am ready to jump up at the sound of Peartree's footsteps, because I don't want him to find me like this. And I think of a girl I once used to know, and I wouldn't mind if she walked in right at this moment. I would show her the forest, I do believe that it is quite beautiful really, and we would sit together in the garden, this spot in the green forest. Then the beer begins to take effect – we drank rather fast, after all – with the result that I want to keep on drinking.

I go outside and see that I have to restrain myself a little because the captain of my ship has also arrived and he and Peartree are discussing business. Settling old orders and placing new ones. I pour another round and join them to show that I am interested. When I finally realize that Peartree is only talking about private business, I go inside again, but this time I walk out at the rear and into the forest. It really is a very beautiful forest with tall trees that are not too close together, although the crowns touch each other everywhere, with the result that the space beneath them is filled with transparent green light. After I've walked for a while it occurs to me that if I keep on walking I will reach the edge of this forest sooner or later, and that I will sit at the edge of the forest and look out over a wide plain. But right now I don't see my house any more, so it is better to go back.

Peartree and the captain are at the gin already and the conversation becomes general, stories about other lonely places, stories about big cities, and then the captain says that he has to keep an eye on the time. We take him to the beach and we've had enough to wave him goodbye when he wobbles in his chair to the prahu. I notice with some satisfaction that the village chief is not one of the bearers. Then we go back to the gin.

I ask Peartree about the forest and if there is an end to it. An edge to the forest, I say. He gets up, goes inside, and comes back with a map on which he shows me where the edge of the forest is, sixty miles north of the coast. He shows me several places along that edge that are easy to reach as far as the vegetation is concerned. He says: You'll want to get away from that forest every so often.

When it gets dark they bring a petroleum lamp. The thing is hung from an ingenious stand: an iron bar that lies horizontally across another iron bar, which is stuck into the ground. Can't fall over, Peartree says. I ask him if they have also lit a lamp inside the house. He says: Yes. I say: Because I have to write a letter. To a girl. He says: The boat is already gone and I say: Yes, but. Well, he doesn't give a damn, Peartree says. I bow to him and go inside. It's quite a problem because I'll never find my stationery, oh well, I still have some letters in my pocket and on the back of an envelope I write with difficulty. I'll copy it tomorrow, sweet darling, sweetest darling.

I tell Peartree about the girl, he tells me about his wife, he is divorced, she ran off with somebody else. We might as well not eat and I tell Peartree about the bottle of cognac that should be somewhere in my luggage and is found by my predecessor's servant, damn it, my predecessor must have drunk himself to death after all, the servant hasn't prepared any food either.

A day later.

Today from eight o'clock on is the first day that is completely mine. This day and the following days are my personal property; I can do what I want with them. Now I can cut through the narrow strip of palm trees to the sea and then walk for some distance along the beach to where there are no huts any more, lie down on the sand in such a way that the shade of the palm trees covers me. Because I've got a head you won't believe. Peartree has left. He was up at six, and so was I, for that matter. He was drinking coffee in the garden and looked very angry when I wished him good morning. Angry and also very haughty. He was put out, of course, about having confided in me yesterday. We drank our coffee together and I wasn't in such great form myself, rather stiff really, because last night I had also revealed my intimate problems to him without holding back, and had sworn that I would follow his advice.

We remained sitting there silently and ill at ease and if Peartree had only said something like: Come on, cut it out, we would have grinned despite our sore heads and would have rubbed our sandpaper tongues against the roofs of our mouths and kept silent and everything would have been all right, except for the emptiness I would have felt after his departure.

But Peartree snapped at me. He called for the village chief, gave instructions, and left at eight o'clock. His attitude spared me the sadness of a farewell. I am beginning to feel better already and think that it's quite nice around here. Even the palms are waving.

The sea is very wide and far, not a ship in sight, that's probably always the case around here. There are a few prahus on the beach, those things you've got to push, with an outrigger, they won't get very far in them and I wonder how the fishing is, to hell with it, I don't feel like getting involved now already with the problems of the village's economy. I'd rather look at the sea, just like that, as if it's the sea, and close my eyes and go to sleep.

I wake up with the sun on my legs and then the feeling of owning this as well as the following days has become burdensome enough that I go to look for the village chief. He tells me all about the prahus and the amount of fish they catch. About what they eat and what the forest produces. How purchasing and transportation are arranged. He tells me all sorts of other things but there's soon an end to what I can take in. So I ask him about the extent of the forest and I point in a northerly direction. I know from Peartree that the edge of the forest is another sixty miles, but I secretly hope that somewhere there will be an open space before that. Because this is one of the few resolutions from yesterday I want to act on: to build a little house near an open space in the forest or better yet at the edge of the forest with a view of the free plain. The village chief looks doubtful. He doesn't know about that, he says. Can't we search for it? I ask. He looks even more doubtful and says again that he doesn't know about that. But I'll get it out of him. I ask him if there are any people living further up north who might know. Oh, he says, I don't know, and this time it sounds so pitiful that I stop trying. It might cost me my popularity.

I walk with him to his village, brown huts, filthy children, and I keep on walking and I make sure that I stay a couple of steps in front of him, otherwise he will take me to his house, his filthy house, to drink filthy coffee out of filthy cups and to sit in a rickety chair on a stinking front porch. But then he suddenly darts in front of me and he points his thumb so politely and obsequiously at a house, his house, that I smile amiably and, thanking him kindly, go inside. He orders coffee, takes the cup from the hands of a boy, probably his son, and puts it down in front of me. He should also sit down, I say. Oh well, blood is thicker than water, for him as well as for me, but the day is no longer my property, I'm well aware of that.

We've become polite neighbours now. I ask the same questions as before, but this time in the affirmative. I say: The fishermen never go very far from the coast? He agrees and nods his head like a village schoolmaster who, years later, has an old student come back to visit him from the big strange world out there. Yes, I say, and the resin from the forest is brought here. By whom? I suddenly ask straightforwardly. By our people, he says somewhat surprised. So they do go into the forest? Yes, he says and he points west. And there? I ask, and I point north, but no, he is not sure about that, he says evasively. And the resin is picked up here by the ship, I say conciliatingly again. Yes, he says. Every six months? Every six months, he repeats with satisfaction. Is that your son? Yes, it is his son, and he's given my empty cup and returns it filled.

In the afternoon, after a meal, I sit down behind my desk, the desk of my predecessor. I take four empty notebooks and write on the first one: Fishery Report. I'll pay close attention to that, the number of fishermen, what percentage they are of the total population. And the amount of fish they bring in, of course. And the kind of fish. In short, a thorough report. On the second notebook I write: Forest Products. About the expeditions they make, the amount of time they stay in the forest, about what they have stored and the different types, about the prices given by the dealers.

The third notebook becomes: In General, and the fourth, I thought that up this morning, is going to be something completely new: Timber Crop. As far as I know, they don't fell trees here, even though it is perfectly suited for it, anybody can see that. There must be a special reason for it, transportation problems or something like that. Maybe the wood is not suitable at all, too light or too heavy or whatever. Now that I think about it more, it does not seem such a great idea after all.

Then I realize something. The village chief is always talking about the western forest and I want to go to the northern forest, he doesn't. But what's in the east? I get up and walk outside. Amazing how cool it stays here in this green tempered light. I follow the demarcation between the forest and the palm trees, with the sea constantly in sight, and I walk this way for half an hour, then everything ends and there's only the sea. The sea, which makes a sharp turn north. Hence there is no eastern forest, which is one complication less and one added obligation, because I have no choice now, I must explore the northern forest. It is always that way in life, fewer complications, more obligations.

When I am sitting in front of my house in the evening, with the lamp hanging from the stand, I think of Peartree for the first time since he left. Peartree is about halfway now. He sleeps in the forest, in the western, not the northern forest, and I turn my chair about forty-five degrees so that I face in that direction, north. After I've sat like that for a while, I feel restless and uneasy and I realize that I'm sitting with my back turned to the door, the door of my world. My world is the forest and the door is the beach, the spot where I came ashore yesterday and where other people too, strangers, can land and force themselves into my existence. I turn my chair back to its former position in order to keep an eye on the door. Everything has its proper place now. The west, that is Peartree, that's where he really belongs. The north, the unknown, what I am looking forward to, that belongs. The east, that is Nothingness, that also belongs. And the south, that is the door, and what lies beyond it must remain locked out. I sit in the night and look and see Peartree, thirty miles further, if he hasn't lied. Annoying Peartree, but you also belong.

A day later.

This morning I invite the village chief to discuss the particulars of my first trip to the forest. While talking, I point west and not north, and he is very happy about that. I hear that we will be visiting some second-rate villages, temporary settlements of the people who gather forest products. We will only be away for two days, staying over only one night, because this is the first time. I don't want to do everything at once and I try to make it clear that Peartree's pace is too fast for me. The village chief, who is my guest now, is completely in agreement with me.

I wonder if we can leave this same afternoon, but I restrain myself just in time, because that would be incredibly dumb and contradictory, to hurry like that. The truth is that the chief's painstaking and endless planning for the trip bores me, because I am not looking forward to the afternoon and evening.

Completely uncalled for: in the afternoon I lie down on a long chair beneath the green with a new detective novel, and for three full hours I read attentively to the end. To the end of a day filled with beauty, to the beauty of the evening, of the silence of the lamp and its light.

Of the silence.

Of the yellow light.

A day later.

This is the day of my first journey. More than ever before I feel the slight but invigorating agitation always associated with travel, because this is travel at its purest, its noblest form, indeed, the form of my journey is noble, ancient and full of tradition.

Up front goes the guide, the scout, walking thirty feet in front of me. In its archaic form this distance would have been a day's travel. My journey is somewhat stylized. This includes where the village chief should be. While he should really be walking a few steps in front of me, he has joined the scout, what one could call the informal style.

I come after him, surrounded by the wall and moat of distinction, I, the prince from the distant court, centuries ago. Respectfully behind me come some lesser dignitaries, members of the village council, if I am not mistaken. There might be some private, well-to-do resin gatherers among them. They have a right, of course, to be part of my retinue. And finally, the train of this retinue is made up of a number of bearers.

We have followed the coast for some time but now, to my great satisfaction, we have changed direction and are heading inland. The forest, as well as the ground cover, becomes denser here, it becomes darker, more ordinary, a less transparent green. In this way we come rather suddenly to our first village. Friendly scouts approach us and there's a great deal of interest when we enter the settlement. I am happy to sit down, but otherwise it's not much around here. The Northwood should be better and more beautiful.

We eat, we rest, do some business, and in the afternoon we go on. Excellent village chief. He has picked a good place to stay overnight. The second village when we arrive in the late afternoon is large and clean, and the gentleman who receives us is almost dignified. An oily, polite, fat and doubtlessly rich gentleman is the chief of this second settlement. He looks as if he knows everything that is worthwhile to know in these parts, and when I invite him and some other gentlemen to have a smoke with me after dinner, I feel that I have to take advantage of this opportunity. Forgive me, village chief of mine, but I cannot pass up this opportunity.

This is a fine and large settlement, I say, almost as fine as the big village. They grin and scratch themselves. I point north-west and ask if there are any more settlements there. Yes, two more. And in the north-east? I ask and I point in that direction and look only at my fat host. He grins and says he isn't so sure.

There's only one settlement there, my own village chief says. Sometimes people live there and sometimes they don't. We don't know anything else about it.

There is something unmistakably sad and disappointed in his tone of voice when he says this, and his manner is really very dignified. That's why I bow politely in his direction and change the subject to something more neutral: the history of his people.

A day later.

I am back home and it is evening already and the lamp is brought outside. It seems there is still some cognac left and I finish it. It's quite a lot of cognac. I sit down with my back to the south, because I have to chase away my fear, I've got to steel myself against fear. Because I have to become a courageous man.

There are two possible courses open to me. First of all, I could go to Peartree and ask him the necessary information about the Northwood. He would do that for me. He will probably tell me that one or more nomadic tribes are to be found out there. If I want to have a closer look at these nomadic tribes, Peartree will either approve of it or think it's ridiculous, probably the latter. The other possibility is not to mention anything to Peartree, and that's what I'll do. Because I don't see how I can make it clear to Peartree that I'm not going there for those nomadic tribes, that I couldn't care less about them, that things would be a lot quieter if they weren't there. I can't make it clear to Peartree that I want to reach the edge of the forest, that I want to walk ten, twenty, a hundred yards into the open plain. Then I will turn around to this green forest. No, I will not turn around, not at first, when I come out into the open onto the plain. Perhaps there'll be a hill, I'll climb it and cheer, I'll shout, as I would never dare do inside the green.

Or I'll be silent and take a deep breath, as I would never be able to do in the green light. And when I have drunk my fill of light and distance, I will turn around, raise my glass and laugh and call out: I see you, green forest.

*

I am having a lot of trees cut, a lot of wood, and I am having a house built, so large and wide that it spreads low against the sky. The entrance on the forest side and a wide terrace on the north side. And a basement, that's a good joke, damn it, I always build houses when I am drunk, damn it all.

A day later.

Today I carefully examine the business affairs of the village, the supply of resin in storage for shipping, the food situation, the general state of health. The village chief accompanies me everywhere. The Northwood is not mentioned any more, the man deserves it. I try to give the impression of being strictly businesslike, the village chief must be able to count on me, he must be able to trust me.

At home I fix up a little office, pull out my notebooks, and begin my reports. I calculate, I estimate, I make plans. I hesitate for a moment when I hold the notebook Timber Crops in my hands. I put it away again. I really don't know anything about wood, and I never will. I don't know the name of even one tree in this area. I'll discuss this matter with Peartree sometime.

In the late afternoon I am overwhelmed by an uncontrollable desire to walk into the forest. It is four o'clock and I decide to walk north for an hour. That way I'll still be able to get back before dark. This walk is a serious matter.

It is remarkable how little the forest changes in this direction. It does not become dense and the ground cover stays the same, the light stays the same, everything stays the same, and I am no exception. When I am in my house, in the village, or during the journeys with the village chief, scouts, and the rest, I change like a chameleon. I am courteous, bored, resigned, interested, miserable, drunk, all depending on the place and circumstances. Here, in the Northwood, the place and circumstances stay completely the same and this sameness becomes intensely evident in the green light.

I wonder how I will mark where I'm going in order to be able to find my way again later, but it's impossible. After an hour I turn back, nothing will come of it in this manner. But after another hour I'm still not home. A compass would be useful here, but I do not have a compass and I am lost. When it is completely dark, I can only grope my way and I am very scared until I see a light shining relatively close by. I stumble in its direction. It is the light from my own house, of course; what else could it be?

Sitting under the lamp after dinner, I consider the possibilities. There aren't many. This afternoon I went about three miles north, that is three out of the sixty that lie between my house and the edge of the forest. If I walk six hours a day, it'll take me a week coming and going, and even then I will have to really work at it. I can't do this alone, I really can't do this alone.

A week later.

I'm going to see Peartree today and I really want to. I make an arrangement with the village chief that we'll take at least three – or if we like, four – days walking to get there. If it's the latter, he says, we have to stay at least once outside a settlement, that is to say, spend the night in the forest. I ask him if he has anything against it. He says: No, I don't but perhaps you do. I can never figure out if these people are serious about something like this or if they hate not sleeping in a settlement. So I say: I don't mind doing it in three days. He says: If you want to do it in three days, we can do it in three days, and sleep in the settlements. But I say: If you'd rather take four days, it's really no problem for me to sleep in the forest. That's that, I've put the burden of sincerity on his shoulders. Hurrying like that doesn't prove anything, I say. No, he says, it doesn't.

Finally I have confided in him and told him that I would actually enjoy spending a night outside a settlement. He has nodded and smiled in a friendly manner. He is really an amiable character.

My retinue is a little bigger than the last time, there are more people carrying provisions. I join the vanguard. Today we are walking to the first settlement, the same one from the last journey. Then we continued in the afternoon, now we are resting. I see that I've made a good decision when I divided the whole journey into four stages. The village chief and the other gentlemen don't like to exert themselves needlessly either, and when we are sitting together in the evening, they are more talkative than last time.

A day later.

We continue in a westerly direction. I think we are following the beach at a relatively short distance. I ask the guide. He says: Yes, the beach is very close. The forest does not resemble my Northwood in anything. It is much denser, including the ground cover. We walk along a worn path, worn by my predecessors, worn by Peartree, worn by his predecessors, on assiduous journeys with gin at the end.

The settlement we arrive at towards the end of the afternoon betrays Peartree's presence. There is a guest house with all kinds of handyman's touches, such as chairs with ashtrays on the armrests, or kobolds by the washbasin holding a stick between them to hang a towel from. A lamp in a corner is again a kobold on a table holding a lantern high. But why should this be Peartree's work? It could just as well be the work of a teetotal predecessor, which is really far more likely. A calm, level-headed person, who puts ashtrays on armrests and who doesn't smoke. He puts a lamp together as if for a joint but he doesn't drink. It is a pretty gloomy place.

I have to meet a settlement chief here I have never met before. This is the third one, a replica of the fat oily host of my overnight stay on the first journey. So here you can still find rest-houses with your typical innkeeper.

We have to have a smoke again, although I'm not quite up to it, I'm not up for anything and I go to bed early.

A day later.

Today, at the end of the day's march, we will spend the night in the forest. I get up early and drink coffee. The village chief comes to ask if I might want to leave already. I say: Fine, and we're on our way. The forest is the same as yesterday but in the afternoon we are walking among palm trees. I ask how that is possible. The palm forest is much wider here than by us, the village chief says. But we are close to the sea, I say. Yes, we are very close to the sea. And how far from the big village? Yes, we aren't that far from the big village any more.

I keep up appearances and nod carelessly, and then we walk another two hours under those damned palms and then we are at Peartree's. I am dead tired and Peartree is loud and jovial.

Go on, he says, freshen up a bit. I was right when I thought that you'd need three days.

I enter his house. I notice that I am putty in the hands of the village chief; that's the way it'll have to be. Peartree's house is bigger and painted darker than mine, brown, rather sombre, but it is divided the same way. It is near a kind of square and the whole place makes a martial impression. Peartree had a square section of forest chopped down, and the soil was turned over, but it's full of weeds now. Among those weeds, right in front of the house, are two chairs and a table with glasses and bottles. A beer, Peartree says. Ha-ha, a beer. He's ahead of me. I sit down, stretch my legs, and take a deep breath. The sun shines low over the trees at the edge of the square. I say: You've got it pretty good here, and I wave at the open space before me.

What? he asks. The forest? And he begins to laugh out loud. I say: No, what I really mean is, that you cut down quite a piece of it. Oh, it was already there when he came here, he says.

You've been here half a year now, right? Half a year, he says, half a year and then another half a year and then we go. Go.

The tour of duty's a year, then? I ask. Peartree scrutinizes me. A year? he mutters to himself. Yes, of course, a year. Just imagine, for Chrissake, if it was more than a year.

I tell Peartree about my experiences with the village chief. Of course, he says, they can't stand long marches, but they'll always manage to get out of sleeping in the forest.

Who put up the guest house where I slept last night? I ask. Don't know, Peartree says. Was there already. For that matter, I also had one put up in the north-west corner of my section.

How do you do that? I ask. What? Peartree asks. Have a house built like that? You give orders, Peartree says. So I give orders. Ah, life isn't all that complicated. The lamp is brought outside. So they bring the lamp outside here too, but damn it,

I'd really like something to eat. I'm starving. Peartree thinks eating is ridiculous, but all right, all right, he will have them get something.

But how can it be so quiet here? Yes, quiet, when the lamp swings back and forth, there are no tree shadows to swing along with it. The lamp swings in a void.

The ship will be back in two weeks, Peartree says, and then five more ships, and I'm on my way. But it's really not so bad around here, right? Visiting each other every two weeks, imagine, every two weeks you have people visit you in your little parlour, it makes you want to swear a blue streak.

A man could damn well take it, if Peartree kept his trap shut. There are even some stars in the sky. Stars flicker and shine. Peartree shuts up. It's not so bad at all if Peartree talks. Let him talk. I ask him: Peartree, that wood you cut here? I didn't, Peartree says. I say, that wood, in short, and I wave with my hands, could it be used for lumber? He doesn't know, he says. I want to cut some, I say. Chop down the whole goddam forest, Peartree yells, beat the hell out of that entire forest! Can it be used for carpentry? I ask. I don't know, Peartree says.

A day later.

But it is still beautiful this morning, that empty piece of land before me, bordered by straight tall trees. Behind me I hear Peartree stumbling around in the house. He comes outside, grumbles when I say good morning, and flops down in a chair. At first he doesn't say anything; we are both quiet, because I don't feel so great myself. It is amazing to see the sun come up and not as at my place, where green light keeps on becoming a brighter green.

Have you been on tour already? Peartree asks. I fill him in on the adventures of my two-day journey to the north-west. That's all? he snarls. There are two other settlements, I say, half helpfully, half guiltily. Peartree sniffs contemptuously. And the other way? he asks. There's another one of those half-deserted places. Didn't you go to take a look? The village chief doesn't seem to feel like it very much, I say as carelessly as possible, but it sounds rather weak. And I feel weak, also confused.

My secret plan to make the Northwood a fairy-tale sanctuary for myself is being roughly exposed. Are you such a jerk that you let some village chief boss you around? Peartree asks. I say: No. I still wouldn't mind going there. I'd do that damn soon, Peartree says. You're gonna get into trouble.

He probably sees me slowly get red, because his last words sound a little friendlier. He's probably thinking: Maybe I was too tough. And now he's afraid that I will get angry. Or he's simply good-natured. But I am thinking something entirely different. I think: Damn it, always the same thing. Because this is not the first time that I clearly miss a chance to realize one of my fantasies.

But it is a passing annoyance. When I reach the big settlement in the evening with the handyman's guest house, I have already fitted the incident into the picture I have of my Northwood. It is and remains a fairy castle with its entrances completely overgrown. Peartree's big mouth has cut a hole in this barrier. Onward.

Two days later.

The rest of my trip back I did in two days and when I come home in the afternoon, I am completely used to the green again and I sit contentedly in my chair in front of the house, when the lamp is brought outside and the play of the tree shadows begins. For the moment I've had enough of ranging in forests. In ten days the boat will arrive. In ten days Peartree will come here. He will ask: Have you been north already? I will say: Yes, I have searched for a suitable spot for a settlement. This is excellent. An excellent plan.

Twelve days later.

The ship has come and gone. I witnessed a replay of my own arrival. Everything was so much like the first time that it frightened me, frightened and depressed me.

Peartree was here for two evenings. In two weeks I will go to Peartree. In a month the ship will come again; third performance.

In the evening I leave my house at the back. The forest is

black and impassable. I wander through the trees along the side of my house to the front. I stand behind a tree and look around the trunk. In front of the house in the forest the lamp is shining, in its circle of light is a table and a chair, an empty chair. It won't be long now before I will see myself sitting in the chair while I stand behind a tree and carefully look around the trunk. I wish that there wasn't a lamp burning but a wood fire, and that a kobold was dancing around it, singing: Nobody knows, nobody knows, that my name is Rumpelstiltskin. It would be more fitting, more natural.

A day later.

I have the village chief come to me. I have been ordered, I tell him, to build three settlements, and I point in the fatal direction. He is frightened and cringes for a moment. He gives me a long, sad look. I say: Well, nothing we can do about it. And then I shake my head a bit. I wish I had never mentioned the Northwood to this man. Until his dying day he's going to regard this assignment as some kind of trick.

The question arises whether there is something I should do myself, but I wouldn't know what it possibly could be. You give orders, Peartree says. Are they going there now and are they taking building materials with them or do they get that on the spot? I would imagine the latter.

A week later.

In the final analysis it all went rather smoothly. I wanted to have the first settlement built about twenty-five miles due north. That would also be just fine, said the village chief, but there was already a settlement around there. When did that happen? I asked. Yesterday or the day before yesterday; maybe I would like to have a look one of these days.

And now I sit under the lamp, and what am I doing? I am singing softly to myself out of satisfaction and relief. The village chief is a good person. He still regards the orders I received and which he passed on as a trick invented by me, but he considers it an admirable idea on my part to do it in this manner, that I didn't bark the order at him to begin the expansion at my very first appearance. He hopes and trusts that we can haggle about the number of new settlements. Surely there won't be more than two, he thinks. And for one of these he has ear-marked the abandoned settlement that is supposed to belong to a nomadic tribe. This nomadic tribe is nonsense, of course, it was those gentlemen all along, until they got sick of it. It was their fear of the unknown forest. The village chief and I, we both have followed the path of least resistance, la di da. But it is much better this way.

Two days later.

This morning I'm going to see the village chief to arrange for my first journey to the new settlement. We are now so polite to each other, the village chief and I, that I think it better to warn him a few days in advance. Then he can prepare things out there at his leisure, because it isn't even half finished, of course. Once again I regard my impending journey as a pleas-ant adventure. I really should go to Peartree, but I am putting it off for a week.

Two days later.

We are on our way. The settlement is some thirty miles away, an impossible distance to cover in one day, but thirty miles means half the distance to the edge of the forest. When we arrive this evening, I will reward the village chief by reducing the number of new settlements to be built from three to two.

I am on my way in my magic forest; I walk between the trunks and look around me. There still is no ground cover and now I know why. The ground is rocky. In any case, a lot of large stones are partly buried in the soil and partly visible above it, it is a marvellous forest. Straight trunks, green light, always the same, and it must be very ancient. It is Time itself, I say, laughing. Ancient, green, and always the same.

We finally reach the settlement, a couple of sombre huts in the darkening forest. I am too tired to eat and I only recover a little in the evening, when I sit on the small porch and stare in front of me into the dark. It is always the same.

*

A day later.

I sleep late, afterwards I take care of the more urgent matters, jot down data, give my approval for the appointment of a settlement chief. Not until the afternoon does the realization of where I am really strike me. This is the Northwood. If I get up early tomorrow morning and head north all day, I can reach the edge of the forest. For a moment I am tempted to call my village chief and give him the order for the journey. It won't work, there are too many problems. And I also have to go to Peartree. Damned annoying, those visits, but I can't back out of them, ridiculous, forsaken by God and man alike, and I have to hurry to pay a visit.

Two days later.

My legs still bother me from that walk of twice thirty miles. I have been loafing and fooling around all day, with nothing to do really. I won't go to Peartree tomorrow.

Twelve days later.

I ended up not going to Peartree at all and tonight, two days before boat day, he comes walking through the forest. I didn't see you, he says. The work in the forest has kept me, I say. It satisfies him. He is simply nervously pleasant.

Four days later.

Today I walked four hours out and back in the Northwood. It is a marvellous forest in all its similar infinity. If I walk here, or if I walk thirty miles further down, it's all the same, nor can I change myself during that time.

Three weeks later.

I am in the Northwood, three miles from the border. The second settlement has been built and I will be at the border in one hour. I walked away quietly this morning. I want to be alone when I reach the edge of the forest, when I cross the border. The forest finally changes. It seems as if it enshrouds itself before it will disclose its secret. There are a lot more bushes and it becomes hilly.

In a while I will see the dawn, the dawning of light. And it is already growing lighter.

I will have a house built out there. It will not have a front or back, no preference for forest or open plain. I will know how to be generous after my conquest of the green forest. If need be, I will have the house built round, that is an idea, a round house with a round porch around it.

And then it is light, then I can see the open plain. I begin to run, I trip, I almost fall, but then it is light. It is exactly the way I pictured it, it is truth, I sing, I shout, I am saved.

I stand still, panting, under an enormously wide sky. This is it, then, so this is it.

A great bare land, with many stones, big stones, hilly, with hazy blue mountains in the distance. I walk on now, but more slowly. I also notice that there is no sun. The light is sharp, I don't notice it otherwise, in the forest. I walk on, I know that I have to go back, that I can't stay yet, for ever, but just for a moment, just a moment longer, like a child before going to sleep. I sit down on a stone. Where have I seen this before? I am thinking.

Stonehenge, maybe, where Merlin stayed, in a picture in a geography book. There are really huge stones here. And those mountains form an orderly and neat demarcation. I have no desire at all to start also constructing a fantasy about what could possibly lie beyond them. Let's leave well enough alone. Now I know what lies beyond the forest and that will have to be enough. I am behind the forest. And then I turn around to the forest.

Three days later.

I just got home. The village chief and the bearers went home. I cannot ask anyone to stay with me. It wouldn't help anyway. I cannot ask anyone to stay, I can't tell anyone what I saw, when I stood outside it and turned around to the forest.

The wind was blowing when I stood there outside. I had not noticed it as long as I was in the forest, but it was blowing.

The sky was a mouldy grey and beneath that sky, against that sky, was the forest, poisonous green in the glaring light of the grey sky, a layer of slithering sliding snakes.

I stood outside it and I was terrified. I wanted to run away to the blue mountains, but it wasn't possible, oh God, of course it wasn't. I had to return, had to walk towards this awful creature with open eyes and enter it, and never, never, shall I know again the peace of the green tempered light, now that I know what is above me.

A day later.

This evening I sit on my bed with my head in my hands and a little later I walk out of the house at the back and go between the trunks to the front. I am not afraid in the evening or at night, because the green snakes above me are then as dead. I stand behind a tree and look at the circle of light of the lamp. A table and a chair. Then I go back again along the same path. It is a game that I play again every evening. I am going crazy, I think. Tomorrow comes the ship.

A month later.

I walked all day yesterday and today, and this evening I'll be back in my village.

The ship has also been, yesterday. I did not think of it, but the ship has also been here.

It is already dark by the time I arrive home. The lamp is not shining and it is very quiet. I sort of counted on Peartree still being there, but there is no one around. It is actually pitch black. Yes, it is pitch black. I take out my flashlight, find the lamp, light it, and take it outside. When I want to hang the lamp from the stand, I see that I can't, because Peartree is hanging from it.

> And now let sweet and low.
> And now let sweet and low
> and now let sweet and low
> Vineflower, swingflower
> Vine in the swing in the vine in the swing in
>   the vine in the swing.
> Vineflower.
> In the flower.

> And now let sweet and low

How dark it is, they all took off, and I have left my lantern behind, back there, I have left it hanging. Oh God, I have left Peartree hanging, for how long, at least half the night, I murdered him. If only he hadn't been dead when I arrived. It was his intention, wasn't it, *rien que pour vous servir, mon très cher. À la lanterne*, Peartree. I am laughing my head off. If, ha-ha, your name is Peartree, then you're going to hang yourself from a tree, ha-ha. Oh well.

But shouldn't he be taken down now? Damn it, I can't find the lamp, I really can't. Otherwise I would have gone to the village chief a long time ago. I can't leave. Wouldn't mind getting out of here. Stop bugging me. I'm afraid, I don't give a shit. I'm afraid. I don't want light. I don't want to see Peartree hanging there. I don't want light.

Hours later.

Oh God, I've been drinking like a lunatic. It is completely light now, perhaps it's afternoon already. Peartree is gone. He's not hanging there any more. They put him down in an empty house. I write a statement and have a couple of witnesses sign it. I let them put down a cross, which isn't right at all, but it will have to do.

I have to have a grave dug, but that's been done already, the village chief says. I ask about a coffin. They bring one. Jesus, that will never do. We'd have to put him straight up, we'd have to put him straight up and give him a good whack on the head so that his knees will give, maybe it will work then. It will never work.

I say: Another coffin and I give the measurements, seven feet long, two feet wide and deep.

They really did make another coffin. Now Peartree has to go in, but I don't see how, I am a creep, a shitface, I don't see how, but he has to, the poor bastard, poor bastard.

We go to the house, the coffin is carried behind me. I've brought a cloth to put over the coffin.

In the house two tables are pushed together, they've put Peartree on top of them, wrapped in a sheet, but his head sticks out. I quickly put a handkerchief over it, it's even respectful.

I ask for a minute of silence and after that we pick him up, with me at his feet, and we put him in the coffin and the coffin is nailed shut.

We carry him to the grave, of course it is much too small, it was measured for the other coffin. They dig. Clumps of earth fly out of the hole and finally it is done.

Two ropes around the coffin and then we let it down. I am standing near an open grave. Our Father, I say, who art in heaven. When I turn around, I notice that my legs are still drunk.

I leave the lit lamp hanging from the standard like before. Because I am still alive.

Translated by Hans Koning

10

ANTON KOOLHAAS

Mr Tip is the Fattest Pig

Mijnheer Tip is de dikste meneer

'Feeling chipper?'

That was the question with which Tip the pig greeted each of his fellow inhabitants of the pen every morning. Tip was a young and cheerful pig and, after he'd asked the question, he'd give the other pig a comically searching look from under his ears, which he'd hold forward at a rather amusing angle, until the answer came. He did this in such an irresistible way that the others always replied and even made an effort to make their responses somewhat entertaining, so that during Tip's tour of the pigpen such cries were heard as: 'Chipper than a chip, Mr Tip!'; or 'Are you suffering from porky trotters?'; or 'Gorge your way through Cheddar Gorge!' and other such witty remarks, because pigs are good listeners and a nod is as good as an oink to a clever piggy.

When Tip had made his round of all thirteen pigs in the pen and enquired after their health, he stood up on his back legs and looked over the partition into the pen next door, the one to the left. That was where the sow Ali 4 lay with seven piglets, who had been born a few months later than Tip, but were already able to engage in a little conversation.

'Chipper than a chip!' Tip would call over the partition, which always filled the little piglets with glee. 'Hello, Tip,' they would call back in a very grown-up way and then they'd come and stand in a semicircle in front of the partition that Tip was leaning over.

'And what have you got going for you?' Tip would ask next.

'Our age,' the seven chorused.

'Are we happy little hoglets?'

'Like pigs in muck! And twice as stinky!' the little ones
would whoop, even though they didn't stink at all badly yet
and were in fact very nice and clean, and, as the hilarious conclusion, Tip would call out: 'What makes a piggy giggle?'

'A chicken with a wiggle,' the seven would cheer. And they
were right to cheer, because it wasn't easy to learn all that by
heart.

At that point, Tip would drop down from the partition and
wait with a joyful heart in anticipation of what always came
next. The seven in the other pen would now also stand up on
their back legs and try to look over the partition. But they were
still too small, and all that could be seen were their little
snouts, dancing helplessly just above the top of the partition,
and then disappearing. This was a most entertaining spectacle
for the pigs in Tip's pen, who watched with great enjoyment
every time, so, at least in those two pens, even though morning
had barely begun, everyone was already having plenty of fun.

After watching the dance of the snouts for a while, Tip
headed over to the partition on the right-hand side. He went up
on his hind legs again and leaned over.

That pen housed Mort, the boar, and the sire of them all.
Mort was always grumpy in the morning, and he made a great
show of his suffering.

'That lot back there are having a great time again,' said Tip,
nodding backwards with his head, as if he had nothing at all to
do with it and thought that he, too, would do better to lead a
life of seclusion, just like Mort.

The father figure groaned softly.

'Must have been a bad night!' said Tip. A muted yet penetrating squeal now entered Mort's groaning. 'I can't piss!' he
whispered, which was certainly not true – anyone only had to
glance into his pen to know that. Tip could see that very well
too, but Mort's declaration still made him sad. 'What a world!'
he said and he stood there looking for a long time at Mort,
who had now folded his ears over his eyes and was irritably
peering out from under those little awnings, preparing for further lamentation.

Tip felt that he should say something else to comfort Mort, but the other pigs in his pen were in such high spirits, having watched their tiny neighbours' attempts to peep over the partition, that Ferry, one of the other pigs from Tip's pen, had stuck his head between Tip's hind legs and kept bumping him up a little higher, so that Tip bounced over Mort's fence and then dropped back down again. Inside, Tip was squealing with laughter, because it was such a crazy feeling and an excellent jape of Ferry's, but it was out of keeping with Mort's morning lament. Tip could sense that he'd have to give in to the fun soon, though, as Ferry was lifting him higher and higher. But at the same time he was somewhat annoyed at being disturbed in his contemplation of Mort, as he was just wondering if, in the balance between venerability and foulness, the former quality stood any chance at all with Mort. There was, however, currently no answer for this issue. The urgency of Ferry's merrymaking was now so intense and bouncy that Tip let out an involuntary little squeal of playfulness, and that caught the attention of Mort, who had not yet noticed the latest party in the pen next door. He lifted one ear from one eye and saw that Tip, gleaming with glee, was being lifted almost up and over the partition.

'We shall have to give the matter some thought,' he heard Tip say, with a tremendous laugh bubbling up in his throat, but that was all he said, as the funny little Ferry was now lifting him very high indeed and moving forward at the same time, with the result that Tip lost his footing and tumbled backwards over Ferry and into his own pen. Mort put his one ear back over his eye, as Tip swiftly disappeared, then he muttered 'sprat louse', and dozed off.

As soon as Tip was back on all four feet again, he decided to bump smack into Ferry and knock him topsy-turvy. There was a dull thud as they collided, but Tip hadn't put enough force into it and Ferry remained standing. 'This is a day for tulip bulbs and wild speculation, my friends,' cried Tip and at that moment the whole dozen other pigs jumped to their feet, and all fourteen of them began lumbering wildly around the pen, crashing, grunting, whirling, and sometimes deftly dodging one another. The game now was for four or five of them to cluster in one corner of the pen, and then pretend they couldn't get back out again. Ferry and Tip had to untangle the knot and it was always so much fun, as they'd call out orders that sounded really crazy. 'Haul that cross-eyed one out of the oil stove,' called Ferry, giving Simon Artzt (the fattest pig in the gang) a whack in the belly so that Simon, shrieking with fake pain, barrelled backwards all the way through the pen and went crashing into the rear wall with his fat behind. It made such an incredibly loud bang that they all laughed themselves silly. Encouraged by this merriment, Simon smashed his bottom into the wall once again, with a frenzy of screaming; to make the chaos complete, he'd then act like a rubber ball rebounding, trotting back, quick as a flash, on his little legs to the tangle in the corner and forcing his way in among the others, where he would stand still as if weak and powerless, his head hanging. If you were to look under his ears and into his eyes, though, you would see that they were shining with fun, as the best bit was about to come. Tip and Ferry set to work at getting him back out of the clump, which involved nibbling the rearmost fold of his ear, where it met his neck, and saying crazy things like: 'It's raining frogs and chocolate logs' and 'Twinkle twinkle little star, legs and wings will take you far', which made Simon Artzt so twitchy and so weak that he started drooling and smacking his lips before throwing himself upwards with a jerk, twisting and kicking and trampling with his front legs over the backs of his friends who were surrounding him, until he was free and standing on his own in the middle of the pen. Then they all called out at once:

> 'Fattybum, who pinched the pig,
> He wasn't clever but he sure was big.'

and, having blissfully listened to it all, Simon would walk over to his corner, where he lay down. At first he'd watched the others capering around for a while, but he didn't have the heart for it these days. And when Tip and Ferry, after Simon had lain down, tried it again and chewed his ear and quietly whispered to him about the chocolate logs, Simon grew sullen and surly and he snarled, 'What do you want? Knock it off!'

This was a game that they always played with the fattest in the pen. Everyone would presumably have a turn, as the farmer would come to the pen from time to time, give the fattest one an approving slap on the flanks, scratch its bristly neck, and then pull it away from the group, out into the barn. That fattest one didn't ever return, and so someone else immediately became the fattest one. Sometimes the fattest-but-one would serve as the fattest one for a few days before the actual fattest one was taken away, as the fattest one would usually stop playing with the others. You could generally sense it coming as, a few days before, the fattest one would start showing less enjoyment as they played, as if he were just going through the motions, and on the first day when he stopped joining in you could do whatever you liked, but the fattest one would only get angry. If you still tried to make him, he'd just snap, 'Get off!' or 'What do you want?' or 'Knock it off!' and he'd try to bite you. Then, the next day, the fattest-but-one would become the fattest and he had to go crashing into the wall and make as big a thud as possible. Everyone would spare the previous fattest one for that whole day and maybe a couple more, until the farmer finally came to take him away. No one could have explained why they showed such deference. You could call it respect, fear, perhaps just ignorance. Because it was always an anxious moment when the fattest one – and occasionally a few of the fattest ones at the same time – was manoeuvred out of the pen. The others watched them go, leaning over the front partition, as they walked slowly past the other pens in the barn, and then disappeared out through the door and into the light. So they knew it was a fact that the fattest ones went outside, where maybe something was waiting for those who no longer wanted to play.

But, whatever the case, why spend too long worrying about it? A new one usually came to join them in the pen straightaway, sometimes a few, who were around the same size or just a little smaller and had to be initiated into the gang's secrets as quickly as possible.

When someone had been taken away, Tip often felt the need to look over the partition at Mort, as Mort was so much bigger and fatter than whoever had just been removed and, in a sense, it should have been possible to tell by looking at Mort (thought Tip) how the future would be. When Simon Artzt had snarled 'What do you want?', effectively announcing his departure, Tip went to take another look at Mort. The progenitor, after Tip's hasty departure, had turned over and was staring aimlessly into space. He was in a mood for becoming deeply melancholy and, with that in mind, he embarked upon one of his most famous feats: a rasping grunt, from deep in his throat, culminating in a little sob. It was a sob as if made by a very young and tender individual, with a sudden fear of being abandoned without protection and being incapable of successfully coping with the situation. Seven of these grunts with sobbing followed, and then came a few variations, the youthful and reedy character of the sobs giving way to a more knowing pain, which was fuller and deeper and gradually acquired some undertones of malice. The sobbing, which at first was an exquisite continuation of the grunting, finally supplanted the grunts completely and became a shrieking wail, wracking Mort's enormous body with panting breaths.

Just as Tip had gone to lean over the partition, the sobs began that reminded him of the sounds he had once made himself when he found a particularly high-quality teat on his mother. That's no reason to sob, you might say; but indeed it most certainly is, as the abundance that Tip found, or the bliss of his own staggering smallness in comparison to the mother mountain, carried within itself the sad awareness that one day it would end. For a young piglet, such happiness is always accompanied by the restless sense of wishing to experience something else for a change, and also with the foolishness of a body that is filling up, before the bliss of fulfilment becomes fixed for ever. And so Tip had always given quiet sobs when he'd found a particularly good teat. Just like the sobs that Mort gave as an overture to his variations.

Tip certainly hadn't failed to notice that Mort was a mess. He looked at the little legs of the enormous, grief-stricken pig, which dangled uselessly in the hurricane of painful squealing. Mort suddenly stopped and tried to see if anyone was looking over the partition. He was most satisfied with the climax he had reached and wanted to find out if it had been appreciated elsewhere. Tip dropped down and didn't know what to do next. He hadn't actually received any insight into what awaited the fattest ones.

Simon Artzt was fast asleep, Ferry was playing at slobbering around in the trough and the others had gone to lie down together, but they were watching, as they were ready for more japes.

'That time with the bucket, that was good fun,' said Tip to Ferry.

'Yes, and that time with Fat Jaap, that was good fun,' said Ferry.

'Yes, and do you remember,' said Tip, 'that time with the rooster?'

'I most certainly do,' replied Ferry. 'That was really good fun.'

'Oh, yes,' said Tip, who was actually quite distracted, and more to keep the conversation going, 'we had such good fun that time, too.'

'Do you remember when Fat Jaap didn't want to leave the pen?' said Ferry. 'Now that was funny. Everyone had such good fun.'

'Everyone had fun,' Tip said, 'except for Fat Jaap.'

'But that was the fun thing about it,' said Ferry. 'Because Fat Jaap hadn't been any fun for a long time. You couldn't have any fun with him at all, but when he left we still had some fun because of him.' Tip didn't say anything now, as he wasn't so sure that it had been much fun when Fat Jaap had finally been dragged out of the pen by the farmer and two of his men. If Tip remembered correctly, no one had really had very much fun at all, as one of Fat Jaap's ears had torn because he'd been dragged about and it was bleeding badly, and besides, there'd been something about the hugely fat Jaap's resistance and about his wailing that had nothing at all in common with Mort's fake wailing.

'It was good fun,' he said, though, to please Ferry, and they fell silent again.

> 'So he mounted the sow and began to play,
> She truly snatched his breath away,'

they could now hear Mort singing in his pen. That meant that Mort expected everyone to join in, but Tip wasn't in the mood. When he compared Mort to Fat Jaap, he realized that he actually hated Mort a bit.

But Ferry wanted to sing. He'd spent long enough smacking his lips in the empty trough now to feel ready for some other kind of entertainment and so he merrily chimed in:

> 'And when he'd scratched his piggy itch,
> He cooled his arse in a nearby ditch,
> The sow folk didn't like to see such muck,
> They . . .'

But he didn't get any further, as before anyone realized what was happening, the farmer removed the front partition and came into the pen. He gave Simon Artzt a kick in the rear, and Simon immediately jumped up and, with no manoeuvring required, trotted over to the trough, without saying goodbye to anyone, and into the barn and then through the door into the light. By the time the farmer had replaced the partition and they were all leaning over it, Simon was nowhere to be seen.

And that was it. He was gone!

'Now you're the fattest,' Dolores said to Tip.

'Me?' asked Tip vacantly, as that was the last thing on his mind.

'Yes, you!' said the others, and Ferry called out:

> 'Fattybum, who pinched the pig,
> He wasn't clever but he sure was big'

and gave Tip a tentative push to see if the new fattest one was enough of a sport to go barrelling backwards and crash into the wall with his behind. But Tip didn't fancy the idea right now. Simon's sudden departure had put him in a very pensive frame of mind. Departure didn't have to happen the way it had with Fat Jaap, but there was something much more eerie about the way Simon Artzt had simply trotted off. Good heavens, they'd had such fun playing with Simon and he'd always been so cheerful. And he had such a carefree way about him, without ever getting angry when they played really rough. Tip felt that he owed it to Simon Artzt's jolly nature to go bouncing into the wall in a particularly funny way tomorrow, as Simon had been so very good at it. But not now, and when Ferry gave Tip another whack, Tip had almost got furious and he'd nearly yelled, 'Yeah? What do you want?', but instead he bit his tongue and said, 'No, chaps, wait until tomorrow morning. I'm not officially the fattest one until then.'

'Hogwash,' cried Dolores, but Ferry calmed the rising discontent and agreed with Tip: 'Fine, tomorrow morning, but then we're really going to make this pigpen shake.'

Tip looked at Ferry and tried to work out whether he might be the fattest-but-one, but he thought it would be Melisande's turn next. Anyway, that was obviously no longer his concern, now that he was himself the fattest. On previous occasions, Tip had always made a big deal of standing in the middle of the pen after the fattest had left and wittily weighing up who was the next in line. He always picked out the most amusing physical peculiarities of all those present. 'What about you, Tip?' the others would cry, and Tip always said:

'Well, my name is young Tip Jones,
And I'm made of twigs and bones.'

and then everything was right with the world. Now that it was Tip's turn, he hadn't thought about his rhyme for a moment, as he realized when he went to take another look over Mort's partition. Mort had finished singing and was having a sleep. He looked very peaceful and particularly filthy. The pigs in Tip's pen weren't dirty, as they were too young for that, their pen was kept clean, and they never went outside. Mort did, though. He didn't have to go into the barn first and then out through the door into the light, as he had a hatch in his own pen that was sometimes opened up. He generally stayed away for a really long time, but sometimes he just popped out and came back in again. Usually he'd return yelling strings of curses. Tip always listened carefully, because Mort was coming from outside. True, it wasn't through the barn's big door that led into the light, but even so it was still from a place that might be connected to it somehow. To wherever the fattest ones went. It was all very confusing, that was for sure, and pigs don't like confusion, but Tip wanted to find out more about it next time he spoke to Mort. Maybe tomorrow, during his morning lament. Then Tip would be able to bring up the subject of whatever lay beyond the hatch. In any event, thought Tip, I ought to know and I shall pretend to remain happy, until I know, because otherwise they might come to fetch me before it's my time. He threw one last glance at Mort, who didn't look as if he would reveal any secrets today, and then Tip stood on all four feet again. The others were lying together, already very drowsy, and Tip wriggled his way in and snuggled up cosily between Dolores and Mr Medlar (as they called one pig who was certainly round but remarkably small) and fell asleep after, without having intended to do so, letting out a small sob.

The next morning, there was no escape. The others all began nudging him before he was even properly awake and they wanted to start straightaway, but Tip said, when he was standing up on his hind legs (which, as he now noticed for the first time, wasn't all that easy for the fattest one), 'Just a moment, chaps. First I'll have my morning conversation with our sire.'

They allowed him to do so.

'Good morning,' said Tip to Mort, who was already waiting for him, 'did the night bring you some relief?' Mort said nothing, but, as on other mornings, quietly groaned.

'It must have been another bad one,' said Tip.

'I have phlegm,' Mort answered calmly.

'Then I wouldn't overexert myself today if I were you,'

advised Tip. And then he asked Mort: 'Are you going out through the hatch today?'

'Bowel brushes!' muttered Mort (a curse Tip had never heard before).

'Is it serious out there,' Tip asked then, 'beyond the hatch?'

'You just stay inside, my boy,' Mort said then, 'Father will swill it all down. Never go there, lad,' he cried, and then he actually stood up. 'You're never going to go there,' he repeated, as if he was very worried about something and was planning to defend Tip.

'I shan't go there,' said Tip nervously. 'But why not? That's what I should like to know, and maybe the others would, too.'

'Out there, it's the leaven of the forked tongue,' Mort mumbled, darkly now, but making no sense at all.

'Oh,' said Tip, who now felt scorching hot over his entire body, which was the fattest body in the pen. That awareness burned within him. Better to be a skinny little diehard, thought Tip fearfully. A skinny little diehard, who never left the pen. But there was little chance of that.

'I couldn't piss again,' cried Mort, who was now rubbing up against the partition just beneath Tip, as he had a bit of an itch.

This trivial announcement made Tip question the gravity of the leaven of the forked tongue, so he replied vaguely: 'What a world!' as he had yesterday and then left Mort, who now had to put up with having hardly any attention paid to his lamentations for the second day in a row. 'Bowel brush,' he called after Tip. 'Dung cockerel.'

But Tip was gone. He was at the mercy of many thoughts as he stood surrounded by the others, who had all taken up their positions for the game. But then he saw the piglets in the pen next door doing the dance of the little snouts. They still had to be indulged. He trotted up to the partition, leaned over it, and called out glumly: 'What have you got going for you?'

'Our age, Mr Tip,' squealed the piglets, who had already heard that Tip was now the fattest one. 'You're the fattest, eh, Mr Tip. That's nice, eh, Mr Tip? You'll bang into the wall harder than anyone ever has before, Mr Tip. We'll listen really hard when you do, Mr Tip.'

Tears filled Tip's eyes as he looked at the delighted little piglets, bouncing busily against the partition.

One of them, whose name was Chervil, said, 'Soon I'll be big enough to look over the partition, Mr Tip, and then I'll be able to see you doing it, at least if you've not already left by then.'

'I'll wait for you, Chervil,' said Tip. 'You can count on that!'

'That's great, Mr Tip,' cried Chervil and then Tip was back among the pigs from his own pen.

Ready and resigned.

'Feeling chipper?' cheered Ferry.

'Chipper than a chip,' replied Tip.

'Are you suffering from porky trotters?' asked Melisande.

'A diehard's skinny little legs is what I call mine,' Tip said solemnly.

'Gorging your way through Cheddar Gorge?' asked Miel.

'My name is young Tip Jones, and I'm made of twigs and bones,' Tip called out as cheerfully as he could.

'My nose,' screamed Ferry, 'my nose is made of wood!' and then he stepped back, and Tip crowded into the corner with five others, and Ferry squealed out:

'Fattybum, who pinched the pig,
He wasn't clever but he . . .'

and he was already starting to trot. '. . . sure was big!' he roared, giving Tip a wallop that really hit home. And Tip merrily barrelled backwards, as required, and slapped his behind into the wall with such a resounding thump that a cry of delight went up in the pen with Ali 4 and the little piglets.

'Record! Record!' Tip heard Chervil shouting.

The pigs in Tip's pen also went wild when they heard such a big thump, and Planta shouted 'Encore' and Tip obediently walked back and began to squeeze his way in among the others. Now it was Planta's turn to do the run-up.

'Fattybum . . .' he cried . . . 'who pinched the pig . . .' But he couldn't go on because he was laughing too much, and he had such a fit of the giggles as he came stumbling up to Tip, that he could only give his body a barely noticeable nudge. But Tip was on a roll! He raced backwards even faster and blasted his buttocks into the wall, like a clap of thunder. It was so bad that he soon felt the blood rushing to his head, and, though he still heard his friends rejoicing, with once again Chervil's cry of 'Record! Record!' loudest of all, he had to take some time to come to his senses. He didn't notice when everything suddenly went quiet. The partition at the front had been removed and the farmer stepped into the pen and, pointing at Tip, he said to the man who was following him: 'He's going to bruise his behind. Come along, lad,' he said then, taking Tip firmly by one ear.

Now all Tip could hear was Mort who, angered by the commotion next door, was cursing away: 'Bowel brushes, stubble stinkers,' all in a filthy tone. Tip wanted to fight back, to scream, to get his ears torn off like Jaap, to stay put, to make a nuisance of himself, to bite, to squeal, to raise merry hell, to curse, to shit, to roll around. He wanted to do all of those things and he wanted to do them all at once. But he did nothing. Without looking back, he trotted out of the pen, into the barn, and through the door to the light. Faster even than Simon Artzt yesterday. Another man stood outside the door beside the lorry from 'Export Meat, formerly Taat Brothers'.

No one had ever seen a pig do that before, all in one go: run out of the barn, dash up the plank into the lorry, and lie down, flat as can be, on the planks, among the other pigs that were already inside. They were also the fattest ones, but from different pens.

There was some confusion in Tip's pen when the partition was safely back in place. No one spoke.

'That Tip,' Melisande said finally.

'You could have fun with him,' said Planta.

'He never got angry. He never got angry one single time, even when he was the fattest,' said Ferry.

'My my, we had so much fun with that Tip,' said Miel.

Now that it was a little quieter, Mort, in the pen next door, began his game of sobbing and shrieking with great gusto.

'Has Mr Tip gone?' asked Chervil, who, to everyone's surprise, was suddenly able to look over the partition today after
all. But he could see that for himself, so no one replied.

'Absolutely, my oh my, we had so much fun,' cried Dolores.

'Mr Tip has the record,' said Chervil, but then he tipped
over onto his back and into his own pen.

'Who's the fattest one now?' asked Planta.

'Ferry, I think,' said Melisande.

'Then we're really going to have some fun,' said Mr Medlar,
and they all looked expectantly at Ferry, who was now the
next in line.

Translated by Laura Watkinson

II

HELLA HAASSE

The Portrait

Het portret

I couldn't remember ever having seen it before, and yet it seemed familiar. The nurse gave it to Charlotte, the day after Father died. She said it had been in his bedside cabinet throughout those last few months. He sometimes asked for it, held it for a while. By then he could barely see.

'Not family, definitely not family,' says Charlotte, and she should know, as she keeps a record of our genealogy. Several times a day, she takes the portrait out from under the paperweight and peers at it through her reading glasses: 'Who could they be? A man with a cap on, in shirtsleeves, with braces, a woman in a hideous shiny black pinafore, and a couple of children. It must be one of Grandfather's servants, maybe a gardener. Someone's written "1915" on the back. Our place in the country was still there back then.'

Bertus reacts with a shrug of the shoulders and an irritated sigh.

'I want to know. I can't bear it,' says Charlotte over and over. 'Why did Father have those people in his bedside cabinet? You know what he was like, never had any portraits around, not even of Mother or the grandchildren. Look, you can see some kind of little house in the background, a brick wall with a window, part of a fence. Was there a gardener's house on Grandfather's estate? You must be able to remember, Bertus, you used to stay there. You were six in 1915, no, seven.'

When Charlotte starts talking like that, Bertus closes his eyes, as if he wants to hide away inside himself. Charlotte knows no mercy; as soon as she notices he doesn't want to do something, or doesn't want to talk about something, she bombards him with questions, rooting around in the protective layers he tries to put up around himself. It's not a desire to torment, and it's not pig-headedness. Bertus's inability or unwillingness to answer often seems to open up chasms of insecurity in Charlotte, and then she requires reassurance. Usually it's about some trivial matter. A frightened child can suddenly be seen inside that elderly woman with the grey hair and the firm gestures. I know how it feels, I'm familiar with that doubt. You don't expect it from Charlotte, though.

Of course, Bertus could not be persuaded to recall any childhood memories at first, a guaranteed means of setting Charlotte off. Then, as a result of her insistence, and with obvious reluctance, a few reminiscences finally struggled to the surface: 'There was an old dog in a kennel. A brick path with dahlias on both sides. And a ditch full of duckweed, where you could catch frogs. Redcurrant bushes . . .'

Charlotte, impatient, unsatisfied: 'But don't you remember anything about the property itself? I mean, the house and the park? There must have been an orchard. Father sometimes used to talk about them eating their own fruit. Of course there was a gardener.'

Bertus glanced at her when she said that, with the look he seems to reserve especially for her, an expression of incredulity and pity. 'Not as far as I know,' he said.

Charlotte wanted to show him the portrait for the hundredth time: 'Here, look at it. Take a good look. Don't you recognize anything? That privet hedge and those spindly dahlias must belong to the gardener's cottage, but you can see tall trees behind the fence . . .'

Bertus doesn't lose his patience very easily, but on that occasion I saw him push Charlotte's hand away in a flash of anger. 'Why should you care, woman?'

Charlotte became visibly more nervous; she spoke to me over Bertus's head: 'Well, do you understand, Elza, why Father wanted to keep this near? He never did anything without a reason. 1915. What was going on at the time? I was two. Wasn't that when Father began expanding the business?'

'You're forgetting that I was born in 1930,' I said. 'I don't know anything about what you and Bertus call "the old days".' I took the portrait from her hand to put it back under the paperweight, a chunk of glass, polished into a hemisphere. I could see the man's face, greatly magnified, and part of the little girl he was carrying in his arms. He looks as if he's just said to the child: Watch the birdie! The smile in his eyes is for her alone, and for the chubby little hand she's pressing to his left cheek. 'A kind man,' I said, but Charlotte was following her own train of thought: 'Father may have had obligations we know nothing about.'

Bertus muttered something behind his newspaper.

'Is that such a strange thought?' Charlotte snapped.

'Not as far as anyone's aware, so don't get yourself all worked up. It's not going to cost you a cent,' Bertus said tersely, a bull's-eye. Charlotte rubbed her handkerchief between the palms of her hands: 'As if it's myself I'm thinking of first and foremost! It's the children I'm concerned about. It wouldn't be the first time Father's given us a nasty surprise.'

Bertus: 'Oh, so you're going to bring that up again, are you?'

Charlotte: 'The boys were only small in 1945, but they could understand enough about what was going on. It's twenty years ago, and thankfully people think differently now, but even so . . .'

Sometimes being blind and deaf would be a blessing.

The execution of Father's will is in full swing. There's little more than his house, the house where all three of us were born and raised. Charlotte keeps bringing it up, saying we should go and live there now. She thinks it's important, 'a legacy for the children', *her* children. Bertus can at least express his discomfort through his usual dislike of change and commotion. He's worked out what it would cost to make the house habitable again, after having been neglected for so long and left partially empty: renovation and repairs, installing an oil-fired heater, maintenance. 'You'll be more comfortable here in the flat with me, Charlotte, we're not getting any younger . . .'

'I wasn't thinking of myself, but the children.' As always,

that's Charlotte's strongest argument, she's the only one of us
to have married and had children, and therefore also the only
one, or so she thinks, who understands life and is qualified
to pass judgement. While she talks and talks, Bertus and I
glance at each other now and then; summoned up by Charlotte's strident female tones, the walls with their dark wooden
panelling grow all around us again; the spiral of the staircase
winds like a snake from the cellar to the stained-glass dome
high on the roof; the symmetry of corridors and rooms, doors,
balconies is as claustrophobic as ever, all the lines vanishing
at a single point beyond the horizon; whatever is close and
within reach is sharp, delineated, cold. In her mind, Charlotte
has apparently reorganized everything, allocating a domain
to each of the three of us; in the remaining rooms she envis-
ages her elder son (in business) receiving clients, her grandson
(later) throwing parties for his fellow students and for his
graduation, her granddaughter (in an even more distant
future) getting married, her second son (now in America doing
laboratory research) with his wife and offspring on a European sabbatical.

'My God,' is all that Bertus says, and then Charlotte starts to
get upset: 'I know that means nothing at all to you as a bachelor, I don't expect anything else, but maybe just for once in
your life you could consider that, having become a widow at
such a young age, I've had to deny the children so many things
they were entitled to. I feel obliged to Sander's memory . . .'

As soon as I came of age, I left. What little self-respect I
have is based on the fact that I succeeded in getting by without
any support from my father and financed my own education. I
don't want to go back to those corridors with their long lines
of antlers, which in the winter seem to continue in the branches
of the trees along the avenue. There were too many locked
doors in that house during the years after the war when I lived
there on my own with Father. The fitted carpets that Charlotte's already planning to install from cellar to attic will never
be able to banish the shuffling echo of the old man's feet, to say
nothing of those other footsteps, before . . .

*

The man in the portrait has bright eyes. His expression is happy yet tired, critical yet resigned. He's holding the child close, he's showing her to the photographer, to everyone who wants to see, and he's telling her to look at what's there in front of her. But there's no awareness as yet to be seen on the round little doll's face beneath the frills of the cap they've put on her, to protect her from the sun, no doubt. The little boy in the sailor suit is standing up straight and holding the woman's hand. He does look aware, though, he seems to be tugging at the hand he's holding, as if he's just persuaded her to come and join them. There's something defensive about her posture, she's pressing her chin down, her brow is painfully furrowed, and not just because of the glaring light. The black satinette gleams over the curve of her chest, the tips of her boots are two shiny squares. When I look through the magnifying glass of the paperweight, I can see more: the rough skin of her large hands, the lines around the man's eyes, the joints and nails in the weathered planks of the fence behind their heads.

We did not take photographs and were not photographed. I never stopped to think about it when I was younger, but took it for granted. It was all part of the strange silence and emptiness of our life at home, and the character of my father, who also adhered to a number of other principles that were as inexplicable as they were rigid. When Charlotte brings up the subject of our old house – as she does repeatedly, in the hope of getting Bertus and me where she wants us – I feel a world without perspective moving towards me: with apparent depths and distances, like the stairwell, the corridors, the view through the series of rooms, the prospect behind the many windows, but in reality a flat surface, a *trompe-l'oeil*. Returning there would mean being forced to exist in a world with fewer dimensions than I need to survive.

By now, Charlotte is pulling out all the stops. During the last discussion her attacks and recriminations became personal: '. . . I'm simply very different from the two of you. Bertus lives like some little bourgeois fellow, I mean, good gracious, just look at those slippers, as long as you can huddle by the fire with your pipe and your newspaper, you don't have an ounce of style, and there is, after all, still such a thing as tradition, and Father's house . . .'

'Mother's, actually,' Bertus said calmly. As usual, Charlotte ignored this remark. She seems to find it shameful that Father moved in with his in-laws after his marriage.

'. . . is, after all, family property, and there's something about it that's . . .'

'Feudal,' I said, completing her sentence, but irony is lost on Charlotte.

'And I don't understand you at all, Elza. You had it the easiest of the three of us, you were the baby of the family, you were allowed to do whatever you wanted. No, don't pull that face; you clearly don't understand just how spoiled you were, compared to Bertus and me. But no, you want the other extreme, you have to go to the slums, rough it, for whatever reason. Your foolish dislike of property, your fear of a normal life, not to mention your illness and your other misfortunes . . . If Bertus and I hadn't taken pity on you . . .'

Mother died of thrombosis soon after my birth. Charlotte was already a married woman with children, and Bertus had grown up and left home, when I was still at primary school. At that time, Father was always engrossed by his business affairs, indulgent out of a lack of interest, generous out of a sense of guilt. But he lives on in my brother and sister's memories as the unrelentingly strict enforcer of authority. The changes that came after the war could not erase that image of him. They rarely returned home, barely knew the solitary figure mumbling away at his desk, the grey-haired old man shuffling from room to room. I don't want to hate my father. I know no name for the shame, the painful compassion I feel whenever I think of him: a man who worked ambitiously and ruthlessly to build his business, and who lost everything that was of value to him, his possessions, his prestige, even for a time his civil rights, because, as he put it, he had 'bet on the wrong horse'.

'I don't want to live there, Charlotte,' I said.

'You and Bertus are hand in glove. He's slack, and you're too highly strung. Such a beautiful house. People like us have

obligations. If Grandpapa and Grandmama's house hadn't
burned down . . .'

Bertus coughed.

'Well, or been expropriated, demolished, you don't know
any more than I do. Come to think of it, what *do* you know?'

Charlotte took the portrait back out from beneath the
paperweight. 'Something tells me this photograph must have
been taken on Grandfather's estate. Bertus, make an effort,
will you? Don't you remember now . . . ?'

Bertus, irritable, rustling his newspaper: 'What do you want
me to say? What am I supposed to remember? I've already told
you everything I know.'

'And all you can remember is trivial things that are of no use
to us. A ditch with duckweed, dahlias, redcurrants, it could
have been anywhere.'

Evening sunlight on the dark panelling. I pass a bowl of
redcurrants across the table to Father. Slowly, he helps himself,
finds an intact bunch among the loose fruits, turns it around in
his fingers, mutters more to himself than to me (usually we ate
in complete silence) something about redcurrant bushes behind
his childhood home, about the cobwebs that tore when you
picked the fruit, about stripping the currants all together. I
interrupted Charlotte, repeated my father's rare remark. He
never spoke about his youth. Bertus looked at Charlotte: 'Redcurrant bushes, that's what I said. Behind the shed. Where I
was allowed to help saw and chop wood for the fire.'

Charlotte: 'The gardener, of course, so you must be able to
recognize him.'

'I don't know anything about any gardener,' said Bertus
gruffly. 'You and your gardener.'

As he disappeared behind his newspaper again, Charlotte
angrily tugged at her embroidery beneath the lamp, a vast
tablecloth with an openwork design for her daughter-in-law, to
be used in the future at dinners to impress the clients. 'You certainly were a most peculiar boy. I can still remember a great
deal from when I was six. If I could have gone to Grandpapa
and Grandmama's when I was that age . . . but they were
already dead by then, and the house had been sold . . .'

'Or demolished. Or had burned down,' I said. Charlotte's eyelids twitched.

Evert and Mary have become involved now too. Remarkably soon after their previous visit, they came driving up, this time without the children, in their perfectly maintained British car, the very latest thing. Charlotte must have alerted them. No courteous preamble, as we're used to from them (they never show up unless they want something), with Evert first trying to engage Bertus in discussions about vertical price fixing, cartels, market mechanisms, and then, together with Mary and eagerly assisted by Charlotte, who is always absolutely delighted by her elder son's infrequent visits, steering the general discussion to subjects such as warm-air heating, private string-quartet evenings at home, cosy farmhouses for the weekend, collections of Japanese woodcuts and Biedermeier furniture. This time they came straight to the point: the ground floor of Father's house for them, thinking of the children and the business; the three of us upstairs; the costs shared.

'It's an ideal house for sharing, in terms of location and layout,' said Mary, warmly persuasive, after Evert had dealt in detail with the financial aspects: 'that extra kitchen on the first floor means you're completely independent, and the attic could be converted into a charming flat without too much effort. You'll have to decide for yourselves how you want to live, Mother together with Uncle, and Elza upstairs, or Mother and Elza on the first floor and Uncle up in the attic . . .'

So, rooms that had been locked and empty for twenty years would be put back into use? All the time I'd lived with Father after the war, I'd always walked across the landing on the first floor as if that section of the house were no longer part of it. Even though I knew I'd never run into them again, those officers in their Feldgrau, and that I would never again have to look in through doors that happened to be open to see rooms forever altered by their presence and the kitchen that had been installed for their billeting; time on the first floor has stood still for me since then, and no new wallpaper or fresh coat of paint can make me forget the runic symbols, the creaking of the boots, the loud voices, the image of that lonely drinker on a '*Feierabend*', leaning against the counter, with unbuttoned uniform collar and glassy stare, his self-pity and vaguely menacing slur disrupting the dreams of my twelve- or thirteen-year-old self for months on end. Seen through the upstairs windows, the wintry trees along the avenue look like naked, mutilated creatures.

I looked at Bertus, who was wearing his wooden face, a mask with pursed lips and dots of colour on the cheekbones.

'Uncle and Elza aren't keen on the idea,' said Charlotte reproachfully, indignantly.

'Come on! Such a delightfully big house!' cried Mary, in the tone she uses with her children when they don't want to eat something.

Evert started from the beginning again, talking in what was, for him, a jovial tone; in other words, throwing the occasional tongue-in-cheek working-class pronunciation into his argument, a student habit he'd picked up, along with taking a tightly rolled black umbrella wherever he went: 'Oh, lass, you know you can go and live in a big posh house again without suffering any pangs of conscience, you'll likely not be teaching no more workers' babbies now, and, God knows, they're the masters in our modern democracy – their tellies, their fridges, and their cars are a lot more important to them than the culture that sweet idealists like you want to share . . .' Neither did he spare me his usual tirades about what he refers to as 'so-called progressive education'. Mary and he are all for discipline and for class-conscious education, children need to learn about authority from an early age, as that prevents misunderstandings in society, where a healthy sense of values . . . blah, blah, blah. People of my generation, a few years younger than I, but just as alien as inhabitants of another planet. As so often happens when Evert's in full flow, I felt as if I were listening to my father speak in a young man's voice, as if the Victorian era had been resurrected in the shape of what the advertisements like to call an 'up-and-coming young man about town'. I unconsciously closed my eyes, but of course I couldn't shut my ears.

Bertus came to my rescue: 'When Elza has completely recovered, and if it's what she wants, she'll go back to that school. I think she's absolutely right. Teaching children to write, to read, and explaining to them what that means, that's quite something.'

Now it was the turn of the vigilant Mary to nip any differences of opinion in the bud: 'But to get back to the house, Uncle. We could call in a friend of ours, who's an architect. That attic, for instance . . .'

Charlotte had told me that Father often used to thrash Bertus as a punishment when he was a boy (Bertus himself never talks about it). 'Up in the attic, in the trunk room . . . with a walking stick. If we'd both got up to mischief together, I had to watch . . . when it was over, he'd give me a couple of hard whacks on my palms . . .' Always those details, imparted by Charlotte with downcast eyes, and yet not without a secret sense of malicious glee, and fear and guilt that she'd yet to overcome. Father never hit me. He was no longer that bothered. Even as a child, I could see the tensions coming to the surface as soon as he was together with Bertus and Charlotte. They were scared of him; he seemed disappointed in them. He would twitch his leg impatiently, or drum his fingers on the arm of the chair when Bertus was slow to respond, or spoke hesitantly with bursts of stuttering. He treated Charlotte with the somewhat condescending courtesy that conservative old men reserve for women, but had no qualms about interrupting when her chattering bored him (which didn't usually take long), abruptly putting her in her place, even in the presence of her husband, the professor, towards whom he behaved almost submissively. That was in the years before the war, when the three of them used to come for lunch every Sunday; we would sit around the oversized table in the oversized panelled room, and after the soup Father would speak only to the professor, as Charlotte pretended to listen or let her gaze – with the haughtiness of insecurity – wander over us and around the room, and Bertus ate in attentive silence, with the occasional quick nod in my direction, and then during dessert he would begin to fold animal figures out of sheets of coloured tissue paper which he always carried in his wallet. Afterwards, he gave them to me, and I had shoeboxes full of them, upstairs in the attic, in the trunk room. I played up there for hours, shifting the old furniture around, rummaging in chests and boxes, murmuring all the while to my invisible companions. Later, during the war years, I would climb up onto the seat in the depths of the dormer window, to do my homework or to read; the trunk room was the place where I felt safest, furthest away from the residents on the first floor. Since I found out that Bertus was punished beneath those slanting beams as a child, I can understand why he never used to follow me when I wanted to show him my domain. When Charlotte brings up those punitive expeditions to the attic, she never neglects to mention 'that one time, I was still just little, so I didn't have to watch, but I was standing at the foot of the stairs, I could hear you screaming, you had to stay up there the whole day, you didn't get any food . . .' and sometimes I can't resist asking: 'But Bertus, what on earth had you done wrong?' Bertus always shrugs his shoulders: 'I don't remember.'

'That house is unfit for habitation.' Which of us is going to say it, Bertus or I?

When Bertus pulls his wooden face, as he is now, it's impossible to get a word out of him. These days, any dissenting opinions that I utter are automatically connected to my illness of a year ago, with what Evert and Mary refer to as my 'depression'.

'Mother, who are they, the people in this portrait? It says 1915 on the back. What a couple, delightful, such an old-fashioned photo. So sweet, eh, that black pinafore, she's all decked out in her Sunday best. Wherever did you find it?'

As Charlotte explained, Evert came to look over his wife's shoulder: 'How peculiar. That doesn't sound like Grandpa! But apparently old people often delve into the past shortly before their death.'

Mary: 'Can we take it with us? I have a black oval frame, I'll put it in that, it'll look amusing on our striped wall, above the dresser with the paraffin lamp.'

Evert: '1915, half a century ago. In the middle of the First

World War. Crazy, to have lived through that time in a neutral land, out of harm's way. I'm sure you must be able to remember those days, Uncle.'

Charlotte: 'You won't get anything out of your uncle, nothing at all. He has no memory.' And Mary again, studying the portrait that Evert is holding, which looks more yellowed than ever beside his very white cuff: 'A man in a cap and a striped shirt, with braces. That woman . . . she has rather a sweet face, I think. Look, Evert, don't you think that's a fine, sensitive face, for that sort of person? And those children, so comical, with the boy's knee-length trousers. They've clearly dressed up the little girl for the occasion; you can see it was an expensive dress, all lacy frills, hideous, but they think it's wonderful. My goodness, so quaint, one of those charming little nineteenth-century workers' cottages, all on one floor, with a brick path to the door . . .'

Charlotte: 'It's the gardener at our grandparents' country house, with his family.'

Mary: 'Well, isn't that divine? Evert, don't you think that's divine? Not having your ancestors on the wall, but their staff?'

'Feudal, feudal,' I murmured, which made Charlotte purse her lips, and Evert and Mary looked at each other with the familiar pitying expression: Ah . . . there goes Elza again.

'Let them hang that thing on the wall!' Bertus suddenly said, his voice loud and harsh. Evert tentatively broke the stunned silence that followed this outburst: 'Given the lack of decent family portraits . . . All we have is from Grandma's side.'

'The house in the country burned down, you know that,' I said. 'So all the portraits will have been reduced to ashes too.'

This was intended as a signal for Bertus, a secret sign of understanding. But he didn't react, just went on sitting, still red all the way down to his neck from his mysterious fit of rage, turned away from us, filling his pipe. Evert and Mary, so steeped in our mythology that it didn't even occur to them to ask questions, didn't respond to my words this time either, following the unwritten rules. They did, however, decide it was time for them to say goodbye. Charlotte shrugged her

shoulders and glared at me as she walked past into the hall. I
followed them.

'How are you doing, Elza? Have you started going out
again, shall we go into town together one of the days?' Mary
was standing in front of the mirror, nimbly arranging her hair
around the brim of her fur hat. I know she feels sorry for me,
and thinks she has to give me special attention from time to
time. Her affectionate tone was genuine; it was also something
of a discreet declaration of independence aimed at Charlotte,
as she disapproves of her handling of my character and situation. To show that I appreciate her intentions, I would have
liked to accept the offer. But the mere thought of the stifling
heat and the glaring lights of December department stores fills
me with loathing. Giant glass cages, vending machines,
through which consumers are sucked; spaces filled with a constant buzzing and banging. I am an unwilling participant,
tormented by the noise, by the tepid scent of soap and textiles,
unable to saunter, unable to rummage along with everyone
else, dizzy in the crush around the counters, through which
someone like Mary purposefully makes her way. It's more than
a physical phenomenon; I break out in a sweat at the suction
that hollows out these people into little figures on a graph,
constituent elements of the economically significant masses.
Passively ascending and descending on escalators, I gasp for
air in a world of noise, colours, obtrusive tangibility, which
will fade away as if it had never existed, already dust, already
mirage. So I declined, and walked back into the living room, so
that I didn't have to see the look that Evert and Mary were
undoubtedly exchanging yet again. I did overhear Charlotte's
whisper, though: 'She still can't cope with crowds. What's
going to become of her? Will she ever be able to teach at a
school again? I have serious misgivings . . .'

They'd forgotten the portrait. It was still lying on the table
inside.

Nineteen hundred and fifteen. That was already the distant
past in the 1930s, which I can vaguely remember. What do I
know about 1915? Workman in the portrait in your striped

shirt, with your merry eyes beneath the peak of your cap, the lines on your face, which could be forty years old, or just as easily sixty-five, no voting rights and no social laws for you as yet. I remember that much from the booklets: you still had years to wait for an old-age pension and health insurance and for the eight-hour working day – if you ever got to see them at all. I don't think you were unhappy, though, you certainly loved those children that you're showing so proudly to the photographer and to the future. You're standing there, no, not in front of a gardener's cottage, it looks more like one of those two-room houses that can still be found in the oldest suburbs of our town; in the twilight between the curtains through the half-open window I can make out a plant in a pot. You had a little garden, just a few metres wide, separated from your neighbours by fences on both sides. It was a sunny day in the late summer of 1915, your dahlias were blooming; it must have been a special day, because you had yourself immortalized (in shirtsleeves because of the heat) with your wife and those two neatly dressed children. Your wife's face shows emotion, and the way you're holding up the little girl is both solemn and touching. What is it about the portrait that I find so touching? That woman on the point of walking away and holding up the black pinafore in front of her eyes, or the man standing there, wide-legged, somehow boldly, naively defiant? Around his house, the neighbourhood, with the smoke from the factories overhead (those trees in the background can't be trees on a country estate); around the town, the land where peace still reigned; around the land, closer than he realized (or am I mistaken?) the trenches, the battlefields.

Later. Charlotte has been restless all evening, sitting, standing, sitting again, busily fussing with things she could just as easily have ignored or done another day. Finally the silence becomes too much for her (Bertus, unseen behind a newspaper that has been opened to its full extent, only answers when he has no choice, and keeps it as brief as possible; he hasn't said anything else directly to me).

'I think your behaviour is extremely childish. Why do the

two of you always have to be so contrary? As if it would be so terrible to live in the house where we spent our entire child-hood. If only out of respect for the memories . . .'

Bertus folds the newspaper in four, shakes his head.

'It's pure stubbornness. You take pleasure in frustrating my plans. I'd feel at home there. And it's important for the chil-dren. Evert's future . . .'

'The first floor, the attic,' I say, angrily stumbling over my words, 'do you think Bertus wants to live where he was beaten and locked up as a boy? And what about me, do you think I'd feel at home in the rooms where the Krauts were . . . ?'

Bertus looks at me, now he must know that I understand, now he'll understand something about me that I can never talk about.

'You're overwrought,' says Charlotte, 'it's just sick emotion-alism.'

Bertus slams the folded newspaper on the table. 'This place is good enough for me.'

Charlotte: 'You're so selfish.'

Bertus: 'Those children of yours want for nothing. Evert will end up where he wants to be, it's in his genes. Keeping up appearances by living in that house – it's an irresponsible waste of money. Let the council buy it for the elderly.'

I could see it coming; Charlotte starts to shake.

'Oh God, you have such a small-minded attitude. Do you want to stay here until you die, in your little flat, four rooms plus a kitchen, your tobacconist across the street, your local on the corner where you go to play billiards? The three of us don't have room to swing a cat, it weighs me down. What kind of man are you? I sometimes understand perfectly why Father got so annoyed with you, you have no ambition, no initiative, you pen-pusher, you petty little man . . .'

'May I?' Bertus's voice sounds calm, but there's something about his tone that should warn Charlotte to take care. 'If you don't like it, you can leave.'

Charlotte is pulling and picking at her handkerchief. As I watch, her face becomes softer, less defined, and the frightened child looks out through her eyes: 'On my own?'

'If I leave, I'll look for another room,' I say.

She turns to me: 'You're just like Bertus. Always that resistance, that false shame, as if it's a scandal to come from a good background, to have standards. You should see yourself. No one would think you were brought up as a lady. Why were you being so hateful again today about the house in the country? You know absolutely nothing about . . .'

We're sitting tensely on the edge of our chairs opposite each other in the living room, a peculiar mixture of Bertus's sober, sombre furniture and the French brocade tablecloths, lamps, and petit-point cushions that Charlotte brought with her when she moved in. Behind Bertus's head, the books are lined up, carefully arranged by subject and in alphabetical order, his only luxury. The clock ticks.

Bertus: 'Where did you get all those ideas about a country estate?'

Charlotte: 'You're acting so strangely. Father said . . .'

Bertus: 'Father never said anything.'

Charlotte is unable to look away from him. Bertus is sitting very straight, both hands flat on the armrests.

'Mother, then. It doesn't make any difference.'

Bertus: 'You wouldn't think so.'

Charlotte: 'Mother said . . .'

Bertus: 'Are you absolutely certain about that?'

Charlotte (agitated): 'We were only small . . .'

Bertus: 'So you don't actually know?'

Charlotte: 'What do you want me to say? You can't remember a thing about it.'

Bertus (with great dignity, which makes irrelevant his bluntness, the helplessness of his slightly turned-in feet in those ridiculous tartan slippers): 'I can't remember any things that never happened and were never said.'

My brother and sister are now leaning in towards each other, like conspirators, or more like children who share a secret but don't trust each other, who'll be the one to give it away, who'll be the one to get punished? I can hear Charlotte breathing. Finally she utters a wail: 'How dare you? How dare you?'

Why do I suddenly remember the hallway at home, the antlers bagged by the men in my mother's family on long-forgotten hunting trips, two lines of trophies opposite each other, from the widely spreading branches of the gnarled showpieces by the entrance to the small plaques with nubs of horn near the garden doors? The rooms are filled with the scent of Victorian complacency and prosperity. The house is a bastion of respectability. My mother, whom I never knew, left everything as it must have been in her childhood, before her wedding, apparently with my father's consent. Their life made no impression on the surroundings; it is as though a generation has been skipped. That does not account for my parents, but it does determine half of why we are as we are, Bertus, Charlotte and I. Half: the rest remains vague, in the dark. Anyone who is troubled by what is missing can fill the gaps with profusion. What should have been there, but what is not, grows in dreams and desires to astounding proportions. Mother's house doubled under its own power, becoming stately and solid enough for two. Beyond the horizon, past the point where all the straight lines converge, a *fata Morgana* emerged, strangely distorted by the shivering layers of air. The antlers, the conservatories full of plants, the mirrors and wooden panelling, the dark green carpets and curtains, the leaf designs on the wallpaper, conjured up avenues, ponds, lawns and copses out of nowhere, solidifying in the distance to form a country estate with a park and an orchard, a legendary ancestral home. No one will ever speak about it in so many words, no lies were told, but it must have been possible to draw conclusions from what was left unsaid, or from what was implied.

Bertus and Charlotte seem to have forgotten that I am there. They have renounced their lifelong roles. Charlotte is no longer the compulsive asker of questions, Bertus no longer stubbornly unresponsive.

Bertus: 'I've always known it wasn't true. I told you so, a long time ago; my memory's that good at least.'

In an unconsciously helpless gesture, Charlotte turns the palms of her hands towards him as if she wants to show him something in them.

'He didn't used to hit you,' Bertus says quietly. 'It was just that one time.'

I am longing for my school, for those little, shining faces above the desks. If I can't go back to work again, I shall go insane, and the images that sometimes insert themselves between me and the real world will prevail. More than memories, something different than dreams, no one can convince me otherwise. I have no name for them. What is it when the boundaries of one's own consciousness fade, when my time, my age, dissipates like a thin cloud, becoming un-time, the omnipresent? There are no red welts on Charlotte's palms now, Bertus is no longer screaming in the attic. When Father hit out, long ago, it was the start of his collaboration with the as yet unnameable force that would much later take shape, and the rooms on the first floor began to grow towards their enemy occupation. There had to be a connection between the runic symbols and the *fata Morgana* of the 'estate'. I can see my dying father's pale yellow head before me, that's all part of it too, the death began long before he so harshly punished Bertus's innocent truthfulness; the agony will continue until we, his children, have become aware of what exactly it was in our home, in the house our mother inherited, that was lacking, that was left unspoken.

I take the portrait from the table and go to return it to its place beneath the paperweight on the mantelpiece. 'For Evert,' I say out loud, 'for that snob.'

Charlotte blanches, but does not protest. 'I don't know who they are,' she confesses with a new humility.

Now Bertus takes the portrait from my hand, holds it out to Charlotte, and points at the two children: 'That's you. That's me.'

Charlotte just stares.

'With Grandfather and Grandmother, behind their house,' says Bertus, more quietly still. I come closer. I didn't even exist in 1915, and wouldn't for some time, but this concerns me too. The albums, the boxes, the folders and baskets under dust-sheets, which no one ever looked at but me, the dark depths of the cupboards under the slanting roof: 'In the attic, it was in the attic,' I say, but they don't hear me.

Slowly, Bertus sits back down. He hangs his head, so that Charlotte and I can't see his face: 'That was the last time. We didn't go back there again afterwards. *He* took us. I could hear him talking to them, inside, in the kitchen. I had to play outside. Later I didn't want to leave. While he waited, they took me aside. They told me that he'd always been the brightest boy in the school, always number one, that he'd come a long way and would go even further, I had to keep my wits about me, grow up to be a fine fellow, do my best, and then he'd be as proud of me as they were of him, parents see themselves rewarded in their children for their hard work and the care and the scrimping and for all the sacrifices, even the hardest ones, it's a great privilege to be able to nurture your intelligence, to learn all those things and to understand, people like that can make the world a better place, I should never forget what I owed him, just as they were sure he would never forget ... He did forget, though, I *saw* that he'd forgotten. And, with me, he got the reward he deserved ...' Bertus has long since stopped talking to us, and is talking to himself. 'He couldn't be proud of me. I didn't want to be like him. I wanted him to forget that I was his son, too. And he always acted like he had. I thought ...' He bends even closer to the portrait on his knee. 'I didn't go to see him when he was dying. I didn't give him the chance to show me he actually did remember after all,' says Bertus, his voice hoarse and surprised.

Translated by Laura Watkinson

12

W. F. HERMANS

Glass

Glas

I had been employed there for just two days, at that sanatorium where nobody could ever recover, when I had to deal with a dying patient. An unusual patient, because he had relatives. None of our other patients had friends or relatives who worried about them as they had all been mutilated beyond recognition; found like that after bombing raids or rescued from burning tanks or planes. Without arms or legs, invariably missing their lower jaws, deaf or blind, they couldn't even say their own names. At the registry offices they were listed as dead, or at least missing. The world makes a fuss about its dead and wounded after a war, but not its missing. They end up in institutions like ours, whose existence governments keep as secret as possible out of humanitarianism. Because even if we organized regular viewing days for the public, like they do with other lost property, it would still be impossible for people to identify their relatives. More to the point: all too many would believe incorrectly that they had found their father or husband. The wards would become the scene of furious brawls like the ones that erupt regularly in foundling-hospitals. Our patients could, in other words, very well have relatives without being able to tell us about them and without the family being able to find out they were here. There would be no way of proving it.

But this dying patient had been irrefutably recognized by his mother: the military surgeon had amputated his remaining arm just below the spot where he had once had his name tattooed.

I sat by his bed all night, listening with my stethoscope to make sure he was still alive. His mother asked repeatedly if there wasn't some way he could say goodbye to her, if he couldn't give her some kind of sign, anything. But his eyes had been burnt out by phosphorus and had finally grown over (he was not dying from his wounds, which had long since healed, but from a pre-existing heart condition), and his lower jaw and tongue had been ripped away. Now and then she would cry, 'Günther, say something!' I knew he was stone deaf, because his eardrums had been shattered by the force of the explosion, and he was unable to move the stump of his arm, the last remnant of his limbs. The only sign of life he was able to give was the beat of his failing heart. Now and then I passed the stethoscope to his mother, so that she could at least hear something from her son and wouldn't have come entirely in vain. But she too was deaf. She took the tube out of her ear and peered into it, but couldn't find the death-watch beetle she was looking for. She tried again and began screaming. There was no risk of her cries waking anyone in the ward, but Sister Elena came over to stand next to us, which calmed the mother somewhat. When I could no longer hear the heart, the superintendent was summoned from his bed. He led the mother away and I took Sister Elena in my arms. She was a blond Italian and her eyes were as blue as blue can only be when set against an abyss of brown. Like all the staff she wore nothing under her tight white tunic, and her body felt like a loaf of fresh warm bread, wrapped loosely in tissue paper. We sat like that for some time on the dead man's bed, the only spot in the ward that was lit.

'You haven't just ended up here either,' she whispered.

'How do you know that?'

'How would I know that . . . ? If you weren't here for some reason, you wouldn't be here.' She kissed me with her whole mouth, or actually it was as if I curled up and became something small on her tongue. Love blew me up like a balloon. I wanted to escape the suffocating heat and asked her to go outside with me, into the park. The sanatorium, which as an institution pre-dated the war, had been evacuated after a bombing raid to this old castle high in the mountains, fifty kilometres from the nearest village. For the time being it would stay here.

But she answered, 'Into the park? It's bound to be raining, and if it's not, it soon will be.' She slid off my knees onto the dead man's bed, the bottom half of which was still free, and pulled me down on top of her. Because of his mother's regular visits, this patient had been allocated a normal-sized bed. Smiling, she said, 'This is something you have to experience, otherwise you'll never adjust to things here.' Her tunic had slipped open and I could see her body, which had taken on the peculiar beauty of a woman who has been had by hundreds of men, a woman who, although young and unscathed, possesses the mature smoothness of the boxwood handle of a burin, polished year in year out by the callused palm of a supple hand. 'What are you looking at?' she asked. 'I'm no nun! A nun is just a woman who's been shaved in the wrong place!'

I asked, 'Do you do this with every innocent newcomer?'

'Innocents never come here . . .'

She stood up – leaving her tunic on the bed – took me by the hand and said, 'Now I will show you what you know. Just like me, you have come here to hide from the world, just like all of us. If you weren't here, you'd be in prison or maybe already executed. To the outside world, it has to be like we no longer exist, like our patients. You know that, don't you?'

I broke out in a sweat, even though I was now naked and should have been able to cope more easily with the suffocating heat that was a constant here. The windows were never opened as most of the patients suffered unbearable agonies when so much as a sheet was laid on their flayed nerves. We didn't have the resources to build tent-like structures around all of them. Many of them couldn't even lie on their beds, but were suspended in ingenious rubber nets. Their exposed, invariably festering flesh blanched with pain when someone simply displaced the air by walking through the ward.

At another full-length bed, she stopped and wrapped her arms around me again. She stroked my throat with her fingertips as if to help her words reach my brain.

'We can't see, we can't hear, we can't speak. We can only

move in this building, between its walls, enclosed almost as tightly as a heart in a body. If you don't know that, you've lost your memory. Kiss me, then I'll breathe it back into you.' I kissed her, but didn't remember anything.

Then she turned the light on over the bed. To my surprise there were blankets on it. She pulled them back. A man was lying there, at least, it must have been a man I was gazing at. It looked more like a hollow tree that had been struck by lightning.

Virtually all of his flesh had been burned away and the scorched skin, as wrinkled as oak bark, was tight over his bones. A rubber mask covered the lower half of his face and his eyelids were closed over empty sockets.

'You know who it is,' Elena said, 'even if you don't recognize him. Wouldn't it be terrible to have a body like that? Wouldn't it be the worst thing that could ever happen to you? What else do we have to believe in, if not the body?

'At seventeen I fought in Spain. I served on every front. Who can still genuinely believe that freedom is what people need? No one would know what to do with it. That's why the Führer took away our pseudo-freedom and gave us a clear conscience instead. Our enemies have defeated us, but their bad conscience will bring them down. They opposed us on the pretext of being better than we were, but they knew they were lying, that they were exactly the same as us, their enemies. The Führer said that he would use lies as weapons and he used lies as weapons. But our enemies said they were fighting for the truth and they lied, because they knew just as well as we did that there is no truth but the body. We believe in the body with the body . . .' She laughed, and at the same time made my body believe as much as it possibly could in hers.

For that one minute I was willing to assume that what she said was true. Then I said, 'But I really don't know who this is. I thought the man who died tonight was the only one with a confirmed identity.'

'You're playing dumb. Fine, I'll tell you.' She put the blankets back in place and turned off the light over the bed.

'It's the Führer, our Führer. When he tried to kill himself after everything collapsed, the pistol shot wasn't fatal; he wasn't burned to death with the petrol they poured over him either. Nobody has ever seen his ashes – and with good reason – because there are no ashes. He was still alive when the fire went out. In fact, he was probably pulled out of the flames beforehand.

'He lived and that's hardly surprising, especially not to you. After all, you're the one who came up with that new ointment for burns. You burned three hundred Jews alive experimenting on it, before developing a therapy that could even save people who didn't have a single centimetre of skin left intact.

'Yes, this is our Führer. He can't see, hear or talk. He can't move, but he's alive!'

I had appraised the patient briefly the previous day, during my first round. It wasn't true that I had burned three hundred Jews alive and developed a new therapy for burns. I didn't know a thing about it, and hadn't noticed anything special about this one patient. Still, I didn't reply, I just looked at her, which she misinterpreted.

'Yes, he's alive, just as he lives in all of us, without any of us being able to talk about it any more, because we have been defeated.'

I said, 'He doesn't live in me, I believe in Jesus Christ.'

She laughed. 'A Christian! The only people who still talk seriously about Jesus are those whose opinions are completely irrelevant. I'd like to hear the views of a professional criminal, yes, a murdering robber who was sentenced to twenty years and pardoned after fifteen, only to be picked up again a year later and dumped in a concentration camp without so much as a court order, simply because he was a born criminal, then stayed alive in the concentration camp for ten years, starved and half beaten to death, until in 1943 he was given the task of pulling gold teeth out of the mouths of gassed Jews. He got an extra ration of butter, cigarettes and brandy, but after he'd been doing that work for half a year they ensured secrecy by putting him down with a rifle shot from the distance. The shot didn't kill him immediately. He lay there dying for, shall we say, ten minutes. I'd like to know if that man thought about Jesus.'

I answered, 'I have always tried to be a good Christian, even if that might not be so very important for someone like me who doesn't have much opportunity to commit evil or suffer it from others.'

'All doctors and nurses are saints in white,' Elena said, putting her tunic back on. 'But what would be even better would be to find out what our patients think of Jesus. Too bad they're no more able to talk about it than the dead about the hereafter.'

I walked back to the charred patient's bed. He was encased in a thick layer of carbonized flesh that had cracked open where his chest moved to breathe.

'There is nothing to show that he's the Führer. If you'd pointed out someone else, I'd have believed it just as much or just as little.' I am not in the habit of telling women exactly what I do or don't believe.

Nothing Elena had said about my past and the experiments I was supposed to have carried out in a concentration camp was true. But I *am* a highly skilled surgeon and, to dispel my boredom, I began experimenting on the patient she claimed to be the Führer. It seemed to me that one of his eyes might be salvageable and, after three months' work, I was able to flatter myself with the hope that he could see out of it again. He could even move it in its socket. I held up a piece of paper on which I had written, 'If you can read this, look up once and then back down.' He did as requested. So he could see again. But what was there for him to see? What did he want to see? We had no way of finding out. There was also no point in communicating anything to him, because he couldn't do anything about it anyway.

In the meantime, I had discovered how they knew that this burnt organism had been the Führer. Two former officers who, even now, five years after the end of the war, were still on the run and being sought by the victors' police, had delivered him to the clinic. They were well-known, high-ranking figures, whose portraits had been in the newspapers weekly before the defeat. Shortly after I had completed the operations on the eye, one of them, Daumler by name, appeared in the clinic.

It was as if he had crawled up out of a crack in the ground. He looked like that, too: pale and sallow, his face damp with perspiration and disfigured by the scars on his cheeks. He spoke in a high-pitched, frantic voice and I couldn't tell if he had always done so, or if this too was a consequence of years of persecution. He was virtually incapable of simply saying something any more; he could only speak in speeches. I came upon him while he was talking to Elena and the superintendent and heard him say:

'But they lie! They claim to believe in the equality of all mankind, but they too have a Führer! Here in their breast! They deny that he rules over them. That is why they are impotent and suffer pangs of guilt, why they forced the war upon him, why they silenced him. They said that we suppressed individual freedom, but they knew just as well as we do that the individual only wants the freedom to reproduce and care for his family. We provided that freedom, in abundance, and more importantly, the opportunity too, something our adversaries were much less keen on. They hate adventurers, artists and madmen as much as we do, but they kicked up a fuss when we castrated the insane. They raised a hue and cry because we gave adventurers the freedom to join the army and fight.

'They say that our Führer ruined us. They are wrong. We emerged from the war stronger than ever, even though our Führer can no longer speak. But he still gives us orders! And we did what the Führer said! Yes, we were unfree, but we are free of remorse – because he was our conscience. Why was he our conscience? Because all the orders came from him! By doing what he said, we could not sin. He bore all our sins. But our enemies, despite knowing this full well, despite having mocked us for our subservience for years, hanged our generals after the war for having done what the Führer commanded. Our generals were free of sin, because they didn't do anything of their own free will. Our enemies knew that full well, but accused our generals of cowardice when they pleaded loyalty to the Führer, and hanged them, probably because Jesus, who had taken *their* sins upon *him*, was out of their reach and couldn't be hanged a second time.'

Here I stepped forward and said, 'It's not true that the war criminals were punished for doing what the Führer ordered. In the concentration camps and occupied territories they enriched themselves by looting and plundering and tortured thousands to death without orders from Berlin.'

Elena then said, 'If that's what they were punished for, it can only mean that they were punished in the name of our Führer. And then they've been punished in exactly the same way they would have been punished if he had been victorious.'

I wrote that down on a piece of paper and said, 'Fine, let's ask him.' At the bottom of the page I wrote, 'When you agree with this, look down with your eye.'

The charred patient read what was written on the piece of paper and looked down. Daumler now puffed his chest up even more and paid me even less attention. I stalked off in a fury. How could anyone know the Führer wasn't lying again now, just as he had always lied as a matter of principle? And also, even if he had been the Führer, he could never assert himself as such again, even if the whole world were to call him back. I burst out laughing at the idea of him pursuing politics by winks alone. He would die the moment he left our clinic. He would never lead anyone again, incapable as he was of expressing anything beyond agreement or disapproval, and despite my skill there was no question of this ever changing. He was no longer a Führer, all he could communicate was yes or no, at the very most he could become that which he had always spat upon: a parliament.

Two months later Daumler sent me one of his own, prestigious decorations and a letter in which he thanked me for the brilliant care I had given the Führer and offered me his apologies for not having asked to be introduced to me during his visit.

The other officer who had helped rescue the Führer, Krantz, appeared before me one day in my office. He had a round head, bald in the middle and greying at the temples, and it was only out of anatomical necessity that his mouth was located in the place where mouths are usually found, otherwise it could just as well have been replaced with an inconspicuous split somewhere else on that roundness. He held out a hand and announced with studied resolve, 'I know that you are a good Communist. I am, too. We can be plain with each other. You may not have known this but, despite being a high-ranking officer, I was a spy all through the war.'

I nodded in agreement, without a trace of surprise on my face to suggest how horribly wrong he was to take me for a Communist.

He said, 'I know the Führer is here and still alive. I myself arranged for him to be brought here. It is of the utmost importance to us that he remains alive. You understand why, I am sure?'

I answered that this was something I did not understand, that it did not actually make any difference at all whether he was what we called alive in our clinic or really dead, as public opinion generally assumed.

Krantz took me by the arm and whispered, 'But his condition can change. It could be of the greatest significance when we eventually announce that he is still alive and that he approves of all our enemies' measures, as they are not doing anything other than continuing his regime by other means. At the moment there are countless prominent figures who could be irretrievably compromised by his declarations. Tell me, how much longer will it take before you've given him back his voice?'

I answered that so far I had only worked on his eyes and that he was more or less able to see with one of them, but that I hadn't done anything for his voice and doubted that anything could be done. I also said that I didn't know if he was still able to think and could not exclude the possibility that he had lost his memory.

The Führer's condition continued to improve – in all ways. My own circumstances had also improved. One of the castle's towers had been fully refurnished for me and connected to the steam heating system used in the hospital's wards. I lived there with Elena and we always walked around naked. Naked, we looked out through the storm windows at the uninhabited surroundings buried in snow. We amused each other by painting our bodies. We never went outside. Her aversion to the park had become mine, too, just as I was free to call everything she possessed my own. The awareness of how extremely sinful we were being gave me a tremendous sense of freedom.

In the confessional I informed the sanatorium priest of every minute detail of Daumler's and Krantz's intrigues, the fact that I hadn't reported them to the police and what I was doing with Elena. But I didn't do the penance he imposed. I noted it down for later, along with the number of times I had lied by telling him I had done penance as instructed.

Due to all my efforts on the Führer's behalf and the gulf in knowledge between me and the other surgeons, the mortality among the patients was extremely high. The superintendent intimated to me that, with such a reduction in patient numbers, there was a great likelihood of the sanatorium having to relocate to smaller premises. He hoped to move closer to civilization. But his dearest wish was to be in the middle of a large city, high up in a building on the main square. The noise wouldn't bother the patients, who were deaf anyway, and the few whose eardrums hadn't been destroyed had lost their tongues. There would be a stock exchange on the lower floors, men and women going out to theatres in the evening, taxis pulling into taxi ranks, streetwalkers looking for customers in the neon lights of the cinemas, all as if there had never been a war, yes, as if nobody could ever even lose blood. And us high above it all! Without anyone below knowing what kind of hearts beat in our beds!

He declaimed it like an actor. He would have drawn just as much satisfaction from it as Elena and I enjoyed when looking out over the snow naked.

Once this analogy had sunk in, I immediately grasped *the system*, the foundation on which both the pleasure the superintendent would find in a clinic on a busy square and my own pleasure at looking out over the snow was based. It was the seeming absence of a quality that was (on the contrary) of crucial importance. It was *glass*. The way glass looks like it does not exist yet protects us from the cold as well as the thickest of walls; this was what made it so fascinating to stand naked behind it before a landscape that seemed full of hidden spies but was never visited by anyone who could observe what Elena and I were doing. In my case it would only take a shepherd to get lost there, in the superintendent's imagined future it could be a postman looking for a bank who inadvertently stepped into our clinic and thought he recognized his father lying there without legs, without arms.

But a susceptibility to this kind of excitement was even more strongly developed in the superintendent than it was in me. One day he grabbed the material of my sleeve between his thumb and his index finger and asked me to walk with him a little. He stuck out his tongue so far he could have used the bottom of it to feel whether he had shaved his chin smoothly enough and said, 'Teuchert, I have to tell you something about your girlfriend Elena.' Doctors, of course, have no qualms at all about discussing the most private of subjects with each other. 'I have been told that at night, when you are occupied in the operating theatre, she loiters suspiciously in the wards. Her walking around naked is neither here nor there, we all do that on occasion and nobody's the wiser. But her being so ruttish as to test to what degree the reproductive organs of the patients who are still lucky enough (he repeated the phrase lucky enough) to possess them are capable of signs of life is going too far.'

I said, 'It's related to an experiment I'm carrying out.'

'Then I didn't say a word . . .' He waited.

I said, 'Regarding ruttishness.'

Him: 'She has taken the testing rather far, to the extreme. There is one patient with whom she has managed that repeatedly, at a fairly high frequency . . . You know which one I mean?'

'Have you seen that yourself?'

He smiled and nodded.

'She hasn't mentioned it to me,' I answered meekly, but coolly, 'probably because she wants to keep it as a surprise, to demonstrate when she has absolute certainty.'

'Surprise her in turn,' he said. 'I'll help you.'

We agreed that he would take my place in the operating theatre that evening and I would conceal myself in the manner that had allowed him to spy on Elena without being seen. The system again, but now in its simplest, classic variant: the ward would appear deserted, Elena would think I was manning the operating table, and meanwhile I would have a front-row view of the things she wanted to keep from me. Glass ... Only through glass is it possible to see things so horrific no one can speak of them.

My head pounded against the glass of the darkened sunroom adjoining the ward. I stared at the Führer's bed. So he possessed a second faculty along with the one I had returned to him! And this second one would allow him to *stay* in a way no one had ever suspected! I waited half an hour but Elena didn't appear. I thought about how silently I could make my rival disappear if I found his relationship with Elena unbearable – one minor slip during the next operation and he would be dead – but he was my most beautiful patient and for that reason alone I wouldn't be able to do it. On the other hand, Elena would have as many opportunities to betray me with him as she wanted, as my duties made it impossible for me to keep a constant watch over her.

But after three-quarters of an hour she still hadn't appeared. I left the sunroom, entered the ward and walked over to the bed. It was empty.

Then I began searching for Elena. I suddenly realized that the superintendent had been less well hidden than he had imagined and Elena's suspicions had been aroused. She had arranged for the Führer to be moved somewhere else! But where? To our tower!

I slipped into the entrance hall, pulled on a pair of snow boots and went outside. On all fours I crawled through the ravine next to the tower, then used the stones jutting out from the wall to climb up to my brightly-lit windows.

Chilled to the bone, I held tight to the window ledge and peered in. There was no one in the room that belonged to this window, but looking through the open door to the room beyond it, I saw Elena's naked legs and the trouser legs of a man lying on the ottoman. It was not difficult for me to slide the windows open and climb in. They didn't hear me. I listened from behind the door. The man was Krantz.

'Are you sure he's a Communist?'

'Darling, why would I tell you that if it wasn't true?'

'I'm not claiming you're lying but there could be some doubt.'

'I'm certain.'

'Then you must know him very well.'

'Silly. Just hearing the word Communist makes me feel sick. Why don't you trust me? Why are you jealous?'

The ottoman creaked. Krantz sat up and looked at the door I was standing behind, as if searching for a reason to be jealous. But he only saw the dark, low-ceilinged room. Emptiness ... He thought he saw an emptiness. The room was almost empty, except for me. Exactly: *except for me!* Krantz lay down again and said, playful but banal, 'If I'm jealous, you can only be flattered. If I wasn't jealous, you could think I don't love you enough.' Kisses.

I now understood why Krantz had claimed to be a Communist the sole time he had come to visit me. He had wanted to test me, to verify Elena's accusation. Glass ... I was as transparent as glass. Nobody could see what I really was.

I no longer believed a word of the superintendent's story about Elena cheating on me with the Führer. He had made a fool of me. It had been Krantz that he was referring to, Krantz.

Numb and unthinking in my excitement, I returned to the window. Rage sharpened my senses and I completed the dangerous descent without once worrying about where to put my feet. I made it back to the main building where I took off the snow boots and ran to the lift. Where could the Führer be? For a moment I thought I might have been mistaken about the bed. That was why I went back to check the ward. Two nurses were busy tidying up. My error was confirmed when I reached the Führer's bed. He was lying in it asleep. But there seemed to be something unnatural about that sleep. I listened with my stethoscope. His heart was beating half as fast as usual. I now pulled the blanket all the way down. His lower body was freshly bandaged and I immediately grasped what had happened. They had castrated him! The superintendent was the only one who could have done it. How had he managed it without protest from the head nurse who always assisted during my operations? I could imagine the head nurse accepting him replacing me that evening (whichever pretext he used). But that she, fully apprised of my plans as she was, would allow this surgery to go ahead was out of the question. I immediately called her in her room. 'Oh, Doctor, are you back again?' she asked after I said my name. It turned out that she, along with the three other nurses who always helped me with my work, had been given the evening off. The superintendent had arranged it all: luring me away with the story about Elena, giving the nurses the evening off and carrying out the castration with another team.

Everyone had their own plans for the Führer, everyone except me, who had done nothing except cure him, without any ulterior motives. I went to the chapel, knelt and prayed for Elena, for the superintendent and for Krantz.

In the course of the next week I learned that Krantz was not an occasional visitor to our sanatorium, but lived there. He only emerged when I was in theatre, disappearing before I returned. No matter how thoroughly I investigated the rooms in the tower, I could never find a trace of his presence. I wasn't able to notice anything out of the ordinary in Elena's behaviour either and I didn't ask her any questions. I didn't ask the superintendent why he had castrated the Führer and I had no idea if this was somehow related to Krantz's presence. For his part, the superintendent refrained from asking me if I had discovered anything the night he sent me off to spy on Elena, though it was clear to me that his reasoning had been: I will put him on sentry duty at the Führer's bed. He will stay there to see if Elena shows up. Elena will not show up. Then he will walk over to the bed and see that the Führer has disappeared. Who will he go in search of first? The Führer or Elena? Elena, of course. Not because she is his lover, but because he knows where to look. Or thinks he knows. The Führer could be anywhere; he will look for Elena in his rooms. When he arrives there, he will find her with Krantz. What will he do? Murder Krantz? Had the superintendent hoped that I would murder Krantz? Could I enlist the superintendent as an ally in my struggle with Krantz? I couldn't rely on it, because if he had not wanted Krantz in his sanatorium, he could have come up with another way of getting rid of him. By adopting this strange strategy he had betrayed himself! I knew why he had done it! I could deduce it by mathematics alone! The superintendent too was a rival! By having me catch Elena with Krantz, he hoped to subject me to the suffering he had felt when he had caught her with me! Yes, he had caught Elena with me first, then with Krantz and perhaps with the Führer as well. Why else would he have castrated the Führer?

These considerations allowed for only one conclusion: I could not find a single ally in the whole sanatorium. Not a single ally in a radius of fifty kilometres!

That was why I took a holiday and set off into the mountains with my snowshoes and a tent. Three days later I reached a small village where I was able to catch a bus to Munich. In Munich I visited a café that was owned by someone I knew to be an acquaintance of the other officer, Daumler. But the café owner didn't know me. Then I showed him the decoration and letter Daumler had sent me. This convinced him, but with the police still on his heels Daumler was not easy to find and the café owner wouldn't tell me what I needed to do to reach him. I stayed with him for a week, unable to undertake a thing. Then one morning he turned out to have contacted Daumler after all. Without saying where we were going, he led me to the post office and told me to wait. He left, but bought a newspaper at the kiosk on the opposite corner and stood there reading to keep an eye on me. I waited twenty minutes. Then I heard someone whistling 'The Song of Germany' in a taxi that had pulled over to the kerb. The taxi was empty. The driver himself must have been the whistler. I went over and recognized Daumler. He gestured for me to get in the back and immediately drove off.

'Why do you need to talk to me so urgently?' Daumler asked, still driving and not looking back. 'You're putting me at tremendous risk. I was able to borrow this taxi for half an hour, cap included. Hurry up and tell me what's going on.'

I told him that if the Führer wasn't soon liberated from our clinic, he would probably suffer an accident, as we had been infiltrated by a Communist who was out for his life. In the mirror I saw Daumler screw up his eyes. The route he was following consisted almost exclusively of curves and he was driving so fast I was being thrown back and forth like a clapper in a bell. I could hardly refrain from adding: 'Krantz has been trying to pass himself off to me as a Communist. I know it's not true, that he's only doing it to put a lie of Elena's to the test, but I'm at my wit's end. I don't know how else to pit you against Krantz. You're my only ally.' But I didn't say it.

Then Daumler said, 'I don't believe there's a Communist alive who would want to kill the Führer.'

'Maybe not, but his presence in our clinic will lead to an accident befalling the Führer. If we don't do it, the Communists will kidnap him.'

I didn't mention Elena.

But Daumler roared, 'I'm sick to death of this nonsense! I know exactly who you're talking about. It's Krantz, isn't it? Didn't you get my message?'

I told him the date on which I had left the clinic. I couldn't possibly have received Daumler's letter. It contained the plan for an attempt on Krantz's life, as I saw on my return when I did find it. Plan might be too strong a word. It was actually nothing more than an instruction for me to immediately liquidate Krantz.

Daumler now repeated this order out loud, gesturing so furiously that he kept inadvertently hitting the horn, accelerating and then suddenly braking. 'Liquidate Krantz! Liquidate him immediately!' It was like he was playing an organ that allowed him to give me a good shaking.

'Liquidate Krantz immediately, make him disappear without trace! Otherwise they'll say it's his child, and it's not his, it is not his! It's the Führer's! The Führer's!'

He braked so abruptly that I flew against the roof of the taxi with my head and slumped back down on the well-padded seat. In the same instant the car door opened and a policeman started yelling at Daumler. I grabbed some money out of my pocket, threw it down on the front bench next to Daumler and got out of the car. With my head spinning, I crossed the large square from the place in the middle where Daumler had suddenly stopped for no reason. From all directions cars shot towards me, stamping on their brakes. When I was finally on the pavement, I could no longer see Daumler's taxi. I didn't know whether he had driven on, whether he was looking for me or whether the policeman had arrested him. I didn't dare go back to the café owner I had been staying with. The safest thing for me to do was return as quickly as possible to the clinic, high in the mountains.

When I arrived there nothing had changed. The Führer's condition was the same as when I left. I studied Elena without arousing her suspicions and it did seem possible that she was pregnant. I kept my fury to myself, but knew I wouldn't be able to suppress it for long. I had gained some valuable information: Daumler was aware of her relationship with Krantz and had ordered me to liquidate him. Daumler was therefore unaware of my own relationship with Elena, otherwise he might have ordered Krantz to liquidate me. And what about the superintendent, who would also be counted as a possible father, once what I already knew for a fact had become general knowledge? Why hadn't Daumler said anything about the superintendent? There were two possibilities:

1) He did not even suspect Elena of having a relationship with the superintendent.
2) He thought I did not suspect it.

Some reflection led me to conclude that the latter assumption had to be the correct one. And with that I immediately understood the plan Daumler and his cohorts had forged against me! Yes, I had to liquidate Krantz and after that the superintendent would be given the task of liquidating me, and when he had liquidated me, he himself would be liquidated by Daumler or a friend of his who was as yet unknown to me. If I wanted to save myself I needed to act quickly. But the outlaw existence that would await me afterwards was anything but appealing and so, until spring, I lived in hope that Daumler had been arrested during his escapade with the taxi and neutralized for ever.

But in April the snow was gone from the slopes and it would no longer be easy to track a fugitive. Then I received the package Daumler had announced in his written orders as containing supplies to use when liquidating Krantz. By that time I had discovered, with great difficulty, where in the building Krantz was hiding. It was the small, bricked-in section of the cellar where the fuse boxes were located.

I announced that I was going to start an investigation into the possibilities for giving the Führer back his voice. I invited the superintendent to attend the first operation. I also made sure that Elena would be one of the nurses assisting. Once we were standing around the operating table, but before the Führer had been placed in position, I gave a brief account of what I was going to do. At the end of my speech I raised a large hypodermic syringe in my right hand – and pressed down with my foot on a button I had prepared in advance, causing a short circuit. After it went dark, it became apparent that the emergency lighting wasn't working. I had disengaged it. I felt the superintendent turning towards me as he protested loudly about the incomprehensible failure of the emergency lighting, and stayed close to him while a nurse phoned the technical department. We waited. I looked at the clock, which had luminescent hands, but it was an electric clock. Two small explosions sounded below us, where I had fitted out the reserve fuses that were always kept there in case of emergency with small cartridges of dynamite, so that the stoker would be killed the moment he screwed them into place. Him and Krantz too, I hoped – and in that same moment I stabbed the superintendent in the throat with the needle, which I had filled with a powerful sedative and an extremely dangerous virus. Just as I withdrew the needle, the overhead lights flicked back on. I saw the superintendent staring with eyes like broken light bulbs, gazing down at the empty hypodermic in my hand. He swayed on his feet and tried to grab hold of something. Suffocating smoke began rising from the floor, which was crazed with cracks. Then the lights went off again. Screams were now

coming from all sides. The nurses began running around aimlessly. I seized the gurney with the Führer and pushed it into
the corridor. Then a third explosion shook the walls. I hadn't
known that flammable liquids like alcohol, ether and acetone
were stored in that part of the cellar, but all the better. With a
sense of triumph I pushed the gurney with the Führer down the
corridor to the large ward to return him to his bed. I was now
his sole owner, I who had respected and supported his life. My
enemies had been eliminated. If Daumler wanted to combat
me further, he would have to face me alone. He didn't realize
how well I had understood him. I had a chance of victory,
albeit a small one . . .

'So, making sure your child's safe?'

Elena must have stolen along behind me. Without answering
I pushed the gurney into the large ward while in the same
instant the fire alarms finally began their wailing. A strong,
cold wind met me. The explosion had shattered the glass of a
great many windows and the moonlit curtains were streaming
inwards. Perspiring in my white tunic, under which I wasn't
wearing anything, I immediately felt icy cold, but ignored it.
Instead, I thought of the patients who suffered the most terrible
agonies when the slightest breeze passed over them. I couldn't
imagine that, even if they had lost their vocal cords, they
wouldn't have some organ left with which to express what they
were now suffering. But I didn't hear a thing, although I kept
listening, even after Elena had wrapped her arms around me.

'Embrace me, otherwise we'll freeze to death. Embrace me,
or we'll die of cold.' She pulled me over to the Führer's bed, the
only one with blankets on it. And in that moment it occurred
to me that she couldn't be allowed to fall ill or die, that the
child she was expecting might not be the superintendent's or
Krantz's or the Führer's, but mine. And I rubbed her warm
under the blankets.

Then the staff began to cover the windows with planks and
cardboard. Workers came to repair the destruction the next
day, but didn't stay long. Half of the patients died that same
night and the rest died in the course of the week, dozens at a
time. I was coughing. By the end of the week I was delirious

with a forty-degree fever. In moments of vague consciousness, I saw that I was in a small room with just two beds and the superintendent dying in the other. He hadn't regained consciousness. I knew that my virus would do for him within a fortnight. I myself had a simple case of pneumonia.

After spending two days in bed, I no longer heard the workers. No hammering, no walking around, nothing. It was as if the whole building was deserted. Nobody came to check on me. Only when I was asleep did they place food and drink next to my bed.

On the fourth day I spent lying there, the sanatorium priest came by. He told me that they were busy clearing out the building as all the patients had died. I asked how the superintendent was, and he told me that he wouldn't last much longer. I asked if the mysterious explosion had claimed any direct victims and he told me that they had dug two bodies out of the cellar. One was the stoker who had screwed in the fuses, the other was unidentified and most likely the terrorist who had carried out the attack. I slumped back down on the pillows, closed my eyes and said, 'Peace be on their immortal souls.'

He then asked if I was sure I would survive my illness and if I had anything else to confess. I said I was convinced I wouldn't die, but that I wanted to confess everything to him anyway, and I confessed everything, including never having done the penance he had given me. He said he hoped I would recover and regain my strength enough to do it after all. I then asked him about the Führer and he said, after some hesitation, that the Führer too had died. I said, 'I looked after him out of respect for life, for no other reason, but others wanted to misuse him.' He replied that he knew that.

Then I asked, 'Where is Elena?'

'She's gone and it wouldn't be good for you to know where. She was a part of your past, yes, of that same past (he stood up and pointed at me threateningly), that same past you always forget! You forget that you burned two hundred Jews alive in search of a treatment for burns! You forget that you yourself were one of the Führer's most fervent followers! But we know, and it's something we've never forgotten!'

I answered that I had only sought my burns treatment out of respect for life, but now realized I should never have let it get out of hand like that. I would never do it again, now that Krantz and the superintendent were dead.

'Take care,' he said, 'don't forget it again and, above all, don't forget that we know. That might be irrelevant, but, if it comes down to it ... maybe not.' He said the last words in a whisper, almost at the door.

A month later, when I was able to leave my bed, I managed to convince him to tell me where Elena had gone. Elena was in Spain, in a convent in Seville. The police were looking for me and I couldn't get a passport. The priest took me across the Swiss border himself. From Switzerland I made my way to Genoa, where I concealed myself on a ship and pondered how to enter Spain. But the ship sank just off the Spanish coast. Three people were rescued and brought to shore near a small fishing village that had neither a police station nor a custom house. I was one of the three and managed to escape before the police could arrive. I crossed the snow-covered mountains on foot, travelling with gypsies and scraping together enough money for food and bus tickets by begging. In this way I finally arrived in Seville.

That afternoon two *guardias civil* armed with sub-machine guns were posted at the convent gate. They are the most terrifying policemen in the world. They scarcely move, only their eyes flash back and forth, and they are lean and emaciated, their walrus moustaches angled down parallel to the straps that cross on their chests on their way to their full ammunition belts. They look cruel and dejected at the same time, so much so that nobody could ever hope to appease them. I thought I was done for when one of them approached me. But he only asked if I had come to visit the convent. I gave him some money. Then he opened one of his bullet cases, pulled out a small bottle of wine and let me have a couple of swigs.

An elderly nun led me in. First to a courtyard lined with three floors of windowless, barred cells where the madmen and women they looked after were lying on straw. 'These are the poor suffering souls,' the elderly nun said. 'We feel great compassion for them. That's not the problem.' Lost in thought, she rattled her keys and led me to the waiting room. Every now and then I felt the membranes inside my body trembling and I knew that, somewhere far away, someone was playing an organ. Another nun came to fetch me and showed me the way to the parlour. I could hear the organ too now, though I was not yet able to make out the melody. Behind thick iron mesh sat a woman who could only be Elena, but I had the sun in my eyes and couldn't make out her features. I had nothing more to say to her and only ran my hand over my head a couple of times to signal to her that she was now shaved in the right spot. Thinking that she might not entirely comprehend the meaning of my visit, I said, 'Krantz is dead, the superintendent is dead and the Führer, too, is dead.'

'You have nothing to fear,' she replied, 'I'm staying here. I'll never come back.'

I could now hear without interruption the final chorus of St Matthew's Passion being played extremely poorly on the organ. The significance of that was not lost on me, but suddenly I refused to submit and asked to speak to the mother superior instead.

I was accompanied back to the waiting room, and half an hour later the mother superior came. Her rustic face was incomprehensibly young and, with her stolid eyes constantly turned up to the heavens, she most resembled the Virgin in Ribera's *Adoration of the Shepherds*.

Her answers sounded as if I had submitted a petition in advance listing all the points I wanted to discuss.

I said that I had come to talk to her about Elena. Wasn't she aware that Elena was pregnant?

'Of course we are. The little treasure.'

'Please help me, use your influence to convince Elena to leave the convent. I am the father of the child.'

'Are you the father of the child? You poor man, if only you knew how many fathers of children turn up here.'

'Not in this case,' I said, 'this is not like other cases.'

'The nameless have an infinite number of fathers,' she replied. 'What is not yet written, shall be written.'

'Fine!' I raged. 'Fine! I'm not the father of the child! The father of the child is the Führer!'

She laughed softly and took her rosary between her fingers. 'We knew that, we have always known that. The sweet babe! The Führer's child! The dear treasure!'

I was overcome with despair that this whole story with the Führer would never come to an end, that it would always start over again, that nobody in the world was serious about wanting to end it, nobody, nobody; if he wasn't dead, he was alive *yet* and if he had died, he had *reproduced,* and that was why I asked, 'If you know it's the Führer's child, what are you planning to do with it?'

'Oh,' she said, smiling at the heavens, 'we don't know yet. We will look after it well if the Lord wants it to stay alive. It can always turn out to be useful! The dear child, the little treasure!' And with that she stood up and left.

The nun who had led me to the room came back to show me out. 'Aren't you hungry and thirsty?' she asked. 'Travellers who come here are always exhausted from hunger and thirst. If you like, you can get a meal and a bed for the night at the monastery.'

I thanked her for the offer and followed her. I could still hear the final chorus of St Matthew's Passion and the clearer the music became, the more obvious it was how poorly it was being played. The nun went through a gate in a high wall and knocked on a heavy door with a knocker. An elderly brother opened the door and let me in. Lighting my way with a candle, he led me down several steps to a room that must have been half underground. The final chorus of the St Matthew's Passion finally stopped. 'You can wait here,' the brother said, holding the door open. 'We have heard that you still have some penance to do. I'd just make a start if I were you. Then you won't get bored.'

I entered a very spacious, empty, but low-ceilinged room, whose barred windows looked out over the pavement of a street. A brother in a brown habit was standing at one of those windows, next to a small organ. He didn't turn towards me, but sat down at the keyboard again and carried on with his wretched music, holding his head so far back that I could

clearly see eternity approaching on the clock face of his ton-
sure. I didn't want to disturb him further and plonked down
on a wooden bench at the back of the room.

The organ the brother was playing so abysmally was
extremely dilapidated. The pedal keyboard had been almost
entirely replaced by loops tied in lengths of all different kinds
of cord: white sisal, grey twine, coloured ribbons like the ones
people tie around presents, home-made rope of twisted cello-
phane. Many of the organ pipes were gone too, replaced with
glass tubes that didn't gleam and were almost invisible in the
dark. But they were still audible and horribly out of tune, like
an elephant's trumpeting.

The brother's back was moving furiously to the rhythm of
what he wanted to play, not what he was playing.

From the street came the sound of a mechanical piano playing a paso doble in competition. A gypsy squatted at the
window, gripped a bar with one hand and used the other to
extend a chipped saucer as far as possible into the room. There
were a few coins on the saucer and he made them clink while
calling out, '*La perrita, la perrita!*' But the monk took no
notice of him and I didn't dare to stand up. I found it hard to
tear my thoughts away from the brother's back, a back that
made me feel as if I had been here before, long ago.

The gypsy left, but the invisible pianola remained, constantly playing that same paso doble. A little later the gypsy
returned and stuck his saucer, which now held more coins,
back in through the window. '*La perrita,*' he said.

This recurred several times, with the monk's playing becoming, if possible, even worse. Each time there was more money
on the saucer. When, finally, there was a small pile lying there,
the monk leaped up and smacked the gypsy's hand, sending
the perritas flying in all directions.

The whole time I hadn't been able to stop wondering what
it was about the monk's back that was so oppressive, and when
he stood up and gave me more of a side view, my stomach felt
as if it had been hit with a battering ram as long as the room
and words that sounded like 'Daumler! Daumler!' escaped
from my chest with the power of explosions.

Before the monk sat down again, he turned half towards me, giving me a clear view of his profile and the scars on his cheek. Sweat was pouring down his face and running in rivulets through his scars. He opened his mouth wide and stayed motionless like that for several seconds, bent half over and with his mouth gaping, before changing his mind and sitting down again to resume playing without answering me.

Furiously he kicked at the pedal keyboard. His legs got tangled in the ropes, but he played on even though many of the organ pipes could no longer be silenced and were constantly whistling. His brown habit was pulled up to his knees. I saw that he was wearing white socks that had slipped down and were now bunched around his scrawny calves in thick rolls.

Translated by David Colmer

13

F. B. HOTZ

Women Win

Vrouwen winnen

It was the autumn of '59 or '60.

Armand was at the wheel, and the other seven were sleeping. His fatigue had reached the point where hallucinations forced him to keep his foot over the brake. After first seeing the disembodied wing of an aeroplane and then a towering ship ploughing down the pitch-black road ahead of him, he pulled the bus over into a parking lane. 'Whaddya doin'?' someone said with a yawn, but Armand had already given himself permission to sleep. His head of curly hair, which women loved, sagged onto the steering wheel, and he looked dead.

Now they all slept soundly. There's not much traffic at 3 a.m., and the few passing lorries didn't wake up anyone. The only sounds in the bus were air drawn into nostrils and occasional childish lip-smacking. The bandleader, riding shotgun next to Armand, slept as straight and stiff as a seated corpse shot through the forehead. One of the brass men clutched his case to his chest like a mother with her child, and the bass player reclined with his head against the canvas cover and his arms around the neck of his bass, which jutted out over the back of his seat. Now and then came the soft sound of wind brushing through the rubber net around the bass drum on the roof.

The sleep of the just – or at least, the justified. Their lives were well spent. They had talent and they used it; they earned – and deserved – the money they handed over to their wives and girlfriends. But more than that, they took intense pleasure in their work, although none of them would ever let it show. It was *bon ton* for them to curse their profession, which was no more than playing around and was even called playing. The griping started out mild – 'How the hell did I get into this business?' – and rapidly grew worse, but always with a half-smile suggesting their true feelings. Sometimes they'd make some old joke about the worthlessness of their profession; they'd pretend to be jealous of a passing baker, bus driver or office worker and sadly say, 'If only I'd learned a trade.' They sometimes used that line on stage too, when they had to play something appalling – a conga, say.

Every aspect of their work was filled with that almost completely unacknowledged pleasure. The trips in their own bus and the group coffee breaks along the roadside were unspoken highlights. All they ever talked about was the wind and cold.

They returned to the dead silence of their houses just before dawn, only to hit the road again a few hours later, yawning, swearing and burping.

Autumn is a fine season for musicians. Their appointment books are full, and they depart mid-morning, as a cheerful sun is cutting through the mist.

That morning was no different; they went to the regular meeting place and greeted each other as usual in front of the Volkswagen bus, nodding slowly and gravely at the cats who were already there and mumbling things like 'Aha, so you made it' and 'Aw, jeez, not you again'. All this was intended and understood to be esoteric language used among friends and incomprehensible to squares.

No one goes to work as light-hearted as a musician, usually after a jocular pseudo-quarrel about the route. Their wives can't join them, because there's barely enough room on the bus for the band and the boss. So there are no watchful eyes, and a day and night of full and satisfying freedom can begin. It's enough to make a one-legged blind man smile. Besides, they could always make room for a cute extramarital hitchhiker along the way.

They laughed and joked as they loaded the bus that morning – a ceremony of theirs, as if they could placate the gods by telling the same old saws over and over again. The bass drum, strapped to the roof rack with its web of rubber cords, shot loose the first time like it always did. 'Why do you guys laugh every time?' the drummer asked. 'The first three or four times, sure, it's funny, but we must be up to sixty by now.' He wasn't really mad, despite all his gloomy head-shaking; in fact, he was clearly honoured that his instrument was the centre of attention.

After searching for a missing oilcan in the street – they imitated the crawling and groping of botanizing field biologists, until it was retrieved, with boyish cheers, from under the bus – they were finally ready to go. Fifteen minutes late, so they drove fast on the main road.

While they waited for the car ferry across the IJ, Tom passed out strong eucalyptus drops. The trombonist spat his out immediately, saying in genuine shock, 'That fucking thing'll cost me my lip.' The other guys chuckled.

'Those are anti-embouchure drops, my friend,' Tom said. 'If you can suck on one of those and still blow afterwards, you know you're a real musician.'

'Don't throw that shit on the floor, it gets stuck in the mat,' the bandleader growled. It was his bus. This nasal tirade inspired several parodies, because when people work and travel together, they develop a need for a common half-enemy. They went on that way for a while, swapping gags that were savoured all the more for their staleness, especially if they had anything to do with the music business.

After an hour, the group began belting out the usual coffee song, their voices wobbling stridently over the constant roar of the engine in the back. The leader warned them they didn't have much time.

Although they were all around thirty years old, they elbowed their way out of the bus like schoolboys and dashed towards the converted farmhouse restaurant, which was flying a cola flag. Inside, they slumped sophomorically in the wooden folding chairs and tossed cardboard coasters at each other. ('Gentlemen!' the leader barked.) When a country girl arrived with coffee, they made lascivious noises until she started to sweat and spill their drinks. They were having fun. It was the same kind of fun they had on every trip, but what difference did that make?

Back on the road, they killed time at closed railway crossings by tapping on their windows at waiting girls and, once they caught their attention, making idiotic, screwed-up faces – a questionable strategy for attracting hitchers. 'Ah, cut it out,' the leader groaned. 'Remember, our name's painted on this thing.'

The bandleader, with his large head full of worries and straight nose – which he sometimes stroked dubiously as if making music weren't all he had hoped it would be – thought many times a day, I take care of the contracts, the rides, the publicity; I repair their instruments and give them advances on their wages; and precious little thanks do I get. They're like children, expecting to be waited on hand and foot. But he was the same as the rest of them; grumbling was in his musical blood, and he no more wanted to be rid of them than they of him. Stray thoughts of a different line of work were quickly suppressed (though often with a sigh). 'Keep your eyes on the road, Armand,' he shouted. 'What are you doing, man? We were supposed to turn right at that corner.' He had to keep an eye on everything.

They acted like fools because they felt superior to everyone else. That included other types of artists, whom they sometimes tolerated and sometimes treated like dirt. At a high-society club in Amsterdam, a renowned poet in a dark jumper had once said to them, 'What you do with sound is like what we do with paint or words.' They had heard that one before, and their only response was, 'Uh-huh.' (They never referred to themselves as artists, by the way, but as hard-working jazzmen.) They were stricter than Calvin when it came to predestination; no matter how goofy they might act, salvation was guaranteed thanks to their musicianship. 'If I happen to feel like lying down fully clothed in a full bathtub,' Armand once said, 'I'll still be Armand B.' That was the essential thing. They believed that their audiences believed it too, and they were usually right. They were magicians and princes among men, although

they may have had that feeling in part because they normally
saw their spectators engaged in that supremely futile, laugh-
able and failure-prone activity – having fun.

But they did have to prove themselves. There was a natural
hierarchy among them, headed not by the eldest, or by the best
stylists or specialists in their fields, but by those with the most
undeniable general skills, the kind of musician who could face
any key signature without flinching, read like a fiend and recite
the chord progressions of 800 standards (a talent subject to
frequent, tiresome demonstrations during rehearsals).

The autumn sun disappeared, and the weather turned cold.
There were shouts to turn on the heat. The second trumpet's
spirits were sinking; he was worried his slow valve would act
up on him. He handed the bandleader his instrument, naked
and vulnerable out of its case in that cramped, moving bus.
The leader unscrewed the valve and then screwed it back in. 'I
don't see anything special,' he said. That infuriated the owner.
'You think I'd say it was sticking if there was nothing wrong
with it?' he snarled at the leader. The others backed him up,
shouting that he was absolutely right. 'Take it easy, take it
easy,' said the leader, 'I'll take a look at that thing backstage
before we start.'

The long drive put a damper on their mood. For a while they
sang children's songs in high falsetto voices, but soon a few of
them lapsed into silence, while others spoke in low tones to
their neighbours about cars, stereo equipment and, above all,
other musicians. 'That guy X doesn't know what he's doing'
was followed by, 'But how about that Y – he's been blowing like
mad lately!' They also knew their classics and spoke with the
refined smiles of connoisseurs about Beiderbecke, Rank, Trum-
bauer, Lang, Nichols, Busse and Mole. It was like they were
performing pages from John O'Hara without even knowing it.

As they neared their destination, they got their second wind,
yapping like kids in a crowded school bus. 'I'm gonna play the
bejesus out of "Body and Soul",' one of them said. 'I hope so,

'cause I've almost lost my faith,' another replied. Once again, sincerity was strictly forbidden.

The bus pulled into the schoolyard. It was ten past nine in the evening – they were about ten minutes behind schedule, but no doubt the usual school play was in progress. They always ran late. They parked in the middle of a cluster of teachers' cars. 'Right this way, gentlemen,' said a pimply-faced boy with a band around his arm.

There were already quite a few students on the stone steps at the entrance, who apparently considered themselves too old for the party inside and were waiting to welcome the band. As they watched the men approaching with their instruments, the girls among them had a brazen, critical look in their eyes – with perhaps even a hint of mockery. They did not lower their gaze as the musicians passed only a few feet away, though a couple of them did blush slightly. A magnificent blonde, who could just as easily have been twenty-seven as seventeen – only her cherubic cheek revealed her true age; the rest put most grown women to shame – whispered to a friend, 'That one looks so grouchy!' She meant Koos, who was still worrying about his instrument.

'You think?' Tom asked, in a not-too-friendly tone, bringing his impressively tall, broad frame to an abrupt halt in front of her. Ordinary citizens of both sexes had to learn to behave themselves around musicians. A certain distance had to be not maintained, but created. 'Watch yourself,' they sometimes said, as if they were teachers. At the same time, it must be admitted, Tom had a degree of enthusiastic, tongue-clacking appreciation for female beauty.

The girl blinked once, with her long lashes, but Tom vented the rest of his indignation on the pimply boy, who had dared to remark, 'You're a little late, gentlemen.'

'Looks like you're a little late with everything,' Tom retorted, taking in the short, scrawny figure from top to toe. After that, the boy kept quiet.

Through a mobbed, dimly lit, insipidly decorated dance hall that smelled like lukewarm cola, children's sweat and floury pudding, they wound their way towards the stage. Holding their instruments over their heads like coolies, they pushed through the crowd, brushing their bodies – some more deliberately than others – against the girls lined up along the wall. Even the youngest ones were whispering to each other about the musicians' looks and clothing, but the teachers hissed at them to be quiet, since the play, as expected, was still in full swing. Armand and Tom saw a number of eyes glittering at them in the dark, as they shouted, 'Coming through!' and, 'Move over, will ya?' You had to use words to keep those pretty little hoodlums in their place. If you tried to be a 'gentleman', they'd just take advantage of you later when you were on stage.

The opening skirmish had not yet been won. Once all eight of them had made it backstage and were putting together their instruments (as the wooden acting continued – they could clearly hear the prompter's despairing whisper), the same blonde-haired girl they'd seen at the entrance came up the stairs, her swaying backside clamouring for attention. She planted herself next to the drummer, following his every move as he adjusted his cymbals and attached his pedal. 'What's buzzin', cuzzin?' he asked in a friendly tone. She gave a start, then smiled again and looked him in the eyes. 'Tom,' he said, 'gimme a hand here, I dunno what to do with this chick.' Tom came over, grabbed her by her fleshy upper arm, pushed her back towards the stairs, and said, 'You belong down there, horseface, unless you're looking for the toilets.' A little crudity never hurt. 'Outta here, sister,' echoed the leader, who was polishing Koos's trumpet. 'Shhhh, shh-hhh!' came angry voices from the audience. But if you let even one of them on stage, before you know it they're all over the place, stomping on the instruments like elephants. And they remembered how, in their own schooldays, the girls could do no wrong; male teachers developed creepy infatuations, and female teachers had half-baked theories about the superiority of their sex. No one cared about the boys. Well, now they had a chance to turn the tables.

Meanwhile, the play showed no signs of ending. The audience grew noisier, and the young actors yelled nervously over the ruckus. Some rowdy pupils were already calling out things like, 'Stop!' and, 'Enough!' The crowd was no longer laughing at the lines, but at their clumsy delivery. An irrepressible impatience filled the hall.

'I can't believe I floored it over here for *this*,' Armand said. A couple of guys wanted to go back out into the dance hall, and though the leader said, 'Certainly not!', off they went.

As the bass player, moving through the mob, passed a smaller, less defiant-looking girl, he ran his hand over her hair. She bent double in a fit of coughing, her baby face turning beet red. 'Shhhhhh,' hissed a teacher. 'They always pick the same girls for that sort of thing,' she muttered irritably to a male colleague. He nodded.

It seemed as though the impatience was rapidly turning into something else. Those halting recitations on stage were bound to stop sometime soon, and then something would finally happen. The mood of nervous infantilism that had settled over everyone would dissolve. Already, the schoolchildren were starting to exude a giggly aura of erotic expectation. And not only the schoolchildren. Teachers looked on from their chairs, wearing the most avuncular expressions possible, at certain girls lined up against the wall, and in the packed hall the musicians got a little gropy, now moving girls out of the way not with their voices, but with their hands. The leader, still standing by the steps in front of the stage, tried to wave to his boys to come back; it seemed to him that the time had come to start playing.

And sure enough, the crowd began cheering in sarcastic enthusiasm and clapping in malicious relief. The young actors – first-formers – and the director were showered in appreciation. There was even a bunch of flowers for the prompter.

But first came the interval.

'Jeez-us,' Armand said again. 'It's already past ten. I'm leaving at midnight, a contract is a contract.'

'Ah, the hell you will,' said the other guys, smiling. They headed over to the makeshift bar, clearly wrought by children's hands.

The caterers who manned this structure were taking orders

from the young student princes with pointed, ironic little
bows: 'Two colas for you, sir?' The hubbub of children's voices
was like a thick porridge running into their ears; there was no
escaping it. The boys crowed hoarsely and the girls squawked.
Someone mounted the stage and shouted – after first moving
his mouth noiselessly in front of a dead mike – that it was time
for the first and second forms to go home. The little girl who'd
been stroked on the head stamped her feet on the parquet floor
in fury. 'Gosh darn it, why now?' she cried with unexpected
volume, considering her small stature, but a much bigger blonde
started shoving her towards the exit. 'C'mon,' the leader said
nervously, as he tugged his boys by their shoulders off the bar
stools, where they'd been silently bestowing signatures on a
clutch of bashful boys.

Meanwhile, even the corridors – especially around the toilets, which were abuzz with activity during the interval – were
laden with an indefinable but distasteful kind of third-rate
nursery-school eroticism. Girls slunk away, peering out of the
corners of their slitted eyes, which were almost invisible under
their demurely lowered lashes. They looked and did not look at
the boys at the far end of the corridor, who were shouting to
each other over the embarrassing splash of water in the sinks
as they went in and out of their designated room. Outside the
dance hall a vague playroom odour permeated the school, as if
the boys and girls still had a few things to learn from their
schoolmistresses about hygiene.

The chairs, the stands and the drum set were slid forward onto
the stage while the curtain was still closed. They were all in
a good mood again; they'd been waiting so long to get to
work that they were raring to go. They put greater flair than
ever into testing their instruments, tuning and warming up. A
microphone was scrupulously checked. 'Ready?' the leader
asked from his seat at the piano. The only one who didn't nod
was Koos, who sat hunched and sullen. 'Koos,' the leader said,
'you ready?' Koos grumbled something like, 'Get on with it,
man.' Looking troubled, he grabbed the mouthpiece of his
trumpet between his index finger and thumb, picked up the

instrument and raised it to his lips, a unique gesture for which he was well known. 'Like baby birdies having sex,' Tom had once described it.

The leader raised one hand above the keys – a last call for their attention – and the others looked tensely out of the corners of their eyes at his foot, which began to tap out the tempo, softly and sharply – just the downbeats at first, then all four, as usual. The band leaped into action like a machine. Finally, the leader smiled. The curtain was slowly raised to applause from the audience.

They played a short signature tune, and the closing bars were followed by raucous cheering. The older teachers looked surprised but forgiving as the fanatical heads of the children screeched with gaping mouths.

The leader stood up from the piano and announced the first set. 'One of these numbers is a special request,' he claimed, and the old trick worked as well as ever: more cheering and grateful applause.

By the third number, the musicians were getting into the groove. The two trumpets bit into the melody with self-important brawn, as if they were a little put out at having to perform such syrupy stuff. But the trombone swelled to the occasion, singing vibrantly in its upper register like a pious orphan girl, modest and mild, but with enough carrying power to make itself heard and felt. Not by the audience, maybe, but by other – imagined – musicians, wherever they might be. The only people here were underage kids and wrinkled teachers. The trombonist fancied himself 'a musician's musician', a phrase he'd picked up from some American magazine.

The children danced earnestly, the girls sagging at the knees like she-bears on every downbeat, then bouncing back – they looked a little like experienced Javanese rice-pounders. But the hips of even the smallest girls pulsed and gyrated like the haunches of panther cubs in heat, forming an absurd contrast to their sickly sweet, often bespectacled, virginal faces. 'The ritual dance of shame,' Tom whispered to Armand, who had just launched into a smart, prissy clarinet solo. The schoolboys clomped arhythmically around the hall, chaste and agitated.

They kept it up until eleven thirty. On stage, guys were exchanging compliments with a sincerity found nowhere else on earth. 'That was one vigorous solo there, Tom,' the drummer said. They smuggled the joys of their music into unsuspecting ears. They played a few requests, but the soul of every number remained on stage. The phrasing, refinement, tone, ingenuity, lyricism, arrangement and effervescent swing were for the musicians; the melody was for the audience.

A short break was announced, so that the students could hold a raffle. The curtain remained open and the band stayed seated, resting their instruments on their knees, a haughty, interior look in their eyes as they stared absently out into the hall – all except for Koos, who was tinkering with his trumpet.

On stage directly in front of them, a robust young woman was standing at the microphone with her back to them. She picked numbers out of a basket and read them aloud, provoking wild cheering by the winners. Once, as she bent all the way forward, Armand stealthily pointed his clarinet at her backside. The other musicians sniggered softly. Tom saw from the side that it was the same blonde he had chased off stage before the show. At that very moment, she looked back at him, and her mature, womanly eyes darkened. She said nothing.

She picked another two or three numbers out of the basket, read them out, and then said into the microphone with a smile, 'One moment, please.' Still sweetly smiling, she tripped off stage.

Meanwhile, Koos was complaining to the bass player: 'Did you hear how shitty I sound tonight, with that stuck valve?'

The bass player looked up at the ceiling pensively and responded, in a cheerful tone, 'Nope, sounded just like always to me!' Koos nodded glumly. He too left the stage, taking his trumpet with him. He wanted to rinse off the valve that was wounding his soul in one of the sinks in the toilets.

At one end of the long, deserted hallway were doors bearing the words 'Girls'. Seeing no others and not having much time to look around, Koos pulled one of them open, revealing an interior filled with sinks and mirrors. Everyone was out in the dance hall, and he assumed they would stay there. And otherwise it would be easy enough to explain what he was doing. Anyone could see he was at the sink with his trumpet, valve and tube of oil.

Scarcely a minute later, the door through which he had entered was closed from the corridor. He could hear the key turning in the lock. 'Hey!' he shouted, but it was too late.

'Where the hell is Koos?' the leader said. The raffle had ended some time ago. Hundreds of schoolchildren were staring at the band in aggravated expectation, and teachers were discreetly but wearily checking their watches. But the band did not begin. 'Let's get on with it, gentlemen!' a deputy headmaster said with raised eyebrows to the bandleader, who responded, on the verge of weeping, that he had lost one of his boys. 'Musta hung himself,' Armand said, aware, as ever, of his professional duty to be a smart-arse. The bass player was told to go and find him; he *did* know where the men's toilets were and wandered around them gamely shouting 'Kobus', but of course nobody answered. On the way back, he noticed that blonde girl at the entrance to the hall, telling a deputy head and an older teacher, 'While I was on stage, they were touching my behind.' Blood rushed to the scandalized teacher's matronly cheeks.

Because the children were starting to chant hateful things – some girls crossing their eyes and sticking out their tongues – and because the headmaster was shooting him questioning looks, the bandleader decided to start without Koos.

Right from the start, the arrangements sounded strangely hollow, almost childish; they had to scrap the two-trumpet special, not to mention Koos's big solo number. That was not such a bad thing, maybe, considering the state of his valve. This train of thought led to a misunderstanding among the musicians, who surmised that Koos had fled because he couldn't face the prospect of his solo. 'He could have used my trumpet for the one tune,' Tom said with a shrug. 'What kinda guy just runs out on his buddies?' (You could almost pick up a hint of the fierce rivalry among trumpet men.)

A quarrel broke out because the leader wanted to go ahead with one tune, for fear that they would run out of repertoire, while Tom said it sounded ridiculous with only one trumpet. The trombonist refused to play too. Armand peevishly struck up a different tune, but the leader insisted and started to count off the tempo. The audience laughed scornfully and started booing. The blonde schoolgirl, now chatting with a balding teacher, said, 'This band sure stinks, doesn't it, sir?'

They made a fresh start and put all their effort into it, but without the usual pleasure in their work. The guitarist cursed as he broke a string; in the music business, as in most other businesses, bad things rarely come alone. In the relative silence of the bass solo – filling in for the temporarily disabled guitar – they could finally hear the sad, pathetic banging on the door in the corridor. The audience and band all laughed in unison.

The guitarist tracked down the source of the sound – followed by a couple of chortling kids – and found Koos, screeching streams of curses behind his locked door. The key was nowhere to be found.

The band stopped. They were outraged. 'Get that guy outta there, or we won't play another note,' they shouted.

It took a long time to find the key. In the end, it was the blonde who, suddenly, with a kindly, authoritarian smile, seemed to recall something about a duplicate. Like a rescuing angel, she set Koos free. With his trumpet clasped foolishly in one hand, surrounded by giggling schoolchildren, his stooped form stumbled back to the stage. The audience jeered as he took his seat. 'Where'd you go off to?' the leader asked snidely, but Koos let out another potent stream of profanity, to the effect that he should shut his ugly mug. The microphone picked up this exchange, and the crowd burst into satanic applause. In this tumult, the blonde rushed on stage, quick as a cat, snatched up the mike, and shrilly announced that for the next bash, in December, they would hire a *good* band. She was rewarded with a standing ovation.

Just as they were hurrying to play again so that they could drown out the blonde, a teacher with a balding cranium and piercing canine eyes strode on stage, spreading his arms wide and gesturing to them to stop. 'You come along with me, mister,' he said to Koos, who gave him a blank look and refused. The man grabbed Koos's arm, pulled him to his feet and hissed, 'Get moving, chum, or I'll call the police.' Tom wanted to fight, but the leader jumped out from behind the piano, calmed the teacher down, and signalled to Koos to go quietly. The audience unleashed a fresh volley of abuse.

The pimply boy with the armband, the one who had met them at the entrance, started jumping up and down awkwardly between the instruments, demanding to know whether they were going to play any more goddam music or not. After he knocked Koos's trumpet off the chair, Tom landed a single punch that sent the boy flying off the stage. There was a moment of total silence in the hall, followed by a tidal wave of hostility. 'Dirty faggots!' two or three breaking voices shouted. 'Perverts!' cried a girl whose face had turned crimson. That last cry was quickly echoed by many other spectators.

Some of the musicians could hear the teacher huffing backstage: 'What were you up to in the girls' toilet? Tell me the truth!' The response was inaudible.

Two or three of the guys ran over to the teacher, shouting and swearing: 'That cat was just cleaning out his horn, not that we expect a prick like you to understand. No doubt you would have gone there for something else.'

'Gentlemen, *gentlemen*!' cried the bandleader, white as a sheet, as he and the headmaster both came hurrying over at once. A young gym teacher, having forced his way backstage, got into a tussle with the bass player and the drummer, who both had highly developed wrists, thanks to their occupations, and made short work of him.

Meanwhile, Tom and the trombonist were packing away their fragile instruments – half precaution, half reprisal. 'I won't play another note in this joint,' they told each other. The others followed their example, once they had liberated their 'buddy' Koos. The baldy stomped off, saying he would call the police, his jaws grinding with rage.

They sat on stage with their instruments in the cases, their arms crossed. The audience was shrieking. The drummer went

on calmly dismantling his set, turning his back and his protruding behind on the furious mob. He dropped his shining
cymbals on the stage floor with a deafening crash, like a loud
declaration of war.

Teachers, waiters and older students with armbands were
wandering in all directions, looking pale. (It was surprising
how many of them were wearing those bands; everyone, no
matter how young, wants to be important.) 'This is a breach of
contract,' the bald man shouted, returning from the telephone
in the headmaster's office. The children, forming a column as
wide as the dance hall, stared at him, and then at the unco-
operative band, and began, as if driven by some Red Indian
impulse from their collective unconscious, to storm the stage.
That is, at least twenty boys started climbing and scrambling
like soldiers on a suicide mission, mounting the glacis of a
fortress.

Tom, the drummer and the bass player, chuckling, defended
their position with the finesse of professional boxers. One
schoolboy after another was slammed back into the seething
throng. Their pain and anger were infectious, and they were
egged on by girls with red faces. With nervous war cries, a new
wave of attackers followed, from a class that had debated
World Peace that very afternoon.

The caterers, with the instincts of the self-proclaimed
oppressed, immediately sided with what they saw as the hired
help, joining forces with the musicians. One tall one with
glasses banged two boys' heads together before hurling them
back into the crowd.

The director raised his arms over his head and tried to reach
the microphone, which was giving off a low, constant rumble.
His shouts were incomprehensible without electrons. A tall girl
jumped on stage, right in front of him, and slitted Koos's face
open with the nail of her middle finger. The bassist grabbed
her head and pushed it down as if holding her under a running
tap. As she tried to wriggle out of his grasp, he felt her panting
mouth warm and wet between his fingers. Then she bit, and he
let go with a shriek, but at the same time thrust one knee into
her skinny behind, sending her flying forward into the mike,

which collapsed onto the headmaster, nearly putting him out of commission. (He limped away.)

'Enough is enough, goddam it!' somebody shouted in an Olympian voice from an otherwise empty balcony directly opposite the stage. They all stopped, but it wasn't clear whether that was because of the voice, or because of what was discovered at the same time in the silent corridor.

Some of the girls were sobbing. On the floor of the corridor lay, unseen at first, a boy from one of the lower forms, having a seizure. A long trail of fluid ran from underneath him over the stone floor, slowly and silently spreading. It was as if the unfortunate boy had sacrificed himself in the interests of reconciliation.

Amid an emotional silence, the figure from the balcony was heard stomping down the stairs. I can't work with that hand, the bass player thought. That's gonna cost money.

The descending man proved to be a broad-shouldered police officer with grey, bristly hair and a sense of drama – a Hindenburg type in a civilian uniform. He ordered the attackers back to their starting position with an outstretched arm and a quivering index finger and warned the musicians to remain calm with a contemptuous curl of his upper lip. 'Back in your seats!' he commanded them, tipping his head at the chairs on stage, some of which were lying on their sides. Only Tom and the bandleader did not obey. Who is this creep? they seemed to ask each other with raised eyebrows, as united as if they were equals in the band.

The policeman took charge with a self-satisfied smirk. The wounded – suffering mainly from lumps and scratches – were led away and attended to. The enterprising blonde turned out to have a first-aid certificate (she didn't mind a little blood), which came in handy, and the gym teacher, too, made the rounds like Dunant at Solferino.

The young patient in the corridor was carefully taken home in one of the teachers' cars. A slightly flushed schoolmistress, with the help of the caretaker, wiped away the shameless fluid on the floor, which suddenly seemed to have acquired a supernatural origin and significance that challenged the very foundations of society. Or maybe it was the lighting in the corridor. The two of them worked in silence.

Meanwhile, the first worried parents – it was almost twelve thirty – were coming through the front entrance and pounding on the main door of the hall. 'What's going on here?' a woman's voice warbled through the glass. The all-knowing police mastermind went up to them, spoke soothing words and kept the dance hall closed. He seemed to be concerned that the pupils would charge the stage again.

The headmaster returned, back in form again and intending to make a speech, but fortunately the microphone had broken when it fell. The teaching staff and the police jointly organized a kind of humanistic tribunal where everyone could 'talk it out' and 'clear the air'. This awakened the musicians' professional cynicism, and the chances of serious dialogue seemed slim. The bass player mumbled something about the United Nations; he had demanded that his attacker personally bandage his hand. 'Could you do my knee while you're at it?' he asked her. 'I didn't know your rear was solid rock.' She tended to his hand without comment, like a seasoned nurse.

The attractive blonde pupil, who had been standing off to one side all this time with a superior smile on her face, testified at the tribunal that she had locked up that scary man (Koos) to protect the younger girls from rape – at the very least. Her flattered captive beamed with pleasure. His musical alibi was eventually, reluctantly, accepted.

Somewhat unexpectedly, the band was required to complete its performance according to contract. Considering all the delays, that meant another twenty minutes or so. Armand suggested that they play the same number ten times in a row; the leader started to turn pale again, until it was explained to him that this was just a joke.

Shaking their heads, the musicians took their instruments back out of their cases, and the pupils – angry, surprised and honoured all at once – no longer danced but looked on like merciless judges. Still, the youngest ones yawned occasionally;

then they no longer looked naive, but moronic. 'Behold the
future electorate,' the trumpeters mumbled to each other.

Koos's trumpet did a kind of inorganic penance by working
perfectly. It put him in good spirits right away. 'You should
have that thing knocked off a chair more often,' the other guys
said in relief.

When they had symbolically fulfilled the terms of their settlement by performing two more numbers, the party was declared
officially over. For a moment, they seemed to be heading for a
serious dispute about remuneration, since the organizers
wanted to dock them fifteen minutes' pay. 'I'll pull down every
damn thing on these walls,' Tom threatened, picturing his
wife's upheld hand. But the whole thing was resolved amicably.
In the end, no one knew exactly who deserved how much
blame, or how much pay. They all wore uncertain smiles as
they said their goodbyes.

A devoted friend of the blonde was waiting at the exit, a girl
a head shorter but clearly determined to emulate her class-
mate's fighting spirit. 'I think that music you play is just
horrendous,' she said with a smile that brooked no rebuttal,
possibly copied from one of her teachers. 'There's no account-
ing for bad taste,' Tom replied, a classic line he reserved for
special occasions like this one.

The band's 'strong and long-standing ties with the school' had
undoubtedly been severed. 'That's another regular job down
the drain,' they said to each other on the way home. In fact,
they were likely to get the cold shoulder from schools throughout that region.

During the long, dark hours of their journey, Koos, with his
long scratch burning, felt like a hero and penitent rolled into
one, but he fell asleep quickly after the group sang a raunchy
song accompanied by rhythmic clapping. The lyrics were
hardly anything more than a string of childish synonyms for
female body parts. The bandleader declined to participate,
shaking his head sorrowfully. He wondered when in his life he
would finally have the chance to work with adults. But he also

smiled a little, because at least these were his own hand-picked boys.

By 3 a.m. they were all sound asleep, except for Armand, of course. The leader, who was fitfully dozing, waved to him to stop at a transport café for coffee.

At their next job, a party in a secondary school in the west of the country, Tom and Armand were friendly to the girls at the door – friendly in the polite sense, I mean. They met their every little demand without delay.

The musicians even considered bringing one or two of their wives along on the next trip – as a kind of superstitious penance, paid in advance. If they all squeezed in a little, there would be room. They might as well bring the ones who'd been whining about it the longest. What the hell, right?

'You cats sure have some weird ideas these days,' said the substitute bass player.

Translated by David McKay

14

HARRY MULISCH

What Happened
to Sergeant Massuro?

Wat gebeurde er met Sergeant Massuro?

BOZ	OFFICIAL
Dept. A Room 3	Ministry of War
Wassenaar	
Netherlands	

It is a calm person who is writing to you, Gentlemen – the calm
that reveals itself when all hope is gone.

I assume that you are familiar with this tone. I don't know
who you are or which Ministry you fall under or what the
initials of your section mean. I have never heard of your Bureau. It wouldn't surprise me if you also fall under a Ministry I
have never heard of. Colonel Stratema, Commander of the 5th
Battalion 124 Infantry Regiment, on New Guinea, gave me
your address and told me I must inform you of what has happened to Sergeant Massuro 'as if I were telling a friend'.

Right, so you are my friend, Gentlemen. You shall hear
what I know about it. I know nothing about it. I just know that
it happened and I was there. However, I have the impression
that you have also received a report from the colonel and from
Dr Mondriaan – and that they know nothing about your Bureau either, except that, I assume, you collect information about
cases like that of Sergeant Massuro.

There are more such cases, Gentlemen? It doesn't surprise
me. Too many? Is that the reason I had to swear on the Bible to
keep it secret? They happen in the Netherlands too? It wouldn't

surprise me. Once Dr Mondriaan had looked his fill at Massuro, he started interrogating me hollow-cheeked about our life in the interior.

'Dear God, Lieutenant, of course it's impossible to stand those inhuman conditions!'

I knew what he was thinking. He thought it was because of fear. Fear is capable of anything. It is a sorcerer like Apollonius of Tyana, a prophet like Isaiah, a political mass murderer and a greater lover than Don Juan. But what happened to Massuro can't have had anything to do with fear.

'I know the interior better than you, Doctor. It could have happened just as well in Amsterdam, in an office, or on a warm summer's evening while reading the paper at the open window, with the radio tuned to Hilversum.'

My panic was different from his, paler, more controlled, but no less intense. I told him that in my opinion it had scarcely anything to do with *Massuro*. That it could happen to *anyone*, to him, Mondriaan, as well as to me – at any moment.

'Maybe it's already at work in one of us, Doctor.'

I saw that he couldn't accept it. He looked at Massuro's remains in bewilderment. He wanted a *reason* – where was he otherwise? And the only thing that with lots of good (and occult) will could pass as a reason was fear. But there was no fear. Massuro didn't have the slightest idea what fear was.

I knew Massuro a little. I'll tell you about it as a friend, Gentlemen, though it's a mystery to me what you will do with it. When he was posted to my section two years ago in Potapègo, I was just chatting to the village headman. The truck from Kaukenau arrived and out of the cab stepped a dark, heavily built fellow with a big head, round eyes and thick lips. I suddenly saw his name on the major's letter in front of me.

'Heintje Massuro!'

He came towards me grinning.

'Afternoon, Lieutenant. Who'd have thought that one day you'd be bossing me about on the other side of the planet?'

I had met him first when I was eleven, in the changing rooms of the gym. He was in the sixth form, I was in the fifth. I'd come to get something I'd forgotten. Massuro was sitting alone

in the sweaty atmosphere of the changing room, as immovable
as a statue among the grubby heaps of clothes. From the gym
came the sound of exercising and a commanding voice that
kept counting to four.

'Can't you join in?'

'I'm being punished.'

'Why?'

He looked at me with his big brown eyes.

'For nothing.'

He already had that heavy and at the same time sharply
defined look. I felt he wasn't lying. I would have liked to
become friends with him, but that wasn't really possible with
someone who was a class higher or lower. Nowhere is there as
much class consciousness as in schools; the Communists could
be proud of that. Sometimes I talked to him, and once he came
and looked at the moons of Jupiter through my telescope.

'The universe is a great bag full of stones and light.'

Two years later we were in the same class at grammar
school; he had to repeat a year. But by then it was too late, the
time for becoming friends had passed. Things like that often
come down to a month or a week; perhaps even a day or a minute. If I had met my wife a year later, ours would have been the
happiest marriage in the world and I wouldn't be here in
Kaukenau in New Guinea now. We almost never talked to
each other: some sort of shame had come between us. He had
few interests: wide rivers of biology and history flowed through
my head in those days. But if I learned one thing about him, it
was that he was not afraid. Yet he wasn't a swaggerer. I never
heard him say: 'Do you dare do this or that' – before performing some exploit. Only boys who were actually too scared and
above all too scared of being seen as scared. Massuro lacked
that fear too. But when it was a matter of really doing something that needed courage, then we'd see Massuro do it, while
we were peeing ourselves. (Like that time when we had to bur-
gle the headmaster's office to find out the project questions.)
But with him it wasn't courage but the absence of fear, and it
was as if that gave him a certain invulnerability. He was always
punished for nothing.

Apart from that he was a perfectly normal boy: Heintje Massuro, ice-cold and cheeky as they come. Should it now appear otherwise, Gentlemen, that is because I am all too keen to refute Dr Mondriaan's fear theory; and because despite myself I am also looking for a reason for what happened to him – which doesn't exist.

Another two years later, shortly before the war, I lost sight of him. He left school and I heard that he had left for the Dutch East Indies with his parents.

'Just in time to be thrown into a camp by the Japs,' he told me in Potapègo, where we celebrated our reunion after fifteen years: I, a lieutenant, he a regular sergeant posted to my section. By then he had completed eight years in the tropics. From the camp he had immediately volunteered for military service; his parents had both died. He had been involved in the whole epic business: the mopping up of the Japanese, the police actions, punitive expeditions on Java and Sumatra ... he seemed to have been involved with Westerling too. I didn't ask any more questions. It was all fairly obscure and impenetrable. I expect you will have better channels to find out more.

Of course, you can look in that direction, but you won't find anything. That is, anything that is directly connected with what happened. I don't know ... perhaps there are such things as 'hidden connections' – quite possibly; but then far underground, around the back, underneath, untraceable. Over the whole planet something indescribable is going on, a kind of process ... The sun shines differently than it did before the war. I don't know how to express it more clearly. Countless new, elusive forces are active; a new kind of people ... In Singapore, Prague, Amsterdam, Alamogordo, Jakarta (and Wassenaar) a whole new breed of gentlemen is sitting around tables in cafés and government buildings: they are the ones with power. Two tables or rooms further on no one knows who they are. It no longer has anything to do with politics. A group of gentlemen drive through Borneo in a column of cars? What language are they talking? No one understands it. But it's *relevant*. Over Ceream a small, unmarked grey aircraft is shot down by an Indonesian battery. It is empty. No cameras on board. Only radio equipment for remote control – or is it itself a living being? Everything is connected. No one yet understands how it fits together, everything that's going on, what is possible, where it's going – and anyone who thinks that it's different at home in Holland is living in a world that no longer exists and is dreadfully wrong.

But Massuro was not scared. He had played his part in that unnameable process – undoubtedly a small part, but a part that could not bear the light of day, a part played with the curtains closed in a play no one knows and with an empty prompter's box. I noticed that he regarded his service with me as a kind of holiday. He was right, it was. It *was*. I wonder if it still is, after what happened to him.

In any case, there was less reason for fear with me than anywhere in the archipelago. I am responsible for law and order in an area approximately the size of London. But the forces ranged against us are not entrenched in the mountains or in the jungles. The poor Papuans . . . they wave our flag and build bungalows for us, they haven't a clue. New Guinea is far away in the Pleistocene, 100,000 years BC. If one of my men shoots a cassowary or a cockatoo, shots are fired, but apart from that – never. Sometimes we discover among the creepers or by a stinking swamp Dutch subjects 1.40 metres tall who have never seen a white man. We name such a village Emmercompascuum, or we give it a name derived from the metabolism: Prickpantsshit, Screwsville. We go through the motions. As long as everything is quiet.

Wherever we go, though, we put an end to quiet; there is shouting and swearing in Dutch, shooting and beating if I don't watch out. We drive around in jeeps and a truck full of provisions, petrol and ammunition. Often we travel round for weeks, in radio contact with Kaukenau. It was right up Massuro's street; he was crazy about hunting and shot the monkeys out of the trees as he drove along. Of course I was more involved with him than with the other seven, and yet at the same time less. Something of the shame that we felt at grammar school because of our missed friendship persisted. I talked to him about different things than the others, about Holland, about nothing. Once he told me that he had four children, two on Java, one on Celebes and one on Halmahera.

When he had guard duty at night, he hummed between the tents or on the verandas of the log cabins that we had had the Papuans build for us here and there. He liked guard duty: he often let the person due to relieve him go on sleeping and took on his shift too. He was resting from something. His music was a big, shiny, trembling globe floating through the night between the tents. He hummed for hours with a throat like an organ and gazed at the mountains or the black jungle, where everything rustled and muttered and shrieked. Sometimes the Stone Age squatted at a respectful distance from him and listened intently.

For two years all went well.

The day that it went wrong we were in Poopjohn Knoll, a hamlet of twenty huts full of dwarves. That was last Sunday, 19 July 1955. We discovered it in May. It was on the edge of the jungle on the bank of the Titimoeka; we hadn't been able to make ourselves understood there.

When I was about eighteen, Gentlemen – in the war – I wanted to be a magician. I held my breath, tried to tie my legs in knots, concentrated on the mark left by a mosquito squashed on the wall, looked at the base of people's noses and read books on 'Personal Magnetism' and 'The Power of Thought'. From them I learned the exercise of recalling the previous day before going to sleep and rerunning it in quick tempo from the moment I woke up. That has become a habit of mine since. If I'm not too tired, I see the smallest finesses again, and even those that had escaped me during the day. In a certain sense I live twice, and the second time more acutely.

Not once, Gentlemen of Wassenaar, but at least ten times did I run that day in Poopjohn Knoll and the way there past me. I remember every branch we drove under, every stone in the foaming Titimoeka, every cry of the black gnomes. I know that that day, apart from an irregularity with Private Steiger, *nothing* special happened, *nothing* that differed from the other days, and in any case *nothing* to do with Massuro.

Because it was pouring with rain, we had left the hamlet of Oemigapa quite late that morning. It was a shower from the mountains; when it stopped it was splendid weather again for half an hour and at twelve o'clock the sun was pounding down on our heads once more. The troop were rather sluggish. We had been on patrol for two weeks and I had promised that Poopjohn Knoll would be our last port of call. Then it would be four days or so before we were back in Kaukenau. I was sitting in the second jeep next to Private Elsemoer: Massuro was slumped across the back seat with his carbine between his legs staring at the tops of the trees. We didn't talk much. I know what we said word for word, but it was of no importance. At about two o'clock I had Elsemoer leave the column for a moment to drive into the fields and have a chat with two kapaukos, who were dragging a dead kangaroo towards the swamps. At four o'clock we reached the Titimoeka and drove upstream along the shady strip between the jungle and the water, half overcome by the smell of rotting plants and leaves. Corporal Persijn in the first jeep discovered footprints in the mud and five of us headed into the pitch-black jungle, but in vain. It was as dense and impenetrable as a city.

Apart from that, nothing happened. As we bumped along, Massuro quickly turned onto his stomach and sent a crocodile to the bottom. At six thirty we drove into Poopjohn Knoll.

The councillor stood waiting for us at the head of the whole tribe. He was the village headman, a naked little chap three blocks of peat tall with a civilized fringe of beard and wild eyes; he had a splendid, yellow, pointed modesty gourd, which stood erect up to his nipples. At his temples he was growing bald in an intellectual way; I had told my men that the Germans called them 'councillor's corners' and from then on that was his name. I suspect him of leading a bunch of cannibals. 'Manowe?' I had asked him the last time. 'Manowe?' He began beaming all over his face; it turned out to be the only word he understood. At any rate with us he had to content himself with corned beef. With two other village bosses he tucked into the welcome meal; on our side it was Massuro and me. The others were busy with the bivouac, while the village looked on reflectively.

During that meal *nothing* out of the ordinary happened.

After the meal a couple of us crept under our mosquito nets, while I made contact with Kaukenau and reported. Later we lay down outside our tent and smoked and listened to the radio. Jakarta had a lecture on Malay poetry, but Sydney was playing dance music. Behind us on the other side of the splashing river everything grew higher and higher and the darkness changed into millions of crickets. When it had become almost completely dark, we put the lamps on and saw that we were surrounded by dwarves squatting motionless listening to the music. Persijn yelled at them, but they didn't go away. When he fired a brief burst from his Sten gun they scampered into the darkness in all directions.

And from now on I'll do it verbatim, Gentlemen, then you can judge for yourselves.

'Where's Steiger?' I asked Massuro. During the meal I had seen him smile and making eyes at a girl of about sixteen, with pretty breasts and a perfect round belly.

'He's in love.'

'Has he gone off?'

'Yes.'

'Did you *know*?'

'Yes.'

'It was your duty to tell me, for Christ's sake. Call him.'

'Steiger!' roared Massuro.

After a few seconds he answered from somewhere behind the vehicles.

'Stick it in your stinking trousers and come here! At once!' Excuse the language, Gentlemen, but that was how he said it, and that's how I'd tell a friend. He did yell in a fairly good-natured way, though. He was on vacation.

I got very worried. A little later Steiger stood before me sweating.

'Were you off again, Steiger?'

'Yes, Lieutenant. I thought you wouldn't notice, Lieutenant.'

'Where's the girl?'

'Ran off, Lieutenant.'

'Did anyone from the village see you go off with her?'

'No, Lieutenant. She was sitting alone under the truck listening to the music.'

That was a weight off my mind, but I was seething.

'You held your hand over her mouth, did you?'

'No, Lieutenant. She wanted it.'

'Hold your hands out.'

He held his hands out. In his left hand there were deep teeth marks.

'That . . . that always happens, Lieutenant.'

'From sucking your thumb, I suppose, eh? Stand there a bit with your hands out.'

I made Steiger stand with his hands out for a quarter of an hour. No one said anything more. The music played softly through the rushing of the river. The insects massed in a thick, crackling, dying layer around the lamps, so that the light lost half its strength. In the jungle on the other bank something began screaming, and suddenly stopped. After a quarter of an hour I rubbed his palm with my thumb. The impressions had virtually vanished.

'Double guard, tonight, Sergeant,' I said to Massuro.

'Right, Lieutenant.'

'Turn in, Steiger, and report to the captain in Kaukenau. You knew what can happen to you?'

'Yes, Lieutenant.'

'Bugger off.'

I could do it with Steiger; nobody liked him, apart from Massuro perhaps. Once he had gone and the others were getting on with their own stuff, Massuro came and sat next to me and silently smoked a fat cigar.

'I know more or less what you think,' I said after a while. 'But still you should have told me.'

'Never done anything like that yourself, Loonstijn?'

That was something new. For the first time in fifteen years he called me by my name; for two years I had been 'Lieutenant' to him. It moved me, probably I had admired him greatly in the past and I suddenly shared confidences.

If that had not been the case, I might have let him do as he wanted.

I felt that he was looking at me.

'You're used to the islands, Massuro,' I said. 'They eat rice there.'

He kept looking at me. I stared at the other bank. There was a rustling sound from the jungle, followed by a soft thud. A tree falling over after a thousand years.

'It happened to me somewhere on the Mimika; when I'd just got here. The same kind of girl as Steiger. I hadn't had anything for three months. What difference did it make – a kapauko girl in the ten-thousand-year-old wilderness ...? I held my hand over her mouth but halfway through she bit me, she started yelling and I had to let her go. When we came back a month later she was no longer in the village.' I looked into his eyes. 'They had slaughtered her and eaten her.'

I don't mind your knowing, Gentlemen of the BOZ. After what happened to Massuro, I have no interest in secrets of that kind. Perhaps your Bureau is entrusted less with investigating cases like that of Massuro – which can't be investigated – than with keeping an eye on those who were witnesses. Go ahead and discharge me, Gentlemen. I have no interest in that any more either.

Let's go on. Massuro asked: 'How do you know?'

I shrugged my shoulders and looked straight ahead. 'They were manowes.'

'She could just as well have been ill, or married off, or simply died.'

'It's possible.' I nodded. 'But Steiger will pay for it.'

There was still rustling and thudding in the jungle – trees that gave way under the weight that suddenly hung on them and dragged other trees with them in a panic of breaking nests and crushed animals.

I didn't know if they had eaten her. At any rate it was possible. But I had never been able to comprehend the thought fully and decide what it would mean to me. (Slaughtering, chopping to pieces, cooking, spices ...)

I looked at my watch – if I close my eyes, I can see the face again: three minutes past nine. On the roof of the truck glowed the cigarette of Persijn, who was on guard. Behind us a few times there was a clear ticking and at the same time a sobbing sound. Massuro sat enjoying his cigar like a farmer in the evening.

Nothing happened that was out of the ordinary.

I had the radio turned off, Massuro shared the double guard duty and gradually everyone went to bed. Only Elsemoer was sitting with his feet in the river some way off. Massuro wasn't a talker and I was in need of distraction.

'Mind the sand fleas, Elsemoer. Otherwise you'll be dancing tomorrow.'

'I'm not touching the bottom, Lieutenant.'

'He's thinking of his girl,' said Massuro. 'Perhaps she's being lured behind the cars in Overschie at this very moment.'

'Don't you want to come and join us, Elsemoer?'

'Sure, Lieutenant.'

Still 'Lieutenant'. He sat next to Massuro like a little boy shaking hands with the queen.

'I expect you were thinking of your girl, weren't you?'

'No, Lieutenant, I haven't got a girl. I was thinking about school.'

'About school? Did you know that the sergeant and I were classmates?'

He looked at us respectfully. I started laughing and offered him a cigarette.

'What were you thinking about, then?'

'Nothing special,' he said in embarrassment, 'as it happened . . . About land-grab.'

'Land-grab?'

As he told me I remembered. A game with knives. Each player is given a part of a square piece of flattened sand. In turns the knife is thrown into a neighbour's land and the piece that can be cut off is captured, provided it is in contact with the attacker's land. Anyone who can no longer stand on his piece of land has lost.

'What have we got to lose?' I said to Massuro. 'Shall the three of us play land-grab?'

Although in various respects I had authority over him (not only deriving from my rank), Massuro somehow still had the measure of me: through the tone in which he said or didn't say something, through a look, through the way he now stood up and opened his pocket knife. He had been through more than me, and experiences play a part in every word and gesture. They always carry more weight than innate qualities of intellect or character. Sometimes I had trouble giving him an order, and then I was surprised and embarrassed by the meticulousness with which he carried it out.

Like an industrious lackey, suffering somewhat from the caprices of his masters, Elsemoer dug the plants out of the ground and provided an immaculate playing area. He must be a guy who could not make love if a corner of the sheet were turned back. Meanwhile it had become pitch black, the lamp shone like a planet and designed against the edge of the jungle a most horrific spectacle of caves, animal heads, grottoes and temptations, which with the best will in the world none of us can be afraid of. So much for Dr Mondriaan's theory.

And now, Gentlemen, I must treat you to a short match report. After all, we are dealing with facts, aren't we?

Massuro threw first and immediately cut off three-quarters of my land. Elsemoer gave the impression of being faced with a difficult dilemma: if he annexed from Massuro, it might result in guard duty, if he annexed from me he was threatened with cancelling of leave. He restricted himself to a small bite of what Massuro had robbed from me, looking at me like a crafty Italian. I had bad luck; my knife repeatedly fell flat on the ground, which Elsemoer always accompanied with a sporting and regretful, 'Whoops!' Massuro flung his knife into the ground like toreador and ate up everything around and kept demanding that we demonstrate that we could still stand on our piece. But, going pale with fright Elsemoer captured almost all of his territory, so that Massuro could only keep upright on the toes of one foot.

I was having a great time. Once Massuro nodded in the direction of the village and I saw the ghost of the councillor. All alone, he was crouching by the river and watching the white men stabbing his land to death with knives and jollity. I didn't like it and I called to Persijn to do something about it. Two shots rang out and immediately he had disappeared.

Massuro won again. Without any prior agreement Elsemoer and I allied ourselves against him, but suddenly Elsemoer was eliminated: after a brilliant throw by Massuro he didn't have a single square centimetre left. With a gesture acknowledging he had met his match and a sigh of relief, he sat down. I stole a small amount from Massuro and then he raised his hand with the knife far behind his back ready to eliminate me too in one throw.

But his arm remained immobile and the knife fell behind him with its point in the ground, outside the playing area. His eyes were becoming larger and larger.

'I can't get my arm down again,' he said.

I stared at him. Above us I heard the deep drone of a rhinoceros bird flying overhead.

It was as if I was dreaming. I went over to him and felt his arm. It was as if there were no joint in it.

'Sit down,' I said.

Meekly Massuro sat down on the land-grab area, right across all the boundaries, arm raised. I began cautiously pulling at it and slowly it gave way, as if he were tensing all his muscles. He had to support his other arm on the ground.

'Pain?'

'No.'

Elsemoer sat watching open-mouthed. Finally the arm was lowered.

'Can you move it?'

He moved it, his fingers too; I saw that it took him a lot of effort. He contemplated it with a worried look.

'Do you have any problems with rheumatism in that arm?'

'No . . . never have.' He was upset, so badly that it surprised me. Suddenly he started shouting at Elsemoer: 'You should have someone put a different mug on your head!'

I heard a sound in his voice that I had never heard before. It was no longer a vacation voice. Elsemoer jumped up in alarm, saluted and disappeared.

'Go and get yourself some sleep,' I said, God knows why. 'I'll take over your guard duty.'

It surprised me that he accepted. (Yes, that was the weirdest thing of all: that he accepted!) Without a word he got up and walked woodenly to our tent. His right arm hung stiffly downwards, but I saw that the left arm was not moving either and that his knees were as stiff as those of a cavalry officer.

'Tomorrow it will be over,' I managed to say.

As long as you know that I am writing with little or no conviction. With what conviction is one supposed to write about an avalanche? One can write about *causes* with conviction: how it could happen, what was done to prevent it. The avalanche itself is just *stupid*, something we have nothing to do with because we cannot defend ourselves against it. And if we realize that there weren't even any causes? Then there's nothing left of us, Gentlemen in Room 3, *nothing at all*.

Massuro slept all night like a log, with his clothes on. I had done the last guard duty with Kranenburg and we had talked about the stars, but in the background there was the constant worry of Massuro. Despite Steiger, everything had remained calm in the village. When I shook Massuro awake at six thirty, I immediately felt panic in my hands: *a human being didn't weigh this much*! I pulled him up, it was like pulling a horse up, a rhinoceros, but the consciousness did not get any further than my hands. Wide-eyed, he stood in the tent wobbling like a robot from one leg to the other. It was as if he didn't see me. He wobbled on stiff legs outside, where the men were washing, and blinked at the sunlight. Beneath my feet pounded the weight of his body. He moved his hand to his face like a very heavy dumbbell, burped and closed his eyes . . .

I felt as if my feet were in my head and my head in my shoes. For a number of seconds I stared at his back. Suddenly it dawned on me how heavy he had been. *Impossibly* heavy. I began to swallow, at least ten times, and finally got out the words:

'Sergeant . . . come in the tent for a moment.'

He looked at me and wobbled back. In the tent I stood opposite him; my hands were trembling.

'Listen, Massuro, you're ill, you hear, you're ill. We'll strike camp at once and make sure we get to Kaukenau as soon as possible.'

He looked at me and said nothing.

'Do you understand me, Massuro?'

'Yes.'

'We'll strike camp right away.'

I looked at him for a moment longer and then left him where he was. Outside I called the men together and said as calmly as I could:

'Guys ... the sergeant is sick. Something to do with his joints ... and with his weight ... I don't know what it is, but it's something dreadful. If we make sure we get to the valley before dark, we can drive through the night and be in Kaukenau by tomorrow afternoon. We'll leave everything behind and take the route via Oegei. We'll leave at once.'

They ran to the tents and I stood where I was. I daren't go back to Massuro. I went to the radio operator, quickly called Kaukenau and told them briefly that Massuro had been struck down by an unknown disease and that we were on our way. I had the captain on the line; he was quite sceptical and asked for more details, but I told the radio operator to create some interference and turned off the transmitter.

I knew it wasn't a disease. Growing heavier isn't a disease. I wanted to get to Kaukenau to be among people, as if I believed that something like this could not persist with other people around.

Ten minutes later we were off. I had no time for the councillor and greeted him from my jeep. The whole tribe was present again with children on backs and breasts. The councillor nodded and held onto his gourd with a grin.

I sat at the back, with Elsemoer next to Massuro. Massuro sitting straight, without turning his head an inch to the left or right. Elsemoer was at the wheel looking as if he was taking his driving test. We did not talk. I did not dare say a word. I had to look at the back of Massuro's head the whole time; I was as scared as I had ever been, and yet ... I couldn't take it on board. Not even a hundredth part. And I never will. Just imagine that in Amsterdam the statue of General van Heutz steps off its pedestal and starts talking to you about Aceh. You'll never manage to take it on board.

At twelve o'clock I ordered a stop so we could eat something.

While everyone got out, I went forward sweating to look at
Massuro. He had blotches under his skin all over his face.

'How do you feel now, Massuro?'

He looked glassily into my eyes.

'I can't feel a thing.'

'Are you hurting anywhere?'

He shook his head almost imperceptibly.

'Don't you want to get out for bit?'

He closed his eyes.

'Just leave me.'

Suddenly I grabbed him and shook his shoulders – an elephant, a car.

'*Massuro, what's wrong with you?*'

He panted and his teeth began to chatter.

My head was spinning. He did not want to eat. I went to get
something for myself at the truck, where the men were sitting
on the ground among empty tins. They looked at me but didn't
ask any questions. I was given my portion and walked a little
way into the dry bush, where I sat down to eat. The vehicles
were empty and parked behind each other, as if they would be
there for ever. In the second one was Massuro's motionless
body. I tried to realize that something impossible was happening, but that was as difficult as imagining that the girl Mimika
had been eaten – though that was still within the realm of possibility. I looked at the sky, too. Something incomprehensible
was at work in Massuro.

We drove on, hour after hour, endlessly. I looked constantly
at Massuro: a heavy neck covered in black hair, a square head.
I had put his carbine next to me. Was I frightened he would
start shooting? We drove fast and his body bobbed up and
down like a tree trunk. I decided to continue on to Screwsville,
where we had a bungalow and could have a hot meal. It was
like a journey from here to the moon; my brain had long since
stopped functioning, it wasn't something for brains, it was stupid, stupid as a stone. We arrived at seven thirty and then it
was as if the time had flown. The village headman came
towards our jeep cackling exuberantly, looking forward to the
greeting meal. I brushed him away and said that we had

someone seriously ill with us. Walking backwards in alarm he
shrank away; the whole tribe started to walk backwards. I
gritted my teeth and started helping Massuro out of the jeep.
As soon as I felt him, I knew that he had got much heavier. The
men looked on in silence. A step at a time we walked to the log
cabin. The steps of the stairs creaked and bent under his
weight. I pushed the door open; a fat toad slipped away. With
both arms around him I lowered him on to one of the rough
wooden chairs. He was completely unable to bend his knees.
Once he was sitting, the chair collapsed under him and he hit
the ground with a shuddering thud.

He started crying.

'*Massuro*,' I whispered.

I was at a loss. I ran to the doorway and started shouting
that we had to move on, that there was no time to cook. The
men must have heard the crash; they sat motionless halfway
out of the vehicles.

I knelt by Massuro. He sat sobbing like a child. Apart from
the blotches on his face there was nothing special about his
appearance, but he must have weighed at least three hundred
kilos.

'What's happening to me?' he wept.

'Christ, Massuro; Christ, Massuro!'

I held him tight with both hands. Fat tears trickled down his
cheeks.

'What the hell is happening to me, Loonstijn? I feel stiffer
and heavier all the time. What have I done?'

'Maybe we'll be in Kaukenau by tomorrow morning, and
you'll get treatment straight away! In the hospital they'll . . .' I
couldn't say any more. 'Hang on, Massuro,' I whispered. 'Lie
down.'

He was doomed and he knew and I knew. He allowed himself meekly to be laid back by me; it was as if I was pushing a
wagon along rails. There was a sweet woody smell in the dusky
hut. If I pushed too fast his legs went up in the air with the
weight of a piano. Suddenly I started crying too. Massuro
looked up at me wide-eyed.

'It's not possible for something like this to happen . . .' he said.

I shook my head in despair.

'No, Massuro, it's not possible.'

'I'm so tired.'

He closed his eyes, and his chest moved heavily up and down. The blotches on his face were clearer than in the afternoon, they came out all over from under his skin as if they were going to break through it. His hands were also full of them. To Kaukenau! To where there were people!

'I can scarcely breathe any more,' he groaned. 'It's like there's a Roman sitting on my chest.'

A *Roman*!

God in heaven, I thought, help Massuro. He hasn't done anything. He's got so heavy a chair collapses under him. There's a Roman sitting on his chest.

But what I should have liked to do was shoot him and bury him on the spot, as deep as I could. Persijn, Elsemoer, Steiger, Kranenburg, they would be as silent as the grave, that much is certain. They would have let him disappear from their thoughts, like a splinter from their flesh.

And now you wet your lips and shift about in your chairs, Gentlemen of Dept. A? Now will come the revelations, you think. Whispered sobbing in my ear! There were none. No confessions. No confession. Nothing. He just lay crying on the floor, growing heavier and heavier and not knowing what was happening to him. Nor did his spirit fly from him in a grandiose flight – far from it. What is the spirit? Sometimes a Napoleon, whose dream becomes reality and engulfs the whole of Europe, and as it slowly recedes leaves behind temporary signs over the whole continent: palaces, obelisks, triumphal arches, dead men, legislation, Holy Alliances and surnames. But mostly a hat that we wear on our heads against the draught; if we meet a woman we take it off politely.

Kranenburg came in shyly with some tins. Massuro still did not want to eat; I wouldn't be able to either. I had them put in the jeep and called Persijn. When he appeared in the doorway and looked in my eyes, I knew that he would make sure that no one said anything if I had killed Massuro.

'Help me with the sergeant, Persijn. Then we'll go on.'

He stopped for a moment. Then he came. Neither of us are wimps, but this was too much. Lips trembling, Massuro looked at our faces as they went red. Groaning, breathless, we finally got him upright. Then the floor collapsed underneath him with an ear-shattering crash between the two of us. Somewhere around our knees he started screaming with a sound the jungle had never heard, smaller than a pygmy, with the splintered planks around his waist. A moment later Persijn brought the butt of his revolver on the crown of the screaming head. It was suddenly quiet; the head did not slump sideways.

I looked in bewilderment at Persijn. My God, Gentlemen! It was as if I had been on an endless journey through France, Burgundy, Trier, Cluny, for the few seconds that that screaming lasted. A vision, a fantastic vision that wasn't connected with anything unless it was via God knows what underground connections. I saw a crowd stretching as far as the eye could see on the square at Reims at the foot of the cathedral, cheering at the execution of a tall blond man in a gold-embroidered cloak, while trumpeters with multicoloured emblems on their chests blew the azure sky endlessly high and empty. I saw a pope heading over the Alps to Germany in the middle of a small caravan, and in the north a king with his family stumbled towards him barefoot through the snow – and above the head of the pope the king's voice floated and said, 'You, Hildebrand, no longer pope but the false monk! I, Henry, king by the grace of God, with all my bishops I say unto you: Descend from the throne, descend from the throne, thou man accursed through all the ages!' And in Loches I saw how a French king weeping and wringing his hands, had a wood cut down, where the news of his young son's death had reached him. Kings, kings tapering streets full of the working of iron on iron, iron on copper, bronze on silver, the churches full of rotting and groaning beggars, trumpets, and in dense gold-brown crowds of common people there are knights on horseback with pieces of meat in their mouths. I saw that all those European lands looked different from now, more fairy-tale-like, warmer, olive green, with weird mouse-grey rocks that grew out of the ground between the houses, growing larger and shrivelling away; trees were slim and light-feathered, idols tumbled from their pedestals in arcs and sometimes an old man walked the same way three times, ten metres at a time, without seeing himself. The third time he met Jesus. I kept seeing cripples from behind, bent over their crutches disappearing behind a hill on their way to the town. And everything, everything, was built up; beyond an olive-green wood rose eight deserted sky-scrapers. It was a different *space*, not just a different time in Massuro's screaming – impossible to fathom. There were rocks that no longer exist, without there being a geological reason.

It must have risen from the depths of my spine. I felt as if I had died. New Guinea. From Persijn I looked at Massuro again. He was unconscious. Four of us pulled him out of the floor and carried him to the truck in silence. Fifty metres away the kapaukos were pressed together and were leaping and barking like monkeys. They must have heard the screaming – but perhaps something else had got into their heads, something for which they had a special organ that made them leap and bark in a different world.

Oh friend, we know as little about life as a new-born baby knows about a woman. If we turn round and get to see a little more, we are immediately brought to our knees.

That night I sat next to Massuro in the pitch-black truck, a rearing block of darkness in a world of roaring engines. I could have switched on a light, but something stopped me. (What stopped me? Paracelsus's fur hat. The sun of Austerlitz.) Massuro became so heavy that he no longer flew in the air when we drove over a stone or through a pothole; I heard no more. I was squatting against the back of the cab and was flung from left to right. My eyes had slid out of their sockets and were hanging in every corner and themselves became darkness. Once Massuro said something, for the last time; perhaps he had been conscious for a long time.

'Loonstijn? . . . Are you there? . . . Just lay me down in the bush, and then they can break their teeth on me.'

It was the darkness that spoke, with a voice like one down a phone line, without depth, one-dimensional. I didn't answer. He was finished – and so was I. Or was it only now beginning? A new kind of human being . . . For the future: calm without hope, suspicious of everything. I was in the complete darkness of the truck; I thought of nothing; that night the darkness became my body.

The rest you know. The following morning when Dr Mondriaan tried to stick his lancet into Massuro for the post-mortem (on the ground, the table would not have supported his weight), the tip broke off. What was left over from his skin he scraped away, a dry, leathery membrane. Massuro had turned to stone. From head to toe, inside and outside. A kind of granite, from light grey to pink. With black specks and dashes like letters. He was sawn open in a native stone works; a piece of grit flew into my eye so that for hours the tears ran down my cheeks. Everyone, officers, doctors, clustered round the two halves of Massuro. Around the fresh cut there was a blue mirror effect. His intestines were preserved in the stone like rare fossils.

'Atrocities?' asked Dr Mondriaan with his dried-out lips.

How well I understood this man!

'Not under my command.'

'But earlier, perhaps. In forty-eight . . . on Celebes?'

'Turned to stone from atrocities, Doctor? Who would still be made of flesh and blood in that case?'

'Not from atrocities – from remorse. A kind of process, a remorse that has stayed below the threshold of consciousness. A particular discharge that was triggered, chemical inversions, a kind of petrifying secretion.'

'Is that scientifically justified, Dr Mondriaan?'

It was as if he acquired a goatee beard and I could smell the plush.

'Everything is possible! Science knows nothing about the area where mind and body communicate, nothing! No man's land. An area as big as . . . the whole of New Guinea! We know nothing about it, nothing.'

But he was wrong. Two and two haven't made four for a long

time. The traffic rolls along the road. A woman finds her man
at the window with his chair collapsed under him, turned into
a statue. In the cities the jungle becomes denser and denser and
the sky is emptier than ever. There are occasional prints of
human feet on the earth, but in the space above the wind blows.
I excused Steiger from his punishment.

Kaukenau, 26 July 1955, Lieutenant K. Loonstijn
New Guinea Sect. G III,
5th Battalion 124 Infantry Regiment
No. 121370

Translated by Paul Vincent

15

JAN WOLKERS

Feathered Friends

Gevederde vrienden

Herbert stands in front of the steamed-up window of his apartment on the fifth, and top, floor. His hands in his dressing-gown pockets, he listens to the rushing in his ears.

I'm in a bit of a state, he thinks. I'm a doomed man, though it may take another ten years. Ten more years with Liesbeth. Horror! I'm perspiring as if I have a fever, yet I haven't one.

He digs his nails into the palms of his clammy hands. The only thing he sees through the foggy window is the Belisha beacon on the opposite side of the road. As if he's standing on a tall mountain and an orange full moon, having just risen above the horizon, is being hidden from view, time and again, by fast-moving clouds. Like he has seen in films run at a higher speed. But the flickering, on–off, is too regular and disturbs the illusion. He takes his hand from his pocket and, fingers slightly apart, he draws long, parallel curves down the moist honeycomb, as though he's caressing a woman's long hair. The Belisha ends up on a post of Liquorice Allsorts; the traffic island with its yellow bollards, poisonous aniline-blue lights burning within, becomes visible. Of the trees in the park only the trunks can be seen. The tops have been devoured by the mist insects. The houses are wrapped in damp sheets. A neon advertising sign loses its purchasing power and acquires a lofty meaning. A red cross on waves of mist. Herbert puts his hand back in his pocket when the door opens behind him. Liesbeth shuffles into the room. She sighs and pokes the fire.

'You've left the vent open too long,' she says. 'The stove's got red cheeks.'

She's now standing by the stove, bent over. Herbert thinks, I should walk up to her and give her squat bottom a shove. A wee taste of purgatory. But she'd scream the place down. I'm wearing my slippers. Before my shoes were on and I was out through the door, the neighbours would be here already.

'Mind you don't go drawing on the windows, Herbert. Once they've dried, I can barely get them clean again. You might wash them for me.'

'I'm not washing anything. I just want to have enough of a view. Let the moisture evaporate: good for the plants.'

'But it's bad for the furniture; it makes them warp, Herbert. Just bear that in mind, would you? Peter, Peterkin! Come here, lad, come!'

That hairy predator approaches to comfort her after the defeat I've inflicted on her, he thinks.

He hears the cat's paws tap the lino. It jumps up at her and climbs up her pinny. She croons over it as over a newborn babe.

Barren womb, yieldless acre, he thinks. Why didn't your womb open itself up to me twenty years ago? Why were you like a pollarded willow that fails to sprout in spring? I would have had a daughter of twenty by now. The scent of young female flesh in the house. Tunes being hummed, the tripping of high heels, rouge to lend some colour still to my old age. Let's think, now let's think clearly.

Herbert leans his torso forward so his head rests against the cold, damp window.

Ah, that's wonderful! I'm in Rome, sitting on a terrace: a hot summer's afternoon. The tarmac's billowing because of the heat. I order a glass of beer, icy cold. I press the glass to my forehead. The cold makes its way through my brain down to my backbone. What was it again I wanted to think about? Ah, yes: why do men always murder their wives in a rage while the balance of their minds is disturbed? Why not a trip to Austria? A hearty walk, a mountain trek? D'you hear that yodeller in the valley over there, Liesbeth? Look, there he is! If I go and stand on this rocky promontory, I can see him sitting there. Where, Herbert? I don't see or hear him. Bend over a bit more! Look, he's sitting there surrounded by columbine, further down the valley. Then a goodly poke with the walking stick and those two hundred pounds souring my existence tumble out of my life.

He suddenly gives a start because of the shrill squeal of tram brakes. It sounds like the screaming of a hare being jumped by a stoat. He looks down. The tram moves off slowly. Then, all of a sudden, there's a woman lying on the traffic island. The parts of her lower legs dangling beyond the kerb are at an angle of almost ninety degrees to the parts on the traffic island. It is as if her instep reaches a tremendous way up, or her knee joint has slid down. Blood runs along the edge of the traffic island towards the rails. The tram halts, grindingly. A conductor runs to the motionless body, bends over it. He shouts something to the driver, steps on to the pavement and enters a shop.

He's going to ring the paramedics, Herbert thinks. Perfectly pointless. Why not quietly leave her to bleed to death? Why must her husband drag out his twilight years behind a wheelchair?

People abandon cars, bicycles, prams, and hurry to the fateful spot. They surround the victim the way carrion beetles do the cadaver of a mole.

Didn't I hear death-watch beetles in the bars of the bed this morning? So it was inescapable. Look: the windows are weeping.

Herbert follows the drops that jerkily draw vertical lines among the curves. Then he turns round.

'Can you see, Liesbeth, what's on that piece of paper in the milkman's window? Your eyes are better than mine. Might even be a special offer.'

Liesbeth sets the cat down on the chair and totters over to the window. Herbert walks to the stove and holds his hands above it in the rising warmth.

Wonderful, those hot water springs in Iceland, he thinks. Would the winter be a severe one? The signs are favourable. Would it be suspect to buy a refrigerator at the beginning of winter? Wouldn't it rouse suspicion? Shucks: there are people who buy a camping tent in January. Didn't I myself once stand beside a girl buying a bathing costume when it was twenty degrees below? But there are indoor swimming pools, of course. And aren't there any houses where the heat's tropical in winter? I can't hear anything by the window yet. Might the mortal ... ehm, might the remaining mother (in-law, grand and great-grand) have been carted off already? That'd be a pity. Haven't heard the siren yet, for that matter. Or are there so many people standing around now that it's as though someone is offering something for sale, just like that, right out in the street?

I must keep a grip on myself, Liesbeth thinks, and with both hands she presses her stomach. There isn't even a piece of paper in the window: he spares me nothing. The blood! She must be draining dry.

She feels the contents of her stomach rise. Quickly, she walks to the door.

'And could you read what was there?' Herbert asks.

He hears the toilet seat being raised with a bang.

A coarse brain but an oversensitive stomach, he thinks.

A siren sounds outside. He walks to the window. A cream-coloured car stops at the traffic island. Hurriedly, two men jump out, pull a stretcher from the back of the car and set it down beside the body. Then they pick it up and put it on the stretcher. The left foot, bobbing up and down, perpendicular in its stocking, ends up next to the stretcher. One of the men shoves it back on with his foot.

Liesbeth comes in again.

'It's busy in the street,' Herbert says.

'That's what I saw too, just now. There seems to have been an accident. I couldn't see.'

'Best thing, too,' Herbert replies as he draws a little landscape with a windmill in the top corner of the window. 'You've got enough of a weak stomach as it is. You'd be upset for days. Assuming it was an accident, then it was caused by the tram. Not a pretty sight at all. Those iron wheels shear the lot off, clean. I once ... Hey, why are you leaving the room in such a hurry?'

Retching, Liesbeth runs to the toilet.

Dinner-for-one this evening, Herbert thinks, rubbing his hands. I'll put the newspaper behind my plate, up against the condiment set. A feast!

When Herbert has reached the top of the stairs, the door to his apartment opens. Liesbeth steps out into the hall.

'Oh, you shouldn't have, Herbert,' she says, ticking him off.

'What shouldn't I have?' Herbert asks, leering with screwed-up eyes at the red face.

'Such a big one, far too much space for a small family.'

'Oh, the fridge – has the fridge arrived? I thought it'd take them hours. Hoisting it up and so on.'

'No, they managed it the ordinary way, up the stairs. But such a big one, Herbert; it really is too much.'

'What rot – this is no ordinary birthday: you turned fifty today. Half a century.'

Too many, he adds in his mind, half a century too many.

'Come on, show me,' he says cheerfully.

He follows her to the kitchen.

'It's a whopper indeed,' he says, once he's standing in the kitchen in front of the gleaming white enamel. 'It looked much smaller in the shop.'

What a magnificent sight, he thinks, the polar ice cap seen from a stratospheric aircraft. It gleams and glistens in the polar light. Now for an axe, and we can start on conservation.

'You would have done better to wait till summer, Herbert; it's cold enough here now.'

'That's just why it's so practical *now*. You won't have to turn down the heating in the evening any more 'cause otherwise your food'll go off. And no waiting for hours in the morning until it's warmed up a bit here. Just take a look,' he says cheerfully, pulling the door of the fridge wide open. 'Just you take a look: the space! I bet you could go and sit in it in summer, when it's hot.'

'Now you really are exaggerating, Herbert,' Liesbeth says, estimating its volume by eye.

'Exaggerate? I never exaggerate.'

With a clatter, he removes the horizontal aluminium racks.

'I think you could take the cat in with you too. No, no kidding: you try it, Liesbeth. My lumbago's giving me gip.'

Blood, blood, he thinks, I'll bring it about without spilling blood. The heavens regard me with favour. There'll be no writing on the wall.

'Well, all right then, 'cause it's my birthday,' Liesbeth says, laughing. 'But it's a strange experiment.'

She sets her bottom down on the floor of the fridge, wraps her arms round her drawn-up knees and swivels herself inside.

'Enduring the worst heat of August would be easier than sitting in this position, I think.'

With a powerful sweep, Herbert throws the door shut. Then he puts the plug in the socket.

I can hear her shouting but I can't make out what she's saying, he thinks.

He walks to the living room, switches on the radio and sits down in the tub chair beside it. Circumspectly, he takes a cigar from the cigar case, licks the outer leaf and presses it down. He twiddles the radio until a nice little tune breezes into the room. From the blue banks of cloud that linger in the middle of the room, the temptations of a life of freedom drift towards him. They spin in the surf of his imagination. He gives them girls' names and those of flowers.

There'll be ice flowers on her pupils; she'll be sitting there, hunched up like the tree mummies of Central American Indians. I could have a hole made in the bottom of my car with a broad pipe through it, reaching down to the road. Then, one rainy day, I put her in the back. On the bumpy rural roads, I shove her down the pipe, head first, so that her hair rests on the cobbles. And then I drive about until there's nothing left but the soles of her feet. I won't take off her glasses. But I won't even be able to straighten her out. She'll have wriggled her way into the most impossible angles. She always did. I'll avail myself of other means to get rid of her, as it happens. Now won't I just, you white-shirts you?

Walking over to the window, he addresses the seagulls diving down into the street, after bread being thrown from a window somewhere.

'I'll be spoiling you, lads! For the time being, your hungry beaks won't be eating dry bread any more: they'll be red with all the raw.'

A grand moment, Herbert thinks, eye to eye with the deep-freeze princess. A fortnight past already: she'll be feeling the cold.

He pulls open the door of the fridge. With a jump, daylight takes possession of polar night. Liesbeth still sits there exactly the way he last saw her. Her hands rest calmly on her tummy, between the hillocks of her bosom and her thighs. Her glasses are covered in a thin, matt layer of ice as though, with its fragile wings, a butterfly seeks to protect her eyes from the cold. Icicles formed by the condensing water, with pointed fingers probe the hoar-frosted shrubbery of her hair. Her mouth hangs open. The pink tongue of land lies speechless, riveted down in the bitter ice of the inland sea of her oral cavity. An elegantly curved little rod of ice runs from her bottom lip to the remnants of food on her chest, as though her last thoughts had been of the fountains of Italy.

Herbert bends forward and looks intently at the food remnants.

Not such a peaceful death as first it had seemed from the resignedly folded hands on the stomach, he thinks. Perhaps that was a whim of the last death throes. Let's take a peek at the eyes.

Carefully, he grips the frame between the lenses. With his fingertips he stirs the cold marble of her forehead and the bridge of her nose. The cold spreads up to his wrists. He has to apply force for a moment in order to free the spectacles. Then he sees what the butterfly was trying to spare him. Her eyes have bulged out so far that, Herbert suspects, the lenses have prevented them from drooping even further. They hang down over the bottom eyelids like infertile, greenish owl's eggs that have been cast out from the red and yellow veined nest of the eye sockets. In blind suspicion, the pupils stare down sideways into the remnants of food. When Herbert replaces the specs, those pupils stare through them like the eyes of a sea monster through the steamed-up pane of an aquarium. He staggers in front of the fridge.

I'm overcome by the cold, he thinks. I must have a drink. I must raise my glass to this memorable fact.

He goes to the living room; he pours himself a glass of genever, warms himself in front of the fire. The liquor warms him all the way down to his digestive tract.

'Now what have we got?' he mutters, taking a sip from the glass at each object he mentions. 'A sharp little cleaver for between the joints, a saw for the bones, a razor-sharp knife for flesh and tendons, a chopping board, plastic sheeting, a nutmeg mill. And a glass for the eyes.'

Triumphantly, he raises the glass aloft. Then he goes to the kitchen, spreads a sheet of plastic in front of the refrigerator and fetches the tools from the cabinet. He goes down on his knees in front of the fridge and tries to turn Liesbeth ninety degrees by her ankles, something he only succeeds in after a great deal of effort, for she is frozen to the sides of the fridge in some places. Then he drags her forward so her lower body ends up resting on the plastic.

To be pruned as soon as possible, he thinks, flipping her shoes from her feet with the cleaver. I'll try to get rid of a leg today.

With an old-fashioned razor he draws a furrow in her right leg, exactly along the seam of her stocking, which he peals from her leg like bark. Then he cuts her clothes away at the hip, the imprint of them visible on her skin as if she is wrapped in thin tarlatan. The flesh is hard and cuts easily. Not without anatomical insight, he severs the leg from the torso at the hip joint, returns the body in the same position to the fridge and closes the door. Then he lets his knife sink deep into the fluvial landscape of her varicose veins and begins to cut off long strips of flesh. The knife makes a sound like skates on mirror-finish ice. When he has divested the thigh and shin bones of flesh, he strikes the foot off with his cleaver. He then begins to cut the long strips of flesh carefully into little cubes he tosses into a large, shallow tray.

The feet are too complicated to bone for my liking. I can simply put them out by the dustbins tomorrow. Perhaps it would be better, however, if I was first to fit them with the antique lace-up bootees. Let's chop things up as small as possible. They're guzzlers; they'll polish things off as they are, too.

With a swing, he lets the cleaver come down on the bunions. The toes hop forward, away from the foot, like small, pale frogs. Purple splinters rain down on the plastic.

I used to sit in the garden like this, Herbert thinks, wiping the sweat from his forehead. The purple flowers of the lilac dropping around me. In front of me in the loose sand were corks in a long row, wriggling insects pinned to them. I let down a woollen thread into a bottle of petrol and laid that across the caterpillars, beetles and locusts. Then I lit both ends. Once the flames met, the insects would be lying there with burnt-off legs and wings. Of some, the body had split open like a roast chestnut. Thick, white goo bulged out. You're worse than Nero, my father said, and he raised blisters on my bottom. You're just like your uncle Louis; he's a bad'un too. Uncle Louis! When there was just a butt left of his cigar, he would walk out into the garden with it. He would stay and wait by the balsam at the back of the garden until a bumble bee came to fetch honey from a flower. Then he'd tap the ash from the butt, suck it so it got a fiery dome at the tip, and put it in the calyx. Can you hear him buzz, little Herbert? he would ask. D'you know what he's saying? He's saying the Lord's Prayer. Soon, when Uncle Louis was staying with us, moist brown cigar butts would be sticking up from all the pink calyxes of the balsam, like arses just about to relieve themselves. Uncle Louis, a sensitive man, stimulating his conscience with the annihilation of little insects, Herbert thinks, touched.

'I've become a big game hunter,' he mutters.

He roots with the cleaver in the splintered heel bone. Then he takes up the board and slides the shattered foot on top of the meat in the tray.

That'll do: they'll devour the chaff with the wheat; they'll make no bones about it.

He takes the tray and walks with it to the hall. He sets it down there, takes out a stepladder and puts it underneath the hatch in the ceiling. He mounts the steps carefully, undoes the hooks and pushes the hatch open. Shrieking, seagulls fly up from the edge of the roof when suddenly his head appears above the antediluvian landscape of tar and shingle.

No one can see a thing here, he thinks: there are no taller buildings in the vicinity.

He goes down, takes the tray of meat and, holding it above his head, he climbs back up. Sliding it across the shingle, he shoves the tray a little further away from the hatch, out on to the roof.

If the dead can still feel anything, she must assume she'll share in the Kingdom of Heaven limb by limb. Come on then, lads, come on! Just you tuck in. Here lies the manna of twenty years' unhappy married life.

Herbert moves down a step, pulls the hatch up over the edge and, through a crack, he watches the seagulls who continue to sit motionless on the edge of the roof in the red light of the setting sun hanging between dark swordfish clouds above the grimy city.

Herbert is sitting on the floor in the kitchen. Round slices of bone are lying around him on the plastic. The electric nutmeg mill whirs beside him.

Liesbeth has no relatives any more, he thinks. Friends and acquaintances have stayed away for years already, driven away by the stale smell she spread. Which leaves the neighbours. When do I actually see the neighbours? Never, surely. Liesbeth hasn't been out in months. Even the shopkeepers no longer ask after her. It'll take years before anyone hits on the idea of asking me how she is. And I will have forgotten it myself by then; my mind'll be a blank. Perhaps, should a seagull be flying over, I'll point up above. And they will say: Oh, she's passed away in peace, you mean. Yes, passed away in peace, I'll then reply – in ice-cold peace.

He presses the button on the side of the mill and so silences it. He removes its plastic lid and puts a disc of thigh bone inside. Then he pulls out the drawer at the bottom, throws the bone, ground to powder, in a pan and switches the mill back on. He picks up the pan, fetches a spoon from the drawer and walks to the living room. He puts a chair in front of the stove, sits down on it with the pan clamped between his thighs and he opens the little door of the stove. Slowly, Herbert stirs the bone meal, makes little mounds and draws Arabic characters in it. In the flickering firelight, it's just as though there's life in it, as if it's a pan full of little, yellow spiders. Then, a spoonful at a time, he sprinkles the meal on to the fire.

It's a bit damp, he thinks. But I could hardly dry it first, now could I?

It emanates sulphur-like fumes, with poisonous blue flames coursing through. He flings the little door shut. The peaceful scent of a village smithy settles in the room.

Herbert wakes up in the morning with the smell of burnt horn in his nostrils.

Ah yes, the bone, he thinks. I was busy till ever so late, yesterday. But I'm rid of the lot. Air the place first in a minute, and then take a peek at what the ash looks like.

He raises his right leg so the cold air streaming in at the foot end wakes his body, and he looks at the bedside table.

'Such a liberation,' he says, yawning. 'Only one glass with dentures.'

Then, in a single sweep, he flings the blankets aside and jumps out of bed. He walks over to the window and draws back the curtains. It's snowing. He stands there ill at ease in the marble light, looks up at the snowflakes floating down like grey ash, to be cleansed only in contrast with the houses opposite.

The meat, he suddenly thinks with a shock, the meat has been snowed under.

He walks quickly to the hall and climbs the steps. When his head emerges above the edge of the hatch, the light blinds him. On top of his head, he feels the chill kisses of the snowflakes. In front of him is the tray. Empty. There's a thin layer of snow on the bottom, tinged pale pink by the blood that has stayed behind on the bottom as though it had stood beneath a flowering sweetbriar. It fills him with shame, shame without remorse. When he removes the tray, a reproachful dark square of tar and shingle remains like a freshly dug grave in the snow.

In the kitchen, he puts the tray in the sink and rinses out the snow and blood with hot water. A few toenails stay behind on

the grid above the plughole. The hungry birds have left no
more than that.

Let's not get sentimental now, he thinks, picking up the
nails and tossing them among the wet tea leaves in the enamel
sink tidy. Raskolnikov was a worthless character. Precisely
because of his weakness, his conscience. Or perhaps one is
allowed to have a conscience but only regarding oneself ... Is
a conscience not the most covert of stimulants? The outside
world, however, must notice nothing of it.

Rubbing his wrists together, he walks over to the refrigerator and draws it open. He halts, rigid with fright. Liesbeth's
sitting just the way he set her down there yesterday, but her
glasses no longer cover her eyes: she's holding them in her right
hand. In a panic, he runs to the door. It's shut; it's even bolted.
Then he walks to the back room and tests the balcony doors.

I must have done it myself, he thinks. I've been sleepwalk-
ing. But no, I surely would have known in that case. I always
know, don't I, when I've been up in the night and what I did
then?

But now he remembers it was Liesbeth who always told him.
She would follow me with a wet floor cloth which she put in
front of my feet. But I would always step over it. And she'd be
picking it up and laying it down in front of me again. Just like
a king being received in state. Where's the cat: where's Peter?

Nervously he goes through the house, searches all the cupboards, but he cannot find the creature anywhere.

Riddles at every turn in this place. Cats disappear, women
disappear, I walk the house at night, my arms stretched out in
front of me like a blind man. Dangerous, too! Tonight I'll tie
myself down to the bed bars. No, I might have an unlucky fall
in that case. Then, suddenly, a story from the Old Testament
pops into his mind. One of ash sprinkled round the altar in
which they found the footprints of the greedy priests next
morning. I'll sprinkle a thin layer of flour on the kitchen floor,
he thinks. I mustn't go imagining all kinds of things. It's too
ridiculous for words. Nobody can get in. And who would
benefit by taking off Liesbeth's glasses? Who'd want to open
her eyes to what I have inflicted on her?

Reassured, he walks to the refrigerator and places the glasses back in front of the half-abandoned eye sockets. Then he drags her round ninety degrees and cuts off her left leg.

It's becoming a routine job now, he thinks. The same actions as yesterday. The two arms tomorrow, the trunk in halves, across, the day after: only leaves the head for Saturday.

Abstracted, he begins to cut into the leg.

Just look what I'm doing, he thinks. Such elegant curves. Yesterday, I began to cut clumsily; as time went by I was cutting splendid, straight strips. Now I'm cutting capricious pieces. Just like in Art. Art, too, is refractory and clumsy at first. Then you get classical harmony, the straight strips of drab-pink flesh. I'm going through the Baroque now. Tomorrow, perhaps, I'll be cutting scrolls and elegant figures and I'll be the Watteau of corpse desecration.

I was at primary school, Herbert thinks, in the fourth form. I must have been ten at the time. I was ten years old when it started. Or much earlier on even: who knows? How is it possible for one to find one's vocation so late? Across from me, at her desk, sat a girl with long, dark hair and spirited, brown eyes. Bent over my work, I turned my head sideways and looked at her profile. Then I looked at her tummy, going up and down like thick, boiling porridge in her tight dress. At night, in bed, I would think of her. I would take her to a lonely house where I tied her hands behind her back. A meat hook hung from an iron bar on the ceiling. I suspended her from it by the roof of her mouth. She sought to speak but I only heard her bottom teeth tap against the hook like a woodpecker hidden in the woods. She wanted to say: You're sweet to me even though you hurt me. I was lying on my belly. With my lower torso I slid back and forth on the sheet. I was covered in a gory membrane in which I threatened to suffocate. Like a child born with a caul. Wasn't I born with a caul? Mother said that at my birth the placenta was stuck to my skull like a Russian fur hat.

When Herbert opens the hatch, the sky, mottled drab and yellow, is stretched above the city like the soiled sheet of an incontinent child. An army of mediaeval knights pokes its helmeted, brick face, smoking, above the white hills of the roofs. Swans float like white islets on the dark pond in the park. Great black-backed gulls sit equidistant from each other on the edge of the roof. When Herbert lets the tray of meat down into the soft snow, they approach, hesitantly. Halting a few metres away from the tray, they stare at Herbert, soullessly, with their fierce, yellow, artificial eyes.

'I'll withdraw, lads,' he says, 'so you can dine in peace.'

He pulls the hatch shut over his head and fixes the catches.

Mind I don't forget to lock everything properly and sprinkle flour in the kitchen before I go to bed. I must have an early night: these are tiring times.

Above his head he hears the frightful shrieking and gorging of the hungry birds.

In the depths of night, Herbert wakes from the cold. He is lying on top of the blankets. He sticks his feet up in the air and looks at the soles of his feet.

'Gotcha,' he says loudly. 'I've caught myself out. Just as if I've got perspiring feet and they've been rubbed with talc.'

He brushes them. The flour sticks to his fingers like dough. Startled, he jumps out of bed.

My feet must have been wet before I stepped in the flour, he thinks.

Quickly, he walks to the kitchen. There are his footprints. His eyes crowd with fear against the top of their sockets. Among his prints he sees a damp square, and another, and the floor cloth in front of the fridge. The cat's prints run alongside his. Hurriedly he goes over to the refrigerator. The meat tray's up against the wall, opposite Liesbeth. He looks at the hallway door. He sees by his prints that he has been back and forth through the door. He sees the cat's tracks too, but just one way. He walks over to the hallway door and opens it. Freezing cold envelops his body. Herbert goes to the hatch; the steps are underneath. When he looks up, he sees the stars in the carbon-black sky. He clambers up and sticks his head into the east wind. Right in front of his eyes, in the snow, he sees the tracks of the cat.

He's been right behind me, Herbert thinks. He knows

everything. He's been spying on me from an untraceable hiding place. But he's up on the roof now. By the tracks I can see he hasn't turned back.

He fills his hands with snow and rubs his face with it.

I must keep a cool head, bring things to a close quickly. But let's tackle the genever bottle first.

He retreats a few steps and closes the hatch.

Warily, Herbert crosses the square, looks up at the windows of his apartment.

It looks uninhabited, he thinks. The lace curtains are yellow with brown rings. Is that something moving there, behind the curtains? He shakes his head and pats his cheeks with his fingers. I mustn't turn into a shying horse. I can see from here the window's ajar. The wind'll be stirring the curtains. How long has it been open? Bad for the plants. I'll shut it before I leave. Liesbeth's head's been standing on the roof for eight hours already. If it's not completely stripped by now I'll leave it there till tomorrow morning; then I'll wrap it in plastic and put it in my suitcase. I'll set it down among the cobbles along the Dordogne.

He feels in his pockets for the key and looks up. The chests of the seagulls protrude over the edge of the roof as though they are part of the building's trimmings.

'You'll miss me,' he mutters. 'Tighten your belts: that's all I can recommend.'

Right by his feet, on the pavement, lies a dirty-white sphere. Herbert bends down and picks it up.

Don't look round, he thinks, I'm just picking something up; everyone does that from time to time. And I've even read that they peck the eyes out of babies lying unguarded on the beach, and devour them.

He puts his key in the lock and enters the dark stairwell.

It feels like the devil's egg of a stinkhorn, he thinks. I'm still able to walk up the stairs, but I've got to take my time over it.

The front door opens behind him. A neighbour comes in; she halts at the letter box.

'Such a long time I haven't seen your wife,' she says. 'Has she got to stay in again?'

'I took her to the train last week; she wasn't feeling too well; she's gone south.'

'Taken the Sun Express to the deep blue sea?' the woman asks.

'Quite, quite,' Herbert replies. 'To the deep blue sea. I'll be following her tomorrow.'

Carefully, he slips off into the dark stairwell.

That eye was as hard as a billiard ball this morning, he thinks, clenching his fingers. Now it's soft and squishy. There's a thaw on: spring has sprung.

Translated by Richard Huijng

16

CEES NOOTEBOOM
Paula

1

Ghosts I do not believe in, but photographs are another matter. A woman wants you to think of her, and contrives to make you come across a photograph of her. The dead, if neglected for too long, can affect you that way. Or perhaps I should say: if they *feel* neglected they can affect you in that way. In my case neglect does not apply, because I still think of Paula pretty often. I don't know about the others, I hardly ever see them these days unless by chance. Gilles is dead, Alexander got his degree in the end and is now a medical inspector for the social services in Groningen, Ollie has moved to the States, and the Doctor's an invalid, last I heard. So that is not much use to her, because she is without doubt one of the unquiet dead. It's down to me, then. Perhaps by default, but nevertheless.

All right then, Paula, here I am, remembering you. I'm good at that, always was.

Because I never stopped. It's an eternity since I've been living on my own. Excess baggage disposed of long ago, but there seems to be no real end to it. I keep finding more. Top-floor flat in a modern building, sparsely furnished, quiet neighbours, peaceful, views over the wide polder landscape. People seldom visit; when they do they look about them warily like cats scanning the surrounds for danger. Bed, table, chair, all streamlined. Minimalist, remarked the Baron with that pale smile of his, that one time he dropped by. He had come on account of an old gambling debt, stood there with the air of a bailiff assessing my possessions in case I didn't cough up. I had no intention of coughing up, not then and not now. I had been expecting that visit for years; I knew he'd turn up eventually. Old habits die hard. I'm not sure how your memory fares these days, but I have no doubt you remember the Baron. Seeing you two dancing together was always a treat, especially to the Rolling Stones. Old men themselves these days. He'd go into a sort of mechanical trance like a wound-up robot, with you rippling and swirling around him, but he always linked up at the supreme moment, and the result was a pulsating machine that drew everyone's eyes. As my eyes are now drawn to you. Your photograph, propped up against my white wall. Well I never, there's Paula, said the Baron when he was there. Long time no see.

Reminds me of a Zen monastery, was another comment he made, but I have never been in a Zen monastery. I just wanted to keep things simple, no clutter, just bare, white space. I'm getting there. I don't entertain, so one chair for reading is enough. Same one for reading and eating. All my walls are white, as you may have noticed. No idea what your sort do or don't see. I detest looking at photographs of me when I was young, but it may not be the same for you. You are incapable of ageing, so you've never looked any different. How many years has it been? Forty? Forty-five? You made the cover of *Vogue* magazine, and we were all bursting with pride, even the girls. Nothing about the picture has aged, not you, nor the photograph itself. Last year you suddenly turned up among some newspaper cuttings from the old days – Provos in Amsterdam, love-ins, sit-ins, all that stuff. It's hard to imagine any of it actually taking place. I was busy for months; it was like a military campaign. Suitcases, cupboards, folders. That steamer trunk with the diaries was the last to go, and that's where I found you. All earmarked for the incinerator, with the exception of the photograph. You standing behind a closed window, left elbow raised against the frame in such a way that the just-lit cigarette between your fingers is slightly higher than your head. You wouldn't see a model smoking on the cover of *Vogue* today, nor would the fingernails be so short. It was a brazen, sexy image then, and that still holds today. Thin, boy-ish body. A white bandeau wrapped around the torso, no doubt a fashion statement at the time. Intimations of a double mastectomy. The boobless wonder, said the Baron. The Writer used a more flowery expression, borrowed from some poet whose name I don't recall. Dark hipster trousers, right hand in pocket, skin sprinkled with the raindrops clinging like tears to the window panes, your face looming out from the dimness beyond, lips slightly parted, gaze directed out of the picture. I can't look at it for very long. There you are in the realm of the dead, and yet you are about to speak. I can hear you now, that voice we will all remember to the end of our days, the hint of rawness, hoarseness, drink, cigarettes, a kind of aspirated prelude to your utterances. Har har, and then you'd be off, working your wiles not one of us could withstand.

A lethal weapon in poker games, that voice of yours, cap-able of turning a lame hand into a full house.

2

I have taken my chair and am sitting in front of you. In a home with only one chair that means something. I have put your photograph up on the window sill with a couple of smooth beach pebbles along the bottom edge to keep it in place. It's wet outside, which fits in with the raindrops on your window pane. This way you have rain in front of you as well as behind. I have this idea you can see me, but I suspect it is not the case. Which is probably just as well, because you might not even rec-ognize me. That is also why I'm not saying these things out loud, although it's in contradiction to our face-to-face arrange-ment. I never hear other people's voices here, and no one hears mine. I think.

It was the Year of Our Habit. That is what we called each year back then, because we were hooked, and we knew it. A shoe-less evening was a waste of time. I can still feel the touch of the cards when I held the bank, I can feel it, and I can hear the sound. When you first arrived I was also holding the bank, left hand resting on the wooden side of the shoe, right hand poised, fingertips on the first card. The game is more generally known as baccarat or *chemin de fer*, but we had our own variant with our own rules, and we called it shoe, that was enough. It was shoe every evening, including that one. The room was dimly lit except for the table, which stood in a pool of light so the only faces you could see properly were those of the players. The door-bell rang, someone went to answer it and those of us who were not playing looked up expectantly. There was a hush, something that only happened when strangers turned up, people we did not know. You arrived alone, which was unusual, but no ques-tions were asked. That was not our style. Much as we disliked interruptions, we broke off to shake hands, that's when we first heard the voice. Cinco had given the address, you said. Cinco, remember him? The perennial loner? Checked tweed cap, used to prop up the bar at Hoppe's? One-time city coun-cillor for Traffic Safety because we had all voted for him. Har har. Cinco, who stopped coming after a while. Dead. This will be my refrain, I'm afraid. Can't be helped, it's part of my life nowadays. I lifted my hand from the shoe and set the stake. One hundred guilders. Perhaps I was just trying to impress you, it was still a lot of money back then. André was sitting to my left. Normally cautious, this time he called *suivi*. I drew the cards, inspected them. Two nines and a six, excellent hand. Over the players' heads I looked at your face, eager, covetous. And I was not the only one: the Baron, Gilles, Nigel, even Tico and the Prodigy were looking, too. This was duly noted by the womenfolk, standing by with hackles raised and claws at the ready. It took a while for you to get them under your thumb. No, that's not right – to get them to love you the way we did. Har har. To the women your laugh sounded different: hoarser, deeper, sweeter. I held the bank ten times or so. Two hundred, four hundred, eight hundred, banco each time, till I could 'take chocolate'. You were a fast learner. *Banco suivi, banco avec.* Get it in the neck. That was ever the Writer's response, we expected it. You lost time after time but in the end, when the stake was back to eight hundred, you called *banco*.

The hubbub subsided. I drew the cards slowly. You held them as you must have seen them do in films, tightly together at first, as if they were one card. You raised them close to your chest, still as one. Only then did you slowly lift them to eye level, spreading them fractionally, just enough to check the values. Har, you said, meaning 'a card'. That was the first time I lost to you. From then on you were one of us.

But that is putting it mildly. It was more like you had always been one of us. Paula? Oh, known her for years.

Years? How long that period lasted I do not know, but what I do know is that everything shrivelled after you died. We followed somewhat from a distance what was going on in the rest of the world: Vietnam, riots in Amsterdam, squatters, cold war, the H-bomb, the Club of Rome with its apocalyptic forecasts, the first oil crisis, Prague '68.

For most people the real war was still quite recent, clearly there were new conflicts that would bring even greater calamities, but, as Nigel would say with cool assurance, those calamities would be on a very different scale from what all the current fuss was about. We believed him, which probably had more than anything else to do with the fact that he always won. Besides, we had other things on our minds. Nigel's field was mathematics, where order reigned. The world was chaos. We were rather vague, the whole lot of us, but the game was crystal clear.

Dodo and Gilles lived in a canal-side house in the southern part of Amsterdam. The canal was a poor imitation of the old ones in the centre, and more of a boundary between the city and the new suburbs that were springing up back then. As the Writer used to say, it was like having to cross a moat to gain access to their castle. Writer was his real name, and that he wrote for a living was a bonus. The Baron had introduced Wintrop, his associate in vague dealings with stocks and shares which they never discussed, not even with André and Gilles, who played the stock market themselves, or had done, that never became clear. Nothing was clear, really. There was no hierarchy. The

Jewish Prodigy was studying to become a surgeon, Nieges dealt in dodgy antiques, and Merel ran a small travel agency with third-world destinations from a little office in the Pijp neighbourhood. Nigel, whose name jarred with his appearance of someone languishing in Dostoevsky's basement, was studying maths, paying his way by playing poker at a private club from which we were barred. Tico was an agent for chartreuse wines and an obscure brand of champagne. The Doctor owed his name to having dropped out of medical school. Remember them? Ollie was with André; she stayed in Texas when he died. Absent friends and the dead, such are my companions.

Merel and Tico are still together, apparently. Like me they lead what I call shadow-lives, or rather, like me, they never came out of the shade. There were those of us who earned real money, those who already had it, and others like me who scraped it together here and here, but money was never an issue. How you got by I never discovered. You did some modelling, but not on a regular basis, and yet you never seemed to be out of pocket. The Writer published books we didn't read, the Baron was a district judge somewhere, the Jewish Prodigy became a successful surgeon though he didn't like to admit it, Merel's agency flourished when immigration from Surinam took off, but money was never discussed, not by any of us. Nigel kept the records of the debts, which amounted to endless rounds of figures being cancelled out against each other. We were all permanently in debt. Every few weeks Nigel would say it was time to settle accounts, which would duly take place the following session.

3

So what is it about remembering the dead? Yes I know, I won't get an answer to that, nor to the question I really want to ask, which is, How is it that the older you get the more your life begins to look like an invention? Hard to say which is worse, getting old or being dead, but then you have never been old and I have never been dead.

I think the reason I have made the place so bare and empty is that I don't want my invention to bear any resemblance to anyone else's, though that's nonsense, of course, because at best it'll only be another invention, one that you do not come across that often. You knew all of those things all the time. You were an avid reader, but there was always a niggle, as if there was something missing. It was from you I got that idea about invention. We had been to see a film, which I found moving, as I remember. Almost the real thing, you scoffed as we left the cinema. Everything is a copy of something else, it's hardly worth living when some guy can come along and squeeze your whole life into a ninety-minute feature film or a book you read in two days. To each his own novel, I say, but even that would take too long. Imitation, that's all there is. I believe I was shocked; in any case I was lost for words. You went on to say something about time being compacted, and I could almost feel it happening. We were walking from Leidseplein to Vondelpark, where the gravel underfoot intensified the sensation. Our steps keeping pace with physical fact struck an accusatory note, as if they were clamouring to be conflated into a film sequence or into a line in a novel like every other. Nigel, who rarely said anything remotely personal, once remarked in the middle of a game, Paula, you're in too much of a hurry to live. Nigel, another conquest. Nigel, who was having an affair with Dodo, who was married to Gilles. A whole pile of novels. You tried us all, tried all the films. Maybe Nigel was the only one you ever really cared about, but maybe not. So mysterious-looking with that white face of his, was all you said on the subject. He was the only one you couldn't have. You had me, easily. There was no mystery about me then, there still isn't. I went all out for you from that very first evening, and that was a story you'd read a hundred times already. The only time we made love you answered my transparency with yours: I don't see what's so special about fucking. *C'est un geste rendu*, no more than that. No less either. And afterwards you said: Evidently you and I were not made for each other. Don't look so miserable, this is only the beginning. Good to get that out of the way. Best friend I ever had. It wasn't you saying that, it was me, and yet I never really knew how you felt about me. Sometimes you gave me a look as if you were hiding something. Three weeks out in the Niger desert, by jeep to Tamanrasset. You came up with the tickets after you'd fleeced us all that unforgettable night when it all went so fast Nigel could hardly keep the score. You were holding a bank that seemed impossible to break, the chocolate steadily melting over the table in your direction. Shoe, *banco*, *suivi*, chocolate. For the unthinkable contingency that you might have forgotten, chocolate was the profit you could take out of the bank if the stakes were too low. *Banco* meant you only wanted to place a bet equal to the bank total. *Suivi* meant you bet *banco* again after losing. The trip was unforgettable. I still spend some time in the desert, any desert, every year. En route you made out with one or two stray men. I won't embarrass you, you said, I'll say you're my brother. In which case I'll have to slit their throats, I said, you don't give your sister up to the first caravan that comes along. But we had agreed: no jealousy. That was the deal.

I spent such evenings writing my own story, alone in a tent, dogs howling all across the oasis. My only pride was that it didn't resemble any stories I knew. Whether you felt the same I don't know. You made no comment, just gave an angry, rapacious look, as if you were left wanting.

Were you unhappy? What a crap question, you'd have said. Then, quickly, an arm round my shoulder, and a whispered – you could whisper, too – I wouldn't have gone on a trip like this with anyone else. Wouldn't and couldn't. If you fancy a fuck just say so, we have all the decor we need right here: heart of Africa, palm trees, camels, stars. Har har.

4

The Baron owed his nickname to his renounced nobility. His grandfather, a believer in egalitarianism, had wrought his own little French Revolution by dumping his title in the dustbin of history. It was a loss that caused his grandson to suffer phantom pain. He still had a family coat of arms, but no title to go with it, so he cherished his surname all the more for its noble ring. You know all that. The dead don't have Alzheimer's.

You needn't listen; I'll carry on talking anyway. For my own benefit. To furnish my space. I don't miss them, for all that they were dear to me. Tico called me Don Anselmo for some reason, I think it had something to do with a film we'd seen together, *El Cochecito*. Tico and Merel. He had a touch of the Indies about him; the formal, overseas accent still lingered. Father in the Colonial army. Sergeant, but no matter, formality assured. Colonial hang-ups. Forever insecure about making the grade. We're from Madura, if you know where that is. Think Bali, Lombok, Soemba, the whole Indonesian archipelago. And Timor, half-Portuguese. People forget that. Tico was friends with Nieges. Ah, Nieges, expert on the patina of age, remember? A question of chemicals. Bury an item in the ground with a drop of this or that and it'll age all on its own in no time. Tico didn't obtain his degree, but he knew enough to be of assistance to Nieges. They saw each other during the day, which I found odd. Alexander was busy with his internships at the same hospital where the Prodigy worked. Merel, Dodo and Ollie were involved in something they'd call fitness now. The Doctor spent his days in chess cafés. I never saw any of them during the daytime, for me they belonged to the evening. The circle of friends, the faces in the yellow lamplight, the smoke. And you. I can see you before me now, nothing to it, one can project any image one likes on the polder. Which reminds me of what you said about time being compacted, because things went too slowly for you. Perhaps it was just a throwaway remark, which I'm blowing out of proportion. And yet. I have the time to think about such things now. The first film I saw by Antonioni was with you. Antonioni and Bergman, both of them dead now too. It's as if I never saw another film since. I lost interest. In those days it was all left-wing radicalism, you were supposed to show solidarity with any number of causes, sign manifestos, march for peace, outrage was mandatory. That didn't bother us much, but the indignation was everywhere. University buildings occupied by students, rebellion in the theatre, sugarcane cutting in Cuba, marches for Cambodia, police crackdowns, and all that time we were busy with shoe and *banco*, a bunch of deserters washed up on an island. No trace of all the general mayhem in those films, which is probably why they made such an impression on me. They were not about social issues, just about people. Individuals. A distasteful word to me even today, but no matter. Solitary souls. Someone riding a tram going down a deserted street. The solitude amid the turmoil. 1964, 1965, I'm not sure. *Il deserto rosso*. Monica Vitti standing with a man at the base of a towering metal scaffold, two tiny figures, so small you would think they were nameless. It was then you dug your fingernails into the palm of my hand. That's exactly it, you said, we don't mean a thing. Who do we think we are? We're being shredded, erased. Our stories are the same everywhere, they have no meaning. I now have that film on DVD, and several others. I watch them at night in here, where I'm sitting now. And each time that scene begins I can feel your hand. Antonioni spins out the moment, the wasteland, the wall, the metal framework, the agonizing diminution. That evening you didn't join us at the gaming table. I was holding the bank with considerable success, and at one point I looked up. You were standing behind the Prodigy, your expression curiously intense, you gave me a little nod and at once made a gesture with both hands drawing in the entire circle, two quick waves and a swipe to the side, as if you were throwing us all out of the window.

After that you left.

5

Our famous escapade took place a bit later. It was the Baron's idea. There was an uncle somewhere near Rouen where he was to deliver something or whose signature he needed, I forget which. So then why not make the most of it and have a go in a real casino, at Deauville? Not everyone was available. The Prodigy had weekend duty, Ollie wouldn't let André go. That left ten of us to pile into two cars: my old Renault 16, the

Baron's cat-back Volvo. Move over, Don Anselmo. You were in the Volvo, next to Nigel. It was strange seeing them all in broad daylight. The Doctor had a mildewy look. Belgium was grey. We made a detour to Saint-Omer, because Nigel wanted to see the church labyrinth there. I have never felt much at ease in churches, least of all Roman Catholic ones. Nigel and you were already there. You were standing at the centre of the labyrinth, which extended across the nave like some strange board game. I still have a postcard of it. From his hand gestures I could tell he was tracing the paths in his mind.

His face was very white; I don't believe he ever saw the light of day.

I was too far away to hear what he was saying, but he was talking a lot, contrary to his taciturn habit. I say, Paula, got some breadcrumbs? called Tico, visibly startled by his voice echoing through the church. I watched you trying to follow the path out of the labyrinth and not succeeding. It's getting dark, folks. That was the Baron. He had been against the detour, but had been voted down, everybody insisted that a labyrinth in a church was not to be missed. Why is this region called Picardy, Dodo wanted to know, there's nothing picaresque about it. Not a knave in sight. Just the lingering smell of war.

Two wars, Gilles said. Graves in their millions around here. And it's not Picardy.

The light was slowly fading. The trees lining the road had white bands painted around the trunks, which lit up one by one. The rain drummed against the windows; inside the car all was quiet. It wasn't until we arrived at the casino that we all woke up. *Il Barone*: ties on. Yessir.

Entrance hall, fitted carpets, chandeliers. Passports, entry forms. I glanced round at my companions. A scruffy-looking bunch. I don't know about nowadays, but back then entering a casino was quite intimidating. There was a gravity about the place, a solemn atmosphere of destiny and fate, addiction and castigation. And of sheer, unmerited luck. I said so out loud, and you, standing in front of me in the queue, looked over your shoulder and said: Some people are born better-looking than

others. Our names were entered in imposing ledgers. I always
think they'll refuse me entry, Tico said. We queued again for
chips. After that we all dispersed, as though by prior agreement. Superstition, not wanting to stand close to anyone you
knew, not wanting to push your luck. Nigel made for the poker
table, which I didn't dare. Casino poker was out of my league.
Gilles and the Baron opted for baccarat, which came closest to
our shoe, while the rest of us sought out the roulette tables.
You stayed by my side at first, watched the bets being placed
and said: Yet another labyrinth. After that we lost sight of each
other. It was a large space, and it struck me that we had spread
out like an army patrol combing enemy territory. Roulette was
a game I think I always played to lose, which was, paradoxically,
the only way I occasionally won. Not that night, though. I did
what I always did, a pathetic combination of adventure and
caution. French francs, a hundred of which seemed a lot of
money back then. Oh, for the days of the quaint old curren-
cies! Guilders, marks, lire . . . I staked a hundred straight up on
twenty-three, and another hundred on red. I knew I'd carry on
like this until I ran out of steam. Twenty-three could be trusted
not to come up at all, and if black came up a couple more times
(*no earthly reason why it shouldn't, statistically speaking,
Nigel would say*) I'd stake all my remaining chips on a random
number. In retrospect I realize I was aiming to lose, just to get
it all over with. Because what I really wanted to do was watch.
Very few people gamble for fun, there's always more to it. You
can tell by the twitching muscles in jaws, the sidelong glances,
the way a player suddenly stands up to leave or gives an
over-generous tip. But the croupiers held a special fascination
for me, the dealers of fate and doom, the spine-tingling under-
tone of metaphysical ennui in their voices. Big words, Don
Anselmo. Sheer boredom, more like. *Mesdames, messieurs,
rien ne va plus*. Still one of the best sentences ever spoken. The
flurry of last-minute bets, split on two-three, split on zero,
then the final, prohibitive, *rien*! The baleful stillness until the
white, spinning ball drops and bounces, a sound without comparison. Two kinds of players: those who look and those who
listen. *Cinq, rouge, impair* and *manque*. What was it you once

said at Dodo's? You were holding the bank, your hand on the cards, no more bets, ladies and gentlemen, here goes: cancer, car crash, divorce, misery, love and passion, a diamond as big as the Hilton . . . Nobody laughed. We weren't stupid, we had already thought of that ourselves.

After half an hour all my money was gone. I saw you in the distance, side by side with your fate, but we were not to know that then. He raised his champagne to you, you clinked glasses. You struck up friendships wherever you went. I did not go over to you, but wandered off towards the other tables. Nigel, white as a sheet, as ever. Dostoevsky in Baden-Baden.

Even he lost. Gilles and the Baron had already left the baccarat table. Tico turned his trouser pockets inside out and held them wide between finger and thumb. The Doctor had a piece of paper covered with scribbled figures, his unbeatable system, but lost all he had. Only Dodo and Merel were still playing. If we all end up losing, said Tico, we won't have any money for petrol. Go and tell that to Merel, we said, tell her to stop, she's still got chips. But Merel refused: she wanted to take her own sweet time going broke.

In the end you were the only winner. The rest of us, losers all, had gravitated to your table. No credit cards in those days, no money out of the wall. Stop now, said the Baron. That was the wrong thing to say. You gave him one of those special looks of yours, took a sip of champagne. We stared at your stack of chips, trying to guess the value. Ten thousand at least. For Chrissake, Paula, save some for our dinner. We didn't much fancy your new friend. He had tattoos on the backs of his hands. Miniatures, a bit like the runic signs they brand into bulls. He said something to you, and you laughed. As if you'd known him for ever. An accent, Spanish or Italian. You motioned to the croupier, circled your finger round the pile in front of you and then pointed to twenty-three, which had just come up. My number. He raked in the chips, totted them up in a flash the way croupiers do (like stirring a pile of shit, the Writer said later) and exchanged them for larger, higher value ones. He held one up to check your approval. It was a gold chip. Everyone was watching now. You nodded. He slid the chip towards you, and prepared to send the remaining, lesser chips after it with that obscene, off-hand croupier's gesture saying it's not money lying there. But it is money. I could hear Tico groaning under his breath when you signalled: Keep the change. Damn, there goes our dinner, he hissed between clenched teeth. *Pour les employés, merci, Madame.* What about us, then? Aren't we in her employ? I have always wondered what sort of relationship croupiers have with money. They don't get their salary paid in chips, after all. Very few of them play. They've seen a thing or two. All eyes were on you. *Faîtes vos jeux.* Tattoo placed a stack of chips on the table. A top-line bet on the zero with one, two and three, to be precise, then he filled the corners, and finally put a high-value chip straight up on zero. You didn't move, just stood there holding your golden chip, and I knew what you had in mind. So did Tico, apparently, because I could hear his stifled moan: No, Paula, no. But you had already done the deed, with slow, almost priestly deliberation. Twenty-three. My number. Zero came up. No one spoke, Tattoo was the only player with stakes on and around zero. So his payout naturally included that golden chip of yours. A thousand francs. Had the twenty-three come up you'd have made thirty-five thousand. The croupier pushed the mound of winnings over the table towards Tattoo, who fished out a gold chip and slid it towards you. You accepted it without batting an eyelid, as if you and he had been at it for years. You did not exchange looks. *Faîtes vos jeux.* Tico let out another moan, a dog mourning its master. Nigel was watching, so was Merel.

The atmosphere was tense. Then came the old flicker of complicity between the croupier and the player, a female player, because it only happens with women, really. A game of eyes. Just a fraction of a second, an attempt at exorcism that everyone knows is futile. The force of the hand sending the numbered wheel spinning round, the ball bouncing, skittering, bouncing again until it finally drops, caught in the small cell with the sacred number.

Twenty-three. Things moved at high speed after that. It still hurts to think that those were the last moments we saw you. You slid your winnings to the man beside you, who slid them back: thirty-five thousand, just sitting there. Tico moaned again, Nigel stared at a point over our heads, Gilles lit a cigarette. You nodded to the croupier, pushed a chip in his direction, divided the thirty-four remaining ones into two equal stacks. Meanwhile Tattoo stood up, waited. You turned round, kissed Tico, kissed Merel, kissed me, ran a fingernail down my neck, handed one of your stacks to Dodo and dropped the other in your handbag. For a rainy day, you said to no one in particular, and stalked off with your man. Much good it'll do her, murmured the Baron as you vanished through the revolving door. We all knew you wouldn't be back. You had left your stake on the baize, pointing to me. I ought to have pocketed it; instead I placed the gold chip on red. Black came up. There are no secrets.

Outside, it was still raining. Someone suggested taking a walk along the beach.

The girls weren't keen, so they stayed behind in a bar-tabac on the boulevard near the casino.

Gusts of wind, and the other sound, that of surf. For a while we stood there getting wet. Then Tico said: I didn't like the look of that guy. Nigel made no comment, neither did I.

Ever woken up in a French seaside resort in the off-season? Hotel Sleepless Nights, hangover, view of the sea, gulls, driving rain. *Petit déjeuner* with apricot jam and those little wrapped squares of butter from Holland. Six months later: Hotel Corona de Aragon in Zaragoza goes up in flames. Pictures of people behind the top-floor windows waving their arms as if there's a party going on. Eighty-nine dead. Nearly all Spanish, a few Germans, a Colombian, and one Dutch national. Just one.

Translated by Ina Rilke

17

REMCO CAMPERT
The Kid with the Knife

De jongen met het mes

You only had to snap your fingers and it was party-time. Summer or winter, it made no difference, the evenings and nights reeked of alcohol. At 3 a.m. anything was possible: you could do a handstand on a genever bottle, fly to New York, get a job as a farmhand and lie in the corn, become stinking rich overnight and, years later, full of champagne, drown in a swimming pool on a moonless night.

In the summer when dawn broke with birds singing and clean streets and a pale sun, you drove to the beach; your hands sweated salt and alcohol and fresh ink from the morning paper. In the evening you returned home heavy as lead, shoes full of sand, your muddled brain bursting with headache: you'd slapped a girl, broken with a friend, laughed and yelled, your dilated pupils were black lagoons swarming with mosquitoes. Your thoughts had disintegrated into isolated words – key words, which you kept on mumbling, because you were afraid you would cease to exist if you forgot these words as well.

And you fell asleep until you were woken up by the next party.

Dick laid his hand on Wessel's shoulder.
'There are some people here who aren't drinking,' he said.
'Where?' Wessel asked.
'There's one over there,' Dick said, pointing to the couch.
'That tall fellow? Who is he? What's he doing here?'
'He's a friend of Erik's. Erik brought him. But that's not

what I'm talking about. It's that he's not drinking. There are limits.'

'You're quite right,' Wessel said.

'Erik,' he said, after he'd tracked him down. 'Erik, there's a tall fellow sitting on the couch who's not drinking. Rumour has it you invited him. Who is he and what's he doing here, if he doesn't drink?'

Erik glanced at the couch.

'He's a really crazy kid,' he said. 'He's a photographer.'

'Where's his camera?' Wessel asked.

'Right,' said Dick. 'There's that too.'

'He didn't bring it. He was afraid it would get smashed.'

'Oh,' said Wessel. 'Was he afraid of that? So he didn't bring it, then? Is he more of a landscape photographer?'

'He's a really crazy kid,' Erik insisted.

'Photographers are never crazy,' Dick said.

'Kids who are afraid of getting their cameras smashed aren't crazy. They're disgustingly ambitious. Kids who are ambitious are never crazy.'

'I only like war photographers,' Wessel said.

'He takes very beautiful photos,' said Erik.

'What does he take photos of, then?' Dick asked.

'The Leidseplein youth,' said Erik.

'The what?'

'The Leidseplein youth.'

'What's that?'

'It's the kids who hang out on the Leidseplein.'

'Why does he take photos of that lot?'

'I don't know. It's what he does.'

'There's never any war on the Leidseplein,' said Wessel.

'Figure it out for yourself, then,' Erik said as he walked off.

Wessel looked at the kid, who was sitting on the couch. He was holding something shiny.

'Dammit, he's got a knife,' Wessel said. 'Do you see it, Dick? He's a kid with a knife.'

'Maybe he is a really crazy kid after all,' Dick said.' But he doesn't drink. I still think that's unforgivable.'

They went up to the kid with the knife. Dick had a bottle of genever. They stopped in front of him.

'I'm Wessel,' said Wessel. 'And he's Dick. I'm the host here. You're a guest. So far so good. But what about you – what's your name?'

'Oscar,' the kid said.

'Dick,' Wessel said, 'ask Oscar what he'd like to drink.'

'I don't drink,' the kid said. He scrutinized the sharp shining blade of his knife.

'You're just sussing out the scene, are you?' Wessel said.

'Not really,' said the kid.

'All you need is your knife,' Dick said.

'That's about it,' the kid said.

'It's a nice knife,' said Wessel.

The kid looked at it as if he was holding it for the first time.

'It's okay,' he said.

'According to your friend Erik, you're a really crazy kid, Oscar,' Wessel said. 'Is that right?'

The kid shrugged his shoulders.

'He feels flattered,' Dick said. 'But he won't admit it.' He put the bottle to his mouth and took a swig.

'Do you always bring that knife with you?' Wessel asked.

The kid didn't answer.

'Do you know how to throw it?'

The kid nodded.

'Is your aim good?'

'Yes,' the kid said.

'Are you sure?'

'Yes!'

'If we choose something for you, can you hit it?'

'Yes.'

'That's what we'll do, then. Come with us, Dick,' said Wessel.

'What are you planning?' Dick asked.

'Something brilliant. Where's Bella? Have you seen Bella?'

'There she is, dancing.'

'Bella! Come here a moment!'

'She's a lioness,' Dick said. 'She's only twenty and she has the face of a posh forty-year-old call girl.'

'And her voice,' Wessel said. 'A fantastically husky sound. It sounds like the voice of an old drunken painter.'

'It's a great party, Wessel!' Bella barked.

'Are you very drunk, Bella?' Wessel asked.

'Drunk?! I've been drunk the whole far-out week. I've gone from one far-out party to another. It's been a far-out week. I mean it.'

'Do you see that boy sitting there on the couch? He's a really crazy kid.'

'A far-out kid.'

'He's got a knife, that kid.'

'Hey, that's far out!'

'He's got a perfect aim. Do you see that spot on the wallpaper? He can hit it if he likes.'

'Okay then, far out. That's a far-out story.'

'His name's Oscar. He doesn't drink, that's why he's so good at throwing knives.'

'That's so far out, that kid with that knife, far out.'

'Now he'd like to show us what a great knife-thrower he is, do you get me?'

'Sure, of course. That's far out.'

'But we think it's much more fun if he doesn't throw it at dead objects. That's not so exciting.'

'No, of course not.'

'That's boring.'

'That's totally boring.'

'We thought it would be more exciting if he threw it at you.'

'At me? That's far out.'

'Yes, I mean not *at* you, but just next to you, at a spot we choose. Like in the circus.'

'That's such a far-out brilliant plan.'

'But you'd have to be naked.'

'Of course. It's a far-out idea. That far-out kid with that knife.'

'Far out,' Wessel and Dick said in chorus. Together with Bella, they went over to the kid.

'You have to aim it at her, like in the circus,' Wessel said.

The kid gave Bella a quick glance and blushed. Then he got up slowly, knife in hand.

'It's okay with me,' he said.

'He's cool,' Bella said. 'He's sooo cool.'

'In the corridor,' Wessel said. 'There's more room there.'

The four of them headed for the corridor.

'Stark naked?' Bella asked.

'Yes,' said Wessel.

'That's fantastic. It's so far out.'

She started getting undressed.

'Turn off the music,' said the kid with the knife.

Dick went into the living room and a minute later the music stopped and the others, their curiosity aroused, started streaming into the corridor.

'Go and stand on the stairs, all of you,' Wessel said. 'And don't forget, total silence. So you can hear a knife drop.'

'Far out,' Bella growled. She'd taken off all her clothes.

Wessel positioned her against the door leading to the kitchen.

'You decide on the distance,' he said to the kid.

'For God's sake, what's going on?' Erik asked. He was standing on the stairs with the others.

'You'll see.'

'She should be blindfolded,' said Dick. He pulled out his handkerchief and tied it round Bella's eyes.

The kid took up position at a distance of twenty paces. He held the knife by the tip of the blade.

'What's the target?' he asked.

'I'll show you,' said Wessel.

'Have you gone quite crazy?' Erik shouted, having finally realized what was happening.

'That's right, quite crazy,' Bella shouted back. 'It's a far-out idea.'

Wessel went up to Bella.

'You should spread your legs a bit,' he said.

He pointed to a spot high up between her thighs.

'That's your target,' he said to the kid. 'As high as possible.'

He scratched a mark in the paint of the door with his fingernail.

'You're tickling me like crazy,' Bella said.

'Stay quite still,' Wessel said. 'Don't move.' He stepped aside a little. 'Don't move,' he repeated. 'Okay, Oscar, when you're ready throw your knife.' Everyone held their breath.

The kid lifted his arm. His face was tense with concentration, but his body was relaxed. Then, with a barely perceptible movement of his arm, he released the knife.

It leaped from his hand almost gaily, did a dazzling somersault in the air, like a fish with intent, slammed into the wood between Bella's thighs and stuck there quivering.

Nobody said a thing. Only when the knife had stopped moving, did they all suddenly start talking.

'Was that it?' Bella asked.

'Don't move!' Wessel shouted. 'Otherwise you'll cut yourself.' He pulled the knife out of the wood and gave it back to the kid.

'Far out,' Bella said, taking off her blindfold.

'It's a pity he didn't have his camera, then he could have taken some photos,' Wessel heard Dick say.

'It's a far-out feeling,' Bella said. 'It's like someone blew on you. Just like someone blowing on you. That's some crazy kid.' She went up to him, threw her arms round his neck, snuggled up to him and kissed him on his mouth.

Afterwards she said admiringly: 'He's totally cool. He just doesn't care. It doesn't make a scrap of difference to him.'

The kid blushed again. Smiling shyly, he laid his left hand cautiously on Bella's bare shoulder; he kept his other hand with the knife in it awkwardly behind his back, anxious not to scratch her with it.

Translated by Donald Gardner

18

J. M. A. BIESHEUVEL

The Shattering Truth

De verpletterende werkelijkheid

I have set myself up in my room and think I know exactly what I want to write.

It's a story about a man who commits suicide and drifts around the universe for a long time before arriving in Heaven. He doesn't believe in God at all, so when God actually puts in an appearance the man says: 'Look, I don't want anything to do with this.'

'Well then, you can just go back into space for another million years,' God says. 'Go on, float around and eat your heart out, and after that you can try again.'

What happens next almost defies description. Desperate loneliness, grinding misery, here and there a little star. No one around for a million years. Fretting until it makes your bones ache. Finally, he gets back to Heaven and appears before God, Elijah, Moses and Malachi.

'You do know you're not supposed to commit suicide, don't you?' God asks. 'You know that life on earth is an ordeal, and that you're not allowed to end it prematurely, right? If everyone did that, we'd have a real administrative mess on our hands. To be honest, I can't really admit suicides into Heaven.'

'Not unless the accused can present a reasonable defence,' Elijah mumbles.

So the story is going to be called 'Rumplala's Defence'.

The man's name is Rumplala. He starts in on an account of his tribulations and disappointments. In the end, God, Elijah, Moses and Malachi are all sitting around weeping.

It was going to be a real Dostoevsky story. About him not

fitting in at his place of employment. About him tearing up all the incoming correspondence. Failing to understand his colleagues. Not being cut out for his work. Stealing money. Going to prostitutes and so compounding his misery. About his guilt complex with regard to his wife. The fears he suffered underneath, all his life, unspecified fears that devour the soul. Finally, the dismissal and the poverty. Then, the Christmas celebration. His wife tries to get him to church at least once. Rumplala goes along with her and sees cripples and invalids, mental cases and little old women. An old man sitting in a wheelchair stares ecstatically at the preacher and at the brightly lit Christmas tree in one corner of the church. There's a frankfurter sausage hanging out of the man's pants. The pastor slurs his words during the sermon. Rumplala gets angry and shouts: 'Bullshit.' Then he runs out of the church. Angst, whoring, his failure at work, his hopeless attempts at making a career, his unhappiness, the rattled nerves, everything one big failure, including the singing, the paintings, the short stories he writes. His friends try to tell him he's not such a bad writer. But the doctor at the health insurance company he reports to every two weeks has never even heard of him. 'Can you recall the titles of the books you've written?' he keeps asking, after Rumplala has spent hours in a stuffy waiting room along with hundreds of sad-eyed workers who mope and sniffle and read old back copies of hokey magazines like *Margriet* and *Panorama*, mumbling to themselves the whole time, or simply staring at a spot on the floor or ceiling. And so he runs through the titles one more time: '*Storm in a Teacup, Murder on the Queen Mary, The Devil's Lamppost* . . .'

'Sounds like a pretty complicated *oeuvre*,' the doctor says. *Backyard with Skyscape*. 'And have these books ever actually been published?' the doctor asks. 'Yes,' Rumplala says, 'you'll find them in any bookstore, but I don't really make any money from it, at least not enough to keep my head above water, my wife . . . the panic attacks . . . getting sacked . . . the time I've wasted . . . the sense of failure . . . my nerves . . . Did I tell you that I went to the whores downtown once too?'

'Tch, tch,' the doctor mumbles, 'oh my, that's really terrible, especially seeing as you're too sick to go to work. How were you able to afford that? What about your nervous state? Are you on any particular medication?'

'You bet your ass I am!' Rumplala shouts, and he pulls out all his little vials and boxes and tosses them in the doctor's face and against the front of his lab coat, one by one. 'I'm taking Trilafon and Dalmadorm and Valium and Nozinan and Serenase and Trofanil!' The doctor just sits there, covered in pills. 'The best thing would be for you to get a little rest. Hopefully you'll find another pleasant job.'

'I've never *had* a pleasant job,' Rumplala says. He thinks back in disgust on the way he shilly-shallied around at the office. Is there anything in life that *doesn't* drive him mad? The drivel in the student papers, in the newspapers. Always the same thing: 'Professor Beiderheide says farewell.' Then you read some ridiculous, cliché-ridden article that talks about gratitude, attentive students, outstanding colleagues, a pleasant atmosphere, happy days, wonderful prospects, yes, there is even something looming on the horizon. Next to it a photo of a man laughing sheepishly as a pair of nurses or students hand him a box of cigars and a book. Rumplala works at the hospital and has been charged with writing a handbook, an intake folder for patients. Anyone in their right mind would have finished it within a week. He has already read hundreds of books and interviewed dozens of people, but he isn't one step closer to being finished. He knows a bit about insurance cover and premiums, all out, all in, doctor out, peignoir, bathrobe or duster with you when you come in, toothbrush, sewing kit and shaving things. If you want a telephone it costs this much more. The lights go out at nine thirty, that's better for you and better for us. It is the patient's responsibility to pay his bills or have his insurer do so. He also has the right to information. He can refuse a given treatment, and if student interns come to his bedside just to goggle at him, he has the right to send them away. Rumplala has been working on this for six months already and so far he's only spinning his wheels. He can't do it. He's already got his first two sentences, though: 'Welcome, dear patient. You've gone through such an incredible amount

of crap in your life and now you've ended up in the hospital.'
His boss thinks those sentences are hilarious. 'This folder is
not going to happen,' his boss mumbles. Meanwhile, Rumplala spends all day thinking about the folder, he dreams about
it at night. About what he mustn't forget to include in it. How
do you spell 'peignoir', anyway? One afternoon he tried out
everything he could think of: 'penuar', 'painwar', 'pignoir',
'peignoir'. He has mumbled the word under his breath so often
that he doesn't even know what it means any more. Coffee
breaks are a disaster. He hears his colleagues conversing, but he
has no idea what they're talking about. 'I told Zwatser that it
will take twenty years before the new wing can be implemented,
that's the government standpoint.' 'So what did Barrestorg say
to that?' 'He laughed and said: "We can always use Plan 2A to
keep them sidetracked, as long as the deputy-minister doesn't
come down with something." There's no milk or sugar on his
table. The canteen is too small. The others don't pass him the
things he needs, they talk and while they talk they read *Margriet* and *Panorama*. Life is a catastrophe. This cleansing
cream penetrates deep into your pores, where it nourishes the
skin and does its curative work. The next time your boyfriend
kisses you he'll say: 'Your skin is as soft as a peach.' A catastrophe, that's what life is. Subscribe to the Winkler Prins
Encyclopedia, your children can use it to do their homework:
a lifelong asset. A welcome addition to your room and your
bookcase. For only two thousand guilders. Revulsion. Her
Majesty wanted to know all about that one particular kiss, the
tabloids said, so you know what that's about. No, what *is* that
all about? Rumplala thinks. What's this preacher blabbering
on about? What kind of rubbish are my colleagues spouting? I
mustn't forget to put this in the handbook too, but it's almost
too much for me to bear: patients also have access to psychiat-
ric counselling. Social workers can come to your bedside.
Disgusting, what a horror, the whole thing, to say nothing of
all the pain you have to go through. 'Chin up, Mr Pinters,' says
the nurse, a young thing who has never had cancer herself.
That is what work at the office is like. Rumplala can't get to
the milk and sugar. The room is too small. They never pass it

to him. He doesn't dare to ask for it. He can't really go crawling over his colleagues to get to the milk and sugar, can he? Why are they talking and reading at the same time? They're not reading out loud, they're talking about work.

Now he gets up and races out of the church, his wife runs after him but can't catch up. 'Frits!' she yells. 'What are you doing, for heaven's sake?' He runs up the fire escape of a high-rise apartment building.

That's where the story begins, in fact. Rumplala has almost reached the roof. He's going to jump, and that will be the start of a never-ending story. His wife is standing down below, he's causing her a lot of pain, but he can do no other ...

Just then the dog starts to bark. My wife is lying in bed. She knows that I'm in here writing. A little boy out on the walkway peers through my window. Hesitantly, by way of greeting, he raises his hand. 'Did you call first?' I ask.

'Yeah, Eva said I could play at your house if my mother wasn't home,' the boy says. Mik, the dog, is now barking to beat the band. My wife comes into my room.

'Why don't you let Maaikeltje in?' she asks. A little later I hear things being knocked over in the living room. Maaikeltje has tossed a tear-gas grenade and two stink bombs into the room, by way of contemporary playthings. He's a natural-born disrupter. The door to my room flies open and a few cats come running in.

'Maaikeltje, don't tease the cats. Maaikeltje.'

Go jump in a lake with your, 'Maaikeltje, Maaikeltje!' I think. Can't you tell I'm trying to write a story here?

Rumplala falls to his death, right at his wife's feet. She believes he's dead. And he is, he's dead as a doornail. To his disgruntlement, though, he has a soul that can survey the whole mess. What a lot of blood, all over the place. Then begins the fall, or the ascension, through the cosmos. The compass he always carries with him has fallen out of his trouser pocket and is floating along beside him, a couple of feet away, the prayer book too. The box of matches, he can't get to it, otherwise he would light up a cigarette right there. Do they expect him to believe that there actually *is* a hereafter? As long as there's no God. Rumplala hopes he'll finally get around to dying. Things can't go on like this for ever, can they?

How is a body supposed to write like this? It's impossible. 'Have you found the hole over there yet?' I hear a strange voice say. Strangers have forced their way into my home. I know what this is about, though. They're here to install the second phone line. 'Be careful, hey, with the pipes and wires,' I hear him say, 'before you know it you'll blow up the whole place.'

Rumplala is falling through space. He fumbles for his cigarettes, but can't find them. Now he notices that he's lost his trousers. As long as he doesn't run into another living soul. He starts weeping, because he is plummeting through the universe in his boxer shorts. That's been going on for hours. Where is this headed, where will it all end up? Frits Rumplala thinks about his mother. Was he a good enough son to her? Hadn't he offended her a little too often? Especially when it came to religion? Had he visited her regularly enough, there at the end? If life is an ordeal, then why does the ordeal have to go on after death too? Has he committed suicide for no good reason? He looks up with a start; there, in the distance, is a lighted gateway with angels flying around it. Please, spare me, Rumplala thinks.

'Hey there,' I hear someone say from out on the walkway. Can I help it that I write during the day and like to leave my window open?

'Good Lord, I almost had a heart attack,' I say. 'What's the idea, going around shouting "hey there"?'

'I heard you typing,' he says. It's Loek, the neighbour.

'I'm working on a pretty complicated story here,' I say, 'could we continue this conversation tomorrow?'

'Don't get your bowels in an uproar,' Loek says. 'There's nothing to get all worked up about. You know what you should read sometime? *The Famous Five*. Man, I laughed till I about burst. How do you like Assoe's new look?'

Assoe is Loek's dog, a gigantic black shepherd. Assoe scares the wits out of me. I stand up with a sigh, walk to the window and find myself looking straight into a cheerful, laughing muzzle. Massive canines. Brown eyes gleaming with pleasure in a

black head like a bear's. Huge paws on my window sill. 'My
God, what a dog,' I mumble.

'Assoe, bark for Daddy,' Loek says. The barking that begins
then is louder than anything I've ever heard. 'Has this dog got
a set of lungs, or what?' Loek says proudly. 'He's going to obe-
dience school these days, all I have to do is say boo and he'll rip
you to pieces!' Loek steps up cheerfully to my window sill and
leans on it. He's like a bar-room regular waiting for me to tap
him a beer. Tilting his head to one side, he peers at the sheet of
paper in my typewriter. 'What kind of a story is that?' he says.
'That's not supposed to be somebody's name, is it? Rumplala?'

'I need to get back to work,' I say. 'Let's continue this
tomorrow.'

'Oh, Mr High and Mighty,' Loek mumbles. 'Doesn't even
have time for a little chat . . .'

'No,' I say irritatedly, 'that's right, I don't, not right now.'

'Hey, did you hear the joke about the Belgian taxi driver?'
Loek asks.

'I really have to go on now,' I say. 'I'm sorry, but this story
is very important to me and you're ruining my concentration.'

Eva, who has been listening from the kitchen, comes into
my study and says: 'Can't you be a little more civil to Loek?
You're being very rude.'

'Oh, okay, I'm out of here,' Loek says cheerfully, 'before you
two lovebirds get into a spat.' He walks away brusquely, taking
his dog with him. I close the window firmly.

What is it that Frits sees up ahead? Could those be the
pearly gates? It's insane, all those angels floating around. And
they actually have wings! Deep in his heart, he'd sort of like to
go in. But he bears a massive grudge against all-powerful God,
who has ruined everything for him. God created him and then
placed him in a hell on earth. He doesn't want anything to do
with God, or with his angels either . . .

Then my study is filled with the deafening thrum of an electric
drill. A few minutes later, pieces of plaster and brick start
falling to the floor. An unshaven man in a baseball cap walks
into my room. 'Yup, right around the corner,' he says, 'is that

beautiful, or is that beautiful? Just pass the wire through here.'
Now there are two strangers standing in my study.

The second one says: 'Excuse us for just a minute.' I go on
typing imperturbably.

Loathing, fear, guilt. Peter is standing in front of him now.
'Listen, leave me out of this,' Frits says, 'I bet you want to take
me to see God?'

'Where's the plug supposed to go?' I hear a voice behind me
say. I point to a spot on the wall.

'Right there, gentlemen, if at all possible.'

So what about Rumplala's defence? Should he start in on
that right away? How would Dostoevsky have done it? No, let
him tumble through the universe for another million years or
so, that will make him see the light. I pick up the typewriter
and carry it into the living room, so I can go on working.

We have eight cats. A few of them are always sleeping somewhere, but two or three of them also spend all day chasing
each other around the house, and then our dog Mikkie gets in
on the act. Mikkie is a nice, handy-sized mutt, not too big and
incredibly sweet, a good watcher too. He barks all the time.

'Maarten, you haven't forgotten that we're having visitors
later on, have you?' Eva says. 'How about peeling some
potatoes?' Meanwhile, the cats have knocked the pages I've
typed onto the floor. The dog sits on them and starts scratching its fleas. As long as nothing gets ruined or lost, that's the
first thing that flashes through my mind. Within twenty-two
minutes I have peeled the potatoes, then I take the machine
and papers back to my study. The telephone has been installed,
the men are gone.

Rumplala is standing before God's throne. So this is the joker
who has made such a mess of his life. Joyful angels are peeing into ponds and singing cheerful songs. This place is really
something. A sweet reward after a life gone to pot. Lovely
chandeliers, ceilings of gold and azure, soft velvet curtains,
crystal tabletops, heavenly beds with silken sheets. Uh-oh,
there he goes, before he knows it he has called God a 'prick
and a scoundrel', now they definitely won't let him in any

more. He hardens his heart and says: 'To be honest, I don't want to have anything to do with you.'

God roars with laughter. 'Not only does he commit suicide, but he's got a smart mouth too!'

Now, from the living room, I hear the sound of the piano tuner. He is just getting started. That's a bit of a distraction. There is nothing I find as ridiculous, musically speaking, as the sounds a piano tuner makes. But we should just be glad he's showed up . . .

'If you don't want to have anything to do with me, well then go back and play outside,' God says. 'And take your time about it, in utter darkness, without anyone you know, through the vacuum of the cosmos, racked by the consciousness of your own self, go on, try it, maybe you'll come back. But it will be a few thousand years before I'll let anyone in who's insulted me like that.'

Suddenly I find myself able to type twelve pages back-to-back. I portray Rumplala's loneliness in space.

Gradually, he starts longing for Heaven. An hour's darkness can seem so long, to say nothing of a million years of falling and falling, with some stupid star flashing by every once in a while. He spends six months at his own house, but he can't communicate with anyone there and no one sees him. Then he continues on his journey. He thinks about the office. How can it be that he never, not once in his life, was able to understand what he read in the papers, in the tabloids and ladies' journals? He hopes that if he comes back, he'll have a chance to speak up for himself. 'So what did Barrestorg say to that?' 'He laughed and said: "We can always use Plan 2A to keep them sidetracked, as long as the deputy-minister doesn't come down with something."' Oh, Rumplala gets it now, if that happened the deputy-minister would discover what a mess things were at the hospital. 'This cleansing cream penetrates deep into your pores, where it nourishes the skin.' Those aren't the kinds of things that would drive anyone else crazy, that would make them commit suicide, are they?

*

Standing in the shop. 'Sir, did you take a number? If you didn't, then you either have to go to the back of the line or else wait here till hell freezes over.'

'What's wrong with *him*?'

'Oh, he forgot to take a number and I told him so, now he's in front of you.'

'Sir, it's your turn now, time to wake up. And what was it you were wanting? Oh, right, that special aged cheese, wasn't it? There's been called in about that, am I right?'

'There's been a call about that, damn it, what's with this "there's been called in"? There's been a call. And why all the numbers when there are only four people in the whole shop?'

'Sir, I'm afraid you don't understand, fifteen minutes from now there could be forty customers in line, and they might start arguing about who's next.' Life is unliveable . . .

'You are my sunshine, my only sunshine, you make me happy . . .' I hear the piano tuner singing along with a stupidly played ditty on the keyboard. You're never going to write that story, I think to myself, because you know nothing about suicide. I sit staring vacantly at my typewriter for a full five minutes.

Then my wife comes back in. 'The guests will be here soon,' she says, 'but the laundryman just showed up, could you come and talk to him?' I like the laundryman; he always has the most wonderful anecdotes. I go to him in the living room and leave the story for what it is.

At a certain point he says to me, while Eva is gathering the laundry: 'The guilder just keeps deprecating, it's bad news, we're going to economical ruin, and then something else . . . my son is starting to go into pubilescence.'

'Puberty,' I correct him, like some kind of know-it-all.

'What's that, pubity?' he asks.

'That's the phase when the nerve bundles develop between one's reason and one's sex drive,' I say.

'All right, whatever,' the laundryman goes on, 'so my son is in pubitescence and at night I can't doze off any more because I lie there thinking about it. The doctor came by a couple of times with all kinds of yaddika-yaddika-yaddika, you know what I mean? The whole thing has kind of thrown me into a dizzy.'

The doorbell rings, the guests have arrived. This is the shattering truth.

There's no way I can write about someone who commits suicide, because I myself am still alive.

Translated by Sam Garrett

19

BOB DEN UYL

War is Fun

Oorlog is leuk

Listen, there's a war on. What more could a ten-year-old boy want? At last, an escape from the rut of going to school each and every day. Never before has the total annihilation of the school, along with all its workbooks and textbooks, been such a clear and present possibility. May 1940: man, these are the days! The weather is fantastic, clear and hot, the air tingles with happy tension. Water mains have been shut off, the windows are covered in newspaper, the blackout curtains are rolled down at night. People are hoarding up supplies like mad all day long; the shelves are being stripped while, a few streets down, they're fighting against paratroopers. Planes come diving down out of that clear blue sky all the time, lovely grey planes with bent gull wings – first they come in, flying in high formation, then they fan out like a song and come screaming down on the city, the bridges, the airfield, the warship moored at Antwerpse Hoofd, the radio is on all day with reports of attacks and counter-attacks, the announcers with their serious, sonorous voices, soldiers are hiding in porticos and shooting at saboteurs. And early each morning that same light again, another clear blue sky – a dream come true. Everyone could die any minute. The national anthem over and over, as though the Holland–Belgium match were kicking off three times a day. On the radio everyone is talking about an ordeal, about trusting in God – what are they talking about? Rumours: we are going to die of hunger and thirst, German paratroopers are being dropped in civilian clothes. British and French troops advancing from the south. Our brave soldiers against the damn

Krauts, and then you've got the dirty turncoats. The boy feels like weeping in gratitude at being allowed to experience this, that God has so clearly chosen him.

The fifth day, the last. Unconditional surrender is the demand. What a load of hooey, Holland is the bravest country in the world, isn't it? The conquest of the Indies, the Zuiderzee causeway, our salvage tugs, that all counts for something, doesn't it? So what if the Queen has fled to England, she wouldn't know how to handle a gun anyway. No, it's like everyone says, we will fight until the Krauts have been driven out of the country. Hundreds of thousands of them have been killed already. Dutch boys, no better lads in all the world when they're fighting for their own soil. Hitler will sit up and take notice. Our army will hold its ground, they were ready for it, they stood firm and they will keep on standing firm, you'll see. Rumours: when the marines on the bridges run out of bullets they attack the Krauts with knives, when they run out of knives they use their teeth. Take that. Soldiers whose legs have been shot off go on calmly priming the cannons. That's the way we fight, and we'll hold the line. Besides: whatever happens, simply going back to school seems so far away now, things will never be like that again. From now on no lessons in penmanship, but in hand-to-hand combat. At home, the boy insists that they whet the breadknife till it's razor-sharp. Funny, though, that you never see any of our own planes, except for a few on that first day. Where are our G-1s? A public-service warning on the radio: boil water for five minutes before using.

The fifth day, the last. The bombardment has been rolling out across the city for an hour already. An unparalleled attraction. At first the boy has to stay inside, the bomb shelter in the park across the street can't be trusted. Concrete slabs leaning against each other, covered with sods, a wooden door, the place smells of piss. The planes perform a cheery, graceful dance in the air, climbing, circling, diving. Tiny cartridges drop from their fuselages, tumble down and disappear in the smoke. A raging thunderstorm. The tension as a plane flies over the house; if he tosses a bomb now, it will land right on top of us! He doesn't, though: barrelling along like a black horse, he flies past the critical point and disappears above the centre of town, amid the smoke and swarm of other planes. What's lighting a little fire down by the Noorder Canal compared to this? The city bellows and cracks, this can't go on much longer. Most of the planes have already flown away. Then a Messerschmitt comes cruising slowly across the northern city, like an exhausted warrior; the boy looks, the bay doors open and the cartridges fall. He runs to the stairwell, where all the tenants are lined up in accordance with the radio instructions: the stairwell is the safest part of the house. The ground starts to quake, people are crying – no reason for it, the bombs are falling all the way at the other end of the street, and against a dark sky filled with greasy smoke the houses begin to collapse and burn. Minor panic breaks out, the families start running as one for the bomb shelter after all, but it's already full to the brim. Here too weeping women, a man shouts furiously that it's about time we surrendered, before everyone is done for. That's strange, why wouldn't you survive this?

One hour later, the bombardment is over. A powerful southerly wind blows the roiling smoke over the house. The sun has vanished behind the cauliflower cloud, ash floats down on the dusky street. Everyone is silent now; the boy stands at the window and looks at the refugees from downtown, pushing overflowing handcarts and carrying mattresses on their backs, looking for safety. The blaze further up in the street throws strange colours against the shadowy sky. 'Some fire, isn't it?' the boy says to his father, who is standing beside him, and gets his head smacked right away. Gradually, he starts to suspect that something terrible may have happened. A man with a head wound is stumbling down the grubby, yellow street. The stench from the fire seeps in through the closed windows. The neighbour lady says this has taken thousands and thousands of lives. The boy thinks about it; of course, lots of people get killed during something like this, how could it be otherwise? An entire city turned to rubble, just think of it. And then a thought rises to the surface, offering new prospects of a better future. Did the teacher survive? He lives somewhere downtown, doesn't he? A war like this, what a blessing. It's hard to believe that a whole war, the whole bombardment, could be happening just to do him a favour, but that's what it's starting to look like. He's dead, he has to be! A fancy funeral, the whole class behind their beloved teacher's bier, it makes tears come to his eyes. There really still is something like justice in the world. He keeps his joy in check. A smiling face could get him into trouble.

A time of uncertainty follows. The boy wanders the neighbourhood aimlessly; he's not allowed to go into town, not yet. Then the day comes at last; in some obscure way his parents must sense that school is starting. There he goes, brimming over with expectation, the miracle will come to pass. Off to that damnable School of the Bible with its walls painted all grubby green, learning psalms by heart and chanting them out loud with the whole group, listening to those worn-out stories over and over again about the Lord Jesus and his disciples, but it will be bearable now that that bastard is dead, dead and buried. Well, buried: maybe he was burned to a crisp inside his house, anything is possible in times like these. The boys standing in front of the school are wound up, telling stories, one wilder than the next, but the boy cuts in line outside the gate. When the concierge opens it, he is the first to run across the playground. Inside the school building itself he reduces his speed, years of conditioning make him do that.

When he comes into the classroom he finds the teacher standing in front of the desks, an erect figure in a brown suit, the broad, disdainful mouth, dark hair combed back in a wave. The boy sits down at his desk and looks despondently at the man in front of him. The other children trickle in slowly, the teacher goes to the door, looks up and down the hallway, then closes it. Silence, silence, silence. He turns to face the desks, folds his hand, looks up at the ceiling and then closes his eyes. The children do the same. The boy folds his hands too but he keeps looking and sees the froggy mouth open and close, 'Our Father in Heaven, in these trying times we place our faith in You . . . help us to do this and that . . . forgive us for such and so . . . that we may not approach our enemies in hatred . . .'

The prayer echoes on slowly. Suddenly the teacher opens

one eye and looks straight at the boy. He feels himself reddening in fright and has the urge to close his eyes quickly, but, to his own amazement, he doesn't. He keeps his gaze fixed on the man, hating. The raised eyelid closes again, the prayer is finished and, after the amen, the teacher remains hunched over for a moment. Then he straightens up and moves deliberately, sternly, with a threat in every step, towards the boy.

Translated by Sam Garrett

20

MAARTEN 'T HART

Castle Muider

Het Muiderslot

When – the only passenger – I got out at a station without an accompanying village or town and gazed at the empty horizon, I could almost hear my father's voice again: 'The old pastor at the Christian Reformed Church didn't write his sermons in advance, but on his way to the pulpit on a Sunday morning, he'd have the duty elder press a scrap of white paper that had been folded many times into his hand. He'd unfold the note as he mounted the pulpit. By the time he reached the top it would be open and he'd read out to the shivering churchgoers the text the elder had written. He'd improvise a sermon around the text, unprepared and off the top of his head. But once he unfolded the piece of paper and there was nothing on it.

' "Nothing," he thundered through the church.

'He turned the paper over and shouted out "nothing" once again before continuing with, "Nothing, nothing! God created the world from nothing." Then he gave such a wonderful sermon that those who witnessed it still talk about it with tears in their eyes to this day.'

Yes, I thought, God created the world from nothing, and the first thing He built was the station building I'm walking towards now, and after that He created the horizon, and He filled the space in between with freshly ploughed fields, and, as frugal as a true Calvinist, He scattered a few scrawny trees around. And then, behind the clouds, He had the sun go up over the righteous and the wicked and brought me to this backwater to spend a whole day trailing a muskrat catcher. What's more, He provided a radio journalist to record everything I and the rat catcher might say to one another, so that it could be broadcast at a later moment.

I had already spotted the small, rather hunched reporter heading towards me on the abandoned platform. He shook my hand and said, 'Your train is fifteen minutes late.'

'Yes,' I said, 'delays. Nowadays, there are always delays.'

'Do you know why that is?' he asked.

'No,' I said.

'Because so many people throw themselves in front of the train,' he said.

'Oh.' I said.

'Yes,' he said, 'a Belgian friend once said it was typically Dutch to throw yourself under a train. Doesn't cost a thing.'

We traversed the consummate wasteland to his car. A while later we were driving through farmland. I was surprised there were even any roads. We drove towards the washed-out horizon. Beyond it lay the town and its station I'd just left behind. Crossing the town we drove towards the next horizon, the reporter saying, 'We need to agree exactly what we're going to do beforehand. We need to make a strict plan and think everything through to the best of our abilities.'

'Why?' I asked.

'Because otherwise it'll be chaos. Besides, we need to present the story to the listeners without giving them anything they can use to come to their own conclusions. We must show the rat catcher and his work as coolly and objectively as possible; we have to leave space for the listeners.'

'It all depends what kind of person the trapper is.'

'No,' he said, 'you mustn't talk like that. If that's your approach, you'll get some superficial and maybe even some reasonable information, but that'll be the extent of it. We'll be staying on the surface and that's exactly what we can't do. We need to furnish them with an interpretation of reality.'

I looked at the moving horizon. If I'd known this, I'd have said no when he asked, I thought to myself.

Unexpectedly, we reached a village that seemed to be comprised of little more than a church. The reporter parked his car on the village green and we headed towards the hotel where we'd arranged to meet the muskrat catcher. Given I'd never even heard of this village before, crossing the green to the hotel was like walking into a vacuum, as if I couldn't actually be there because the village didn't exist. Neither was I surprised to find that the hotel was completely empty – how could a muskrat catcher ever be waiting there for us? It felt strange to go into that silent hotel so early in the morning. The grandfather clock next to the bar wasn't ticking. From an unseen corridor came the clattering of buckets and when a door opened, we saw that the corridor was flooded and that in the water was a reflection of a window at the end of the corridor, through which a brief ray of sunshine fell. The water glistened. It looked just like a river was running right through the hotel. Then the door closed again and I suddenly noticed, above the bar, a collection of deer's heads with big antlers. The dead deer were staring at me from under their antlers.

The door to the corridor opened again and a woman with a mop peered around a coat stand and asked, 'Can I be of assistance, gentlemen?'

'We're meeting a muskrat catcher here,' the reporter said. 'He doesn't seem to be here yet; we'd arranged to meet at half past eight and it's now almost nine. Have you seen anybody?'

'No, there hasn't been anyone this morning.'

'I simply don't get it. Could you get us two coffees for the time being?'

'Yes,' she said, and carried on mopping.

We sat down at the only table that still had chairs around it.

'I'm sure it was half past eight,' the reporter said nervously.

I was about to say that the rat catcher was probably doing a preliminary tour of his traps to get rid of any unwanted animals but the reporter said, 'Now, first of all, let's agree on exactly what we're going to do. I'm imagining the following: we'll go around with the trapper as he does his work. You'll walk next to him and I'll walk behind you, and whenever you say anything particularly interesting to each other, I'll poke a pair of microphones between your shoulders. The point is for you to have a proper argument. No trivia or funny anecdotes but a conversation that cuts to the core. Preferably something dramatic that you both entirely disagree on, but keep your distance too, don't let yourself be drawn in – that'd be disastrous.'

The mopping woman interrupted her work and came over with two cups of coffee. When I tasted the liquid I wondered whether she hadn't simply squeezed out her mop into my cup, but I thought: She's not wrong, coffee *is* disgusting, why not just serve up the used hot water?

As I sipped cautiously, a little old man appeared in the doorway. He came towards me, his hand held out. He didn't smile but around his dark eyes, hundreds of wrinkles appeared that all pointed towards the stubbly, grey hair that was closely cropped to his skull. He shook the reporter's hand too and took off his coat. Then he sat down opposite me and immediately started up about muskrats. He kept on screwing up his eyes, and, from time to time, a gloomy expression would cross his face. He got out a pipe and calmly began to fill it.

'So,' he said, 'I'm to tell you a bit about my work and you'll come out with me for a day. Well, that's fine. But before we go out, I want to give you some background information. Listen, rat catchers are still employed on a regional level, and as a consequence, different provinces pay different salaries. This causes jealousy, of course. It all should have been nationalized long ago, but that's another issue. Until now, the trappers have fallen under the Ministry of Traffic and Water Management, just like the muskrat itself, but it's long been apparent that muskrats are more damaging to agriculture than to the waterways. So now they don't know where we belong – ach, well, that's always the problem with animals.'

'You're right,' I said, 'the stickleback doesn't fall under anyone.'

'What do you mean?' he asked. 'How do you know?'

'Oh,' I said, 'I once wanted to make a film about sticklebacks so I called the film fund at the Ministry of Culture and asked whether I could apply for a subsidy. Yes, they said, but the stickleback falls under the Ministry of Agriculture and Fishing. You'll have to apply to them, and they gave me a number to call. So I called. I got a man on the line who asked, "What

kind of fish is it? Fresh water or sea?" "Well," I said, "in the
breeding season it lives in fresh water and outside of that, in the
sea." "Oh, then it falls under sea fishing," the man said and gave
me a number. I called the number and told my story. "Is it an
edible fish or not?" the man asked. "Sir," I said, "I don't know
if you've ever seen a stickleback, but if you had, you'd know it
wasn't edible." "Oh," he said, ' "then it's not our department."
As a result, the stickleback doesn't fall under anyone, it isn't a
freshwater fish because it swims to the sea in the autumn and
it isn't a sea fish because you can't eat it. But that's not really
relevant here. We're talking about muskrats.'

'Yes,' the trapper said, 'apart from it not being clear which
department it belongs to, there's another problem. Catching
muskrats isn't an official profession. Anyone can do it. You
don't need any qualifications. That's why it's so poorly paid,
even though it's a hard job that actually requires an enormous
amount of expertise. Otherwise it all goes belly up because
you get too much bycatch.'

'Bycatch?' the reporter asked. 'What's that?'

'Well, other animals than muskrats in your snares and
traps. Common brown rats or water voles or ducks.'

'Or little grebes,' I added casually.

'Yes,' he said, all of his wrinkles vanishing in a flash and a
certain vigilance appearing in his dark deep-set eyes. 'Yes, our
biggest problem, grebes. They dive deep for a long time and go
far – they like to go through the culverts under the roads. There
isn't a single other animal, besides the muskrat, that does that.
Well, the otter does it too, but where do you still find those?'

He lit up his pipe and said, as he shrouded himself in
blue-white smoke, 'We had a scandal here once. Five grebes in
a single snare.' He drew on his pipe and commented, 'But now
we've got better traps and the snares are extra protected by a
latch that only the muskrat can open, so that problem's in the
past. The rats come swimming along at such a rate of knots
we've been able to adapt our catching methods to their speed.
Shall we get going?'

He got up calmly, put on his coat and left the hotel before
the reporter had time to gather all of his equipment.

'Interesting,' I said, 'this promises to be fun. Have you recorded anything yet?'

'No,' he said impatiently, 'we'd agreed to do the recording outside, walking along, hadn't we?'

'But why not now? It's pretty fascinating those rats not falling under anyone, isn't it?'

'Oh, what does that matter? Those are facts. What can facts tell us? It's about the interpretation of facts. We need to carefully select the facts. We can't just go recording willy-nilly. It'd all get mired down in mundane chitchat.'

'Yes, you can say that again,' I said. 'I once had a student, a sociology major who wanted to do an ethology minor and was going to observe stickleback behaviour. He turned up on the first day, sat down in front of a fish tank and his test case was startled and darted behind a plant. My student waited a while but when the stickleback still hadn't reappeared after ten minutes, he went away. The next day he came again and his test case darted behind a plant for the second time. The same thing happened all week long because a stickleback stays shy unless you sit in front of it for days at a time. During the second week, the student said to me, "I'm struggling to do any observation but that doesn't matter since it's really about the ideas, insights and their synthesis. Maybe you can just carry out the observation for me and I'll take care of the ideas."'

'Quite right too,' the reporter said, 'he'd understood how it works. Did you do the observations for him, then?'

'No,' I said.

'Why not?' the reporter asked in astonishment.

But I didn't reply, I walked out of the hotel and joined the trapper who was pulling on a pair of tall boots. After he'd done that, he pulled another pair of boots for me out of his car boot. After that, he got behind the wheel. The reporter got into the back and suddenly, as the trapper started up the engine, thrust two microphones between our shoulders.

'Ready, you can start now,' he said.

'Mild for the time of the year,' I said to the trapper.

'Yes,' he said, 'almost seems like spring. The winter jasmine is already in bloom.'

'Do you think we'll get any sun today?' I asked.

'It's not impossible,' he said, 'this morning they predicted breaks in the cloud and the occasional shower.'

The grey microphones disappeared and I heard the click of a tape recorder being switched off behind me.

'Now you need to take a good look in the ditches,' the trapper said. 'I'll drive slowly. Then you can see for yourself. The farmers have to plough a metre and a half from the sides of the ditch; if they don't, their tractors sink into the holes running into the earth all along the ditches. Can you see?'

'Yes,' I said, as I studied the black holes visible on and above the waterline. 'If the water levels weren't so changeable, you'd have fewer holes,' I said.

'That's right,' the trapper said, 'they always dig on the waterline. If the water rises, they dig higher, if it sinks, they move down with it.'

'Might it be possible to come up with a drainage system that maintains the same water levels so you only get one horizontal set of tunnels?'

'How would you like to organize that?'

'It must be possible,' I said.

Behind us I heard that distinct click again. The mouse-grey microphones appeared between us like a pair of dormant little chinchillas.

'Carry on,' the reporter said, 'this is good.'

I looked at the omnipresent horizon and said nothing.

The old trapper said, 'They always start in a corner and colonize the entire ditch from there.'

'They've found the perfect spot here,' I said, 'the Netherlands is made for muskrats.'

'You can say that again,' he said, 'water everywhere and agriculture too and all kinds of regulations they just don't fall under, and they've not even spread to Zuid-Holland and Noord-Holland where they'd have it made. If they got there . . .'

The rat catcher paused to avoid a muck cart.

'Then what?' I asked.

'It'd be end of story,' he said, 'they'd sink the whole ship.

The dams and dykes are terribly vulnerable. Yes, there'd be just one solution.'

'Which is?'

'Squatting houseboats,' he said.

The microphones disappeared and it was as though the trapper had been waiting for this because he braked sharply. He got out immediately and climbed down the bank of a ditch. He turned up the cuffs of his waders and stepped into the water. With a casual gesture that betrayed that he already knew what he'd bring up, he lifted up a trap. It contained a young rust-coloured muskrat with a pale grey belly. The rat catcher opened the trap, threw the young animal at my feet, cocked the trap and put it back. Then he got out of the ditch, grabbed the rat and cut off its tail with a knife. After that, he threw the dead animal onto the ploughed field that extended from the other side of the ditch to the brightening horizon.

'Ask him something then,' the reporter hissed behind me.

Was I, an unpaid interviewer, supposed to dance to the tune of this reporter? I wondered. I didn't want to think up any more questions and waited calmly for the trapper to move along. But he pointed out a reddish plant to me and said, 'Coltsfoot. Coming up already.'

Then he straightened up and stared at the horizon.

'Shame it isn't less misty,' he said, 'it'll probably take them a while to discover I'm here.'

We looked at the charcoal sky, which was turning a lighter grey to the south.

'Yes, there they are,' he said.

I saw a couple of black dots approaching fast from the sky to the south-east; they gradually began to look more like birds, birds which approached with large wing beats until suddenly they were circling the field where the rat lay.

'Two buzzards,' I said.

'Yes,' he said, 'they find them as delicious as I do, they're at their tastiest at this time of year – we share them out equally; if I catch six in a day, we have two each.'

The buzzards slowly circled the dead animal that lay on the farmland like a rusty stain.

'They won't dive until we've gone,' the old catcher said, 'and they'll gulp him down in the blink of an eye. They usually follow me all day, tidying up everything I catch. Well, reincarnation! When I return from death, I hope I'll come back as a buzzard. No one hates them or envies them or needs them. They're never distressed or in danger, and as long as they eat carrion, they don't need to kill anyone to stay alive. And you can bet on it becoming a paradise for them here. The muskrat will keep submerging the Netherlands until there are no human descendants left of those folks who once invaded the place on wooden floats. Then it'll be exactly like it always was here. Muskrats will flourish in this brackish delta, as will the buzzards that'll save them from having to bury their dead. And then the otters might come back. Did you know there's no pet more faithful than an otter? If their owners die, they die too. In the Middle Ages, poor people who couldn't afford to keep a dog kept otters and they were lucky to have them too, they're the most affectionate animals under the sun. I witnessed that in America.'

He stopped talking, rubbed his eyes for a moment and I heard the reporter whisper behind me, 'No use to me, this.' He turned off his recorder as the trapper ambled off, quietly muttering, 'They don't know how lucky they are here. I've seen them in Alaska and Canada, in the middle of the winter when it was bitterly cold and they could still survive because they have such great pelts, and even at minus forty, they manage to keep one bit of water open as a group, but they don't need to do that at all here. They're like pashas here, it's the Promised Land, no otters or eagles or lynxes or minks.'

'But don't the polecats get them, then?' I asked.

'No, they don't like getting their feet wet,' the trapper said.

'And foxes?' I asked. 'They've spread everywhere, haven't they?'

'You're telling me, but foxes don't like water either, although they do sometimes catch the odd young, foolhardy muskrat. But look: muskrats rarely venture onto land. There's plenty of food in and along the edges of the ditches; they only have to tunnel in from the waterside to run into white beets and potatoes and beetroot or other crops and they can go from Vlissingen to

Groningen without having to cross a single dyke. Hang on, there's another trap here.'

He climbed down and put his hand into the water. A muddy rat came up with the trap; the catcher quickly took it out and cut off its tail.

'Ask him why he keeps cutting off the tails,' the reporter whispered.

'I don't need to ask,' I said, 'I can just tell you. He does it to stop anyone who finds the rat cutting off its tail and giving it to him. He has to pay a bounty for each tail. It used to be five guilders, but I don't know if that's still the case.'

'Yes,' the rat catcher said, 'the bounty's still the same.'

'Then it's been five guilders for fifteen years,' I said. 'My father killed one in the graveyard in 1963 and got five guilders.'

'During that harsh winter, I'll bet? Yes? Must have been an old codger. Elderly males go wandering off on their own. Probably looking for a suitable place to rest its head for good.'

'How odd the bounty hasn't gone up,' I said.

'No, it's not odd,' the trapper said, 'it's about five times easier to catch a muskrat than it used to be and everything has got five times more expensive since they first came swimming down the Rhine.' He threw the dead, mud-caked rat into a field. Black dots approached silently in the sky.

'Maybe this is interesting for you. About three years ago, some unknown fellow was handing in between ten and fourteen tails a week to me. So it was costing me about fifty to seventy guilders a week. This went on for almost a year and I was amazed that I never saw that lad out in the fields and neither did I have any clue where he was catching those rats. But, well – it didn't matter to me; I didn't have to pay the bounty out of my own pocket. One day I was chatting to a colleague and he told me that each week some young whippersnapper was handing in ten to fifteen tails to him. "With one of those stick-on moustaches?" I asked. "Yes," he said. "And hair that looks like it's had clay brushed into it and then combed out again?" "Well," he said, "I wouldn't describe it like that, but it looks a lot like Elvis Presley's hair." "Then it's the same one," I said. "I don't get it, if he looks like that guy you just mentioned, why doesn't he stand in front of a microphone and open his mouth? You can make a fortune doing that these days, especially if you don't know a damned thing about singing and have a voice a market trader would be ashamed of."

'We got in touch with some other colleagues. It was the same story everywhere: a lad of about twenty handing in tails all over the place. So, reluctantly since I was against it, we got the police involved. After a good eighteen months – still rather quick, don't you think? – it turned out that some poverty-stricken Count was living on a vast estate with a pond under each big tree. He'd released muskrats onto the estate and aside from that, he was rearing them in his empty stable block. Don't ask me how, I wouldn't have a clue. Every day he caught a few rats from his ponds and he cut the tails off some of the rats he'd bred in the stables (I still have to pay five guilders a tail, a rat's a rat) and he sold their pelts to the fur industry because in Belgium they're still very active in the muskrat fur trade, while here in the Netherlands it's been banned, and he sold the contents of the pelts to seafood restaurants along the coast as water rabbit, and he sold the tails to that lad for fifty francs a piece. Since in Belgium you get absolutely zilch for a tail, the lad would smuggle a couple of saddlebags full of them over the border on his moped each week.'

The reporter hadn't even gone to the trouble of switching on his tape recorder, but I asked, 'Why is it illegal to sell muskrat fur here?'

'Because a muskrat's pelt isn't worth the same all year round. It's thickest in the autumn – getting ready for the winter. If you wanted to trade in them, obviously it would be in everyone's best interests to only catch them in the autumn and leave them alone in the spring and summer. And what you get then is that not wanting to drive them away, but actually profiting from their presence. More rats, more fur. It's a sensible measure. And now I just have to check a culvert here.'

He stepped into a ditch and pulled a mesh trap out from under a small dam. There were two muskrats in the trap.

'So, these are undamaged. They simply drowned. Mine, for tonight; there's no tastier meat than that of the muskrat – full-flavoured, tender and spicy like the best game and yet not

as dry; it's even more delicate than yearling venison. I'm not
surprised predators devour them so eagerly. It's almost
unbelievable they managed to escape from Czechoslovakia,
where a prince who'd brought them with him from Alaska first
released them into the wild. Yes, a wonder they managed to
spread everywhere, while everything and everyone that can eat
finds them tasty. They have to be excellent breeders. Offspring
all year round!'

'Yes,' I said, 'so it sounds like a hopeless task ever getting rid
of them.'

I heard a click behind me. The silent grey microphones
appeared between us again.

'I never have to worry about being out of a job,' the man
said presently and then ambled further along the bank of the
ditch. I walked behind him and the reporter walked in front of
me and behind the catcher and held one microphone to his
mouth and another to mine and I thought: How long is he
going to keep this up? We were just walking along, the old man
slowly, almost trudging, and the reporter wading through the
ditch like a heron anticipating a catch, and I followed him and
said nothing and saw, out of the corner of my eye, the black
dots slowly flying through the sky.

'You can start,' the reporter said.

I looked at him and thought: He's just like a walking scare-
crow with his arms spread out, and those black trousers and
that black jacket. It's as if a silhouette were walking along,
actually it's as if he wasn't there but had sent his shadow, and
again I heard him say, 'You can start now.'

'Steady on,' the rat catcher said, 'we've got the whole of
eternity ahead of us.'

We walked on further in the deadly silent, wintry desolation, along a ditch, along a second ditch, the catcher pointing
out to me each time the holes or footprints of the muskrats, or
the tiny red crowns of coltsfoot peeking through the mud. I
marvelled at the fact that the catcher and I had understood
each other without needing to say a single word. We simply
walked, along ditches that continued to bend and from which
side channels issued and the black dots followed us at a slow

pace that kept them from catching up. The reporter turned off his tape recorder and said, 'Well, now I have enough background noise.'

We walked from one trap to the next and not a single trap was empty. The catcher kept on bringing up full traps from the culverts and I thought, If he always catches this much, the country must be swarming with muskrats. There were three common brown rats in one of the culverts, and one of the traps threw up a tailless animal ('I'll get that back soon for five guilders,' the catcher said). The morning passed and a fine, chilly drizzle descended as we walked back to the trapper's car. We headed back to the hotel, its corridor was now dry, and ordered some sandwiches, sitting down at a table that looked as if it had been laid for dinner.

I asked the rat catcher, 'How did you end up in this job?'

'It's a long story,' he said, 'but what it comes down to is that I tried pretty much everything a man can do before slowly realizing that, actually, the oldest profession a man has ever had still provides the most satisfaction, even though I practise it with traps and snares rather than a bow and arrow. But the difference isn't that great and I soon found out there's no better way to check whether previously clean ditches haven't been taken over by rats than to ride up to them and study them on horseback. Today I took the car because you were coming, but usually I do everything on a horse, although the ministry I no longer fall under does find it odd that I'd rather have oats than petrol. I started off studying forestry in Wageningen but I didn't finish my degree because I got the chance to go to Venezuela. I chopped wood with the natives for a few months. Every day I'd go into the jungle with forty of the fellows. They went barefoot and pretty much every day one of them would tread on one of these tiny moss-green snakes that would bite them. Within two minutes, the native would've contorted so much, his feet would reach his afro hair and we'd bend him straight again and hang him on a stick and two men would lay the ends of the stick across their shoulders and carry him. I kept on asking my boss for shoes for the natives. But he said it was pointless. So I saved up and bought forty pairs of shoes in one go. They were so happy! Forty black men wearing eighty shoes in the jungle and not a single death that day! But in the evening they started gambling – the shoes were the stakes! They played until one man had won all the shoes. The next day we go into the jungle again and one man had tied forty pairs of shoes together and hung them over his shoulder. Well, that day we had another contorted body. Then I came back to the Netherlands. I couldn't find anything here that suited me. I worked in catering and even in construction for a while. I've done everything, but the thing I liked best was being a forester. So when the rats started to turn up here, I became a trapper right away. Since then I've been quite happy, particularly out here in the sticks where you don't come across a soul. I have everything I need: a horse, a roof above my head, no women around, a bucket of oats, a bit of baccy when it suits, an old jerrycan to make coffee in, and varied outdoor work. But what do you do actually? I understand you work at the university and apart from that you write, the radio man told me?'

'That's right,' I said.

'Yes,' he said, 'I've met a few writers in my life. Often they come up with all kinds of important reasons for writing. Ostensibly they can't do anything else, they have to, it's a compulsion, it's a need, a necessity, and if they want to mystify you even more, they say they want to bring about change with their writing, but my impression is that they were unfortunate enough to be born liars. Every writer is a born liar and while you don't get very far in this society, or in any other, as a trickster they make a virtue of necessity. But anyway! If you're a writer, I've got a good story about muskrats for you. A bit more than six months ago, the owner of that castle, Huys Hooghgelegen, asked whether I'd like to drop in for a look because he suspected his estate was infested with muskrats. So I went there and we walked around his enormous estate together and he told me that increasing amounts of flowers were disappearing from his flowerbeds. At first he thought his children were picking the flowers, but since they kept denying having anything to do with it, he began to suspect that somebody else must be stealing his dahlias and sweet williams. He

didn't manage to catch anyone at it, even though flowers were
disappearing on a daily basis. What he did notice was they
were mainly being picked in the vicinity of his biggest pond. In
the pond – yes, sometimes rich folks come up with crazy things
to keep themselves entertained – he'd had built a scale model of
Castle Muider, with a bridge and thick walls and towers and
turrets and little canons mounted on the walls. He kept hearing noises in the castle. It seemed too small to house a real
ghost and since he didn't believe in dwarf ghosts, he surmised
that rats or mice must be taking advantage of his hospitable
lodgings and called in a regular rat catcher. But he couldn't
find any droppings or teeth marks or nests and this was why he
ended up thinking that muskrats might have taken up residence in the Castle Muider. As we walked towards it, I could
see from a distance that he was right. The pond around his
hobby was full of waterlilies. But there wasn't a flower or even
a bud to be seen. If you know that muskrats love to fill their
bellies with waterlily buds, you can guess that it was a cut and
dried case for me: muskrats had moved into the castle. The
only thing I found strange was that they'd chosen that Castle
Muider. It didn't look like suitable lodgings for muskrats at all.
I came to the instant conclusion that a lone elderly rat had
taken up residence; he'd cut himself off from the pack and gone
a bit funny in the head. We inspected the castle in so far as that
was possible. And bingo: you know muskrats bung everything
up with humus. I soon saw that the old, invisible fellow had
filled in the doors with humus bungs and closed off the windows with humus bungs and blocked off the gun turrets with
humus bungs. Even the little canons had been loaded with
humus bungs. I laid snares, not just under the castle bridge but
also next to all the other holes I could find in the castle beneath
the waterline. But I didn't catch anything.

  'The count telephoned me again recently, to tell me he'd
managed to catch the animal at last. One night he'd heard
noises coming from his swimming pool, which was empty in
the winter, and following the noise, he'd discovered a muskrat
that had fallen in and could no longer get out. And this will
demonstrate how frightened people are of muskrats because he

poured petrol over the creature, lit a newspaper and threw it at it. Horrible!'

'Why are people so frightened of muskrats?' I asked.

'Because they're big and they come at you.'

'Really?' I asked. 'They do that?'

'Yes, if you're in a field with one, he'll calmly come walking up to you. They're not at all afraid and if you don't go away they'll try to bite you. People are scared to death of them. But now I'm going to leave you for a minute and then we'll go and look at a dyke and you can see what kind of damage they do.'

He wandered off and the reporter whispered, 'We really have to go about this differently, otherwise it'll be worthless.'

'Didn't you record that nice story about the Castle Muider?'

'Nah,' he said irritably, 'silly anecdotalism. It can't be true. Gun turrets. You get those in airplanes, not castles. What's the point of stories like that? We need insights, we need to confront the listeners with ideas about muskrats and a discussion about both your ideas. An exchange has to come out of it; the muskrats are just a means – the aim is to use this phenomenon to gain an insight into the structure of our society. It's about a clash between the interpretation of yours and his realities, in which the rat is the catalyst. What can we learn from all that information? All those facts? All those silly stories? The point is the ideas, the syntheses, the summaries!'

'You've said that,' I said.

'Yes,' he said, 'we need to make a programme that appears to be about muskrats but actually penetrates deeper. The muskrat has to be as big as the world.'

'A mammoth muskrat?' I asked guilelessly.

'Exactly,' he said, 'from now on stop asking questions and start discussing, don't go after the man's experiences but his opinions, otherwise it will keep being superficial and anecdotal!'

The rat catcher returned. We got up, paid, and soon were driving along in the greyish January afternoon haze. The microphone popped up next to me again, but I didn't ask any questions and I didn't speak. I simply looked at the ditches along the road, recognizing the signs of their presence. From now on – I'd almost spoken into the microphone but kept it to myself just in time – I'd always be able to recognize these spores, even though up to today I'd failed to notice them. It was as though I could hear somebody else, who'd temporarily taken over my thoughts, remarking: *And that's the hardest thing, being a good observer. It's something only a child, not yet corrupted by having ideas, can do. Because everything you think is a kind of tax on sensory perception, paid for by your reason, because your brains have to function somehow. What it comes down to is not the functioning of the brain and the perpetually and necessarily incorrect falsifying and superficial philosophy they issue, but the ability to process all that excess ballast, that material in your brains produced by thought, and to replace it with a unique, always one-off receptivity to one-off sensory impressions, because in your entire life there is nothing that is completely identical, so that each moment has its own value, and that value is registered through your senses and so that, actually, there isn't even any time left to think.*

We stopped and walked along a small river, not for half an hour or an hour, but the entire afternoon. I suspected the rat catcher had deliberately taken us on a long walk, yes, that he was trying to test our powers of endurance. He walked tirelessly ahead of us, despite his advanced years, and most of the time the reporter walked between him and me, inserting his microphone into position from time to time, to no good effect. Sure, the catcher and I sometimes chatted, and once an argument even threatened to develop because the trapper casually said that the muskrat's holes don't collapse until they've been unused for two years and I said, 'Obviously. It's not in their interest for their holes to collapse when they're still living in them, so they won't collapse unless the rats are caught and can't keep their holes in good condition.'

'Nonsense,' he said, 'they dig so much and so deep, there's always a risk of collapse.'

'But you just said they don't collapse until they've been empty for two years.'

'Yes, but not if a tractor drives over them.'

'Then they do actually collapse?'

'Sometimes.'

'Often?'

'I don't know.'

That was the moment the reporter swung into action. The microphones were held to our mouths again and he said, 'Would you have that argument again, please?'

'Sure,' the catcher said, 'like I said: there's always a risk of collapse but the risk is larger when the holes have been empty for a long time.'

'That's undoubtedly true,' I said and we walked further along the river that had burst its banks in some places so that we had to wade through the reflections of clouds and the reporter recorded the sound of our squishing feet –'Nice to play at the beginning of our programme,' he said, 'sets the scene' – and the melancholic January afternoon light that rises up from the earth when it's not quite freezing. It grew chilly, my hands began to shake and my feet were blocks of ice, but it didn't bother me because I was walking along still waters in which the reflections of pollard willows formed ghostly, silent silhouettes.

When we reached a dyke on higher ground, the muskrat catcher said, 'There was a danger of the dyke breaking here last summer. The rats had dug through so that when the river rose, water ran through it. The local water board had to use some pretty heavy machines to press the holes shut.'

I listened carefully to what he was saying and thought: You see. Those holes are so well built they don't collapse. They needed heavy machinery to press them shut. But I said nothing because the reporter, who didn't seem to have ears to hear with, didn't grant me the argument I might have had with the old trapper about it.

We continued on our way past the willows, along the small river. I missed the black dots, but noticed a goldeneye at a bend, which, strangely enough, swam past on its own and dived under for a moment with that irresistibly supple ease that even a grebe can't equal. We saw two little grebes not much further up. The trapper paused for a moment and pointed at them. I smiled and he said, 'Two of them, though.'

'Two of what?' the reporter asked.

'Two dabchicks,' the trapper said.

'What are they, then?' the reporter asked.

'Little grebes,' the trapper said, 'look, see them swimming there.'

'Where?' the reporter asked and the rat catcher pointed at the water. The little grebes dived under and the reporter said, 'I can't see anything.'

We walked on. A dyke rose up ahead of us and behind it glittered a lake fringed with fields and a wood. Then the sky lit up briefly for the second time that day, even though it was almost dusk, because the sun unexpectedly broke through the clouds before disappearing again at once. As we climbed the dyke, I heard the lost cry of a curlew and a little later, I suddenly saw five fly up at the edge of the grey woods. They didn't all fly up at the same time but one by one. While the first had already left the woods, the last one still had to stretch its wings.

'Look,' the old trapper said, 'the dyke broke here a year or two ago because it was weakened by muskrat tunnels. It's the only dam structure in the area that doesn't fall under the local water board. When the dyke broke, they were here in a flash to repair it. And that's where we're heading, here in the Netherlands, and that's why I've brought you here because it would be criminal not to show you this. Here, to thirty centimetres below and forty centimetres above the waterline, they've put in a stonework facing to stop the muskrats from digging again. I hope you'll see for yourselves how ugly it is, and sooner or later, they'll still break through. But before that happens, the civil servants on those boards and committees will discover that stone facings are effective in stopping them from digging and they'll build stone banks everywhere, until long after the first rats have broken through, because before that gets through to those boards and committees, the rats will have multiplied thirty or so times and all of our richly vegetated, reedy riverbanks will have been sacrificed.'

Then he stopped talking. He stared gloomily at the other side of the small lake that, at the bottom of the stone dyke, good-naturedly cast small waves again and again against the bluestone cladding. Further up, the water was as smooth as a mirror. It ran over almost imperceptibly into a meadow where thousands of black coots stood, all of them looking in our direction. As we descended the stony banks, they turned their heads then their black bodies forty-five degrees and began to walk off. It was something you'd never forget, all those white beaks that were suddenly no longer visible and all those black bodies that moved away from us so calmly and controlled, although it was unnecessary because, once we'd reached the waterline, we stopped to watch the slowly retreating coots that suddenly, all of them at the same time, looked back so that all those white beaks became visible again, and then stopped in their tracks, just like us. The sun broke through again, momentarily sweeping a ray of light over the coots, which lit up, shining, one by one, and then extinguished again as the ray moved on, brushing us briefly as it went.

The reporter came to stand behind us and wrangled two microphones between our shoulders, whispering, 'Carry on,' but the old man laid a finger to his lips and then allowed the same finger to tilt forwards until he was pointing at the coots with it.

'Pay attention,' he said so quietly that it felt like I'd gone deaf. I looked across the water at the coots, saw the dark clouds clearly and yet threateningly reflected in the smooth surface of the middle of the lake which rippled around the edge. Because I was just staring and staring at those deep clouds under water, it took me a while to notice, even though it had been going on for a while, that the coots in the middle of that gigantic flock of birds standing motionlessly were moving apart to allow through something that moved rather slowly and steadily towards us. When whatever it was that was approaching was halfway, I saw how calmly and almost nonchalantly the coots granted it brief passage, before closing up again. I had even stopped blinking, so keen was I not to miss a single moment. I looked intently at the moving hole through the flock of coots nearing the waterline. The reporter whispered behind me again, but I pushed away the mouse-grey microphones. The last coots moved apart, briefly revealing in the already dark,

misty twilight a long, flat, black shape that inserted itself into
the water and begin to splice the reflected clouds. It left behind
ripples that became ever wider and flowed back towards the
coots, as it reached the place where a small part of the already
deep-red, but mainly obscured by clouds, sun was reflected in
the water. It swam across the sun, turning the sun into ripples
that ran to the left and right behind it and soon faded away,
and in the meantime it was coming towards us. At the same
time, it didn't really seem to be moving; it was as though someone was pulling it through that silent, charcoal lake. When it
reached the stony bank, around ten metres from where we
were standing, it hesitated for a moment. Its head disappeared
under water and it soon came up again about five metres further along, and there it climbed the bank, not even dripping or
shaking itself out, before walking immeasurably slowly away
from us across the shiny, stone-clad bank.

'He does that every evening,' the rat catcher whispered.

'Louder please,' the reporter said, 'I won't be able to record
it otherwise.'

'He's here every evening,' the rat catcher said, turning
towards me to give me the opportunity to lip-read his silent
words.

'He always comes here around this time, when the curlews
fly up and the last starlings seek out trees to roost in. I think
he's one of those lonely old chaps.'

'What does he do here?' I asked, as quietly as possible.

'I don't know. Maybe he inspects the bank to see whether
there isn't a place he can dig a hole just for himself, here where,
for the time being at least, there's no chance he'll be disturbed
by others.'

'You're not tempted to catch him?' I asked.

'I can't bring myself to do it,' he said, 'he can't do anyone
any harm any more. He doesn't impregnate any females; they
don't want to mate with a knackered old muskrat like him.'

He stopped moving his soundless lips and just gazed at the
large dark patch that was moving without any haste towards
the point where the stony bank stopped and the lake ran into
the ditch.

'You can tell he's approaching the end of his life,' the rat catcher said, 'he does everything slowly as though eternity were within hand's reach.'

The animal waddled slowly along, taking the time for each separate stone. I was sorry he was already so far away because now I couldn't see much more than a vague black shape that wasn't just walking away but also slowly dissolving into the increasingly nocturnal dusk.

'No,' the short, grey-haired man who'd been to Venezuela said, 'no, I can't and I won't catch him. I come here every evening to see whether he's still alive and every evening a jolt of happiness goes through me when I see he's still there – and then I think the world can't be such a bad place if coots still part for a lonely old man and if that fellow is still able to find a place to rest his head for the night.'

Translated by Michele Hutchison

21

HELGA RUEBSAMEN

Olive

Olijfje

Olive and I moved into our last shabby attic room because we'd been kicked out of all the nice lodgings. We were old but high-spirited and we liked a tipple. To be honest, we no longer cared where we spent the winter. We'd gone from the bottom to the top and taken a fast train back down again. We'd seen it all. We'd misbehaved in Marlot Park and we'd been called hussies on the banks of the Zieken canal; we'd lived like fine ladies on Count Loeki's loot until he'd breathed his last breath; we'd sailed Holland's inland waterways and the Seven Seas in the seaworthy barge of retired Rear Admiral Hendrickx – with a 'c, k, x' – and we'd sold chips on a stall at VUC Den Haag's football grounds, sleeping under the counter, all three of us, including Pimmy the dog. In short, we weren't that fussy any more.

Apart from saying that if there was a drink for the taking we'd be there, gossips said that Olive and I were an item. Maybe that *was* the case sometimes, but we had a lot of other stuff on our minds, for example, how, at our age, old but still too far from our pensions, we could get hold of some cash. We drew benefits, of course, picking up eighty guilders from the Beierse Bank every Monday morning, but that was a basic allowance and we couldn't live in the manner we were accustomed to on it. We did a few cash-in-hand jobs now and again, but as few as possible because there was little satisfying work of that type to be had, and we scraped together ten guilders here and twenty-five there – which still added up even though it was peanuts compared to the free pickings of the past. We didn't complain about it. Our needs had diminished too. It was no longer as important to dress up, to primp and preen. In my case, it was no longer worth it. It had never been much use anyway, as far as I was concerned.

Olive had deliberately stopped dolling herself up, otherwise I'm sure she could have put on a good show, better than a lot of those young things, slender and chic as she was. But she'd had enough, she said. All of her previous earnings, which were not insignificant, had blown away like ashes in the breeze, so why would she go to more trouble than she needed to? Olive could have been rich and well-married, to an aristocrat if necessary, if she hadn't been too kind for that – and too indifferent. Her motto had always been: It's all Swings and Roundabouts. By this she meant that if, for example, she had married Count Loeki, she'd probably have been harassed to death by his relatives by now, and if she had looked after her money better, she'd have had a house, but no happy memories, only all the worries that come with ownership. That was the way Olive thought about things, and so did I, naturally.

The people who called Olive a harlot were wrong. She was simply open to any suggestions and if it happened to pay, she wouldn't say no. Rather than whorish, she was just curious – more than anyone I'll ever meet again, alas. Where money was concerned, she always put her personal pleasure first and never did anything out of pure calculation. The way I got to know her was proof of that. Thirty years ago.

I was going through a tough patch and was sitting in my attic room one miserable Sunday afternoon, complete with drizzle and pasty faces outside, struggling to keep body and soul together. That's what you went to high school for, my mother would have said, but one of the reasons for my despair was the five years I'd had to spend there, steering a middle course through the dangerous rocks of that girls' school, without mentioning some of the female teachers with their sultry gazes and not even thinking about my confusion when we attended parties with the boys from the boys' school opposite. The only attractive thing about those boys was that they casually smuggled in bottles of booze and when I'd been allowed to take a few sips from them, my confusion would disappear and I would go and sit on the wooden bench with the wallflowers, where it was cosy and warm.

On that Sunday afternoon, there was half a tin of sardines that I was going to share with the cat and not a drop to drink, apart from tap water. Little by little, it still turned five o'clock and I was lying stretched out on my bed, periodically going over to my record player to play my one record by Big Bill Broonzy and then I'd pace around and roll my forty-seventh ciggie and wonder why the hell I'd bothered to get dressed. The cat was sitting by the window counting raindrops, as happy as Larry, and I envied her, and I decided that she could keep all the kittens she was carrying so that I would be surrounded by beauty and insouciance and *je m'en foutisme*.

Then my downstairs neighbour, a tomboyish girl who worked in an acrobatic group that performed in nightclubs, came upstairs and said, 'Tell me, have you got the pip or something? You're pacing backwards and forwards and that's the sixteenth time in the last hour you've put that darky on. Isn't there anything you want to do?'

Nothing with her, I thought.

'Do you fancy a beer?' she asked.

She was actually quite sweet, but back then I was still jealous of those kinds of girls who spoke so frankly and didn't seem bothered by anything.

'Come with me to Olive's,' she said. 'These days she even has a good spread on Sundays.'

I wanted to put on my one smart skirt instead of my corduroy trousers but the girl said, 'You needn't bother for Olive. Just come along quickly because once her gentleman arrives, we'll have to leave.'

I didn't see much point in a visit like that, but as the tram rode through a posh Scheveningen neighbourhood, the girl told me that Herr Doktor Von So-and-So, Consul General, had been keeping Olive for the past few months. She'd got to know him through his driver, Gentle Willem; the girl knew Olive in turn through the nightclub circuit where Olive would turn up after the regular bars had shut and was always extremely generous and open-hearted. Von So-and-So was a dignified, shy gentleman with a bald pate, gold-framed glasses and teary eyes and Olive always felt sorry for everyone and everything, which was why she was perpetually surrounded by stray dogs and cats and tramps and other unfortunates, of which this gentleman was one, Olive had said, because he was weighed down by many complexes. Olive, who rarely went into indiscreet details, had told her that she absolved him of his complexes and, in exchange, he absolved her of her material concerns.

After hearing this story, I became more interested, but when we found ourselves in front of a *fin-de-siècle* mansion, I wanted to go back because we weren't dressed for the occasion. The rain had made the hair of the acrobat, an athletic negress, expand into a feather duster of a million frizzy curls framing her impudent face. Her leotard, decorated with pink and pale blue flowers, clung to her body so that you could see she wasn't wearing anything underneath, not even a pair of knickers. In the tram, she'd kept her bright red raincoat over it, but now she was strolling insouciantly, and as they say, worse than naked, up the manicured garden path. I was dressed, albeit in a pair of stained corduroys and a dirty blouse, but that was as far as it went. Half of my hair was white blond, its original colour, and half chestnut brown and it hung in slithers around my face, which looked like an old-fashioned drawing of Oliver Twist. What's more, my hands and lips were trembling.

But Charmie said that Olive would welcome us with open arms.

She did too and I was astonished. She looked like a Spanish donna, her ink-black hair piled high, and she was wearing a long, black velvet gown with a white lace tucker and cuffs and she had on dangly earrings and ruby and diamond rings. She had stuck a tortoiseshell comb into her hair, also studded with rubies. If she hadn't rushed up to us with such immediate enthusiasm, I really would have curtsied.

'How nice that you've come to cheer me up, Charmie. This weather makes me need a drink and it's a Sunday and I can't drink alone, you know.'

She shook my hand and said, 'Is this your girlfriend? Who is she, your little Oliver Twist?' That's what I'd thought just before, and now she was saying it, and then I hoped – well, what exactly? – it's hard to reconstruct after thirty years, perhaps I hoped, even then, that I would never lose sight of that marvel Olive, not for the rest of my days, even if I could only observe her from a distance.

Once we were inside a great many bottles and crystal glasses appeared on the table and Olive said we could eat whatever we wanted, but for the time being we didn't want food, I almost didn't even need a drink because the cheerful Charmie and the shining Olive made it seem like the sun had risen in this ostentatious room. Charmie and Olive launched into a pyrotechnic show of stories and I limited myself to laughing, which I could at least do here heartily, and everything was going wonderfully well. Although, drinking more slowly than the enraptured women, I noticed that Olive's stately appearance was slowly beginning to show fine cracks. Her hair came loose, the tortoiseshell comb hung somewhere between her ear and her shoulder and she'd unbuttoned the tucker and rolled up her sleeves. The black velvet gown was covered in cigarette ash and wine stains, but she had a flush to her olive-coloured cheeks and her eyes sparkled. When you drink you lose track of time and it must have been seven o'clock in the evening when a civilized bell tinkled. 'Holy mother of God, it's him!' Olive cried, not frightened or startled, but simply like a person who'd forgotten they had a date. 'He'll let himself in with his key. Well, don't worry, Charmie, grab the bottle and your glasses and sit in the window seat. I'll hurry things along.' She took us to a large, deep window seat, set down some bottles and glasses, threw us a couple of cushions and closed the curtains. We found ourselves in a tiny recess, closed off with velvet and glass. Olive stuck her pretty face through the curtains again for a moment and put her finger to her lips.

We heard Herr Doktor Von So-and-So coming in and some pleasant chit-chat in German between him and Olive. He asked whether she'd had guests – well, that was a polite question – and whether she'd enjoyed herself. Olive said yes to everything and nodded her head and I couldn't tell whether she was behaving differently from usual, but I was under the impression she was responding rather hastily and eagerly to his advances and when I peeked through the chink in the curtains, I saw that she was practically shoving him towards the massive sofa which was right in my line of sight.

Doktor Von So-and-So danced an excited little jig, I repressed a giggle and Charmie pulled me away so that she could spy on them too. She was less good at repressing her giggles than I was and I had to push her back onto the window seat because she was making the curtains billow. But I couldn't hold her back and she got up again to watch and I took a couple of nervous sips and looked too and choked on a spluttering laugh. In a short period of time, the doktor had stripped off completely, aside from his gold-framed glasses, and it was a pretty sight, this pear-shaped gentleman whom we'd seen pictures of in the newspaper, naked and pink with a few tufts of grey, spiky hair, like a dignitary transformed into a boar as punishment. He polished his glasses with a lilac cloth, put his glasses back on and carefully rubbed his pate, which was already shining like a mirror, with the same cloth. I had an excellent view of all of this because his head was facing our way on the canapé. Olive had stepped out of the black velvet gown and was undressing herself from the midriff down. She kept on the top half, her tucker waving like an SOS flag, her sleeves rolled-up, her fella clearly didn't care. He was snorting like a pig, lying on his back, his hands folded atop his belly, which bulged out on either side. Charmie stood there as though she were at the races, on tiptoes, her neck outstretched. 'What's going to happen now?' she whispered in her hoarse voice. 'The doktor isn't going to be able to perform, you can see that, can't you?'

Olive was clearly having a tough time of it, I saw her lingering next to the sofa and her shoulders were shaking. It looked like she was struggling not to laugh too. Both Charmie and I were now peering through the chink, pressed against each other, our glasses in our left hands. Then Olive mounted the sofa with determination, she squatted above the doktor's face and he opened his mouth wide. Olive looked at us helplessly, hiccupping and grinning, and suddenly peed like a cart horse, over the shrieking little man, who raised his hands angrily and begged, '*Bitte, bitte, tropfenweise*.' Please! A slow trickle.

This was the last drop that maketh the cup flow over because although Charmie and I tried to keep each other in balance, we both toppled the wrong way. The curtains burst open and the two of us tumbled into the room: two colourful, drunken harlequins, tripping over each other's feet and waving glasses. The duchess collapsed too, she wavered for a moment before, rendered helpless by urination, burying Herr Doktor Von So-and-So's head beneath her buttocks. I later heard that his gold-framed glasses didn't survive. We exited the room at a hop, step and a jump and hid somewhere else. Olive fetched us again, giggling, half an hour later. We'd already heard the front door slam.

She left everything behind. Even the ruby-studded tortoise-shell comb lay trampled on the ground. Nevertheless, we did transport all the bottles to my attic room in a string bag.

Back then already, Olive didn't care about going from a down-filled four-poster to a damp mattress with broken springs overnight. She'd whistle as she made tea in the morning and beautify herself with my cheap rubbish in the steamed-up mirror above the sink. Herr Doktor got in touch and wanted to restore relations, but Olive said that after the incident she could no longer absolve him of his complexes in good faith and that was the end of it. By then she was already thirty plus, had neither kith nor kin and was afraid of nothing. Apart from one thing, which she confided to me in a rare moment of sombreness: she was never any good. Because whatever she did, she said, the eyes of the world would always look down on her.

We weren't together all the time but our paths often crossed and whenever Olive saw a chance to involve Oliver, as she'd started calling me, she did. And so I came to laze about in country houses and sailed the Seven Seas and saw in the Alhambra a colour photograph of Olive in the same kind of black velvet gown she'd had on in Scheveningen and with almost the same comb in her hair, probably one without rubies but you can't see that from the photo, and I've seen Delos by moonlight and played ghosts there with Olive, to the outrage of our host, a cultured ship-owner – who cried out in desperation: 'You're trampling on history, girls!' – and we rode in Count Loeki's barouche, he was one of the last, one of the nicest, aristocratic alkies, and it was one of the last barouches in the country, pulled by four white horses through Amsterdam where we were cheered and booed because people thought we were royalty. But those kinds of bizarre memories are really no more valuable to me than the ones of our chip stand at the football ground, a stand that became a financial fiasco because of Olive's inability to show hungry cats, children, dogs and vagrants the door. Until it was packed with free chips freeloaders, and when we started to sell beer as well, that was the end of it.

I also remember one of our many nights as down-and-outs when Olive and I walked through the snow, feeling at every car door and finding an open Mercedes-Benz in Surinamestraat with a pile of plaid blankets on the back seat. It was such a long time since we'd had a good sleep that we awoke on the move and sat up screaming somewhere near Leiden where we promptly ran into a crash barrier because our driver was rather too abruptly confronted with his passengers. Luckily the damage was minimal and the driver, a neurologist, employed all kinds of ruses to ensure we stayed out of the firing line and out of prison. But we didn't let him treat us.

We spent some homeless summer nights in a small, pretty wooded park with a hexagonal gazebo built in the middle of a pond. It was cold waking up on the floor, but that would soon be forgotten because we'd see waterlilies opening up in the first rays of sun and, as we lay there slowly rousing, young ducks would swim around beneath us and it hardly seemed possible that we were in a stinking, screwed-up, office-block city. At least, that's the way I think of it now. I picture the waterlilies opening like in a slow-motion film. I saw that then too, but I think the chances are I was mainly feeling cold and miserable. It's only now, when I'm even colder, that the memory exudes warmth.

One night when we were making our way to our gazebo in Arendsburgh Park, we saw a figure in the bushes. We froze at once. After a long time, we realized that the figure was probably doing the same. 'He must be frightened too,' Olive said and we hurried on and saw the figure running away from us like a great white stag. This piqued our curiosity and we ran after it and if he hadn't stumbled, we would never have known that the person who was running away from us so valiantly was the invincible Hessel Pietersma, who claimed to be a descendant of Pier Gerlofs Donia, the great Frisian warrior.

'Two old women out in the woods at night; you two should be ashamed of yourselves,' he said in a thick accent, relieved to have recognized us. Then he removed the brown paper wrapping from an oil painting, for which the description 'an oil' was more than sufficient, to check whether the wares that were supporting him hadn't suffered from his flight and fall. He repeated that two old women should be ashamed of themselves and testily withdrew.

This occurred shortly after Count Loeki's death and we can't have been so terribly old, no more than in our late forties, but it got me thinking one way or another. And Olive perhaps too, although we never discussed such thoughts because, however you look at it, they make you feel glum. You ask yourself what's wrong with you – you live in a civilized city like The Hague where at least half a million people live and work and have families and even gardens and clubs to spend their free time in, and you have to sleep in a park where, stupidly enough, you have to get off your bench before the cock crows because the early-morning walkers will be coming along with their dogs, and school children. It was like we were still children ourselves. But other women of our age would go to work in the mornings or into town and like us they'd have coffee at eleven but not in the railway station waiting room because the friendly waiters didn't kick you out of there, however unsteady your step. At one o'clock they'd have lunch; they didn't have a liquid lunch like us in a café in the hope that sympathetic acquaintances might be found there. At six o'clock they'd prepare a meal and weren't tipsy like us and they didn't stand next to a jukebox arguing, or cheat at cards to earn money. Their dogs got their own bowl of food every day and didn't get, like our

Pimmy, a meatball out of a vending machine. And that, I thought during those bouts of self-pity, was a shame for Olive who could have been a countess and fabulously rich in the bargain. After such thoughts, we'd spend our last cents hiring a room, without saying anything else about it. Then we'd start to feel like we were getting somewhere.

And so one evening we were sitting in a room on the Hobbemastraat, one of those filthy, cramped streets reeking of nasty business, in the midst of The Hague with all its greenery and fancy airs, and there we sat in a room with piss-coloured wallpaper and a grey-blue torn linoleum floor, one chair, one bed and one sink for thirty guilders a week and I said, 'I'm going to enrol at a temping agency tomorrow as a typist.'

'Me too,' Olive said and despite the fact her talents lay in other areas, she had good intentions.

'Let's get an early night,' we said and we'd already got undressed when the landlady banged on the door and asked whether the lady with the dog had left yet.

'Left? What do you mean, left?' shouted Olive, who could come across as very vulgar if she wanted. 'The lady with the dog has rented the place.'

The landlady opened the door, saw us standing there naked on the linoleum floor and Pimmy tucked up at the foot of the bed and screamed such a torrent of abuse that we'd got dressed, put the dog on the lead and were on our way down the stairs before she'd finished heaping burning coals on our heads.

There we were, thirty guilders poorer and homeless again, and after that, you're not going to work the next day. And then we'd sit somewhere, on that next day or one of the many other next days, in an East Indian café, for example, eating corn-cakes on tick. And on one of those days, a very yellow, jovial East Indian chappie joined us at our table and invited 'me and my girlfriend' – he'd addressed me to my utter astonishment – to go to his house and taste his home-made brandy. He lived in a spacious house in Segbroek and in his living room crammed with Djokja handicrafts, we gazed out over the dunes and drank arak from tiny porcelain eggcups. But the problem was he'd set his sights on me. I looked reasonable for my age,

perhaps because I'd calmly frittered away all those years, my
hair was still white blond and I still had the smooth face of a
hungry young boy. Next to Olive's indestructible, proud beauty
I was nothing, and as long as we were together, I rarely had to
fear male advances. Besides, once she noticed that I was in a
predicament like that, she'd hurry to my aid and the assailants
would invariably change their minds. This time her attempts
were futile, Desiré – 'call me Desi or Deetie, whichever you
like, Roosmaryn' – stubbornly continued to court me.

He was sitting on the edge of my chair, playing pat-a-cake
and after hearing Olive's account of how we'd been drifting
from hotel to hotel because we couldn't find anywhere suitable
to live, et cetera, et cetera, he'd offered us lodgings, 'if necessary, for life', beaming and winking at me. I kept shooting
Olive pleading looks and she did her best when Desi asked,
'Why, for the love of Mike, does your crazy friend call you
Oliver, Roosmarynie?' to which she responded with affected
meaningful intonation, 'Well, you know some women really
hate women's names. The ones who've always wanted to be a
boy.' Understanding nothing, he cried out, 'Rubbish! Absolute
twaddle! Stuff and nonsense. Roosmaryn is a lovely name and
suits her perfectly.' Olive gave up and it was true, we were in a
worse than wretched state and I saw no other way out.

It's the only time she let me down, by the way, if you can call
it letting me down. And actually, I let her down because I
couldn't manage it with Deetie. After all, Olive was my whole
world and I don't know whether you can call our relationship a
relationship since she wasn't like that, and I considered and still
believe now that it didn't matter to me if she was a woman or a
man. I was the one who'd called her a marvel when I saw her for
the first time. I loved her as a matter of course, I was convinced
that everyone loved her and luckily they did too in general,
apart from that time at Deetie's, blinkered as he was. Of course,
Olive with all her generosity couldn't understand what torture
it was for me. She was totally amazed, but very sweet when I
climbed into bed with her in the early hours, crying and shaking, not under the bedclothes but on top of them because I'd
just got out of Deetie's disgustingly wet and dirty ones. 'Blimey,

Oliver,' she muttered, kissing my neck and stroking away my tears, 'the little monkey can't have been that rough, can he?'

'If only you knew what he did,' I began, stopping because I realized that with all the experience she had, it'd be old hat to her. She seemed to understand because she said sweetly, 'Yes, the things they get into their calcified brains,' and then she comforted me at length, even though I pushed her away at first because I didn't want her going into the places the monkey had left traces, but she said, 'No, no, we'll share everything and I'll get rid of all of the stains and you'll be just plain Oliver again.'

Deetie came across us during the comforting, all of a sudden there he was in the doorway and light slowly dawned in the east. '*Tiens, tiens,*' he said, '*c'est la vie. La vie est belle, le ciel est bleu.*' And then he jumped on top of us and nestled against me. '*Continue, continue, ma chérie.*' If Olive hadn't burst out laughing, I'd have whacked him and hard too. She danced up and down on the bed. '*La vie Parisienne,*' she cried. 'Fancy that. *A Paris à Paris sur un petit cheval gris.* Listen to the horny traveller amongst us. We'll make him the mayor, Oliver. *Monsieur le Maire de Paris.*' Rocking cheerfully, she threw back the covers, revealed my miserable genitals and began her industrious handiwork, while I noted to my astonishment that the monkey was taking pleasure in this, panting blissfully, and no longer showing any interest in me. Well, Olive said later, men are like that, Oliver, as meek as little lambs, babes at that. But I had my own thoughts about it.

I can dig up memories for hours. I remember everything that happened to us. Even those things that happened during dark, drunken moments well up from my unconscious but not, as they used to on occasion, like poisonous gases from a swamp. I can call them to mind very calmly and pretty much pick and choose, the way a miser takes out precious coins he's been saving for years in a big chest. He hasn't looked at them for years, he no longer knows what the long-outdated coins look like and as he feels his end approaching, he opens the chest and studies them one by one. That's what I'm doing because I've got nothing else left; I can find nothing from the years before Olive, it's a compact tin of years, that's all. I can't say I can feel my end nearing, unless I put an end to things myself and I'm too cowardly for that and God knows what I'm to do with my life now that Olive has gone.

I found Olive in a pool of blood, no, not a pool, there were thick, fleshly globs on her white kimono, as she lay on the couch and the television blared out and a blue-lit comedian with rabbit's teeth looked into the dark room – he look grinning at Olive and she looked with one eye back and the other one was turned away. At first I thought she was no longer breathing but then there was a noise like something from a subterranean vault and it continued for five, six seconds and after that, deathly silence. And after half a minute the noise came again.

After that it was to hell at a quickstep. We didn't have a telephone. Our landlady didn't want us to use her telephone, besides, she'd already let us know she was against 'unnatural friendships' and she hated Olive because, old as she might be, she wound the landlady's much younger man around her little finger, so I didn't even knock. I walked down the street to a phone box, there was a listless young man in it, after waiting a long time I finally opened the door and said, 'My friend's dying.' I wanted to say more but he replied, 'Then there's no hurry,' and pulled the door shut again.

I went into a café, ordered a beer and asked whether I could use the phone. I could. I called the local health authority and they said someone would come but it might take a while. I called the Zuidwal hospital and there too they said someone would come, only they didn't know when exactly. I called the GP whose name was on our health insurance card and his wife said her husband would come as soon as he returned home. I'd begun every cry for help with 'my girlfriend' and then I got what we all get sometimes – the feeling that they keep our type hanging on because they don't care for us, so I picked up my beer, called the health authority again and said in a broken voice that my husband had had a terrible accident and had dragged himself home bleeding, I gave the address again and they said they'd come and when I arrived home at a run, an ambulance was just drawing up and that must have been a lucky coincidence. They asked for Mr X, Olive's surname, the landlady had already opened her hateful mouth, but now they were there, I could deal with it, I herded them upstairs and they took my Olive away.

I wanted to go with them and they asked, 'Family?'

'No,' I said and upon further consideration nothing else and after that they did let me come along as far as the hospital and then to a waiting room. A nurse came and wanted to know everything about Olive, her profession and religion and so on and I told them everything, making it sound as respectable as possible.

'Where is she?' I asked.

'We have to wait for the test results,' the nurse said.

'Where is she?' I asked. 'I'd like to see her for a moment. I've got the feeling she's conscious.'

The nurse began her dutiful chit-chat about family and the whole sourpuss goddamed rest of it, but she was a young nurse, pretty too, and all of a sudden I could handle her and, what's more, she was kind. I said grimly that Olive had neither kith nor kin and asked whether that was enough and she said, 'Go on then, come with me.'

Olive lay in a bathroom on a stretcher and wrestled herself into a half upright position when she saw me, groping about desperately. 'Oliver,' she cried and her eyes were as big as plates, 'what are we doing here, for God's sake, let's get out of here at once.' At that she vomited up a garland of blood clots, which she looked at hopelessly. Once I was inside, the nurse had closed the door after me, she definitely didn't want to be found responsible, so I held one of those metal kidney dishes under Olive's mouth and said, 'Don't worry. It's all as right as rain.' She vomited blood until I thought there was none left inside her and in the meantime I wiped her lovely hair from her eyes and kissed her forehead and her mouth with its black, crusted lining which I licked away and then two male medics came in, the oldest of whom asked, 'Hello, what's the meaning of this?'

Again I wanted to say, this is my girlfriend, but I thought,

Let me not be a coward for once in my life and not so arrogant either, let me rattle their conventions humbly, which is why I said, 'She's my girlfriend, Doctor, but that's the same to me as if she were my husband and that's why I'm here and the reason I want to stay here.'

'Oh, I see,' he said, 'go to the waiting room then, please.'

I saw the other one, the younger doctor, a thin blond man, glance at us. He said, 'There's not much we can say right now, but you're welcome to wait.' And for a moment I was able to take off my blinkers and see ourselves and everything more clearly, even if for just a moment, thank God. I saw Olive, lying back flabbergasted because she didn't know what was happening to her. Her lovely black hair was dark grey and hung in greasy strands, her proud face was the pointy, shrunken skull of a witch. I had always considered her eyes to sparkle and mock, but now they were bulging and the irises swam in a jumble of red blood vessels and the places they had burst, in the corners of her eyes, were red and yellow. Her lips were flaccid and blue, they hung open, her cheeks hung too, covered in dirty pits and purple patches and the skin pulled taught across her excessively pointed chin fell in enormous ochre folds to her throat. Her hands, which she had laid across her belly, looked like the yellow horny claws of a dead wild duck.

She hadn't got like this because she was ill, she'd already been like this yesterday and the day before, when we ate crab sandwiches, she'd been like it the entire previous year, who knows how long she'd been like it.

But I would never have admitted, not even to myself, that my beautiful Olive was no longer my beautiful Olive, because even under that grimy impasto of old age, she was still her. A Spanish duchess with a proud face, even though it was hidden beneath layers of yellow fat and purple algae.

She was wheeled into a room and a bottle was attached to her, which slowly drained into her so that she could live a bit longer.

She writhed and groaned but no longer responded to me.

She conducted entire conversations with other people, in a different world, I thought, which is why I no longer felt excluded but stayed at her bedside, wetting her lips with cotton pads until they sent me away.

The next morning, I was at her bedside again and the situation was unchanged, writhing, groaning and having mysterious conversations. Now she wasn't attached to a red bottle but a white one and now I no longer had to contend only with the hundreds of strangers surrounding her, but with three very present people in the three other beds. Next to us was a strict woman with ivory paws reading a library book with a hard red cover; on the other side of the room two young creatures with angry, neurotic faces sat upright in bed listening to a portable radio turned on full blast and I, the only visitor from the outside world, was subject to constant hostility. It was like a wordless third degree, which didn't stop until all kinds of males bearing flowers and dragging children streamed into the room. No wonder Olive remained caught up in her endless private conversations and appeared to find no rest.

It wasn't even a fit end for a horse.

I plucked up my courage again and forced my way into the medical director's office. He turned out to be the same arrogant, jovial man who had examined Olive in the bathroom.

I said, 'I think my girlfriend should be alone.'

'As soon as a place is free, your . . . er . . . the lady will get her own room.'

'Doctor, to me she's like . . .' I wanted to say 'a husband' again, but, God forgive me, I couldn't get the words out. By now I'd gone along with the hypocritical mess for long enough and if they couldn't understand using idiotic comparisons, they'd never understand, which is why I ended with a timid, 'She's everything I've got. And vice versa.'

'We do understand that,' he boomed amicably. 'We're doing our best. We'll keep you informed.'

But when Olive was moved to a room because she was keeping the others awake with her delirious ramblings, they didn't warn me and when they gave her up as a hopeless case they didn't warn me either. I wasn't family and we weren't married so they'd rather leave her to die like a dog alone.

It was only because I slinked past the hospital at night like a stray cat, having forced some Dutch courage into myself, and because the doorman turned out to be human and found me at the front door, my teeth chattering, and only because of random and trivial reasons, that I got to find out which room she was in.

I found the room in a dark corridor, right next to a back exit which filled me with despair because there's a reason they put you right next to the back exit, and just then a young neurologist skipped into her room, I accosted him and he cheerfully showed me to a waiting room with a defunct television, where a tiny green light glowed. Why a waiting room? I wondered. He didn't go to the trouble of turning on other lights, he spread his hands and said, 'Alas,' in a professional tone of voice they probably had to take an exam in.

He took me to her room and lifted up her wrinkled eyelids, which had tumbled down like crumpled, withered leaves; it was amazing that they didn't crumble between his thumb and index finger.

There was no sign of a reaction from her pupils and he said, very satisfied, 'See for yourself.'

In the days that followed, I began to think about death in my own inadequate way. But I didn't get further than dead is dead and the end is the end and that's why I was happy that Olive was in a coma and we'd been spared a ludicrous deathbed scene at least. I even began to worry she'd regain consciousness. Olive had been raised a Catholic and even though she'd long since abandoned her faith, you can't predict how an attack like this is going to pan out. Severe illness often has the same effect as a fire, the strongest steel constructions can get contorted. I didn't want my Olive to have a deathbed, ringed by conjurors and illusionists making the longed-for rabbits and coloured handkerchiefs appear from nowhere, I didn't want her to lie there pitifully praying for the attention of a higher being. I loved her too much for that and I had too much respect for her.

But it all turned out quite differently.

*

'Well? Isn't it wonderful your girlfriend can go home again? All of us here in the wing thought it was a miracle.'

This was that pretty, kind nurse from that terrible evening, who had also come to collect me at the door on a very differently tinged, but just as terrible afternoon, when I'd loitered and lingered in the hope that a miracle would take place.

May God stick a hairy paw through the ceiling and drag me away from here, if necessary in agony, because I'm having sinful thoughts. If these aren't sinful thoughts and if I'm not annihilated now, well then, put any hope of salvation out of your mind.

Oh Olive, if only you'd been murdered.

'Come on now, she's been looking forward to seeing you for so long.' The nurse pushed me through a labyrinth of corridors to the waiting room, the same one I'd cursed the neurologist in, with its defunct television and the little light, the same no man's land I'd inhabited like a drowned person on the seabed amongst indescribable and incomprehensible plants and fishes called 'convalescents'.

No one recovers from life, some smooth-talker or other claimed, but be vigilant and stop believing what they tell you, you can recover from anything. Some of those creatures carried a new body part with them, a plastic bag into which their wounds could suppurate. It was welded onto them with a plastic tube and if they sat down to have a nice cup of tea, they would carefully hang their transparent anal toilets over the back of their chairs, the way women do with mink stoles. Olive, in a dressing gown at the time, was one of them and even further estranged from me than when she'd lain on her sickbed, whispering and laughing with her unknown friends.

I said I was headed to hell at a gallop when I found her in her white kimono covered in blood clots on our couch. I don't know how often since then I've muttered the words *do not go gentle into that good night*, it became a magic charm. But against what? Why?

Now she was waiting for me, all jacked up for the outside world again.

Do not go gentle, because why, for Christ's sake, was she waiting for me? Couldn't Count Loeki have risen from the dead and where was Herr Doktor Von So-and-So or any of the thousands of others?

I didn't even recognize her. Olive had left me on her sickbed, when she'd begun to talk to the other people.

The jovial doctor came to take leave.

'You know the deal, don't you?' he babbled, patting her on the shoulder. She didn't even straighten her back but peered up at him, at me. She even covertly moved her head in my direction, a gesture of conspiracy between her and that arrogant old clodhopper.

They'd put her thin, grey hair into a bun. And they'd reduced her black eyes to ashes.

He took me aside. 'If I were you,' he said paternally, 'I'd take things easy. It'll be more comfortable for your girlfriend.'

God forbid. Now that they were forcing on me this witchy, grim-faced creature with her bun and her toothless maw, she was suddenly my girlfriend.

'What do you mean?' I asked haughtily. It was my turn to be arrogant now, if they wouldn't have it, they could keep her as far as I was concerned.

'Go easy on the drink,' he replied politely, as I stood there stinking like a vat of methanol.

'As far as madam is concerned . . .' aha, so he'd felt it, 'she has to stick to her diet without exception. She's got the list and she has to stick to it exactly. And not a drop to drink. Not a drop.'

I raised my eyebrows.

'A hepatic coma ain't no joke,' he said, suddenly coarse and sniffing slightly. In the old days it really would have got to me, now I didn't give a damn.

But what's the point of raking these things up now? Because the long and short of it was that this unfamiliar woman and myself moved into the apartment, that last shabby attic room that Olive and I rented.

What else could I have done? Left her next to a bin on the way home?

We lived together the way my mother and I had lived together once. She didn't want me to bring in sick cats off the street. She searched the cupboard under the sink and threw away my bottles of booze. She chewed each bite of our meals a hundred times, meals I prepared with an almost hostile feeling of love and she complained and complained. Too salty, too greasy, too bland, disgusting, cold, inedible, am I allowed to eat that, I'm not allowed to eat that.

She didn't listen to what I said because she was busy complaining and nit-picking and complaining. And if one of my comments did happen to sink in, she'd suddenly double over and start making vomiting noises. 'A bleed, another bleed, I'm done for,' she'd groan. That kind of trick stops working after the thousandth time and sometimes I'd pray, 'Lord, please give her one and make it good and proper.'

I wasn't allowed out without her and she inched along step by step as if she were heavily disabled, giving a running account of the passers-by in the voice of a deaf commentator.

There was nowhere to go; everywhere we went the smoke got into her lungs, even in cinemas where you weren't officially allowed to smoke. She forbade me to smoke and held my packets of tobacco under the tap. She kept tabs on me, even when I went to the toilet three flights down, an alarm clock in her hand. If I'd popped to the kitchen to fetch something she'd ordered – whatever it was could never be found – she'd sniff my mouth when I returned and turn away in disgust. In the evenings we tried to watch television and she'd zap from one channel to the next, still complaining to herself and not taking me into account at all, making it impossible to follow any show properly. One day she let me go out shopping on my own and when I returned she'd smashed the screen with a hammer and she said innocently that one of the cats had run into it. 'But what does it matter?' she said. 'We talk so little to each other, now we can.'

If only that had been the case. Night after night she did nothing but stare into space and when I finally managed to read something, in that atmosphere you could cut with a knife, I'd realize that she was staring at me.

What did it matter? She'd been critically ill and I'd let her down by staying healthy, so I did understand her thought process and I may have grown accustomed to this new life in time and become satisfied with it, because we'd known each other for a long time and even a relationship like ours, I thought, was for better and for worse.

But for yesterday.

I cleaned and dusted the living room, every nook and cranny, because she'd claimed I was keeping her in unhygienic conditions and slowly murdering her with dust bunnies and cat hair. I paused while dusting the book shelf to look at the portrait of the duchess in the Alhambra. The colour photo, which I'd taken of that heaven-sent beauty, was now being sent back through hell.

As truthfully as I'm writing this and as old as I am now, tears appeared in my eyes and that was a sensation I'd long forgotten.

'What are you secretly up to there?' she screeched from the couch.

I couldn't reply because I had a lump in my throat so I gave her the photograph.

She looked at it and then asked, with something strange in her voice, cunning I think now, but I don't know, 'Well, what do you think of that, then?'

I shook my head because I still couldn't say anything.

'Good-looking woman, wasn't I?'

I nodded.

'You liked that, didn't you?'

From that moment, I let her words flow over me, at least I hoped they'd flow over me like all her other malice, but in reality, it would have been better if, from her couch, she'd thrown a number of knives into my back.

'I've always know you were a wrong 'un, you know. Even though you were too lily-livered to openly admit it.

'The very first time I saw you, I thought, There's one of those stupid dykes.

'You were a cheap date to drag along, though, you were used to not having much, you didn't have a stale crust to eat. And it paid off, I looked good next to you, admit it. It always worked well too because it didn't do you any harm, did it? It's quite a sensation, a real woman next to a dyke.'

She looked at the photo again. 'But well,' she said dreamily, 'it was having to make do. If only I'd been able to get myself a Moorish slave girl.'

Translated by Michele Hutchison

22

MENSJE VAN KEULEN

Sand

De spiegel

He raised the blinds, and his wife turned her back to the late sun slanting into the room. He paused a moment, registering the ginger hair partially hidden beneath the collar of the bathrobe, the hand elegantly holding the glass of red wine, the bottle in the middle of the table. He sat down across from her and picked up the newspaper.

'I think I wouldn't mind having a mirror in the elevator,' he said.

She lifted her eyebrows. 'What on earth for?'

'You often see them in elevators. A mirror makes it seem less cramped and oppressive inside, because there's the illusion of a window. Besides, it lessens the feeling of being at the mercy of technology.'

'We're at the mercy of technology all day long. Doesn't bother me, I can't imagine how else we'd manage.'

He spread out the newspaper. 'It's even more oppressive with other people in the elevator. Sometimes I just don't know where to look.'

'I don't want to see myself in mirrors all the time. How old I look, I'll think whenever I take the elevator – my face has gone all weird.'

'But there's the mirror in the bathroom, and the one by the hallstand – you see yourself in those, don't you? You can even see yourself in the toaster.'

'What makes you think I would look in the toaster? Is that what you do, Theo? Look at yourself in the toaster?'

'It's an automatic thing. It's shiny, that's all. Like catching your reflection in a window when it's dark outside.'

He stared at a picture showing a group of oriental girls in bright-green work clothes. He tried to guess whether they were happy or sad.

'I didn't know you were so vain.'

'It just happens, like in the evenings when you go over to the window to close the curtains and you see the room reflected in the glass, with you yourself drawing near.'

'Not me; I don't look.'

'You mean you don't take any notice, but neither do I, not deliberately anyway. I just see it, whether I like it or not.'

The caption said the girls were Chinese workers at a factory producing ski and mountaineering wear in Bucharest.

'From what you said just now it's obvious that you do notice yourself. Which means that you're vain.'

'Oh.' He read that the girls preferred working six days a week instead of five.

'I don't notice myself,' she went on, 'I just don't see my reflection.'

'Like a vampire.'

'What was that? Vampire? I heard you all right. So now you're comparing me to a vampire.' She sniffed audibly, tightening the belt on her bathrobe.

'No, I didn't mean it like that,' he said. 'I was thinking of those stories about vampires.'

'What stories? What are you getting at?'

'Oh, you know. Stuff about vampires not having reflections.'

'How odd to discover after all these years that you're vain. It explains a lot. People who are vain have eyes only for themselves. It also explains why you don't see me.'

'Why do you say that? Of course I see you, I'm talking to you.'

'Not talking, really. We never talk; we just go through the motions. For a time I thought that we did talk, I thought you listened to what I had to say, but you always manage to twist things around so it's all about you. Like now. You didn't respond when I said I didn't want to see myself in mirrors because it'll make me think I'm old and ugly. You didn't even register what I said. Either you agree about me being old and ugly or you're not listening, but either way you don't care. You want to rabbit on about mirrors and elevators, you won't admit that you're vain, you just want to score points. But I do listen to you, I smile, I'm supposed to be understanding and sympathetic about everything: the bad feelings at the office, or your latest craze, whether it be for green olives, a black car or a custom-made dress shirt.'

'You shouldn't exaggerate so.'

'Your shiftiness. Your unfaithfulness. I think that's what really gets me: that you were unfaithful.'

He pressed his knees together, spread them again, said, 'Don't go down that road, please. We agreed that it wouldn't happen again.'

'I can't help being reminded. Being unfaithful has to do with vanity, too. It was your own fault, it's the way you behave.'

'What's wrong with my behaviour? I spend all day at work and then I come home again, like millions of other people.'

'You know what I mean.'

'No, I don't know what you mean,' he said gruffly. 'I thought we'd agreed that it was all nonsense and that we wouldn't talk about it any more.'

'It keeps coming back. I can't help it.'

'But it was ages ago – must be about a year, I think, and anyway, I wasn't unfaithful to you.'

'Hey, you left something out,' she said, jerking her head up. 'Normally you always say "not *really*, I wasn't *really* unfaithful to you".'

'Stop it, Gemma.' He stood up, took a bottle of water from the fridge. 'Want some? Better than all that wine, anyway. How many glasses has it been? I gather there is no dinner in the works? Never mind, I'll go out for some takeaway, you might feel like a tortilla, or pasta, or some of those corn rolls. Whatever.'

'So how did it go, then? Tell me. That is, if you don't want me ever to think of it again, ever to mention it again. It's up to you. Help me to get it out of my mind for good.'

'Why bring it up, then? Why be so hard on yourself?'

'Tell me the truth. I don't think you've been completely hon-est about it, or rather, I think you've been hiding things from me, for whatever reason, like not finding the right words or something. Why else would it keep coming back to me?' She rapped her knuckles on the side of her forehead. 'It's horrible, and lately it's been getting worse, goodness knows why. When you get home later than usual with some excuse I can't bring myself to believe you, or when you suddenly go off in the mid-dle of the weekend to pick something up from the office, least of all when you come back with a batch of papers. Just tell me once more what happened. Perhaps by now you can talk about it with a bit more detachment, and you'll be able to find the right words. Then it'll be clearer, something that's over and done with, so I can at least let it rest. There are still a lot of blanks, and I can't help filling them in, picturing you and her in that house, in all sorts of rooms I've never seen, in bed together. Perhaps I get too carried away by my imagination, but I can't stop it . . . I'll tell you what I know. She had some job in your office, she was a young widow, younger than me, and she had a child. I expect she pretended to be lonely, think-ing she could reel you in with a sob story. You went over to her house to put up some shelving. Tell me why you had to fix those shelves and why it took such a long time, why you kept going back. All I know is what you've told me, and that isn't much. That time you came home with a blue thumb, a big bruise where you'd smashed your thumb with a hammer – did you do that on purpose, to make it look like you'd really been doing carpentry? Because that's what I suspect. I think those shelves had nothing to do with it. And I don't want to think like that, I don't want to get all tangled up. I want to get the story straight, I want to round it off, as something small and insignificant. I wish you'd help me do that.'

She sat as though transfixed, but in her green eyes he thought he could see the tears building up, and even a tangle of dark threads.

'Stop tormenting yourself,' he said calmly. 'Nothing hap-pened for you to worry about. I don't feel like raking it all up again, I probably wouldn't even remember everything exactly any more. I never even think about it. As far as I'm concerned it's gone, faded into the background, like an evening out or a dinner with so-and-so.'

Leaning against the sink, he gazed out of the window. The apartment block across the way had balconies of grey-blue glass. On the balcony directly across, a woman stood smoking a cigarette. Each block in the new suburb was based on a different concept; the architects had indulged themselves. A groundbreaking project, harmonious, idealistic, challenging: a waterside adventure. Successful, too: none of the flats was ever vacant for long.

'I want to know. I *must*.'

'All right then, if you think it'll help. Just one last time . . . She had heard about me lending people a hand, like Arno and Peter, remember?'

'Why don't you just say her name?' she broke in. 'Her name's Lucy. Go on, call her Lucy, I don't mind.'

'Lucy,' he said, and he felt a flicker of something spreading through his body. 'I can't see why you want this, but if you think it's necessary, so be it. She, Lucy, had a part-time job as a receptionist. She greeted visitors, answered the telephone, put people through. In her kind of position you get to know all the staff pretty quickly, and she was talkative by nature. One day she must have said something about needing a bookcase, and that it had to be made to fit, as she lived in an old house with uneven floors. She wanted the shelves to extend across the whole wall.'

'So she had a lot of books, did she?'

'I don't know. She said she had boxes and boxes filled with books, which bothered her because it felt as if they were dead and buried.'

'Trying to be funny, I suppose.'

'She might have been serious.'

'Serious type, was she?'

'I don't know. I don't know what she was like.'

'Did you help her put the books on the shelves?'

'Some.'

'You never mentioned that before.'

'I probably thought it wasn't relevant.'

'What kind of books did she have?'

'What kind of books . . . ? Most of them were her husband's, I assume. Graham Greene, I remember, and a bunch of travel guides and photography books, including one about the First World War and one about pygmies. Rather interesting.'

'You just said you didn't know if she had a lot of books.'

'I didn't. I didn't see them all. What difference does it make?'

'You keep saying "she" and "her". You've stopped saying her name. Not that I want to hear you say it again – the way you pronounce it, oh it makes me cringe.'

The woman on the balcony flung away her cigarette and leaned over to follow its fall with her eyes, or she might have been looking down for the return of her husband, a balding man invariably dressed in black and to be seen on Saturdays carrying a sports bag with a tennis racket sticking out.

'Tell me about the little boy.'

'Gemma, please.'

'How old was he?'

'Gemma.'

'Eight or nine, wasn't he? So he'll probably be ten by now. Nice kid, was he?'

He took a sip of water and said: 'I hardly saw him, so I wouldn't know what he was like.'

The flood of recriminations that was about to ensue would be too much to bear in the kitchen, or in the entire flat for that matter. He detached himself from the sink, took a step forward.

'There you go, running away again. You always run away.' Her eyes brimmed with tears. 'Do you know how I feel?'

'You're drunk,' he said. 'I'm not in the mood for this.'

She refilled her glass. 'And you're vain. So how do you think I feel?'

'I'll go and have a bite to eat somewhere, leave you to it.'

'Like this,' she said, and promptly poured her wine glass over the front of her bathrobe, causing a stain shaped like a bleeding heart. 'This is how I feel.'

He stopped on the way to buy a couple of sandwiches. Caprese. Tuna with capers. With the two brown paper bags beside him he drove to the sea. He pulled up at the far end of the boulevard by the pier, switched off the headlights, left the radio on without listening to it, and downed his first sandwich. Wiping his mouth with the provided paper napkin, he realized that he hadn't tasted anything. As though he were in a world of his own, as they say. But he wasn't, it was more like being sucked into a void, cut off from all sensory perception.

The moon hung like a small hook in the sky, and the sea was still lined with a thin stripe of red. Behind him, a little to the side, a man in a white apron was closing down a snack bar. It was the end of the season, most of the beach cafés had already been dismantled. A few parking spaces along stood a delivery van, grey or beige. On the boulevard he saw a walking couple and a man with two Labradors. The dashboard indicated 68.9 degrees inside, and 48.2 outside, which was one degree down from when he set off. As he took a bite of his second sandwich, registering the taste of fish and capers, he noticed someone running from the pier in his direction, waving his arms. The man tapped on the car window and put his face up to the glass. A dark, frizzy lock of hair hung over his forehead. Brown, round eyes, not unfriendly. Could you help? He wasn't sure if he'd actually heard the man or if he'd read his lips.

'What's wrong?' he mouthed, with a questioning shrug.

The man tapped harder on the glass, pointing to the beach with his other hand.

He switched off the radio, lowered the window a hand's breadth.

'It's my dog,' said the man. 'He was with me a moment ago, and then he suddenly took off. He's very young, and I don't know what to do.'

'A Labrador?'

'Labrador? No, much smaller than that, a Jack Russell, very frisky. If I head off in one direction I'm afraid he's gone in the other, and vice versa. Could you possibly help me? Because I don't think he can be far away. I'm at a complete loss. Do you have a dog yourself? Do you understand the position I'm in?'

'No, I don't have any pets, but I do understand how you feel.'

'Some people would say don't worry, it's only an animal, but I'm not like that. And there's my wife, too, and the kids . . . Christ, I can't go home without him, you see.'

'I haven't got a coat with me, but I'll drive along the boulevard to take a look.'

'Thanks a lot.'

The man retraced his steps and waited twenty-odd metres away beneath a street lantern. He was lanky, but not thin. He wore a leather jacket, a black scarf and baggy jeans almost obscuring his white running shoes.

'I really appreciate your help. If you knew what I was in for if I came home saying I'd lost him . . . She wouldn't believe me, either. And then the children, they'll all start bawling, I can already hear them now. Oh Bennie, Bennie. They'll insist on coming out with me to hunt for him, with their coats on over their pyjamas.'

'Your dog's called Bennie?'

'The dog? Yes, his name is Bennie. Didn't you hear me call him just now? I've shouted myself hoarse. By the way, I'm John.'

'Theo.' He was used to introducing himself with his first name at work, but felt uncomfortable doing so now. He turned up the collar of his jacket, held the lapels together at the neck.

'You're a good sort, Theo.'

It sounded too familiar somehow, almost embarrassingly so. He would avoid addressing the man as John.

The man faced the sea, shouting, 'Bennie! Bennie!' He cupped his hand to his ear and shook his head. Slowly he walked on.

'It's very dark, though, isn't it? Not much of a moon, I mean. You can hardly see a thing, except when the lighthouse bothers to flash its beam. Bennie!' The man halted, pointing to the right. 'Hey, I think I can see him.'

He stared, saw nothing but the pale swirling of the surf. 'In the water?'

'No, Bennie's mad about paddling in the sea in the summer, but it's too chilly for him now. We'd better take a look down on the beach in case he's still there, and can't hear me calling him because of the waves.' He unwound his wool scarf. 'Here, take this, Theo, or you'll catch cold.'

They went down the path veering away from the bank of basalt blocks. He thought of the sand getting blisteringly hot on sunny days when he was a boy. All those times he had kicked off his sandals and put them on again on the way back, making sure there was no sand sticking to his bare feet. He was glad not to be going barefoot on the beach in this weather, but worried about sand getting into his shoes along the tops and the laces.

It was even darker on the shore.

'God, where can he be?' said the man. 'I'm sure I caught a glimpse of him just now.'

'Shall we each go in opposite directions?' he suggested, meaning to turn left himself so he would only have the short distance to the pier to go. He couldn't wait to discard the itchy, matted scarf.

'I've been there already. I think we need to go in the other direction. If we keep roughly to the middle, one of us can keep looking to the left and the other to the right, that way we can cover the ground together.'

'I don't have very much time.'

'I suppose they're waiting for you at home too?'

'Yes, that too.'

'Wait a minute . . . Bennie! I thought I heard him. Let's stop a moment.'

They halted. The man held his hand behind his ear again, then pointed to something in the dark that looked like a shed. Close to it there turned out to be a mound of stacked panels, windows and planks covered by a tarpaulin.

'There, at the back, I can hear him whimpering, very softly, can you? He must be somewhere behind there. Bennie?' The man vanished behind the tarpaulin. 'Jesus! Look at this! I think they've tied him up.'

Now he caught the sound of whimpering, too, and went round to the back.

'Is it bad?' he asked anxiously, leaning forward to peer over the leather shoulders of the man crouching down.

'Depends ...' The man sprang up and jabbed both his
elbows back.

The searing pain in his belly made him double up. He
gagged on the taste of fish and bile in his mouth, swallowed a
soggy lump, gasped for air.

'Depends on what you call bad,' said the man, swinging for
the next blow.

The fist hit him on the jaw and neck, and the next thing he
knew he was grabbed by his hair, forcing his head down.

'Don't move, Theo. I've got a knife.'

He staggered, flailing his arms for support.

'Hands off. I told you I had a knife, want to see it? Or do
you want to feel it?'

His contorted position sparked the old backache he thought
he'd got rid of after all that physiotherapy last winter and
spring. He sank to his knees.

'That's better. Now you can see Bennie for yourself. Drop
your arms. Don't move. The only one moving here is me. And
Bennie, of course.'

The man pulled his head towards him, he felt the denim
against his forehead, the open zipper.

'You're going to give Bennie a good time. Here he is. Smell
him? Feel him?' Whimpering faintly like a puppy, the man
brushed his cock along Theo's cheek, his nose, his lips. 'I told
you he doesn't like the cold. Bennie wants to go inside. Bennie's mad about fucking and that's what he's going to do, yeah,
he's going to fuck you, but first he wants to be nice and warm
and wet. He needs love, you gotta give him love, gotta give him
a whole lotta love, you know why? Because you think I'm
black.'

'No, that's not what I thought,' he said.

The man laughed. 'Listen, honey, that's what they all say,
but they don't mean it. And I am black, that's to say, my father
was black. My mother was blonde, blacks like them, though
I'm not so keen on them myself. I prefer Latinos, so in that
respect I'm not black but more like my mother, who fancied a
bit of colour. Do you follow me? You're not saying much,
which is just as well, because Bennie isn't one for chit-chat right

under his nose, and he's getting cold and wants to go in. Open
your mouth. Bennie's crazy about white guys, and he thinks
you're cute. Put your hands down, or keep them behind your
back. I said open your mouth, you shit, if you don't I'll slice it
right open for you ... There, that's better, that's what Bennie
likes. One two, one two ... no spitting now, no messing around,
just let Bennie get on with it, that's all ... What's the matter
with you? You won't suffocate – nobody does, at least not in my
experience. Bennie's having a bit of fun, he's swelling up with
it, that's what ... Good, that's good ... one two, one two ...
And now you can use your hands to take your shoes off and
drop your trousers. Just the shoes and the trousers, mind, go
on then, you can start with the trousers so Bennie can see your
pale little dick, maybe they'll want to play together, no, that
would be too cold for Bennie. Hurry up with those trousers. I
bet you thought to yourself: Just let the black guy come in my
mouth and that'll be the end of it, but no way, Theo. Bennie
wants the real McCoy, this was just a starter. Tonight I'm a
big, strong black guy ... One shoe off is enough. Down with
the rest of your trousers, whitey. Turn around, I tell you, turn
around, gimme that saggy white ass of yours.'

A stinging blow to his ear, a shove to his back. He lost his
balance, felt something scratch over his thigh, a fingernail or
the point of a blade, he couldn't tell which. Now and then the
beam of the lighthouse swept past, but no one could see them
in the shadows behind the tarpaulin.

'Now bend over, hold on to those planks, legs wide, but not
too much now, or Bennie can't reach ... Virgin, eh? If you
shout I'll cut your throat. That would be a shame, and unnecessary. You know what? Put that scarf over your mouth, go
on ... First I'll soap you up some, you tight-assed shit.'

The scarf smelled of ash. He heard the man clear his throat,
he felt the wetness slide down between his buttocks, felt the
cold air, the touch of a leather jacket on his skin, a hand gripping his hip. The man panted, breathing obscenities, but from
the moment he was split open and a rasping pain filled his
lower body he no longer heard the words.

He fixed his eyes on the shoe and sock he stood in, and

pictured himself walking along the sea, leaving footprints that would fill with water, one after the other in a long trail, dozens of footsteps; he imagined the spaces in between, the shells, wisps of plastic, seagull feathers, but most of all the sand, here and there in ridged banks interspersed with long pools which he skirted around. On and on he went, past the pier, to the next stretch of shore, past beach huts, through dunes overgrown with marram grass. He found himself in a friend's garden, where a birthday party was going on. A warm evening, women with bare arms and legs. He had been tipsy, in a combative mood. One of the women had laughed and shaken her head at him, saying he was like a schoolboy, and he had felt attractively boyish, with a casual smile that would never fade. That night he had made love like a boy, too, carried away by the swift vigour of his loins, and Lucy had flashed into his mind, and a sister of one of his friends, young, sweet, unreachable. Afterwards Gemma had dug her nails into his shoulder.

The pain had become narcosis, his back a rigid right-angle, legs dangling underneath.

He unscrewed the showerhead from the pipe and, crouching down in the shower stall, tried to hose himself as best he could. There was a little blood, too little to tinge the water round his feet, but in a wave of panic he thought: I might be infected. And then, with calm indifference: So what?

After his shower, he realized that the glass door had been ajar. He mopped up the puddle with a towel from the laundry basket and wrung it out over the tub in which Gemma had left her bathrobe to soak. The fire in his behind had returned and he dabbed himself with one of Gemma's face creams, which felt greasy although it promised hydration. He rinsed out his socks until all the sand was gone, and stuffed them along with his underwear into the laundry. His jaw was red, he had bruises on his legs, there was a gash at the base of his left thumb, must have got caught on a nail or a splinter. He tipped it with disinfectant, but the skin was already sealed and he felt nothing. He took a sleeping pill: six hours of respite.

Gemma lay on her side. He switched off the bedside lamp, which she had left on with the shade turned away so the light didn't shine in her eyes. He slid between the covers beside her, lay still on his back. His breathing was shallow.

'Why did you take a shower? You always shower in the morning.' Her voice sounded soft, but not sleepy. 'Been with her, have you?'

He laid his hands on his chest and slid them down to his belly. The soreness there resembled muscle ache. He said: 'What?'

'I didn't mean that,' she said. 'Not funny, sorry. I was so upset when you left. Where have you been? I thought you'd walked out on me, and I could see why – nobody would put up with me when I'm like this. And I think you're right about having a mirror in the elevator, it's bound to be an improvement. I've been crying my eyes out, I look a mess. I don't know why I brought up the subject at all, why I get in such a state, about her, about the child, I get so miserable, and then I want to leave you, but I'm scared of losing you and I just don't know what I want any more. It's strange, I thought people who don't have children were extra close.'

'I drove to the shore,' he said. 'I went for a walk on the beach.'

'I thought you hated the sand. Is that why you showered? I'd quite like to have gone with you, actually. Fresh air. I won't drink any more, not during the day anyway. I'll stop, I promise.'

The room seemed to become airless; the panic returned: I've been infected. It's nestled itself deep inside me, spreading already. He said: 'Say "no".'

'How do you mean, "no"?'

'Please, Gemma, say "no".'

'No. But what for? Oh, how horrible all this is, life can be so cruel. I know, I know, we should never have moved here. It was a mistake, I want to live on the ground floor. It's so windy up here. The whole building sways to and fro at night, as if it wants to rock us to sleep, but I don't want to be rocked to sleep all the way up here, it scares me to death. What are we to do, for goodness' sake?'

'Not now,' he said. 'I fell, you see, and I'm feeling a little shaky. I want to sleep, I've taken a sleeping pill.'

'You fell.'

'There was a man who'd lost his dog. I went looking for it with him, and I tripped over something, don't know what, and fell against a stack of wood. A dismantled beach pavilion, I think it was.'

She touched his arm and his entire body grew tense.

'Even that hurts?' She fumbled for the light switch on her side of the bed.

'No light, please,' he said. 'I'm almost asleep.'

She lay back, waited a moment, then said: 'Theo? That dog, was it found?'

He could hear that she was close to tears.

'Yes, it was found.'

'Thank goodness for that.' She sighed. 'I'll say "no" again for you, if you want. No.'

He reached for her hand. For a long time they lay side by side, staring up in the dark, as though some revelation were in the offing . . .

Translated by Ina Rilke

23

NICOLAAS MATSIER

The Minnema Variations

De Minnema-variaties

I

In the abstract I have no problem with him. His description is as follows. He has the form and attitude of the doomed poet. A coat that flaps about; I can scarcely imagine him without wind. He always looks battered, always ready to absorb the next blow, never discomfited. He feels as if he is the representative of something. Something has chosen precisely him, and no one else, as a mouthpiece. Something that cannot do without him.

He is the ravaged young man that one has sometimes seen sitting in cafés. At the reading table, but not reading. The young man who – totally oblivious of his surroundings – pursues his thoughts with his ballpoint pen, and now and then watches crestfallen as they disappear in the distance round a corner that, on foot, he will not be able to reach soon enough. Other customers, who while having a surreptitious drink – which is entirely unnecessary! – glance at him, ascribe inspiration to him at those moments, or think their own thoughts about the exhibitionist. Meanwhile, he, the poet, is in despair: something escapes him once and for all.

He is the detached young man sitting completely alone in a Chinese restaurant that does takeaway meals. From outside a passer-by might be able – it is pouring with rain – to see the title of the book lying next to his plate (*La pratique du Zen*). Inside it doesn't interest the man behind the counter at all that he, the doomed poet, occupying only his own place, is slowly eating white rice, and nothing but white rice. His luggage consists of two plastic bags. His coat, which he has kept on, is thin and torn like himself.

Obviously he has no fixed abode or base. He lives and works everywhere. He is constantly on the move. When he arrives somewhere, it is only to be able to set out from there again. As he leaves he is sure of returning here.

Not only for me but for him too it is a mystery how he comes by something as simple as money. As if in a dream he does temporary work in some office, which is in fact simply a backdrop for his thoughts, his breathless thoughts. He is also constantly occupied with creating. He has no idea of the names of his colleagues or what they look like. His creative urge does not relate to trivia like places and people, or other things with names. His love for himself and for the universe coincide.

All he possesses are writing materials. Varied, as his different moods require different felt tips and many sizes of paper. This is the only thing that really matters, and of course the only thing that doesn't count. If necessary he writes on cigarette papers, flyleaves, more or less blank pages torn out of telephone directories, and menus.

What bothers me is that he is no longer nameless. What bothers me is the by now overwhelming number of proofs of his existence. What bothers me is the complete monotony of that existence, which imposes itself powerfully on me.

2

Our doomed poet is called Minnema. In our head and later in our conversations he began unobtrusively as 'someone', who was succeeded by a 'a certain Minnema', who in turn evolved into the present, unmistakable, simple Minnema one couldn't get rid of, whose first name we shall know for ever without ever using it. The sight of his initials evokes a gamut of emotions, including: jollity, boredom, murderousness and resignation.

The first letters from Minnema didn't strike me as exceptional at the time – for the obvious reason that then, in the autumn, they were not *first* letters, but just letters. Letters from someone or other . . . Who of course had some name or other, an address and so on . . . Letters from a pile of correspondence that I was going through without interest. Going through says it all. It was, so to speak, only the later letters of Minnema that ensured that there could be any question of 'first' letters. What is important is the quantity of Minnema's letters, the weight in kilos.

Minnema is the man who sends 'work', or – a word he uses even more frequently – 'material'. If we had kept Minnema's work or material, and he was dead, we would now have the complete Minnema. The collected Minnema. But Minnema refuses to become complete. He refuses to regard his work as finished! All we are constantly confronted with is the creative process of Minnema's work. His work is never finished, all versions are provisional, or worse still: fragments of provisional versions. Hence *material*. Yet he sends constantly and indefatigably, often many times a day, all those versions to us, although we long ago made it clear to him that his work or material does not interest us in the slightest, leaves us cold, and irritates us. First in neutral terms, then in downright rude and then in insulting ones. When we had informed him that further submissions from him would no longer be dealt with, he continued to praise and follow our work. He continued, as our colleague and most loyal contributor, to follow and compliment us, down to the most recent publications and most obscure interviews, and he continued to ask us to give attention to his material. When we had informed him that his work would henceforth be returned unopened – since the absence of a reply turned out to give him grounds for hope – he started putting his work through the letter box *in person*, without an envelope, hence as it were already opened. When we had informed him that with immediate effect his work would go into the waste-paper basket, his submissions doubled. We don't know what to do about Minnema. We don't understand what we are for. We don't understand what Minnema is for.

3

I'm an editorial secretary. People should be careful not to have too rose-tinted a vision of my activities. Like everywhere it is a matter of manoeuvring, self-importance, humble work, stealing postage stamps, drinking company coffee, genial conversation with the other – really nice – staff, and more particularly reading other people's work. Let me be clear about this once and for all. About that reading, that is. I read *as if* – this cannot be emphasized enough – as if what I am reading interests me *personally*. And what do I read *as if* it interests me *personally*? A lot! Poems, an unending stream of poems. Long ago I calculated that one in ten of my countrymen writes poems. And one in thirty essays. And what a joy it would be to read all this writing *really* personally and fascinated and intrigued. And certainly I am a warm supporter of people formulating things for themselves and in that way becoming a little less perishable for each other. Welcome, all you who wield the pen. Welcome and more than welcome. All of you, write about your experiences, which in that way can become ours.

But the accompanying letters ... Of which, by the way, I have established an archive so as to be able to devote a comparative study to them afterwards. The humble, the hopeful, the confident, the okay, the naive, the neutral letters. Handwriting, spelling, letterhead. At a glance I can see whether I am dealing with stubbornness, quality, imitation. But I don't leave it at that one glance. Humbly, confidently, naively I read through all that work, as if I have not realized long ago what is wrong with it. I read. I read on in a disciplined way, so as not to formulate or blur any judgements that are not mine.

To be honest – I interrupt the work frequently for a visit to a neighbouring espresso bar. Sometimes I take work with me. For some reason it is easier for me to take cognisance of those outpourings in a somewhat tarnished environment, amid the spluttering of the espresso machines, conversations, ladies who leaf through magazines like ours with well-concealed boredom. Cultured lunches! I also chew cautiously on a roll with a fantasy name understood only here, while I, equally cautiously, study the hopefully submitted copy. Just as relationships between people become unreal in espresso bars – comfortably furnished vacuums, where time does not exist and where the staff is of an equally great if not greater spiritual nobility than those who are being absent-mindedly served – just as, I was trying to say, relationships between people evaporate in such bars, so my relationship with the texts I have brought with me evaporates. I like espresso bars.

Back at the publisher's, once I have finished reading, I take a pile of envelopes, I take a pile of photocopies, I fill in the date and after *Dear* I write a name with a hurried pen stroke. (I must have at one time filled in the name *Minnema* there.) One of my first actions as secretary was that, making two hundred of those letters. I think with melancholy of my humane, existential predecessor, also a good actor. Who always answered in person: warm, direct, careful! I however turned out not to be able to keep myself in check. Hence I resorted to the cool copies and I stopped pretending, extending the pretence that I read the copy personally to the pretence that I was personally replying to those involved.

So I expect I sent some submitter of worthless poems the following mechanical text:

(*date*)
Dear (*Mr Minnema*),
We regret to inform you that we do not consider your submission suitable for publication in our magazine.
Yours faithfully, on behalf of the editorial board,
(*my signature*)

4

Minnema for his part returned my rejection.

Now the phenomenon of a troublemaker is well enough known. I expect that I didn't pay particular attention to some letter from some meanwhile completely forgotten submitter. It was, though, a strange letter that I took out of the envelope. In a fraction of a second I actually thought it was addressed to *me* . . . The way that one immediately starts treating someone who is the spitting image of a very good friend with blind sympathy, I expect that the handwriting, for a moment, inspired me with confidence – my own handwriting filled in the photocopied rejection of a certain Minnema. I am not now remembering that name but the letter. In amazement I turned it over. On the back was written: 'What do you mean by "not suitable", if I may ask?' Or words to that effect. I tossed it in the waste-paper basket with a smile.

Subsequently, I now know, a 'collection' of Minnema's must have arrived, entitled *Reunion*. The fact that these poems were sent by the same Minnema, the same at that time completely nameless Minnema of previous forgotten poems, must have escaped me. And would probably have escaped me just the same if the sender, whether or not deliberately, had *not* omitted his name and address. The ring-binder sheets, written on in ballpoint pen, were held together by a thick woollen thread in which a knot had been tied. I looked, I remember, at that thread. It gave something benevolent, something caring to the whole. Not that the poems held together by it gained in consistency or quality (questions of identity, wordplay, what was worse: seriously pursued wordplay). But that thread. That thread made me uncertain for a moment. Because that thread reminded me of a woman I had known. She was also in the habit of bundling papers like that. I hadn't treated that woman in a way . . . But why am I telling you this anyway?

I used to keep such stray papers in a special folder to be able to send them back as soon as the forgetful writer got in touch. Which, in fact, never happened: foundlings. Hesitantly I threw the ring-binder pages in the waste-paper basket.

Suddenly Minnema acquired his name. Probably this was the direct result of my silence about the 'collection' *Reunion*. Minnema interpreted my silence as consent. Precisely the omission, whether or not deliberate, of name and address – led Minnema – only now has that become clear to me – to emerge from his relative anonymity. At high speed his identity was created. That is, his identity in relation to us. This sounds contradictory, I must admit: identity-in-relation-to-us. Nevertheless, I don't think Minnema has any other identity.

Minnema acquired a name because he started sending numerous letters every week. I got to know his handwriting . . . With a sigh I opened one letter after the other. They followed each other so quickly that I did not feel like returning them in the same breathless tempo. They piled up, Minnema's letters. And increasingly they irritated me. His tone! His constantly repeated autobiographical comments ('still have no house', 'the writing has now entered a new phase', 'am currently unemployed'), his familiar tone. In virtually every letter, strangely enough, there is an allusion to a forthcoming visit to the editors, a contact to be followed and maintained. *As if he knew us!*

Minnema's letters piled up – a bundle of paper, kept somewhere apart, in expectation of something, as it were in quarantine, so as not to infect the other items of post. Minnema's letters arrived constantly, by now he was familiar to all the editors. In the space of a few weeks he had established a place for himself. He had acquired the same unasked-for and ignored axiomatic presence as the renowned works of art hanging in the editorial office. Minnema had been able to lend himself a kind of inevitability, that we gave a wide berth . . . It had got to that point already, where we pussy-footed around him!

Meanwhile, it seems obvious that Minnema, having prepared his presence forcefully, should appear in person.

5

Thank God I had just finished my work. I was on the point of leaving when a man of my age came in – resilient was the dominant impression, if it was not cat-like, the way he put out his hand: '*Nanne Minnema*'. The way he said that! As if we had known each other for years. As if this introductory ceremony were taking place years after the event . . . Pen pals! I meet my pen pal from Southern Africa. Practically speaking we know all about each other. All too late in the day. The only thing we don't know about each other is what we look like in the flesh.

Minnema was curious, and at the same time full of anticipation. There was a presupposed mutuality in his behaviour. Something he presupposed was mutual. His behaviour was through and through that of an equal. It wasn't *I* who looked at *him* in anticipation, meanwhile, *he* looked at *me* in anticipation! As if I had taken the initiative for this meeting. He stood in our office space (approximately 6 by 7 metres) perfectly relaxed, as if he were a friend, a brother. Minnema was fully present. Not a trace of embarrassment!

I told him we were going to leave the premises, as I had just finished work. He seemed to find every suggestion quite normal.

He waited cheerfully until I had completed a number of insignificant, winding-up, more or less ritual actions. In accordance with the company code I emptied the ashtray, put a cover on the typewriter, slid my cup into a washing-up bowl, pushed the drawer of a card index closed, put the telephone book back in its place, locked a filing cabinet, put the outgoing post into a tray, pushed my chair under the table, moved the stapler from the centre to the edge of the table, and put on my coat. I did all those things as if Minnema was not there at all. Hectically, absent-mindedly. I was simply on my way home. And Minnema, for his part, waited. Just waited. I went outside, with Minnema behind me, but as if no one was following me. However, since I simply couldn't escape the fact that it was Minnema following me, I slowed down. So that he caught up with me. And so the two of us walked on side by side. Minnema in the previously described cheerful and resilient mood, from which he occasionally looked at me from the side. I, on the other hand, looked straight ahead. And I walked, partly, as if Minnema was not walking next to me, and partly as if he was walking next to me. And so the three of us as it were went into the espresso bar where – who can say? – I had perhaps read Minnema's work for the first time.

For that matter, why is it that I cannot possibly recall Minnema's appearance? I can more or less remember our vacuous conversation in that espresso bar. But what he looks like ... Is that because from the very first moment I *negated* Minnema, because he tried to weave me into a sticky web that he picked up every day anew? Would I only be able to recognize Minnema in order to avoid him, to be able to look the other way in good time? The way one cannot remember a pain, but can recognize it.

What increasingly surprised me was that Minnema seemed to find everything that happened normal. Constantly, during the whole conversation, he seemed to be in conversation with exactly who he *wanted* to be in conversation, and the things that were said seemed to be exactly the things he had imagined. *Everything* had his constant consent. I gasped for breath.

For my part I left no stone unturned – no effort was too great – to convince Minnema, to impress on Minnema and to persuade Minnema that his work left the editors entirely indifferent. Nevertheless, Minnema talked about his material as if it interested us both equally, as if I were an initiate in the same mystic cult. I think that, even if I had wanted to understand anything about it, I still would not have been able to understand a thing. Minnema was unfathomable. His individual sentences did not sound strange. Each of them could have issued from other mouths. But collectively it was impossible to get a handle on them. Minnema simply indicated, but defined nothing. As a result there was no connect between his utterances. Quicksand.

He referred to 'a certain way' that he 'must go' ... He informed me that various possibilities 'were now becoming ever clearer' ... He preferred not to talk about 'certain things', which 'had recently come to his attention' ...

I told him I didn't understand a thing he was saying. He, for his part, went on talking, not only as if I had not said this, but on the contrary had made it clear that I understood him perfectly. In order to unburden myself of at least some of my discomfort, I suggested that he, Minnema, was undoubtedly a very religious person. I must say that he reacted in a very alert way. He must have heard in my words or seen in my face *this* aversion, and no other, because he reacted as if to an affront.

He enquired – the only sensible question he asked! The only question at all, now I think about it, Minnema made only statements – he enquired whether I had anything against religion. Which I fully confirmed. *Whereupon I suggested he might enter a monastery.* Saying that, he seemed like a mystic to me. I was making fun of him, and he knew it. While Minnema completely ignored all my direct rejections – it was in fact impossible to reject Minnema, this one indirect remark about religion and monasteries seemed to him to be hostile in intent. He must have sensed infallibly that I meant madness and asylums.

This finale of our conversation produced the only silence on both sides that satisfied me. The haziness of our dialogue – conducted in broad daylight, solely between actors of flesh and blood – had lasted exactly as long as I needed to drink my cappuccino without too much hurry. Minnema's cup was still half-full. He saw that I saw that his cup was still half-full, and to my amazement that was enough. I could not deny Minnema a certain elementary development of character. A little later then we were in the street. Subsequently too Minnema would have accompanied me anywhere at all – we had only exited together – if I had expressed the wish. For there was no end to his adhesive capacity. So I said, 'I'm off now.' And I went. On my bike. Minnema was on foot. I did not look round. It was windy. Although I did not look round, I have a clear picture of Minnema's figure, his long strides, his coat hanging open and flapping, his bent head.

6

Min-ne-ma . . . A monument to failure that does not know itself. I had not heard his name for the last time, had not seen that ghost for the last time. Minnema went on existing unimpaired, sending material, and keeping in contact with us on his side.

A curious phrase cropped up regularly in his letters: 'Certain steps would now seem logical, in view of the preceding.'

What steps, why they were logical and what had preceded them, and especially who was to take them – Minnema left all that unspecified.

I think that there is no room in his head for more than one idea at a time. An idea that takes possession of him in all its intensity and wears him out. An idea that he circles around and continues circling without realizing that it is *the same* idea. Until the idea in question is suddenly replaced by another idea, after which the process begins anew. And I think that that sudden replacement of one idea by another corresponds with, if it does not coincide with, Minnema's departure for another town or another island. Every move is a transmigration of the soul for Minnema. From each new address he sends us new material.

It is not improbable that the absence of 'certain steps' heralded his next, extremely short visit. I had already on several occasions found memos on my desk indicating that a certain Miedema or Meinsma had asked after me. As I parked my car in a parking spot, I already saw Minnema. Instinctively I stayed in the car. I considered driving straight off again. I got out. Minnema made energetically for me.

'I'm leaving for Paris this evening.'

'Have a good trip,' I mumbled. I stayed by the car.

'You've still got material of mine.'

I did not say yes or no.

'I need to take it with me.'

I offered to send it back today or the next day. 'I don't have much time,' Minnema insisted.

With reluctance I saw him standing in our office again. I looked for his papers. I said sourly that another secretary would have long since thrown away his work, which had no return postage enclosed. That I, strangely meticulous, kept all correspondence for a year, I didn't really know why myself. That he had absolutely no right of return. That we did not want any further work.

Minnema looked through the papers. He seemed to know his work by heart.

'The letter from Schiermonnikoog is not here.'

I raised my eyebrows. For form's sake I leafed through the file a little further.

'And my first collection, where is that?'

'Collection?'

'*Reunion.*' It didn't occur to him that his own interest in his own work might be more detailed than mine, and that my question was not a request to activate my memory by mentioning a title.

Like an unpleasant counter clerk I looked at Minnema. 'Everything you sent was in this file. I have given back to you everything that was in this file.'

'Can I have a look for myself?'

'No,' I said, as I had already looked twice.

Minnema left. And I thought, of course, that we were rid of him. I knew vaguely that there was something wrong. Why that reluctance to give him back his stuff?

Meanwhile, Minnema did not leave at all – on the contrary, he intensified his relations with us. What he did was to initiate an exhaustive telephone enquiry into the whereabouts of his vanished poems. He was suspicious and persistent. He went to work very systematically. After his visit to me he rang editor N., who in a very friendly way denied all knowledge of the poems. Then he rang editor O., who if possible denied with even more sincerity and amazement having anything to do with these poems and advised him to contact the secretary. Subsequently Minnema rang me again. I told him, but not benevolently like N. and O., that we had discussed this subject previously. He didn't believe a word we said. That is, he did not know what words he *could* give credence to. Perhaps he was inclined to believe the last speaker but one. And since he was tossed to and fro between his need to believe and his passionate longing for his poems, he found himself obliged to continue his telephone assault. So he rang editor N. again, whose amazement this time transferred from the vanished poems to the poet, who was all the more present. And so he rang editor O. again. And so he rang me again.

I realize now that these telephone conversations were not just irritating, but also somehow painful. Minnema missed his

poems like an amputated limb that retains its feeling. Like a
dog he trotted to the place where his master's stick yet again
does not fall, because the latter, his boss, has again made a
feint. Minnema's telephone conversations were like the umpteenth search along the same cupboards, under the same beds,
behind the same sofas, along which, under which, and behind
which one has already searched, but not well enough. We were
the places where Minnema was searching for something.

The telephone conversations ended increasingly curtly. The
series ended where it began: with me. Minnema suspected me
most, partly because the round of investigation had begun
with me and hence it was my turn to start the new round. He
rang in the evening.

'This is Nanne Minnema.' Very resolute. 'I'll be in the K.
restaurant next to the Concertgebouw until eight o'clock, and
I'll expect to see you there with my poems.'

Because my fellow editors, N. and O., had been worrying
me for days with questions and requests for measures to be
taken, I had thought about the matter. By pure chance and
concentration I had been able to retrieve the image of the
ring-binder sheets held together by a woollen thread, and of
the waste-paper basket, in which it could have lain for more
than a day. I explained carefully that there had been no name
and address. I put plenty of feeling into my voice. I looked in
vain for another expression than 'er ... threw them away'.
With one word, I made comprehension possible. But Minnema
was implacable. He kept repeating that he wanted his poems,
thrown away or not, back *now*. After I summed up the situation again, with much less feeling in my voice, and in different
words, and he on his side started from the beginning, I said:

'So you'll have to go to the dump.'

'So you won't be coming?'

'No.'

'Then I shall be obliged to make this a police matter.'

'You must do what your heart tells you,' I said, and hung up.

For the first time I had the completely absurd idea that
Minnema might have a knife. Min-ne-ma ... Knife in my
stomach.

7

Minnema next distanced himself from us – literally, by going travelling. But what he could not help doing meanwhile was to emphasize his absence. In a nocturnal phone call from Paris he wished editor N. *success* with his work. He did not send any material, but did send postcards from significant places like Arles. We hoped fervently that he would continue his journey in a southerly direction and that it would be a one-way journey. But from Marseille he complained that he wasn't producing much. Perhaps, I could well imagine, his desperate gaze had fallen on that bell . . . in the wall of the fort in the Vieux-Port. Where foreigners can lose their identity day and night by enrolling in the legion.

After his return everything began anew: thick envelopes, sent from quickly changing addresses. With one difference: he now focused exclusively on editor N., in whom he presupposed an equal degree of interest in his, Minnema's, work, as he, Minnema, showed for N.'s work. 'The work is streaming off me,' Minnema wrote to him quite superfluously. Naturally N. soon lost interest, he left the letters unopened and asked me to settle the matter.

However, I could not resist opening Minnema's absurd communications. Poetry (the collection *Reunion* II . . . the collection *About-Face* . . . the collection *Return* . . .) and letters on poetry, and letters about our silence with regard to the letters on poetry, and letters about them in turn. A self-generating and self-perpetuating work. A work that read itself. This was what fascinated me, that Minnema tried to communicate by means of a completely self-contained system – his *oeuvre*. I studied the symptoms of Minnema's lunacy. I took his letters home with me.

But it did not escape Minnema that his friend, editor N., was not responding ('you can regard the previous letters as unread'), but later asked him to pass on the material to editor O., 'who will understand, as he is a real poet' (the latter words double underlined). On following submissions he wrote:

'For O. who is a *poet*'. In this way the work kept changing position while it was in my folder the whole time.

When O. did not answer either – as was said, because I did not bother him with Minnema's material – Minnema stressed that he was not aiming for a 'breach'. After that he began to complain in secret language. That is, there were things in his letters that O. the poetry-writing editor could not possibly understand, but which I did. There followed veiled threats.

He was torn. On the one hand he sent more and more material, and the other letters in which he demanded all his work back – sometimes with the statement that he was now in contact with a publisher (the last word double-underlined). Some letters carried as a kind of motto the words: 'Whoever understands it keeps it.' I think that in Minnema's logic distorted by will-power, there is no difference between 'Whoever understands it keeps it' and 'Whoever keeps it understands it'.

Whatever the case, I kept the material. I kept it until Minnema began to be a nuisance again. By this time he enjoyed such celebrity at the publisher's that I heard from various quarters that he was pacing up and down in front of the building. He did so in a strange way: he did not walk on the pavement but past the bumpers of the cars parked at an angle by the waterside, which gave his route, according to the staff of the publisher's, a meandering, capricious quality. One day he met me as I walked along. He asked for his material. I promised I would send it on. He wanted to take it with him immediately. I first had to collect it, I assured him. He said he had time. I said I didn't have time until tomorrow.

Again that reluctance, I thought to myself. The same day I photocopied a few of his letters, *secretly*. The machine had a problem with the colours of Minnema's felt tips. Listening for possible footsteps of members of staff who might be able to see me in this strange activity, I traced Minnema's blurred signature and I *heard* the words resisting and I felt my heart pounding, and I was glad when I could turn the light out and leave.

8

I sent his work back, with a hard-hitting letter in which I pointed out to him yet again that we firstly had no interest in his work, and secondly had no interest in his person; that we, more particularly, were not his friends or psychiatrists; that even if we were his friends we could not help him; that further submissions would go irrevocably into the waste-paper basket; and that finally we were considering taking legal action because of persistent harassment.

But – my God! – Minnema goes on. His letters *can* no longer be returned, as he no longer gives any address. To be precise he first writes some address or other at the bottom left on the envelope, *then he crosses it out*, in such a way that it is actually illegible.

As if to emphasize this state of affairs he also sends us a change-of-address slip filled in as follows:

> Name and initials (*Minnema*)
> Occupation (*dash*)
> Further details (*dash*)
> Previous address (*dash*)
> Town (*dash*)
> New address (*I'll go then. Shall I go then? But I'll go.*)
> Plus a dash through the rest.

He doesn't need to give our address, as he stuffs all his letters personally into the letter box up to five times a day. At top right he draws stamps. Sometimes he rings the bell. I hear that Minnema has been at least twice removed by staff with a minimum of force.

Once he rings the bell when I am alone in the building. I do not open up. He looks in through the window. It is snowing that day. He gesticulates. I silently shake my head. He gives me a melancholy look, and makes a writing gesture with his hand. Again I shake my head. He casts an indescribable look at me, and disappears into the snow.

Just before Christmas he sends a bunch of flowers, which stand in the unheated editorial office while the publisher's is closed.

Only now do I have the chance to look through his production of the last few days. With each letter the handwriting becomes more vigorous and less controlled. There is less and less on a page. The number of sides rises to sixteen. Through a fog of images I have the impression that Minnema is an adherent of Manicheism, the doctrine of continual conflict between two separate principles of good (light) and evil (darkness). Vague allusions indicate that I am the prince of darkness. The letters and envelopes are decorated with numerous suns (eyes?). In the poetry there is a door that remains closed, and a window. Some letters are signed with my name. There are indications that I am an executioner in Dachau (sketch of chimney with a plume of smoke). I suspect that Minnema is talking about me when he writes: 'Like ash/ he will be/ in more fiery ovens/ like ash ash ash ash ash ash' (across the whole width of the page). And about me, when he writes: 'Press my fingers/ into you so/ drink you completely empty/ sharpen the knife.' These furious pages alarmed me.

9

It is the first working day of the New Year. (There are two letters from Minnema.) I am busy all day catching up with a backlog of work. Post has piled up. I read items in an espresso bar. I have telephone conversations. (On Minnema's letters are two real, not drawn stamps.) I send copy to the printer's. I enquire about the rights for a translation. (As address of the sender Minnema gives our editorial address: 'sorry'). Now and then I look outside. At this time of year, as is well-known, it gets dark quickly.

Reluctantly I finally open Minnema's thinnest letter. To my surprise the official letterhead is of a firm of solicitors. What on earth was this? Very carefully typed. A number of sections divided by a space.

'Useless for the useless.'

'I'm washing my hands of it, with the result that you will be left with soulless material. Any further infringement will have direct results for you personally.'

'He kept my voice for months. Now he is not home.'

'If I appear in his work, everything will be automatically fixed. Fear the sun.'

A drawing of a head on a thread, and an opened pair of scissors.

'Bye-ye.'

I study the letterhead, which strikes me as vaguely familiar. Those solicitors' names, their address, nearby. I check in a file. Sure enough, it is *our* firm of solicitors. How did Minnema come by this paper? Is this coincidence or has he spun a net, comprehensible only to him, around me. It must be coincidence. It must be investigated. Outside dusk is now falling.

It is the first working day of the year. The office has been closed for a week and a half. It has struck me a few times that Minnema, if he is clever, will come by today. It is dark now, there is nothing more to be seen. I, however, am clearly visible for anyone taking the trouble to bend down and look into the basement, between the volumes displayed in the window. I have finished. And in a cheerful mood; the story I am writing and from which only the ending is missing is making progress. I perform the ritual actions. I empty the ashtray, put the cover on the typewriter, lock a filing cabinet, put the outgoing post in a tray, push my chair under the table, move the stapler from the centre to the edge of the table, and put on my coat. I turn off the fluorescent lights. I am on the point of leaving. Something occurs to me at the last minute. Without putting the lights on again I go back to my desk. Feeling my way I dial the internal number of a higher floor. As I stand there by the desk, in the dark, with my coat on, I of course look at the only point where light is coming from: the window. I stand and listen to the ringing tone.

I stare, and suddenly someone is *there outside* on the edge of the pavement. Standing still. I cannot see the head. I keep the receiver pressed against my head. Outside someone comes closer, and studies the display window it seems, which is not lit. I still cannot see the head. Someone is studying the display window it seems and then brings his head very close to the window and looks inside. I stand motionless in the unlit basement. I have my coat on. I don't move a muscle. I listen to the telephone. It has long since dawned on me that there is no one left in the building. I hold my breath and do not blink. My heart pounds. Outside is that head, of which I can see only the outline, against the glass. And here am I, a coat in a dark room, a telephone to my ear. My heartbeat is now irregular.

He is outside, I am inside. Neither of us moves. I shall stay inside for as long as Minnema is outside. I'm sweating and I'm cold. I coincide with my physical perceptions. I have been reduced to an immobile body, caught by Minnema's look. If it is him. If it is Minnema that I can see.

I have the feeling that we shall never leave. It's as if I'm dreaming. *Where am I? Is anybody there?* It is like the congealing of a pursuit dream into a single image, so frightening that the dreamer can only wake in order to realize slowly, slowly – sitting up, peering at a doorpost, the outline of a window, a chair over which his clothes are hanging – that he is at home, having escaped this time too, that they are his own clothes.

Translated by Paul Vincent

24

FRANS KELLENDONK

Foreign Service

Buitenlandse dienst

The only reason I don't have a peephole is the large window of the office building just across the road. I can observe him in it at my leisure every Tuesday morning at twenty past eight as he stands waiting at my front door. Our arrangement is that he will come to my home at precisely half past the hour. Too impatient to stick to this agreement but not wanting to arrive early, he waits a while with his chin lifted gruffly, his arms crossed loosely over his stocky form. A long moment after eight twenty, too long for any clock to quantify, his arm rises, yearning and threatening like a snake extending towards the charmer's flute, and presses the button so forcefully that the plastic cap falls off the bell in my front hall.

He has come to clean my house. By that time I have straightened my desk, picked dots of hair off the floor in the shower, scrubbed out the toilet with bleach, made my bed, rinsed off the previous night's dishes so he won't have to see the remains of my food – in short, expunged any trace of my bodily existence that could possibly arouse his disgust or hurt his pride, which is the size of an ostrich egg.

I push the cap back in place, rush downstairs and open the front door with a broad wave of welcome. Every week, he recoils. 'Were you in the bed?' Did I oversleep, he means. Then, 'Are you on the holiday?' And finally, 'Are you ill of the flu?'

These are reminders – the kind you might receive for a bill paid long ago – of the three times when I was unavailable and he came to my door for nothing. Three times in the three years he has worked for me. Let me add right away that I cannot call him to cancel – he has no phone. He moves from squat to squat, so I'm told, commanding a territory the size of his mattress in one corner of a kitchen or landing, the border demarcated by an old curtain. His name is Gamal. What more is there to say? Even if I knew, I'd have to keep it to myself, because he's here illegally. He comes from Egypt.

His country and mine: the open palms of two great continents, their fingers glittering with ports. Both are swampy deltas, dammed and dyked through endless drudgery. His forefathers, like mine, wrested every clod of earth from the water and belaboured it year after year down the centuries. And we are both exiles. That is where all similarity between us ends.

'No, no,' I say jovially, as if I cannot sense that he will bear his three grudges all the way to his Mohammedan hell. 'Come on in.'

'Not early?'

He knows very well he is too early, even if he doesn't wear a watch. As for me, I know he knows because he is *always* ten minutes early – on the dot. 'Oh, no, not at all.'

If my collar is up, if I have a dollop of shaving cream next to my ear or if the look in my eyes is a bit morose, as it can be on occasional mornings, then he takes another shirking step back, moving his flat hand back and forth to ward me off like a devil or the immigration police. 'No! I wait! One quarter hour.' He will not budge an inch, no matter how much I plead. In the large window across the street, I see his mirror image waiting by the door again, in his old sports jacket, faithful to his post, come hail or pouring rain. The reason he has not yet deemed our dismal climate worthy of a coat is, I suspect, that he wishes to see the Netherlands as a temporary matter; and if, under these circumstances, one quarter hour lasts no more than seven minutes, that too I can understand completely.

As soon as he's in the house, he hangs his jacket – and, in the winter, his jumper – over the back of a chair. He pulls his shirt out of his trousers, takes off his shoes and socks, sets his glasses on the table and wobbles into the cold kitchen on laggard feet. Anything else I have to say will go unheard. Time for me to go now.

He doesn't like to be seen at work. Does he drink the coffee I keep warm for him? I don't know. The first time he came I left a sausage roll in the oven for him, only to find it in the rubbish bin that evening. The piece of mocha cream cake I left him for my birthday – 'Look, Gamal, a piece of mocha cake. For you.' – same story. 'You please to go now.'

Every Tuesday morning, I leave my flat as if an angel with a flaming sword is in hot pursuit. It is no small task for me to spend a whole half-day away from home. I am fiercely attached to my little walk-up flat, which has become a part of me, all the more intimate because I share it with no one. It is a second body.

There among my furniture, books and tropical fish, I am a model member of the unemployed. Every night I sleep exactly seven hours and thirty-five minutes, without fail. My health has never been so good. Like the pale idiot in the asylum, the dowager wearing her life away in her straight-backed chair, I stand a decent chance of reaching one hundred. And all my love goes to my things, my books, my prints, an old ashtray and a box of wine corks not excepted, mute things that do not strain my affection, caught in their prisons of hardened emotion like amber.

I used to be a teacher. It's not a time I recall with pleasure, to be sure, but I did exist, then. These days I am a person whose letters and filled-in forms lie for weeks in a corner of a bureaucrat's desk until they finally glide off unnoticed and I vanish. I ultimately exist only for myself. This is not normally unbearable, but sometimes I feel like one of the living dead. I occasionally toy with the idea of plotting a graph of my good days and my bad days, to ascertain statistically whether growing old is what I have come to suspect it may be. But every time, I decide it's wiser to remain ignorant. I dutifully try to make a life out of my good days. From time to time, my bad days show the undeniable tendency to recur at shorter intervals. Then I spend a week with my sister in the countryside. When I return home, my little life again seems not unbearable.

In short, I can certainly leave the house for more than half a day if required, but I would prefer it not to be Gamal who does the requiring. Whenever he cleans my house, I feel anaesthetized, sick with a pain I cannot feel, as if I am being cut and poked inside. If you'd like to know how a soul looks without a body, you should follow me some day on my Tuesday-morning wanderings through the city. I first spend an hour in a coffee house, bowed over the morning paper. Newspapers, especially morning papers, cause a guaranteed dip in the graph of my days, but on Tuesdays I read the morning paper anyway, because what else can you do in a coffee house before 10 a.m.? Half-dozing, I read of the triumph of my way of life, the percentages rising month on month, the million mark coming ever closer. In just a few years, the unemployed will outnumber the women. In the foreseeable future, my way of life will be the most common human condition. Yet my fellow outcasts and I have yet to adjust to this new reality. As we stand waiting at the entrance to the public reading room, a few minutes before ten, we all do our best to look gainfully employed. I always make sure to have a folder with me, filled with papers. Others bring two pairs of glasses or fill their breast pockets with colourful rows of ballpoint pens. As soon as the doors open, we all rush for the magazines, each of us intent on the same glossy paper, the same full-page colour photos that admit us to the gardens of Schönbrunn and Sissinghurst, the temples of Tikal, the treasure houses along the ancient trade routes. Or did you think we have no need to travel?

When the weather is fine, I forgo the reading room and stroll around the marketplace instead, buying one bargain after another so I feel I have money to burn. I indulge myself shamelessly. I have fifteen bars of soap in my cupboard at home, enough razor blades and shoelaces for years, piles of underwear in pristine packaging, all because of my intense self-pity on Tuesday mornings. I stop by the house at some point (I live in the city centre) to deposit my carrier bag full of purchases at the bottom of the staircase. Then I linger there for a moment, listening, in the hope of hearing the soothing roar of my vacuum cleaner. There are times when I hear nothing – no industrious footsteps, no dull thud of a bucket or stepladder being moved. A breathless silence reigns, despite the thin walls of my home, the silence that surrounds a person in hiding. I've never had the heart to take a look upstairs. Once or twice I've called my own number because I'd forgotten to tell Gamal I was expecting a package. He did not answer. With every ring of the phone, I sensed his hunched shoulders like a physical presence in front of me.

At twelve twenty, I am allowed to re-enter my home. I suspect Gamal insists on that time because he has to pray at the stroke of noon. I usually find him seated, waiting motionlessly, his hands crossed over his belly and his nose turned up obstinately, as it is whenever he is not cleaning. As I enter the room, he springs to his feet and does not respond to my greeting. Once in a while he is still at work, singing in a high, throaty voice, and it takes a moment before he notices my presence. Then he mutters some kind of apology and finishes his work in silence, at breakneck speed. Meanwhile, I light a cigarette and pretend to read my letters. 'I'm not looking, see!' my whole averted form calls out to him. When he is done, he washes his hands and feet, gets dressed, and assumes a standing position in front of the same chair where he normally sits, without a sound – not even the faintest warning cough. He will not let even his gaze brush up against me.

The moment when I pay is easily the most awkward in the whole Tuesday-morning routine. I have tried to dodge it by leaving the money on the table in advance, but he painstakingly dusts around it, unwilling to lay so much as a finger on it. Nor am I permitted simply to hand him his twenty-five-guilder bill. I am supposed to place it on the edge of the table and then make it clear that I have forgotten all about it. Only then, while my attention is supposedly elsewhere, does he deign to pick it up. Pinching it between his thumb and index finger, apparently worried that if he slipped it into his pocket it might make a cashy crackle, he hurries off without a word of farewell, his head hanging in defeat. I have a fearful suspicion that he utters a curse every week as he passes over my threshold. When he pulls the downstairs door to the street shut behind him, the door to my apartment swings open on its own. He has pulled down the handle with such hidden force that it takes three days for it to right itself. 'Who's there?' my neighbours hear me shouting for days, because until Friday, the slightest draught in the stairwell can make my door fly open.

When I turn around to face my agitated interior, it's as if nothing will ever be the same again, as if I had gone to the station that morning to bid a final farewell to someone I love dearly. On the floorboards, damp spots dwindle. My prints seem shaken. My dusted knick-knacks have, with gross insensitivity, been put back in the wrong places, and in the aquarium, the guppies cower behind the rocks. The electric clock on my desk is running a quarter of an hour behind, the quarter of an hour that he used the socket for the vacuum cleaner. By adjusting and restoring it all, I reclaim my personal domain. My second body regains consciousness and immediately falls into a post-narcotic depression. In the kitchen, I survey what Gamal put away incorrectly after he did the washing-up, and I separate the ceramics from the glass, the flat plates from the deep dishes, the knives from the forks from the spoons. He has declared one kitchen cupboard off-limits. Whatever came out of there, he will not put back. It holds a few cups, bowls, serving dishes, nothing special, but he avoids it as if it were a tabernacle, my holy of holies, simply to show me his unrelenting discretion.

This is how it has been between us for three years now. Maybe I would be better off with a new cleaner, or, better yet, no cleaner at all. It would certainly save me some time to do the work myself, considering all my preparations, my adjustments after the fact, and the lost morning in between. But I have no reason to economize on time, thank you very much, I am drowning in it. The twenty-five guilders would be a better reason, the mental agony I would avoid a better one still. Even so, I spend half the week eating thin soup with stale bread so that I can pay this son of the desert his wages. It is my only source of pride. No one else can put that money to such good use. I know for certain that he will not turn over a single cent to profiteers and warmongers. As long as he has that money, no banker or taxman will ever see one bit of it. I envy him that freedom and feel privileged that I can help, in some small way, to make it possible. Best of all, thanks to him, I, one of the unemployed, have become an employer. The two of us form our own little economy.

That is what makes it so excruciating that our dealings are bogged down in rules and habits. Rules make each day identical to the last. My whole life ebbs away into routine. *My days are swifter than a weaver's shuttle, and they come to an end for lack of thread.* I leaf back through my diaries and notice that the order of events has slipped my memory. When did I find the broken-winged starling on my doorstep? It could have been this morning – but I have to go back five notebooks. Years ago. Nothing that happens to me has a history.

I do take notes, very thorough ones, on this experiment in the laboratory of loneliness. Only people like me, who never experience anything, who are on the ash heap of history, as Trotsky once said, have the time to keep diaries. Mine are about encounters that never took place, missed opportunities, nostalgia for the daily trials of my time as a teacher (students I am only now beginning to see; a freight train passing through a railway crossing at a slow crawl, preceded by a man with a red flag; the condensed breath of the impatient cyclists; a view of Centraal Station from Kattenburg Island at seven in the morning, when it caught the first rays of sun and shone like Byzantium). I turn my memories into keepsakes, capturing them in the amber of my hardened love.

A few of those notes are about Gamal. I have reproduced them here to melt off the amber and give these incidents a sequel, a history. Do not expect this tale to be resolved. I am writing it down in my search for a resolution, a reconciliation – or if necessary, a quarrel. The conclusion is on the far side of the silence after the final sentence. I will make sure that Gamal has the chance to read these pages. I will leave them on the table. The lure of his own name will be too much to resist. Then he will see himself through my eyes. I am your friend, Gamal! Earlier stories have merely described life; this story must change mine.

*

This time he does not remove his jacket right away when he comes in. He reaches into his inner pocket and pulls out a letter, which – after quickly checking whether it's still the same letter – he hands to me. I can see myself standing there for ever and ever, world without end, my eyes wide and happy, pointing at my chest. For me? Of course I would like nothing more than to correspond with him, if that is how he prefers to communicate.

But he says, 'Correct, please.'

The letter, I learn, is addressed to a person named Dolly. I can instantly picture her from head to toe: long, bleached-blonde hair, a tight, faded T-shirt and tight, faded jeans. Her rear slides back and forth on a bicycle seat; the denim over her left buttock is adorned with a coarsely stitched, hot-pink heart. A Dolly and a prudish Arab – no good can come of that.

'Isn't this letter a little too personal to show to me?'

'Correct, please.' If only I would just do as he says.

Two lined sheets of loose-leaf paper, covered with green ink from a felt pen. Ellipses and exclamation marks where words fail him. I promise to take the letter with me to the reading room and give it back to him at twenty past twelve.

'Correct *now*, please.'

I hold the sheets of paper some distance away so that my reluctance will not go unnoticed. The address '1 Souk el Selah St – Cairo' hovers like a vague promise in the upper right-hand corner. He tells the Dolly that he still has both his ears and furthermore is a little older than six. 'The bad ones' have spread rumours about him. 'To love a dummy brings many troubles,' he sagely observes. The Dolly has resisted his advances. He brandishes his romantic feelings like a threat: 'Love needs water . . . from two hands . . . one hand alone can almost never feed the plant . . . !' He must have come up with that on his mattress, behind his curtain. She is his moon-beam in the sorrowful night. 'Without you everything and Nihil become friends,' he concludes. Gamal has a head for languages and likes to speak them all at once. The letter is signed 'God'.

There are a couple of points that require clarification. I also ask him, casually, what the signature means. I am told it is 'too difficult for Dutch'.

'But how can I edit your letter if I don't know what you mean to say?'

'Correct, please.'

I shift the words around a bit, replacing 'dummy' with 'foolish woman' and then changing it back to 'dummy'.

'Is it a marvellous letter, you think, Misser Job?'

I assure him that it is a marvellous letter. He beams. His cheeks glow, his eyes go blind with happiness, and he emits a noiseless cry, revealing the gap where there once was a front tooth. For a moment, I see Gamal as a baby in his mother's arms in that corner house in Souk el Selah Street. Gold coins jingle on her plump wrists, telling of a bright future.

'I ask again later, Misser Job?' Of course, the *effendi* would be delighted to do him a similar favour again in the future, free of charge. 'You be so kind,' he says, and pauses before resuming, 'to say if I have in me – hmm, how do I say it?' – (he rolls his eyes and twiddles his fingers) – 'if I have in me, you think, to be her lover?'

What a pedestal he has put me on! He seems sincere in his belief that my mere Dutch nationality gives me insight into the feelings of a Dolly I have never met. 'I have no idea, Gamal,' I reply honestly, to make it clear to him that in this and countless other respects there is no difference between us. He doesn't care for that answer; his face falls like a flag without wind. I take a different approach, trying to be helpful. 'Maybe you should flatter her a bit more. A moonbeam on a dark night – that probably doesn't mean much to her. List all the things that make her beautiful in your eyes, and say why. Start from her toes, don't leave out a thing, and she'll know for certain you love her and no one else.' I should have patted him on the shoulder, I realize, and wished him the best of luck with his conquest. He bows his head. 'Thank you, Mr Job.' The letter shrivels between his fingers.

When I ask him the following Tuesday whether he managed to win Dolly's heart, he tells me curtly that he never sent the letter. Why not? Because I corrected it in red pen. Red, he says, is the colour of hate. A strange superstition, all the stranger because his accusation is imaginary: I wrote in soft, easily erasable pencil. 'I don't hate you, Gamal!' He also noticed, he continues, that I got in touch with Dolly and told her 'things' about him. How did you notice that, Gamal? Did a dove land on your shoulder and whisper it in your ear? He becomes confused, mumbles that he saw 'signs next to her door'. And now he would prefer to start cleaning.

After that, everything returns to the way it was.

On a Tuesday in December, months later, after he leaves in defeated silence as usual, after the door swings open in his wake and my apartment briefly seems to teeter on the edge of the stairwell, I find another letter of his on the landing outside my door. This one ('For me?') is addressed to 'Misser Job'. The letter is perched half over the edge of the uppermost step; he has dropped it accidentally-on-purpose, 'despite myself', as he says when he breaks a glass.

'It is the third year that I work at your house. We are now at the doors of a new year. You have make some promise but you do not satisfy ... You gave me nothing back, you brought me nothing more. I have done my best, but sometimes the means are disabled to accomplish anything. This is a truth that the Dutch and you and the others cannot know it!

'I love the Netherlands very much. Oh, what beautiful country with green and red and with water ...! In the Dutch, the soul is big with love of goodness, but also there is the war of the soul and the greediness and then the greediness wins. Bananas for their owners! In Egypt the soul is small with poverty. I am shy of the Dutch, Misser Job. They have open my letters and use my thoughts. The Dutch hates me.

'Sometimes the translation from inside comes wrong on the outside. And the only difference between the woods and the other human one is that the animals can not speak ... Unlucky! Then some safety goes away in the understanding. (Black pen means nothing ... it just happens!) You are what you understand.'

I grab my coat from the hook and rush outside. He is wrong to say that speaking can only lead to misunderstandings. I am touched by his confession, although a shadow passed over my tender heart when I saw that this letter, too, was signed 'God'. But I will drive away that shadow. It's probably a worn-down compliment addressed to the Most Gracious, Most Merciful One. Allahu Akbar, God is great, both East and West belong to Him – it must be that sort of thing. No need to be concerned. If I hurry, I may catch up with Gamal. I think I know where he's squatting. I must speak to him now. We have much more in common than I always thought. I, too, am a stranger in this beautiful country, am I not? I may have a home of my own, but society has cast me out. I cannot stand all the indifference around me, any more than he can, and so I too console myself with the illusion that I am hated. His sorrow is my sorrow's twin, I am what I understand. Isn't it possible that our solitudes could bring us together?

Poor Gamal! If he thinks the Dutch hate him, he overestimates them. The Dutch cannot hate, any more than they can love – all they can do is threaten him with their sluggish indifference. You are the one who hates, Gamal! I too feel hate. The Dutch are so indifferent because democracy has turned them into slow-witted slaves. The politicians call it 'the least of all evils'. They call that an ideology. They dare to call it a credo! In the Greek *polis*, the citizens knew each other. That was a place where you could make decisions together. But how do we go about that in this country? Here we are governed by the anonymous power of numbers. The majority rules, but the majority is no one, and no one can hold it accountable. Its delusional decisions are natural disasters against which there is no defence. I'll take a despot any day of the week – then at least assassination would be an option. The majority declares the Dutch to be enemies of the Russians, but no one feels they are our enemies. The majority threatens total annihilation. If I did that, I would be a misguided fantasist, a madman. The majority has decided that I may no longer practise my profession, while every Dutch person I talk to says it's a crying shame. Look at all those books I have at home. I've read them all, some of them three or four times. I know long passages of Georg Wilhelm Friedrich Hegel by heart. The wisdom of the ages! Declared null and void by the majority. Democracy is a disaster. Madness has taken power; the state is the greatest threat to the citizen.

Have you ever met the couple who live upstairs, those two inflated torsos with small, superfluous heads, arms and legs? Those two are unemployed like me. They stopped talking about it years ago. They open their mouths only to shovel food into them. Before long they are likely to come crashing through the floor. Each day the thud of their footsteps grows duller; each day the boards over my head creak more menacingly. They are dutiful people. They take the money the state holds out to them and dutifully convert it into shit. Two digestive tracts, that's what they are, two tubes connecting the authorities to the sewers. In times of heavy rain, the plumbing can't handle their excrement – that's how much effort they put into it. Then the turds float downstairs, through the entranceway, over the doorstep, and into the gutter.

Two men from the city sanitation department come by with long bamboo poles, which they screw together. One of the men uses them to poke around in the sewer. 'Is the sludge coming out yet?' he asks the other one, who is staring down into the next hole over. He keeps poking and prodding until the sludge comes out and the money can start pouring in again.

The two of us, Gamal, have an economy on a human scale. The problems of the other economy are easy to solve. We'll abolish supply and demand. Away with the unreliable consumer. We'll hook up the factories directly to the destruction centres. Right in the middle we'll install a taxation system, and we'll turn the whole thing up as high as we please. *Our* sado-masochism has a friendly face!

When I arrived, bubbling over with joy, at the corner where his squat should have been, I found a sandpit, fenced off with wire. Of the lives that had been lived in that house, a cross-section remained, projected onto the side of the adjoining building: here and there a patch of wall tiles, a washbasin at an unattainable

height, the outline of a stairway zigzagging upwards, and a
square of wallpaper, now more than ever purely decorative,
against which a lamp cord was whipping in the wind.

The Gamal I see the following Tuesday, climbing the staircase
ahead of me, does not wish to have written that letter. He splays
his legs into a broad, ridiculous pose. He stamps his feet. With
every step, he puffs mechanically through his nose. He puts on
a parody of the wage slave's walk. He sniggers to himself.
'Look at me walk!' I translate. 'Step-stomp, step-stomp, like
an ambling old horse, with my master trailing behind me.
What a pitiful fool I am! But I laugh at myself. I think Gamal's
a riot, Misser Job!' At the top of the stairs, when I look him in
the face, the merriment leaks out of his eyes and he turns away
like a schoolgirl, his face slightly red.

'Is something wrong, Gamal?'

'No, no, is fine,' he splutters, 'is fine.' His Egyptian blush
has a hint of orange. He must be embarrassed. To reassure
him, I tell him his letter touched me, touched and disturbed
me. 'No, no, is fine,' he says, and he giggles. 'It's just a
Molièrism.' Beg your pardon? A Molièrism, that's right. My
own part in the conversation seems just as bewildering to me
when – after a hard-won victory over my more passive self – I
go ahead and pour out my heart to him. My sincerity discon-
certs him. He nods and agrees with everything I say before I've
said it. He studies the sole of his shoe, a sole full of holes. It
feels almost as if I'm scolding him. His hair is in short tufts
pointing every which way, like a chick newly hatched. It has
just been cut. Somebody must have done that for him; he's too
clumsy to have managed it himself. I see him in the chair as the
hand snips away, his eyes narrowing with contentment. I bring
my rambling to an end. If he has someone to cut his hair for
him, what use could he have for me?

The giggling becomes a habit of his, and I notice it is not always
entirely cheerful. Under his glasses, his cheeks are sometimes
wet. Over the past three years, has he become a little alien-
ated? His stooped, wordless existence here, the bestial burden

of poverty stunting his soul, the huge portions of tedium we Westerners cram ourselves with – it must gradually have become too much for him, and some of the safety in his understanding has slipped away.

There is also a 'Mrs Liesje', the friend who put me in touch with Gamal. We have tried all sorts of things to persuade him to drop the 'Mr' and 'Mrs', but he clings firmly to them, and to be honest, we don't even mind, it sounds respectful, grateful, and makes us feel somehow noble. Liesje has a busy medical practice and a labour-intensive household, with three whippets and a husband. He goes there twice a week. I call her and ask if she's ever noticed anything odd about Gamal. Her voice sounds comfortable, she's in the mood for a nice chat on the phone, and although nothing springs to mind immediately, she takes her time to reflect on what she might find odd about Gamal. He occasionally breaks a plate. He breaks a plate almost every week. He once scrubbed her carpet, and she had to put the whole thing in the wash. A month or two ago, he locked himself out of her house in the morning, and when she came home that evening at six, she found him on her doorstep, barefoot. 'Why?' she asks.

I read her his New Year's letter. How could I ever have thought it was the outcry of a kindred spirit? The ravings of a maniac with a persecution complex, that's what it is, there's no mistaking it. Unfortunately, that's no defence against his accusations. I cannot refute them, precisely because they are figments of his imagination. *Non liquet*. I tell Liesje about his romantic obsession. She clicks her tongue pityingly and does her best to recall other incidents. Oh, yes, he once consulted her about stomach ache. Apparently most of his diet consists of candy. There were also sexual problems, which he didn't care to explain in any detail. And has she ever noticed his colour fetishes? Why, now that I mention it, she has a red sofa cushion that's always missing after he comes by. She finds it in the strangest places – under her bed, or in the meter cupboard.

We are now a majority of two, Liesje and I. We chuckle about him in voices filtered by telephone wires, and then one of us, I forget who, says *let him go*. Only as an impossibility:

'And a fellow like him . . . of course it would be wrong to just *let him go*.' One of us must have said something of that nature. And once these words have been spoken, Gamal's fate hangs by a thread, like a yo-yo in my hands, as I sit by the phone. Up and down goes his fate as we contemplate the pros and cons. Wouldn't it be in his best interest if we let him go and he had to return to Egypt? He has no future here. He would have to spend the rest of his life here cleaning houses and shuffling from squat to squat with his mattress and old curtain, his back bent with scrubbing, not a tooth left in his mouth from all the chocolate he eats. Liesje points out that trouble awaits him in his homeland. She vaguely recalls something about a pregnant girl he left behind – the neighbour's daughter? During our first conversation, long ago, he mentioned that his opinions were considered subversive in Cairo. Hadn't he been expelled from his university? We wrap him up and box him in with our gossip. Although all we have done is speculate, he is practically ready for shipment by the time I hang up.

I am the crocodile. I lie in the mud, encompassed by willows, covered by the shade of the lotus. When I sneeze the light dances, but I am tender and loving when I hold my jaws open for the crocodile bird, which wanders over my teeth, picking out scraps of food and leeches with its long beak. You are that bird, Gamal! Every Tuesday I meet him at the door with the firm intention to let him go, but the right moment never arrives, so strict are the rules that prevail between us.

Almost every day, I go out for a stroll around seven in the evening. Most people are having supper then, and I have the city to myself. Today wind from various directions sweeps veils of elm blossom through the streets. The petals pile up like tissue-thin tokens along the kerbs, and I walk through the gutter dragging my feet till the mounds of blossom reach above my ankles and then kick the stuff into the air, where the wind catches it again. Gravity seems suspended. Above me clouds glide past and over each other, and there are heavenly revelations and a fierce sun that blinds me and gives me the feeling that I am made of pure

light. It's as if after a long illness I have come outside again for
the first time, and I think about dying, the way a boy sometimes
thinks about dying, with a yearning that is so intense only
because it will stay unfulfilled for so long.

Then, on the other side of the canal, I see Gamal walking
ahead of me. It is the first time that I have run into him outside
work. If I go to him now, we will have to do without the deep
grooves of our rituals. This is our chance to start afresh. I see
his black hair, one arm of his glasses, the legs of his trousers
resting on his shoes in weary creases, heavy with dust and
ashes from the streets. From his hand – only the fingertips
emerge from the sleeve of his sagging jacket – there hangs a
plastic bag with lettering that has almost worn away, the same
one he's been carrying for the past three years. 'Fresh from the
butcher – always the best', it used to say. He walks without
looking up, hastily, as if on his way to work.

When someone behind you calls your name, even if it's
someone you wish to avoid at all costs, your legs betray you,
snapping to attention – but as my voice echoes from the house
fronts, Gamal trudges on, the bag in his hand swinging in an
unchanged rhythm. I put my thumb and index finger to my lips
and whistle. 'Gamal!' He walks on without a twitch of hesitation, as if stone deaf. I remain standing by the canal-side. For
a moment, I feel the urge to run across the water to his side
over the thick layer of blossom.

I am weighed down with guilt, sunk in grief. No, I have not
yet come close to putting my affairs in order. That moment
when death seemed welcome was entirely premature. Sorrow-
ing over Gamal, I take a right into a narrow side street. I
wander over a bridge and past a row of shops and turn around
with a start, because in the front window of an ironing service
I glimpsed his form passing through a landscape of snow-
white shirts, as absent and mechanical as ever. How could he
have overtaken me so quickly? It can't have been more than a
minute ago, it seems, that I was standing beside the canal. But
maybe I was daydreaming there and lost track of time. 'Gamal!
Just a second! I need to talk to you.' He does not answer. The
sun gleams from the lenses of his glasses. No waters run

between us now. Three swift strides and I've caught up with him. When I try to grab him by the arm, it's as if we're two identical magnetic poles – I can't do it; I have to let him go.

For the rest of my walk, which as usual follows a route so haphazard I could never retrace it (but always the very same route, I'm sure of that), I am repeatedly struck by the feeling that he is still nearby, like a guardian tiger, a feeling that always turns out to lack any perceptible basis. So it's all the more surprising when later that evening I'm back at home, about to close my window, and I see him pass again in the street below. What kind of person are you, Gamal, not to remember your house of bondage with a single look?

Translated by David McKay

25

OEK DE JONG

The Motionless Man

De onbeweeglijke

Although I do not like other people and avoid meeting them, I entered his room one evening and asked, 'And what about you? How do you occupy yourself?'

He didn't answer immediately, but after some time he spoke with a sigh, and it seemed like the final part of a longer answer: '. . . and with nothing in particular.'

That somewhat surprised me, as I had always regarded him as an active and enterprising man. How many times had I seen him roaming the stairs and hallways with strangely sparkling stones, books or small dead animals? I didn't know the man's name. I called him Tze.

I turned my gaze on his curved back and his head, which he'd propped on his fists, piling up the flesh of his cheeks. He'd slid the chair he was sitting on almost halfway under the table and bent so far forward that only fifteen centimetres of space remained between his face and the bare wall. Even out of the very corners of his eyes all he could see was the wall. There was not a trace of strangely sparkling stones, books or small dead animals.

Tze's room was remarkably small. If I stretched my arms above my head, I'd touch the ceiling; if I took a step forwards and reached out my arms in front of me, then I'd hit the opposite wall; holding out my arms to the side to their full length was only barely possible.

Without the slightest movement, Tze now said quietly, 'And you, sir, what is your name, and how do you occupy yourself?'

'Kalk is my name, and I occupy myself with writing an

account of myself, though without any particular need to do so. I regard it as a pastime.'

'And have you been working on your attempt at this account for long?'

'For over seven years now, with many interruptions.'

'And why is it that you interrupt your work?'

'I don't actually know what precisely the interruptions are: the days when I work on my account or the days when I don't. Let's just say: I fast for five days so I can gorge myself for two, and find both activities unimportant, but prefer fasting to eating.'

'Yet after five years of fasting, you must be approaching a point where you can formulate your wisdom briefly and simply.'

'That is true. Two years ago I completed my account, and it ran to many thousands of pages. Then I began rewriting and after every day's work there were fewer sheets remaining than the day before. For a while now, there has been just one sheet left. What is written upon it encompasses but a few seconds of my life, and yet its entirety.'

I waited some moments, looking intently at Tze. During the course of the conversation, he gave an occasional shiver, as the words increased in number. He pressed his stomach even more tightly into the edge of the table now, hooked his feet behind the legs of the chair, opened his fists and folded them firmly around his head like large leaves. Then he sat motionless again, and I continued, 'On that one sheet of paper is described what I once saw, in the middle of the night, on the cusp between waking and sleep: I am sitting in a room that has no obvious character, although it is not empty. A man enters; in the embrace of his arms he is holding great bunches of flowers, brightly coloured and of many different varieties. He lays them on a table, makes up bouquets, and puts them in vases, of which there appear to be a great number in the room. Then he leaves. At first I'm delighted by the beauty and the fragrance of the flowers, but then their presence becomes unbearable. I pull all the flowers from the vases and throw them out of the window. The room is empty now, and the scent of the flowers slowly fades. I feel as if I've been liberated and have escaped from a great danger, but at the same time I'm deeply saddened.

'The next day, the man returns, bringing the flowers. Again, I enjoy them at first, but then I become afraid and throw them all out of the window. I am relieved but sad. This same event is repeated over and over again.'

Tze said nothing, so I stood there feeling awkward. After a long time – I was just about to leave – he said: 'If I understand the profusion of your words correctly, life is both appealing and terrifying for you, and that saddens you.'

'That is true. I avoid people now and become involved in life only when necessary.'

'So is there some necessity for your presence in this room?' asked Tze, and I heard something defensive in his voice.

'Every principle requires an inconsistency, or it cannot be a principle; and that inconsistency makes the principle all the more desirable.'

'That sounds very fine,' said Tze. I suspected he was smiling with gentle irony.

'In youth, one is more voluble, yet emptier,' I apologized.

'That sounds very fine indeed,' replied Tze.

I deemed this moment of agreement a suitable one to approach him a little more closely. Very cautiously, I left my place by the door, where I had been standing until then, with the intention of catching a glimpse of his face. But no sooner had I moved than Tze said, 'Be so kind as to remain still. Even my own movement is unbearable to me. I hate motion, things changing makes me ill. I used to occupy myself with small dead animals, but they rotted away in my hands. So I read books. Twice I would read the same page, and twice I would find something different written there. Finally I sought my answer in the stones. But I could never see their sparkle in the same way twice.'

I understood now that his aim was to be motionless, and that the sight of the wall was as much as he could bear. I began to question him about his motionlessness, but he no longer answered. The peculiar shivering of his body slowly ceased.

*

And no matter how keenly I watched him, I could not detect any movement. So I left the room, without a sound.

A week after that first meeting I returned to Tze and from then on I visited him almost daily. By then I knew my way blindfolded through the maze of stairs and hallways that made up most of the house. In his room, I stood by the door, as still as possible. Tze sat motionless in his chair, and we spoke to each other.

Sometimes he would stretch his stiffened arms and legs for a moment, but always with great reluctance and considerable effort, as the clothes he wore were exceptionally tight and close around his body. I used those moments to shift my weight unnoticed from one leg to the other.

Tze was the only person with whom I had any contact. And I actually tried to win him over by keeping my words to the point, and every now and then remaining silent for a while. My account was finished, but it had merely brought me to a dead end. I now had no direction or aim, and was in a state of great uncertainty.

One evening I asked Tze to leave his room and accompany me on a walk. After much hesitation, he agreed. He pushed back the chair and, with difficulty, stood up. For the first time, I saw his face; it was narrow and sharply chiselled. His face skimmed past, close to mine, then towered high above, up against the ceiling. Tze was a giant. He must have been thirty centimetres taller than me. His chest was almost as wide as the door, and he could have grasped around my neck with one hand if he'd wanted to.

We found our way through the darkness of the stairs and hallways and, after some time, arrived outside. Then we followed a narrow path, which twisted among bare, undulating fields. We walked for a long time, constantly descending. The path was so steep in places that we had to brace ourselves so as not to fall.

It was a great effort for Tze to propel his lumbering body forward. As he walked, he panted heavily and at first all his joints creaked. He'd tilted back his head to look up at the dark,

star-strewn sky, which always remained there above him, no
matter how he walked. That made it bearable for him. He
allowed me to take his arm and guide him down the path.

We came to a river, which flowed broadly onwards. The
water swirled and splashed, whipped up by a strong wind. On
the other side, very distant and barely visible, were mountains.

Tze stood with his back to the wind and shook my hand
from his arm.

'I can hear that you have brought me to water,' he said bitterly. 'A lake or a river.'

'It's a river. But I didn't do it intentionally. I didn't know
where the path we were following would lead. Like you, I'm a
stranger to these parts.'

'Rivers are unbearable,' said Tze, 'one never steps into the
same water twice. A fine place you've chosen for my farewell!
You should have taken me to the mountains instead!'

He seemed indignant at me for persuading him to leave his
room. So that our only walk together would not be spoiled by
an unpleasant silence, I told him the first thing that came into
my mind, remembering the mountains he would have liked
to see.

'Perhaps you've heard the story of the man who left his
house one morning, just with the clothes he was wearing, and
headed for the mountains in the distance. He arrived towards
nightfall, and he lay down like a bridge across a narrow yet
deep ravine. There he remained, seeing only the deadly depths
below, and enduring the heat of the day and the cold of the
night without complaint. He thought he had achieved perfect
motionlessness, and hoped to turn to stone and become a natural bridge. But spring came, and the snow on the mountains
melted. A stream went tumbling down the slopes, searching
for the lowest point and, furiously swirling, it flowed beneath
the man and through the gorge. Now he saw constant movement and change. Finally he could bear it no longer, so he
stood up and cast himself into the ravine.'

Tze was silent.

'The same will happen to you,' I continued. 'There will
always be movement somewhere to make you shiver and feel

restless. Why not step into this river in order to achieve perfect motionlessness? Do it now, the moment is right: there is no one to rescue you against your will!'

'No,' replied Tze. 'I want to live motionlessly.'

'That sounds like a paradox.'

'It is a paradox. But the paradox is the only way,' Tze cried, incensed and inconsolable. 'It's easy for you to talk, with your paradoxical understanding of life, which does not oblige you to anything.'

I wanted to respond with a torrent of words, as uncertainty makes a man speak. But no sooner had Tze said this than he turned his back on the river, lowered his head, and began to climb the narrow path. He did so with such great strides that, within just a few moments, I stopped trying to keep up with him. I stayed by the river, on my own.

After this incident, I didn't dare to visit Tze for a few days. I felt that it had been foolish to tempt him to take a walk, but even so I cursed him and decided many times to leave him alone in his motionless state. I even considered seeking solace among others. But it was becoming increasingly difficult to suppress my longing to see him, and finally I returned to his room.

Tze had used screws and nails to fasten his chair immovably to the table and the floor. He'd secured himself to the arms, the back, and the legs of the chair with leather straps. His head, chin resting on his chest, was now all that he could move. But it was immediately clear to me that he would never do so again, any more than he would speak. I took up my familiar position by the door.

'You must forgive me for that walk,' I said, 'it was foolish of me to urge you to do it. If you forgive me, remain motionless. If you do not, then make a movement, and I will leave.'

And so I assured myself of his company, and prolonged my indecision. I spoke to him again as I had before, but now without interruption, and answering my own questions. By doing so, I came to have some remarkable thoughts. But eventually my imagination was exhausted and I began to repeat myself. Then I tried to recall all the conversations we'd had and to repeat them word for word. To practise this exercise, I changed the order of the conversations and recited each of them from back to front. But when that, too, no longer required any effort, I fell silent. For a few days, I considered acquiring a chair and sitting down beside him – there was still space at the table.

Then I tried again to leave him alone in his motionless state, as I had many doubts and reproached myself for having brought about Tze's demise with that walk to the river. But I had become so attached to him and his presence gave me such deep peace that I continued my visits, standing silently behind him for a few hours every day.

One day, just before the end of a visit, I heard a buzzing and a gentle tapping on the walls and ceiling of that quiet room. I looked around and finally spotted the insect on Tze's neck. Without thinking, I took a step forward and crushed it with my hand. The giant head fell sideways and the neck ripped open. Legions of insects now emerged from his clothes and advanced towards the tear.

Sadly, I left his room and the house. Outside, I began to climb the path, although my heart drew me to the river.

Translated by Laura Watkinson

26

THOMAS ROSENBOOM

Tincture

Tinctuur

'I have poison. If you want poison . . .'

In my fear, I never forgot where Mattij was. During the school day I saw him in class; after school he would make his slow way to the bicycle shed as it rapidly emptied out. His friends would cluster around him then, a dense throng, and Harm was with them, not as a friend but as their possession. Sometimes it took more than an hour before they were done with him. When they finally let him go, he barely had the strength to mount his bicycle. From behind an advertising column, I could see Mattij and his friends come out of the shed a moment later. I would wait until they too were out of sight before riding off to the closed brickworks between the edge of the woods and the river. There I would build a fire, sit out on a wing dam and fish, wander the scrubby hills, or walk along the channels in the water meadow with my hand net.

'I haven't made it yet, but I could start right away . . . Just let me know when you want it.'

It was unclear why Harm was the one they had chosen for the bicycle shed, but still, I could understand it. He had certain qualities that almost invited it, and those qualities grew more intense the longer he played his role . . . You might say he grew into it.

*

But the other thing I understood was that I had the same qualities. Once they got tired of Harm, I would be the obvious
replacement. That was why Mattij filled me with panicky fear,
why I always knew where he was, why I could not stop staring
from behind that column out over the empty schoolyard at the
seemingly long-deserted bicycle shed. From the very first, I had
parked my bicycle next to a tree near the column, so that I
would never have to go in there. Not daring to give the slightest impression of a connection between me and Harm, I hadn't
said one word to him ever since it started. All I knew was what
I could see from the outside.

'You can use it on animals ... It affects the heart. You
interested?'

My fear continued to grow. I sorely wanted to escape Mattij's
grasp by giving him something, something to create a bond,
something bad, and in doing so I would become bad myself, on
the same side as Mattij, as safe as a crow among crows. But I
had nothing to give, until one day at the brickworks I was
taken by surprise by a couple out walking their dog.

The weather was fantastic, and I was dozing in a ventilation
shaft when I heard them. I took a cautious peek around the
corner and saw them right away. They were walking along the
forested edge of the overgrown site, towards a patch of purple
flowers that had been in bloom for a couple of weeks and stood
out against the tall trees behind them. A little dog ran ahead.
The woman called it back; it wouldn't listen. She told the man
to call the dog.

'Why?'

'Why? Don't you see those purple flowers on the tall spikes?
Those are foxgloves!'

'Well, what about them?'

The woman's snort resonated as far as the shaft where I lay.
'You don't know the first thing about flowers, do you? Foxgloves are poisonous ... what if he eats them?'

A couple of hours later, back at home, I found confirmation

in the *Flora of Europe*: 'Common foxglove (*Digitalis purpurea*): forest edges, marshy soil ... contains digitoxin, which stops the heart but can also be taken medicinally in a diluted tincture of oil.'

The very next day was the first time I offered him the poison. Mattij said nothing. But I raced to the brickworks on my bicycle right after school to get started. I had everything I needed.

The long spikes of flowers still looked the same, but not to me: they were poisonous now. I threw my bicycle against the shaft, put on my mother's housecleaning gloves, and holding a pair of scissors in one hand and a plastic bag in the other, I moved in closer.

It hadn't rained in a while, but the soil around the foxgloves was soaked with water that had trickled down from the hillside. The weather was still amazing, a loud buzz hung over the purple spikes, and no sooner had I reached towards the first flower with the scissors than a bee came flying out. From the uppermost flower, a whole head taller than me, to the dark green rosette of leaves on the ground, I did not stop until the stem was bare, surrounded by a growing swarm of bees from the purple goblets, which were dotted with red and white on the inside.

Back at home, I stashed the full plastic bag in the barn. After dinner I retrieved it and started making what, after consulting the dictionary, I understood to be a tincture. I decided to use petroleum, the most volatile oil I knew of, so that it would evaporate down to a concentrate more quickly. I didn't know, then, that Mattij would continue to turn down my offer for weeks. I ground the flowers to a pulp between two paving stones, left the pulp for a few days to dry into a powder, added the powder to a pan of mineral oil, and whisked the viscous mixture until it was as purple as the flowers had been.

'Maybe you don't need it right now, but I've started working on it anyway – you know what I'm talking about ...'

*

The purple grew deeper by the day as the oil evaporated. I eventually sealed the lid with tape so it wouldn't vanish completely. For two weeks I went on offering the poison, without ever receiving an answer. That didn't change until one day in chemistry I took the next step and ventured a concrete proposal.

'I made a tincture. It's ready . . . If you want I can give you a bottle tomorrow. It's your business what you do with it. Tomorrow during lunch break . . . at the front gate, okay?'

For the first time, Mattij seemed to hear me; he nodded; a giddy wave swept through me. Then he actually smiled, but again, without looking me in the eyes. That must be how it was with those boys, I thought; they kept their distance, didn't get too close to each other, wouldn't be too quick to touch you. My heart swelled with a feeling of safety as I returned to my desk.

That night I crept back into the barn. I had poured the nose drops out of a bottle and removed the label, and I'd smuggled a pipette out of the chemistry lab. I pulled off the tape, removed the lid from the pan, and saw that it still held too much of the purple petroleum. Above a burner, I warmed the liquid until there was just enough left to fill the small bottle. But every constituent of the flowers, including the poison, was still in there. The vapour rising from the pan still smelled like petroleum and nothing else, so I concluded that all that time nothing had evaporated but the oil. I dipped the pipette in the oil, filled it, and squeezed it out into the bottle, thinking how incredibly concentrated it must be.

The more important an appointment is, the slower time passes while you wait, and I had an appointment with Mattij! To avoid breaking the fragile bond between us, I didn't so much as look at him all that slow-footed morning. Then the buzzer sounded for lunch.

My hand on the bottle in my trouser pocket, I wound my way across the already teeming schoolyard towards the gate. Though I tried as hard as I could not to hurry, I got there first. Just as casually as I had strolled through the crowd, I glanced over my shoulder at the groups in conversation, but

Mattij came from a different direction and was suddenly standing in front of me.

'Ha ha!' I laughed nervously, but I immediately composed myself, even going so far as to lean back against the brick gatepost. I slung one leg over the other as if about to light a cigarette, took the bottle from my pocket, and held it out to Mattij.

'Here you go, but be careful – it's highly concentrated!'

Mattij did not move, yet the bottle was taken from me . . . At first I saw only the hand, and then the man; it was the headmaster, who from outside the gate, around the corner of the post, reached into the gap between Mattij and me and then emerged completely from his hiding place.

'Well, I'll be . . . You were right!' he said, looking back and forth between Mattij and the bottle in his hand.

'He's been bugging me about it for two weeks,' Mattij said with a sigh. 'I ignored him at first, but when he said it was ready, I thought it could be dangerous . . .'

'Good idea to tell somebody,' the headmaster said.

'I wanted you to see for yourself that I didn't ask for it. He just offered it to me anyway. That's how it was from the start.'

'Sure, sure, I understand, Mattij. We'll have one of the chemistry teachers analyse the contents. I'll keep you informed. Thanks!'

Without a word or even a glance in my direction, the headmaster vanished around the corner with the bottle. Mattij turned in the other direction, and the next moment he too had vanished among the groups in the schoolyard. Tingling from top to toe, I remained slumped against the post, certain of nothing except that every word Mattij had spoken was true.

I'd offered him the poison, again and again, for two weeks.

All that time he took no notice.

As my blood went on slowly curdling, I sat through the rest of the school day. After the last buzzer I could barely move. But a few minutes later, I was crossing the schoolyard as if nothing had happened. I wanted to go straight home, but first I took a quick look back from behind the advertising column. Just then Harm came riding out of the bicycle shed, standing on his pedals, stronger than ever. Still, nothing could surprise me any more. I walked on to the tree where I always left my bicycle, but it was gone.

Bewildered, I circled the trunk, looked all around – in my excitement that morning, maybe I'd propped it up against a different tree. Or was I so dazed that I'd picked the wrong tree now?

As I glanced around again, two of Mattij's friends came out from behind a van and, with smiling faces, solved the mystery.

'Can't find your bicycle? Don't worry, we put it in a safe place for you,' one of them said.

'Why do you always leave it here? That's what we have a shed for,' the other one continued.

'We moved it for you this time, but from now on you'll have to park it there yourself,' the first one added.

'Come on, let's go get it ... Mattij is there too,' the other one concluded.

Waving his arm invitingly, the first boy urged me on ahead, as the other one lifted a hand in silent insistence in the air behind my back. Untouched but thoroughly boxed in by my escorts, I started walking, back to school, growing dizzier with each step, tottering from one leg to the other.

Ahead of us gaped the deserted bicycle shed. By the time we went in, there was nobody else coming out.

Translated by David McKay

27

A. F. TH. VAN DER HEIJDEN
The Byzantine Cross

Het Byzantijnse kruis

'Hinge scissors are not of European origin, but were probably
imported from Byzantium or the Islamic world.'
(From: *Excavations in Amsterdam*, Fibula-Van Dishoeck, 1977)

The other day I bumped into an ex-girlfriend in the street. She
had just got back from Karachi, where she had been working
for a while as a nurse in a home for the mentally handicapped,
run by nuns. Out of pure altruism or out of a feeling of guilt –
you sometimes can't tell with those boarding-school cows – she
told me a few things. Nice mess, over there in Pakistan. They
have no notion of the mentally defective. Only those possessed
by the devil. The mentally handicapped are hidden away anxiously by the family. Chained up in kennels behind the house.
Often beaten. In the slums of Karachi the nuns sometimes
trace them and transfer them to their institution. One day they
found one with a group of travellers. A boy of about twelve. He
was chained in a barred cage, and could not move a muscle.
Naked. Swarms of flies obscured his open wounds from view.
His skin was one big relief map of scars. The nuns did not
manage to take him with them. Out of the question. But that
same night he was left, cage and all, as a foundling at the gate
of the institution. Once he was released, he turned out not to
be able to walk upright. The nuns had to drive him ahead of
them like a monkey to the bath. He allowed himself meekly to
be fussed around. Until one of them appeared with a pair of
scissors to clip his nails, which were ten centimetres long. When

he caught sight of the things, he lost control. He went berserk like an animal.

'We had a terrible job knocking him out with sedatives,' she said. 'And once we'd pumped him full, his nails were clipped at top speed. As if he could come round any moment, with a heavy dose like that in his body. We cut his hair, too, as it was also too long. And full of vermin. Man, you should have seen him when he came round. Completely disorientated. He realized at once what had happened to him. He kept looking at his hands and grabbing at his head with his hands. He was in a panic. Not because he had lost his nails and his hair, no, because he saw that we had used scissors on him. *That* panicked him. He was frightened of scissors. Frightened to death. And he stayed that way. I've never seen anyone driven into such a corner by a simple utilitarian object. He only needed to suspect the presence of some somewhere, and he went up the wall. He shied away from everything that even gleamed like a pair of scissors. For example, there was no point in approaching him with cutlery. A fork could upset him for hours. I was once with him when he was completely calm. Really no trouble at all. He was playing at my feet. Suddenly his head jerks up. Immediately he sits absolutely still. Just like an animal getting a whiff of danger. I see his eyes darting back and forth. Until out of the corner of his eye he keeps peering at a particular corner of the room and starts trembling all over his body. I go and look. What's there? An open safety pin. Something shiny immediately gave him the shivers. It drove him completely wild. It was as if he was repelled with the same force that a magpie is drawn to it. For that matter, there was something about him like a magpie at the end of its tether. Now that I mention it.'

A real chatterbox, that cow I had bumped into quite by chance. But she finally shut her trap for a moment and gave me a long, enquiring look. Then she quickly asked what kind of life I had been living recently. Was I still studying?

'Not any more,' I said. 'I've packed it in.'

'What does the future look like now?'

'My future? Darling, you've just given a striking image of it yourself. No, really, no kidding. I couldn't think of a better one off the top of my head.'

And that was enough for her. We'd said all we had to say. For ever.

Pusher, dealer . . . I hate those words. I hate them. They're slippery words. You let them slip. I never use them. There's no Dutch equivalent. They no longer belong to any language. And they don't seem ever to have been part of any language. They came out of nowhere. They were heard and remembered. They are so often used that they have lost all flavour. They have rolled off the tongues of so many nationalities that they are not even words any more. They are sighs. They are indictments. And they are only heard by those who have ears to hear. They are associated with endless calls. Phone calls, house calls – in telephone boxes that don't work and on steep steps. Endless and in vain. Again and again. Hour after hour. Up huge flights of steps. You know exactly where the bell is. You can find it blindfold. Unerringly. Your howling arm knows the way. That poor, helpless, porous arm of yours. It knows the way. It hooks up. It connects. In vain. Late in the evening, at night – they keep you ringing. At night, at night and again at night. And early in the morning, at the end of everything. Huge great steps, towering houses. They often live so high up that you can't even hear the bell ring. So that you never know if the thing is off or not.

And if, to be on the safe side, you try listening at the flap of the letter box while you're ringing, then you can't reach the button. It's so high up. You're so small at that moment. You've simply got to ring and wait. When you have waited long enough and are fed up, you go to the next address. And on to the next. That can go on for whole nights. If you have three addresses, the city is reduced to a triangle, consisting of the shortest distances between those three addresses. The city disappears into that triangle. It fits precisely into it. It *is* that triangle. And the night is the incessant passage from angle to angle. En route you leave colourless vomit behind. Luminous puke of a lunatic dog. You've puked all over all their doorsteps. You've stood there in the cold, sick and helpless. All night long.

And they see you. Somehow they can see you. If they're sure you've got dough, doors open for you. Even at night. Preferably at night. They open up in sunglasses. They pull the ropes to let you in and stand at the top of the stairs with sunglasses on. Even the evenings are too bright for them, the night isn't dark enough. Their stairs are high and steep. They've disappeared again before you've reached the top. For a second you saw him hanging around in the stairwell. You saw the light of the street shining in the lenses of his sunglasses, and he's gone again. You've got to knock. Again. Louder, louder. And again. A conversation through the door. He doesn't trust you. Suspicion is the name of the game in those circles.

There are other addresses too. Usually in back streets. That's where your money comes *from*. That's where you flog what you've been able to get together on a day like that. Complete car interiors are sold on. At a heavy loss for you and a fat profit for him. You accept what they offer. You're in a hurry. If what they offer isn't enough, you've still got your scissors. Then you score half a fix, and move on. Then you scrape a little more together. Bags of addresses. You weigh things up and ask and sell till you have enough bread for the next half fix. You hustle and you sell and buy till you have enough for the whole day. Then either you sleep or you don't, and then you start over. Again and again. You've got your scissors.

If anything typifies us, it's this: an open pair of scissors in a closed hand. It could be our emblem. Closed fingers and points and rings poking out on all sides. The narrow blade with the pointed tip between the index and middle finger. That's the key. The only usable part of the scissors. That is the barb that works its way into the safest locks. A bit stiffly to start with, but gradually more supply. It gets notches in it that make things easier.

At right angles to it, between middle and ring finger, the wide blade with the blunt end. Unusable as a key, indispensable as a grip. One ring pokes out from behind the thumb, the other presses into the palm of your hand. Or against your wrist – depending on the length. They are mostly big scissors. You carry them interwoven through your fingers. Like a cross. That gives the best grip. They arm your hand. They hold your hand straight. Your limp, helpless, trembling hand. They form its skeleton. They are anchored in it. Provided you hold them firmly.

There are people (I know them) who take their scissors apart and just keep half. The narrow part. They take them to bits. Not for me, a gruesome little thing like that. It doesn't give as good a grip. It keeps slipping. Particularly when you are getting to the end. When you're in a hurry. When you start getting the shivers. Give me the whole pair of scissors. So I can feel the wide part gripped firmly between my fingers. A clenched fist with a cross of steel, I think to myself. Not a cross of honour, of dishonour. All the better, and beautifully chrome-plated. Gleaming treacherously in the torchlight.

Too treacherously. I paint mine black these days. With cheap satin sheen from the Hema store: colour C108. Except for the point, beyond where it can't go any deeper. That's too sensitive. That must stay pristine. That's what I earn my crust with. The rest I paint black. First I go over the chrome with abrasive paper. Otherwise the paint won't stay on. Then I brush it on.

At the first attempt I didn't allow for the drying time. I was in too much of a hurry. Back then it was the only pair of scissors of the kind that I possessed. I walked around for two weeks with black rings round my fingers, with black lines in my palm. I felt like I was arousing suspicion. They took a long time to wear off, those strange criss-cross marks that went up into my sleeve. Since then I've been more careful. I now rub the scissors down so that the paint takes better. And I let it dry until it can't get any drier. If they're new, only the chrome-plated side of the narrow blade occasionally catches some light. A spark of light that leaps up. That bounces over the shiny car for a moment and then leaps up. Across the canal or up the face of the houses. It reminds me of the pocket mirrors we used to have at school, with which you could make the sun dance through the room. If you use them often enough they do wear out. With each lock the smooth point roughens. It becomes covered in scratches. It lets the inside of the lock make grooves in it. It absorbs the combination. Very subtly. By means of burrs. A pair of scissors like that has a good memory. It gets to know and distinguish

locks. It recognizes them. It adapts. And fits. It transmits sig-
nals to my hands through tiny jolts. It trembles in my hand. My
fingers follow it, fractions of millimetres. Left, right. Forward,
backwards. A little deeper then back a bit. Crick crack. Open.

But as the scissors adjust the risk of breaking increases. The
notches become too deep. A breaking point is created. The
blade breaks all the more easily. You are asking for it. The point
is usually left intact. An absurdly thrusting barb. Indicating
that the owner can keep his stuff. For as long as it takes, that
is. I must make sure I get rid of the remainder of the scissors as
soon as possible. I've thrown lots in the canal, broken scissors.
Funnily enough always in the same place. I've dreamed about
them too. Teeming over each other like handicapped crabs
when a tour boat disturbed the water. Crippled scissors, eyes
on stalks. They were snuffling about the body of my melancholy Aunt Stientje, who had once thrown herself off the bridge
there. Aunt Stientje who drowned herself because she didn't
like the fiancée of her only son Sjorsje. Gas hadn't worked and
she had survived crying too. Then one night she stole out of the
house and stepped off the bridge. In my dream I saw her exactly
as she was, Stientje. I could clearly make out the node of nerves
on her right temple. That blueish bulge, that purple egg, which
made the police suspect a violent attack. Uncle Sjors was able to
refute this. It was a knot of nerves. She lay very peacefully on
the bottom of the canal. Until that boat came over and my
mutilated scissors started snuffling at her. They scuttled around
her and over her. They prodded and pricked her. Her breasts,
her thighs, everywhere. They snapped at her toes and nipped her
ears. Until one of them spotted her nerve bump. At that moment
they all snapped shut and headed for it like a shoal of herring.
There was a riot of snuffling and pricking and snapping. Aunt
Stientje started gabbling as she lay there dead. Saying that I
could have Sjorsje's toys, because it was all over now. And
more of that nonsense. A little later my next pair of scissors
plunged into the canal. Still unbroken. They fell in a closed
state directly downwards and hit Stientje right in her purple
egg. Clouds of yellow liquid started rising from it. She got up
in a rage and tried to clamber up the quayside. Scissors were

hanging from the hem of her dress. As I saw her surfacing, my
dream suddenly stopped. She called my name. I woke up.

I always have a spare pair of scissors in my pocket. They are
in a calf-leather case, intended for an aluminium pocket comb.
I carry it in my wallet, in which I also keep a series of cut-out
profiles. Black and white. I bought them from one of those
quick-fingered clip artists in Montmartre. In the Place du Ter-
tre. Failed and rejected profiles. For almost nothing. The price
of a drink. A transaction with a shrug of the shoulders. He
didn't understand what I wanted them for. I didn't need my
own profile cut. *Non, merci.* He couldn't for the life of him
understand what I saw in them. Anyway, the owners of those
profiles had all long since gone back to America. And Japan. I
told him I was going to deliver them to all those people. That I
would search until I had found the matching profile. He
thought I was an oddball, but was happy to let me have the
worthless things. Clipped profiles. Black and white. To have
an artistic alibi to hand. To justify my carrying so many pairs
of scissors in my inside pocket. A forged hairdresser's diploma
was impossible to come by. No one need notice that my scissors were rather large for that delicate, nimble-fingered work.
And if at the station they wanted a cut-out of the superintendent's head, I can always refuse. 'Uniforms make me nervous.'
(Come to that, I left Paris again straightaway. The cars there
were just as easy to break into as in Amsterdam. The haul was
often even richer. But I didn't know where I was supposed to
get rid of the stuff. I had no addresses. And I was too impatient
to wait and see for any length of time. In the last car I opened,
I chucked all the stuff I had collected meanwhile on the back
seat. Just like that. The world turned upside down.)

I tried to build up a stock, of that special type. As has been
said, they are inclined to break. On average I lose one a week.
I hoard them. There is really only one particular type that I
can use for my work. They're quite expensive. Something
about the length, the width, the thickness, the sharpness, the
strength – *something* about the damn things makes them ideal
for my purposes. I was given the tip through a contact. Nothing distinguishes them from run-of-the-mill kitchen scissors.

Except for the price. And a slightly more luxurious appearance. But that may be me. I pick them out automatically. They are used a lot. Worryingly often. Almost everyone uses them. Of course there are other methods, but give me the scissors any time. I ask you, I can see myself standing there with a great bunch of car keys. And trying them out one after the other. The more delicate finger work. There are people who do that (I know them) but it's not for me. You need nerves of steel for that. And I haven't got them. At least my scissors know the way. By themselves.

No one knows who started it. Who exactly discovered and used that type. You'd expect him to keep it to himself, lucky dog. Each to his trade. Or at least to apply for a kind of unwritten patent on it. But perhaps he was very altruistic. Or perhaps it was the actual dealer himself who had the idea. And he passed on the tip to his customers. To put them under an obligation, the swine. Perhaps he insisted that they pay him in kind ... These are just speculations. What is certain is that those steel blades sell like hot cakes. When I went to get some recently, they were out of stock. Sold out. And at my regular supplier at that. I had just been through my supply. The last one broke off in the lock of a Mercedes. I shan't let it get to this point again. Ever again. I took preventative measures, and not cheap ones either. I dragged round half the city. I did not rest until I had collected a dozen. They turned out to be available in more places than I thought. The best thing is to direct your buying mania at department stores. There it is less noticeable if you buy five or six of a particular product at a time. In a bag, receipt, and off you go. Still, it is better to buy just one, for example every other day. But in the Bijenkorf the other day, the penny started dropping. They have bright girls. At the till that serves the scissors department and others, there is one with shrewd eyes.

'Well, well,' she said. 'You do wear out a lot.'

I just smiled a bit, I think. I'm very good at smiling. The next time I tried to pay at a different till. But I was referred to her. I considered putting the thing back, but that struck me as really suspicious. I felt cameras directed at me from every direction. It was busy at the till I needed. She won't notice at all this time, I thought. There are so many people. When it was my turn, the young madam said cheerfully and loudly: 'Another pair of Lothar-Sciss? What on earth do you do with them?' I replied quickly that all she had to do was come out with me one evening. Then I'd tell her.

And at that she looked at me as if something began to dawn on her. As if she wanted to say: Oh, there's no way I'm doing that. Do you think I'm letting myself be skewered on a pair of scissors costing forty-nine guilders fifty?

In the fanatical zeal with which I hunt for my type of tool, I've become completely obsessed by them, scissors. Not just that one type, no, other types also awaken my desire. Larger ones, smaller ones, slimmer ones. The other day in a department store I came across a tray full of scissors for toddlers. They were plastic, hard plastic, but they were such sweet colours that I couldn't resist them. The melancholy air of lemonade straws. Milkily translucent. I bought one of each colour. Not even expensive. They are unusable, but great to look at. I've got them here on a white plastic plate. And I have big ones too, bigger than I'd ever be able to use. They are monsters. They are scattered casually around. Like malevolent pets. But I've got silver ones too. Operating scissors. The slim instruments of the surgeon. Mostly stolen. They are in matching beakers. Sometimes they are straight, sometimes curved. Bent inwards, bent outwards, bent sideways. I have all sorts. They are nice to take out of their beaker and run through your fingers. Unusable for me, but with a divine grace. I like them almost as much as my small Perspex scissors. They are my absolute favourite. So finely polished that they are a joy to hold. The blades are kept apart by a small double-headed screw in black plastic. On the wide blade there is something written in fine white lettering. Japanese. I can't read it, but imagine that it must be an infinitely tender word. It is like a caress.

But anyway, occasionally a broken-off tip gets left behind in a car lock. So there are scissor fragments in *their* possession. It must be child's play to check what type they come from. And what if today or tomorrow they get it into their crazy heads to take that special type off the market. To see whether car break-ins can be reduced a little? It doesn't bear thinking about. We would be dealing with yet another extra black market: Lothar-Sciss. Dealers lending them out to their regular customers. And of course illegal manufacture. Anyone who can duplicate keys can do the same with scissors. They would change hands for a lot of money. The damn things would be unaffordable. And they would stay just as breakable. You can scarcely insure yourself. You would have to break in to twice as many cars to be able to finance your tools. Little would change, thieving would just get a lot more inventive. But would the manufacturer take his products off the market when he sees that they are doing so well? Come, come – he's not stupid. He could even manufacture them, those dream scissors of his, in such a way that they break a little sooner. The principle of built-in wear and tear. He would immediately see the difference in his turnover. Then he really would be rubbing his hands with glee. I even considered contacting him. Via the suggestions box. His name is etched by the hinge of the scissors, next to the screw. I would put the plan to him of supplying *pre-formed* scissors. With notches in the right place. Various sizes of burr mixed together. For different locks. 'Tested on all current makes of car.' And still usable as household scissors. They should be sprayed black. Silk sheen. I can already see them hanging by their rings on steel hooks, ready to be wheeled on racks hundreds at a time into the oven. No maker's name must be stamped into them. This is true under-the-counter work. It takes place after working hours. The workers do well out of it. Delivery is directly to me. I sell them on. Yes, I'd know what to do. I wouldn't have to lift another pair of scissors for myself.

But by the time tools cease to be a problem, you'll see that the minerals you're after will become exhausted. You'll always see that. That's how it is in this country. Anyway, there are already enough signs pointing in that direction. You need to have an eye for them. I ask you. Someone may allow his car to be emptied twice, but definitely not three times. He's not as stupid as that. Not even in the Netherlands. After the first time he may buy a new radio. Second hand. Nicked, of course. But when that disappears, no more. When everything has been stripped out that can be stripped, except for the seats, the motorist will park on the canal without qualms. Right, there you go. There it is. Nothing more to finish off. Unless we make off with the whole vehicle. But that's another story. That's not our territory. Those Amsterdammers are a crafty lot. They start catching on. They are irritatingly sharp. But stubborn as they come. You've got to strip the fur from the driver's seat two or three times before they think of putting back the old plastic cover. But sooner or later the penny does drop. When that happens the car is reduced to its old familiar proportions: a thing to drive in. That's our virtue, albeit unintentional. We rely increasingly on tourists. They don't suspect a thing, until it happens. Then it ends in tears. Tourism is becoming our main source of income. In that respect we are true Italians.

When I was much younger than now, I did a lot of hitch-hiking. I hated it, but I had to. I often couldn't afford a train ticket. Cars that wouldn't stop – I've seen more drive right past me than anyone. Perhaps it was at the side of the road that I acquired my addiction to swearing. I learned to swear marvellously under my breath. I dreamed up the loveliest curses. And once I was sitting down, when someone had finally stopped, it simply continued. Behind my front teeth. Inaudibly, but certainly not unnoticeably. I couldn't stop. I liked it, swearing. And I still do. I just go on. There will never be an end to it. In the grave I shall still be gross. A requiem of curses. 'May the pox be with you.' But in the very beginning, when I was a lad, at the very beginning I called them 'islands of domestic bliss', those cars that refused to stop. Particularly at night. And when it was cold. 'Islands of domestic bliss gliding past.' Gradually I learned to despise them, those disappearing islands. It happened faster than I thought. Finally I didn't want to hitch-hike at all any more. Even if they offered. I *couldn't* any more. I'd had enough. The people with their simple-minded questions about your studies. Their endless drivel about the capacity of the engine 'which is not at the front but behind'. It was made all too easy for me in my contempt. I found all their pettiness

and small-mindedness combined in their cars. From small service to glove compartment, the whole works. And the irony is
that what I have always considered the most contemptible
thing in a world where it was so hard for me to find my place
is what I break into by stealth to hustle a crust. That's no
longer irony, that's pure cynicism.

Yes, those shabby Fords have become my main source of
income. I keep body and soul together with them. I've got a
special key for them – one that is wrong in every way. I carry
them clenched in my fist over my heart. I open them before I
leave home and grip them in my fingers. Then I place my hand
holding the scissors over my heart and button up my coat like
a one-armed man. That gives you something to hold on to. For
the next few hours that key is the axis around which my world
rotates. There, inside my hand, is the turning point of the
world. My grip never relaxes. The whole time I am out, my
fingers are clenched tightly around the scissors. I can see that
from the indentations I find afterwards. And with that cruciform key I penetrate the affluent world of cars big and small
(Volkswagen versus Mercedes: the level to which the discussion on the fairer distribution of incomes has moved in the
Netherlands.)

Point thrust forward, I wend my way. Blankets are usually
on the back seat. For some reason they always evoke in me the
image of an old man in an invalid carriage. It has to be a very
bad day for me to take them. They fetch scarcely anything. I
just hate walking with them over my shoulder like a gaucho.
They are often full of hairs from some dog on heat, which is
now at home in its basket.

When I break into a car at night, I sometimes take it easy. I
prefer to sit in the front passenger seat. Inside the sun visor with
the hinged flap there is often an extra mirror for the ladies.
For checking their make-up. I leave it where it is but can never
resist having a look in it. The way I look when I break into a
car. (Always different.) The glove compartment. I take lighters.
Often very expensive ones. The other day one from Australia.
On one side there was a coloured map of the continent and on
the other the depiction of a platypus. Definitely an expensive

item, but it didn't fetch much. Michelin Guide, Shell Guide,
motoring guides, reading matter for passengers or concubines –
often whole libraries. I save Michelin guides. For trips I shall
never take. Sponge and chamois leather. Rubbish, of course.
Peppermints, paper handkerchiefs, condoms, cosmetics, pocket
combs, sunglasses, driving glasses. All rubbish. I only take the
lipstick. For girlfriends who never actually use it. Sometimes
I'm able to get one to put on lipstick just before we go to bed.
I'm so crazy about the flavour.

I know at once when I'm in a woman's car. I smell it. Often
it turns me on. I'm not a fetishist anywhere but there. But when
I find one of those openwork imitation-leather driving gloves in
the glove compartment, it makes me kinky. I can't help pulling
them to pieces. A purse or wallet left behind can make my day.
At least if there's something in it. Passports are welcome too.
Doesn't happen much. Car radios and tape recorders are of
course the most interesting items. They fetch the most. So I pick
my way through the creepy-crawly world of imitation-fur covers, neck rests for the driver, and dolls dangling from rear-view
mirrors, official adjustable safety belts, adjustable child seats,
removable mats, ashtrays, umbrellas, magazines, the chaos of
the cat tray, removable steering-wheel covers, wrist bags. With
my razor-sharp cruciform key I penetrate it infallibly. With a
flick of the wrist.

Translated by Paul Vincent

28

MARGRIET DE MOOR

Sunrise Day

De dag van Zonnegloren

It was still dark when she noticed him getting up and starting to potter around the room.

'Come back to bed, Jacques,' she mumbled. 'It's too early.'

He didn't respond, but groped for the linen cupboard and opened the door. He rummaged around inside.

'I need a wash,' he said. Even tucked up in her blankets and sheets, she could feel that it had turned cold in the night. A strange silence hung on the other side of the curtains. Maybe it had snowed. The shower began to roar, and she dozed off again, to vivid dreams.

When she awoke for the second time, he was sitting on the bed, now dressed. The curtains were open.

'No, not those socks.'

She nodded at the window. In the dim light, the houses across the street were just visible. A layer of snow covered the roofs.

'It's cold. Wear the blue ones, my boy. The thick woollen ones.'

She got up, took the socks from the drawer, and sat down beside him on the edge of the bed. She was a fat woman with a fine complexion and watery, pale-blue eyes. Age indeterminate. Maybe sixty, maybe seventy. As she put his socks on for him and gave his big feet a quick rub with both hands, the man sat there, bolt upright, staring calmly ahead. He had blue eyes too, dark and deep-set.

'Go and have a shave,' she said.

It was nearly eight o'clock when they sat down for breakfast. She'd squeezed oranges, and she'd fried eggs. She passed him the bread basket.

'How many am I allowed?' he asked.

'As many as you like. Just you enjoy them.'

He took two bread rolls and put them next to his plate. As he began to cut into a third, she put on her glasses and opened up the newspaper. She took her time over the articles, reading all of them; she had no preference. She ate nothing but drank the entire contents of the teapot. Every now and then she glanced up to meet his eyes. He was chewing away, his whole face in motion.

This big man had always eaten well. He was a glutton by nature. Young though she had been, she'd understood that right away. With those hands. With that wide mouth. 'I'm going to marry her this summer!' he'd proclaimed, looking around the family with ominous cheer, and the silly goose was pushed in the direction of two elegant sisters-in-law. The goose sat all evening in a straight-backed chair, transfixed by his booming laugh, his drinking, the bloody nose he accidentally gave his brother, the winks across the crowded room that were intended for her. That big man opposite her had to be the happiest man in the world.

She looked outside. The daylight was hazy. The car was covered with snow. Across the street, two doors opened at almost the same time. Men in dark coats emerged. They walked to their cars and began wiping the windows. One of them had problems starting. Then the car sat there with the engine running for a long time. Steam drifted down the street.

He'd finished eating now and sat watching her with his usual pained expression. The anxiety of recent years had made his features sharp. It was as if he wanted to hide his eyes, they lay so deep in their sockets, and two deep furrows now ran beside what had once been the nose of a gourmet, but was now an angular beak. His mouth was dotted with crumbs.

'We'll be off soon,' she said. 'We'll just wait until the rush hour's over.'

He stood up to go and wash his hands and face.

'Where are you taking me?' he asked when he came back in.

'You know where, don't you? It's Sunrise day.'

But of course he had no idea. Why should this hunter, this

fisherman, this half-gipsy have any understanding of how to make ashtrays? Of the scorching-hot oven they were fired in? Of the red paint he was required to apply to them?

He thought for a moment.

'I want to stay with you,' he said.

Suddenly she felt intensely guilty. Not because she was taking him to the day-care centre, as he was no worse off there than at home. It was her own foolishness. This morning she had the sneaking feeling that her simplicity was criminal. Why couldn't she follow his trail? Why couldn't she see with his eyes? What was the terror that he couldn't live with?

'I'll come and fetch you this evening, sweetheart,' she said helplessly.

He stood there before her, broad-shouldered. She helped him into his coat. Gently, she led him down the garden path. As she walked around the car, clearing the windows, the small vehicle seemed to be crammed full with a hunched-up bird. Two eyes followed her movements with the incomprehension of an animal.

They drove out of the village. Alongside the road lay the white, silent fields. Did he remember the gunshots, the excitement, the triumph? When he got home, he would put his day's kill, with the bloodied fur, the bloodied feathers, in the shed. He was very skilled at skinning and plucking. The animals arrived on her kitchen counter, clean and tidy. A humble offering. She'd always been good at preparing game, and it was a crying shame that, for years now, he'd refused to eat any kind of animal whatsoever.

She drove cautiously. There was little traffic, but it might be slippery in places.

'Look, Jacques, isn't it beautiful?' she said as they approached the lakes.

He stared at her profile for a moment.

The narrow road was no more than a dyke between the lakes. A hazy sun gave the air and the water the sheen of metal. In the distance, the villages were just faint silhouettes. Beautiful, indeed, for those who could see it. She was briefly startled by an unexpected event: a flock of birds skimmed across the road with wild cries. Above the water, the creatures fanned out a little, but stayed together. Then, suddenly, they were gone. Flawless. Resolute. Entirely aware of their position in space and time.

He was her husband. She knew the rhythm of his breathing. She could smell his scent. Without looking aside, she knew how the shadows were falling on his face. The sense of doom had returned, even worse than it had been at home just now. She suspected it was not solely his present secrecy that was shutting her out as if she were from a different planet. He'd always been a stranger to her. Even, especially, on those nights when he overpowered her with his body.

Who had she spent her life with?

It was getting on for ten. Bright sunlight broke through the clouds. The lakes to the left and the right began to shine like mirrors.

There had been a few winters when she had not been pregnant. They'd skated here. She'd gone on ahead, a good deal faster than him, superior for the first time. In the middle of that flat expanse, beneath a sky that promised snow and storm, with that demon trudging after her, she'd felt her body change, right down to the smallest molecules. She knew for certain that she was beautiful. As beautiful as the reeds and the ice and the deep blackness gleaming beneath her. The whole combination was perfect. She was not at all startled by his grasp when he caught her after all and kissed her so hard that her lips split and started to bleed.

At the beginning of the next village, there were traffic lights. It was not yet time for people to do their shopping. Slowly, they drove along an empty street of modernized shops. Neon lights shone everywhere. She noticed that he'd started to look around: and yes, there was the colourful sign outside the sweetshop on the corner.

'Would you like a treat, Jacques?'

He nodded in delight. She pulled up, walked around the car, and helped him out. In front of the shop window, they conferred. Finally, he chose a simple chocolate figure. Once inside, they had to wait for the sales assistant to finish arranging a line of white chocolates in the display cabinet, but she was very friendly when she came to help them. The chocolate figure was packed up in a gift box and presented to him. The two women smiled at each other across the counter. But he was reluctant to leave. He walked around to the assistant and took her to one side.

'There's a possibility that my coat may have brushed against those peppermint sticks,' he explained. 'I certainly came very close to them. So maybe it's not such a good idea to sell them.'

Back in the car, he started eating straightaway. It was just a few bites. She picked up the clean handkerchief in readiness and handed it to him as soon as he'd finished. With a frown on his face, he wiped his hands, his wrists, and each individual finger. Then he put his hands back on his knees and gazed down at them with his chin on his chest.

She looked along with him. His hands lay there like heavy, unfamiliar objects. Then a sense of horror washed over her: she felt that she could see the same as him. Pity shot through her, as fierce as physical pain. She went to take hold of his hand, but he pulled away and gave her a look that was so raw and so terrible that her breath caught in her throat. For a moment she thought she was absorbing his actual fear.

'Let's go,' she whispered.

She started the engine, jerked the car into gear, and sped off.

The village gave way to the next one almost without inter- ruption. The narrow road cut through the social strata like a jagged knife: to the right were the big houses in their parks with their old trees, to the left were the workers' homes, lean- ing against one another, with backyards that opened onto the canal. The composition of the local high street was imbal- anced: 'Laundry', 'Dry-cleaning', 'Wash-o-matic' said the signs. They must do an incredible amount of washing in this village.

Cars were lined up in front of the hotel, with white ribbons and white flowers attached to the aerials. People, as colourful as birds, were walking down the steps outside.

She pointed.

'Look, Jacques, a wedding.'

She hoped he would forget the church among the houses a couple of hundred metres away.

But his sharp eyes had already noticed the open side door.

'I want to confess,' he said.

There was no point objecting that he'd already been to church once this week. That last week he'd visited two, three other churches. That every priest for miles around must be aware of his secret story by now.

The thick layer of gravel crunched beneath their feet. Inside the porch it was ice cold, but once they were through the heavy revolving door, the temperature was pleasant. You could feel that the place was well insulated. Whatever happened here did not escape, but lingered in the form of scent. And that scent did not fade.

They walked along the side aisle and came to a door from behind which they could hear quiet noises. Footsteps. The clink of dishes. She knocked. 'Yes?' someone called. The door opened, and a young man in a red jumper appeared.

He looked at the man and woman, a question on his face.

The old man put his head forward.

'I need the priest,' he said.

'I am the priest,' the young man replied with a smile.

The old man stood silently for a moment before repeating: 'I need the priest.' Then he added, 'I have to confess.'

The young man's gaze slid away from the couple and he looked around the church. In one of the side walls were a few doors with stained-glass panels at the top.

'Wait a moment,' he said to the man before disappearing again. He left the door ajar.

He was back surprisingly soon, in his cassock and white surplice. As he straightened the purple stole around his neck, he motioned for the man to follow him. The woman joined them.

The priest opened one of the doors. Inside the small dark room was a vacuum cleaner, a pile of books with red covers, and a few sticks with limp velvet bags attached. The priest bent down and began to move everything, including the books, which weren't really in the way. Eventually the kneeling rail became free. The priest and the man, who had stood motionless as he waited, each disappeared through a door.

She sat down in a side pew. It was absolutely silent. Not a sound penetrated through the doors. Her gaze wandered before coming to a stop on the icon in the alcove in front of her; she looked at the familiar image of the crucified man with the bloodied hands, the bloodied feet.

When had it begun? Maybe as long as ten years ago. She'd recently remembered his strange behaviour on the day of his retirement. They'd laid on a lovely party for him. The alderman had given a speech. About his great services to the village. About how indispensable he was, in fact. There'd also been a few allusions to the last winter of the war. His courage. His cunning. No one had known the hiding places in the peatlands like he had.

Yes, nice things had been said. But Jacques had been too drunk. He'd started an argument afterwards. A friend who'd wanted to shake his hand had found himself on the receiving end of some nasty insults and had slunk off, astonished. Ah, that good, good man didn't want to be turned out to pasture. That was all.

Suddenly, directly above, she heard a few hesitant chimes. Every ring summoned forth another, louder one. A column of sound piled up on her head. A column of triumphant peals. The wedding . . . At the front of the church, a man in a grey suit appeared and began to light the candles in the huge candlesticks.

The doors beside her swung open. She turned her head to see the priest rapidly retreating and the bowed figure of her husband, who was waiting for her. Unchanged.

'Come on,' she said, in a loud whisper. 'Now we really do need to get a move on.'

At the exit, he spread his hands, one at a time, in the basin of water.

It was almost eleven o'clock. Inside the car it was nicely warm. Snug. Almost like in bed. These trips were not at all unpleasant. She looked at the trees along the village road. They were birches of some unusual variety, which, with their broad white trunks, bore a certain resemblance to plane trees. In a quarter of an hour they would be in town.

'Are you comfortable, Jacques?' she asked kindly. He didn't respond at first, but when she turned to look at him, he mumbled, 'I don't feel well.'

'What is it? What's wrong?'

'I feel sick.'

She changed gear and slowed down, but there was no way she could stop there.

'Just keep calm. It'll soon pass,' she promised.

But suddenly he began to sigh, his hands searching around, groping for the door and for the plush fabric of her coat.

As she turned off and looked for a parking spot – it was break time at the school and the young people wouldn't move an inch out of the way – he slumped to one side with a quiet groan.

She managed to make it through the crowd and to park the car. Then she got out and walked to the other door, thinking: Fresh air, he just needs fresh air. As she opened the door and was about to lean towards him, he fell. She reached out her hands to catch his head. The weight of his body was suddenly enormous.

'Jacques! Jacques!' she cried out.

He was now lying half on the street. Crouching down, her hands still cradling his head, she looked around. She could see no one except for a handful of schoolchildren who were standing some distance away, watching. Her hands were caught between the warmth of his hair and the icy paving stones.

A young man arrived on a bike. He dismounted, resolute, as if he'd known where he needed to be. His large head, shaved almost bald, filled her with confidence. Together, they laid the heavy body neatly beside the car.

The young man removed his scarf and made a pillow to go under the head. Then he lifted the eyelids and felt for a pulse. She watched, with wide open eyes. These vital actions had a calming effect.

'My husband is confused,' she said.

The man seemed to ponder her words for a moment. Then he stood up and looked right at her.

'Your husband is dead,' he said.

Then everything became very busy. As she was still sitting there on her haunches, staring curiously into that suddenly dead face, she heard sirens approaching. Doors slammed. 'Over here!' someone called out, and: 'Out of the way!' A few louts in brightly coloured jackets had finally come closer now and had to step aside to let the stretcher through. The paramedics tucked him in very carefully, with blankets and straps, and then slid him into the ambulance with ease.

A policeman made her stand up, and asked her a number of questions, of a personal nature, which she answered precisely.

How strange that they prevented her from getting back into her own car when it was all over. Even though her grief had yet to surface. Even though no one could have claimed that her senses were not working in accordance with the expected patterns, because look: there, beyond the curve in the road, were the white fields and the white trees and the sun, the ice-cold sun above elongated pale-purple clouds.

Translated by Laura Watkinson

29

P. F. THOMÉSE

The Southern Continent

Zuidland

1

If he closed his eyes, he could hear the roar of the sea. He was convinced that if God had a shape, He would be the sea, rolling meaninglessly in His immensity. So awesome was His expanse that no coast was beyond His reach, even the unknown ones at the end of the world. But no sooner was He there than He retreated and people lived there without knowing Him. God was indifference and Jacob Roggeveen felt that knowing this made him one of the elect. Formerly he would have propagated this truth to prove everyone wrong who laughed at him and saw him as a failure; today, however, he kept it to himself and it gave him a secret satisfaction. In the presence of others he often deliberately closed his eyes. While the people he was talking to uttered their futile words, his thoughts were putting out to sea en route to that immense calm. On the quays of Middelburg too, which he was accustomed to visit every day, he felt his omnipotence. Initially he heard the sounds of the harbour, the harsh rattling of cart wheels, the rolling barrels and creaking ropes; but then the waves of the sea broke and roared majestically over them, swallowing up every separate thing.

2

As a boy he feared the sea. It was as if the seals of all the horrors of the Apocalypse had been broken: the devastating violence of whirlpool and hurricane, the crushing majesty of rocks and reefs, the ship reeling defenceless over the unfathomable depths that teemed with invisible shoals of sea creatures lurking for him – and no safe haven anywhere, only primeval forests or wildernesses that were home to devils incarnate, cannibals, pangolins, griffins and fire-breathing dragons and overgrown with poisonous plants as all other vegetation had been blighted by locust plagues.

His father often talked about the sea, although he had never sailed himself. His tales of the wonders of Babylon and Egypt, of eternal snows and mountains of ice, of pearls and gold, of tropical countries where it was always summer and cold ones where night reigned eternal – he listened to them as prophecies of doom.

The harbour, which he visited every week in the company of his father, felt like the gateway to hell. The warehouses were chambers of horrors, the ships dismal prisons. Above all, the ominous East India schooners, towering over the quays with their gallows-like masts, filled him with dread. Deep inside them, in the narrow passages where there was neither light nor air, in the crew's foul cribs with their sweaty bedding and in the hold full of sour-smelling casks, musty crates and stinking small livestock he felt oppressed . . . He had to bite his lips at the thought that he would have to pass his whole life in a floating coffin imprisoned in the infinite emptiness of the ocean.

His father had preordained him to be a captain with the East India Company. He had initially planned this profession for his other son, but the latter proved a sickly child, unfit for life at sea.

How often had Jacob prayed to God to inflict him with a painless but incurable ailment? He kept his dread of the sea to himself, knowing that his father wouldn't want to hear about it. In secret he invented excuses, but no matter what he conjured up, his future life loomed ahead of him like an ineluctable hazard. His only hope was that God would swiftly summon him to Himself, because dead children were enlisted as angels with trumpets in the Heavenly Hosts.

He dreamed of a golden trumpet.

Because the Lord had given him no sign of having heard

him, he had asked his father if he could join the boys' choir. Their singing made him think of heaven and he knew for sure that God listened to them on Sundays. At all events their hymns seemed a better way to Him than prayers, which were so silent he could not imagine them being heard. He would have preferred to declaim them out loud under the naked heavens, but for whatever reason, that wasn't permitted.

Did God in fact know that he existed? He was by no means sure of that – and he sometimes doubted whether he would be saved were God to pour a new Deluge over the land, providing an ark for the pious. He saw the parson and the boys' choir already there, standing at the railing to welcome the animals: stallion and mare, bull and cow, billy and nanny goat, boar and sow, cock and hen, two of each animal, except for the fish because they could swim. And if he should humbly beg that a place be granted him too as he shuffled cautiously amidst the caterpillars, beetles and larvae, he would be refused one with the words, 'The Lord knoweth you not.' The preacher would pull the gangplank up from under him and the boys would launch into a hymn to the greater glory of their Lord as the waters rose visibly, with household goods and church pews washed down the streets and there would no longer be any escape for him anywhere.

His father rejected his request to join the choir with a laugh: 'My dear boy, if you were to sing, the sky would fall on our heads out of fright.' Later on he had tried to persuade him to buy him a trumpet, but he didn't comply with that request either. Permission to enter the ark was denied him for good. His fate was sealed: he was destined to be a ship's captain, a prisoner on his own ship, and to sail to the end of the world, beyond the icebergs to the land of everlasting night.

3

His father regarded voyages of discovery as the crowning glory of creation. If yet another East Indiaman sailed into the harbour, he seized every occasion to look at it. He knew all their names: the *Gilded Dragon*, the *Four Winds*, the *Great Voyage*, as well as those of ships of former times. Their figureheads were familiar faces to him. As an assayer he had to inspect all their cargoes. But rather than descend into the hold, he preferred to stay on deck, where he pictured himself sailing forth sometime.

He knew all the sea routes to the East, from the safe one along the coast of Africa to the wide arc across the ocean, blown onward by the trade winds. And the captains often asked him in astonishment if he wasn't a sailor himself and he always answered, 'Yes, of course,' believing it as he spoke. Strolling from one deck to another, they went on to discuss distant coasts, because when seafaring was the subject, the talk was of land. They exchanged facts about climate, vegetation and commodities, and it was not uncommon for one of these captains to learn something new from him about the country he had just returned from.

He always postponed his descent into the hold as long as possible. It was only when the captain invited him to view the cargo that he went meekly below deck. There was always a huge crush there, with seamen coming and going, harbour staff, East India Company officials and casual hands. The petty officers guided him neatly through the labyrinth, opening doors and hatches, going on ahead up stairways and down passages, and showing him the barrels and jars, the crates and sacks. For a moment he fancied himself a rich merchant as he fingered the linen or porcelain as it passed his inspection; it was then that the petty officer, whose sole wish was to return to shore as soon as possible, became impatient and coaxed him onward to view the spices.

The inspector took a bushel of everything. Before stuffing each sample in his bags, he crushed a little and held it between his fingers to sniff. With that, he hastily packed up his samples. Back in his harbour office, sitting at his desk of polished teak, he subjected the spices to a meticulous inspection. Most of the smells and tastes were strong, so that it was a while before he was restored to his former state without flavour or odour. He carried out the work of smelling and tasting in turns: first he bit into a coffee bean from Java, after which he sniffed a clove from Ambon. But there too there had to be an interlude, because it was impossible to separate smell and taste. The art of tasting required one to summon up old sensations. As he was letting the coffee grains roll over his tongue and past his palate, he tried to think of other experiences – preferably unpleasant ones, because these were much more distinct and meant such an onslaught on his sensitivity. What was pleasant gave him a feeling of harmony with his surroundings and was thus hard to distinguish: a feeling of bliss was always a generalized pleasure and the role of taste in it was not always plain. His tongue drove the coffee round the inside of his mouth as long as was necessary for him to detect the qualities of bad coffee – too bitter or else an insipid, sandy flavour. Then he rinsed his mouth with water and decided on its quality, noting it in his register. To test the smell of something, he took a handful of the spice, pressed his nose cautiously in his palm and breathed slowly in and out. He must not sniff because that meant it might hit his throat, ruining the pure sensation. After smelling something he sucked in the fresh air in order to rid himself of the smell. Some items had to be smelled and tasted: pepper and nutmeg from Ternate. He always kept the pepper till last because it made his nose smart.

He loved testing spices. It was beautiful work, calling for great precision. He was fond of everything that required precision, because that implied that he was a master craftsman. He was master of an invisible world: even if he were blind, he would know the way – a blind captain who could smell his route over the seas of the world and who could tell from the scents carried on the wind whether he was approaching a country and if so which one.

Afterwards he felt a little sad: those smells and tastes that he recorded so meticulously when he was testing them left him with a bittersweet longing after they had vanished. For a moment they had transported him to their land of origin. It was as if after assaying them he had returned from a long voyage.

In the study in his silent house he spent long hours perusing the atlas he had compiled himself, with dozens of maps, executed in watercolour and ink. Leafing through it, he always made the same voyage: west-south-west to the Azores, south-south-west across the Equator, south to Brazil, then along the coast past the dreaded forty-degree latitude where Cape Horn lay, and finally west, west, west into the Great Ocean en route to the final map, still empty, but soon to be filled with the contours of the undiscovered Southern Continent.

There were maps of the Southern Continent. The oldest was by Claudius Ptolemy, depicting a huge image of *Terra Australis Incognita*. These maps, however, were not reliable – some geographers, for instance, had not hesitated to draw palm trees in spheres enveloped in eternal frost. A modern cartographer did not work with his fantasy, but with the navigation of the sextant and with mathematic calculations. He sometimes felt that this was a shame, and he envied the voyagers of old who had boldly set course for the void, with nothing but the dream of a paradise lying beyond the deserts of Africa and Asia. Their little craft often bobbed up and down on the infinite ocean, becalmed because they did not yet know about the swift trade wind route; or else they searched for harbours along strange, hostile coasts, scanning the night sky in search of familiar constellations and relying by day on sun and hourglass. Today all people had to do was to follow the familiar shipping lanes and the coasts of the Orient were well explored by merchants and soldiers.

Only a few people had as yet set their course across the western hemisphere. The Spanish shuttled to and fro between Peru and the Philippines and buccaneers had explored the South Pacific but no one had as yet ventured to reach the coasts of the Southern Continent. All his love went to that unknown land on the far side of the globe, the final void. To sail there – that would be to make the glorious era of the great seafarers live again. To sail in that great emptiness, with only that dream in their thoughts: that one day the unknown coast would loom up, capricious as a chimera, the continent of our opposites, the undiscovered Southern Continent.

He knew the travel diaries of his predecessors, Drake, Quiros, van Noort, van Spilbergen, Schouten and Tasman, and had noticed that none of these voyagers to the Southern Continent had set their course below the fortieth latitude, except Tasman. He, however, had stuck too close to the Indian archipelago.

Arend Roggeveen was sure of his route and couldn't wait to set sail.

Up till now his voyage of discovery, however, had only taken him past the numerous institutions that the Dutch Republic vaunted: from the Estates of Zeeland to those of the province of Holland, from the Estates General to the West India Company and from there back again to all these Estates. On each occasion his request was referred to someone else, so that he gradually began to feel like Vasco da Gama on a tow barge. The West India Company seemed to be the chief obstacle. This irritated him beyond measure: the Company did not even have a monopoly and what had it ever done for seafarers? All it did was to live off former glories. Expeditions were no longer equipped; all the Company did was to maintain a cargo service – black slaves were sent over there, sugar was brought back.

And yet Arend Roggeveen did get his charter. In exchange he had to promise the Company the riches of the Southern Continent. What was left over would be his, but that was of no concern, as fame was worth more to him than riches. It proved impossible, however, to get merchant companies and bankers interested in the enterprise, and the attitude of the West India Company was that it did not intend to participate directly except for taking its share of the profits. Once again the prospective explorer felt obliged to travel by barge round the towns of the province of Holland. He wrote a fund-raising brochure in which he guaranteed that he would in any case discover 'some land', although he felt unable to promise any 'precious jewels'. He returned from his mission a disappointed man. He cursed the fact that he had almost reached the end of his life without having realized his dreams. He persuaded himself that his sons would have to carry on his work: if he couldn't complete it himself, at least there would be one Roggeveen on the roll-call of famous discoverers.

By a trick of fate his invalid son turned out to be a passionate connoisseur of geography and astronomy; on many occasions

Jan had even rescued his father from a perilous calculation. The absent-minded Jacob was more of a thinker than a future naval hero and under a happier star his father would certainly have designated him for a career in letters. But due to his brother's illness, Jacob was doomed to leave everything behind and sail to somewhere he didn't want to go.

To familiarize him with seamanship, his father brought him time and again to the harbour and instructed him in navigation, geography and astronomy. To his father's exasperation he proved to have only an average talent for these subjects. He asked the wrong questions every time. After completing a classical education at school, he was sent to Leiden University to study law. The history of patents had taught his father that the admirals in the Dutch Republic were no longer those who had sailed the seas from childhood, but rather those who were adepts of inkpot and goose quills.

4

And so the young Jacob Roggeveen set out from home. It was his first journey and he left with great expectations – above all, of escaping his father's pressure and embarking on a new life. He took letters of recommendation with him so that he would be hospitably received on his way and in Leiden by family members he did not know and scholars with unfamiliar names. He was also expected to deliver his father's brochure to a number of addresses, as his father hadn't yet abandoned all hope. This bag full of letters and quarto notebooks gave the son the sense of being a person of weight – he had a task to fulfil. He had no difficulty in forgetting that all this was intended as preparation for becoming a voyager, because he had an excellent gift for seeing only what he wanted to see.

Travelling across the waters of Zeeland had suddenly made life on board ship seem eminently bearable. The waters were calm and the seascapes were restful on the eye, framed as they were by views of the coast. He took pleasure in the clearly outlined surfaces of land, sky and water and decided that ships were a fine invention after all: they turned an obstacle into a convenience – the seas and rivers had become the squares and streets of a metropolis of God. The meaningless flow of the waters and the senseless blowing of the winds had acquired a purpose – namely the progress of mankind. It did not occur to him that his reconciliation with the sea was purely temporary – a gathering sou'wester would have blown it away at once and without ado.

In the horse-drawn barge on his way to Delft he couldn't believe his eyes as he gazed at the landscape of South Holland. The water in the canals was high, sometimes higher than the surrounding countryside – it was a dyke of water surrounding the subsided peat moors. He saw barges gliding across the landscape on these dykes of water. Everything here had to do with water – the people, the cattle and the crops. When he saw the windmills with their sails, his admiration was complete. Everything here shifted and glided and revolved without any effort. Only the nag on the towpath had to do any work. It was as though God's plan had been revealed, creation as a *perpetuum mobile*.

On arriving in Leiden he talked to his uncle non-stop about his experiences on his way. He ended his hymn to technology by expressing his desire to be an engineer. Building bridges, digging canals! His uncle patted him on the shoulder, 'Young man, wasn't it law that you came here to study?'

The study of law bewildered him, however. Man-made laws were complicated and numerous. Privileges, institutions, family connections and inheritance, renting and leasing, excise and tolls, punishments – there were more punishments than there were crimes. He learned that nothing was the same and that there were terms to describe all these differences. He toiled through folios full of verdicts and treaties. They were the account books of human activity; everything was recorded, but the sum total was lacking. His mind could not cope with this branch of study. What he missed was a governing principle. He found one in the Bible instead. God's laws were marvellous in their simplicity. Put your trust in God: all you have to do is submit to His will. Compare that with the meaningless toil of humanity, of which the study of law was so faithful a reflection!

He noticed, however, that he could not fill his days with resignation. So he started reading zealously about God because everything else paled into insignificance. Nowhere did he find the severe simplicity of Ecclesiastes or the true faith of the Evangelists, except in Spinoza's *Ethics*. He did not understand everything about the latter's geometrical reasoning – to be honest he understood only one thing – that God's existence could be *proved* even by earthly reasoning. Without letting his father know, he began to study theology. But this study also didn't bring him what he had expected. His professor dictated so many rules and regulations that God, if He had indeed decreed them, would probably never have got round to creating the earth. Two years later he returned to Walcheren. He had found his guiding principle, but as yet it hadn't led him anywhere.

5

He envied his sick brother, who went on living without having to go anywhere. From time to time Jan's illness deprived his lungs of oxygen to such a degree that he seemed to be choking. He breathed in with great gasps then, his chest heaving like a pair of bellows, but it didn't help: his air pipes were blocked. After a while he turned red, the veins in his neck and cheeks swelled, his eyes bulged in their sockets, his tongue lolled from his mouth and his arms swung helplessly: every part of his body that wasn't affected by his disease seemed to want to escape it.

Sometimes Jacob thought his brother was playing a superior game, because the blockage that stopped him breathing vanished every time miraculously. But even if the illness was real – which he did end up accepting – it still felt enviable, as it brought so many advantages with it, despite the temporary bouts of asphyxiation. Jan's illness absolved him of all the duties that made life unbearable. He was not obliged to earn a living, nor did he have to fulfil any expectations. He could opt out of unwanted meetings and bring any irksome conversation to an end: all he had to do was to start coughing. And yet, should he need it, everyone rushed to help him.

Jacob even thought that the invalid was at a great advantage knowing what he would die of. This certainty must give one great peace of mind. Each new day that was such a trial to a healthy individual was a godsend to the invalid. While someone who was healthy was faced with the vagaries of fate every day – not to mention the ever-present danger of death from which no one was ever safe – the invalid could lie calmly in bed and only had to ponder matters of the greatest importance: life and death and God.

Jan Roggeveen, however, did not seem to be aware of his privileged state. He invariably lamented his fate and was jealous of Jacob, who would get what was withheld from him – a career as ship's captain. To free him of his jealousy, Jacob told him, while stipulating that he kept it strictly secret, that he had no desire to go to sea. Jan, however, did not believe him.

Jan Roggeveen spent all his days studying the voyage he would never make. He spoke of the Southern Continent as though he had already visited it. Where his father had always been cautious enough to speak of 'some land tract', Jan had drawn up entire lists and tables from the safety of his bed, and had calculated with the aid of statistics how great a likelihood there was of some vegetation and what might be the nature of its soil, its raw materials and climatic conditions. For his calculations he made use of all possible data about countries that had been discovered round the fortieth latitude in both northern and southern hemispheres. He classified this data according to a variety of organizational principles. He also made an estimate of the surface area of the Southern Continent with the aid of the comparative method and the premise that there was as much land on the earth as water. He ended up producing a *Provisional Description of the Southern Continent*, illustrated with a map, of which he was extremely proud.

In order not to disappoint him, his father behaved as though it was a work of great scientific value. Jan went on to insist on its publication so stubbornly that in the end his father had it printed at his own expense. The edition had a run of three copies, one for each member of the Roggeveen family. The author, who considered that his work should be read throughout the world, felt richer than a king. He asked Jacob what people thought about it in Leiden. And because Jan wasn't in a position to discover the truth, Jacob lied. 'Interesting, extremely interesting,' he told him. The successful author thought that nothing stood in his way now and asked his father when he was planning to set sail. The latter, who hadn't dared admit that he had given up hope, avoided the question. 'Soon, my boy, soon.'

6

To elude his father's wrath, the flunked law student pretended that he had passed and was looking for a job. It was the first of many plans for his life that he'd think up, not for himself but to satisfy other people's expectations. And just because it seemed to have nothing to do with him, he was able to invent prospects with the greatest of ease. He also had no problem offering advice to others when asked. He noticed that a good intention was much more appealing to people than actually implementing one. It was a long while before people were required to answer for what they said – a seemingly disastrous situation that one could, however, get out of by accompanying the failure with a new good intention.

His father expressed his delight that his son had embarked on his studies with such enthusiasm, and asked with the utmost confidence in his son what sort of position he was seeking. The latter declared that he would first have to think about matters carefully, because one should not approach one's future too lightly. His preference would have been to leave his future as it was – blank, in other words. Because, before you knew it, you had exchanged your future for a past. The drawback of a past was that it was set in stone. With one's future all directions were possible.

When he spoke to his father he used a more cautious formula for this idea that he held for the greatest wisdom, 'The future offers you a variety of things, but you only get one past.' His father could easily agree with this, thinking of all the years he had spent testing exotic products – while he had never been on a voyage, although that had been his great dream.

After his father had encouragingly patted him on the shoulder, Jacob launched on his first plan. First of all he divided human labour into two categories: the static and the dynamic professions. The static ones consisted of repetitive transactions. Their advantage was that not a great deal of commitment was required: after all, the part of the body that carried out such things functioned independently, so that the rest, especially the mind, remained free. Their prestige – and that was after all his first concern – was little, however. The 'dynamic' professions were much more respected. These consisted of constantly changing activities which required all one's energy, both mental and physical. But if one prepared properly, one could realize such esteem with little effort. Esteem, after all, was acquired by something that was *seen*.

But what?

A procession of generals, grand pensionaries, navigators, aldermen and kings passed his mind's eye. But none of these professions seemed destined for him. Then he saw one that was hidden behind the others and barely visible in this display of power – he could be a spy. A spy – or, in public life, a diplomat – was someone the nature of whose work was not to be seen, but in such a way that everything he did, no matter how trivial, appeared to conceal something of great importance.

His father regarded the diplomatic service as a splendid profession, since it meant that his son would be moving in superior circles, something that would prove favourable for financing a later voyage of discovery. He did, however, wonder how Jacob thought he would realize this plan. The latter had no idea and just shrugged his shoulders; at the same time he put on a meaningful and secretive expression and he must have done this quite effectively as his father gave him a conspiratorial smile. That's how these things work, Jacob thought with satisfaction.

For a while he took pleasure in his reputation as a prospective diplomat, which he had acquired with so little effort. From one day to the next his decision meant that he was no longer anonymous. On his strolls through Middelburg, with which he occupied his empty days, people asked him enquiringly when he would be leaving for the capital to receive instructions from the Estates General for his first mission. With a smile he answered that political affairs, as one could easily imagine, were conducted behind closed doors and not on the street. An answer like this made him appear even more distinguished and the people he met gazed after him for a long while.

Unexpectedly the prospective diplomat left for France. He explained to his father that he could give him no information about this as the assignment was a confidential one. In actual fact he went there to accompany a preacher who had been banished to Dordrecht. (He had met this preacher on one of his walks and was profoundly under the influence of his religious ideas.) Due to a curious twist of fate he ended up in France anyway as the preacher proved not welcome in the province of Holland either and the only acquaintances still willing to give him shelter lived on the Loire.

Jacob set great store by his inability to make a decision; after all, it had brought him what he had longed for – a life in the service of the Lord, escape from his father, who had prepared a fate for him that he would never have chosen for himself. Henceforth he would devote his days to walking and to the musings that originated in the rhythm of his feet. Once a day, he would preach a sermon full of fine words and that would be it. God knew no limits. He stretched out lazily across the world and left everything as it was.

The preacher, a man called Justus van Oyen, seemed like a wise man. He spoke little and listened a great deal. How many people – and he had his professor of theology at Leiden in mind – thought that they knew better than their Creator. God's laws were simple and those who needed a lot of words to explain them had understood nothing. Justus did not care to speak about God. If Jacob made a remark about religion, Justus pointed with a sweeping gesture to the surrounding countryside: please be silent; He is here in our midst.

He preferred to listen to Jacob talking about what he intended to do in life. And Jacob, who spoke about his plans openly for the first time, could barely hold his tongue. His words always led to new words and, to his own astonishment, he came up with ideas that to his knowledge he had never entertained. Beyond Arras in the rolling hills of Artois, his torrent of words had led him to a lucid life principle which consisted mainly of not having any plans, so that everything remained possible. Justus's response was a huge belly laugh that was reinforced by the shaking of their coach.

On reaching Saumur on the Loire, Jacob began for the first time to doubt the piety of his travelling companion. On their way he had viewed his reticence as originating in a pious awe for the works of the Lord. He felt it strange, however, that Justus remained silent in his new abode. A preacher after all was supposed to preach. When he remarked on this, his companion roared with laughter. Do people learn from their own mistakes? he asked and proceeded to laugh even harder. All this gave Jacob pause for thought.

Justus spent the whole day at home with his friends. They spoke in a jargon that Jacob didn't understand. A slattern brought them food and wine and willingly let herself be felt up as she brushed past them. She made Jacob nervous and he preferred not to stay in the house too much. He roamed around the countryside, but no matter where he was, under a bridge or on the castle walls, God's eye was on him. Why was He pursuing him? Was He angry, because he had let the preacher drink wine instead of urging him to preach His name? Only later did he realize that God had foreseen it all: Justus was no preacher, but an adventurer, which was a euphemism for a confidence-trickster. The friends turned out to be pickpockets. As for Jacob, he continued to chant the praises of the Lord and His good works if only to drown out the jingling of their ill-gotten coin.

*

The road back home was beset with obstacles, because little remained of his money, which he had shared with Justus. He travelled alone, trusting no one. Nor did he knock on anyone's door to ask for lodgings; he slept under the skies and of necessity he stole from the farmers while God watched him anxiously. He thought he would never return home, but one day to his astonishment he saw the coast of Walcheren.

With his tattered appearance, the former envoy attracted a lot of notice in Middelburg. He was greeted noisily with compassion, while malicious amusement whispered stories behind his back. He didn't need to offer any explanation, because they already had one. He had been robbed. And it was true; he had been robbed, although they had no idea what of. Every word he spoke and every step he took in his life added to his disappointment. Why couldn't everything stay as it was? If only everything just began and went no further. Because things that come to an end are worthless.

Was it God's purpose to deprive him of everything?

He awaited his fate with resignation.

8

The day came that his father passed away; he died peacefully in his sleep. Initially Jacob felt betrayed: without so much as a word his father had gone on ahead, leaving him to his fate. Things had taken place that he had no part in. Members of the family turned up and they carried the deceased out of the house. (Jacob had proposed that his father should be granted a seaman's grave, as a final honour, but his suggestion was dismissed indignantly.) After that he was entirely alone. What could he do without his father; what was there left to avoid? He was unwilling to believe that his father's decease was final. There had to have been a misunderstanding. He remained sunk in his thoughts – how could he have ceased to exist?

An unbearable compassion overwhelmed him. He felt an inexplicable loss. It was as though he saw things through his father's eyes and he was filled with a strange longing for the things around him, which seemed to have undergone a profound transformation – it was as if he was seeing everything that he saw for the last time. Instead of his father who had 'fallen asleep' so peacefully, it was as if he was the one who had to say farewell. The tears welled up in his eyes when he pictured his father up there in heaven, surrounded by all those strange souls, and thinking of all those things and people dear to him whom he had had to leave behind: his own body, his sons, his maps of the world, the little port of Middelburg with its ships sailing out without him. Perhaps from where he was now he could see the Southern Continent. Poor father in heaven gazing for all eternity at a world that was able to get along without him. He was inconsolable at the thought of his father's loneliness. The dead man had been cheated in perfidious fashion: it wasn't he who had gone, with everyone waving goodbye, but the others who had departed, all of them together, leaving him alone in his tomb.

Jacob considered it his sacred obligation to cherish his father's memory: if he stopped thinking about his father, he would vanish into the bottomless pit of oblivion. He alone was responsible for his destiny. To his astonishment, however, he observed that when he thought of the dead man, he was really only picturing himself. He could only summon up his father by imagining him as himself. He missed being alive and cursed the work that had never been completed. And the reason why he had experienced his father's death as such a shock was because he saw it as a harbinger of his own death.

Members of his family found a position for him with the East India Company, because he had to earn money for his own livelihood and that of his brother. He accepted the work gratefully. He had the feeling that in this way he could at any rate pay off part of his debt to his father. This debt consisted of everything that his father had expected of him and of which he hadn't paid back one jot. The balance had been drawn up and the debt was insoluble.

During his life he had never respected his father and he had rejected everything he represented. Any plans he had made for his life were evasions: he was determined never to become like his father. He wanted to be nothing at all. His preference had been to let everything stay the same, just a host of possibilities. Many lives were possible; only one could actually be lived. Posthumously he strove to live up to his father's demands. To reject them would mean that he had confirmed that his father was irrelevant. Only through respect could he compensate for all he had lost.

Jacob worked hard for the Company, where he held the post of notary: his task was to draw up and annul contracts. In the evening he studied his father's plans for discovering the Southern Continent. He overcame his dread of the sea, because his own wishes no longer counted: he sacrificed himself without stint. With Jan, his invalid brother, he discussed the chances of fulfilling their father's dream. He wasn't enthusiastic, but it seemed to give meaning to his father's death if he trod in his footsteps; he continued where his father had left off and they would achieve their goal together. He had taken on a task that was greater than himself; he had a destiny now. At least that was what he told himself – but without realizing it he was already planning a new evasion, one however that was doomed to failure, because how could he escape someone who was dead? There was nothing he could do about his father's incomplete legacy.

9

The Company sent him to the East Indies and despite his reluctance he went to this remote region, because he had no choice. He already felt homesick in the harbour and when the ship sailed out he gazed behind him the whole time – it was a horizon that held ever less promise. He saw himself vanish: he was only a dot in the ubiquitous blue around him. At last he had become something; he had made one choice out of the endless possibilities life offered: he was an insignificant little penpusher, entirely lost behind the immense form of He who is all things.

He experienced disembarkation in the trading post of Batavia as something miraculous: he had followed many paths and in each case he had visualized the end. It was nothing like this, yet here he was. He saw that everything he undertook led to something else, something that he neither knew nor had expected. And strangely that gave him hope. There had to be something that would release him and his father from that cursed Southern Continent.

But what could it be?

He still remained spellbound by the idea that there actually was something. Faithfully the official went through his dossiers, in full confidence that the true meaning of this futile work would one day be revealed to him.

Nothing was what it seemed. He found proof of this everywhere. He was maddened by the sounds that surrounded him, yet when he looked he saw nothing. The façades of the buildings looked so Dutch, but they were set in a strange dazzling light. He saw himself sitting in the offices of the Company, but he also saw himself watching himself sitting there – he couldn't work out where he was seeing himself from. Perhaps it was from above. He could not find God anywhere in this desolate realm. If he thought of Him, he thought of Middelburg, and he found Him there too – in the grey spaces offshore.

Year in year out the notary worked with great zeal and diligence, but the true reason for his stay on earth was not revealed. He was often visited by memories of his father and then he felt a deep compassion, because his father had never found what he sought. Then he returned yet more determinedly to his work. In this way he hoped to repay the debt he owed, even if the task seemed impossible: no matter what one did, it was always too little.

He thought of the story of the fortune seeker who arrived in Eldorado. He found so many diamonds and gold ingots there that he could not take them all away. He grasped all he could till his arms were full and he had to lift his thigh to prevent his spoils from slipping out of his grasp. Standing like this, stooping a little and with his leg raised, he saw so much more gold and diamonds gleaming, that the gold and diamonds he already had seemed like a sorry amount. He would leave with that poor amount but he would always think of that which he had not been able to carry off. And so he dropped his spoils and thought as he stretched out his empty hands towards the horizon: All this is mine.

10

Jacob Roggeveen returned to Middelburg empty-handed. It was his umpteenth return, but it was also no new beginning. True, he remained the same person he was – he had always had the impression of being at the start of something new – but his surroundings changed constantly so that he was like someone who always joined in a conversation too late: he understood the words exchanged, but could not figure out what was being discussed.

Jan was overjoyed to see him again, and Jacob himself seemed contented. They talked about the Southern Continent, as this was their way of talking about their father. Jan remained convinced that his brother was going to discover it. How could Jacob explain that he was hoping for something quite different, something that didn't exist, but which as soon as it did materialize would reveal everything in a different light?

He lived for a year on money he had saved in the Indies, after which he had to return to work. He set himself up as a notary. How easy it all was: you called yourself a notary and that was what you were. In this way his life continued without effort. If things became too difficult he closed his eyes, and peace descended on him. The fortune seeker stretched out his empty hands. Closing his eyes, that was his favourite gesture.

But his sense of guilt towards his father didn't leave him. Like the fortune seeker, he might think that all this was his. But this thought was constantly contradicted by another, that his father hadn't enjoyed it. Jacob cursed his father who had taken up his abode in him like a tapeworm devouring everything insatiably, so that nothing was left over for him.

Nothing had changed; he saw everything in the same light, or else it was a grey light, which robbed everything of outline and colour. It was so long since he had cherished any thought of escaping that the whole notion of it seemed to belong to another life. One life was behind him and the other lay ahead and in no way did they resemble each other. He was not worried, however, unlike his brother who was very concerned and behaved as though he was his father's representative on earth, admonishing Jacob time and again. Jacob in turn was happy to be rid of any responsibility and obediently did what his brother told him. He had to bring his father's life to completion. Without him realizing it, it was the perfect escape: he was living someone else's life. His own life was unlived; it was as empty as if it had never existed.

Did that make him happy?

No, he wasn't happy.

He was indifferent. Like a stone that is worn down by the life that passes it by.

In the early evening after a day at the office, spent as usual in drawing up and dissolving contracts, he met God. Jacob hadn't prayed to Him; yet suddenly there He was. He shook his head. He didn't say anything. All he did was shake His head.

Then everything became plain. What he was looking for didn't exist. All his evasions were due to fear – fear of belonging and being something, which would have made it impossible for him to be everything else. He had behaved like the fortune seeker who had spread his arms out wide, not to take, but to show what he was able to take. But no matter how far he pointed, like the fortune seeker, he was no longer able to point to his father.

When the West India Company at last approved of his – or rather his father's – plans for the discovery of the Southern Continent, it no longer meant anything to him. He could picture his father after receiving this news standing on the waterfront, his gaze penetrating the distance, as though he could already see the Southern Continent waiting for him. For his father this would have been his great day; for him it meant nothing.

He stood there on the waterfront and gazed into the distance. Very far off, across seas and continents, through the rain and mist, he could see a little dot: it was his own back.

Urged on by his invalid brother, he equipped a small fleet. He named the flagship after his father. And on 1 August 1721 he set sail.

He could just as well not have gone.

Translated by Donald Gardner

30

MARCEL MÖRING
East Bergholt

Translated by Donald Gardner

She asks how far it is now to East Bergholt. When he says they'll be there by nightfall at the earliest, her face darkens.

He looks straight ahead, at the non-existent traffic, on this road leading to the coast like a tired river that in the endless rain – it's the third day of rain – seems wet enough to sail on.

'Nightfall?'

'Nightfall.'

She wraps her hands more tightly around the wheel.

Endless rain.

No, no, she'd said, for her it wasn't about the, let's say, literary aspects of courtliness, the whole courtly system (she pronounced the word with a slight German accent, 'Sustum'), but about any theological, religious implications that courtliness may conceivably have had for people's lives.

May conceivably have had.

My God, he'd answered (said – he didn't speak to her, to anyone, he fixed his eyes on a vague spot on the brick wall in the foyer outside the lecture theatres), my God, he said, reception theory has made it all the way to theology.

She blushed. That surprised him. He nodded slightly, as if trying to peer over his glasses (which he wasn't), and took stock of her, this tall, long-legged, long-curly-haired theology student. Under his scrutiny she shifted her weight from her left leg to her right. The bluish strip-light shone in her glasses.

Was he taking her seriously?

Very seriously, he said. Very seriously.

He's as little understanding of maps as he has of church fathers; at six in the afternoon they drive into East Bergholt. Without saying a word, without a hint of triumph or disdain, she turns right, off the main road, into a cluster of pastel-coloured bungalows. In a long gentle bend, rain-flattened grain to the left, the inimitable English ugliness of the bungalows to the right, the village unfolds. He's just about to ask where on earth they're supposed to sleep when they plunge into a country lane.

'That was the village,' he says. He stretches and looks back.

'There's a hotel,' she says.

The car swings sharply to the right, onto a car park surfaced with gravel. He's flung against the door.

'Boom,' he says, as the bumper gently nudges an oak.

I know nothing at all about theology, he'd told her, and I'm not planning to learn anything either. My own field, he said, is hazy enough without any holy triumvirate and immaculate conception.

Trinity, she said. Holy Trinity.

Even if it was a duet, he said, I flatly refuse.

But she'd talked, as they strode along corridor after corridor, right to the top of the building, where his room was, directly under the restored seventeenth-century roof, which in summer let in too much heat and in winter too much cold. She sat across from him, on the far side of the desk with its fishbone-patterned veneer, and argued endlessly, her eyes gleaming behind her glasses, her cheeks red.

Young lady, he'd said. He'd already forgotten her name. Young lady, courtliness is something very different from what you suggest, it's not some exalted, serene form of worship, it's deferred sex.

This time he didn't look at her as she blushed. He unscrewed his fountain pen, took a piece of paper and asked for her name, address, phone number, previous education – everything he could get out of her, in other words. When he'd filled two pages with illegibly small handwriting, he made her blush for the third time.

Greta, he said (Margaretha Theodora Maria van Groningen, he'd written on the first page), two things, before you can count on my support. The first, he lectured, was that the period she was talking about was typified by married priests, with or without a whole host of children, not serene piety. The second was that love takes many guises. And when I say love, he said, I'm talking about sexual love.

As she coloured, he suggested a number of titles.

Hadewijch wants to be fucked by God, he thought as she was walking away.

Later he said in a teacherly voice that courtliness was a matter of structure, only rarely of morality.

After four days of privation, the Hare and Hounds is an oasis of peace and refinement, especially culinary refinement. In the bay window of the mediaeval taproom they're served splendid steaks on matt-brown plates. Beside the meat are a handful of bright green peas, fresh and plump, flanked by a creamy-white cabbage leaf. He cuts off a piece of steak with a sharp knife for the first time in ages. A crisp crust encloses beautiful pink flesh. He watches as she, careless, absent, slices the cabbage leaf in two and stabs it with her fork.

Margaretha Theodora Maria van Groningen, he'd read at home. Twenty-eight years old, born in Harlingen, living in Amsterdam. Middle school, high school, university entrance, university (broken off), convent, university. A year and a half, that convent. I wasn't ready for it, she'd told him. When will you be? he thinks. Her interest concerns the courtly aspects of mediaeval theology. Hadewijch? he asked. She shuddered. Not Hadewijch. That's not theology, that's mysticism. Her words. What is it, he'd asked, that makes you want to be a nun? She shook her head. Wanted, she said. Want, he said. Again that shake of the head. Want, he thought, leafing through his notes. Want. Hadewijch wants to fuck God.

*

He's got a certain reputation. One that has less to do with his work than with how he works. He'll be remembered fifty years from now, if he's remembered at all, as a man who behaved in this or that way, not as a man who taught this or that subject. As he realizes. He realizes he doesn't represent academia but rather the manner in which certain academic knowledge is passed on. Why, he thought, did she come to him with her peculiar ambition? Was she, unconsciously, seeking form?

They sleep in rooms of wood in a little house behind the inn: The Cottage. He couldn't have come up with any other name for it. The building exudes the steady calm he so admires in the English. It's the kind of environment where you immediately feel at home and where you know: whatever happens, it won't happen here.

When their hostess leaves them after exhaustive explanations and instructions (breakfast at nine thirty, fried eggs with bacon and tea for madam, French rolls with cheese and coffee for sir), they stand in the large room that will be hers. He goes to sit on the edge of the huge double bed and sinks almost up to his hips in the mattress. While she lays her suitcase on a small table and slowly begins to unpack, very orderly, very neat, he leans against the ornately carved foot of the bed and takes stock of the room.

A polished wooden floor.

Walls lined with wood panelling.

Ancient beams in the ceiling.

Two linen cupboards of gleaming cherry wood.

At the window overlooking the inn, a small writing desk covered with a cloth embroidered with roses; beside it a straight wooden chair with floral upholstery. On the desk a French mantel clock of cracked walnut showing nine o'clock and a romantic lamp on a spherical ceramic foot.

'What,' he says, in the languid tone that so appeals to him in Waugh, 'do you say to a short walk through the village?'

She turns round, one of her navy-blue pleated skirts over one arm, lamplight in her flaring hair. She nods.

She says so much when talking about Aquinas and Augustine

and Ruusbroec yet so little during their extracurricular conversations.

Once he awoke with a tepid, wet sensation on the skin of his abdomen. Thirty-five years old, he thought as he took a shower in the bathroom, and my first wet dream. Later, when he wiped the condensation from the mirror and saw the familiar splashed face that always stared back, he realized with shock what (or rather who) had given rise to the dream.

He had walked with her through the long corridors of the old faculty building, to the narrow stairs that spiralled upwards in one corner of the complex. She went ahead and he watched her legs rising and falling, rising and falling. He followed the haughty curve upwards, long, long, long, all the way to the miraculous, incomparable roundness of her buttocks. He was directly behind her. His hand under her skirt, along the inside of one of those delicate legs, upwards. He felt the soft dampness of her vagina, while his thumb slid up along her thigh, into the cleft of her arse, and his forefinger stroked her clitoris. At the very top of the stairs she bent down, propped on her hands against the floor. He flung her long skirt up, a blue frame to her delightful backside, opened his trousers and slid into her. He fucked her, his hands resting on her hips. Oh God, she'd said.

God wants to fuck Hadewijch.

Young lady, he'd said (he called her that from time to time to get her attention), what do you do in the summer months?

The story of her life. Bursary, therefore not much money, therefore summer jobs. A succession of them. The bulb fields, potato farming in Groningen, tour guide, clothing retail.

And this summer?

A shrug.

He presented his proposal. His plan to mount a search for the source text of the Utrecht Baptismal Vow, a text originally written in Old English, based on a Latin sacramentary. The original, he'd said, eyes on the wooden ceiling, head back, hands on his crown, is in all probability Northumbrian. There is assumed to have been a Yorkshire version.

So?

Whether she, for a fee, would like to assist him.

He twisted her objections (she's studying theology, knows nothing of literature and . . .) into a series of suitable qualifications. Perfect for a theology student, with a knowledge of church archives and theological textual criticism, and wouldn't she break the ice brilliantly and didn't she have a driver's licence?

Yes.

Well?

When did he want to go?

The fascination, for him as opposed to his colleagues, is not the significance an old text may have for the archaeology of language. To him it's all about the poetry, the fragmentary nature of found documents, the incomplete, often simple language. He savours a good description: *folio seventeen recto tattered, scorch marks and water damage, lines four through fifteen partly illegible, preamble in red ink*. Give him a textual reconstruction with lots of square and round brackets and alternative readings and he'll savour it like a Haut-Brion 1974.

The Baptismal Vow. What he so enjoys in the short text is the sing-song responsory.

Forsachistu diobolae end allum diobolgelde end allum dioboles uuerkum . . .
    Ec forsacho diobolae end ec forsacho allum diobolgeldae . . .
    Golbistu in halogan gast
    Ec gelobo in halogan gast.

Halogan gast, holy ghost, which he wants to read as holy guest.

He's looked out of the window and seen the inn. It gleamed like a tombstone in the rain. Now the rain has stopped. They lock the door to the cottage and walk down the garden path, past the inn, onto the street. Street? Road. One car wide, man-high hedges on either side. They walk in single file, he in front, she behind, towards the village.

It's a beautiful road, more so than it seemed on arrival. It twists around an enormous beech that leaks rainwater into their hair. After the bend the roadway is spanned by power cables. The air is so damp there are sparks between the wires.

Nothing is said.

What is his life? An endless trudge along beaten paths. Mindlessly rumbling onward to the rhythm of a train to the horizon. No friends, no wife, no direction. Mahler, Sweelinck, Orlando Gibbons, James Brown, The Cure, Guns N' Roses, Beckett, Gogol, Salinger, Auden, Pushkin, burgundy, vodka, a few fragments of faith, here and there a little thermodynamics, liberal left, Malevich, Kiefer, Heda, Vermeer, the Flemish primitives, Richter. The tablets of stone, that's what he is, but after Moses has smashed them. A pile of rubble, a disorderly grab bag of information. His life, he, is like the texts he researches: *folio seventeen recto tattered, scorch marks and water damage, lines four through fifteen partly illegible, preamble in red ink.*

He's the one to blame for the fact they're in Essex, instead of Northumberland. Blame in this case in the literal sense. He deliberately booked the boat to Harwich. But just as she discovered only on looking at the map what a long drive it was to York, he discovered only in East Bergholt that the purpose of his ruse (to see the place where Constable painted) concealed a deeper desire.

Now they're standing in front of Constable's house, a grand country seat with a garden open to visitors in daytime. He looks at moonlit patches of the garden and listens to the bickering in his head.

'Well?' she says.

'Constable lived here. In the garden he painted the river.' His point: the central importance of the River Stour in the life of the early Impressionist Constable.

He hears himself speak. He wonders how tiresome a man can be before he makes himself sick.

*

The strange thing, he'd thought, is that she doesn't give off anything that seems directly erotic. On the contrary, she looks quite respectable: blue woollen sweaters with the white collars of blouses, long pleated skirts, penny loafers and tights. All the same, the clouds of long hair, the dark eyes, the hint, under all those modest clothes, of a magnificent body. Despite never having seen more than her wrists and throat, he knows for certain that all that wool covers a body that steals out of bed at night like a predator.

One time, in his office, he crouched beside her, to point something out. As he inhaled the fragrance that rose from her clothes and sensed the warmth radiating from her, he felt his balls grow and his sex sluggishly stiffen. He talked and talked and the craving for her body boiled in his breast. When she looked at him for a moment and he saw her face as if under magnification, he felt a drop trickle out of his penis.

She doesn't speak, not at all. He, not exactly a waterfall himself, doesn't know what to say, can no longer say anything. In this silence every word takes on a thousand meanings.

He walks ahead of her, half stumbling as those eyes jab into his back. Twice he contemplates turning round, grabbing her shoulders and saying: I love you, I want to push you up against that tree, right here, and I want to feel the breasts under that woollen sweater and I want to pull up your skirt and fuck you until you bite my neck and say you'll stay with me, for ever, here, my wife, my love, my heart, my yearning heart, quenched and fed.

But here they are, at the cottage already. She puts the key in the lock and opens the door. He goes upstairs, to her room, where he sits on the edge of the bed in the dark and stares straight ahead.

The remarkable thing is, before they left he wrote a poem describing an extrapolation from the situation in which he finds himself now.

The situation in which he finds himself now. That is: hungry for love.

In his monthly letter to his father, blithely freewheeling in sunny Florida, he wrote that he was so busy he wouldn't be able to come, not this summer. He received a postcard in reply, one of those big floppy American sheets of card with poison-blue waves, and on it: 'OK.' Anyone else would have thought that single word masked a clamour of disappointment. He knew better. The family he came from was like a book of etiquette. A bunch of handshaking, crystal-knife-rest-arranging diplomats, whose surprise was detectable only to those trained in reading the English stiff upper lip.

Father, my house has burned down, my wife has run off with a lesbian lion tamer and the manuscript of my research on the north-eastern Lower Rhine Prudentius annotations has been swept away in a flood.

How annoying, how unpleasant.

The circumlocutions of civility.

Would a different son, from a different family, have written to his father that he wasn't coming to Florida because he preferred to roam around England with a strapping theologian than spend a month among blue-rinsed old biddies?

His 'prophetic' poem, if he adapts it (the rain, the cottage), is a fairly accurate description of what would happen if they were to . . .

The Bridal Suite

> In the room with the low roof, ceiling
> of wood, floor of wood, all the walls
> wood, the glass of happiness breaks.
> Naked on the bed she turns round.
> He smiles in the soft half-light
> and thinks: this was the signal to start.
>
> He walks to the window, looks
> at the hotel, a mountain
> that shines in the evening rain,
> and thinks of their reception,

the cause of all this:
'The cottage, the bridal suite,
the only room free.'

Behind him he hears the rustle
of linen. She leaves the bed.
From the sound of running water
and the shifting of a few
little things he can tell
that she is preparing a bath.

Once, he thinks, long ago, this was happiness:
a wooden room, low light, me,
and in audible proximity she, a woman,
languidly preparing a bath as a prelude
to the things that are yet to come.

Never been happy with women, he thinks, standing next to the
bed, bare feet, bare legs, and he wonders how he'll ever get to
sleep at such an impossibly early hour. He shrugs, walks around
the room and tries to distract himself with memories of past
affairs. He goes to stand at the window again and looks at the
hotel through a gap in the curtains. A mountain that shines in
the evening rain. Then he shakes his head, grabs his trousers,
shirt, socks, jacket and gets dressed again. Holding his shoes,
he creeps outside, Old Shatterhand in England.

Hands in his pockets, collar up, he walks along the dark
road to the village. Between the high-tension wires, sparks
still fly.

A very serious young woman, said Johannsen (On literary for-
malism in Aquinas' *Summa Theologica*). They were sitting on
the ground against the glass back wall of the squash court,
panting, dripping with sweat. Four white legs side by side on
the shiny wooden floor, the smell of tennis shoes and wet chalk.

They got to their feet, slowly, with effort, and flipped a
racket. He won. As he kneaded the ball in his hand he asked:
Serious in what sense? He served low, just over the line, slightly

off-centre. The ball passed close to the wall near Johannsen, who took a swipe and hit the wall with his racket.

Are we bullshitting or playing? Johannsen asked.

They played.

In the changing room, under the shower, he repeated his question.

Not really a great academic talent, Johannsen replied, not a strong researcher, but very serious.

In what sense?

They got out of the shower and dried themselves, skip-hopping.

Difficult, Johannsen said. Difficult to say. I think she's one of the few – if not the only – truly religious student I have.

She was in a convent, he answered.

Johannsen shrugged: six months or so.

All the same.

Then Johannsen looked at him. He rubbed his red beard thoughtfully with a towel and said: Why the interest?

She's rather mysterious.

Johannsen nodded.

A remarkable young lady.

Johannsen nodded again.

Very odd.

So you have a bit of a weakness for icy frumps from the north, Johannsen had said.

There's a pub, somewhere round behind the church, but the door is locked. He moves the door handle up and down a couple of times, then just stands there for a moment, thinking. Strange English closing times. But then comes the sound of a key in a lock, the door opens slightly and a surprised face looks out through a gap the breadth of a hand.

'Yes?'

Apologies, he'd forgotten that pubs closed so early in this country. He didn't mean to disturb.

'Not at all, not at all.'

The head sticks out through the door a little, looking to left and right.

'Come in.'

He follows, eyebrows raised. A friendly, greyish man looks at him with a smile as he stands in some kind of narrow hallway, offering his apologies again. They walk on, across a courtyard and into a kitchen. Laughter breaks out when he stares open-mouthed at the gathering inside. About fifteen or twenty people are standing and sitting in the large kitchen. Candles are burning, there are pints of beer on a wooden table and someone is pouring whisky into wine glasses.

They're having a party. The landlord's birthday. It's after closing time, so they've moved to the kitchen. What would he like to drink?

'I didn't mean to break in on a private party.'

No, no, the more the merrier.

He orders a pint of lager, introduces himself, wishes Morris, the landlord, many happy returns and is swallowed up by the party. There's singing, someone recites a poem, he gets chatting with the teacher at the village school and talks about the purpose of his trip. Half an hour later, for want of repertoire, he sings 'Egidius, Where Art Thou?'. At five in the morning he dances his Russian squat dance on the kitchen table.

When he wakes he feels as never before, strong, healthy, cheerful. He takes a hot bath, shaves, gets dressed. Then he knocks on the door to her room, twice, three times. After a moment's hesitation he opens the door and sees the yellow sun shining across the freshly made bed.

In the breakfast room he eats his French rolls. There's even instant coffee. The hotelkeeper tells him that 'Miss Ven Kronning has gone for a walk'.

An hour later he strolls down the country road to the village. The rain has made the grass fresh and green. Birds warble in the hedgerows. An English summer.

He wanders through the village, not spotting her anywhere. When he eventually gets to the church, which looks old enough to be interesting, he decides to make a half-hearted attempt to find her in there.

It's a church like all others, cold, damp, dimly lit, the same dull pews, worn gravestones under moth-eaten rugs, glum-looking saints, their bodies impaled. He walks around for a while, shivering in his jacket, then feels a gentle tap on his shoulder.

Behind him is a small man wearing slippers.

Is he a visitor or . . . ?

A visitor.

And what do you think of our church?

A bit cold, but otherwise . . .

'Ah, let me offer you a nice strong cup of tea.'

He begins a stammered series of self-effacing objections, aware they'll be to no avail. English hospitality demands fulfilment of the holy task of pouring tea for every wanderer, even for those who'd prefer coffee. So he follows the shuffling verger in his green cardigan and threadbare trousers across the rugs and the worn gravestones to a door behind the altar, along a corridor, into a kitchen. There a middle-aged woman (My Wife) with the look of a matron, arms folded over her bosom, stands and looks at them.

When they're sitting at the big kitchen table drinking tea from big mugs and talking about the Battle of Arnhem (I was there. Near Amsterdam), he asks whether anyone has perhaps seen a young woman, also Dutch. They haven't seen her. And the vicar, then, might he have . . . ?'

'But I am the vicar.'

'You . . . Excuse me, I . . .'

He invents an excuse. He thought this was a Catholic church, and seeing as you're married . . .

A broad smile breaks through.

The dean of the faculty hadn't thought much of his plan.

'Source text, source text. You don't go looking for things like that, you come upon them.'

A powerful argument. He defended himself by pointing out that a) he was doing the research in his free time and b) it couldn't hurt to go and take a look. It wasn't as if the institute carried out all that much archival research.

The dean raised his eyebrows.

Just when, hand on the doorknob, he was about to leave the room, he heard his name.

'It says here,' said the dean, waving his application, which was written in triplicate, 'that you intend to take an assistant with you?'

He nodded.

'And who would that be, then?'

He'd been thinking about one of his doctoral students.

The dean looked at him with pursed lips, then raised his eyebrows again.

'Van Groningen. Theology. She's researching the religious implications of courtly culture. A sort of reception theory,' he lied.

'Is this the lady Johannsen was talking about?'

'I don't know who Johannsen has been talking about,' was his stiff reply.

The dean had rubbed his brow. Then his eyes cleared. 'Yes, that's the one. The ice queen from the north. I say, you've got it bad all right.'

He didn't have the feeling he'd got anything, good or bad.

He finds her in the canopied rose arbour in Constable's garden. She's sitting on a stone seat, sunlight blotching her blue sweater.

'I lost you,' he says.

She doesn't look up, doesn't answer.

'Hello,' he says. 'I'm Dutch too.'

'You weren't there, last night.'

He opens and closes his mouth without any words coming out.

'I couldn't sleep,' he says eventually.

She nods.

He argues furiously in his head. How can she know I wasn't there last night? She came to my room. No. She heard me on the stairs. No, she didn't hear me. But she can't have come to my room either. Why not? Because she wouldn't do a thing like that! But it's a logical supposition. Yes, it's a logical supposition. He has to admit: it's a terribly logical supposition.

'There was a party,' he says. He tells her.

She continues to stare straight ahead, through the portal of rose bushes that gives onto the slowly passing Stour, the river John Constable had to thank for his entire *oeuvre*.

'And now?' she says, when he's finished talking. 'Now that we've seen East Bergholt, what now?'

As if nothing remains to us in this world, he thinks.

He stands up and beckons her. Together they walk around the garden. They admire the beds of rhododendrons, the trimmed conifers, the huge oak standing next to a pond with aquatic plants and reeds, leaning slightly out over the water. Then it starts to rain. Suddenly, without any real beginning. Water patters down on the leaves of the oak. They stand under the crown of the tree and look at the garden, grey beneath a cross-hatching of raindrops. The pond bubbles and splashes. He feels clammy cold penetrate his clothes. He takes off his jacket and lays it around her shoulders and thinks: The longer I'm in England the more English I become. She stands next to him, slightly bowed, shoulders hunched, her clouds of hair dark with the wet. Drips glisten on her skin.

He'd like to fall to his knees and kiss her shoes, her soaked, blessed, sacrosanct penny loafers.

The evening before his departure he'd gone to dinner with his mother and her new boyfriend, Alexander. The new boyfriend had walked back and forth between the table and the sound system. There were Bach fugues with the chervil soup; Strauss's *Vier letzte Lieder* with the main course. The dessert was zabaglione, prepared by Alexander to the accompaniment of an old Miles Davis record. As he stood in the kitchen whisking, his mother looked at him with amusement.

'In bed he's just like he is in the kitchen,' she said.

He'd stared at her in shock.

She shook her head. 'What a prudish boy you are. Sometimes I think you were brought up by someone else.'

He could imagine. His father had got rich on a rather simple invention and as soon as the money began to pour in he'd bought himself out of the bosom of the family, without divorcing. He rang his wife once a fortnight, transferred a generous sum to her account every month and beyond that fulfilled his mission in life in the beds of women half his age. His mother, from a family where money was never a problem and divorce more the rule than the exception, had accepted her new marital status with mild contentment. She'd remained alone for years, aside from the occasional companion, and at last she'd permitted herself the luxury of a new partner in life. 'I don't care what you think of him,' she'd said, 'as long as you don't say a word.'

But he did like Alexander, a lover of music, a good-natured type, the kind of man who makes desserts.

The zabaglione was fantastic. He looked across the table at his mother and caught her exaggerated smile.

Over coffee she'd asked him what he'd be doing in England. He explained, fire inside him taking hold. That evening the Utrecht Baptismal Vow seemed to him the highest achievable ambition in his boring life. He accepted Alexander's cognac, absent-mindedly emptied his glass and told them, as Alexander poured him another, about the beauty of those ancient half-Dutch, half-Latin sentences, the sing-song rhythm, the overwhelming impression the Vow must have made on the man or woman who recited it when joining the church.

'Yes, yes,' his mother said and she nodded and then asked whether he might be in love, he was speaking so passionately.

He choked on his cognac and had to walk gagging to the kitchen, where a concerned Alexander came over to slap him on the back and give him some water. He took the glass and looked at the manicured hands of his mother's new boyfriend, pink nails with neat white cuticles, a modest steel watch on a black leather strap round his wrist. He drank and went on observing him, the V-necked sweater, the white shirt with open collar, the corduroy trousers, the hand-made moccasins. A meticulous lover, he thought, without knowing exactly what he meant by that.

When they came back into the room, his mother was smoking a cigarette. He sat down and asked her for one. She pointed to the pack and as soon as he'd lit up she said: 'Alexander, would you pour us another?' He wanted to refuse, but his mother looked at him, eyebrows raised. They drank a toast, to his research. And slowly he got drunk, politely, without becoming loud, without throwing up on the designer sofa, but drunk. Drunk enough at any rate to kiss the cheek his mother proffered to him as he left and suddenly say that he was indeed in love, God-awfully in love, with a student, but that he didn't know what to do and was afraid it would go wrong and ... God, so awfully in love.

At home he sat at his desk for a long time, smoking a cigarette cadged from his mother. In front of his gritty eyes floated the image of her creamy body.

As the shower of rain subsides, they walk back. The same old path. She shivers, still in his jacket. He feels the cold sink into his chest. In the cottage he takes his jacket and goes to his room. He removes his wet shoes and socks and decides not to put on fresh clothes. A hot bath, that's what he needs. He undresses and wraps a towel around him.

When he opens the bathroom door, clouds of steam pour out. Before he can turn round, he sees her leaning over the bath. Her long legs are just as he imagined, her buttocks firm, not too big. He feels a rising erection press against the towel round his waist. Oh God, he thinks. Out. Out. As he turns he catches sight of her stirring the hot bathwater. In his room, seated on the edge of the bed, he walks over to her and lays a hand on her naked back. She bends down over the warm bath and he fucks her and thinks of the stanza by Hadewijch, the stanza he looked up after they first met.

> Ah! However I cry out and lament my woe,
> Love may do with me what she pleases
> I want to give her all my days
> Praise and honour.
> Ah! Love, if only you had eyes for my faithfulness.
> I am heartened, however, when I relate
> That first towards your high levels
> Your balm attracted me.

Later, in the bath, as his thoughts wander across the wooden bathroom, he recalls a number by The Beatles. A very fitting number, he thinks, and he sings it softly. 'Norwegian Wood', it's called. About a girl who lived in a wood-panelled room.

The rest of the day is taken up with lunch and an afternoon walk. Somewhere outside the village they walk side by side in silence. In front of them is a hill. As they climb he watches the sun go down. He points and follows her unmoved gaze.

'Let's run to the top,' he says. 'Then we'll just be able to see the sunset.'

They start walking more quickly; the sun sinks faster and faster. They step up their pace and reach the top out of breath, half laughing. The sun glows on the horizon. Panting, they stand and watch.

On the way back they drink a glass of earthy-tasting beer in a small pub at the roadside in the middle of nowhere. The landlord himself pulls the pints. They stand in the bare space, on the worn wooden floor, exchanging pleasantries with him. It is indeed a very nice day.

Once, shortly after he was appointed, there'd been a student who came and settled a denim-clad buttock on his desk and looked at him with a provocative smile. Could the door to his room be locked? Yes, he'd said, and the windows can open. He stood up and went over to the light switch. And this, he said, is a switch for turning on the light. Actually, he said, this whole room is full of gadgets. She shook her head, gathered her papers and left. That entire year, whenever he came upon her in one of the corridors, she shook her head.

Women, he'd said to his father during one of his annual visits, I wish I could figure them out as quickly as an early mediaeval text. His father had pushed his straw Bing Crosby hat back on his head. He wasn't having any problems, was he? No, Dad, no problems. Did he want another Manhattan?

Manhattans and straw hats. How, he'd been asking himself for most of his adult life, could two people differ so much? His father, whom he could characterize no differently from the way a newspaper had done, as the mattress king (his invention had something to do with mattresses), had over the years come to resemble the stereotypical American from a television series, a spruced-up version of Walter Matthau. His mother was still who she'd always been, a woman who consumed her pleasures with relish. He didn't know which he preferred, but he did know whom he took after.

In the evening they sit in her room, in soft, wood-muffled light. He opens the bottle of vodka he's brought from the Netherlands, fills two water glasses and talks about himself. Which is to say, he drinks two glasses of vodka and then begins to talk about himself. About his love, the fragmented text, about his mother and her dessert-preparing boyfriend, about the mattresses that made his father (who now makes himself useful only on mattresses), about the odd poem he writes now and then. She looks and listens. He stands up, holding his glass, and recites one of his poems, without saying that he was thinking of her when he wrote it.

> This evening you were here and every time
> I tried to kiss you something broke
> between us and I pulled back.
> How ashamed the heart can feel
> of what it does not receive.

She drinks her vodka in little sips, but no less quickly than he does.

'It's a beautiful poem,' she says.

He looks at her in astonishment.

She laughs.

The bottom of the bottle comes in sight. She continues to sit unmoved in her chair, while he stands up again and again and explains things, glass in hand, gesticulating, in an incantatory voice. Then, the glasses empty, the bottle in the waste-paper bin, his heart sinks in his chest. He no longer knows what to do. He stands up, his face taut, lips thin, and walks to the door.

Later, on his way to brush his teeth, he passes her room. The door is ajar. A strip of yellow light fans out into the hallway. He turns his head to one side and looks in. She's sitting on the edge of the bed, hands together, head bowed, wearing a long white nightdress with tiny flowers. He goes on looking until she's finished and stands up to turn off the light. Then he realizes that she sleeps with the door open, that she did indeed hear him leave the previous night.

The next morning it rains. He runs through the downpour to the main building. The hotelkeeper brings him coffee.

'So you're leaving too?'

He looks up and considers this.

'That's what Miss Ven Kronning said when she left.'

'Yes. Yes, of course,' he says.

The bus to Ipswich is a boat that glides along a smooth, straight river.

Endless rain.

Translated by Liz Waters

31

MANON UPHOFF

Poop

Poep

Once there was a nice, tall man who was very poor and never had a great deal to spend. He liked to go walking along the city's canals in the early-morning air. At that hour the light from the houses burned a watery yellow and the canals were still smooth and taut. The gentle sound of the leaves and pebbles beneath his feet made him feel almost content, as though for a moment the water, the canals and the houses were his. His poverty, however, stung him, but there was not much he could do about that.

One day the nice, tall man set out again to walk along the water. Having reached the very end, where the big canal bent sharply and turned back on itself, and where the old trees were covered in mossy green, he stopped to pick up a few stones. These he skimmed across the water as low as he could, then watched until they sank and left the surface taut and unperturbed once more. He breathed in the water's calm and sighed deeply. A little further along he settled down on a wooden bench. The bench was in front of a lovely white house. A house with a stately entranceway – with tall stained-glass windows and bright yellow silk behind the panes. A house with a charming garden, the kind of garden that went with a summery England or France, but which in Holland always strikes a rather aristocratic and defiant tone.

That kind of house, mused the man who had so little to spend, in a house like that, with a garden like that, that's where I should be living. I could give a house like that what it needs – why doesn't that house belong to me? It made him feel sad and almost rebellious, but he spoke firmly to himself and went back to staring at the water and the leaves, which lay along the banks in gold and yellow and red.

At that very moment the door of the lovely house opened and a lady came out with two large dogs. The dogs tugged briskly at their leashes and dragged the lady behind them in their eagerness.

'Ah, me,' the lady said a little later. She had let the dogs run free. They were two huge, extremely well-groomed Great Danes. Their short fur gleamed and their pinkish-red tongues lolled happily from their broad jaws. They danced through the piles of leaves and chased each other cheerfully.

'They're so strong,' the lady spoke. 'At times I can hardly hold them back.'

She panted as she said this, and sat down beside the poor man on his bench. You could see that everything about her had cost a great deal of money. The leather of her little boots fairly crimped with softness in the chilly autumn air, and her long coat smelled of beavers. Her hair had been washed and rinsed until it resembled gold filament.

'I always come here with the dogs,' the woman said. She pointed over her shoulder. 'It's so convenient, I live so close and this way the darlings don't bother a soul.'

'I like coming here too,' the man said, 'it's lovely here.'

'Oh, isn't it, though?' said the lady, fairly gasping with pleasure. 'There's such an absolutely gorgeous view of the canals from the orangery. It's only a pity one sees passers-by so often. I mean, people who have no business being here, who are incapable of appreciating beauty.'

She laid one neatly manicured hand on the knee that showed beneath her warm coat.

'Do you come here often?' she added, with a smile kept perfectly in check.

'What's often?' the poor man replied. 'Maybe two or three times a week. As I said, it's lovely here and your house is truly beautiful. Very impressive, that white amid the greenery.'

'The house is very expensive to keep up, but it's worth it to me. It belonged to my late husband. Oh, one lives here in such wonderful calm. A house like that makes everything easy. Is your home attractive as well?'

'I have a room downtown. It's small, but I can live in it.'

'Oh yes, a house like mine means a great deal in one's life, really, it makes up for all the misery.'

The poor man could no longer contain himself.

'You're so right!' he cried. 'So very right! What I wouldn't do to live in a house like yours. There are no words to describe it.'

As he spoke these words, the Great Danes sprang boisterously into the canal. A few minutes later they struggled back onto the bank, barking excitedly. They ploughed through the piles of leaves with their moist noses. Then – as though on command – they stopped and squatted beside each other on their haunches to deposit, with an expression that resembled prayer, two huge piles of poop on the moist embankment. A distance of about a dog-and-a-half lay between the two mounds, which steamed in the autumnal morning air.

The lady, huddling in the depths of her exclusive fur coat as she reflected on the man's words, suddenly developed a peculiar gleam in her finely made-up, silvery-blue eyes. A strange, but not entirely unpleasant tingling began at the tips of her toes and ran all the way up to her tummy.

'Perhaps I could make you a proposal?' she began. 'Did you see what my two darlings just did?'

'They jumped in the canal,' the man replied. 'They are fast, athletic animals, as anyone can see.'

'Along the embankment,' said the woman, pointing. 'There! You could hardly call them rabbit droppings.'

Her mother-of-pearl nail directed his gaze towards the two gleaming, dark-brown piles of dog poop.

'If you eat both of those, I will give you my house. The house of your dreams, with the garden and everything along with it.'

The poor man who had so little to spend looked at the woman, and from the woman to the two piles. The dogs were far away now, barking at a dachshund on a short leash.

The morning was of a purity that almost pained him, and then to have to hear such a ridiculous proposal from someone who wallowed so lavishly in her own wealth.

'Both piles. Completely, without spitting out any of it, and then I will give you the key to my house.'

The woman rummaged about in her leather purse and pulled out a keyring. She removed the largest key from it and held it before the man's eyes.

'Both of them,' the man said quietly. 'Every last bit, and I'm not allowed to spit out any of it? And if I do you'll give me that key?'

'That is the long and the short of it,' the woman said.

She slipped the key back into her bag and looked out contentedly across the canal's smooth surface.

The poor man stood up, stretched his stiff legs a bit, took a deep breath of fresh air and headed for the two enormous turds, which seemed to summon him mockingly: 'Eat us, eat us.'

I'll do it, damn it, the man thought. I'll eat them both; it's only a pair of lousy turds.

In two strides he arrived at the place where it would have to happen. He squatted down, bent far over and stuck his finger into one of the piles. Then quickly, and without thinking, he began to eat, one bite after the other.

From the bench the woman stared in a mixture of horror and silent amazement at the hunched back of the man as he gobbled and gulped down the stinking meal. The dogs, looking startled, came padding over.

She saw his shoulders heave and heard him gag heavily after the third bite.

The lengths people will go to, she thought with the tranquillity of the well-to-do. Wait until I tell Lidy, Cecile and Margaret about it this evening. They won't believe what one finds walking about here, even in the better parts of town.

So occupied was she with her own thoughts that she failed to notice that the man was already bolting down the second half of the bolus. He was trembling violently now and she could hear him making strange noises – noises that sounded somewhere between a sob and chuckle.

Gradually the doubt came trickling in, and though her disbelief grew with every bite he took, along with that disbelief a simple truth now came to her as well. A truth almost too horrible to entertain: he had almost finished his first turd!

One more and she would have to turn over her lovely house to this idiot.

The poor man who had so little to spend was overpowered by the feeling that he had been eating poop for years on end. Life as it stretched out before him now had only one colour: dark brown, and only one flavour: the flavour of dog shit. He didn't dare to think about the next bite, and didn't dare at all to glance to the side, where yet another hideous pile was waiting for him.

He couldn't! He couldn't! Sweat was pouring down his back.

Come on! he shouted silently to himself. One more turd, just one more, and you can call yourself the owner of one of the loveliest houses in this city! But he couldn't. His stomach, his gullet and intestinal tract had taken over, and their decision was unanimous. It was over. He couldn't do it any more.

Exhausted, and having grown old and bitter in the space of five minutes, he stood up. He tossed the lady, who was still seated on the bench with her hand over her mouth, a glance she interpreted as triumphant, but which in fact was one of deep fatigue.

'Stop!' she cried out. 'Stop!'

She ran over to him and placed herself between him and the second, still-untouched pile, as though to guard it.

'Wait! For God's sake, wait! Can we make a deal? This is impossible. This isn't right. You're a person of flesh and blood, like me. What am I to do without my house? My lovely home. You don't really expect me to give up everything, do you? What if I take that second pile? I'll do the same thing you did, and I won't skip any of it. I won't spit out anything, I swear. Then the house will still be mine. Would that be acceptable to you?'

The poor man could barely make out what she was saying, his head was pounding too loudly. The poop was wreaking grim havoc on his taste buds. But he nodded; he realized she had asked him something, and whatever she wanted of him could not possibly be worse than this.

With almost girlish optimism the lady unbuttoned her fur coat and tucked it up behind her.

Come on, she said to herself.

On her knees in the wet leaves, she too bent over now and began to eat, in great haste, afraid that the man might change his mind. The two dogs circled around her hesitantly, not entirely sure of themselves. They both barked once, brief and shrill.

The woman saw and heard nothing more. With all the strength within her she tried to imagine roasted chicken, sugar-coated almonds and toffees, but the taste of the turd was more powerful than her most powerful flight of fancy. Her shoulders, too, began to shake.

Such a filthy stench, she thought at one point, such a hideous taste.

Yet the fear of losing her house was greater than her disgust, and so she ate faster, faster and faster, until not a smidgen was left. The same exhaustion that had overtaken the man now settled over her as well, and she leaned back in the grass.

The house seemed smaller to her now, much smaller and of much less consequence than it had ever seemed before. She didn't want to look at the man beside her. After a few minutes she rose to her feet, coughed and shook the leaves from her coat.

'Aaron!' she called out. 'Atlas!'

The two huge, well-groomed dogs came running back to their mistress and snuffed her tenderly.

'Down!' the woman shouted. Her voice had grown high and harsh. She hooked the leather leashes to their collars again and pulled the two dogs forcefully along behind her. Without looking back, she ran through the wet leaves, up the path and into her lovely garden. She locked and bolted the door behind her.

Inside, in the warmth of her English-style living room, the woman sat on her soft couch. Before her on the walnut coffee table stood a stiff glass of cognac. Her feet were tucked away securely in thick woollen slippers. Yet still the woman trembled. She picked up the snifter, but the trembling grew worse and worse, until she had to put it back on the table without a sip.

Why did I eat poop? she thought as the cognac gleamed golden in the glass.

Outside the man rose to his feet. He stared for a long time at the spot where the two boluses had lain, then turned his gaze from that spot to the house.

The canal curved smoothly and calmly through the city. A little further along, the old trees stood green and unperturbed. He could hear the pebbles crunching beneath his feet. It was very quiet in this part of town, but the man covered his ears with his hands to protect himself from the noise that came from within:

Why in God's name did I eat poop? said the pounding at his eardrums.

Why did I eat poop?

Translated by Sam Garrett

32

JOOST ZWAGERMAN

Winnie and the Innocence of the World

Winnie en de onschuld

The love song of a clandestine guardian angel

Ten minutes ago Winnie was still thinking the world should simply end. This morning she had a fight with someone I don't know. I expect it's one of those clever dicks trying to claw their way up the ladder at that rubbish advertising company that has taken her on as a temp. The spat wasn't serious, but believe me, less significant incidents have been known to send Winnie into a broody spin over corruption, mortal sin, violent revolution, environmental disaster and total annihilation. Winnie is one of those people who at the first little setback console themselves with the thought that everything on earth will inevitably come to a crashing end. But it's the height of summer, luckily, and she's walking down the street in a T-shirt (white) and jeans (skinny, ripped at the knee), and the sun, which is, after all, blameless, makes her skin glow, so it's no surprise that Winnie is already thinking of other, more appealing things: a glass of beer, a shady terrace, a filter cigarette.

If you really want to know: I was once in love with Winnie. Once. Now I just love her the way, on a day when I'm ready to face whatever I have to face, I also love the sun. It was one of the few things we had in common, Winnie and I: we loved the sun. On summer days in the village where she and I used to live together in my rundown garden shack, half the inhabitants would rush off to the beach to scorch themselves in the sun alongside the tourists. On those days we would ride our bikes along the quiet streets, exhilarated. Winnie perked up when there was less traffic, with all the cars parked at the seaside blinking in the sun. Winnie despised cars, and especially their drivers, but as soon as they were out of sight and the hatred inside her ebbed, she became receptive to the love I was always so keen to smother her in.

On those pure, quiet days she would sing improvised ditties as we pedalled past the camping and the restored pancake house, to where it was even quieter, the dunes, which were only accessible from the bicycle path, to observe the seagull colony. If Winnie was happy and relaxed, I was too, and was prepared to slap at flies all day long as we lay stretched out on the sand drifts in the middle of the dunes, the middle of nowhere, and savoured on each other's lips the aftertaste of the vanilla ice cream we'd just had at the wooden coffee house, next to the sheep pen that had no sheep in it but tons of shiny bikes locked with the kind of flimsy AA padlock you haven't seen in the city for years because anyone can smash them open with a single well-aimed kick. At night we'd eat spaghetti and get a bit tight on the wine from the supermarket, and before going to sleep in our shack I'd apply After Sun to her back and shoulders, because not a summer's day went by when the sun we so worshipped didn't manage to set Winnie's shoulders on fire.

She was twenty-four, I was three years younger, and of all the things I didn't know then, the thing I knew least of all was that there was no point getting jealous about her past. Shortly after she came to live with me, Robert would sometimes phone her. He was the bloke Winnie had lived with for two and a half years in a student flat in Diemen. They'd been in the habit of bashing each other over the head with various chipped pots and pans before making up with a hot passion that even now, retroactively, I wish I could have prohibited. I believe most of their friends and acquaintances called them 'the perfect couple', an empty phrase people like to employ to describe a popular, attractive pair. In truth they weren't at all well suited. In spite of her thoughts about the world ending, Winnie has what in chick-lit is known as 'a sunny disposition'. As for Robert: his temperament doesn't let in even a flicker of sunshine. Cheerfulness and optimism are déclassé in his book; good moods are for chumps. That contrast wasn't particularly good for their relationship. Whatever Robert was against, Winnie was for, so that they often lost sight of the fact that they actually agreed on just about everything. Where Winnie was *for* starting a student protest action, Robert was *against* the neo-feudal administration of the academic overlords. Winnie was *for* radical reforms and the further democratization of South Africa, Robert was *against* the clandestine terror operations conducted by the white state apparatus still in power at the time. Winnie was *for* abortion and euthanasia, Robert *against* the Evangelical Broadcasting Company and the Dutch Christian Fundamentalism it advocated, which was proving a more stubborn holdout than anyone had thought possible.

So they were on the same page on everything, which is always a great plus. Yet to Robert, Winnie's optimistic attitude was nauseatingly chirpy and upbeat, whereas what really annoyed the hell out of Winnie was Robert's dogmatic negativity, which had intrigued her when she first got to know him, but which she later found smug and extremely unsexy. When the world showed its positive side, Winnie just couldn't persuade Robert to rejoice about it; and whenever anything went wrong, even in the most godforsaken corner of the earth – and of course there was always some disaster happening somewhere – Robert couldn't seem to make her see that it had been *bound* to happen. If one day the world did actually end, Winnie would be having a full-scale panic attack and Robert would be proved right. Come on, be honest, which would you rather have: authentic, heart-stopping fear, or the glib, smug knowledge you were right?

I met Robert just once. It was at one of those parties that some officials, but mostly our less exalted fellow citizens, tend to find outrageous. In the halogen-lit recesses of a second-floor flat on one of Amsterdam's central canals, once a squat but long since renovated, some Arabic-looking boys were suavely, I'd almost say flamboyantly, snogging with other Arab-looking types. Nobody knew whose party it was, but the guests were the sort that aren't fussed about who exactly invited whom. So that's where I ran into Robert, who Winnie had told me was 'in spite of everything' 'quite inspiring, really' and besides that, just 'good-looking'.

Robert wasn't really supposed to be there either. Let's just say there are parties you're not invited to, but still somehow wind up at, if you get my drift. The only thing Robert and I had in common then was that we both felt a bit awkward about being there, and our discomfort may have been noticeable – although for different reasons. Robert, as a blatant heterosexual, probably felt out of place in that almost intimidatingly trendy company; for my part, I just felt too unattractive to be there – when it comes to insecurity and inhibition, I am a flagrant pansexual. A hired funk band was playing too loudly for me to hear Robert say anything 'inspiring', but no one at the party would have denied he was 'good-looking', although I was happy to see two gross ginger-coloured warts sprouting in his neck. The warts were as big and round as shirt buttons, and you could somehow tell he often scratched at them. Our exchange must have lasted no more than five minutes, tops. Shouting to be heard over the music, he asked me how Winnie was. I answered truthfully (yelling back) that she liked the life in my village, where there was nothing much to do but go for walks, go out for coffee, hang around and count the clouds. Robert stared at me and his face took on a waxen expression. He was practising looking inscrutable, which was probably supposed to disguise profound disdain. He must have thought (and probably still thinks) that he 'formed' Winnie, 'educated' her, 'raised her consciousness' – I don't know how exactly he would describe his influence on her, but the fact that Winnie, in the time she lived in that student flat with him, had turned from a ditzy adolescent into someone who could make your jaw drop at the things she said, the things she did and (to be fair) the way she looked was something Robert probably ascribed to his own, indubitably lengthy, list of talents and attributes.

At the risk of being accused of being spiteful (which, believe me, I am not – not really), I think I have every right to despise Robert, his personality, the two button-warts in his neck and every minute Winnie ever spent in his company. The more bastards you get to know, the more it seems that you ought to have the right to deprive them of any happy memories.

I met Winnie about a month after she'd left Robert. It was in a Chinese restaurant behind Amsterdam's Centraal Station. She was on the phone – talking to her parents, she told me later. I was eating rice and beans, and when at some point she discovered that her linen handbag had been nicked – wallet, cash cards and all – I gave her money for the payphone and the food she'd ordered, and went with her to the Warmoesstraat police station to report the theft. Two weeks later she moved into my shack, to live the way I was living. And so we contentedly observed all the ways nothing in the North Holland dunes ever changed, and twice a week went swimming in the sea, spring, summer and autumn, always after eight at night, taking no notice of rain, cold or other people, and whenever we weren't outside, we'd be indoors watching B-movies on the telly with the patience I'd taught her to have, the patience of angels, or reading hefty yellow-edged American paperbacks about rootless geniuses who, if they weren't lolling about somewhere sucking on a joint or opium pipe, were always walking in the rain or waiting in airports for couriers or accomplices or loved ones that never showed up.

Winnie and I, we lived on fresh air, because it was always extremely draughty in the social services office with the one desk where I had to present myself once every three months to fill in forms specially designed to put you off. Once, when she had been staring at me for a long time with throat-constricting intensity, I literally felt it in my bones: all the flesh of my body tensed up, seemed to contract, ready to dissolve and expose my skeleton for Winnie to chisel her love into. I wouldn't have minded, actually: she a teenager with a knife and I a piece of tree bark into which she solemnly carved a wobbly little heart. Without her knowing it, she was drilling her way into my very marrow, I would dizzily tell myself. Who can blame me for being happy with her, and having my innards, my sinews, muscles and joints demanding their share of that happiness?

After eighteen months and twelve days, Winnie decided that neither the fresh air nor I came up to her dreams or expectations. She went back to the city, where instead of spi-ralling into drugs, fundamentalism, fornication or Robert, she finished her art history studies in one intense but perfunctory spurt, and, notwithstanding a lackadaisical attitude, produced a rather brilliant thesis on Mark Rothko and Zen Buddhism. Shortly after graduating she got a job at that crummy ad agency and a small council flat near the Tropics Museum, to which, once every five or six weeks or so, she would lure some punk kid she had picked up in a smoky disco (after Robert they all had to be younger) to share her bed for the night, never longer, involving one or two condoms in the night and three or four croissants in the morning – they were always big eaters, those boys, and unlike her girlfriends' reports, the boys always went at it for an inordinately long time, not the eating, of course, but the fucking, as if they were keen to break all kinds of personal records so that they could brag about it later to their mates. In short, Winnie lived the life most of the people around her were living: dull, uninspiring and mundane, with-out even a speck of selfless devotion or unconditional love. Winnie was wasting her splendour; it was hard for me not to miss her.

In the initial weeks of her return to the city, I had to train myself to deal with being alone once more. With the help of alcohol and self-taught meditation, I focused my mind on her life, which was playing out some fifty kilometres south of me. The fact that she was getting on with that life quite openly, without any noticeable trace of the past we'd shared, astonished me at first. But after a month or so, I discovered how alarm-ingly easy it was for me to feel almost literally transported into her presence. I didn't even have to close my eyes, drink myself into a stupor or with Orphic absorption hum myself into a trance in order to behold her in my mind's eye: I was so close to her that after half a year of this I was aware of all her comings and goings, what she was thinking and what she was feeling. Without ever having to leave the house, and without her having even the slightest inkling, she had never left me; I was with her more than ever before. That is how I became Winnie's clandes-tine, outcast and utterly powerless guardian angel.

I decided the sensible thing was to accept this new role and be satisfied with it. However, I was often anything but sensible, and therefore felt terribly unfulfilled— because although I was closer to her than ever, it was impossible to make contact: she remained deaf and blind to my compassionate presence. If I touched her, it was the wine (or the one-night-stand city-boy who'd wound up in her bed); if I spoke to her, it was the trees (or her boss, at lunch); if I smiled at her, it was whatever she fancied was going on with the wind and those trees. She was like the sea, into which I could bellow as loud as I liked what I wanted, over and over, without any effect. My despair, my desire and my besotted love began to fade, the nature of my love changed, I was starting to love her like the sea – or, as I mentioned before, like the sun, which, like a pet, so generously lets you adore it, and which I couldn't blame for anything either, not even for the existence of clouds.

Winnie and the sun. Even on a sunny day like today, for instance, she won't think of the traffic-free afternoons in the village, when we used to ... Right, I already told you about that. And yet in the end it is the sun that is drawing Winnie and me together, for as she's walking down the street, having nearly forgotten all about this morning's spat and her conse-quent brooding about the end of the world, we are both feeling the stinging yet balmy caress of the same sun on our skin, I in my garden, hunched a bit awkwardly over some flowering Poor Man's Orchid and at the same time invisible, but none the less tenacious, at her side; and she, Winnie, in Leiden Square, walking towards the American Hotel – because the thought of an outdoor terrace, a beer and cigarette hasn't left her.

Look, just a few more steps, and Winnie is taking a seat on the terrace across from two apple-tart-eating ladies who are thinking about the gossip they're about to exchange. And as she sits down and smiles at the waiter and smiles at the ladies and smiles at a boy with a trendy pair of sunglasses perched on the tip of his nose riding by on his bicycle, she hasn't the foggiest – is completely oblivious of the fact – that Robert, whom I just saw buying two tickets for tonight's show at the Cinerama box office on Marnix Street, and who very shortly, in less than

three minutes, in the space of time it would take to warn
Winnie – if only I could – to get out of there, to go home or, I
don't care, to go to the park; oblivious of the fact that in less
than, now, two minutes, Robert will have spotted her; the shock
settles in quick, cool waves in Robert's stomach, upon which he
rallies with characteristic speed, plucks up his courage –
scratches the warts, perhaps? – realizes with relief that Winnie
hasn't noticed him yet, has time to rehearse some clichéd
pickup line and decides to feign surprise as he walks up to her
and utters the prepared text: 'Jesus, Winnie, it *is* you! How the
hell *are* you . . . ?'

What can I say is happening, about to happen? *Of course*
Winnie waves her hand and Robert sits down next to her. *Of
course* they immediately start talking 'as if they never lost
touch'. *Of course* he's flirting suavely and she's gaily (and nauseatingly, so fucking nauseatingly) flashing her expensively
whitened teeth as she laughs, hahaha, as she laughs at his little
jokes . . . Forgotten are the knockdown, drag-out fights of the
past, forgotten is the snooty tone of voice in which he used to
lecture her, forgotten the dreary fucking in the early morning
when her thoughts were elsewhere and she was dry as a bone
and the only thing he was after was to come, to come . . . There
are no awkward silences; neither one has to search for words.
Robert tells her about his world travels, about his mother who
(lowered voice, lowered eyes) was ill and is now dead ('Oh no,'
says Winnie, sincerely) and about how good he is at keeping up
with international developments in computer science; Winnie
tells him about Mark Rothko and about Zen, about raves
and the income gap, about cool restaurants in the Jordaan,
about the housing shortage and the job market and about me.
They're talking about me and Robert says something like, I
once met him, at some dreadful party, he didn't seem your type
at all, he was so quiet and droopy and was he good in bed I bet
he wasn't good in bed . . . Winnie orders two beers and answers,
grinning – ah, forgive me for turning away for a moment, for
inspecting my little garden, for burying my nose in the Poor
Man's Orchid and stuffing my index fingers in my ears; for toppling headlong into the flowerbed, coming up with a forehead

smudged with soil, a twig between my teeth, a flower in my hair I'm not here I'm with Winnie in the dunes I am the girl-ocean called Winnie . . . What can I say is happening?

Well. What's happening doesn't surprise them at all, really, me even less. I'm hovering over their café table like an invisible, impotent third wheel and have a clear view of, for example, Robert's hands (flat on the table top, not a dirty fingernail in sight), of Winnie's eyelashes (mascara'd), eyelids (eye-shadowed) and cheeks (kiss on the cheek, from me, from the wind). And whether I now focus my attention on a hand gesture of hers, a glance, a charming little laugh, or a slight frown meaning 'I'm listening to you attentively', it all points to what Robert and Winnie (and I) both (all three), already know yet at the same time are carefully leaving unspoken . . .

Don't call me a voyeur; if the two of them were reunited by happenstance, it is my fate to have to watch it happen. I can't help it. I may have secured for myself a place close to her, but how do I *rid* myself of her, of the irresistible look of her, of Robert's seduction tricks, which she seems to be so gladly tolerating? When I close my eyes I am immediately aware of every little thought that flashes through Winnie's brain, and believe me, at this moment I would rather have Winnie's exterior in my mind's eye than what's going on inside her head. No matter which way I turn, or make myself think about mice in the house, about soggy overcooked rice, or the dentist's laser drill, I am incapable of *not* knowing what Winnie is doing, seeing, saying, thinking or wishing. And so I have to witness Robert settling the bill, the two of them trailing (not yet in complete lockstep) towards the tram stop, the Line 2 tram jangling to a halt, the two of them scoring a seat, teasing each other (Winnie's dreamy throat-laugh continually pealing out) and how everything, every interaction, gesture or topic of conversation (and corresponding hesitations) is but the prefatory scrimmage to the event no mortal will be astonished to see coming: *a striking sexual encounter*, as I once saw it formulated in one of my yellow-edged American paperbacks.

Will anyone be surprised if I choose to give as brief an account as possible from this point on? Any elaboration would

give me – seeing that I am already deep into American termin-
ology here – *the blues,* as defined by some potbellied crooner:
the blues ain't nothing but a good man feeling bad.

So: there's a restaurant, haphazardly chosen by them upon
getting off the tram at the Koningsplein stop. There's a menu
(wannabe haute cuisine) and there's a wine (Bourgogne Pinot,
1990 – well, well, R., laddie, aren't you the big spender?). Before
the main course is served, there's Robert's hurried phone call,
at the back of the restaurant: 'Alice, let's go see that film tomorrow night, shall we? I bumped into some mates downtown, yes,
I know, sorry, sorry . . . Yeah, yeah, you're a doll, bye, love, bye,
Alice. Kiss kiss.' There's brandy with the coffee, and a right
moment for one of them (Winnie) to confess to the other she's
'a wee bit tipsy'. Throaty laugh. There's a short stroll to Rembrandt Square, there's unvoiced speculation as to whose
place . . . There's Café Schiller, where Winnie artfully manages
to dodge several people she vaguely knows. There's a last glass
in an all-night café down the street. There's . . . But perhaps it's
best if I tell myself it's all an elaborate hoax, that it's just television, the fortieth repeat of an episode from some American
series, and that I'm a detective and I've been assigned to tail
Suspect A (Winnie S., of Amsterdam), who at this very moment,
hesitantly, is responding to the proposal of Suspect B (Robert
What's-his-name, also of Amsterdam) who's wondering if . . .
if maybe . . . Ah. No? Uh . . . well, then a hotel? OK? Good?

Pension The Three Princes on Dam Street, a shabby doss-
house with junkies decoratively draped in adjoining doorways
and giant grey rubbish bags, most likely tossed down from
three floors above, nestled against the broken streetlights. Suspect B, flushed, stands at the desk to pay in advance. Both
suspects take the stairs without exchanging a word, and upon
reaching the fourth floor thread their way along the corridor.
Suspect B breaks the – now nevertheless tense – silence with
some inconsequential mumble about a dried-up ficus tree in an
alcove. Suspects enter designated hotel room. Place of delict
carries the number 406. Both suspects inspect hotel room. Suspect B smiles and closes door. Suspect A silently curses stubborn
lump in throat. Suspect B takes initiative in commitment of

crime. Warm hands under Suspect A's white T-shirt. Muttered sweet nothings. Surprisingly uneasy sigh from Suspect A, who whispers wouldn't it be better if ... or, isn't this crazy ... Suspect B prevails over Suspect A by snuggling his head against her shoulder with a guileless but unequivocally pleading look in his eye; Suspect B is making himself small, helpless – in the trade we call this the 'little-boy tactic'. Suspect A responds to the look by stroking his hair, nestling her hand in his neck. Suspect B tightens his grip on her. Suspects undress themselves and each other.

It is 03:16 hours when the crime is committed on the bed that was changed that morning by an underpaid Dominican cleaner. A few details to note: the bedsprings sag, one of the two bedside lamps is broken, and the tap over the rusty sink drip-drip-dips – didn't I tell you this was television? Most important detail: neither suspect makes a sound; the offence takes place in complete silence. This last has no – I repeat *no* – religious significance, it is merely the silence of pleasure alloyed with fear. After changing position three times, it is Suspect B who at 03:41 hours breaks the silence and with short, rather nasal bursts of breath announces his orgasm. As for Suspect A: the crime fails to bring about the culminating physical explosion in her. (Stop lying, arsehole, you're neglecting to mention the shrill, high-pitched sob you heard just now; and didn't you see her back arching, the way she started glowing all over, or the pinkish flush welling up in her neck and along her shoulder blades? Did this ever happen to her when she was still yours, all the blood in her body bottling up beneath the surface, turning her skin red?)

I happen to know that many detectives train themselves to put on what they call 'a steely expression', and that they possess the same cold efficiency also encountered in politicians, TV presenters and certain local dignitaries. All in all I don't think I acquitted myself very well in my brief stint as detective. May I please be taken off the case? May I please be excused? May I *please* be allowed to leave the Room 406 battle scene? Won't some almighty supreme being, I don't care which one, please return me to my own grotty little garden and make me be like everyone else on this earth – unaware, uninformed, oblivious? And could someone please tell me to whom and where to apply for membership in the Society for the Advancement of the End of the World? Those who would deprive me of the right to have such unfriendly thoughts or feelings can just go find themselves a self-made guardian angel of a more tolerant stripe. To those who decide to stick with me, I'll confess that I was extremely gratified to know that Robert was feeling depressed and rather sad just now, consistent with post-coital law, and that, faithful to that same law, he fell asleep without putting up the least resistance ... I mean, I don't blame Winnie for leaving him sprawled on that pathetic three-quarter bed; nor for collecting her clothes and boots in the dark, splashing a handful of water on her forehead at the sink and sneaking out of there.

Granted, as he lay there fast asleep Winnie did kiss him goodbye, she did kiss the corners of his mouth and – ever so gently – his left hand, which she then cautiously picked up and moved to his chest, so that our friend Robert now lies there like an operetta singer, eyes closed, clutching his heart. Now she's even writing her phone number on a paper hankie she's fished out of the back pocket of her jeans, and leaving it ... on the pillow, or should she leave it on his clothes? Unable to decide, she stands there, paper and pen in hand, before slipping the tissue, folded and all, into one of his shoes, the right one. Love filters right down to the toes, did you know that?

In the lift she reads what is scratched into the four walls: that Howard loves Jeanette and Chris loves Ineke; that Ajax is forever and God is a football team and even that 'good old Killroy was here'. Behind the desk stand a young man and a no-longer-so-very-young woman Winnie hadn't seen earlier that night. Neither deigns her a glance, since they assume Winnie is one of the hordes of semi-desirable lady guests who by reason of their profession come and go at dubious times of the night, ordered from an escort bureau by some randy hotel guest in a fit of boredom, preferably a married man from the sticks whose wife has temporarily kicked him out. But anyone paying the least bit of attention will notice, as I do, that

Winnie is making her way to the exit with a skittishness that does not accord with what in the circles of those same married men is known as 'a young lady of easy virtue'. Hastily, and with suppressed-panic stealth, she slips out of the hotel. It is long past midnight, the sun set so long ago that you'd almost forget it exists; less than a kilometre from my shack the oily, ink-black North Sea has for hours been the land's fearsome bogeyman, and I, I am like the night whose presence not even Winnie can ward off. She finds herself gazing at the tacky, outdated neon signs over the storefronts, at the waiting-room-yellow street lighting in front of the hotel. And Winnie pretends to herself that there's no rubbish piled against that streetlight over there and that the shivering drug addicts in the dark doorways aren't junkies at all but sentinels disguised in rags; courtly, true-blue depressives with whom she might, perhaps, share her suddenly awoken angst.

On the Dam the night-time traffic whooshes by; only a couple of taxis are required to revive Winnie's car phobia. The aversion is so strong that all other feelings and emotions are clean forgotten. And as Winnie's hatred of cars and drivers raises its ugly head even at this late hour, and she wishes a fatal traffic accident on every single cab driver in Amsterdam, an equally unpleasant dream-wish pops into my own head, one I'm rather ashamed of, granted, but which *would* be a convenient way to release me from my increasingly unbearable guardian-angelship.

Because if Winnie does indeed harbour such intense and heart-stopping hatred for anything with an engine and four wheels, then surely there ought to be a stressed-out taxi driver somewhere, or some reckless undergrad with a brand-new driving licence in a shiny new Fiat, who could run her over, preferably with a fatal outcome? Couldn't some double-seeing, blotto intellectual come chugging along in a Lada and mistake the Rokin's zebra crossing for a poorly marked acceleration lane? Isn't there some other miscreant out there with his foot on the gas who'll notice Winnie just a fraction too late, so that she's tossed in the air, hurled to the ground, crushed, maimed, mutilated? Is it really so despicable of me to conjure up a tragedy, to daydream about the ambulance, her parents' despair, the brief paragraph in the paper, the obituaries, and finally the low-budget but lovingly produced docudrama about 'Winnie the accident victim', shown six months after her death on the hippest commercial TV channel? Is it, in short, so criminal of me here to confess that a fatal accident would come as a welcome relief? I mean, if the only thing that compares to my all-seeing gaze glued onto Winnie is a continual living death that's driving me insane, can't I be allowed, just this once, to indulge in the thought of Winnie in a deadly accident – my only possible salvation? Can't Winnie and I be allowed to part, to be divorced from each other, I stone-dead in my stone-dead little garden, my nose buried in the crematorium-pink Poor Man's Orchid, and she simply gone, wiped off the face of the earth?

Allow me my brief rhapsodizing about her death. Allow me my morbid flirtation, allow me to wallow in my own shittiness, allow me my garden melodrama. If I'm making myself look clownish, pathetic, despicable, aren't I also proving myself harmless? Because in reality *of course* the cars stop in time – one by one, all in a tidy row. Wherever Winnie goes, she invites respect. Cars spontaneously bow before her. One vehicle reverently flashes its headlights at her, short–long–short, an SOS serving as an improvised headlamp aubade. Save Our Souls, Mistress Winnie . . . And as in her glorious oblivion she crosses the street longing for a cup of camomile tea, the newspaper and then a good sleep, even the morning brume appears to be moved. The way you can tell is that suddenly everything and everyone in the city is shrouded in mist, except Winnie. Winnie is striding purposely through the town, straight through the light and straight through my heart, and never before have I felt *this* certain that there is an innocence in all that she does, thinks, doesn't do or doesn't think, an innocence she will never lose. It must be the innocence of the world.

Translated by Hester Velmans

33

HAFID BOUAZZA

Ghost Town

Spookstad

'Sibawayh!'

The silence shifted uneasily like a bashful woman in male company.

I called again. It was always the same ritual, ever since the day he had exchanged his place on my cot for the stable down below. Perfidious Sibawayh. My impatience, his maddening sluggishness.

'Sibawayh!'

This time I tap-tap-tapped with my tremulous walking stick (silver-knobbed) hard on the floor.

Silence.

Some commotion, a cough, the a-metrical creak on the stairs and suddenly my gloom was filled with evil-smelling, swishing Sibawayh: he was undoubtedly adjusting his hurried clothing. Brusquely he helped me into my cloak.

'What a stench . . . what a stench . . .' I muttered, leaning on his low shoulder. He slipped 'those-yes-yes-those' babouches on to my feet and smoothed the hood of my cloak. 'Now go and saddle the mule,' I told him.

There was a time when mule and harness were matters of grave concern to me. Like all men of rank I had a predilection for the female animal, preferably dappled, sleek, nib-eared, the mane and tail plaited, the croup drum-sized. As for the harness, the caparison had to be brocaded, or at least veined with the illusion of gold thread. Scrofulous beggars with watery eyes, hands ever cupped, would gape at the silk and gold of bridle and stirrup as at the splendours of after-worldly promise. Both legs had to rest over the left flank, swinging gently from the knee, the cloak arranged in even folds, the feet shod in velvet-covered slippers. It was quite an art to affect boredom while holding the reins between thumb and curved little finger, and not only to conduct one's mount with delicacy but also (when accompanied by two servants) to keep the eyes fixed ahead, over the pitching gait of the slave holding the bridle, and never to allow idle thoughts of vanity to draw one's gaze to the black sun-soaked parasol-bearer at one's side.

But now it was night and for various reasons I only visited my physician after sundown. Sibawayh returned to the stable. I stood in the room and waited, a quaky old man. Memories are unpredictable, except at moments of pitiful helplessness. A blind elder, a couple of centuries old, with shrunken untoothed jaws, is invariably both helpless and to be pitied.

Sibawayh's youthful sullenness had, as was entirely to be expected, worsened over the years. Yet life (and here the wheels of memory turned again) had so indulged this once hollow-backed, round-bellied, blinking, half-naked slip of a boy. From the far end of a cramped blundering darkness (Sibawayh swore as he stumbled down the stairs) a slanting sunbeam of memory flared in my mind's eye: a prismatic burst of blinding sunshine and blazing colours, meandering multitudes, tumult, a grimace of sunny cruelty. The slave market: bare heads baking in the sun, vivid turbans and canopies, corrupt shadows. Beyond the slave market stood the great azure mosque, its back unaccountably turned to us. Slaves, both male and female, stood on display in a long gallery, running the gamut of pale and luminous to gleaming black; warm nipples, cool bellies. And there he stood, dazed, eyebrows knitted against the glare, a hint of orphan's sorrow around the corners of the mouth, arms folded behind the back (weathered elbows), jutting shoulder blades. There stood Sibawayh, nakedly exposed, obedient to the hands of the deafening broker invoking the sun's help in his exposition of the state of the four-foot-high young Sibawayh's health: the imperfect teeth, the endearing little pouch, the promise (unkept) of muscular development in his tender arms.

Mule-high, I gazed out over the multitude, my parasol-bearer at my side. I fell, forgive me, very nearly to the ground. Suddenly my precious dazzling white robes struck me as hopelessly cheap and unsuitable. By some miracle I managed to conclude the transaction without unseemly haste. Overcome with emotion, I yanked the reins and left the market. A servant followed behind with Sibawayh.

And since that day, the day when (moneybag on my right hip lightened, loins weighted with ample promise of ecstasy) I first led him, Sibawayh, to my dwelling, where I bathed him (his sun-brined skin warm as sand) and then took him, naked except for a fine mousseline wrap, smelling of apple orchards, to my cool room – since that day he had been nothing but intractable, runty, all elbows. His body grew more slowly than the sores on my skin. Amid draperies patterned with hunting scenes, spent after my exertions for a shameful Venus, the stout goat of my loins lolled on my belly, soiled, reeking of Sibawayh's puckered profundity. Propped up on his bleached elbows he lay silently weeping, the nape of his neck furrowed and a trough between his jutting shoulder blades. The cleft of his hillock was smeared with blood – and the goat resumed his grazing.

My spacious and tastefully appointed suite, from the steamy kitchens to the awninged gate, put him in good cheer. Daubs of light and shade had free play with him when he ran about in the courtyard during the siesta (the only time he was permitted to leave my side). Only rarely did he slide an anxious, inquisitive glance into the gold-dusted stable. He never wore the pretty pampooties I had given him, and would weep when forced to put them on. No doubt he still felt the stony plains of his fatherland under the soles of his feet.

In my blind state this period of my life is a playground of sunny reminiscences, a pool of light in my greedy memory. In my private darkness Sibawayh eluded me, like a mouse too swift to be seen. He existed only in so far as he breathed, moved about or spoke, which he did less and less in my presence and more and more (in that same order), alas, in the stable, that nether world where he made his belated rediscovery of youth.

I heard him curse the mule. I heard him shuffle about. I heard a door open and then shut. I heard a heavy key drop on the flagstone with a clear high clink. I heard his step-step-step on the stairs.

I held out my hand for him to guide me and leaned on him as we proceeded through the corridor and down the naked stairway past empty rooms. Along the gallery, across the roofless courtyard, past the defunct fountain into the vestibule and then down the steps to the main gate: a cautious progress through a languishing house, as smooth and perfect as a womb.

At the gate I heard the jingle-bells on the old mule's bridle. He guided my feet into the stirrups and hoisted me effortlessly on to the saddle, whereupon I shifted from one buttock to the other with a lamentable lack of grace, while keeping both legs over the left flank: a shrivelled fruitlet of life.

The house of our renowned Jewish physician was a few streets eastward, beyond the great mosque. He had subjected me to various treatments, all to no avail; salves and ointments redolent of summery lavender – a physician's cunning sense of poetry. And all the while my skin continued to break out in suppurating sores while Sibawayh felt smoother than ever to my infrequent touch. I knew what he was doing on the pallet in the stable; I knew how he lured ungodly maidens and beggars' daughters to celebrate his long-dormant lust. Each thrust wounded me. Indifferent to my heartache, he kept thrusting to the hilt.

My days of noble pursuits are over, my pride is awash in threadbare purple, the fool has vanquished the king, my writing quivers, I live in a portable darkness, my bowel movements give cause for concern. My prose resembles the spectres of my memory: empty vessels, truncated epithets drifting soulless in a ghost town where even my language is dead.

'To the physician,' I said.

He took hold of the reins and we set off at a slow pace. The mule shook its head and evaporated in a thousand tinkles. I turned back the edge of my hood. I laid my right hand open-palmed on my lap and crossed the heel of one foot over the instep of the other.

An inexplicable repugnance stirred in me. Suddenly the road dipped and my stomach lurched. This must be the alley frequented in the daytime by beggars trailed by ragged broods, their souls bared in a bowl or cupped palm. Some of them – legless, sightless, or in some other way disorderly – spent the night huddled in doorways and nooks. Some, too, persisted sleepless in their labour.

We would soon pass the door that had been painted a livid green to signal the resident's pilgrim status, to summon the mumbled blessings of beggars. The pilgrim himself had recently died a dishonourable death, leaving his reprobate sons to care for their aged mother, who had previously lost her first husband, likewise a pilgrim, and who would survive her two sons as well.

The night was a veritable poem of sounds, from Sibawayh's footfall to my hoofs: a lullaby to the pounding in my old temples. To my right sounded the far-off clamour of a demon's wake – travesties of the sense of hearing. There was a cave on the mountain of Tawbad, which backed the town, where a spring slumbered and monsters and prophets were born.

'A pittance, lord!'

The road had suddenly acquired a voice and hands, and began to tug at my cloak.

'Alms,' the hand begged, 'a pittance for a man in need!'

I am repelled by beggars, particularly beggars whose rags belie their rhetorical skills. Here was a true poet of the wayside, a master if you will of mendicant eloquence who, glutted with inspiration, awaited with hungrily bated breath the passing of audible riches. He was also desperate, and hung on to my precious slippers for dear life. The scuffle did not last long. Sibawayh came to my rescue and the ghost made off with my babouches. Both of us barefoot now, we proceeded on our way.

The streets narrowed and I sensed that we had entered the Jewish quarter. Ivied archways sent down fluttery tendrils like rabbis' beards. A salvo of sensory stimuli: a cascade of flying vermin, the rank smell of the dungheap, a sudden braying, feathery whirrings, squawking, barking and howling. Hurried footsteps – an interrupted dalliance?

We were nearing the end of the street. As I trailed my fingers along the walls, doors sank warily into the secure embrace of their ancient arms, which soon reopened to form a modest square. Our shadows flitted to the other side.

We entered a gently sloping street. Other cobbles, other sounds. A final turning and we found ourselves in the main square, where the slave market was held by day in the cheer of the noontide sun. Beyond rose the mosque, from which a side alley to the north-east led to the hell of tanneries and abattoirs. Running off the square in a north-westerly direction was a back street where those in the know could locate a small brothel, low-entranced and lavishly creepered. A rain butt by the door stood on guard, lidless and wrinkly.

Each time I touched the water in the butt before going in it would break out in a smile, believing my fingertips augured a shower. The old men in the mosque went through the same motions, with a different cistern.

This was the brothel to which I had paid many a hooded visit in the course of a nonchalant, manicured stroll – always with young Sibawayh in attendance. At the other end of the courtyard, guarding the much-frequented latrine, stood another rain butt, and yet another in the corner. They seemed to have taken the place of watchdogs. Even the host (corpulent, immaculate, a rosary in his fastidious hands) had the size and girth of a rain butt.

In my memory, images of this brothel glide by in a wheeling masquerade: the swish of clothing, gleaming buttocks, well-turned calves. My moist nose, my dry throat. A smeared crack. My rhythmic spasms in the swaying dark, the room draped with tapestries depicting a young doe eyeing the hunter across her shoulder, the hunter standing scissor-legged, with a relaxed proprietary air while aiming his spear, and then Siba-wayh's face crumpling up in a grimace of searing pain.

Why did I always think it was raining when I was secluded in those dimly lit rooms? I even fancied I could hear the patter of raindrops – only to step outside under gold and azure.

One day I took Sibawayh to a garden at some distance from the town. On a little stream in the sun-glanced shade he watched a duck with a downy flotilla in her wake, and she had splashed and plopped so madly that he had been afraid the poor thing was drowning. I can still see his eyes, in which the tears and the dragonflies and the sun had cut diamonds.

Further off, outside the garden, in the hellish glare, a shepherd and his flock slept away the bleached, baking noon.

Was midnight upon us already? We went past the mosque and after a while we approached the physician's tall house. Behind it loomed the awesome mountain of Tawbad. It was on that mountain that a leprous fool, a self-professed prophet, had sought refuge from the world – no prophet without a mountain. The hostile populace had pelted him with stones, which had moved him to put a curse on the town before he fled, broken and bleeding profusely. His sole companion was a donkey. He had not returned since – a farcical ascension to heaven.

We halted in front of the physician's door. My repugnance was undiminished. A sense of tedium came over me. There was nothing left to be distracted by – my memory had come to rest, it was spent. What did it matter? What of my affliction and what of Sibawayh – above all Sibawayh? What was there to stop me from grinding everything underfoot and having done with it? When all is said and done the end is only a question of dignity.

And at that moment, out of nowhere, a stick, glowing with malignant ardour, struck my brittle spine, and while the pain still throbbed in my head there came a second blow, this time to my shoulder. I had hardly the time to savour the ecstatic stiffening that pain can induce, for the blows came hard and fast, methodically aimed now at my left side and then my right. It all happened so quickly, there was no distinguishing between the pain in each limb. After a blow to my neck, the expert beating proceeded crown-wards. Eventually I surrendered to the unrelenting thwack-thwacking. For a split second of weightlessness (tumbling backwards off my saddle) the safety of the ground seemed dizzyingly far away. A leaden ball turned in my gut as I cowered on the ground trying to call out for Sibawayh, but my stiff tongue could not dislodge the words from the gush of vomit.

Translated by Ina Rilke

34

ARNON GRUNBERG
Someone Else

Iemand anders

He's considered a good catch, he's got a job with status, he's a psychiatrist, still fairly young (38), childless, never been married, he's not bald; he has, he realizes as he stands at the mirror shaving in the morning, almost no physical defects, and he takes good care of himself. A nourishing cream here, a massage there. Aron Barshay has less reason for dissatisfaction than a lot of people.

Aron Barshay doesn't look like your typical psychiatrist. He doesn't wear glasses and he doesn't have a beard. At bars and restaurants, they often ask him whether he's a yoga teacher, or else maybe a fitness trainer. He has resigned himself to looking like that, not like a psychiatrist, more like a yoga teacher.

On rare occasions he speaks at conferences, but not as often as he used to. He once took part in a research project dealing with the connection between adolescent suicide and antidepressants. Barshay's contribution was modest, but he knows that. He doesn't try to make more out of that contribution than it really was, not to himself, not to others. More than anything else he is realistic, about his own life and those of his patients and colleagues. Vanity is a pastime he has abandoned.

He's an associate at a hospital where he is well-respected. It has been years since he felt the urge to try to become the director, to *move up a notch*, as they say.

Barshay doesn't allow himself to be driven by ambition, at least not any more. He takes time to play tennis, to go out, sometimes he flies to Paris or London for a three-day weekend. Or he visits his sister in Los Angeles; Barshay's parents are no longer alive. Occasionally he'll have a girlfriend, occasionally a friend will hint at the advantages of a stable relationship ('when you get to a certain age, it's embarrassing to be a bachelor any more'), occasionally Barshay considers such a serious, stable relationship, only to reject the idea. Occasionally Barshay goes out dancing and uses recreational drugs. The world is foundering in chaos, but Barshay is good at keeping chaos at bay.

On the evening of Saturday, 6 November, Barshay and a friend go out to dinner at a Spanish restaurant in the Village. They have an eight-thirty reservation. Barshay puts on a red turtleneck, even though it's actually too warm for a turtleneck, and a pair of black suit trousers. Even his nonchalance has been thought through. Barshay thinks about everything, without letting it cripple him. He thinks about things and draws a conclusion. Sometimes he modifies certain conclusions he has drawn in the past. It's not like him to be melancholy about missed opportunities. Not that Barshay has never missed an opportunity, but he refuses to glamorize those opportunities. Some opportunities have to be missed. People, too, live according to the laws of statistics. There is no greater whole that masks the meaning of all the details. There are no big meanings, only little meanings. What's more, the individual's failure can be a blessing for the group. In melancholy, in other words, Barshay catches a whiff of the lethargy he detests.

His friend teaches modern American history at an elite university, and publishes regularly in prominent magazines.

They sit across from each other. They have both ordered paella. They haven't seen each other for more than four months.

Barshay tells him that he's thinking about adopting a Chinese child. You can do that these days, even if you're single. He's already attended three information evenings at the adoption agency. Barshay was the only unmarried person there. After the first meeting, a couple took him aside. 'We could introduce you to someone,' they whispered.

They sounded concerned, worried almost. Barshay told them that wasn't necessary, that he was perfectly capable of introducing himself on his own.

'I don't know,' says the friend, who is divorced and has a five-year-old son. 'An adopted child, that almost always generates problems, doesn't it?'

'Almost always,' Barshay concurs. 'But what are the alternatives? An orphanage in the Chinese countryside, do you have any idea what that's like? And they're almost all girls at those orphanages, because girls aren't wanted.'

'Why so sudden, then? Are you feeling lonely? You could buy a dog, couldn't you?'

'I could,' Barshay says. 'But there are so many children no one wants, and I have a big apartment. Someone else will just have to take care of the dogs no one wants. And it's not all that sudden. I've been toying with the idea for years. I've always felt an urge to care for the unwanted. I suspect that's why I wanted to become a psychiatrist in the first place. Back when I still thought that psychiatrists cared for the unwanted.'

The friend sighs. His divorce cost him a bundle. Getting married was expensive, but a divorce even more so. He had to start all over again. Financially speaking, that is. Sometimes he wonders aloud whether the investment was really worth the trouble. How much is one's freedom actually worth? In fact, the freedom is a disappointment too, now that he can enjoy it so boundlessly. Unlike Barshay, the friend does not have an athletic build. No one ever mistakes him for a yoga teacher. They see him for what he is: a university professor.

The friend stretches, he's finished eating. He looks at Barshay, they've know each other for twenty years already. Barshay was a witness at his wedding.

Aron Barshay goes on eating calmly, but with relish. When his plate is empty, he says: 'They've been to my house already, the adoption agency, to see whether I can be trusted. So far, apparently, I can be trusted.'

They both laugh. The friend laughs perhaps a bit too loudly, as though he has to convince himself that this is funny, even though he doesn't think so. Barshay with a Chinese baby.

After they've called for the check, and split it, Barshay proposes that they go somewhere else, the way they used to. His friend hesitates but, when he sees that it has started drizzling outside, he decides quickly. 'There's an article I still have to work on,' he says. 'Some other time.'

They say goodbye out on the street.

'Let me know how it goes with the adoption,' the historian says with something like a laugh, although not a mocking one. His misgivings seem to have vanished. Perhaps he sees adopting a Chinese baby as something like a divorce, troublesome and costly but not without certain advantages. 'Maybe you should find a wife first, and then go for the adoption. That's the way it's usually done, Aron. Why should you be any different? Why do you have to act like you know better?' He turns and leaves quickly, he doesn't wait for an answer. The historian is not dressed for walking in the rain.

Later that friend will think back on this evening, the way people think about evenings when they've seen and heard something without knowing exactly what. And the more they think about it, the more they wonder 'what did I see, what did I hear, for God's sake?', the less chance they have of ever finding out.

Aron Barshay is wearing a raincoat with a hood. He puts up the hood and starts walking. He wants to go out dancing, but he doesn't know where. It's Saturday night. Standing in line for half an hour first, he doesn't feel like that. At a deli he buys a pack of Marlboro Lights. Barshay tells the man behind the counter: 'And a box of matches, please.' He's an occasional smoker, he doesn't carry a lighter.

Under the awning of a closed restaurant, he smokes a cigarette. He feels satisfied, it was good to see his friend again, the food was nice, the conversation lively, lively enough in any case for a Saturday evening in November.

Barshay lacks for nothing.

Maybe he should go home, read the newspapers, lie in bed

with a book, watch a DVD. He wonders which film he should rent, but then he remembers the Soho Grand. It's been a long time since he was there, an evening two summers ago. A fine evening.

On Saturday night there is always something going on there, and it's not far.

He tosses away the cigarette and starts walking. Calmly at first, then faster and faster. Excitedly.

Around midnight, Barshay arrives at the Soho Grand. The lounge is packed, just like he'd expected. There's nowhere to sit, but he doesn't mind standing. He manoeuvres his way to the bar, orders a glass of wine, then withdraws to a corner. Across the room he thinks he recognizes a former patient, but when he takes a better look he sees that it is a former colleague.

Barshay has been reading a book about angels. He can't seem to finish it; on reflection, he doesn't have much of a feeling for angels. He looks at his former colleague and he is reminded of that book. Apparently there's something about that former colleague that reminds him of an angel. The glassy gaze, perhaps, the pale skin, the flaxen hair. Barshay knows that the former colleague has seen him too, but they both pretend they haven't.

After a second glass of wine, Barshay feels the urge to smoke. He goes down the stairs and outside, beneath the canopy, he pulls the cigarettes from the pocket of his raincoat. The hotel doorman runs to a taxi with his umbrella, to keep some guests from getting wet. Life is wonderful.

Barshay can't find his matches, so he turns to a girl who is standing beside him, smoking. She pulls out her lighter without a word and hands it to him. The lighter goes out three times in a row. Barshay has to hold open his raincoat to win the fight with the wind.

He inhales, while she puts the lighter away. He looks at her and asks: 'Do you feel like dancing?' She takes the cigarette out of her mouth, but says nothing. She looks at the hotel, as though checking to make sure where she is.

'Or are you here with someone?' Barshay enquires. This is

Aron Barshay at his best: energetic, prepared to go far to make
the best of things, unconventional but never threatening, the
driver of a glorious coach who makes his horses gallop as
though it counts, as though he has someone important in his
coach, a VIP.

She looks back at the hotel one more time.

'Not really,' she says.

'Then let's go somewhere and dance.' Barshay smiles. A
smile you can trust. In the end, that's what it's all about: gen-
erating trust, in both patients and women.

'Okay,' she says, 'let's.'

They run through the rain to a taxi, and Barshay puts his
left shoe down in a puddle. The water splashes up high.

Only when they are in the cab does it occur to Barshay that
they haven't decided where to go yet. He leaves it up to her.
She's bound to have a better idea about that. It's been a long
time since he went dancing.

'Let's go to the Meatpacking District,' she says, 'we'll find
something there.'

Barshay thinks that's a good choice. The taxi pulls away
from the kerb.

'Do you want to know my name?' he asks.

'What you mean is that you want to know my name.'

'That's right,' Barshay says. 'That's what I mean.'

She tells him her first name: Madison. He had a patient once
called Madison, a long time ago, one of his first patients.

Barshay tells her his first name. Last names are for later,
maybe for never.

The left leg of Barshay's trousers is soaking wet.

'Why aren't you wearing a coat?' he asks.

'This *is* my coat.'

Barshay looks at the piece of cloth, that seems to him like
something in between the jacket of a tracksuit and a cut-off
piece of bathrobe.

The nightclub they go to is one Barshay's never been to
before. The club is new, maybe hip as well. Barshay is sceptical
about hipness, he is sceptical about all the things people tell
themselves.

They dance for half an hour. Madison dances well, with abandon, rhythmically. She dances differently from the way she talks. More youthfully. Bolder. Effortlessly.

Then they go to the bar for a drink. They both slip through the crowd like professionals, like people used to noise, used to sweat, used to physical contact.

'So tell me about yourself,' Madison says once they've reached the bar and ordered their drinks.

He wipes the sweat from his forehead. What is there to tell about himself? What does he want to say about himself? That he looks like a yoga teacher, but that appearances are deceiving?

'I'm in the process of adopting a Chinese baby.'

'A what?'

'A little girl. From China.'

'Why?'

'I like children, and I have enough time. And money. It seemed to me like the right thing to do.'

It sounds a little formal; he wishes he could talk about the adoption a little more ironically.

Madison grins. He hadn't meant it that way, but he grins along with her.

'I'm adopted too,' she says. 'I don't usually tell people that, but I can tell you, because I'll never see you again.'

Now it's Barshay who starts grinning.

He says nothing for a few seconds, then asks: 'Have you ever met your real parents?'

'My biological parents? No, never.'

'Do you know anything about them?'

'My mother was young when she had me. Fifteen. Barely fifteen. She kept it to herself for eight months.'

'That's young,' Barshay says. 'And your biological father?'

'He was older.'

The music is so loud they have to shout.

Their drinks arrive. Madison had asked for a Kir Royale. She tastes it and makes a face. 'Taste this, would you?' she asks.

Barshay tastes it.

'That's disgusting,' he says. 'Let's get out of here.'

They walk to the door.

'So now what?' Madison asks once they're outside.

He looks at his watch. He has no idea. That's not like him at all, he always has ideas, plans, suggestions, but right now he doesn't know where they should go.

'Most of the children in Chinese orphanages are girls, because no one wants them. At least not in China,' he says in the hope that he will come up with something, if only he keeps talking.

'If I had been a boy, I don't think my mother would have wanted me either,' Madison says with a pride that Barshay finds touching.

He leans over. He kisses her, and she lets him. She tastes like lemonade concentrate. There's still a wad of chewing gum in her mouth. The chewing gum doesn't get in their way.

After the kiss, they walk rather aimlessly in the direction of 14th St.

'And why haven't you ever tried to find your biological parents?' Barshay asks.

'I was afraid we wouldn't have anything to say to each other.'

Once again, her reply touches him. Of course, imagine you met your parents and then a silence descended. A painful silence. It could happen. They kiss again. Longer this time. Less carefully. As though they've been doing this for a while.

He notices that she has taken out her chewing gum, without him seeing it.

'Now what?' she asks finally.

Is he responsible for her entertainment? Is he her chaperone? She is little, but pretty, that's true. And she touches him. Her answers. Her boldness.

'I've got wine at home. I can make a gin and tonic. And I've got some good port.'

'Port,' she says.

It is two thirty in the morning, Sunday, 7 November.

'Have you ever actually been to China?' Madison wants to know, in the taxi on the way to his apartment.

'Not yet.' He looks at her in the semi-darkness of the cab. 'You're different,' he says. It sounds like a confession.

'Different from who?'

He should really say 'different from the other women I've taken back to my apartment', but he doesn't.

'You're special,' he says. 'I'm a sceptic, I don't often say that to women. I've never said it before. You're special.'

'You're different too,' Madison says.

They kiss again.

'Who named you Madison, anyway?' Barshay asks after another kiss and a brief silence. 'Your real parents or your adoptive parents?'

'My adoptive parents. I didn't have a name yet when I came to them. My real mother didn't give me a name, because she knew she was going to give me away.'

She takes a compact out of her purse and looks at herself in the little mirror. 'And who named you Aron?'

'My parents. I'm not adopted.'

'Too bad.'

When they get out, he has to help Madison. The heel of her shoe is stuck somewhere. She worms her way free.

Barshay lives in Central Park West.

The night porter greets Barshay coolly. He watches as the psychiatrist walks past. Watches how he stands with the girl, waiting for the elevator, how they enter the elevator.

For a moment, Barshay is afraid he knows what the night porter is seeing.

'I'm going to go change my trousers,' Barshay says once they're inside.

Then he lights three candles, that's all he has, and dims most of the lights.

He changes quickly in the bedroom. A different sweater, a different pair of pants. No shoes, no socks.

Madison is sitting on the couch, waiting for him.

He pours two glasses of port and sits down next to her.

'Am I allowed to smoke here?'

'Rather not. Unless you really have to. Do you really have to?'

'Not yet. Maybe later.'

She sips at her port.

'This reminds me of my grandfather,' she says, after tasting the port. 'He used to put cherries in it. How old is this port?'

He looks at the bottle.

'Twenty years. About as old as you are.'

She looks around. 'So this is where the Chinese baby is going to live?'

'Yeah,' he says. 'This is going to be the Chinese baby's house.'

He shows her the room that is reserved for the child he will adopt.

They walk past the freshly painted walls like a couple looking to see whether this house might be something for them.

'Do you think she'll like it here?' he asks.

'Adopted children are satisfied with almost anything.'

They kiss, they undress each other, they make love, standing up first, then on the floor, in the room reserved for the Chinese baby.

After that she lies down on the couch in the living room, she says she's hungry. Barshay offers her an apple and a slice of melon.

She eats the apple first, then the melon. They make love again.

Barshay feels like he's in love. He declares his love to her. She laughs.

They have another glass of port.

It is seven o'clock and growing light out when Madison says: 'I have to go.'

She puts on her clothes.

'I want to see you again,' he says. 'We could go to a movie. Cook something together. Do you like cooking?'

She takes a pocket diary out of her purse, tears out a page, writes her phone number on it and gives it to Barshay.

'You have to come back again real soon,' Barshay says.

'Then we can cook something together. What kind of food do you like?'

'I'll eat anything.'

Before she gets into the elevator she turns and blows a kiss to Barshay, who is standing half-naked in the doorway.

Fifteen minutes later he sends her a text message. 'I miss you,' he writes.

Contented, Barshay falls asleep. He is a man who will soon be a father and who, in the face of all probability, has also fallen in love just before he turns forty.

At two in the afternoon he wakes up. It has stopped raining.

He cleans up the living room. A piece of melon, apple peels, an almost empty bottle of port, an empty pack of cigarettes, burnt-out candles. He does it thoroughly, as though by cleaning up he is also clearing away the memory of her.

A pile of old newspapers and magazines he throws away as well; he's not going to read them now anyway.

It all goes into big plastic bags that he takes downstairs, where he talks to the porter a bit about a leaky tap that needs fixing.

Then he takes his car out of the garage. He feels like going for a drive, out into the woods. It's nice weather for walking.

On the highway, he sends Madison a text. 'What are you up to?' he writes. 'Are you awake already?'

Outside Tarrytown, Barshay parks the car. He walks for more than hour through the woods. It's quiet, he doesn't stick to the path.

He walks, following his intuition, zigzagging through the woods. You couldn't get lost here anyway. The sensation of being in love grows stronger. You can also save adopted children by starting a relationship with them. Or isn't being in love the same thing as wanting to save someone?

After his walk, in a restaurant in Tarrytown, he orders a cup of hot chocolate with whipped cream, and sends another text message to Madison. 'What are you doing?'

It is Sunday evening, a little before six.

Barshay leans back, he looks at the other customers, there

are only a couple of them. He imagines how he and Madison adopt a little Chinese baby together, then he starts fantasizing about a vacation. A luxury hotel, a swimming pool, Madison on the diving board. Does she like diving boards?

At ten past six the phone rings. A masked number, he sees. It isn't Madison, a man has dialled a wrong number.

The disappointment doesn't last long. He lets his thoughts flow on to destinations where he might go with Madison. Not like a daydreamer, more like someone who works at a travel agency. Which hotel would be best, how long a flight would be justifiable for a week's vacation. In any case, he doesn't want to take her to Florida. He's been there too often. Miami is done with, there's nothing left for him to do there.

By nine thirty that evening he still hasn't heard from her. He drives home and calls out for Thai food, which he eats on the couch, hurriedly and in deep concentration.

On the floor of the room set aside for the little Chinese girl he finds an earring. He places it beside the alarm clock on his nightstand, as though it were a religious ritual.

On Tuesday evening Aron Barshay attends another information meeting at the adoption agency. 'You will pick up your child at the airport, she will have a little suitcase with her,' a lady tells them. He is annoyed by the condescending tone in which the lady from the agency speaks to the prospective adoptive parents. As though they were toddlers.

During the break he confers with the other prospective parents.

A few of them agree with him, others have no problem with the way things are going. One couple is afraid to say anything; they're worried that they won't be given a Chinese child if they do. Barshay appreciates their honesty.

The enquiries into the persons of single parents are more exhaustive than those for the couples. The prospective adoptive parent has to pay for the investigation too. It costs a fortune. But Barshay doesn't mind. He makes another appointment with the interviewers, who will come to his home in two weeks' time for an in-depth interview.

On his way home in the taxi he sends Madison another text

message, the sixth one since her visit to his place. She hasn't reacted to any of them yet. He has already called her twice, maybe the text messages aren't getting through, but she doesn't answer and her voicemail box is full.

The next afternoon, after a meeting that was almost exclusively about money, Barshay's secretary announces that he has visitors. It's important, apparently. Urgent even. Madison, he thinks. How did she find him? Was it supposed to be a surprise?

But once again, no Madison, and no unexpected visitors from the adoption agency. A man and a woman. About his age, maybe a little older. They apologize a few times for disturbing him at his work, but they were unable to reach him at home.

'What can I do for you?' he asks.

His desktop is almost bare. Barshay likes an empty desk. Once Barshay told a woman: 'I'm empty inside.' That shocked her. It's not a nasty emptiness, though, it's a tidy emptiness. Inside Aron Barshay, everything is nice and neat.

'We're here about a missing person,' says the woman.

Barshay looks at her; a look that some of his colleagues think looks rehearsed. As though he's acting. Which may very well be true. A psychiatrist often has to act.

'We've been hired by the girl's parents,' the man says. 'The police are slow.'

From a white envelope, the man produces a photo. Almost tenderly, he shows the photo to Barshay.

'This is the girl,' the man says, 'do you recognize her?'

Barshay looks at the picture.

He looks at the man. Not a man of whom you'd think: He tracks down missing persons.

Then he looks at the photo again.

'Why are you asking me this?' Barshay asks.

'Because we think you saw her recently,' the woman says. 'Is that right? Did you see her recently?'

The woman slides the photo over closer to him. She is more forceful than the man. More aggressive.

Barshay picks up the photograph. Even though he doesn't

need to. She's very recognizable, but still totally different from the way he remembers her.

Barshay rummages in a drawer, pulls out a stick of lip balm and rubs it on his lips.

The photo of Madison makes him melancholy, sad, and that surprises him, that annoys him. What annoys him is the feeling that he misses her. He doesn't like to miss people. Missing people is more dangerous than a messy desk; it is an illness, the start of an obsession.

'That's right,' he says. 'I saw her last weekend. Met her, actually.'

The man and woman glance at each other.

'Where exactly did you meet her?' the man asks.

Barshay looks at the photograph again. She's not wearing earrings in this picture, she does have a necklace, though. He recognizes her effortlessly, but in this picture she looks like someone else. Not the girl he met in front of the Soho Grand. Younger, even younger, brazen, even more brazen, a look that says *fuck you* to everyone and everything. Barshay likes that look. He wishes he had a look like that. First the scepticism, then the middle finger held up to the world, to fate, to culture, to science, to the gods, to the dead heroes, to the woman from the adoption agency, to China.

'How did you actually happen to come to me?' Barshay asks. 'How did you find me?'

The man smiles. 'That's our job,' he says. 'People leave tracks. They can't help it.' He says it with a certain melancholy, as though it would be better if people didn't leave tracks.

'I'd really like to help you, but could we continue this conversation in two or three hours, say? Maybe somewhere other than this building? I have some urgent business to attend to.'

Barshay mentions a time and the name of a cafeteria where he eats lunch sometimes, when he doesn't feel like going to the hospital canteen.

Once he is alone again he pulls a report out of a drawer, a report a colleague wrote; he's supposed to correct it and comment on it. He reads, but he can't concentrate on the text.

Barshay takes out his phone and sends Madison a text

message, cheerful but urgent. 'Where are you? Give me a call. I need to talk to you.'

He writes her name on a prescription pad, twice. Then he tries to go back to his colleague's report on the function of memory among patients suffering from PTSD.

Barshay doesn't feel like going to the cafeteria, but he goes anyway. He has nothing to hide. He has never had anything to hide. An immaculate sceptic, that's Aron Barshay.

'Was she actually alone? When you met her?' the woman asks after Barshay has told them how they met. The Soho Grand. The rain. The nightclub.

Barshay thinks about it.

'There wasn't someone else? Someone talking to her, maybe?' the man asks.

'No. I'm the only one she talked to, as far as I know.' It sounds proud coming from him, it sounds like an achievement. 'She was standing outside, smoking.'

'You know that she's fifteen?' the woman asks.

'Jesus.'

He stirs his coffee, he adds a little milk.

'She never mentioned her age. I thought twenty-two, twenty-three, something like that. Twenty, maybe. She seemed grown-up. We're talking about the same person, aren't we? I can barely imagine that, fifteen. That must be a mistake. No one asked her for ID, not even when we went to dance. She wasn't fifteen.'

Barshay keeps the account of what happened that night to a minimum. He mentions the melon and the apple and the port, but not the lovemaking. He goes into detail about the Chinese baby he is planning to adopt.

'And that Sunday? What did you do then?' asks the man.

'I went hiking, out by Tarrytown. In the woods.'

'Do you do that often?'

Now it is the man who will not let go.

'What?'

'Walk in the woods?'

'Not often, but often enough not to get lost.'

*

Barshay takes the subway home. He runs water in the tub and lies in it. He reads the paper. Nothing about Madison. That puts his mind at ease.

Then he leafs through folders from restaurants that deliver. He is unable to choose. He calls his friend, but hangs up after letting it ring twice. Barshay lies down on his bed. He feels more in love than ever.

The people from the agency that looks for missing persons don't come back to him. Maybe the case has been solved. Still, Barshay doesn't dare to contact Madison. It's up to her now, he figures. You shouldn't force yourself on a fifteen-year-old. You have to give adolescents the time they need.

Again and again, he thinks back on the evening when he fell in love. The dinner with his friend, the hotel, the wine. The recklessness, the enthusiasm that had come over Barshay. The invincibility. The power, the pure power that being in love had given him, that Madison gave him, the way he was touched, the adoption. He wishes he could go travelling with her, he wishes he could say to her: 'Now we're going to adopt a baby together, and we won't leave it at just one. The unwanted children who have no name because they're so terribly unwanted, we'll take care of them. You and me. We'll give them a home. When you think about it logically, we're all unwanted. Unwanted people who are stuck with an unwanted God, that's what we are. So don't feel unwanted. I mean, feel as unwanted as you like, but feel welcome. With me.'

One Thursday evening he calls his travel agency. He books a brief but all-inclusive trip to a Caribbean island.

Two days before his departure for the Caribbean island, he takes a bath in the evening and then goes to lie in bed with a bowl of peanuts. He watches TV, the local station, the news. Sometimes he dozes off, awakes with a start, eats a few peanuts.

At a little past nine thirty a man appears on the TV, talking about a girl they've found close to Tarrytown. Her photograph appears on the screen.

Aron Barshay sits straight up in bed. The bowl of peanuts falls to the floor.

He sees men carrying away a bag.

Aron Barshay looks at the TV, he looks at the photo of the girl on the TV. He looks and he looks and he looks, he tries to remember her, he tries to remember himself, the friendly sceptic, the sceptic in love, the psychiatrist who looks like a yoga teacher, but he stands before his own memory as before the gates to paradise, where he is not allowed in.

Translated by Sam Garrett

35

SANNEKE VAN HASSEL

Indian Time

The long seat was empty. She sat down and put her cardigan beside her. It had been hot for days. The leaves of the plane trees barely filtered the sun. Frightening, how all that green had kept itself hidden for months and was now bursting forth. Everything was shooting up out of the ground. Growth – she wanted it to slow down, so you could get used to it. Every month she sorted the children's cupboards, removed clothes that had got too small, selected, took some to the container on the corner, kept too much yet again.

She pulled a pile of exam papers out of her bag. She'd mark a few, then she wouldn't have to do it this evening. In the canal a duck quacked. It swam away, disappearing behind the bronze Rodin sculpture standing almost directly in front of her. '*L'homme qui marche*' she read on the plinth. The man's legs were long, his buttocks firm and round. He had no head or arms and his prick was obscured. Only his steps mattered, keeping going, putting one leg in front of the other.

Out of the corner of her eye she saw a man coming towards her. She quickly looked down at her papers, working: no empty chatter with guys who were just hanging about in the city.

His shadow reached to her shoes and led to a pair of suede moccasins, then above them the legs of leather trousers with fringes down the side seams: the Indian suit she'd bought for Heintje as a St Nicholas present. The man came to sit next to her. Annoyed, she picked up her bag, put the exams back into it and placed it between them. On this long bench, with room for an entire school class, he had to come and sit right here.

The idiot. Although Heintje would like the way he looked. She peered sideways at the black hair hanging halfway to his shoulders. He was wearing a leather wristband with a turquoise gemstone on it, set in silver. He'd crossed his brown arms.

'Could I ask you something?' His voice was soft.

'Certainly.' She looked at him. His eyes were very dark brown.

'Do you know where Ahoy is?'

'You need to take the metro to Zuidplein. There's a stop along that way where you can get on.'

'On the Ahoyweg, it said in the directions.'

'From the Zuidplein metro station you just follow the signs.'

An empty Coke cup floated past the water's edge. The duck poked about in the litter with its beak. A tram passed on the other side of the canal. She noticed that on one of the big old houses it said 'Mariners Centre'. On the building next door was a sign: 'Stop suffering'.

'Off to a concert?' she asked.

'No, I have to work. I'm already late. I wanted to walk there but this city is bigger than I thought.'

'You've got a long way to go. It's on the other side of the river.'

A Japanese couple came to stand in front of the Rodin statue. The boy asked if they would mind taking a photo. He'd used gel to make his hair stand upright.

'Better not get me to do it,' she said. 'Mine always come out blurred.'

The Indian took the camera.

The boy and girl put their arms round each other. Next to the legs of the walking man they looked like a pair of dwarves.

'You only have to press.' The Japanese was becoming impatient. His smile was artificial.

The Indian took his time, changed position, rotated the lens, pushed one or two buttons. The boy was clearly struggling to resist switching places and taking the photo himself.

When the couple had gone, they laughed together. Then it was quiet, for several minutes. The sun shone all along the bench. Holidays in the past, the sense of timelessness you felt walking home from the beach.

'I have to go,' said the Indian.

From a clock on a lamp post she saw it was already five. The crèche was on the other side of town, there was a vegetable box to pick up, they'd run out of nappies. 'So do I,' she said. 'If you like, I can walk to the metro with you. I'll show you the stop.' She blushed.

'Yes, please,' he said.

Together they walked along the shopping streets, past people with sunglasses and full carrier bags, past buggies issuing high-pitched wails. It was busy; the fine weather had drawn people out of their houses.

The metro station was a dark hole in the ground. At the top of the steps they stopped. 'You need to go down there.'

He asked if she had a pen.

She found one in her overstuffed bag.

He tore a corner off a free newspaper, wrote something on it and gave it to her. Then he adjusted the collar of her blouse. For a second his fingertips touched her throat. Before she knew it, he'd disappeared into the ground. Bewildered, she read the note he'd given her.

She dashed into the crèche, panting for breath. The children didn't seem to mind too much that she was so late. She stuffed them into their coats. Heintje dragged his backpack along the pavement. At a rocking duck he stopped and tried to haul himself onto it. 'Just keep walking, darling.' She clamped Nora to her side. In her free hand she held the note with his phone number. He was called Justin. What a name. The area code didn't look familiar. Did he live in one of those outlying suburbs? Hadn't he got a mobile? At the glass doors to the block of flats she crumpled the note and threw it into a litter bin. For a moment she had an urge to walk back, stick her hand in and pull his number out from among the crisp packets and ice-cream wrappers.

The lift glided upwards. The long half-hour they'd spent sitting on that bench together. His eyes. Relief at having disposed of the note didn't come. The children whined. Heintje wanted to press all the buttons; Nora pulled her earring out.

Inside, Heintje made straight for the fridge. 'Ice cream, ice cream.' He tugged open the freezer compartment. His little sister crawled after him.

'We're just about to eat.' She sighed and gave them each an ice lolly.

It was stuffy in the flat. She slid open the balcony door. The pansies she planted in the window box last week could do with some water.

She gave the children their dinner and loaded the dishwasher. Hugo was late. Recently he'd started talking about a third. When you had two already it didn't make all that much difference, he said.

He didn't get home until they'd finished dessert. He'd gone for a quick game of squash with Carel after work. Carel had seen an adviser about his pension, Hugo told her as he poured a glass of wine. 'He thinks we ought to invest in real estate. You pay all the costs out of the rental income. You should see what you can build up over ten years.

'I'd rather just put something in a savings account,' she said.

'Go ahead. Two per cent interest, nice subsidy for the banks.' Shaking his head, he poured another glass and said nothing.

At eight thirty the children were finally in bed. Hugo was sitting in front of the television. He looked tired, his eyes were dull, his skin greyish. He'd barely reacted lately to anything she said.

She sat down with her laptop and looked up the Ahoy website. A Western Fair was starting, with Indian dances and rodeo demonstrations.

Suddenly she felt Hugo's hand on her shoulder.

'In need of a bit of adventure?' He chuckled.

She quickly clicked away the page and opened her university email account.

When he was settled in front of the television again, she went back to the Western Fair. Photos of men with cowboy hats and guitars, of sun-reddened blonde women line-dancing back to back. A stage with the Stars and Stripes as a backdrop and, six times as big, the Dutch flag.

There were just two photos of Indians, one of a dance group and one of a warrior with a headdress of white feathers. Didn't he look a bit like Justin? Their faces were painted with black-and-white stripes. She doubted the authenticity of the brown underneath.

She clicked on the opening times. The Fair started at nine thirty the next morning and lasted for two days. Her first appointment at the faculty wasn't until eleven. She could be at the Centraal Station at nine, at the front exit, where all the passengers came out.

It was cool in the bedroom. Hugo was already in bed; he'd set the air conditioning running. She didn't switch on the light, he didn't like it.

She slid across to him. 'Little furnace, so here you are.' Eyes closed, he pulled her towards him and kissed her. She turned onto her side. Tomorrow morning she could work on her research for two hours instead. She hadn't got much done recently. Compare the results of the surveys she'd got her students to carry out after the summer.

She couldn't sleep. Every time she shut her eyes she saw Justin, his eyes, the skin of his arms, his fingertips touching her collar bone before he disappeared into the maze of the metro station.

Hugo snored. She got out of bed and took a homeopathic sleeping pill in the bathroom. That couldn't do any harm. She lay down again. Before she knew it she was standing on a wide-open plain, summer freckles around her nose, hair in a ponytail. The sun burned. The sky was blue. Someone was coming towards her out of the arid distance, forcing his way through prickly scrub.

For fifteen minutes now she'd been standing at the ticket machine. She'd picked up a newspaper. Combing the crowd with her eyes, she pretended to read. The station clock said it was ten past nine – still less than twenty-four hours since she met him on the bench by the canal. Had it been a hallucination? How long was

she going to stand and wait? It began to get hot. Her silver
sandals pinched. She loosened the straps a little and rocked
from one foot to the other. She wondered what to cook tonight,
spaghetti carbonara or penne with peas and ham.

Behind two men in suits, he emerged from the pedestrian
tunnel. Justin. His long hair was tied in a ponytail. He came
straight towards her. He didn't hurry.

'There you are again.' He touched her wrist.

'I saw you were going to be working at the Fair,' she
stammered.

'Yes,' he said. 'I've got a stand there with handicrafts. We
set it up last night.'

Perhaps he could tell she was nervous. He calmly went on
talking, to allow her to settle, get used to his voice, to the fact
he was there. 'I sell tapestries and pots, but not many, transport is tricky. Jewellery's better, not big, not heavy, always
good. Dutch women are crazy about turquoise.' He raised his
arm a little to show her his leather wristband with its blue
stone set in silver.

'Is that from America?'

'How does Taiwan strike you?' He laughed.

'Are you also in the dance group that's performing this
afternoon?' She blushed.

'I'm hopeless at dancing.' He gave a little jump, making
other passengers briefly look up. She didn't believe for a
moment that he couldn't dance.

'Come on. My treat.' He stuck out his hand.

She took it. This can't happen, she thought, holding tight.

Between hurrying commuters they strolled towards the
centre of town. At the bottom of one of the city's tallest buildings he asked her name.

'Maidie,' she said.

'Then you'll never grow old,' he said.

They walked along the canal, past the Rodin statue near
where they met, the man who was mainly legs. He stopped.
'Beautiful.' His hand skimmed a bronze ankle. The metro station came into view. 'I really only wanted to say hello. I have
to go to the university.'

'Phone not working?'

'I lost your number.' In a bin, to be precise. His note had probably already been swallowed by a dustcart. She blushed.

He asked whether she'd have time soon. After.

Hugo was collecting the children from the crèche today. Just for once she could get home a bit late, a couple of hours. He often rang to say he wouldn't be in for dinner. And there were still fish fingers in the freezer. Urgent meeting, she'd say. No, she was going to the theatre with a colleague, unexpectedly. They'd eat something in town first. It wasn't worth coming home. 'I can make five o'clock,' she said.

The rest of the day was a disaster. She forgot an appointment with a student, wiped part of a draft and jammed the photocopier so badly they had to ring the manufacturer. At three the lecture 'Governance in the Public Sector' began, a course she was giving for the first time. 'The world in which policymakers attempt to implement changes is often more complex than they anticipate.' She laid another sheet in the projector. There was total silence. 'Excuse me, but either you're in the wrong place or we are,' a student called out. The whole room laughed. On the large screen behind her it said 'Methods and Techniques of Qualitative Research'. Red-faced, she hunted for the correct sheet.

At four thirty she grabbed her things and hurried to the metro. Below ground she used a window as a mirror. She undid her hair, tied it into a ponytail, then released it again.

On the dot of five she reached the spot where they'd parted that morning. She put on her sunglasses and looked around nervously. It was so busy; the whole city was adrift. As long as no one she knew happened past. Justin's a colleague, she'd say. It didn't sound very good. She didn't know anyone on the university staff who wore fringed leather trousers. A friend from America, that sounded better.

She took up position on the corner, in front of a place where you could make photocopies twenty-four hours a day. Then she went over to stand on the kerb, a little higher than the street. Her eyes kept wandering to the clock above the counter. At five thirty he still hadn't arrived.

She was just about to leave when he ran up to her. 'Sorry. I was just packing away when this big group of women suddenly came up to the stand. There wasn't a soul all afternoon, but right at the end I sold three hundred euros' worth. Necklaces and earrings. Hand over fist.'

'Business before pleasure,' she said. How stupid that sounded. She tried to wink as she said it, which no doubt looked like a nervous tic.

They went to a Surinamese place she used to call in at sometimes after a night out. A semi-basement, it was hot and damp inside. Fiery Caribbean sounds came from the loudspeakers.

He had two rolls with roast pork and a large bowl of soto, eating quickly and with concentration. She stabbed a little at her rice and beans and couldn't swallow a mouthful. In every sense he was unlike the men she knew. His imperturbable gaze. The skin of his face, his arms, which seemed to shine.

Ten past six. Right now Hugo would be lifting the children out of the car. She'd left a message on his voicemail saying a colleague had a spare ticket for the theatre. A very lengthy performance. 'There are still some fish fingers in the freezer. And sorry, but my phone's almost dead.' Then she'd switched off her mobile.

Plates of food and bowls topped with foil were slid through a hole in the wall. Behind the hatch, illegal immigrants worked here, Hugo had once told her. The last time they ate out he'd added that all the bars in the city centre were terrorized by the Turkish mafia. He liked to tell her things like that right at the start of the evening. She'd be unable to get them out of her head and he would casually order some special wine or other.

'Delicious.' Justin wiped his lips.

She prodded at the beans some more. A few ended up next to her plate.

He looked at her, then said: 'Shall we go outside?'

They walked in silence towards the river. A cool breeze got up as they stood at the waterside. A freight barge passed. The cage on top of its cargo hold had a playhouse and a slide inside it. They walked along the quayside. Justin sang a song with words she didn't know.

She used to come here with boys from her class. First sweethearts after school hours. Her grandfather had stood here too; his brother left for America from the building on the far bank. Long afterwards he'd come to this spot and watched the bridge being built. A few days before it opened, he died. A month later, in a force-six gale, the whole structure started to sway. The cables had insufficient resistance.

On the open deck of a tourist boat stood an elderly couple. The woman waved her handkerchief. Justin waved back. The evening sun lit up the flats and warehouses on the other side. The buildings were sharply outlined against the pink sky.

Suddenly she felt his hand sliding up from her wrist, past her elbow. Her breathing quickened. She swung round to face him. She kissed him, taking hold of his leather jerkin.

Her clumsiness.

His hands on her back.

A car tooted. They were standing at the edge of a parking place.

'Come on.' Justin pulled her after him over the cobblestones. The sun had gone, the buildings on the opposite bank had faded. He led her with him, into an avenue. As if she could no longer walk by herself. A row of historic houses was being restored. Green gauze flapped from deserted scaffolding. An overhanging wisteria was attached to a front wall with rusty wire. That sweet smell, as if out of a bottle.

At the road junction they stood still. He pointed to a hotel across the street. She nodded.

In the lobby an aquarium was built into a wall of lacquer. Little fish swirled about, blue, yellow, fantails. The fish came towards them and then swam away.

They took a room. Number 304. 'Beautiful view,' the receptionist said. She paid. As they were going up she realized that the credit card she'd used was from her joint account. 'Sorry.' She ran back down: 'Can I still cancel that payment?' The receptionist shook his head. She turned round and walked slowly upstairs.

*

He was sitting naked between the white sheets, upright, his legs apart. The legs she'd felt around her. She leaned against the wall. Dark tresses slid between her fingers. She made his hair into a thick plait, then undid it again. From the corridor they heard the voices of other hotel guests. The balcony doors were open a crack. It was getting dark, but the birds were still singing, high in the tall poplars along the street.

'Where do you live?' she asked.

'In Emmen,' he said.

She laughed. 'An Indian from Emmen.' She ran her fingers along his spine, from bottom to top.

The muscles of his shoulders hardened. 'Just shut up about Indians.'

'Sorry.' She withdrew her hand.

'Maidie, little girl . . . You shouldn't say the first thing that pops into your head.' He laughed. There was a tiredness to it. 'My father was American. In 1954 he came here with the air force. He was stationed at Soesterberg and he brought us with him, his whole family. As a boy I often played on the moorland there, I knew all the paths and rabbit holes.'

She laid her hands on the base of his spine and gently pressed.

He spoke quickly. 'My father was born in Navajo Nation but he didn't grow up there. A government programme paid for him to go to a boarding school where the aim was to turn the Navajo into good citizens. At seventeen he joined the army.' He looked off to one side, at his clothes hanging over a chair. 'My father wanted to fly, to look out across the world and see what people were making of it.'

The evening sky was grey with pink stripes and a pale crescent moon. He turned round and took her by the shoulders. He pushed her firmly onto her back and lay on top of her. His touch was no longer exploratory. He forced himself into her, screwed her for a long time, five minutes, ten minutes. She grew dizzy, felt the mattress move, grabbed the side of the bed. He went on like that until she couldn't think about anything any more. Hold on to his upper arms, that was all.

Afterwards he lay motionless beside her, like an exhausted animal. Outside it was dark. She pushed him away and wrapped the sheet around her, covering the loose skin of her belly that the children had left.

He stood up and opened the balcony doors so that the cool of the evening could come in. His warm, hard body. She wanted to pull him back into the bed, to feel him against her, but she did nothing. With strangers you had no right to intimacy.

He went into the bathroom.

She rummaged in her bag for her phone and turned it on. No messages, not even from Hugo. Had he believed her excuses? Hugo wasn't easily worried. His attitude was that you shouldn't have to check on each other. Seeing it was almost twelve, she picked up her clothes from the carpet next to the bed. She buttoned her blouse, could smell her own sweat, the scent of arousal.

'You're leaving.' He stood leaning against the doorframe.

'Justin,' she said. 'I'm sorry . . . Yes, I have to go. And you?'

'Don't worry about me.'

'Stay. I've paid for the whole night. Tomorrow's your last day here.'

On the website she'd read that the Western Fair would be moving to Ermelo the next week. As an extra attraction a rodeo would be added to the programme there.

Without speaking he got dressed and held the door open for her.

As she walked down the stairs after him, she pictured the children, lying in their little beds, Nora on her back, stretched out, the blanket thrown off; Heintje with Mag the Rag.

On the pavement outside they stood facing each other. 'You look perfect,' he said, as she pushed her tangled hair back behind her ears. The first time, the day before yesterday, the way he'd straightened her collar, the scrap of newspaper with his number, a note that was now ash, particles of soot in the sky over the city. Tomorrow she had to invigilate three exams. Orals.

Fleeting kisses. Two. He turned and walked off in the direction of the river. Surely he wasn't going to sleep on a bench at

the quayside? He didn't look back, crossed the road, a ghostly
figure between the tall trees.

She was standing directly under the lamps that lit the pavement in front of the hotel. She hesitated, unable to think clearly,
then took a few steps to one side so she was out of the light.
She had to get moving.

Rain poured down the windows. To her right the bed was
empty. Shit, the children, they needed porridge, clothes on, to
the crèche. Almost seven thirty, the alarm clock said. Hugo
had let her sleep in.

She leaped out of bed and went to the kitchen. He was sitting at the kitchen table in a bathrobe reading the paper, the
children playing at his feet. They were still in pyjamas. It didn't
look as if they'd eaten anything yet.

'Mummy!' Nora called out enthusiastically. She rubbed her
knee for a moment and crawled away under her chair. Heintje
briefly glanced up, seeming to look right through her. Then he
carried on playing. He made his plastic elephant jump onto the
pedal of the bin so that the lid rattled.

Hugo looked up from his paper. 'Hi, lazybones.'

She went to sit at the kitchen table, needing to find the
energy from somewhere to open the kitchen cupboards, warm
the milk, get the whole show going.

'How was the performance?'

'Quite beautiful.'

'Filthy weather, eh?' Hugo nodded at the window. The sky
was a flat grey expanse and the rain streamed down the glass
as if it would never stop. 'Quite a contrast to last night. We had
a sunset here, really spectacular.' Hugo picked up his camera
from the table and waved it in the air. 'I took some incredible
photos.'

'I know, I saw it too,' she said before he could thrust the
camera under her nose.

'You were in the theatre, weren't you?'

'It was a site-specific performance.' She picked up the
newspaper and attentively studied a special offer for new
subscribers.

Hugo was no longer listening. He was looking at the photos of twilight he'd taken from the balcony. Pinkish-red kitsch skies.

'That nature has such colours in it,' he said.

'You sometimes see them on postcards from seaside resorts,' she said.

He raised his eyebrows. 'Hey, something else,' he said then. 'Rob Beers has invited me for a project in Croatia. We're going to train prison officers there, show them what we do here, how to handle inmates. It's in an old monastery. When you get there you wonder where on earth you've landed up, Rob says, but it's a really beautiful place, with all the modern facilities, even a wellness centre. It starts on 28 June and lasts for two weeks.' He gave her a questioning look.

'Seems to me you should do it,' she said.

'Great, fantastic,' he stammered in surprise. 'I'll have to see straight away today whether I can still apply.' He'd probably been expecting complaints, a cynical remark, after which he'd go anyhow. 'Perhaps your mother can come.'

'Yes, perhaps.' She stood up to take a shower.

As she passed he grabbed her shoulders and kissed her on her mouth. 'My sweet,' he said.

She walked on to the bathroom. There she turned on the shower good and hot. She stretched, rinsed her armpits, the water dripping down her sides, over her belly, between her legs. Justin's fingerprints – they were everywhere. Off in the distance she could hear Hugo urging the children to get a move on. She shut her eyes. Another fifteen years and she'd go travelling, for a long time, alone.

'Where are their backpacks?' Hugo's voice blared through the bathroom. He was the one who'd fetched the children yesterday afternoon.

'In the living room, somewhere near the sofa, I think.'

The wall of the shower was a mosaic. Tiny tiles, all identical, all made by tiny fingers. Supposedly glued onto the wall one by one. Why had she found that attractive two years ago?

'I can't see them.' Hugo's voice, distant now.

'I'm coming.' She turned off the shower and grabbed a

towel. The rain had stopped. Beams of sunlight were reflected in the mirror-clad block of flats opposite.

Heintje laughed loudly, then came screeches of delight from Nora. They were doing something in the hallway, probably something that would damage the walls or their clothes.

They'd be late, all of them.

Suddenly Hugo stuck his head round the corner of the shower. 'Found! You just relax, I'll take the children myself.'

'Okay.' She nodded in surprise. A little later she stood waving at all three of them near the door to the lift. She went to sit on the sofa in a bathrobe, legs drawn up. On the coffee table was an ashtray they'd bought five years back in Andalucía, before they had children. Olives were painted on it. It fitted into her hand perfectly.

Translated by Liz Waters

36

JOOST DE VRIES

A Room of My Own

Een kamer voor mezelf

Henry Kissinger had a small flabby mouth he was fond of using to make droll comments, like calling power the ultimate aphrodisiac, an aphorism he repeated so many times people started to believe it, encouraged by his own tendency to pose for the paparazzi at dinners and cocktail parties with a platinum-blonde socialite or an aspiring starlet on his arm. Looking at those photos now, you see a square tuxedo with a man stuffed into it. A bulging face, no neck to speak of, tiny eyes behind enormous glasses, classic wavy hair. And one of those Barbarella babes next to him in a delirious dress, her teeth bared by a smile so strained it looks like she's putting her face through an aerobics workout.

'Power is the ultimate aphrodisiac.' He was referring to those women, but didn't think his theory through enough to realize it applied to him too. In the run-up to the presidential election of 1968 he'd called Richard Nixon 'unfit to be president', but when President Nixon called him three weeks after winning to make him National Security Advisor, he didn't hesitate. He too felt his knees quiver and his heart pound when faced with the true power of the White House.

'Will you be my National Security Advisor?'

'Oh, I will, Richard. Yes, I will.'

We recognized him from some thirty metres, maybe more. He was walking towards us from the Louvre. A small, elderly man with a walking stick, flanked by three much younger men who were obviously security. On our right, the Seine. Left, the Jardin des Tuileries, the Orangerie, the Rue de Rivoli with its palatial hotels and Armani stores. Behind us, the Place de la Concorde with Napoleon's enormous Obelisk and, further in that direction, the Grand Palais, the Champs-Elysées with the Arc de Triomphe, which even Hitler marched around, rather than through, out of respect for the tomb of the Unknown Soldier. We were surrounded by echoes of the past.

It had to be one of the most touristy spots in all of France. Close to the museum's inverted glass pyramid, one hundred and fifty metres away from the undocumented Liberians and Senegalese trying to flog Eiffel Tower keyrings to indifferent tourists. If you had two hours to kill in Paris, this was the place to go and that was why we were here – one and a half hours before we were due to report at the Gare du Nord – but the tourists rarely left the main route through the former palace gardens, so you could still stroll peacefully along paths of fine gravel of the kind that is undoubtedly very good for playing boules.

Look, could it possibly, surely not, is that, could that really be, we said to each other, but there was no doubt in our minds. It had been some four decades since he'd held a cabinet post, and more than not being able to remember the last time we'd seen him on TV, we couldn't remember *ever* having seen him on TV apart from archival footage.

He was walking slowly and we too slowed our pace. We wanted to delay that moment, the moment our paths would cross and we'd be able to look him in the eye. Ten metres, six metres, three metres and then – to my surprise – my brother stepped over to him.

'Excuse me, Mr Kissinger, could we please take a picture?' Immediately adding, 'I am such a big fan of your book, *Diplomacy.*'

The security men held back for a moment. 'Ah well, ah well,' mumbled the former Secretary of State, who didn't come up to my brother's shoulder. He seemed to be amused. My brother put on his big, fake, photo grin, while one of Kissinger's assistants smiled professionally and said firmly, 'Please, just one picture.'

Their faces were next to each other on the screen of my

iPhone. I knew Hugo's all too well, but Kissinger's was a feast for the eyes. His facial skin was leathery and crumpled and angular, like an old leather travelling bag. Gravity had taken hold of his eyelids and not let go; they were watery and drooping. The same for his lower lip. Once so strong, his face had collapsed. It was past it, but his eyes were clear and icy blue and burning through the lenses of the square glasses that rested on his potato nose like twin television sets.

In that moment I thought about all the things you could know about him. In the thirties he'd fled Germany with his family to escape the Nazis, he'd become a brilliant academic at Harvard, joined Nixon's government in the late sixties, successfully pursued detente with China and the Soviet Union, let the Vietnam War escalate (squandering tens of thousands of lives) so he could de-escalate it later on his own terms and win a Nobel Peace Prize for it.

The peace negotiations had been held here in Paris. Anyone who might see him walking here in the Tuileries knew that. History personified – war and peace. This old man supported fascist regimes in Latin America, probably had Salvador Allende murdered, delayed informing the president so he wouldn't mediate in the Yom Kippur War, deliberately left thousands to starve to death in Bangladesh. And here he was.

Click, said my camera.

'Thank you, thank you,' said Kissinger. 'Good day, good day.'

'Great meeting you, sir,' we said.

We didn't walk on, but watched him walk away with his support staff. They left the gardens a little further along, heading out to the road where a car was undoubtedly waiting. We didn't say anything. I could imagine that he'd done some shopping, that he had his regular addresses on the Rue Saint Honoré, the Place Vendôme.

'Wow. Henry Kissinger,' Hugo said at last.

'Yes, smashing,' I said.

'Super.'

'Absolutely.'

We looked at each other once again.

'He should have been chucked in prison years ago.'

'On bread and water, the bastard.'
We laughed, of course.

For the first sixteen days of June it rained as if God was trying to wash a stain from the earth, but on the seventeenth the clouds parted and a forgiving sun shone down on the hills between France and Belgium. Summer revealed itself, a promise fulfilled. There were faster ways to get from Amsterdam to Waterloo, but we had signed up to a regiment – 'regiment' was completely the wrong word, but that was what we called it – with lots of British re-enactors, who gathered at Gare du Nord, where the train from London arrived and a small fleet of coaches were waiting to take us to our encampment in Belgium.

There were people who spent their first hour on the bus completely preoccupied with the lights and vents over their seat. There were men (and there were only men) who immediately grabbed fat historical works and started to read or pored endlessly over maps, but most of the passengers immediately leaned forward against the back of the seat in front of them, instant male bonding. There were conversations about what we could expect, planned events, everything that had been announced on the various web forums of the official Waterloo Day, beginning tomorrow.

For those who wonder what kind of man travels to Waterloo to re-enact what once happened there, what kind of men were sitting in the bus, I can only say: correct men, men who haven't forgotten how their parents raised them, men who know life's rules, who have arranged their pension and their fire insurance, who probably have a letter in a drawer somewhere that's been there since their fortieth and contains instructions for their funeral 'in the event of', men who buy the same pair of shoes every year. Some of them had brought their sons with them, timid boys who still spent Saturday night at home in front of the TV. They were the kind of men who are very easy to mock, with their Gore-Tex boots and their zip-off trousers, their fleece jackets and their bum bags – but that's doing them an injustice. They were probably men who spent hours in their attics making trees out of foam paper, papier mâché and ice-lolly sticks, constructing miniature chateaux and inns, creating entire landscapes for the tiny tin soldiers they had painted under a magnifying glass. Toys that are not toys, but meant for reliving history. These men put hundreds of hours and thousands of euros into it. In short, men I am jealous of in a very fundamental sense, because every man should have a room of his own where he can shuck off work and family, and play and be happy in a way that is usually reserved for boys alone.

'Bonjour, tout le monde. Bonjours, soldats heureux.'

The voice coming over the speakers was unusually slow for a Frenchman's, enunciating each syllable.

'Welcome, everybody.'

It was coming from the first row where a man had stood up. Holding onto the luggage rack with one hand, he raised a microphone to his mouth with the other. Tall and elegantly slim, he was wearing a jacket that came down almost to his knees, a kind of doctor's coat. While speaking he looked down shyly at his shoes, which had a certain charm, given that he must have been at least sixty and had such striking, rugged features that he could have been a colonel in the Foreign Legion.

'Welcome to the Battle of Waterloo.'

He was going to explain to us where we had to register for the camp-ground, where we could pick up our uniforms, what time tomorrow we had to report. But first he wanted to give us a special word of welcome, considering that we, British and Dutch, were being so chivalrous as to fight on the side of Napoleon's France. Smiling, he raised a fist in the air, 'Vive l'Empereur! Vive Napoleon!'

'Vive l'Empereur! Vive Napoleon!' we cried in reply.

Of course, he continued in his irresistible camembert English, afterwards we would all be hanged as traitors. Aff curz, afzerwarts, ol of you shell be hang-ed as tray-tors.

We all laughed loudly and our guide took that as a sign of an excellent esprit de corps and passed around a box of booklets with the programme for tomorrow's battle.

Nobody on the bus hesitated before plunging into his booklet, which meant an immediate end to the moment of easy-going solidarity; the excursion had become an object of study again. Next year it would be a real celebration. 18 June 1815–18 June 2015. The French army had already promised several cavalry regiments, the president would be coming, maybe even the British queen, the Dutch king in any case. Stands to accommodate tens of thousands of visitors would be erected. All over Europe grown men were already taking riding lessons in their free time because they had been lucky enough to be assigned official roles by lot – not as Napoleon or Blücher, whole casting agencies had been deployed for those, celebrities were being flown in, Benedict Cumberbatch had apparently already committed to playing Wellington, but as minor colonels and captains who had made it into the history books with their name and rank by falling horse and all on the day itself. But that didn't make us any less serious today.

So we studied the costume store, the camp-grounds, the scheduled outdoor readings, the tours . . .

'Hi, I'm Raymond, by the way. From Rotterdam.'

The giant next to me had set in motion, holding out a coal shovel and telling me that he had spent the weekend visiting all of the Napoleon-related monuments in Paris.

'His tomb in Les Invalides.' He put a hand on his heart. 'Goosebumps.'

'Beautiful, isn't it?'

'It's so immaculate, so clean. As if they only interred him there yesterday.'

'Or like he's been there for ever,' I said. 'As if he's always been there and will always stay there.'

'He'll be there for ever, take it from me. Nobody's going to move him.'

I always loved things like that, his 'take it from me'. I decided that I liked Raymond the way you can like a taxi driver – because you have nothing to do with him but are still putting your life in his hands. The bond was strengthened by Raymond's wearing a shapeless, greyish-purple jumper with a geometric pattern that was just like the ones my favourite teacher at my Protestant primary school had worn. He had a large, bald head and cheeks like saddlebags, but a narrow, hard and pointy nose, pure cartilage – you could imagine sticking a nose like that into a lock and jiggling it open. The dark bags under his eyes looked like they'd been there for decades.

'First time in Waterloo?'

'First time I'm fighting. You?'

'First time. Always wanted to give it a go. Now I've got the time.' He slapped himself twice on the chest. 'Lungs. No good.'

I told him that my brother was in one of the buses a couple of hundred metres behind us; he'd booked later and, my God, the organizers were strict. Raymond laughed: the French weren't leaving Waterloo to chance. His wife and two sons had already driven there with the collapsible caravan. His daughter preferred to stay at home because, yeah, you know, women and Waterloo, they just don't go together.

Out came the iPhone. Photos of monuments, selfies of him in front of monuments, selfies of him next to a blue plaque on the ground. 'Marshal Ney, Prince of the Moskva, was shot here.' That's what happened, huh, he told me. When Ney saw that the battle was lost, he went in search of a heroic death, but though horse after horse was shot out from under him, he was saved – only to be executed by the new regime after Napoleon's flight – heartless, Napoleon's most faithful commander.

'*Le Brave des Braves*,' I said.

'He gave the order to fire to his own firing squad. They don't make 'em like that any more.'

This firm sense of history triggered something in the men around us, as if it was a signal for them to join the conversation, and they presented their own nuggets of information about Ney and Murat and Talleyrand and Fouché – and why not? We were here because we had something in common, something in the distant past, out of reach. The more we talked about it, the more realistic it became, the less we felt we were on our way to do something embarrassing. I turned back to the window, the motorway and the green hills beyond.

I died almost immediately, as one of the first.

We were advancing up the hill in three lines of fifty men, towards the British artillery. Thirty metres to one side another

three lines were advancing, next to them another three. We
were the first wave. In complete accordance with the historical
course of events, our charge would be followed by a much
larger frontal assault with cavalry on the flanks; another two
thousand French devotees were already in position. That
morning we had collected our uniforms from a big barn. They
came in two sizes: too big and too small. My trousers were so
big and hung so low they looked like they'd been lifted straight
from a *Yo!* MTV *Raps* video. Hugo's hat slipped down over his
eyes. The boots flapped with each step. You felt every pine-
cone, every branch through the soles. On the hills of Waterloo,
Hugo's boots produced a weird squeak, it sounded like he was
breakdancing – that morning we'd almost split our sides over
it, but we weren't laughing now.

Nobody spoke. Somewhere someone was playing a drum,
a two-handed ruffle that seemed to be working very slowly
towards a climax, the kind of sound that makes you march
taller and stare ahead.

We focused on the men two hundred metres in front of us. I
tried not to think about them in too much detail. They too
were wearing uniforms they had made themselves or hired
here. The midday sun was burning our necks. The stiff, cheap
material of my uniform chafed against my skin. The sky was
as clear as blue ice and made the grass look greener than it
already was.

I had got up very early that morning. I had dreamed I was
being pursued by a film crew and had to interrupt my flight for
a piss, but was afraid they'd film it – and woke up with a nag-
ging, swollen bladder. The taste of the rubber of my airbed was
in my mouth, my brother was snoring quietly and rhythmically. His greying, wiry hair was stuck to his forehead, his
mouth was so far open I could see the ridges in the roof of his
mouth.

Quietly I unzipped the tent flap and stepped out over the
guy ropes of the surrounding dome tents. I could hear others
snoring too, a reticent sun was just poking its head over
the horizon, there were tents and caravans almost as far as the
eye could see. I relished the quiet. It was nice to stand there

awake, surrounded by all those sleeping people, as if the day was mine alone, as if I knew something they didn't.

My piss was rustling on the dry pine needles with a sound like crackling ice when suddenly I was startled by a horseman. Though he was already close by, I hadn't heard the hoofsteps. A man in a French cavalry uniform on a grey horse, with a sabre and all, a cigarette in his mouth and a coffee in one hand.

'*Bonjour, monsieur*,' I said.

He nodded (the slightest of gestures, gruff really, as if my presence disturbed him, perhaps he wanted the day to himself too), spurred his horse, and before he'd fully disappeared around the corner of the amenities building, at least another twenty cavalrymen had galloped past.

James Salter wrote that the irresistible thing about being a fighter pilot was that everything revolved around *you* – the aircraft carrier put out to sea for you, the mechanics on board, the technicians, the radio operators, the cooks, the cleaners, they were all there so *you* could take off.

I've had that very feeling my whole life: the family I grew up in definitely revolved around me, the schools and universities were there for me, the newspaper existed for me, the bookshops, the literary festivals – but the cavalry rode past and ignored me as if I was invisible. The ground shook, a horse snorted, they swished their tails, the riders sat straight but relaxed, they didn't deign to look at me – but I stood there with the happiest grin on my face.

The British frontline was now a hundred and twenty metres away. Just as I tried not to think about the British soldiers, I tried not to look at the spectators, who were a hundred and fifty metres away behind orange tape with their zooms and binoculars. I wondered if Raymond's family was among them, I wondered just how bad his health really was, with his 'Lungs, no good'. He was a few metres away from me, but I didn't want to look at him.

I was able to concentrate exceptionally well on the here and now, existence, my uniform, the way we were marching, the tension in my back, which I was holding so much straighter than usual. As if a wet rag had wiped the blackboard of my mind clean. That's how much a part of the line I felt. It was almost physical, a tingling sensation rising from my spine into my brainstem. Gradually feeling myself dissolve into a dream.

We were now marching downhill. The valley between us and the Brits was more difficult because you had to hold back to avoid going too fast and breaking formation. This was the moment the British opened fire. One thirty p.m., of course, just like one hundred and ninety-nine years earlier. *Le baptême de feue,* the baptism of fire.

A cannon directly in front of me fired in my direction, as if someone was sneezing in my face, the sound already whooshing past before the white plume had emerged from the barrel. The crazy thing was that all the time I had a sense of having experienced this before. The clouds of gunpowder smoke from the blanks merged until the entire British line was hidden from view and wouldn't reappear until we were seventy metres away, and Marshal d'Erlon on his horse behind us blew a whistle and we knew it was our turn to attack.

'*Vive la France!*'

'*Vive l'Empereur!*'

'*Allez, soldats heureux!*'

Suddenly I realized I was about to die – we'd agreed in advance that at eighty metres we would speed up and come within the historic range of fire and that five soldiers would fall per ten metres. 'Volunteers?' our guide from the previous day had asked. I had raised my hand and only now did I understand why.

Men rushed over the grass, holding their jolting muskets with both hands as if they were oars they were using to propel themselves forward. We could see the Brits taking aim, our drums sounded much louder now, our rented boots were in even more danger of falling off, a British officer raised his sword, we reached fifty metres, our neat lines broke up, we reached forty-five metres and saw the sword coming down, the first loud bangs sounded, we saw the flashes of fire and plumes of smoke rising from the British muskets – and I let myself fall forwards at full tilt. I held my musket in front of my chest with both hands, my face hit the grass, my hat went flying, I tasted earth.

I had offered to die because it felt like it was supposed to feel, as if I was making a sacrifice. The soldiers in the lines behind me stepped over me without a backward glance and again I felt a tingling through my whole body, it was something psychosomatic. I was lying there deliciously inert in the soft grass, I felt the pull of gravity, I felt the world turning and I felt hopelessly, infinitely alone. It was a pleasant, unmelancholy kind of loneliness, the sense of being in a crowd without being absorbed by it, and feeling more individual as a result. The further away from me the French soldiers ran, the happier I became. It was really like that: I could feel myself becoming truly happy, as if someone had injected me with a serum, I felt it passing through my body.

France – this country had given me so much. It had been so long since I had experienced this. It was summer, it was France, the setting for the happiest weeks of my life. So uncomplicated. My brother's being here heightened that feeling, as if I'd gone back in time. All those summer holidays. From our regular campsite to the nearest village was a five- or six-kilometre hike, a winding road up a mountain. There was almost no traffic, lavender grew in the verges, invisible crickets made their scratchy sound, you passed a small farm where you could buy jars of jam. The farmer was nowhere in sight, you had to leave a few francs, there was faith in human honesty. Almost every day I walked to the village in the blazing sun, mostly with a towel over my shoulders to keep them from burning.

I told my parents I was going to play football with friends or going to the river, but I didn't. I never had any purpose. I walked and wanted to do it by myself. I never took a Walkman with me. In the invariably sleepy village I bought a roll of Mentos at most and then walked back. I got so brown, so blond, I was so skinny. I wanted it all to myself: the country, the days, my life.

At the weekly karaoke evening, I sang Blondie's 'The Tide Is High' with Hugo, with friends I played six thousand games of round-the-table on a tilting concrete table-tennis table behind the toilets. During our first holiday I got to be a linesman for the annual football tournament, once I'd turned sixteen I was allowed to play in one of the teams. We listened to Phil Collins's *Greatest Hits*, to the Rolling Stones' *London Years*, the only CDs we had with us. We visited markets in nameless villages, bought bags of fresh herbs, sent two dozen postcards each. We never bought ice lollies, but stopped at supermarkets where we'd buy a tub of vanilla ice cream we'd eat with the disposable plastic spoons we'd brought with us for that purpose, shovelling it in so fast it gave us all brain freezes. I remembered summer holidays and how my father asked me if I wanted to go for a drive and how we'd cruise the provincial back roads without any destination at all, criss-crossing the countryside, passing tiny villages, drinking a Coke somewhere. My father drummed on the steering wheel, I stared out of the window.

In the summer before my eighteenth birthday I lost my virginity to a French girl, although I never really liked the sound of that 'lost'. I didn't lose anything, I gained something. That's how I saw it at the time, that's how I see it now; she gave me a present and that present was her and I treated it with appropriate haste and awkwardness – just like immediately ripping the wrapping off a gift you're very happy to receive – but cheerful, grinning. She grinned too and said that we just had to wait a little and try again. And that's what we did, almost the whole afternoon, until her parents came home from doing the shopping.

Afterwards we went to the small river that flowed past the campsite and floated on our backs hand in hand, letting the current carry us downstream. The blue sky, the sun, looking up through our lashes at the mountains on either side of the Gorges du Verdon. We went so far that we ended up having to walk back five or six kilometres in our bare feet, but we were together, just the two of us, and holding hands and when we got back it was already dinnertime. Doing the dishes, I shed a few silent tears, I remember, because the day was over, because I had let it slip through my fingers.

Lying on the grass I felt the drone of the horses' hooves,

which must have been similar to the sound of a small earth-quake. I heard shouting, but it didn't get through to me – I wasn't lying there in my role because my role felt more real than anything else. I was in the past, completely, just not the past that was being fought out here, but something much smaller, a much less distant past.

France – this country had given me so much. That was what I was thinking as I lay there, until I realized I wasn't in France at all: Waterloo was in Belgium, a country whose history was somehow profoundly forgettable, a country where I had never done anything I really enjoyed. But I was lying there in a French uniform, fallen for the glory of the French empire.

The agreement was that you had to stay where you fell; medical orderlies would come to kiss you back to life as it were. The re-enactors were then allowed to return to the start-ing positions and take part in a subsequent charge. Let them take their time, I thought, let me lie here as long as possible.

Out of the corner of my eye I coud see other casualties on the ground, metres away. I could have tried to see if there were any familiar faces among them, but I closed my eyes. A heli-copter flew overhead, quite low. I assumed a foetal position and concentrated very contentedly on my own death.

Translated by David Colmer

Author Biographies

A proponent of Dutch Naturalism, **Marcellus Emants** (1848–1923) was influenced by Émile Zola and Ivan Turgenev, with whom he corresponded. He wrote in a sober style, expressing a dark and pessimistic view of life. After the First World War he left the Netherlands for Switzerland, where he died. His most well-known work is *A Posthumous Confession*, published in 1894 and translated into English by J. M. Coetzee.

Louis Couperus (1863–1923) was catapulted to prominence in 1889 with *Eline Vere*, a psychological masterpiece inspired by Flaubert and Tolstoy. It depicts upper-class life in The Hague, where the author was born, though his work also contains impressions of Indonesia (where he lived in his younger days) and Italy, Africa and China – fruits of his extensive travelling. Writing in a rich and sensitive style, Couperus was the greatest novelist of his generation. His *oeuvre* also contains novellas, short stories, poetry, travel stories, fairy tales, feuilletons and sketches.

Arthur van Schendel (1874–1946) was born in the Dutch East Indies and moved to the Netherlands when he was young. He wrote twenty novels in all, as well as stories and essays. *The Johanna Maria* is one of his best known books, along with *The Water Man* (1933) and *The House in Haarlem* (1934). In 1947 van Schendel was posthumously honoured with the P. C. Hooft Prize, the most prestigious award for Dutch literature.

For many years, **Nescio** (J. H. F. Grönloh, 1882–1961) was a one-book author with only a collection of three world-weary, poetic stories (1918) to his name. Nobody knew who Nescio was until fifteen years later, when the author revealed himself only because his work was falsely attributed to someone else. His output may have been small, but his name is legendary and in recent years, Nescio has been translated into many languages, English included (*Amsterdam Stories*).

A lawyer by profession, **Ferdinand Bordewijk** (1884–1965) made his prose debut in an unusual genre uncommon for the Netherlands – three compilations of *Fantastic Narratives*. Three subsequent short and futuristic novels secured his reputation as an author of highly original prose, with short sentences and an abrasive style. A frightening father and son story set in the legal world, *Character* (1938), is another highlight in his *oeuvre*, the film being awarded an Academy Award in 1998.

Maria Dermoût (1888–1962) was born on a sugar plantation in the Dutch East Indies and educated in Holland. She then returned to the Indies with her husband and spent thirty years living in, as she later wrote, 'every town and wilderness of the islands of Java, Celebes, and the Moluccas'. Only in 1951, at the age of sixty-three, did Dermoût publish her first book, a memoir called *Yesterday*. Her celebrated novel *The Ten Thousand Things* was published in 1955.

Born in the small Frisian town of Harlingen, **Simon Vestdijk** (1898–1971) studied medicine in Amsterdam, but turned to literature after a few years as a doctor. As legend has it, Vestdijk could write faster than even God could read: he published more than two hundred books (no less than fifty-two of them being novels). A classic is the Anton Wachter series, a eight-volume set of novels about an obsessive youth love. Apart from prose and poetry he was also a foremost essayist with important publications on religion, art and music.

Belcampo (Herman Pieter Schonfeld Wichers, 1902–90) was an admirer of E. T. A. Hoffmann and used one of Hoffmann's characters as his own pen name. In 1922 he started writing stories, mostly of a fantastic and bizarre nature, which became his trademark. In 1958 he published his best known work, *The Great Event*, an apocalyptic novel situated in Rijssen, the town where he grew up.

A writer, journalist and translator, **A. Alberts** (1911–96) travelled to the Dutch East Indies to work as a civil servant. After the Battle of Java (1942) and his internment by the Japanese from April 1942 to September 1945, he returned in 1946 to the Netherlands. In 1953 he made his debut with *The Islands*, a collection of short stories about an imaginary archipelago, based on his experiences in Guinea and Indonesia. He wrote a classic *oeuvre*, consisting of short stories, novellas, novels, memoirs and historical studies.

Father of architect Rem Koolhaas, **Anton Koolhaas** (1912–92) started writing as a journalist on foreign affairs and since his first story appeared in a newspaper in 1936, he wrote many literary books of animal stories. In addition, he wrote about human beings as well, but there was always a major role for animals. Some of his novels have been filmed. He was also the director of the Dutch Film Academy, wrote film scenarios and directed one film.

The grande dame of historic fiction, **Hella Haasse** (1918–2011) was one of the key figures in postwar Dutch literature. She made her debut with the novella *The Black Lake* (1949), a story about a friendship between a Dutch and an Indonesian boy, based on her experiences of growing up in the Dutch East Indies. Haasse received many prestigious literary awards, among them the Dutch Literature Prize in 2004, and her work has been translated into many languages. *The Tea Lords* was the first work of hers translated into English for fifteen years.

Willem Frederik Hermans (1921–95) is another key figure in Dutch literature; a writer of many novels, short stories, essays, drama and poetry. He wrote two classic novels about the Second World War and the Dutch resistance, *Tears of the Acacias*

(1949) and *The Darkroom of Damocles* (1958), and a novel about a young man's search for a meteorite, *Beyond Sleep* (1966, filmed in 2016). The last two have been translated into English. Lesser known, but equally important, are his short stories and novellas, such as *The Safe House* (1951).

F. B. Hotz (1922–2000) started to write in the early 1950s when he was playing the trombone in a jazz combo. When finally he sent his story *The Tram Race* to a literary magazine, it caused a stir of excitement: never before had the editors read such an accomplished debut. With his polished style, he quickly became a cherished author of short stories and just one novel; much of his work was set in the depression era of the 1930s.

Harry Mulisch (1927–2010) was born to a Jewish mother and a German father. 'I didn't so much experience the war; I *am* the Second World War,' he once famously claimed. One of his most successful novels, *The Assault* (1982), is about the Second World War. The author further gained international fame with his *opus magnum*, *The Discovery of Heaven* (1992). In addition to novels, Mulisch wrote plays, poetry, political pieces and philosophical studies. He was one of the most illustrious authors in the Netherlands. His work has been translated into more than thirty languages, including English.

Author, sculptor and painter **Jan Wolkers** (1925–2007) became famous in the 1960s for his literary work, which caused a commotion because of explicit scenes. His Protestant upbringing is a theme in much of his work. The 1969 novel *Turkish Delight* became his biggest success; it has been translated into many languages and made into a movie, directed by Paul Verhoeven. In his later life, he lived on the island of Texel, concentrated on painting and less on writing and also presented a popular television show, explaining the wonders of nature.

Cees Nooteboom (b.1933) has written a huge body of work, consisting of novels, stories, poetry, essays, journalism and translations. He is one of the most successful Dutch authors internationally, especially in Germany, where all his work appears simultaneously in translation. He witnessed the revolutions in Budapest (1956), Paris (1968) and Berlin (1989), about each of which he wrote accounts. His novels include *Rituals* (1980), *The Following Story* (1991), *Roads to Santiago* (1992) and *All Souls' Day* (1998). The author lives in Amsterdam and on the island of Minorca.

Remco Campert (b.1929) is one of the most popular writers in the Netherlands, who started writing poetry and short stories in the 1950s as a member of the legendary experimental group De Vijftigers. In comparison to his friends, his work was more accessible – always balancing dry wit and melancholia. He is also a widely read columnist for *de Volkskrant*. In 1976 Campert was awarded the P. C. Hooft Prize and in 2014 he received the tri-annual Prize for Dutch Literature. In recent years he has found inspiration for new novels, including the successful *A Love in Paris* (2004).

J. M. A. Biesheuvel (b.1939) became a sensation with his debut, the short-story collection *In the Upper Berth* (1972). After that, he published a large number of story collections and novellas. In 2007 he was awarded the prestigious P. C. Hooft Prize for his complete oeuvre. Suffering from depression, Biesheuvel has published little in the last decades. In 2008 his collected works appeared, followed by a couple of newly written short stories in literary magazines.

Bob den Uyl (1930–92) was a writer of short stories, with a famously ironic, observant and deadpan style. In his later work, the focus of his writing shifted to more autobiographical and travel stories, mostly concerned with bicycle trips in neighbouring countries. Several collections of stories have been published posthumously; 2008 saw the publication of the biography of this cult figure in Dutch letters.

Trained as a biologist in zoology and ethology, **Maarten 't Hart** (b.1944) has been one of the Netherlands most successful novelists since the 1970s. *Flight of Curlews* (1978) was his breakthrough novel. His books have been translated into many languages, notably in Germany where he has a large readership. Protestantism, nature and classical music are recurrent themes in his work.

Born in Batavia, present-day Jakarta, **Helga Ruebsamen** (b.1934) was on a visit to the Netherlands when war broke out and her family could not return. In 1997, she published a bestselling autobiographical novel about her colonial youth and the contrast with the Netherlands during occupation, *The Song and the Truth*. Apart from this novel, she has published many short stories, most of them about people suffering from alcoholism, poverty and/or madness, in a witty trademark style. She was awarded the Anna Bijns Prize in 2003.

Mensje van Keulen (b.1946) made her debut with *Bleeker's Summer* (1972), now considered a modern classic, followed by collections of stories and poetry, novels and children's books. She is a subtle storyteller with an eye for significant, slightly bizarre details that give her work a melancholy atmosphere and a touch of suspense. In 2011 she was awarded the Charlotte Köhler Prize; in 2014 the Constantijn Huygens Prize.

Nicolaas Matsier (b.1945) is the author of many children's books, short-story collections, essays and two novels: *Closed House* (1994, written after the death of his parents) and *The Forty-Eighth Hour* (2005, about illegal refugees). He has translated work by authors including Lewis Carroll, Stefan Themerson and Xenophon and for many years was an editor for literary journals *De Revisor* and *Raster*.

During his short life, **Frans Kellendonk** (1951–90) created an *oeuvre* of novels, short stories, essays and translations. From his debut *Ruins* (1977) to his novel *Mystical Body* (1986), Kellendonk won the admiration of readers and critics; with his intelligent and adventurous prose he is considered one of the most important names in Dutch literature. In 2015, his collected works and an edition of his letters were published.

Oek de Jong (b.1952) made his breakthrough with the bestselling novel *Billowing Summer Dresses* (1979), followed by three novels, and collections of stories and essays. In 2012 he published his *opus magnum*, *Pier and Ocean*, which was awarded the F. Bordewijk Prize and the Gouden Uil. De Jong's books have been translated into nine languages. His most recent publication is an essay on the state of the novel, *What Only the Novel Can Say* (2013). His story *Motionless Man* was first published in 1975.

Thomas Rosenboom (b.1956) has written novels, short stories and essays. Historical fiction is his trademark, with *Washed Flesh* (1994), *Public Works* (1999) and *The New Man* (2003) being prime examples. He is the only author to have won the Libris Literature Prize (best novel of the year) twice. Controversial was his essay on the decline of educational standards, *Thinking About Holland* (2005).

A. F. Th. van der Heijden (b.1951) is the author of two novel cycles: *The Toothless Time* and *Homo Duplex*, both of them spanning thousands of pages, which rank among the highpoints in Dutch literature. He has also written four memoirs, the last of which is about his son who tragically died, *Tonio*. The book became a bestseller and won three of Holland's most prestigious literary awards. It has also been translated into English.

Margriet de Moor (b.1941) had a career as a classical singer before becoming a novelist. Her debut novel, *First Grey, Then White, Then Blue* (1991), was a sensational success across Europe, winning her the AKO Literature Prize, for which her second novel, *The Virtuoso* (1993) was also nominated. She has since published several other novels, including *Duke of Egypt* and *The Kreutzer Sonata*. Her books have been translated into twenty languages, including English.

P. F. Thomése (b.1958) was awarded the AKO Literature Prize in 1991 for his first collection of stories, *The Southern Continent*. *Shadow Child* (2003) spent several weeks in the list of top ten bestsellers, was nominated for the NS Readers' Book of the Year Award, and was longlisted for the Libris Literature Prize. The book was his international breakthrough and has been published in nineteen languages. Since then he has written prize-winning novels, short stories, essays and novellas to wide acclaim. His novel *J. Kessels* has been adapted for the screen. His most recent novel – the bestselling *The Underwater Swimmer* (2015) – has been nominated for both the ECI and Libris Literature Prize.

Marcel Möring (b.1957) has published novels, stories and essays. He received the Lubberhuizen Prize for his debut novel, *Mendel's Legacy* (1990), while his second novel, *The Great Longing* (1992), was awarded the AKO Literature Prize. It quickly became his international breakthrough, with translations into many languages, including English. In 2007, his fourth novel, *DIS*, was awarded the F. Bordewijk Prize. His most recent novel is *Purification Mountain* (2014).

Manon Uphoff (b.1962) is especially known for her short stories and novellas. She made her debut with *Desire* (1995), followed by a novel, *Missing* (1997). The story included in this anthology, *Poop*, caused a stir upon publication. Her most recent book is *The Sweetness of Violence* (2013), also a collection of short stories.

Joost Zwagerman (1963–2015) was a novelist, poet, essayist and editor of several anthologies. He started his career as a writer with bestselling novels, describing the atmosphere of the 1980s and 1990s, such as *Gimmick!* (1988) and *False Light* (1991). In later years, he concentrated on writing essays – notably on pop culture and visual arts – and poetry. Suicide was the theme of the novel *Six Stars* (2002). He took his own life just after having published a new collection of essays on art, *The Museum of Light*.

Hafid Bouazza (b.1970), is a Moroccan-Dutch writer of novels, stories, drama and essays. He received the E. du Perron prize for his 1996 debut *Abdullah's Feet*, which was translated into English. He edited and translated an anthology of Arab verse. Later works include the 2004 novel *Paravion*, which won him the Golden Owl Prize. His last publication is the novel *Meriswin* (2014).

Arnon Grunberg (b.1971) is a prolific and versatile writer of novels, essays and columns, living in New York. He made his debut in 1994 with the novel *Blue Mondays*, which critics hailed as a 'grotesque comedy, a rarity in Dutch literature'. The acclaimed novel *Tirza* was Grunberg's first book to be made into a movie, after winning the Libris Prize and the Golden Owl. His work has been translated into thirty languages, including English.

Sanneke van Hassel (b.1971) is the author of four collections of short stories, which have been praised for their powerful atmosphere and economical style. In the summer of 2010 her first novel was published, *Nest*. She is the organizer of an international festival of short stories, Hotel Van Hassel. Together with Flemish writer Annelies Verbeke, she compiled an anthology of contemporary short stories from all over the world (*To the City*, 2012).

Joost de Vries (b.1983) is a writer, editor and literary critic. He made his debut with *Clausewitz* (2010), inspired by the work of Harry Mulisch. His second novel, *The Republic* (2013), which won him the Golden Owl and several nominations for other literary awards, will be translated into nine languages, including English.

Acknowledgements

Every effort has been made to trace copyright holders and to obtain their permission for the use of copyright material. The publisher apologizes for any errors or omissions in the below list and would be grateful if notified of any corrections that should be incorporated in future reprints or editions of this book.

Introduction copyright © Joost Zwagerman, 2016, first published here.
Translation copyright © David McKay, 2016.

'Een zonderling' ('An Eccentric'), by Marcellus Emants, first published in *Mensen* by Querido, 1920.
Translation copyright © Paul Vincent, 2016.

'De binocle' ('The Opera Glasses'), by Louis Couperus, first published in *Proza* by L. J. Veen, 1920.
Translation copyright © Paul Vincent, 2016.

'De groene droom' ('The Green Dream'), by Arthur van Schendel, first published in *De pleziervaart* by J. M. Meulenhoff, 1951.
Translation copyright © David McKay, 2016.

'Titaantjes' ('Young Titans') by Nescio, first published in *Groot Nederland*, 1915. First book publication: *De uitvreter, Titaantjes, Dichtertje*, J. H. De Bois, 1918. Reprinted with the permission of Nijgh & Van Ditmar.
Translation copyright © Damion Searls, first published by New York Review Books, 2012.

'Vrouwen winnen' ('Women Win') copyright 1976 by F. B.
Hotz. First published in *Dood weermiddel en andere verhalen*
by De Arbeiderspers.
Translation copyright © David McKay, 2016.

'Wat gebeurde er met Sergeant Massuro?' ('What Happened
to Sergeant Massuro?') copyright © Harry Mulisch, 1995.
First published in *De versierde mens* by De Bezige Bij.
Translation copyright © Paul Vincent, 2016.

'Gevederde vrienden' ('Feathered Friends') copyright © Jan
Wolkers, 1962. First published in *Gesponnen suiker* (Col-
lected Stories) by J. M. Meulenhoff.
Translation copyright © Richard Huijing, 1993.

'Paula' copyright © Cees Nooteboom, 2009. First published in
's Nachts komen de vossen by De Bezige Bij.
Translation copyright © Ina Rilke, 2011. First published in *The
Foxes Come at Night* by MacLehose Press.

'De jongen met het mes' ('The Kid with the Knife') copyright ©
Remco Campert, 1993. First published in *Nacht op de kale
dwerg* by De Bezige Bij.
Translation copyright © Donald Gardner, 2016.

'De verpletterende werkelijkheid' ('The Shattering Truth')
copyright © J. M. A. Biesheuvel, 1979. First published in
De verpletterende werkelijkheid by J. M. Meulenhoff. Reprinted with the permission of G. A. van Oorschot.
Translation copyright © Sam Garrett, 2016.

'Oorlog is leuk' ('War is Fun') copyright © Bob den Uyl, 1968.
First published in *Een zachte fluittoon* by Querido.
Translation copyright © Sam Garrett, 2016.

'Het Muiderslot' ('Castle Muider') copyright © Maarten 't
Hart, 1981. First published in *De zaterdagvliegers* by De
Arbeiderspers.

Translation copyright © Michele Hutchison, 2016.

'Olijfje' ('Olive') copyright © Helga Reubsamen. First published in *De ondergang van Makarov* by Contact in 1971. Reprinted with the permission of Atlas Contact.
Translation copyright © Michele Hutchison, 2016.

'Zand' ('Sand') copyright © Mensje van Keulen. First published in *Een goed verhaal* by Atlas Contact in 2009.
Translation copyright © Ina Rilke, 2011.

'De Minnema-variaties' ('The Minnema Variations') copyright © Nicolaas Matsier, 1979. First published in *Onbepaald vertraagd* by Querido. Reprinted with the permission of De Bezige Bij.
Translation copyright © Paul Vincent, 2016.

'Buitenlandse dienst' ('Foreign Service') copyright © Frans Kellendonk, 1983. First published in *Namen en gezichten* by Querido. Reprinted with the permission of Athenaeum-Polak & Van Gennep.
Translation copyright © David McKay, 2016.

'De onbeweeglijke' ('The Motionless Man') copyright © Oek de Jong, 1975. First published in *De hemelvaart van Massimo* by J.M. Meulenhoff. New and revised edition: *De onbeweeglijke* by Atlas Contact, 2002.
Translation copyright © Laura Watkinson, 2016.

'Tinctuur' ('Tincture') copyright © Thomas Rosenboom, 2006. First published in *Hoog aan de wind* by Em. Querido's Uitgeverij.
Translation copyright © David McKay, 2016.

'Het Byzantijnse kruis' ('The Byzantine Cross') copyright © A. F. Th. van der Heijden. First published in *Gentse lente* by Querido, 2008. Reprinted with the permission of De Bezige Bij.

Translation copyright © Sam Garrett, 2016

'Indian Time' copyright © Sanneke van Hassel, 2012. First published in *Ezels* by De Bezige Bij.
Translation copyright © Liz Waters, 2016.

'Een kamer voor mezelf' ('A Room of My Own') © Joost de Vries, 2014. First published in *Vechtmemoires* by Prometheus.
Translation copyright © David Colmer, 2016.

Every effort has been made to contact Richard Huijing, translator of 'Funeral Rights' and 'Feathered Friends'.

WHY READ THE CLASSICS?

Italo Calvino

Why Read the Classics? is an elegant defence of the value of great literature by one of the finest authors of the last century. Beginning with an essay on the attributes that define a classic (number one – classics are those books that people always say they are 'rereading', not 'reading'), this is an absorbing collection of Italo Calvino's witty and passionate criticism.

With thity-six essays – including thoughts on figures like Homer, Hemingway, Borges, Tolstoy and Twain – *Why Read the Classics?* represents Calvino's own canon of great works and is full of the fascinating insights of the mercurial, incisive mind of a brilliant reader, as well as a writer.

'A classic book at bedtime, a seductive invitation to forgotten opportunities or rereading' *The Times*

PNIN

Vladimir Nabokov

Professor Timofey Pnin, previously of Tsarist Russia, is now precariously positioned at the heart of campus America. Battling with American life and language, Pnin must face great hazards in this new world: the ruination of his beautiful lumber-room-as-office; the removal of his teeth and the fitting of new ones; the search for a suitable boarding-house; and the trials of taking the wrong train to deliver a lecture in a language he has yet to master.

'Nabokov writes prose the only way it should be written, that is, ecstatically' John Updike

ALONE IN BERLIN

Hans Fallada

Berlin, 1940, and the city is filled with fear. At the house on 55 Jablon-ski Strasse, its various occupants try to live under Nazi rule in their different ways: the bullying Hitler loyalists the Persickes, the retired judge Fromm and the unassuming couple Otto and Anna Quangel. Then the Quangels receive the news that their beloved son has been killed fighting in France. Shocked out of their quiet existence, they begin a silent campaign of defiance, and a deadly game of cat and mouse develops between the Quangels and the ambitious Gestapo inspector Escherich. When petty criminals Kluge and Borkhausen also become involved, deception, betrayal and murder ensue, tight-ening the noose around the Quangels' necks . . .

'A classic study of a paranoid society. Fallada's scope is extraordinary. *Alone in Berlin* is . . . as morally powerful as anything I've ever read' Charlotte Moore, *Telegraph*

PERFUME

Patrick Süskind

Jean-Baptiste Grenouille is abandoned on the filthy streets of eighteenth-century Paris as a baby, but grows up to discover he has an extraordinary gift: a sense of smell more powerful than any other human's. Gradually he learns how to exploit this gift in the art of creating the most sublime perfumes in France. Yet there is one odour he cannot capture: the scent of an innocent young virgin. In order to perfect his experiments, he must have this final ingredient – at any cost. A cult international bestseller, *Perfume* is a bewitching, darkly humorous fable of desire, obsession and death.

'Witty, stylish and ferociously absorbing' *Observer*

SIDDHARTHA

Hermann Hesse

Siddhartha, a handsome Brahmin's son, is clever and well loved, yet increasingly dissatisfied with the life that is expected of him. Setting out on a spiritual journey to discover a higher state of being, his quest leads him through the temptations of luxury and wealth, the pleasures of sensual love, and the sinister threat of death-dealing snakes, until, eventually, he comes to a river. There a ferryman guides him towards his destiny, and to the ultimate meaning of existence. Inspired by Hermann Hesse's profound regard for Indian transcendental philosophy and written in prose of graceful simplicity, *Siddhartha* is one of the most influential spiritual works of the twentieth century.

'Hesse sensed, decades before my generation . . . the necessity we all have to claim what is truly and rightfully ours: our own life' Paulo Coelho

METAMORPHOSIS AND OTHER STORIES

Franz Kafka

'When Gregor Samsa awoke one morning from troubled dreams, he found himself changed into a monstrous cockroach in his bed'

Kafka's masterpiece of unease and black humour, *Metamorphosis*, the story of an ordinary man transformed into an insect, is brought together in this collection with the rest of his works that he thought worthy of publication. It includes *Meditation*, a collection of his earlier studies; *The Judgement*, written in a single night of frenzied creativity; 'The Stoker', the first chapter of a novel set in America; and a fascinating occasional piece, 'The Aeroplanes at Brescia', Kafka's eyewitness account of an air display in 1909. Together, these stories reveal the breadth of his literary vision and the extraordinary imaginative depth of his thought.

'What Dante and Shakespeare were for the ages, Kafka is for ours'
George Steiner

HOWL, KADDISH AND OTHER POEMS

Allen Ginsberg

'I saw the best minds of my generation destroyed by madness, starving hysterical naked'

Beat movement icon and visionary poet, Allen Ginsberg broke boundaries with his fearless, pyrotechnic verse. This new collection brings together the famous poems that made his name as a defining figure of the counterculture. They include the apocalyptic 'Howl', which became the subject of an obscenity trial when it was first published in 1956; the moving lament for his dead mother, 'Kaddish'; the searing indictment of his homeland, 'America'; and the confessional 'Mescaline'. Dark, ecstatic and rhapsodic, they show why Ginsberg was one of the most influential poets of the twentieth century.

'The poem that defined a generation' *Guardian* on 'Howl'